Kim Wilkins was born in ⟨...⟩ Australia at the age of fou⟨...⟩ books began soon after, ⟨...⟩ at school to ameliorate her painful lack of popularity. After trying the daytime nine to five as an office clerk, and the night-time nine to five as a misunderstood rock pig, she opted for the flexible hours of university life, and in 1998 graduated with first class honours in English literature from the University of Queensland. Her first novel *The Infernal* won the 1997 Aurealis Awards for best horror and best fantasy novel. Her plans for the future are not firm, but she will be happy if she can spend the rest of her life with her nose in a book—either studying one, reading one, or writing one.

Also by Kim Wilkins
The Infernal

KIM WILKINS
GRIMOIRE

VICTOR GOLLANCZ
LONDON

First published in Great Britain in 1999 by
Victor Gollancz
An imprint of Orion Books Ltd
Orion House, 5 Upper St Martin's Lane,
London WC2H 9EA

A CIP catalogue record for this book
is available from the British Library

ISBN 0575 06786 1

Printed and bound by
The Guernsey Press Co. Ltd, Guernsey, C.I.

If you would like to write to Kim Wilkins,
her e-mail address is:
kimwilkins@uq.net.au

More information about Kim and her work
can be found on her website:
http://welcome.to/kimwilkins

This book is lovingly inscribed to Princess Katelyn.

ACKNOWLEDGMENTS

I wish to acknowledge the following for their help and support.

Selwa Anthony, as always, has been a rock, but a very gentle and loving one. Kirstyn McDermott has been an adviser, a co-conspirator, and a friend on my creative journey. Janine Haig, I am forever in your debt. *Merci* to Nicole Ruckels for providing me with the story of Mr Buchmann (it's all *true!*). Charles Samuel in Jerusalem and Dr Wally Wood in the Anatomy Department, University of Queensland, provided invaluable assistance with my research. Claude and Polly were fantastic lap warmers on cold, inspirationless days. Mirko Ruckels has made more cups of frustration-easing tea than I care to count and has always reminded me tenderly that one bad writing day does not mean I've lost it forever. Others I would like to thank include my teachers at the University of Queensland and my friends, especially Drew Whitehead, Davin Patterson, Dansex Johnson, Boris Ruckels, Allison Gallagher and, of course, my beloved mother and brother, who love me even though I continue to bring the family name into disrepute.

Most of all for this book, however, I wish to acknowledge a debt to Kate Morton who, with her love and her irrepressible vivacity, has made me discover parts of myself that I had forgotten in adolescence. For all the times we've dressed as fairy princesses, for all the pizza and red wine we've consumed, for all the celebrity-obsessed TV and magazines we've devoured, for all the creepy stories we've told or read to each other, and for animating my imaginative life with childlike energy, this book can only be dedicated to her.

Let Love clasp grief lest both be drowned,
Let darkness keep her raven gloss.
Ah, sweeter to be drunk with loss,
To dance with Death, to beat the ground,

Than that the victor Hours should scorn
The long result of love, and boast,
'Behold the man that loved and lost,
But all he was is overworn.'
ALFRED, LORD TENNYSON

I gotta keep movin', I gotta keep movin' . . .
There's a hellhound on my trail.
ROBERT JOHNSON

PROLOGUE
1867

PC Hallam was a long way from his beat. The bitter smell of the Thames, the dark shadows leaping in the gaslight, the wharf-hands swearing as they loaded the crate onto the spar—a stark contrast to the fashionable, genteel streets of Faraday Square and Milton Close, the new estates which he usually policed. Perhaps it wasn't such a good idea to be down here at the Docks, huddling in the gloom out of uniform.

But he had to be sure.

'Easy . . . easy . . .' called a foreman from the boat—a hundred-foot barque headed for the colonies. The crate threatened to spin off the hook, then hovered over the wharf as it swung on the derrick to the deck. It cast a block of shadow which momentarily darkened the faces of the workers. Men on the boat were guiding it into the cargo hull.

The chill night air chafed Hallam's cheeks and he rubbed his gloved hands together. How strange that he should be pining for the comfort of his beat when it was there that he had experienced the garish nightmare that continued to haunt him. He shuddered as, once more, the sickening vision squirmed its way into his reluctant memory.

It had been a Thursday evening—brisk, but not too cold. The fog was rolling in for the evening and a young couple had stopped to ask him directions. He had just sent them on their way when he had heard screams from 13 Milton Close. Peter Owling, the resident, was a well-known eccentric, usually dressed in flamboyantly coloured silks which drew attention to his obesity. Hallam had run up the stairs and hammered on the door. No response—only a loud sobbing. He broke the window in the door and fumbled for the lock on the inside, burst in and followed the sound of the voice until he came to Owling's opulent dining room, decorated lavishly with deep red wallpaper, gilt-edged picture frames, an extravagant chandelier.

And there, the nightmare.

It looked as though guests had been expected for dinner. The dining table was heaving under the weight of dishes—a ham, a roast turkey, bowls of cooked vegetables, tarts, bottles of wine—and in the centre of it, illuminated by the dim, flickering candlelight, the dead, naked body of Peter Owling.

Hallam had scanned the room. The sobbing came from a boy in the corner—Christian, Owling's young friend. He was about seventeen, a beautiful lad with an angel's face, and the target of a lot of gossip about the exact nature of his relationship with Owling.

'My God, what happened here?' Hallam asked. Though he didn't really expect an answer. It was well known that Christian was a mute.

Christian sobbed, pointing senselessly towards the body.

Hallam approached the dining table. Owling's massive white belly was criss-crossed with deep, thin lines of gore, as though some cruelly fine, sharp instrument had been used to inscribe a message of hate in the pallid flesh. The back of his head, Hallam could see, was mashed and bloody, as though he'd been slammed onto the table with great force. And lying on his chest, pinned there with a dagger which had clearly been driven into his heart, was a book. Or rather, a section torn from a book. Dark blood dribbled in sticky drops off the table and pooled on the floor.

'Dear Lord,' Hallam muttered.

'Next time he will destroy us all.'

Hallam spun around. The boy had spoken. He stared in astonishment at the lad, silent for years as far as he knew. Was it the shock that had given him back his power of speech?

'What happened here, Christian. Who did this?'

'Next time he will destroy us all.'

'Did you do this?' But as soon as the question left his lips, Hallam knew that Christian could not be responsible. Owling was all the boy had.

'Next time . . .'

'You're not making sense, lad.'

Then a thin, keening wail as the boy turned his tear-stained face heavenwards and lapsed again into mournful sobbing.

'Next time he will destroy us all.'

Hallam shook his head to clear it of the visions. The last crate of books was being lifted onto the barque. Owling's books. He had been nearly insolvent because of the lavish lifestyle he had led, and he had owed a rich banking family—the Humberstones—a fortune. They had emptied his home as part payment. And in one of those crates was the book that had been pinned to Owling's chest. Hallam knew for sure because he had put it in the crate.

He had seen enough of the pages to know what kind

3

of book it was—backwards writing and invocations, impossibly complicated drawings of circles embellished with ancient languages, pentagrams and hexagrams. Something unholy, something he wanted as far away from London—from himself—as possible. And no doubt it was the unholy magic that stopped the thing from burning when he and two other constables had set fire to it in an attempt to destroy it. Owling's front door hadn't yet been fixed, so it had been easy to break in, to jam the thing in one of the crates between the other books, send it to the colonies where it could do no harm. Because next time—

A scream broke through the rimy night air and Hallam turned to see a pale figure approaching in the dark, running down the pier as though the devil were on his tail.

Christian. His white face was contorted in terror, his long black hair flowed behind him.

'No! No!' the lad screamed as he pelted towards the barque.

'Christian!' Hallam called, stepping out to stop him. Christian pushed him out of the way and made to run up the gangway and onto the boat. The commotion had caused confusion among the handlers. The last crate had already been let off the derrick and the spar was swinging back over to the dock. Hallam felt his body tense as he saw what was going to happen.

Christian's head collided with the hook. There was a spurt of blood as the heavy iron crushed into his temple. The men were rushing towards him, but he staggered a few paces, then plunged unconscious off the gangway and into the black water.

Hallam turned his back on the ensuing commotion. He knew they would not find the boy before he drowned—not in the murky depths between the wharf and the boat. Perhaps his sad grey body would be pulled from the water in a day or two, floating to the surface after the fish had already feasted on its extremities. Perhaps it would never rise, but stay eternally, like a pathetic secret, in the silent depths.

Hallam sat heavily on the edge of the dock. He waited all through the evening, shivering in the bleak October wind, watching the half-hearted rescue attempts from his place in the shadows. He only felt he could breathe again when the barque finally drew away and set sail for Australia. The ends of the earth. Then he pulled himself to his feet and began the long walk home.

He shoved his hands into his coat pockets and huddled deeper into the warm material. Poor Christian—a second victim of Owling's unholy dabbling. Hallam shuddered as he remembered the strange, empty look in the boy's eyes when he'd been released from police custody after questioning. Half mad with grief and shock, he had relapsed into his dumbstruck ways, never telling what had happened to Owling.

But then, Hallam wasn't really sure he wanted to know.

CHAPTER ONE

....

~

The pleasure was exquisite.

Hot, moist trails of bliss in arcs and spirals on her skin. Deeper, deeper. She groaned in her sleep. The feather-light touch of warm fingers on her thighs—soft, slow, creeping boldly upwards, gathering intensity.

Holly shuddered then woke with a gasp. For a moment she was disoriented, couldn't remember where she was. The lamp over her desk sent the shadows huddling back into their corners. She was alone in her office at the college. It was very late and she had just had an orgasm while dozing over a book.

'Great,' she muttered, 'wet dreams, like a teenage boy.' She swivelled round on her chair. There were two other desks as well as her own in the office. One was for Prudence, the aloof, purple-haired girl whom she had met briefly this afternoon. The other was for somebody called Justin who hadn't yet arrived at the college.

Holly checked her watch and thought about going home. Her heart sank. Another sleepless night battling with the bugs and the cold draughts, with the musty smell of the place and the noisy plumbing. She berated herself once again for not inspecting before she signed the lease—it was just that she'd been in such a hurry, so eager to find a place, any place, so excited about her scholarship, so desperate to be away from Daybrook and start a new life.

A shadow seemed to move on the periphery of her vision. She turned quickly, but saw nothing.

'Afraid of the dark, Holly?' she said aloud, and her voice sounded very hollow in the empty room. It was the dream that had spooked her—her imaginary lover's touch had seemed so real.

Yes, definitely time to go home.

She leaned over to switch off her study lamp then paused, realising that it would plunge her into total darkness. Surely it wouldn't matter if she left the light on overnight. Her keys jangled in her pocket as she pulled her jacket on. The sound comforted her, broke the silence. She eyed the telephone and thought about calling a cab. Ridiculous, it was only two blocks home and only nine o'clock. Hardly the witching hour.

The hallway was dark and Holly had to stand still for a few moments while her eyes adjusted. Every other sane student at the college must have gone home hours ago. The wonderful smell of the place—old wood and dusty books—cheered her a little. So she had left behind her family, her friends, a secure job and a comfortable home to live in a bug-infested flat behind somebody's house—what did it matter when she had this opportunity to start her Masters in Victorian literature at one of the most elite institutions in the southern hemisphere? She locked the office behind her and headed for the stair tower, bounding down the steps two at a time to the front door. A muted red light from the Coke machine in the cafeteria glowed in the darkness. The door handle was cool under her touch as she pushed it to let herself out. It locked behind her with a thud and she emerged into the reassuring glow of security lights over the front entrance.

The two ancient fig trees that stood sentinel on either side of the front path cast shadows in the moonlight. Holly paused as she stood beneath them, turned to look at the front of Humberstone College, its narrow arched windows and crumbling balconies lit from below by two bright spotlights. A massive Victorian building in dirty sandstone, it stood on the rise of Sheldon Street in South Yarra, one of the moneyed suburbs of Melbourne. From the west tower was an uninterrupted view of the city, shrouded in haze. The building had some kind of fantastically interesting history. Professor Aswell, her thesis supervisor, had elicited a reluctant promise from Prudence to relate it to Holly over the next few days as she settled in.

Again a shadow moved in the corner of her eye. Holly felt her heart start as she spun around. This time there was definitely a shape moving towards her from the road. She stood frozen for a moment, not sure what to do.

'Get a grip, girl,' she said under her breath. She peered into the darkness and realised it was a young man. If she went on her way she would walk straight into him. If she ran back and locked herself in the building she would look like a fool. Chances were he was just another student anyway. She decided to stay where she was and watch him as he approached.

'Hi,' he said when she was close enough to see him well.

'Hi,' she replied nervously.

'Sorry. Have I frightened you? I just came to look at the college. My name's Justin Penney.' He extended his hand.

Justin. The third student sharing her office. 'Oh, Justin. I'm Holly Beck—we'll be sharing a room.' She shook his hand lightly. Holly noticed he didn't smile, and found she was smiling too widely to compensate. He didn't respond. She thought it odd, as he didn't seem unfriendly otherwise.

He looked up at the front of the building. 'Wow. It's great, isn't it?'

'Yes. You should see inside. And it smells fantastic.'

'I'll have to wait until tomorrow, I suppose.'

Holly almost mentioned that she had a key but stopped herself at the last moment. She didn't want to go back inside the dark building with a stranger.

'Yeah. They'll give you a key to the main entrance and your office, provided you've got the security deposit.'

'Why are you up here so late?' he asked, turning to her. He was only a few centimetres taller than her, with a shoulder-length mop of brown curls and dark eyes behind small round glasses.

'I fell asleep over a book.' She felt her skin grow hot as she remembered her dream, and was glad that it was too dark for Justin to see her blush. 'I haven't been sleeping so well at home, so I find I'm dozing in the oddest places. How about you?'

'I just stepped off a plane about two hours ago. I've been with my aunt and uncle and I needed some breathing space. I'm staying with them.'

'Where do they live?'

'Just up the road. Mayberry Street,' he replied.

'I'm in Lincoln, round the corner. I'm just on my way home.'

He hesitated a moment, then said quietly, 'I'll walk with you, if you like.'

'Thanks. I know it's only a short way but ...' She shrugged and left her sentence unfinished, not wanting to admit that she was a bit spooked.

He took another look at the college and turned back towards the wide driveway. 'Are you from around here?' he asked as they advanced towards the road.

'No. I'm from a little sugar cane town called Daybrook, about fifty kilometres out of Townsville. How about you?'

'I'm down from Sydney.'

'Are you on a Magnus Humberstone scholarship?'

He shook his head. 'No. It's a little complicated to explain why I'm here.' He fell silent. It made Holly uncomfortable, as though she might have asked the wrong thing.

'I'm on a scholarship,' she offered quietly.

'Really? You must be good—apparently they only offer two a year now. What's your dissertation on?'

'Tennyson's *In Memoriam*. Death and spirituality. And you?'

He buried his hands deeper in his pockets. 'Still deciding. This is ... ah ... a last-minute decision. Coming here, I mean. This time last month my world was very different.'

Again he fell silent. Holly reminded herself not to ask him any more questions. She was already feeling like an unsophisticated country hick, the last thing she needed was to make too many social gaffes.

They were approaching the junction of Lincoln. 'There's another girl in our office,' she said, trying to fill the silence.

'Yes. Prudence. I've heard about her.'

'Oh.' Holly wondered how he knew, but didn't want to risk another uncomfortable silence by asking.

'She started her dissertation last year—apparently they put new students in with the old. She's supposed to help us adjust. Like a prefect.' His lips twitched into a faint smile, but he soon resumed his sombre aspect.

'Well, she doesn't look like a prefect. She has purple hair and a nose ring.' As soon as the words left her lips, Holly realised how conservative she must sound. 'Not that there's anything wrong with—'

'Is this your street?' Justin stopped.

'Yes. There's my place.' She pointed across the road to a large restored Edwardian villa.

'It's nice.'

'That's what I thought. But my flat is behind it, like a converted garage, really. It's draughty and there are bugs.' She shuddered, but she didn't tell him the rest. She didn't tell him that the kitchen smelled bad, that the pipes howled if she turned the hot water on, that the bathroom had no door, and how she had wept when she realised it didn't matter because she was all alone and didn't have to worry about anyone seeing her undress.

'I'm sorry to hear that. Perhaps you should buy some insecticide.'

She shook her head. 'Mrs Partridge—that's my land-lady—won't let me. She says her cats are allergic to it.'

He shrugged. There was a moment of silence as he contemplated Holly's front yard. Finally he said, 'I'll see you tomorrow.'

'Okay,' she replied. He was already turning away. 'Thanks for walking me home.'

'No problem,' he called over his shoulder.

Holly watched him go then turned to head home, feeling like she'd got off on the wrong foot but not sure why.

The airconditioning shuddered and wound down, ticking in the dark until finally there was silence. The long halls and winding staircases of Humberstone College were dark except for the finger of light from one room where a lamp had been left on. All was still.

Then a slow, soft groan bled into the gloom, lapped off the walls and sank into the carpet. The sound was unearthly and mournful, expressive of some kind of unending sorrow. A shape, somewhat blacker than the darkness around it, shivered and faded. The groan sounded once more, distantly, then died away.

Lucien Humberstone awoke screaming and thrashing. The cool, dark reality of his bedroom eased into his consciousness. His wife Emma was leaning over him, her blonde hair straying from the neat plait she wore to bed.

'Lucien? Are you all right?'

He sat up panting, put his hand to his chest. His heart was racing. He waited, taking deep breaths, and it began to slow.

'More nightmares?' Emma asked, leaning across him to switch on the lamp.

He nodded.

'Perhaps you should go to see a psychologist,' Emma suggested. 'It's not normal for—'

'Emma, I don't need to see a psychologist. I've dealt with this problem for long enough, I'm sure I can manage without some nosy pseudo-scientist spouting platitudes at me.'

She looked taken aback, but not angry. 'Can I get you something? A cup of tea?'

'No. No, I'll be all right.' But, as always, the nightmare had reminded him of his worst and most inescapable fear.

The dreams always started in his hands. A shape pressed between his fingers, sticky and elastic. An abyss opening up inside the shape. Frantically he tried to mould it between his hands, give it boundaries, make it square, self-contained, safe. But every time the abyss spilled through his fingers. He had to look away or risk going mad. Turning his face upwards he saw a tiny pinpoint of light miles above, the blackness closing over it like the moon eclipsing the sun. *Am I in my grave then?* The elastic abyss was distorting and stretching outwards and sideways. He dropped it at his feet and started scrabbling at the walls of the pit. Moist soil under his fingernails, darkly glistening creeping things in his hands, the shapeless blackness opening up at his feet, swallowing him, returning him to oblivion.

Emma switched the light off again and gave him a kiss on the cheek. 'Goodnight, Lucien.'

She curled up next to him and within moments was drawing deep, regular breaths. Sinking back into his pillow, he pulled the covers around him and lay staring at the dark ceiling. His flesh seemed to tingle and creep, his mind overwhelmed by the thought that awoke his unspeakable dread.

The thought that one day he would cease to exist.

CHAPTER TWO

⁓

Prudence Emerson and Dr Laurence Aswell shared a cigarette on the west verandah of Humberstone College. They had just had sex over Aswell's expensive mahogany desk, the blinds drawn to keep out prying eyes and the cruel morning sunlight, which Prudence knew made Aswell conscious of his 46-year-old body next to her 22-year-old skin. He needn't have worried, she was besotted with him. His wife and teenage son were all that stood between her and total happiness.

'I liked you better blonde,' Aswell said, touching her hair lightly.

'Boring. I needed a change for the new year.'

'Yes, a new year. What are we going to do about your dissertation, Prudence?'

She raised her eyebrows at him. 'It would be a good start if we didn't shag every time I came to see you.'

Aswell looked around nervously. 'Yes, I suppose you're right.'

'I'll come up with something. Soon.' Prudence handed the cigarette back to Aswell and moved forward to lean on the iron railing. A gentle morning breeze caressed her hair.

She always hated the half-hour or so after sex with As. She was so overwhelmed with emotion that she wanted to hold him, to tell him she loved him and to hear that he loved her. That didn't happen, of course. They were always dressed and out for a smoke on the verandah within five minutes. And he didn't love her. Perhaps he was fond of her, but it wasn't love.

He came to stand beside her and she looked across at him. His blond hair was cut with a long fringe that flopped in his eyes—he was trying to look younger, more hip. He gazed out over the garden. Prudence smiled at his profile, then remembered something she'd been meaning to ask him.

'As, I thought you said that Randolph was in York.'

'He is.'

Prudence noticed he lied without blinking. She supposed he got plenty of practice with his wife. 'I saw an envelope on your desk,' she said. 'A letter from him, from Israel.'

The short silence was almost imperceptible. 'Israel? Oh, yes. Yes, he had a stopover on the way there. A week's holiday. But he's in York now.'

Again Prudence knew he was lying. Professor Randolph Humberstone had been gone six weeks. The postmark on the envelope was dated only a week ago. She didn't pursue it. She would hear the whole story eventually—she always did. Aswell was notoriously bad at keeping secrets from her and she had a talent for prising the most profound confessions out of anyone.

He turned to face her. 'So what do you think of your new room-mates?' he asked.

She shrugged. 'Holly seems okay. I haven't met Justin yet.'

'Holly is a very smart young lady.'

Prudence felt a twinge of jealousy. Holly was also very attractive, with honey-blonde hair, wide green eyes and the kind of slender figure that Prudence had always envied.

And Aswell was her academic supervisor. 'I gathered that. She's on a scholarship, isn't she?'

'Yes. The best application I've ever seen.'

'She's from up north, right?'

'Apparently. Married, or at least separated. I think she left her husband to come here.'

'Married? How old is she?'

'About twenty-five. You'll be the baby. Justin's twenty-seven.'

Prudence fished in her pocket for another cigarette. She offered one to Aswell but he refused.

'And what's the gossip on him?' she asked, taking a drag.

'Be nice to him. He's well connected.'

Prudence grinned. 'For a moment I thought you were going to say well hung.'

'You and your filthy mind,' he said fondly. 'He's living with his uncle and aunt, who are none other than Lucien and Emma Humberstone.'

Prudence's eyes widened. 'Get out of here.' Lucien and Emma were the owners of the college. They had a billion-dollar bank balance and a billion-dollar opinion of themselves to match.

'It's true. Apparently he's some long-lost relative.'

'How intriguing. I'll have to pump him for info.'

Aswell shook his head. 'No, don't. I've been instructed by Lucien not to ask too many questions. He's just been through some kind of family crisis. He didn't know he was related to them until quite recently.'

Prudence smiled. 'And that's supposed to stop me from wanting to ask? Don't get my imagination going, As. You know it's dangerous.'

He took the cigarette from her and pressed it between his lips. 'Yes, I do know. And speaking of your imagination, when you fill Holly and Justin in on the college, leave out the bit about the ghosts.'

'Oh, come on. Noni in the library has always said she thinks it's haunted. There has to be at least one ghost in a building this old. It used to be a convent, for Christ's sake. Maybe there's the spirit of a mad nun roaming the corridors.' Or at least Prudence hoped so. She found the notion wildly thrilling.

'You've been reading too much, Prudence.' Aswell flicked the cigarette butt off the balcony and watched it arc into the garden.

'You'll all change your tune when I'm proved right.'

He ruffled her hair. 'Silly girl, there's no such thing as ghosts.'

Justin stood at the door to room 205, his new office, taking deep breaths and preparing himself to turn the handle. *They don't know, nobody knows.* Everything would be fine. The girl he'd met last night, Holly—she was pleasant, friendly. His aunt was affectionate, even if his uncle could barely conceal his impatience with his newly found nephew. Dr Jane Macintyre, his academic supervisor, had seemed nice enough on the phone. None of them had asked too many questions, he hadn't aroused any excessive interest, all he had to do was relax and get on with his new life. Easy.

Just as he reached for the handle, the door burst open and he found himself confronted by a pretty, hazel-eyed girl with violet hair.

'Sorry,' she said, 'I'm just going downstairs for a Coke. You're Justin, right?'

'Yes.' He tried but he couldn't twitch the corners of his mouth into a smile. *Give me time.*

'Prudence,' she said, extending a hand with glitter-painted fingernails.

Justin took her hand, and rather than shaking it she pulled him down the corridor with her.

'Come on, come with me. Holly's not in yet. Do you want a Coke? I hate financing the multinationals but I'm addicted to the stuff.'

'Um . . . okay.'

'Have you seen the cafe? It's a bit pov but they make great food.'

'I haven't seen anything, I just got here.'

She was leading him down the staircase and into the front foyer. The woman behind the administration counter raised her hand and waved.

'Hi, Prudence.'

'Hi, Allison. This is Justin.'

Justin had time to wave a quick greeting before Prudence dragged him across to the cafeteria and up to the Coke machine. A group of students were laughing loudly at a table nearby. To his relief, Prudence finally dropped his hand.

'What do you want? I'll shout.'

He looked from Prudence to the Coke machine and back again. 'Whatever you're having.' He didn't even feel like a drink, but he sensed that it would be rude to refuse.

She fed some coins into the machine and two cans of Coke clunked into the tray at the bottom. She handed one to him. It was ice-cold.

Prudence leaned her back on the machine and turned to face him as she opened her can. 'So.'

'So.' As uneasy as he felt, he did his best to appear relaxed and natural. He had been acting all his life, really. Sometimes he wondered if there were a real Justin in there—some poor, stunted embryo of a whole person.

'I'll show you and Holly around today. Holly's the other girl sharing our office,' she said.

'I know. I met her last night.'

Prudence raised an eyebrow. 'Last night?'

'Yeah, I came up to have a look just as she was leaving.'

'At night? What time was that?'

'Around nine o'clock. She said she fell asleep over a book.' Justin had the feeling he was saying more than he should, but he didn't know why.

'How interesting.' A smile lifted the corners of her lips. 'She's pretty, isn't she?'

'Sorry?'

'Holly. She's pretty, don't you think?'

'Well, I . . . Yes, I guess so.'

'And smart too. Or so I'm told. Did you know she used to be married? She seems too young to have a broken marriage behind her.'

Justin shrugged, unsure if he was supposed to comment or not.

'You haven't touched your Coke.'

He looked at the can in his hand. 'Sorry.'

'That's fine.' She drained her can then crushed it expertly with one hand. 'Well, I've had my morning sugar fix. I suppose I'd better let you see your office.'

Justin followed Prudence back towards the staircase. Narrow, grimy windows on every floor provided an outlook to the carpark and the street beyond. He paused on the first floor to take in the scene, but Prudence had stopped a few stairs above him, waiting. A solitary exploration would have to wait until some other time.

She showed him back to their office. Three desks were arranged around the room. Prudence's was under the window, looking out over the back garden. Justin's and Holly's were in opposite corners. The room was newly carpeted in a nondescript beige, but the fancy scrollwork around the skirting and that indefinable musty smell of past years betrayed the building's true age. Holly's desk was already stacked with books. Prudence's was largely empty except for two books, an oil burner and a collection of half-melted coloured candles. A huge Tea Party poster was pinned to her noticeboard.

'So, do you like your new office?' Prudence was asking.

19

Justin sat down at his empty desk and placed his Coke can on the top. 'It's fine.'

She perched on the edge of his desk. 'I'm writing about Oscar Wilde. How about you?'

He looked up at her. She asked so many questions it was starting to make him feel uncomfortable. But the way she looked at him, her eyes so unwaveringly focussed on his, that friendly smile playing at the corner of her cupid's-bow mouth—it was impossible not to answer. 'I'm still deciding. Coming here wasn't in my grand scheme, it's all been a bit of a surprise.'

'Oh?'

'Lucien and Emma were kind enough to offer me a place when my . . . other plans fell through.'

'You know Lucien and Emma?'

'Yes. I'm a relation. A nephew.' He looked down at the desk top before he said too much. Condensation beaded the outside of his drink can and was starting to form a little puddle on the wood. Prudence seemed to sense that she'd probed far enough for the time being and moved back to her desk.

'When Holly comes in I'll show you both around. Okay?'

'Okay. Thanks.' He heard her settle behind her desk and open a book. The room fell silent for a while. He could hear a lawnmower outside in the distance and the slapping of a wire against a flagpole.

'Justin?'

He looked around. 'Yes?'

'Are you going to sit there staring at the desk all morning?'

'I . . .'

She strode across the room to Holly's desk and grabbed a book which she handed to him. 'Here. Entertain yourself.' She dropped down again behind her own desk and went back to scribbling notes in a folder.

Justin opened the book, a complete works of Tennyson. On the inside front cover 'Holly Beck' had been inscribed, then crossed out, with 'Holly Torrance' in its place. Clearly she hadn't yet got around to changing her books back to her maiden name. Justin wondered how Prudence had come by the information of Holly's failed marriage so quickly. He needed to be wary of what he said to Prudence. He had too many secrets to keep. If she got near the edges of one she'd haul it wriggling into the daylight, those pretty eyes smiling benevolently all the time. He had to take care.

Holly found it hard to get going in the morning on only four hours' sleep. Perhaps it was idealistic to expect things to fall perfectly into place so soon, but surely a good night's sleep wasn't too much to ask for. Unused as she was to any kind of cool weather, the early morning draughts that crept under her door were like icy fingers prodding her as she tried to sleep. And it was only March—winter was going to kill her. As soon as her first scholarship payment went into her bank account, she had to get out and buy herself the fattest doona on the market. Until then, she had barely enough to buy bread and milk. She tried not to think about the old Queenslander she and Michael had been renting back home, the long humid summer days spent on the verandah watching the cane fields shimmer under the vaulting, endlessly blue sky. Tried not to think about Michael at all, and that awful pain in his eyes when she told him it was over, that high-school sweethearts didn't always live happily ever after and that there was something in the world beyond him which she needed to make her fulfilled. She busied herself getting showered and dressed in order to distract herself from that sad little ache in her chest. How tragic that all she had to offer Michael in the end was pity.

Locking the front door of her flat behind her, Holly stepped into a soft autumn breeze. Fat white clouds scudded overhead. She walked up to the college grounds and admired it from the winding driveway, framed by trees. What a perfect moment of promise, thought Holly, looking at the elegant, high-Victorian lines of the building standing proud between bowing trees, the wide green garden basking in the gentle autumn sun. Perhaps she could get used to any kind of discomfort to have moments like this—she could just *exist* in between them, and really *live* when her senses suddenly awoke to the beauty around her.

The deep, woody smell of the place enveloped her when she got inside. She stopped at the drink machine and agonised for a few moments about the dollar it would cost to buy a can of lemonade, before deciding against it and heading upstairs to her new office. She had already planned what she would do today. There was a stack of articles she could photocopy out of periodicals in the library, then she could spend the afternoon and the evening going through their bibliographies, highlighting references that looked like they may help her. Tomorrow she could start some reading. She had a couple of empty notebooks waiting and her fingers were itching to fill them, to possess that enormous sense of gratification from putting the first marks on the page with a new pen. The start of the process, the moment of infinite promise.

Prudence and Justin were already in. Prudence was sitting on the deep window sill with her back against the glass and her feet on a chair. They both looked up as she came in, but Prudence soon turned her attention back to her notebook.

'Hi,' Holly said to both of them and neither of them.

'Hi,' Justin answered, standing up. 'Here, I borrowed this.' He handed over her complete works of Tennyson and she took it with some surprise.

'Oh. Thanks.'

'You look like you've got a good start,' he said, indicating her desk with a dip of his head.

She looked to her desk then back at his, which was completely empty except for an unopened drink can. 'You do know where the library is, don't you?' That didn't sound like an insult, did it?

'We've been waiting for you to come in. Prudence is going to show us around.'

Holly looked over to Prudence. 'Do you have time? I can show Justin the library and the catalogue if you'd prefer.'

Prudence shrugged. 'I've got time, I suppose.' She lifted herself off the window sill. 'Wait here, I'll go get the master keys off As so I can show you the clock tower.'

She whisked past them and out into the hallway. Justin watched her go.

'I don't think she's too excited about giving us this grand tour,' Holly said.

'It's strange. I thought she was looking forward to it. She was bouncing around all morning until you came in.'

Holly felt her stomach dip. Great, Prudence didn't like her. 'I don't know what I've done to upset her. I only met her yesterday.'

Justin turned to her. 'I wouldn't worry about it. It's probably something completely unrelated to you. Did you have trouble with the bugs last night?'

'The bugs?' She was momentarily confused, then remembered she had told Justin about her miserable flat. 'Oh. Yes. Something landed in my hair at around one a.m. and I couldn't get back to sleep until after sunrise. I've only slept about four hours.' Her mind was elsewhere, trying to figure out why Prudence wouldn't like her.

In a whirl of silver jewellery and purple tie-dye, Prudence came back into the office. She dangled the keys in front of them. 'Come on,' she said. 'You're going to love this place.'

The three of them stood on the narrow walkway that skirted the roof of Humberstone College. The maintenance crew used it to access the crumbling tiles and the modern airconditioning duct, which was shoved unceremoniously through the ceiling past the clock tower. They were up high enough to catch the sweet autumn breeze, and the sun glinted off their hair.

'Okay,' Prudence said, pulling out a cigarette and offering the packet around. Holly and Justin refused. She lit up and gazed out over the rooftops of the surrounding villas for a few seconds, preparing to give the spiel that she'd been given by As nearly a year ago.

'Okay,' she repeated. 'Humberstone was built in 1857 as St Anne's Anglican Convent. The guy who designed it was Howard Humberstone. He was running from some scandal in London where he was a well-paid architect, and decided to try his fortune in the colonies. Most accounts paint him as a bit mad, but that's the Humberstones. Years and years of marrying your cousins and . . .' She paused, suddenly remembering that Justin was part of the family. 'Just ignore that last remark,' she said.

Justin look momentarily perplexed, then seemed to realise that she was talking to him. 'Oh. Don't worry. I'm hardly part of the family, really.'

'Part of the family?' Holly turned to him curiously.

'Yeah, Justin's uncle is Lucien Humberstone,' Prudence said to fill in the gap created by Justin's resolute silence. 'Sorry, Justin. I didn't think it was a secret.'

'It's not a secret,' he said, almost too quickly. Prudence knew the signs. There was a secret all right. She could smell it.

'Please continue,' Holly said, sensing Justin's discomfort.

'Right. So the convent didn't go so well. A bout of typhoid wiped out half of the nuns in 1864, and most of the others were relocated to Sydney. The Humberstones back in London heard about it—they were a big banking family with squillions of pounds—and they decided to buy the building. At the time they were buying up all of Howard's work, I don't know why. They sent over heaps of books, mainly the overflow from their own libraries which they were cataloguing, and by 1867 it was Humberstone Library and it stayed that way for a long time.'

Prudence mashed her cigarette butt into the railing and flicked it into the garden. 'Want to see the clock tower?' she asked.

'Sure,' Holly said. 'You're going to tell the rest of the story, right?'

'I guess. Come on.' She led them down the walkway to the tower, then fiddled with the bulky set of keys, trying to find the right one. This was the first place she and Aswell had made love. They had been staying back late, sharing a cigarette on the balcony and discussing Oscar Wilde. She had been slow to fall for him—after all, he was more than twice her age and she usually preferred the young, dumb ones. But he was intellectual and accomplished and self-possessed, and he had a way of looking at her—grey eyes just burning into the back of her skull, a half a smile that made her catch her breath. He had proposed a visit to the roof. For the view, he'd said. They'd sat on the maintenance path with their legs dangling over the railing, comfortably close, talking in low voices, with the lights of the city spread out like jewels on a dark carpet before them. During a particularly long silence he'd caught her eyes with his—one of those electric moments. Twenty minutes later she was getting her gear off and taking a tumble behind the dusty work-ings of a 140-year-old clock.

She found the key and opened the door to let Holly and Justin in. She stood leaning at the door. 'This thing is always breaking down. Once a month on average. Won't be long before—' She stopped, realising again that she was limited in what she could say in front of Justin. The fact was, Lucien Humberstone was so tight with his money that he made repairs reluctantly and cheaply. She had no doubt that one afternoon the clock would stop at four and stay there until Judgement Day.

'In the twenties the Humberstone fortunes took a bit of a downturn. They couldn't afford to maintain the library so they had it boarded up. It stayed like that for about forty years, until one of them could be bothered to have a look at the place. In the sixties, Magnus Hum-berstone came over and catalogued the volumes. He found it to be a wellspring of material—fascinating Vic-torian tracts and treatises on every topic, priceless first editions, books long out of print. At first he allowed other universities to use the library for research, then he got the idea that he'd like to spend some of his millions on making it a college. But none of the Australian univer-sities were interested in a centre specifically for Victorian studies—art, literature, history, politics—which is what he was really into. He had two PhDs, wrote about twenty books on Victorian culture. He had a passion for it, I guess, and he wouldn't compromise his plans. Anyway, the upshot is he cut a deal with Kingsbury University in York to auspice the college for a fee. That's why we're part of the British education system, and that's why Hum-berstone has such a reputation for elitism. That and the fact that only the very rich can get in if they're not very smart.'

Justin had made himself comfortable cross-legged on the floor. Holly stood beside him, her arms folded in front of her. Prudence ached a little seeing how pretty she was. And she seemed nice too. Perhaps too nice. Perhaps a bit of a wimp. Surely As would never be interested in a wimp—he admired guts, verve. The things Prudence knew she had in buckets.

'Is he still around?' Holly asked.

'Sorry?'

'Magnus Humberstone. Is he still around?'

Prudence shook her head. 'He died in 1994. A real pity, because apparently he was the driving force behind everything. He established the scholarships; there used to be ten a year but now it's been cut back to two. And now most people pay to come here. Like me. My father pays for me to be here so I don't embarrass him by joining a circus or something.'

Justin had clearly seen enough of the back of the clock. He pulled himself to his feet and squeezed past Prudence at the door to take a wander up the other side of the path. She watched him go—strange, sombre thing.

'I'm on a scholarship,' Holly said.

'I know.' *You'd be surprised what I know.* 'Congrats. They're hard to come by. Unfortunately my sister got all the brains.'

'I'm sure you must have brains, too.'

'She passed her law degree at the top of the class. I flunked very early and had to change to arts. It sucks being twins.' Prudence watched Justin as he slowly turned and headed back towards them.

'Do you like As?' she asked Holly. She had to know.

'As? I'm sorry, who's As?'

'Laurence. Laurence Aswell, your academic supervisor.'

'Oh. He seems nice. He spoke very highly of you.'

A warm tingle washed through Prudence. Maybe her worry was unfounded. Perhaps Holly wasn't a threat at all, perhaps she could even be an ally.

Justin rejoined them and stood looking at Prudence

27

expectantly. 'Go on,' he said. 'After Magnus?'

'Graham, his son, took over. Kept things running pretty much the same but he didn't last long, unfortunately. Went out fishing one day and never came back.' She noticed Justin flinch slightly. Bingo. Justin must be Graham's son, illegitimate or something. This was getting more and more interesting every moment. 'They never found the body, but it was assumed he'd drowned. Lucien, his brother, took over. Have you met Lucien yet, Holly?'

Holly shook her head.

'He's okay, I guess. But perhaps we should ask Justin for the low-down.'

Justin shrugged. 'You've known him longer than me. Ask me again in a couple of weeks.'

'Sure.' Prudence took a last look over the rooftops. 'Okay, let's go downstairs.'

They clattered down the stairs to the bottom floor and Prudence took them past the cafe and over to the opposite stair tower. Fading yellow tape marked the area off and a danger sign hung limply from it. Prudence took a look over her shoulder, then lifted the tape and ducked under it. She turned to see the two of them staring at her from the other side.

'Come on,' she said.

'What's the danger sign for?' Holly asked warily.

'This part of the tower is crumbling. The stairs are a bit dodgy. But we're not going up the stairs. Come on, before somebody sees.' She beckoned again. Justin and Holly looked at each other, then seemed to decide at one accord to follow her.

They went into the tower and around to the bottom of the stairs. Prudence led them to an alcove on the other side of the stairwell. Rather than being decorated with plants and pre-Raphaelite prints like the other stairwells, this one was marked by peeling wallpaper and creaking floorboards. Around the side of the stairwell was a door. 'It goes to the cellar,' Prudence said, sorting through the keys again.

'Is it safe down there?' Holly asked.

'Probably.' She inserted a key into the lock and opened the door. Holly looked sceptical. 'Hey, relax. We're not going in. It's just a dingy room that smells funny.'

'Sounds like my flat,' Holly remarked dryly.

'You can see it fine from up here.' Prudence felt around on the inside wall for a light switch. There was a flick but no light came on. 'Great, the bulb's burned out.'

'Is it used for storage?' Justin asked.

'No, it's not used for anything. It's tiny and there's rising damp.' She swung the door closed again and locked it. She turned to look at them earnestly. 'But I bet the nuns used it to store bodies.'

There was a moment of stunned silence as they tried to work out if she was serious or not.

'Bodies?' Holly looked amused.

'Sure. Aborted foetuses. Wicked nuns that would bring disrepute on the convent.'

'How Gothic.'

'So you think there are ghosts here, Prudence?' Justin asked. He seemed deadly serious, but she was getting used to that.

'Without a doubt. What old building doesn't have them? People have already said the library's haunted. You can check the stacks before closing time and all the books will be shelved, then come in the next day to find two or three books on the floor. Probably some tragic nun with a broken heart.'

'Or some tragic post-grad with a deadline,' Justin remarked. He still didn't smile. Prudence was intrigued by him, utterly, utterly intrigued. Perhaps this year was going to be good after all. Perhaps she could even make a friend or two, that would be novel.

'Right,' she said, shoving the keys into her pocket. 'Who fancies a coffee?'

CHAPTER THREE

⁓

Midnight.

Drizzle misted over Lucien and Emma as they huddled under a black umbrella and scurried towards the back entrance of the dark college. Emma held the umbrella while Lucien found the right key for the door. The sky was heavy with clouds and it looked like the rain was going to set in for a few days.

The door sprang open and Lucien ushered Emma in before taking one last look around outside to check that nobody was watching. He locked the building behind him. Emma shook the umbrella and leaned it against the wall. They went up the stairs to the third floor where Lucien kept an office which he rarely used. Jane Macintyre was already waiting outside the office door, yawning.

'Good evening, Jane,' Lucien said, unlocking the door and reaching for the light switch. The bright light contrasted with the dark, wet street outside.

Lucien entered the room first, laying his expensive leather briefcase on his desk.

Jane went to a cupboard. The door squeaked open. 'I'll get the candles,' she offered.

'In the very bottom at the back. Behind the books.'
He turned to Emma. 'Go make us a pot of tea, Emma.
Laurence should be here very soon, unless he's slept
through his alarm again.'

Emma nodded and left the office. Lucien heard her
bustling about in the kitchenette next door.

Jane emerged from the cupboard with a handful of
black candles. She was an attractive brunette in her late
thirties, with a tight little body that Lucien found his eyes
drawn to over and over again. Emma was getting too big.
She insisted on living on a diet of the most voluptuous
foods. He found it offensive that she could exercise no
self-control.

'Found them,' Jane proclaimed, placing the candles on
Lucien's desk. 'Hey, I met your nephew today. I liked
him a lot but he's a bit too serious, don't you think?'

Lucien felt himself stiffen. His nephew. If it wasn't
for that clause in Magnus's will, Justin would have
remained forever unknown. By Magnus's eightieth
birthday, when he realised there were going to be no
other heirs to perpetuate his branch of the family tree,
the old man had started talking obsessively about Graham's son. It was only at Lucien's persistent urging that
Justin wasn't contacted immediately. The mother had
only been a brief fling for Graham, and a substantial
payment for her silence and absence had already been
made. Fearing more demands, Lucien had decided to
wait until her death. It had come sooner than expected.
Now with Justin here it felt like there was a crack in
the system somewhere—the lad was a wild card. 'Don't
get too attached to him,' Lucien said. 'He's young and
he's not sure about himself. He could decide tomorrow
that he wants to run off to trek in Nepal.' Wishful
thinking.

Emma was back with a tea tray. 'Justin's mother died
recently,' she said to Jane as she poured a cup of tea. 'He's

having some difficulty bouncing back from that. We need to treat him gently.' She cast an accusing glance at Lucien, who ignored it. It was evident that Emma had a soft spot for Justin. Lucien sometimes wondered if she deliberately disagreed with him over small things just to annoy him.

The door swung inwards and Aswell stepped in, his hair drenched. He extricated himself from his raincoat and hung it over the back of a chair as Emma hurried over with a cup of tea for him.

'Sorry I'm a bit late. The car wouldn't start. It's bucketing down out there.'

Lucien went to the window and stared out. Beyond his reflection he could see the rain was now coming down in sheets. He sipped at his tea gratefully and Emma snuggled under his arm. Jane and Aswell were talking in low voices by the desk. It felt good to be inside while the weather outside was so inclement. In a rare moment of tenderness, Lucien kissed the top of Emma's head and gave her an affectionate squeeze. Maybe he could relax. Maybe everything would turn out all right. He wished he could see just one year into the future, because surely by this time next year the deed would have been done and he would not be waking to dreams of torment any longer. That inescapable dread would have left him for good. Only a few hurdles to get over in the meantime, and he could face anything—he knew he could—if the result was an end to his fear of death.

He let Emma go and turned around, handing her his teacup. 'Laurence, pull up a few chairs, will you? We'd better get started or we'll be here till dawn.'

As Aswell arranged a few chairs in a circle, Lucien went to his briefcase and flipped it open and, with some reverence, retrieved the remains of Peter Owling's book of shadows.

Kept in a black leather folder, the dirty pages were well

worn and almost ruined with age. Through a large part of the book a bloodstained puncture defaced the writing. The fragment that Magnus Humberstone had stumbled across in an antique store in New York was in the best condition, while the pages Magnus had spent twenty years and thousands of dollars tracking down from Peru to Guyana were, in some places, unreadable. Lucien shuddered to think what condition the fragment Randolph was pursuing in Israel would be in, but he just hoped it was the last piece. How could he bear it if there were another ten years or more stretching out ahead of him as they searched for more?

The others were sitting down, looking at him expectantly. He snapped the briefcase shut and came to sit with them, the book in his long pale hands. He stole a glance at Jane, who sat opposite him, her legs crossed demurely.

'As you know, I've been working on pages 255 to 289, the last part of the Guyana fragment. Though it's barely legible, I made a breakthrough this week. We can safely say that the method for summoning entities outlined in the first fragment was superseded in his later work. Clearly this book is a living record of his work, so we shouldn't be surprised to find such an unprecipitated change of technique. Here, see this word?' He carefully turned the volume around so that the others could see the word above his fingertip. Aswell and Jane leaned in to peer at it, but Emma glanced at it uninterestedly before gazing vacantly out the window. Lucien felt a barb of anger.

'What's it say? Is it a name?' Aswell asked.

'Tro . . . No, is that a "u" or an "r"?' Jane's eyebrows drew together.

Lucien turned the book back to himself. 'Traitor. It says traitor. This word casts light on the remaining thirty pages of the Guyana fragment, and makes me twice as eager to see the next part.'

'If Randolph finds it,' Emma interjected.

'Randolph will find it,' Lucien replied sternly. He knew he sounded more confident than he felt.

'I have a letter from Randolph,' Aswell said, fishing a soggy envelope out of his pocket.

Lucien had to bite a breath back between his teeth. Between Emma, fat and docile in the corner, and Aswell, bedraggled and halfwitted across from him, he wondered how this project was ever going to be successfully completed. Only Jane still had her mind on the subject. She offered him a reassuring smile. Ah, the delight of unspoken communication between like minds.

'We'll get to Randolph's letter,' he said patiently. 'First things first.'

'What does Owling mean by "traitor"?' Jane asked.

'As I said, this marks a radical shift in Owling's approach. Unfortunately it's accompanied by a radical shift in his handwriting. I've been deciphering his work for so long, it's been hard for me to readjust. But I think there's a reason for the change in his writing too. I think that Owling had started receiving material help at this stage.'

'Material help?' Jane asked.

'Yes. Of course we know that much of Owling's work was dictated to him by a variety of spirits, but it seems by this stage one of the spirits was guiding his hand.'

'You mean automatic writing? Like Led Zeppelin?' said Aswell.

'Except this isn't "Stairway To Heaven",' Jane remarked dryly. 'I rather think we may be heading in the other direction.' She turned back to Lucien. 'Go on.'

'The spirit is certainly not one of the Klipothic demons. Its name is not recorded and Owling's own handwriting resumes in parts to write of his frustration with the being. But it appears to have offered some important insight to Owling with his project. The idea of a traitor.'

'I don't follow,' Aswell said.

Lucien was unsurprised. Aswell had been staring at Jane's thigh for the last three minutes.

'In the New York fragment, Owling made it quite clear that the Klipothic entities work together, forming a safety net around the source of their power. Even when they are summoned singly, they have a sense of group solidarity. The being that Owling has made contact with mentions the dark Klipoth, or the shadow demons. I thought that this was just another name for the entities about which we already knew, but evidence that I've just decoded suggests otherwise. There is another group of entities, jealous of the primary Klipoth's relation to their monarch, waiting in the wings.'

'Demons-in-waiting,' Emma noted indifferently. Her scepticism about the project was wearing Lucien's patience thin.

'Demons-in-waiting, maybe, but demons lacking a consistent code of ethics. Demons who may be persuaded to betray their monarch. To play the traitor and deliver Satan himself into our hands.' At moments like these, Lucien always wished that other people weren't such impenetrable oubliettes. What were they thinking? These meetings had been happening for years. They dated back to Magnus's time, though Jane and Aswell hadn't been around then. Emma was sceptical, but went along with Lucien out of duty. Aswell was loyal and hardworking, but sometimes Lucien wondered if his interest was born out of boy's-own-adventure fantasies, rather than any firm belief in the benefits of Satanic ritual. And then there was Jane. Smart, decisive, gutsy, never flinching at what needed to be done, her generous mouth set firmly as she accepted the most grandiose and ambitious of Owling's suggestions as though they were pure common sense.

'Do you really think we can do it, Lucien?' Jane asked.

'There is nothing more important to me than this,' he replied, his naked honesty surprising even himself. 'We

35

must try, at the very least. Better to regret what we did do than what we didn't, don't you think?'

She smiled at him, a little too kindly, and he realised he must have seemed too intense, had maybe even betrayed his powerful attraction to her. He slammed the grimoire shut and hastily turned to Aswell.

'That's all for now. I want to look over the rest of that fragment again with this knowledge in mind, and I'll report to you next week. Randolph's letter?'

'Ah, yes. He's in Jerusalem.' Aswell was unfolding the letter and smoothing it out on his lap.

Lucien could feel his pulse beating too hard in his throat. Desire was an uncontrollable child, screaming and kicking and demanding to be noticed at the most inopportune moments. He reminded himself that Jane was not important, only the grimoire was important.

'Go on,' Lucien said. 'Read us the letter.'

'Okay.'

Dear Laurence, et al.

I have come to Jerusalem on the advice of a very strange fellow I met in Eilat. He was a one-eyed Jew, whose grandfather practised magic in Germany before moving here prior to the Holocaust. The old man is dead now, but apparently he had often mentioned to his grandson the existence of a strange set of papers—the 'dark fragment', he called it—which were supposedly somewhere in the Old City of Jerusalem. Unfortunately that was the limit of his knowledge, but I have given him my address should he find out anything further.

I arrived here yesterday and I've rented an apartment called Lev Yerushalayim *in the new city. It's a lot cleaner and safer here than the Old City, I think, and I'm still close enough to spend plenty of time in there exploring, provided I can abide the smell of the taxi drivers for the duration of the ride.*

The Old City is like a warren designed by dyslexic rabbits, but I took a stroll around the ramparts today to get a better idea of its size and scope. It's not a big place, but its topography is going to make it very hard to find anything. I think six weeks in Israel is starting to wear me down, and I hope I'm not placing an unnecessary faith in my informant. I want to find this fragment and bring it home.

I will write again soon to let you know how I'm faring.
Yours, Randolph.

Lucien was excited. The search had been narrowed down to one city, and a small one at that. He took the letter from Aswell and quickly scanned through it again.

'Good, good. Now we're getting somewhere. We are all . . . getting somewhere.' He readjusted his glasses on his nose and rubbed his hands together. 'Time for a little ritual?'

The others began to move their chairs out of the way while Lucien carefully laid the grimoire back in his briefcase. Then Aswell took one end of Lucien's desk while Lucien took the other, and together they heaved it about a metre from its original position so that the ends of the Persian rug on the floor were completely exposed. Jane bent to roll up the rug and pushed it into a corner. It was evident now that a neat square had been cut in the carpet. Aswell picked up the corner and began to roll it back, exposing the floorboards and the huge symbol painted on them. It was a large circle with a snake coiling three times at its outer perimeter, some ancient Hebrew inscribed on it in yellow paint. Inside the circle was a series of five- and six-pointed stars, and outside was a triangle with the words *anaphaxeton*, *primeumaton* and *tetragrammaton* written on each side. It was a fairly standard Goetic circle, except for the special addition that they had made on the advice of their long-dead mentor. Barely visible against the floorboards, beneath the circle, each one of them—Lucien,

Emma, Jane, Aswell and Randolph—had written in their own blood: 'I revoke my saviour.'

Jane had placed the black candles around the room and lit them. Aswell hit the lights and they were plunged into candlelight. Jane, Emma and Aswell settled cross-legged on the floor around the circle. For a few moments it was very quiet, except for the rain beating on the window.

Lucien came to join them and eased himself down to the floor. Everyone was silent as they centred themselves, then Lucien's voice cut through the gloom. 'Emma?'

Her voice soft around the edges, like her body: 'I revoke my saviour.'

'Laurence?'

'I revoke my saviour.'

'Jane?'

She held his eyes momentarily, her pupils enormous and black in the candlelight. Then plainly, assuredly: 'I revoke my saviour.' She smiled. 'And you, Lucien?'

His saviour. The one who withheld the most dire information from him with only the flimsiest of assurances that he would discover the truth, and then only after he had suffered the agony of unknowing, the terror of mortality.

'Why, of course. Of course I revoke my saviour.'

Prudence was very, very pissed. As she fumbled at the front door to get her key in the lock, she started to suspect that she had just given the cab driver a ten-dollar tip, and that was after he had spent the entire cab ride trying to convert her to some fundamentalist Christian religion.

The lock gave and she stumbled inside out of the rain. Julia hadn't left the light on and she found herself groping in darkness for the switch. She banged her shin on the edge of a coffee table.

'Ow, fuck.' Okay, so she was a long way from the light switch, but she must be close to a lounge chair. She felt around and eased herself into a chair, put her feet on the coffee table and closed her eyes. A coloured wheel of memory rolled out in her mind's eye. Had she really let that guy grope her tits? Well, he was kind of cute, but she had her doubts that he was over sixteen. The Pit was notorious for being lax on under-age drinkers. Never mind, at least she hadn't fucked him. Partly because she was incapable of undressing herself in this state.

Suddenly lights blazed on around her and she warily opened her eyes. Julia stood in front of her, looking like she knew everything. Like she always looked.

'Hey, I was just dropping off,' Prudence protested.

'Yeah, well, I was fast asleep until a herd of elephants woke me.'

'A herd of . . .? Oh, sorry. Was I noisy?'

'You can't sleep there, Prudence. Look at you, you're soaked. Have a warm shower and go to bed.'

Prudence shook her head. 'My fingers won't work.'

Julia sighed and leaned over to pull Prudence to her feet. 'Come on. Jeez, Prudence, I don't know why you get yourself so wasted.'

'It's Sunday night. The Pit does dollar drinks.'

'It's Monday morning. The sun'll be up shortly.' Julia was marching her towards the bathroom. Prudence loved her and hated her. Loved her because she was smart and successful and capable; hated her because she was a constant reminder of how Prudence looked before she had started experimenting with hair dye, make-up and facial piercing. Looking at her was like remembering what a boring person she really was underneath it all.

The bathroom light was too bright. Prudence leaned on the basin while Julia turned the shower on and let the water heat up.

'You're good to me, Julia.'

'Yeah, right. Here, get out of this thing.' Julia untied Prudence's red velvet bodice and began to pull the laces out. 'Oh, Prudence, I think you've spilled wine on this— it smells awful and there's a big stain on it.'

'God, no. It cost over a hundred bucks.'

'Well, if you're going to buy expensive clothes you really should take care of them.'

'Fuck. Why are you always *right*?'

'Don't swear.'

'Fuck, fuck, fuck,' she said as Julia stripped her out of her bodice and long black skirt. 'Thanks, Julia.'

'You're welcome.'

'What would I do without you?'

'You'll soon find out.'

'Huh?'

Julia took a deep breath and sat down on the edge of the bath. 'I'm moving out, Prudence. I've been offered a transfer to the States. Boston. I got the call this afternoon.'

'You're . . .?'

'I'll be leaving at the end of March. You'll have the whole house to yourself.'

Prudence shook her head. 'What, is this a conspiracy or something? Has the whole family been planning since birth to desert me?'

'Don't be silly. Get in the shower, Prudence, and wash that make-up off. You look like a raccoon.'

Prudence stripped out of her underwear and stepped under the warm water, pulling the shower curtain across. She turned her face up to the shower head and let it wash her make-up away. 'So can I get a housemate?'

'You know Dad and Mum wouldn't like that.'

'They're in fucking Hong Kong. They wouldn't even know.'

'What? I can't hear you.'

Prudence leaned out from behind the shower curtain. 'They're in Hong Kong. As if they'd find out.'

Julia shook her head. 'They'd want you to be mature about this.'

'They wouldn't want me to be lonely.'

'You lonely? You've got a million friends.'

'But no close ones. You're the only person I can really talk to.'

Julia smiled. 'That's sweet, Prudence, but I'm going back to bed. We'll talk about this tomorrow—I mean later today. Goodnight.'

'Yeah, goodnight.'

Julia left and Prudence sagged against the tiles under the shower. Great. First her father had to go and get a professorship at Hong Kong University, now Julia was moving to America. And Prudence was going to be left alone in the family home—six bedrooms and an en suite of misery. She was only twenty-two—she wished people would stop treating her like an adult.

'"Alone, alone,"' she murmured under her breath. Perhaps a law degree would have got her a stable career, but studying English literature was always good for finding quotes to describe various states of melancholy. '"All, all alone."'

CHAPTER FOUR

⁓

When the shadows started to deepen around her, Holly realised she had been reading for four hours without a break. Justin had left at three and Prudence hadn't been in at all. The silence had been conducive to uninterrupted work, but now as she reached up to switch on her desk lamp she noticed a tight feeling behind her eyes. Perhaps she'd overdone it.

She surveyed the notebook in front of her, its pages filled with her neat, exact writing. She picked up a pen and began to doodle in the corner of a page—a little creature with two fat feet and a round body. A vast yawn stuck in her throat. Sleep was still eluding her at home. Maybe she needed to get out from behind her desk and stretch her legs.

The corridor outside her office was gloomy but not yet dark. The college was quiet, and Holly wondered if she were the only person left for the day. It was a delicious thought, having the whole building to herself. Rain beat heavily on the roof and eaves. She took the stairs up to the third floor and walked past Dr Aswell's office. No light under the door, he'd probably gone home a long time ago. Right down the end of the corridor was Lucien Humberstone's office. Prudence had said it was palatial: 'Like the tardis, man, bigger on the inside than it looks on the outside.' Holly had seen neither the inside of the office nor Lucien Humberstone himself, though Prudence said he'd be hard to miss if he passed in the corridor—a towering man with pale skin and a halo of thick curls.

She kept walking. What a relief that Prudence hadn't been in today. She rarely stopped talking for a moment, and seemed not to care at all about working on her dissertation. The previous morning Holly had had to take refuge in the library for a few hours because Prudence was upset about her sister moving overseas and her chosen form of therapy was to bitch about it continually. It wasn't that Holly didn't like Prudence—she did—but she seemed a little young and a little spoiled, and she required so much attention it was almost exhausting. Very different from the stand-offish girl she had appeared to be at first. Perhaps it would have been better if Prudence had stayed that way.

Be careful what you wish for.

She came to the stairwell and began to descend, stopping as she reached the grimy window to the outside world. Justin was a lot easier to deal with than Prudence. Probably because he was older and kept to himself so much, but also because he seemed intuitive and empathetic. Justin had a first degree in art history, so he had decided to work on Dante Gabriel Rossetti. He had quietly asked Holly for a recommendation on Rossetti's poetry that afternoon, and she had lent him one of her anthologies, her favourite pieces helpfully marked with stick-on notes. His very sincere thank-you was almost touching—not embarrassingly profuse, just the gratitude of a person who seemed unaccustomed to receiving help.

Sighing, she sank to the stair and leaned her forehead on the glass. Twilight was well advanced outside and the rain looked like it would never stop. Her eyes felt heavy.

All she wanted was to put her head down, somewhere with clean, fresh linen, somewhere warm where the space around her was her own and not encroached upon by creeping bugs. The raindrops flashed silver and gold in the beam of the security lights. She was dreading the walk home, dreading getting home too. The damp seemed to be rising out of the ground and into her flat, making the whole place cold and dank. She yawned again, stood up and began to walk back to her office.

Prudence had a large, fat cushion on her chair which Holly lifted off and placed on the floor. She grabbed her complete works of Tennyson and lay down on the carpet, glad to take the pressure off her neck and shoulders. Tucked up on her side, she opened the book where she had last marked it and began to read. Twenty minutes later she realised she was dropping off to sleep. She forced her eyes open and concentrated on the page. '"I think we are not wholly brain,"' she read aloud, as though her voice could ward off the dozy feeling. '"Magnetic mockeries; not in vain."' Her eyes closed again, but this time she relished the darkness. Perhaps it was no use fighting. '"Not only cunning casts in clay,"' she murmured. Scrambled thoughts bled into her consciousness—the divine warm shadow of approaching sleep. Half a dream, blurred edges. Holly collapsed into it willingly.

A warm, moist pressure moving around her throat, her ears. Feather-light touches across her skin. The poem had made her think of clay, that's how she felt. Like a clay creature being moulded by the irresistible firm hands of a lover. His hot fingertips crept up her skirt, inched under the elastic of her underwear and were lost in the soft folds of her flesh. Was that somebody groaning in the distance, or was it herself? Wakefulness was rushing on her too fast and she fought to keep its tide at bay.

'Who are you?' her dream voice asked, her clay tongue heavy.

No answer. A hot mouth over her nipple, as though he were moulding her breasts with his lips. Those fingertips at first maddeningly light, then recklessly bold. The pressure built and built until suddenly it felt as if the world were a sand dune collapsing beneath her, and she shuddered in orgasm.

'Who are you?' she asked again, realising her body was not clay, ascending into consciousness.

The lips closed over hers and he whispered his name into her mouth. Then there was a cold space where his mouth had been and Holly opened her eyes to find she was alone.

She sat up slowly and looked around. The muscles in her thighs were twitching and she could smell the faint scent of her own arousal. Tennyson lay open on the carpet next to her. Already the dream was retreating down a dark alley in her mind, but the sensations reverberated through her nerve endings.

She felt slightly foolish, yet pleasantly satisfied. They were a nice way to deal with her lack-of-sex problem, these spontaneous erotic encounters with a skilled dream lover. And he had a name—what was it? She closed her eyes again, remembered the pressure of his lips on hers, the warm breath that spelled his name.

'Ah, yes,' she said to the dark. 'Christian.'

Holly's heart sank a little the next morning when she saw Prudence sitting on the window sill, dressed all in green velvet. Did this mean she was going to spend a day listening to a steady litany about her sister's imminent departure? She braced herself, but Prudence merely looked up from the book she was reading and smiled, then went straight back to it. Holly dropped her books on her desk and started work.

Forty-five minutes later, when Prudence still hadn't

said a word, Holly started to get curious. Prudence had never given her undivided attention to something for so long before.

'Prudence?'

Prudence looked up. 'Yeah?'

'What are you reading that has you so engrossed? Found something relevant to your dissertation?'

Prudence sniggered. 'Hardly. Come have a look.' She shifted across on her window sill and patted the space next to her. 'Come on, it's fascinating.'

Holly dropped her pen and crossed the room to wriggle into the space next to Prudence, nearly knocking over one of her candles by accident. Prudence flipped the book closed, jamming her thumb in it as a bookmark. 'See?'

The book was called *Architects of the Victorian Age*. 'Architecture?'

'Sure. I got it on inter-library loan from Melbourne Uni. It's got a whole chapter on Howard Humberstone.'

'The guy who designed this college?'

'Yeah. It's fascinating.' She opened the book again. 'He was completely mad, but unbelievably wealthy. He was committed once, but only for about a month. There was even a rumour that he murdered a prostitute. Don't you love it? Like Jack the Ripper or something.'

Holly was examining the pictures of other buildings on the page. 'These places all look pretty normal to me.'

'Ah, but they're not. He built subterranean passages under all these. Look.' She turned over the page and there was a black and white photo of a tunnel leading off into various doorways. Holly had to admit it piqued her interest.

'So you think that maybe . . .?'

'Sure I think it. This building was built in the latter phase of his career. Between 1850 and when he killed himself in 1861 he didn't build a place without at least one underground chamber.'

'But wouldn't the Humberstones—I mean, the current Humberstones—wouldn't they know?'

'They probably do know. They probably just don't mention it.' She slammed the book shut. 'God, Holly. I am just going to *die* if I don't go look for a tunnel.'

'I'm sure it can't be that injurious to your health.'

'You don't know me. It's like the curiosity fills me up and threatens to split me open.'

'So what are you going to do?'

Prudence shrugged. 'For now, nothing. But I'm going to work As, I'm going to see if he knows anything. I'm going to get down into the cellar soon, look for an entrance.'

'Will you be disappointed if you find nothing?'

'I'll find something.'

'Perhaps your ghostly nun,' Holly said, then regretted it. She hoped Prudence didn't think she was making fun.

'Perhaps,' Prudence replied without blinking.

Holly considered her for a while. Prudence was studying the cover of the book. When she looked up and found Holly gazing at her, she smiled. 'What is it?'

'Do you really believe in ghosts?'

'I believe in anything.'

'Do you know anything about dream interpretation?'

'Are you kidding? I'm the dream queen. Is there a dream bothering you?'

Holly started to regret bringing it up. 'Yes. But I think I'm about to make some intimate revelations of a grand nature. The dream's a bit . . . personal. Perhaps I shouldn't tell you.'

'Oh, don't feel uncomfortable.' Prudence's gaze was locked on hers. Prudence had the prettiest eyes, her lashes long and curly. 'You can be frank with me. Being frank is what I do best.'

'I don't know.'

'Have you had lunch?'

'Lunch? I only just had breakfast.'

'It's eleven-thirty. Come back to my house for morning tea—I've got some fantastic books on dreams. You can look it up yourself if you like. I just live down on St Angelo Crescent, on the other side of the park.'

'I don't know, Prudence, I just got in.'

'All work and no play makes a girl a lousy lay.'

Holly had to laugh. Perhaps spontaneity was lacking from her life. 'Okay then, why not.'

Prudence dropped the book in her lap and clapped her hands together. 'Hurrah. Come on, let's go.'

Prudence chattered merrily all the way down the stairs, out of the building, down the hill and across Fawkner Park to St Angelo Crescent, which was quite some distance. The rain had eased to a miserable drizzle, but all was still very grey and gloomy. Holly noticed that Prudence's street was a millionaire's row of fantastic houses. Up each side of the street was a perfect row of old elms, obscuring Edwardian villas and newer glass-and-concrete mansions. 'Do you live with your parents?' she asked.

She shook her head. 'No, I live with my sister. That is until Friday when she leaves. It's my parents' house, though. They live in Hong Kong. Dad works there at the university, and Mum's a painter. You'll see some of her paintings inside.' Prudence led Holly through a black wrought-iron gate, up the front path of a double-storey, restored, red-brick home. She searched in her bag for the key and let herself in.

'Julia!' Prudence called as they stepped inside. 'Are you home?'

No-one answered.

'Your sister's name is Julia?' Holly asked.

'Yeah, why?'

'Were your parents Beatles fans?'

'Oh God yes, incurable hippies.' Prudence shut the door behind them. The sunlight coming through the stained glass made a coloured pattern on the terracotta tiles.

'On *The White Album* there's a song called "Julia" and another called "Dear Prudence".'

Prudence regarded her with a look of astonishment. 'What? I'm named after a Beatles song?'

'I'm surprised you didn't know. Have you heard the song?'

'Yes, but it never clicked that . . . Well, that just tops it all off.'

'Your parents never told you?'

'My parents told me very little unless it was designed to get me out of their way.' She went to the bottom of the stairs and called up again. 'JULIA! If you're here, come down.'

'I guess she's not home,' Holly said after a few more moments of silence.

'Good. Follow me.'

Holly followed Prudence through the kitchen and down three stairs to a cellar. Prudence switched on the light. Hundreds and hundreds of bottles of wine lined the walls.

'It's my dad's hobby,' Prudence said, beginning to search through the bottles. 'White, white, white,' she murmured as she checked the bottles and slid them back into their pigeonholes. 'Ah, here we are. A 1982 Château Latour Bordeaux. This will be worth a fortune.' She took it from the rack and headed back towards the door. 'Come on, let's go to my room.'

'Are you going to drink that?'

'*We* are.'

'But it's your father's wine. Doesn't he have an inventory?'

'He won't be back at least until Christmas. Didn't even make it home for Christmas last year. As long as Julia doesn't find out, I can put off my day of reckoning indefinitely.'

Prudence collected two glasses from the kitchen on the way through, then led Holly up the stairs to her bedroom.

'Mother, Mother, Mother,' Prudence said, tapping the glass of a number of simple and colourful paintings hung beside the staircase. 'She earns almost more than Dad these days. And that's a lot. You have no idea how it feels to have incredibly intelligent and talented family when you're just an ordinary girl.'

'There's nothing ordinary about you, Prudence.'

'Perhaps I don't look ordinary, but my brain is very ordinary. You'd fit in with my family better than I do.'

Holly didn't know what to say. Prudence let her into her bedroom. Spacious and carpeted thickly, the room was nevertheless impossibly untidy, with clothes in piles on the floor and an overflowing ashtray on the bedside table. Ceiling-high bookshelves lined the walls, with half-burned candles dribbling wax in random patterns all over the pine. Given the lack of wall space, Prudence had pinned posters to her ceiling, of bands and weird underground films that Holly had never heard of. But her eyes kept being drawn back to the books.

'Wow, what a library,' she murmured in astonishment.

'Yeah, it's such a good scam. My parents were concerned about my health, thought I needed to get out and play a sport or something. I told them I'd join the gym if they paid the membership fees for an expensive ladies' gym in Toorak. They send me the money monthly and I spend it on books. I'm no healthier, by the way.' She flopped onto the unmade queen-size bed among a purple tie-dyed quilt cover and dirty red satin sheets, and reached into a bedside drawer for a bottle opener. 'But I sure have got a lot of books.'

Holly took a slow circuit of the room, glancing over the spines. History books, classics, dozens and dozens of books on psychic experience, demonology, witchcraft, alien abduction, occult psychology. 'All I can say is wow,'

Holly said. 'I'm so jealous.' She turned to see Prudence reclined on the bed, offering her a glass of wine.

'I don't know, it's early and I don't usually—'

'Prudence's rules. It's my bedroom, after all.'

Holly sat on the bed and took the glass. 'Thanks.'

'Look, here's Sooty come to say hello.' A black cat was miaowing cautiously at the door. Prudence leaped off the bed and scooped it into her arms, kicking the door shut behind her with a thump. 'Come on, Sooty, meet Holly.'

Holly reached out and touched the cat's head. Its fur was soft and fluffy. 'She's beautiful.'

'It's a he.'

'He's beautiful.' She took a cautious sip of her wine. It was divine.

Prudence nuzzled at the cat's neck then let him drop to the bedspread where he settled between the two girls.

'So, Holly. Your dream.'

'Ah, my dream. It's actually a . . . you know . . . a sexy one.'

Prudence could barely contain herself. 'A sexy dream,' she squealed. 'You're so lucky! Did you come?'

Holly looked abashedly into her glass. Perhaps she should have drunk it all to fortify herself for this conversation. 'Yes, actually.' She looked up again. 'Both times.'

'You've had it twice? The same dream?'

'Well, not exactly the same but . . . the same dream lover. He even has a name. Christian.'

'Oh, how *intriguing*.' Prudence gulped down her wine and refilled her glass. She offered the bottle to Holly, who refused it with a shake of her head.

'What do you think it means?'

Prudence shrugged. 'As you'd imagine, with a name like Christian it has to be something to do with religion. Ever been fucked over by religious freaks?'

'Actually my ex-husband's family were very strict Methodists. Their disdain for my interests and ambitions was one of the reasons the marriage failed.' Holly felt a little disappointed that such a rich and sensuous dream could be reduced to such a flimsy and colourless meaning.

'Look, we could go through one of my dream psychology books, work out a whole bunch of stuff about your dream and what it means and what your subconscious is trying to tell you, etcetera, etcetera, blah, blah, blah. But—and this is a bigger but than my butt—if we do that you might stop having the dream. And I'm betting you don't want that.'

Holly could feel herself blush. 'I . . . well, no I guess not. It's kind of pleasant.' Holly was glad she hadn't told Prudence that she only had the dream when staying back late at the college. Her academic enthusiasm might start to be read very differently.

'So is that what happened to your marriage. Evil in-laws?'

Holly sipped her wine. It always went straight to her head. 'No, not just that. The horrible, tragic truth is that I just didn't love him any more.'

'But he still loved you?'

'Yes. He still does. That's why it's been good to get so far away. It's awful, Prudence, feeling pity for somebody. Pity's a kind of tyranny.'

'Were you married for long?'

Holly shook her head, once again telling herself she was stupid. 'We should never have married, I should have known better. We were high-school sweethearts—he was my first boyfriend, my first kiss, my first love—'

'Your first fuck?'

Holly tried not to look shocked. 'That's a rather more complicated story.'

'I love a complicated story.' Prudence adjusted the pillows behind her head and scooped Sooty into her lap.

Holly laughed. 'You're incredible, Prudence. I'll leave out the details for the time being. The upshot was that after

I came back from getting my degree we married and I started teaching. I should never have gone back to Daybrook, but I was under an enormous amount of pressure, from him and from both our families. The marriage lasted two years. I was desperately unhappy for about eighteen months of that time. I applied for the scholarship here without telling him, and when it came through I left.'

'I'm sorry. Do you want a smoke?'

'I don't smoke.'

Prudence lit up and pulled an ashtray onto the bed. 'How about a refill?'

Holly looked at her glass and realised she'd drunk the whole lot. 'Sure, why not.'

Prudence passed Sooty to Holly and reached for the bottle. Sooty curled in Holly's lap, purring like a warm engine. 'What a beautiful cat. He's so docile.'

'That's because he's spoilt. Isn't this a great way to have morning tea?' Prudence was filling Holly's glass.

'I must say I've never had red wine for morning tea before.'

'Then you haven't lived.'

'Enough about me. Tell me about you. All these books, have you read them all?'

'I've read most of them. It's a lot easier to buy them than to read them.' She reached under her pillow and pulled out a large paperback. 'Here, this is what I'm reading at the moment.'

Holly took the book from her. The cover said *Ghostly Encounters*.

'It's true stories of ghosts from all around the world,' Prudence explained.

'True?'

'As true as anything else that's said to be true.'

'Have you ever seen a ghost, Prudence?' The wine was really starting to go to Holly's head now. She felt decidedly fuzzy.

'I think so. I was very young.' Prudence leaned forward, her voice taking on an edge of urgency. 'Do you want to hear the story?'

'Of course.'

'Okay. Well, we were living on the Gold Coast in Queensland. Dad was teaching at Bond University. We had a big property in the hinterland, with a little creek running through it and a bridge crossing it. Mum had this student in one of her art classes who I was terrified of. He always wore this musty old overcoat, and he was German. His face was red and he had a—what do you call those things? A carbuncle? Like a shiny tumorous bump on his forehead. He had one glass eye and it would look in completely the other direction while he talked to you. His name was Mr Buchmann, and he was so stern and so weird-looking that I was just scared to death whenever I saw him.

'So, back then I was in about grade six and the school bus would drop Julia and me off at the bottom of our property and we'd have to walk up and across the bridge to get home. On Mondays Julia had piano lessons and I had to walk alone. One Monday, as I was approaching the bridge, I saw Mr Buchmann. He was leaving our place, just coming over the bridge to where his car was parked. I'd never been alone with him before, and I was always afraid that he'd wrap me up in that horrible over-coat and steal me away somewhere. So rather than going towards the bridge and home and passing him, I ran away in the other direction. I ran back down to the road and across to my friend Tammy's house and I played there until my mother called, frantic, trying to find out what had happened to me.' Prudence paused to put out her cigarette and take another gulp of her wine. The row of silver rings on her fingers clinked against the glass.

'Well, Mr Buchmann called Mum that night and told her that I'd run away from him, and I was chastised roundly for being such an impolite girl and I think Dad even gave me a big fat smack. Now I was not only terrified of Mr Buchmann, I was terrified of being rude to him.

'I didn't see him again for ages. Until . . .' she paused for dramatic effect and lit another cigarette, '. . . one weekend I had been staying with my grandmother and she took me straight to school from her place on the Monday. As I was coming home that afternoon, I saw Mr Buchmann standing on the bridge. I was scared, but I wasn't going to get in trouble again, so I walked right up to him and said good afternoon. He just turned and looked at me with his good eye and said nothing. I thought he was being rude to me on purpose to punish me, so I just put my head down and kept walking. He remained standing there on the bridge, watching me.

'When Mum got home that afternoon, I told her that I'd seen Mr Buchmann on the bridge and I'd said hello to him like a good girl. I was pretty damn proud of myself. Mum went pale and ran out of the room crying. Julia and I were sitting at the table having Tim Tams and lemonade. I asked her what was wrong and she shook her head at me and said I was being horrible to Mum. Mr Buchmann had had a heart attack on Saturday morning right there in Mum's art class.'

Holly listened, feeling like a little girl at a slumber party. 'He was dead?'

'Died on the way to hospital.'

Holly shivered. 'You've given me goosebumps.'

'I saw him, Holly, as clear as I'm seeing you now.'

'I believe you. Jeez, I hope that never happens to me. I'd freak out.'

'I did freak out. I never slept comfortably in that house again. Luckily we moved down here a few months later.'

Just then the phone started ringing, jarring both of them out of their spooky reverie. Sooty jumped up and stood miaowing by the door. Prudence disengaged herself from ashtray and wine glass and ran out of the room to answer it. Holly picked up the book and flicked through the pages. One of the stories caught her eye and she skimmed it casually. It was about a young mother who had made contact with a ghost that was bothering her child. She summoned it up with the aid of two candles and a mirror, had a nice long chat to it and asked it to leave the kid alone, to which the ghost had gladly agreed. Holly thought Prudence's story was far creepier.

'Just some guy selling cheap holidays,' Prudence proclaimed as she came back into the room and tossed a cordless phone onto the bed.

'Did your parents ever believe you about the ghost?' Holly asked.

'No. My parents never listen to anything I say. They thought I must have heard about Mr Buchmann dying and made the story up. I didn't, I swear to you.' She settled back on the bed.

Holly wondered if the years between now and her childhood could have played with Prudence's memory, but said nothing.

'I guess we should go back to the college at some stage,' Prudence said, draining the last of her wine glass. 'We've nearly finished the bottle.'

'Really? A bottle of wine at midday—I feel so decadent.' Holly held out her glass as Prudence shared the last few drops between them.

'A toast,' said Prudence, raising her glass.

'Okay. A toast to what?'

'A toast to having a far more interesting year than last year.' Their glasses clinked together. 'Bottoms up.'

CHAPTER FIVE

'**W**ell, are you coming?'

Prudence looked up from her book to Julia, immaculately dressed in a three-piece red wool suit, her hair tied back with a black velvet ribbon. Her going-away party at work was starting in half an hour and Prudence was invited.

'I don't know, Julia, I've had a bad day.'

Julia sat on the coffee table in front of her sister. 'Why, what's up?'

And how was Prudence supposed to answer that? How was she supposed to say, 'I saw As today down at the newsagent with his wife and teenage son and he smiled at me politely, like he barely knew me, and didn't even introduce me to his family'? How was she supposed to tell anybody, even Julia, that As's wife was attractive and attentive and all the things As had said she was not? It sucked, having an affair—nobody to bitch to about boy problems.

'I'm just a bit down, that's all.'

'It will cheer you up if you come. You can wear something outrageous and shock all my co-workers.'

'And you won't mind?'

Julia smiled. 'Of course I won't mind. I'm flying out on Monday, I'll never see them again.'

'Can you give me twenty minutes to get ready?'

Julia checked her watch. 'Sure. They can't start the party without me anyway.'

Prudence raced upstairs, pulled a long black satin dress out of her wardrobe and combined it with a black velvet jacket that still smelled a bit smoky and beery from the last time she had worn it. Getting to the dry-cleaner was a Herculean task for her, so she got used to wearing things rumpled, stale-smelling or stained. It drove Julia mad. She lined her eyes thickly with black, and changed her modest silver nose stud for a more ostentatious ring. Julia was standing at the bedroom door waiting for her as she finished her lipstick.

'That's a nice shade, it matches your hair,' Julia said.

'You said I could be outrageous.'

'So I did. Come on, I've got a cab waiting outside.'

Prudence laced up her boots and followed her sister down the stairs.

Macmillan and Bourke Solicitors had decked out their softly lit, mahogany-coloured main foyer with streamers and balloons in tribute to their departing wunderkind, Julia Emerson. Prudence, after the initial embarrassment of being told repeatedly, 'You're nothing like your sister,' and biting back the reply, 'Now *there's* a comment I've never heard before,' settled herself down on a couch with a couple of bottles of wine and got roundly soused. Everybody bugged her—all dressed so bloody neatly, all so fucking polite and terminally unfunny.

A small stage had been set up in the corner for a duo who were going to play boring love songs for the duration, but Prudence was watching the sound technician as he ran leads and checked microphones. Long black hair tied back in a ponytail, pale skin, tight leather pants and a loose white shirt. She had stopped mentally undressing him twenty minutes ago, and was now onto far more detailed fantasies.

'Prudence, don't drink too much,' Julia hissed as she whirled by with a group of friends.

'Too late.'

'God, can't you exercise some . . .?' Julia trailed off.

'Some what? Some prudence?'

Julia shook her head and moved back into the crowd. 'Go ask Frank to be more frank,' Prudence muttered, gazing into the bottom of her glass. As was happily married. As had pretended he barely knew her. As's wife was a real human being, not a nameless harridan with a personality disorder. Julia was heading to Boston and Prudence had no friends. The longer she looked into the wine glass, the more depressed she got. The duo had climbed up onto the stage and were launching into a bad version of 'American Pie'. The sound tech had adjusted the levels and now sat back to watch, looking like he didn't fit in amongst this well-dressed, well-bred crowd of smart rich people.

'We're meant to be together,' Prudence said under her breath as she pulled herself out of her seat and walked over to him.

'Hi,' he said as he saw her approaching. 'I saw you before. You look about as comfortable as I feel.'

'We're meant to be together,' she said again, because she couldn't think of what else to say.

'We're meant to be away from this godawful music,' he replied, just as the crowd began to sing along with the chorus.

'Can you leave your post? I mean, what if something goes wrong?'

'As if this mob would notice. Come on.'

He grabbed her hand and they went through a door marked 'Staff Only' and found themselves in a rabbit warren of small offices.

'It's dark,' Prudence said.

'Yeah, and you can barely hear the music. Great, isn't it?'

'We should have brought some wine or something.'

He led her into an office that had a lockable door and locked it behind them. 'I don't think you need any more wine,' he said.

'Great, now you sound like my sister.' Things were getting decidedly hazy. The contrast of the quiet darkness with the whirl and commotion of the party was messing with her head. She realised that he was kissing her neck. She sighed and leaned her head back, closed her eyes.

'You think I'm just some drunk, easy slut,' she said.

'No, of course not.'

'Yes, you do. I'll have you know I'm studying for a Masters degree in literature.'

'I don't care what you do. I don't think you're a slut. I think you're gorgeous.'

'I could recite poetry for you: "We caught the tread of dancing feet, we wandered down the moonlit street . . ."' She trailed off and opened her eyes to look at him. He was attractive, but he smelled a bit sweaty.

He was smiling at her. 'I don't even know your name,' he said.

'I guess it doesn't matter.' Her jacket was off and her dress was being unzipped. His hands felt very cold against her hot skin. 'Only, let's not do it on the desk. I do it on the desk with As all the time. Just once I'd like to lie down and do it like ordinary people, in a bed.'

'There's no bed.'

'Ah.' Prudence sighed. 'No bed.'

He took a step back. 'Wait here.'

Wait here. As if she was going anywhere. As if she ever went anywhere. He disappeared out of the office for a few minutes—it seemed to Prudence to take forever—and came back with two huge cushions under each arm.

'I got them from the armchairs in the waiting room,' he said as he organised them on the floor. 'Look, just like a bed.' He stood back to admire his handiwork.

Prudence slipped off her dress and collapsed among the cushions. 'Ah, sleep. I could go to sleep right now.'

'Not yet.' He was unlacing her boots and she realised he was naked. She hadn't noticed him undress, and hoped that didn't mean she'd blacked out momentarily. Surely she hadn't drunk that much. A bottle and a half, maybe? Or was it closer to two and a half?

She reached her hand out to run her fingertips over his skin. Undressed he wasn't quite the young Adonis she had imagined—a chest too hairy, a notable set of love handles—not the fantasy man she had been mentally fucking all evening. Never mind, she was hardly a super-model herself.

'Do you have a condom?' she asked.

'Sure do.'

'You've done this before, haven't you?'

'Not with you.'

Prudence laid her head back and closed her eyes. As he lowered his body onto hers, she found herself imagining it was As and silently accused herself of being a sick bitch.

Justin was constantly amazed by his uncle and aunt's kitchen. He had never seen anything so clean in his life. Enormous and echoing, with white tiles, a stainless-steel fridge, not a smudge or a speck anywhere to embarrass its mistress, Emma, who kept it this way. If it weren't for the country kitchen touches—a framed sampler, a wood-and-iron baker's shelf, a spray of dried flowers over the entrance—it would have looked like a morgue, and the gleaming fridge door he was now opening would provide him with a selection of bodies rather than a selection of soft drinks. He reached for a bottle of lemonade and sat down at the bench. The lemonade was down to its last flat dregs, so he screwed the cap off and began to swig directly out of the bottle. The clock on the microwave blinked as the seconds went past. One-fifteen a.m.

He remembered his mother's kitchen—never clean, food scraps left out for roaches, grease caked on every element of the stove. There had been one day when, sickened by it, he had spent four hours scrubbing and tidying. She had come home from the pub and vomited in the sink, washed the contents of her stomach rather haphazardly down the plughole, and left a thin film of bile over the taps before toasting herself a cheese sandwich. It had burned and then sat untouched except by ants while his mother lay in a drunken stupor nearby. She had laughed at his efforts. The only place he was allowed unpolluted tidiness was his own bedroom, which he had wisely fitted with a padlock.

'Justin?'

He looked up, and the contrast of seeing his soft, pretty aunt standing at the doorway after thinking about his harsh, sallow mother almost overloaded his senses.

'Hi, Emma,' he managed to say.

'Why are you up so late?' She came to stand next to him, reached over to brush his hair out of his eyes.

'I got thirsty. How about you?'

She cast her eyes upwards, as though she could see through the ceiling to her bedroom above. 'Lucien's had a nightmare. I'm making him a cup of tea.' She turned to switch on the electric kettle and went to the cupboard for a tea bag. 'Would you like one?'

'Um . . . okay,' he said.

She set up three teacups and settled on the stool next to his, sighing deeply. 'I don't know what to do about Lucien. His nightmares are always waking me up. Perhaps

I should sleep in a room of my own. It's not as wonderful as it's rumoured to be, sleeping with the same man for twenty-six years.'

Justin had no idea how to respond to this, so he didn't respond at all.

Emma let him sit quietly for a while, then gave him a sympathetic smile. 'Do you miss your mother, Justin?'

He shrugged. 'Sometimes.'

'I hope you don't blame yourself. There was nothing you could have done.'

A cold hand clasped Justin around the heart and squeezed. 'Of course. I know that. She was . . .' He almost thought for a moment he could tell Emma how tyrannical his mother was, how the notion of missing her was almost absurd. But he didn't.

The kettle had started whistling, saving him from finishing his sentence. Emma made him a milky, sweet cup of tea, as if he were a child. He accepted it and took a sip.

'Do you like the girls in your office?' she asked as she sat down across from him with a cup of her own.

'Don't you have to take Lucien his tea?'

'I'll get there. It's nice to be able to talk to you.'

'They seem friendly enough. I get along with them okay.'

'They're both unattached as far as I've heard. A handsome boy like you would certainly interest them. Have you thought about that?'

Justin, taken aback, looked at her blankly.

'I wouldn't be surprised if one of the girls—if not both—was interested in you. Maybe they think about your eyes, or your hair.' She reached out again and touched his face softly. 'Or your lips.'

She dropped her hand and Justin turned his attention to his cup of tea. When he glanced up again, Emma was still looking at him fondly. Perhaps more than fondly.

'Thanks for the tea,' he said.

'You're very welcome. Do you think about either of them? Holly's a very attractive girl, according to Laurence Aswell.'

'I don't normally drink tea. This is nice.'

She smiled at him. 'I'd better get back to my husband. Goodnight.' She leaned over to kiss Justin on the forehead. Just as she did, Lucien stepped into the kitchen, wrapped in a rich red dressing-gown.

'Emma? My tea?' he said, eyeing Justin coolly.

'Yes, of course,' she replied, 'I'm coming right away.'

'I'm going to bed,' Justin said. 'Thanks, Emma. Goodnight, Lucien.' It felt as though he should call his uncle sir. He resisted the urge and turned to go back to his room. He could hear a silence behind him, as though Lucien were waiting until he was out of earshot before saying anything to Emma. As he opened his bedroom door, he heard Lucien's voice, lowly yet urgently chiding his wife. He closed the door behind him, kicked off his jeans and flopped down on his bed. Not expecting to be able to sleep, he pulled the quilt around himself and drifted off almost immediately.

It seemed only a short time later that he was being awoken by someone—a female—calling his name. It blurred on the edge of his dream momentarily, and for an instant he thought he was back home with his mother calling from the other side of his door in one of her drunken fits of affection. But gradually the voice became more insistent, and he woke and sat up, looking towards the window.

'Justin.' A harsh whisper.

'Who is it?'

'It's Prudence.'

'Prudence?' He was already untangling himself from his quilt, pulling on his jeans, hurrying to the window and casting the curtains aside. Prudence stood outside, hugging a velvet jacket tightly around herself against the cold. He lifted the latch and slid the window up.

'What are you doing here?'

'Can I come in?' she asked. 'It's pretty cold out here.'

He could smell alcohol on her breath and the scent temporarily filled him with a kind of sick dread. But he could hardly leave her outside in the drizzle, so he pushed the window up all the way and helped her in. She squeezed between two overgrown bushes and unceremoniously clambered through the window.

'What are you doing here?' he asked again as she stood readjusting her clothes.

'It's a long story. I can't go home, I'm in disgrace with my sister.'

'You're drunk.'

'Very, very drunk. Do you mind?'

What could he say? With an effort, he shook his head. 'How did you find me?'

'I've been here before. With As. We came to pick some books up and Emma showed me through. I guessed Lucien would tuck you away down here on the ground floor. I would've gone to Holly's only I don't even know where she lives. Could I sleep here? I'll just sleep on the floor or something.'

'Why can't you go home?' He was irritated but wary about showing it.

'You're cross with me. You think I'm an idiot.' She stuck her bottom lip out and flopped down on his bed. 'I'm not an idiot.'

'I don't think you're an idiot.'

'Julia does. That's my sister. I did something very bad this evening, very, very bad, and now she thinks I'm . . .' she trailed off, as though she were afraid she'd said too much.

'Listen. You really should go home. I can walk you if you like, if you don't feel safe.'

To his horror, she began to cry. This was starting to

take on a nightmarish resemblance to the long nights with his repentant mother. He found himself trembling, unable to offer her the comfort she probably needed. He quickly handed her a pillow. 'Okay, okay. Sleep here. I'll get you a blanket.'

She took the pillow and sniffed a strangled thank-you. Justin went to the wardrobe and slid open the door, rifled around and found a thick quilt. When he turned back, Prudence had passed out on his bed. He walked back over and shook her lightly. 'Prudence?'

She muttered but did not stir. He liberated the pillow from her grasp and got her boots off, trying to rearrange her into a more comfortable position. She curled gratefully around the quilt as he spread it over her and settled in with some babyish noises of slumbering comfort. He watched her for a little while, the rising and falling of her chest, her jaw slack and her purple hair spread out around her.

With a shrug he gathered the spare pillow and quilt and made himself cosy on the floor, dreading the awkward scene awaiting them both in the morning.

'Nobody here, thank God,' Prudence muttered under her breath as she let herself into the empty office. She dropped her keys on her desk and sat down heavily behind it. She didn't want to face Justin yet—she had embarrassed herself so spectacularly on Friday night that when she came to on Saturday morning she had decided to sneak out the window before Justin awoke, rather than try to apologise for her behaviour. She hadn't seen him yet, and she wasn't looking forward to it.

Leaning forward on her elbows, she gazed out the window. A plane went by overhead and she wondered briefly if it was Julia's, but of course Julia's had left hours ago. Her sister had shaken her awake at four a.m., given her a brief teary hug, then disappeared in a cab to the airport. 'See you at Christmas,' she had said. Well, Prudence had heard that promise before.

Eleven o'clock. Hopefully Holly would be in soon. The scene with Justin would be a lot smoother with another person to mediate. She wondered if it was the stupidest thing she had ever done, but then remembered that shagging the sound technician at her sister's going-away party was probably far stupider. She did some mental calculations in her head and realised that she was dangerously close to a double-dozen of sexual partners—twenty-three. She was overwhelmed by an unbearable sense of vulnerability as she momentarily imagined them all standing in the room with her. Luckily, Holly opened the door and came in, dispatching them all back to history.

'Holly, I'm so glad you're here.'

Holly closed the door behind her. She looked pale and miserable. Her mouth barely twitched into a smile. 'Hi, Prudence.'

Prudence slipped out of her chair and came over to grab Holly's wrist. 'God, you look terrible. What's wrong?'

Holly shrugged. 'I . . . I've had a letter from Michael. It's upset me a bit, that's all.'

Prudence led Holly to her seat and sat her down. 'Can I get you something? A cup of tea or something?'

Holly shook her head. 'No, I'll be fine. Maybe later, when Justin comes in. It would be nice to spend an hour in the cafeteria with some good company.'

'God, Justin,' Prudence groaned, hiding her head in her hands. 'I'm not looking forward to seeing him.'

'Why?'

Prudence looked up. 'Oh, that's just my stupid problem. Yours seems far worse.'

'No, tell me. It'll take my mind off things.'

Prudence perched on the edge of Holly's desk, nearly knocking over a stack of books. 'Okay, but promise you won't think I'm an idiot.'

Holly smiled weakly. 'I promise.'

'Friday night I went to my sister's going-away party at work, and I kind of got . . . intimate with a guy there. The sound technician.'

'How intimate?'

'Let's just say that my sister's erstwhile boss found us in naked post-coital bliss right about when some dickhead knocked the sound desk over and made it feed back into infinity. Very loudly.'

'How embarrassing.'

'Very embarrassing.'

'But what's it got to do with Justin?'

'I was in disgrace with Julia, which was kind of ironic because she *had* said I could be outrageous, but I guess she didn't mean getting-shitfaced-and-being-found-naked-with-a-stranger outrageous. We had a big fight in the cab on the way home and I ordered it to stop and I got out and . . . Well, I didn't want to go home and I didn't know where you lived, and I didn't have my keys to the college so I—'

'Went to Justin's?'

'Yeah. I'd been to the Humberstones' place once before. He let me in a window and I passed out on his bed. And left the next morning before he was awake.'

Holly chuckled. 'What a mess, Prudence. Are you going to apologise?'

'I don't even know if I'll be able to look him in the eye. Do you think I'm a fool?'

'No. And I bet he doesn't either. You didn't tell him about the sound technician?'

Prudence shook her head. 'No. At least I don't think so.'

'So do you think you'll see him again?'

Prudence was momentarily perplexed. 'Justin?'

'No. No, the sound technician.'

'Oh.' Prudence was suddenly acutely aware that there might be a difference in sexual morality between herself and Holly. 'Well, no. It was just a . . . you know, a one-off thing. I didn't even get his name.'

Holly merely nodded, and Prudence wondered if she was repressing her shock, or if it really wasn't that surprising to her. 'Well. I'm sure Justin doesn't think badly of you.'

Prudence stood and stretched, went back to her desk. Holly swivelled round on her chair to look at her.

'Want to hear my problem?' Holly said.

'Sure, if you want to tell it.'

'Michael's threatened to kill himself if I don't come home.'

Prudence drew a quick breath. 'Ouch. What are you going to do?'

'I'm not going to do anything. I'm not going back of course. It's just so unlike him. He was such a—I mean, he *is* such a pragmatic person. I think he's trying to scare me.'

The room fell silent for an instant. Prudence thought about how petty her problems seemed compared to Holly's. An ambulance siren raced past in the distance. How petty her problems were compared to everybody's really. 'I'm sorry. It must be fucking with your head.'

'Yeah. Fucking with my head. Fucking with my life.'

Prudence hadn't heard Holly swear before. The words seemed to come out uncomfortably, like a foreigner taking the first nervous steps in a new language. 'You're probably right about him trying to scare you. And anyway, I know it sounds cruel but what he does isn't your problem any more.'

'Technically, he's still my husband.'

'Hell, technically I'm supposed to have written about

half my dissertation by now. Technically means nothing, it's all in the actually.'

Holly caught her bottom lip between her teeth and looked like she was fighting with tears. 'Yep. That's right. I guess I should just get moving on this divorce business.' She sank down on her desk. 'God, I'm too young to be planning my divorce. How on earth did I get my life so out of whack?'

Prudence sprang up and dragged Holly out of her seat. 'Come on, Holly. Let's go down to the cafeteria. We can leave a note for Justin to meet us there.'

'I don't know.'

'You can't work in this state.' Prudence squashed the feeling that she was leading Holly astray down the dark path to terminal procrastination.

'I guess you're right. I need something strong and caffeinated.'

Prudence led her out of the office, conveniently forgetting to leave a note for Justin. That was a problem that could wait until later.

CHAPTER SIX

~

'**Y**ou'll do well, Holly,' Laurence Aswell said as he leaned back in his leather chair. 'Your ideas are already very coherent and I can tell you're enthusiastic about the project.'

'Thank you, Dr Aswell. I am very enthusiastic.' Holly was pleased with herself. It was only her second meeting with him and she already had a number of interesting ideas to go on, and he had noticed. She wished she didn't feel as though she had to justify her scholarship by doing brilliantly, but she had a nagging worry that she had to convince the college that they hadn't wasted their money.

'Call me As, everybody does.' He rummaged in his drawer for a packet of mints and offered one to Holly, who refused. 'I wish your enthusiasm were contagious. Prudence could certainly do with some.'

Holly was aware that discussing Prudence in her absence was disloyal, but she too was worried about how little Prudence did regarding her dissertation. 'I'm sure she'll get in the swing of things soon,' she murmured. Though Holly doubted it. The last she had seen of Prudence was Monday morning in the cafeteria. She had spontaneously decided to take the week off so that she didn't have to face Justin just yet. 'Never do today what you can put off until doomsday,' she had said. Holly had to admit that she was a little lonely without Prudence around. Justin was so serious and sombre.

'I hope you're right. That girl has brains enough, she just has no motivation.' He leaned forward. 'Sorry, I suppose I shouldn't be saying that to you.'

Holly shrugged. Aswell was blond and good-looking for a man his age, charming and affable enough. But there was an edge of professionalism missing from his attitude. As though he wanted to be a 25-year-old student himself but didn't know quite how to turn back the clock. Holly reshuffled her notes.

'Well, I'll look up those books you suggested and see you in a fortnight.'

'Sure. But feel free to drop in any time if I'm in my office. You know, if you have any problems.'

'Thanks Dr—thanks, As.'

'See you, Holly. Keep up the good work.'

Holly let herself out and walked back to her office. The small digital clock that she had set up on her desk blinked at her. It was nearly five o'clock. The afternoon was overcast and dreary. She switched on the lamp over her desk. Justin had gone home. His desk was now nearly as laden down with books as Holly's. She hovered over them and sorted through a couple of volumes, looking at them. Open on his desk was the fat anthology she had loaned him. She picked it up. He must have been reading Dowson's *Cynara*.

'"But when the feast is finished and the lamps expire,"' she read aloud, '"Then falls thy shadow—the night is thine."' She placed the book back on Justin's desk, returned to her own and pulled out the letter from Michael.

She wished it didn't grate on her that the damn thing

was so badly misspelt. Michael was not cerebral or bookish like she was, and she had long ago repressed the wish for him to be her intellectual equal. *Holly, I'm dying without you. You don't even relise what you've taken away from me. Your everything to me.*

'I'm sorry, Michael,' she whispered, leaning back in her chair and closing her eyes. 'God, I'm so sorry.' She had read about Catholic monks punishing themselves by wearing a hairshirt—that's how her pain felt. Like something constantly rasping against her, not allowing her a moment's repose. The fact that she didn't even miss him made it worse. The guilt sat on her chest, heavy as the Atlantic. A warm tear trickled from the corner of her left eye, tickling her cheek.

Almost imperceptibly, something brushed softly across her cheek, moving as if to wipe the tear away. She snapped upright, looking around. The room was empty apart from herself, and she quickly managed to convince herself that she had imagined it. She was clearly overwrought.

She picked up the sheet of notes she had taken in As's office. Desolation and rising damp awaited her at home, especially on a drizzly Friday afternoon when the rest of the world was preparing to go out for dinners and cosy get-togethers. She burrowed under a pile of books, looking for a photocopied article she knew she had, pulled it out and uncapped her highlighter pen. Perhaps a cosy get-together with some complex critical theory was what she needed to sort herself out.

It was fully dark outside by the time she had finished the article, and there really wasn't any further reason to stay. The weekend stretched out in front of her, long and dismal. She thought about calling Prudence to arrange to go see a movie, but making the first step into extra-curricular activities was always difficult. A girl like Prudence would probably have a million friends, and the last thing Holly needed was to put her self-esteem on the line trying to compete with them all.

She grabbed her coat from the back of her chair and put it on, collected the books she wanted to take home with her and reached over to switch off her lamp.

Once again, it seemed something brushed against her, this time across the back of her neck, gently caressing her hair. She left the lamp on and spun around, her pulse thumping hard in her throat. She had to fight back the urge to call out, Who's there? because she could see quite clearly that nobody was there. She reached her hand out towards her desk to steady herself and took a deep, shuddering breath.

'There is nothing here,' she said aloud. It made her feel marginally better, so she said it again, this time more confidently. 'There is nothing here.' She waited a few heartbeats, as though she had issued a challenge to the empty room and was seeing if it would respond. Nothing.

She turned back towards the desk. Suddenly, a sound like a sharp intake of breath rushed past her ear. She couldn't help letting out a little shriek of fear, over-balanced and had to grab her chair to stop herself from falling. She eased herself into the seat and took deep breaths. Prudence's ghost stories suddenly became far more frightening than they had sounded before. Her voice quavered as she gulped, then said, 'Is there anybody here?'

As if in answer, the open book of poetry on Justin's desk shifted a few centimetres, teetered on the edge, then fell to the floor. The sound of the book hitting the carpet took on monstrous proportions in Holly's mind. She cried out, sprang from her chair and raced out of the room, slamming the door behind her.

The hallway was dark and silent. All she could hear was the sound of her own ragged breath and the thump of her heartbeat as she leaned her back against the wall.

Her keys. She had to go back into the office to get her keys. She knew this, but at the same time felt that she could never walk into her office again.

'Maybe the book fell off the desk for another reason,' she muttered. 'Maybe I didn't put it back properly. Maybe I'm imagining this. Maybe this is some kind of post-traumatic hallucination.' It was no use, she couldn't bring herself to go back into the office. Her stomach had turned to water and she thought of the safe, bright haven of the ladies' toilets on the next floor.

She dashed up the stairs, pushed the door open and reached for the switch. Everything was bathed in harsh yellow light, including her shaking hands. She spent a few minutes regaining her composure and splashing cold water on her face. Over the basin hung a large antique mirror, the silver worn through at the corners, in an ornate frame. She gazed at herself for a moment—she looked exactly the same, not like somebody going mad.

Okay, so what the hell was it all about? Where had the touch, the noise come from? Holly felt her flesh begin to creep as she thought about her dream lover, how real he had seemed. She turned her back to her reflection and leaned against the basin. Prudence's book, the woman who had contacted the ghost—suddenly she couldn't stop thinking about it.

'This is ridiculous,' she said as she turned and put her hands on either side of the mirror frame. 'Absolutely ridiculous.' She lifted and felt the mirror's weight suddenly transferred from the hook on the wall into her hands. She pressed it against her body, screwed her eyes shut as she reached inside herself for the last shreds of her courage, then opened her eyes and headed back down to her office.

The room was empty and looked quite ordinary. Her lamp cast a friendly pool of light over her piles of books. She leaned the mirror against the wall over her desk, propped a few books against it to keep it in place, then turned to Prudence's desk and prised two candles out of their waxy foundations and set them up on either side of the mirror.

As she rummaged in Prudence's top drawer for matches, she reassured herself that nothing was going to happen. It was merely an experiment, to prove to herself that there was no ghost lurking around her office, that it was just her hysterical imagination working overtime. But if she was so sure, why did her hands shake as they closed around the matchbox, as they lit the two candles and reached out to turn off the lamp?

Muted darkness, the two tiny flames dancing slowly, carelessly. She looked at herself once again in the mirror—her pupils seemed huge. Her throat was so dry she had to lick her lips to make a sound.

'Christian?' she said softly into the dark.

Heartbeats ticked by. 'Christian?' she said again, starting to feel very relieved, if a little silly.

In the mirror she suddenly noticed something move over her shoulder. Upwards from the base of her spine and out to her arms she could feel gooseflesh spreading over her skin. She didn't turn around, but focussed intently on the shape.

'Christian?'

A moment of silence, a moment of stillness. The shape perhaps just another shadow in the dark. But in an instant, with a low rushing sound filling her ears, the figure of a young man shivered and materialised over her left shoulder.

She shrieked and spun around. Nothing there. All her nerves were screaming. She grabbed her keys and her bag and, turning back only long enough to extinguish the two candles without looking in the mirror, raced out of the room and locked the door behind her, clattered down the stairs two at a time and raced into the driveway. She didn't stop running until she was at the corner of her street.

Bending over and panting, she reached out to a street sign for support. A light drizzle descended. She realised she was crying. Standing in the dark in the rain, she felt almost at home. It seemed nowhere else offered her much comfort.

Straightening up, she pushed her hair off her face and started up the hill for her flat. She didn't have to be at the college alone at night ever again, she could make sure she only went there during daylight. Problem solved. And she could pretend that tonight had never happened.

But his face—so sad, so lost. Ah, God. It was too late.

She had seen Christian, and he was beautiful.

Lucien cherished his Saturday mornings with the house to himself. Emma always went shopping early and he had convinced her to start taking a reluctant Justin with her. Even in his locked, hushed study, the knowledge that somebody else was in the house always grated on him, as though there were no place on earth that he could just be by himself. But Saturday mornings he felt free and weightless.

The clouds were starting to clear outside and patches of weak sunshine fell on his desk. The room was large, but bookshelves took up a great deal of the space. Behind a painting which he now removed was the face of the safe in which he kept the grimoire. He dialled the combination: 34-28-36. These had been Emma's measurements in inches when they had just married and moved here. When he had still found her attractive. He doubted any of the measurements still held. All had been stretched out of shape by her excesses.

He pulled out the grimoire and settled behind his desk, determined to decipher at least some of the last pages of the Guyana fragment before the weekend's meeting. With no news from Randolph for a few weeks, and hardly any new transcriptions from the grimoire, the meetings had become short black masses, where Lucien sometimes felt about as effectual as a teenage boy experimenting with a ouija board. If it wasn't for his powerful attraction to Jane, he would probably cancel the meetings until further notice, even if Owling did recommend regular ceremonies to train the mind and harness the darkness.

It was the handwriting that was baffling him. He looked over the pages again and again, vainly hoping for one or two words to jump out. The spirit who had had hold of Owling's body while he wrote these pages had an erratic hand—'y's looked like 'j's and all the vowels seemed to be represented indiscriminately by one skinny loop. Lucien sighed, picked a page at random to work on, pushed his glasses firmly onto his nose and prepared to concentrate.

Around eleven o'clock, after hours of grindingly hard work, he had a breakthrough. He noticed a slight difference, small but crucial, in the way some of the letters were formed. Everything began to fall into place, slowly but certainly. Soon he had a whole paragraph transcribed, made no easier by the lack of punctuation and the peculiar syntax the being used. He copied out the paragraph before trying to read and make sense of it:

> to traitor must needs be given much young youth
> beauty need body undone body the young like
> chrysalis break forth with traitor full lush needs
> body of young so orphan boy most often required

He read it over. It seemed to be proposing the price that needed to be paid to the traitor demon, but beyond that it made little sense. He kept working, picking apart the letters and transcribing them carefully in his own neat, round hand:

traitor comes by ease you must promise break none
of as . . .

This part of the manuscript was obliterated by an elaborate burn mark, as though a sigil had been burned into
the very page, destroying the words around it. It continued a little further down:

must of course break own to father of us who goes
to hands of magus hands of magus quake not strong
be need no doubt

Lucien sat back, his mind already overworked by the
effort of deciphering the impenetrable handwriting. Again
and again he cast his eyes over the words. They could
mean everything or nothing, he really had no way of
knowing. He bit back the frustration, swallowed it down
and compressed it in the dark place he saved for all those
useless feelings that would undo him if he let them. He
flipped through the next couple of pages to the end of
the book and used his new key to decipher the last paragraph in the fragment:

find orphan male and ask again all then will told to
magus of finding traitor and by steps brought to
Father Shadow

'By steps brought to Father Shadow.' Lucien said the
words aloud. So often he had looked at the last words in
this fragment and been unable to figure them. Father
Shadow—for the last two years those words had eluded
him, sometimes seeming to read 'either swallow' and
sometimes seeming nothing more than a collection of
meaningless consonants, as undecipherable as the meaning
of life. Father Shadow. And the need to find an orphan
male. He browsed over the rest of his transcription for
the morning, came back to the line that read: 'like chrysa-
lis break forth with traitor full lush needs body of young
so orphan boy'. He tapped his pencil on the desk slowly,

felt the warm shiver of hope creep up from his toes and into his heart.

In the distance he heard Emma open the front door and call, 'Lucien, we're home!' Normally he would cringe at such a contemptible interruption, but not today. Because he knew that Emma had brought his orphan boy home with her.

Monday morning. The worst morning of the week. Why had she been stupid enough to choose this morning to sort out the tangle of her emotional life? Prudence half-heartedly pushed open the door to the office and was surprised to find Holly in.

'Holly? You're in early.'

Holly looked up with half a smile. 'Hi. I had a few things to take care of. This place smells funny first thing in the morning, doesn't it?'

'Especially after being locked up all weekend.' Prudence sighed and dumped her bag on her desk.

'I missed you last week.'

Prudence turned around, barely able to conceal her smile. 'Really?'

Holly suddenly looked embarrassed. 'It's a bit dull when you're not here.'

'Thanks.' Prudence collected a few books from her desk, pleased that Holly seemed to like her. She knew she was manic and overwhelming and she was just hopeless at making friends, despite what Julia always thought. The people she saw at clubs were just people with first names and no outside existence to her, sometimes fun to dance or drink with, but usually as interchangeable and expendable as buttons. 'I hope As feels the same way. Perhaps my interesting personality will make up for the fact that I've done virtually nothing since I saw him last.'

'Do you have an appointment this morning?'

'Yeah.' She sighed. She knew that she had to start doing some serious work soon, not just mucking around with finding sources and photocopying things that she was never going to read. But there was too much else to think about; for example, what, if anything, she was going to say to As about the way he had snubbed her last week. 'I'd better get down there. If Justin comes in can you let him know that I'll be back in about an hour, and I'll have that long-overdue apology ready for him. Don't let him sneak off to the library or anything.'

'Okay, I won't.'

Prudence moved towards the door, then turned to look at Holly. She looked pale and there were dark shadows under her eyes. 'Are you okay, by the way?'

Holly shrugged. 'As okay as I can be under the circumstances.'

'I shouldn't have deserted you last week,' Prudence said guiltily. 'Not after what you told me about Michael.'

'Really, I'm okay. Let's have lunch together today, the three of us.'

Prudence smiled. 'Okay. I'll see you soon.' She closed the door behind her and headed up to the third floor to see As.

'Come in,' he called as she tapped timidly on his door.

'Hi,' she said, closing out the hallway behind them and, out of habit, flicking across the lock.

'Prudence. How are you?' He didn't get up, eyed her appreciatively from where he sat behind his massive desk. The curtains were already half drawn, heavy dark green drapes blocking out the intrusive morning sun.

'I'd like to say I'm fine but I'm not.'

He raised one eyebrow. 'Oh?'

'You ignored me completely.'

'Ignored you?'

'When I saw you at the newsagent's. With your terribly attractive wife.'

He shrugged. 'You think she's attractive? You haven't seen her first thing in the morning.'

'You haven't seen me first thing in the morning.'

He fell silent.

'Well?' she said, feeling her heart racing. It was the first time she had acted like anything but a pliable sex toy around As.

'I'm sorry. I saw you and I freaked out.' He stood and came around the desk to Prudence, touched her cheek gently. 'I sometimes feel like I'm living in two different worlds,' he said, sighing. 'In one I'm an English teacher and I have a beautiful, sexy girlfriend, and in the other I'm a boring old man with a boring old wife, a high-school dropout for a son and all the problems in the world. When I saw you the other day, it was like the two worlds suddenly collided and I was terrified. I didn't know what to say.' He leaned forward to kiss her fore-head. 'I should have introduced you to Mandy. I'm sorry. I know you wouldn't have given the secret away.'

Mandy. It was the first time he had ever used her name. He usually referred to her as 'my wife', reducing her to the status of an easily disregarded object. Prudence closed her eyes and leaned into him, felt his lips moving on her face, across her mouth. But she didn't respond, could only stand still and try to feel nothing to stop herself being overwhelmed.

'Prudence?'

'I'm sorry, As. Not today.' She stepped away from him. He shrugged and returned to the chair behind his desk, putting two metres of mahogany between them.

'I haven't done any work to speak of since last time,' she admitted, 'but I will try to start writing something this week. It's good having Holly there, she's a great example.'

'I'm glad. I'm worried about you.' Did he sound pissed off? Just a little, perhaps? He had probably been anticipating some young hot flesh all weekend. *Suffer*, she thought.

'I guess there's not much point in me staying then,' she said. 'What say I come to see you on Thursday, sort things out before the Easter break?'

'Thursday? You know you can come sooner if you like.'

She shook her head. 'No, I want to have something to show you before I come back. So Thursday should do.' She was getting an uncomfortable power surge from seeing his agitation.

'Well, if you need me don't hesitate to—'

'It's okay. I won't need you.' She nodded curtly. 'See you Thursday then.'

He had turned away from her to his bookshelf. 'Sure. See you then.'

Prudence left the office not really knowing who had won.

Holly's nerve almost failed her as Justin prepared to leave that afternoon.

'Are you staying?' he asked as he shrugged himself into his overcoat.

She looked up. 'Um . . . yeah. I've got a little bit more to do.'

'Your dedication is frightening.'

'It's not really.' She wasn't sure what to say. And she desperately wanted to leave, not to be alone in the office.

But no. *Determination, Holly.* This could be excitement, not terror, making icy patterns in her bloodstream.

'Hey, I'm glad Prudence finally spoke to you,' she said, changing the subject. 'I was beginning to worry that she'd be avoiding you for the rest of the year.'

Justin's mouth twitched into one of those half-smiles that Holly was getting used to. 'I'm glad she spoke to me, too. I had started to think I'd imagined the whole thing. I'm happy to say my sanity is still intact.'

Holly felt her own smile fade on her lips. Imagination and sanity. Just what was she trying to do anyway?

'Okay,' she said. 'I'll see you tomorrow.'

'Bye, Holly.' The door closed softly behind him and Holly returned to her reading, waiting for night to fall.

At around eight o'clock she could stand it no more. Not one word she had read had made any sense whatsoever, but she was sure that she was now alone in the college again. She stuck her head out the door and listened. All was quiet and she could see no lights on anywhere. She padded up to the bathroom in the dark, pulled the mirror off the wall—she had re-hung it very early that morning—and returned to her desk, her heart thudding.

He wouldn't hurt her, she knew that. If he wanted to hurt her he would have done so already. She just had to see that face again, she had day-dreamed about it all weekend. The pale oval, the dark hair flowing over his shoulders, round blue eyes laden with an eternity of sadness. Over and over she had recreated his image in her mind's eye, overwhelmed by the desire to see him. Speak to him. Even if it was just once.

Once again she retrieved two candles from Prudence's desk, her nerves singing in an anticipation that was more than a little sexual, though she could barely admit that to herself. Once again she faced the mirror in candlelight and breathed his name.

'Christian?'

This time the feel of his hands on her body came first. Confidently sweeping up her ribcage to enclose her breasts. She kept her eyes focussed in the mirror, fighting down the panic that had seized her brain and threatened to undo her. His thumbs goaded her nipples into peaks. She felt warm breath on her neck, hot kisses behind her ear.

84

'Christian,' she said again with a shaking voice. 'I want to see you.'

The hands left her body, and with that same uncanny rushing sound the air behind her left shoulder seemed to waver and reform into his shape. Her first impulse was to turn around, but a voice that seemed to come from everywhere and nowhere at the same time, said, 'Don't. You can only see me in the glass.'

Her eyes bulged as she tried to come to terms with what she was seeing. An achingly beautiful young man in a deep red frock coat, not a ghostly apparition in a white sheet. Her heart was leaping about in her chest like a wild thing.

'Oh my God,' she breathed. 'What have I done?'

'You've done nothing. I've always been here. We're just meeting at the limit of our planes.' His voice was becoming more focussed now, as if he were speaking just behind her instead of out of the walls.

She gathered her wits enough to ask the only question she could think of. 'Who are you?'

'I'm Christian. You know that. Who are you?'

'I'm Holly. I mean, what are you doing here? At Humberstone?'

'I'm bound here. I'm looking for something.'

It was all Holly could do to stop herself laughing hysterically. She tried to choke out a few words but found them stuck in her throat. Finally she managed to say, 'I'm frightened.'

'Of me?'

'Of the fact that I can see you. I . . . I keep wondering if I'm going mad.'

'You aren't going mad. I'm here.' She saw him turn his eyes downwards, that aching sadness touching his lips. 'Would that I weren't. Would that I were still with Peter.'

'Peter?'

'My protector. My father. My lover.'

'Who is Peter? Is he here too?'

Christian shook his head. 'No. I don't know where he is. Perhaps too far away for me ever to see him again.' His accent was upper-class British with well-rounded vowels. Just occasionally the faint reminder of some other accent touched his voice. Holly was bewitched by his voice, his face. But at the same time, she felt as though events had spun ever so slightly out of control, as though she might be losing her grip on reality.

'I don't know what to say. I don't know what to ask,' she said.

'We could make love. You'd have to close your eyes.'

'I'd . . .' A million emotions welled up inside her, temporarily stupefying her. 'No, not yet. Tell me how you got here. Tell me about Peter.'

'It's quite a long tale.'

She glanced at the clock on her desk. Eight-thirty.

'I have all night. Please, begin.'

CHAPTER SEVEN

'**M**y mother and I were very poor. I never knew my real father,' Christian began with a slow tilt of his head. 'All through my childhood we lived in squats, or sometimes on the streets in summer. Occasionally my mother would meet a gentleman and we would move in with him briefly, but those occasions always ended badly, with my mother beaten and thrown back on the streets.

'When I was about eight and old enough to be left alone, my mother started leaving me for short periods— a day, two days—and she would come back with milk and fresh bread, or sometimes a little trifle for me. She said that she had been out working and I think I knew, even at that tender age, that she meant she was selling her body. Sometimes when she came back she'd be bruised and walking stiffly, but she would not complain.

'One winter, just after my eleventh birthday, my mother found us a new room to live in. She said it would be our permanent home. It was a grim place with filthy walls and cold draughts which we had to plug up with paper, but it had a fireplace and a bed big enough for both of us. We had only been living in it for two weeks when Mother left for work and never came back.

'I waited for a week, but by then our landlord was bothering me about rent. I pleaded with him to let me stay until Mother returned. He allowed me a month, but I did not see her again. I was thrown out on the street, with a belting from my landlord for the trouble I had caused him.

'Of course I knew how to endure a London winter without a home. I knew how to beg, how to steal, where to find an abandoned building to shelter in. I had never known any better, so I did not burn with injustice or weep for my lot. I merely survived.

'I found I was quite successful as a beggar. People usually hate the appearance of poverty, but I was repeatedly told I had the face of an angel. And they could hardly leave an angel to starve in a doorstep. While I watched other children around me racked with illnesses and dying from hunger and cold, I lived on at least one modest meal a day. There was never any question of sharing my food with others. I am afraid I knew no charity myself, nor did I have a sense of fellowship.

'It was one of the coldest winters in a hundred years, and every morning on my rounds I would find at least one body—either a child or an old person—with their frozen hands stretched out before them. Remembering it now feels like remembering a very old nightmare that haunted me in childhood. The images still have the power to unsettle, but they are felt at a remove, through a veil, and are easily dismissed from my imagination. Have you ever felt really cold, Holly?'

'I . . .' Holly was brought back to herself. She had been lost in his words, in watching the motions of his exquisite face in the mirror. 'It's cold where I live now. Colder than I'm used to.'

'That winter, Holly . . .' He trailed off and sighed, then

began again. 'Imagine a cold that seems to turn your bones to ice in your body. Imagine air so frosted that it seems to shatter around you as you move. Imagine stumbling when you walk because you can no longer feel your feet. Imagine an icy net cast around your mind, freezing out any hope that you will ever be warm or dry again. And then imagine standing outside a house with small windows glowing amber from the fire roaring inside, the sounds of laughter heard muffled through the walls, while you know that only half a foot of brick and mortar separates you from relief. Half a foot that may as well be a freezing, stormy ocean.

'I was begging down near Whitechapel when a gentleman, dressed like a dandy, offered me money on the condition that I come back to his house to get it. Of course I followed him, but rather than leading me to a house he led me into an alleyway and forced me up against a wall. The brick was cold against my face, but his hands were hot on my back and my legs as he pulled down my ragged trousers and raped me. I suppose it must have been painful, but I hardly remember the pain. I remember the salty taste of his palm against my mouth as he stopped me from screaming, the sounds of his guilty pleasure, the warmth of his body pressed against mine, and the hot trickle of his semen mixed with my own blood. And of course the money. He threw a few coins at me and left me there. I redressed myself, bought some hot bread, and embarked upon a new career.

'That angel's face which kindly people had hated to see pinched with starvation became a fine lure for those looking for street trade. One evening, I paid a young thief to break into a tailor's and steal a good coat, knowing I would attract richer men if I did not appear to be little more than a ragged beggar. My face has been my fortune, Holly.'

'It's a beautiful face,' she murmured. Every time the

full knowledge of what she was experiencing screamed into her mind, she pushed it away. *Just go with it.* She might wake any moment and find it all a dream, and until then she had to burn the memory of the beautiful boy into her mind.

'It kept me alive. I rented a filthy, squalid room and lived through another two London winters there. And then Peter found me.

'At first I thought he was just another client. He was dressed outrageously, clothed in purple and gold silks, with a long red woollen overcoat. He had an air of decadence about him, like a degenerate Roman emperor or a dissolute Catholic bishop. He was large even then, though he would grow fatter over the years, and he had an enormous hooked nose and dark shadowy recesses beneath his eyes. An ugly man, yes, but strangely compelling.

'He was merely walking past when he spotted me and stopped to gaze at me. I smiled at him, as I did to all potential customers, and he smiled back and went on his way. I saw him again the following day, and finally on the third day he put his hand out to me and said, "Boy, come with me." I followed him to a carriage and he took me to his house. It was the first time I had ever been to the house of one of my gentleman clients, and certainly the first time I had ever been in a place of such extravagant grandeur.

'He led me into the sitting room. A red marble fireplace warmed the room, red and gold wallpaper covered the walls, lavish oriental rugs were laid out across the floor. He sat me in a leather armchair in front of the fire and told me to wait for him. I looked at the ceiling and even that was ornate, with a decorative pressed-metal pattern curling and swirling on the plaster. I gazed around me, trying to take it all in. He returned with a tray of hot soup and bread which I wolfed ravenously, washing it down with a bitter glass of wine. I was intoxicated instantly, having never tasted alcohol before. I sat in a muted daze, all my cares floating somewhere near the patterned ceiling. Finally he spoke to me.

'"What is your name, boy?"

'"Christian, sir."

'"I'm Peter. Do you like it here?"

'"Very much, sir."

'He took the tray from me and gently pulled me to my feet. His hands worked at my buttons, deftly but tenderly stripping me. My skin was warmed by the fire. When he had me completely naked I reached out to remove his own clothes, but he pushed my hand away.

'"No," he said, "don't touch me."

'He turned me around, ran his hands and his fingers all over me, almost as though he were inspecting me. His warm hand cupped one of my buttocks and he sighed softly.

'"You're an exquisitely made creature, Christian," he said.

'"Thank you, sir."

'"Would you like to stay here with me?"

'"Yes sir, I would like that very much," I said, though I do not think what he had asked me had sunk in properly. I thought perhaps it was the offer of a man transported with desire.

'"You will have to call me Peter if you're going to stay with me," he said.

'"Yes, Peter."

'"Very well. Now you are mine." With that he gave me a tender kiss on the forehead and cast my beggar's clothes into the fire. And from then on I was, indeed, his.'

Christian stopped for a moment, turned those sad, sad eyes downwards. Instinctively Holly swivelled around in her chair, intending to touch his hand or offer some other gesture of sympathy, but he was not behind her. The voice had scattered again, seemed to be coming from the walls all around her. 'Turn around, Holly, you can only look at me in the glass.'

She turned to the mirror again and he was there. 'I thought I'd lost you,' she said softly.

'No, I'm still here.' His voice had already refocussed. Just as if he were really there. She was starting to get a headache. A sick feeling of dread weighed down on her.

'What happened? Did you stay with him?' she said, trying to fill the strange silence.

'Yes I did. He lay down his red overcoat in front of the fire and told me to sleep there. He came with blankets and a huge feather pillow, but it seemed he did not wish to bugger me. He treated me rather like a new pet, stroking my hair and my body, muttering little noises of comfort as I fell asleep. You have no idea, Holly, how it felt to be surrounded by love and warmth after my hard years on the freezing streets.

'It seems I slept forever, and I didn't dream. When I woke, I noticed from the clock over the mantelpiece that the next day was well advanced. I could not have judged the time by the sunlight because there was none. The windows were blocked up by heavy drapes and not one courageous glimmer of sunlight drifted in to illuminate the scene. He had candles burning even during the day.

'I lay for a while in front of the fire, unsure if I should rise and search for him. Finally he came in with more food and wine and I gulped it greedily. I'm afraid I had no manners of the table, I had spent too many years seeing food as a rare gift to be jealously guarded. He pulled me into his lap and petted me again. I sat silently. This was the first time anybody had ever touched me gently and kindly and I found it strange and wonderful.

'"Can you read, Christian?" he asked eventually.

'"No, sir."

'"I'm not surprised, you can barely speak."

'I was offended. I tried very hard at the time to speak properly, and I saw myself as something of a valuable trinket in my trade—a beautiful, well-dressed, well-spoken lover. Of course I still spoke in the harsh tones of the gutter that I could not disguise.

'"Well, I shall teach you how to read and how to speak, Christian. You will be my pupil as well as my pet. I have no spare rooms so you will have to sleep here in front of the fire. You can make yourself at home down here, but stay away from the upstairs rooms. If I find you up there I'll flog you."

'"Yes, sir." I could not believe how fortune had smiled upon me. He was serious about me staying with him, I would have a warm bed in front of a fire every night and food every day. "What will I have to do, sir, to earn my keep?" Here is where I assumed I would be put to work, either as a servant or as a bugger-boy.

'"Nothing," he said. "Nothing but remain beautiful. Do not grow old, do not grow fat, do not grow ugly. Be beautiful."

'I was barely fourteen, so this task seemed entirely possible. "Yes sir," I said obediently.

'"Good," he said. "And remember, you must call me Peter, and you must always do exactly as I say. There are many secrets in this house."

'Again, as a fourteen-year-old urchin who was faced with the prospect of secure tenure for the first time in my life, I hardly cared if Peter was the devil himself. So his talk of secrets barely made an impression on me.'

Holly pressed her palm to her forehead. A sharp pain had started throbbing over her left eye and nausea was rising in her belly.

'Are you all right, Holly?' Christian asked.

'I'm not feeling well. It's probably the shock.'

'It's me, I'm making you ill. It comes from being so close to me. I should go.'

'No!' she said, too quickly. 'Please, I'll be all right for a bit longer. Tell me more. Did Peter teach you to read?'

'Yes,' Christian resumed, a light smile playing on his lips as he remembered. 'Yes he taught me to read, and to write and to speak, as he said he would. We would sit in front of the fire in the late afternoon and early evening going over letters and words. And he bought me new clothes, fantastically expensive outfits in rich colours and ornate patterns. He was very gentle with me, Holly. Only once or twice did he lose his temper and hurt me. And then I deserved it, I deserved it very much.'

'What did you do?'

'That was later, much later. For now, I wish to recall those nights sitting at his feet, his gentle voice, the strange musky scent of him. He had no housekeeper, and did most of the cooking and cleaning himself. Well, the cooking at least. The house was filthy—a thick film of dust covered everything, and the upholstery and carpets were stained and dirty. Weeks went by. It was almost two months before I realised there was another person in the house.'

'Another person?'

'Yes. She lived in an upstairs room. I knew I was not allowed to go up there, but when I began to get used to my surroundings and to take Peter for granted, I would lurk at the bottom of the stairs, looking up, wondering what was up there. Peter would disappear upstairs for hours every day. I knew he was doing some kind of work but I knew not what. I was standing on the first step, my hand on the dusty banister, gazing up into the dark, forbidden place, when a small, pale creature appeared. She paused at the top of the stairs and looked down at me, gave a startled cry and ran back into the darkness.

'I nearly ran up after her but I was conscious of behaving myself. She was a girl about my age in a blue muslin dress, with pale golden hair in ringlets gathered in bunches on either side of her face. And she was pretty. I wondered if she was another of Peter's pretty pets, and I felt a pang of jealousy imagining that I might not be his only darling.

'Try as I might, I could not forget about her. Weeks went by and I did not see her again, nor did I mention to Peter that I knew of her existence, afraid that he would be angry with me.

'Then one day, Peter left early in the morning saying he was going out for business and I was to stay home and practise forming my letters. I sat in my favourite armchair, carefully copying letters in the gloomy house. I could hear it raining heavily outside, the water dripping off the eaves and onto the street. The clock ticked loudly in the quiet room and I could think of nothing but that it may be my only chance to explore upstairs and find the girl.

'I put aside my book, my stomach weak with excitement. Only a few months before I would have thought nothing of exploring the house, taking some expensive items and hocking them out on the street. But Peter had begun to civilise me. Even more than that, I had grown so dependent on his love and his attention that I could not imagine having to live without it ever again.

'So it was with great trepidation that I approached the stairs and started up. The runner was worn through in places. I put my feet carefully one in front of the other. It was strange. All the outward signs suggested I was home alone but I knew she must be up there, her warm little heart beating just as mine was beating. I reached the top of the stairs and knew not which way to turn. I wavered, peering left and right, then finally took a deep breath and veered to the right.

'It seemed impossible, but it was even darker upstairs than downstairs. All the doors to rooms were closed and no daylight at all filtered through. My eyes had to adjust to the darkness and I felt along the wall until I found a door handle. My heart was racing as I turned the handle and pushed the door open. I found only an empty room, the curtains drawn and a dusty smell hanging in the air. I closed the door and advanced up the hallway.

'I listened carefully, but could hear nothing that indicated any sign of life. I began to think that perhaps I had imagined the girl, and my heart sank. I opened the next door I came to. Clearly it was Peter's bedroom. It smelled very strongly of him, a slightly sweaty, masculine scent. I backed out and kept moving, opened the next door and found myself standing in another dim room. My eyes had grown used to the dark now, but I still rubbed them and looked twice because the room was decorated so oddly.

'Bookshelves lined two of the walls, and on the third, where a window had been bricked in, a large red star was painted. Numbers were formed around it, and letters— some strange letters I had never seen. I drew closer to look at them, managed to decipher a few but not others. Turning, I took the rest of the room in. It reminded me of something but I couldn't think what. A book was open on a long low table and candles were arranged in neat patterns all around the room.

'Then I remembered. As a small boy my mother had often taken me into various churches to receive charity. The room was set out similar to a church, and the long low table seemed to be some kind of altar. But something about the room disturbed me, whereas I remembered the churches I had been in as places of light and love. This place was dark, cold. There was something sinister about the strange painted language and a thick, unpleasant smell breathed from the walls. I backed out of the room and closed the door warily behind me, a million questions that I knew I would never be allowed to ask forming in my mind.

'Only one door remained in the hallway, but I had convinced myself by this stage that I would find nothing behind it. I twisted the handle gently and pushed the door in.

'And there she was. The light in her room dazzled me after so long in darkness. The curtains were drawn open, revealing a low grey sky groaning overhead. I can only imagine that I would have been rendered blind if the sun had been shining. She sat upon her bed, gazing up at me with violet eyes, looking like a frightened rabbit.

'"I will not hurt you," I said, advancing towards her.

'She squealed and cowered from me, but I sat next to her on the bed and took her hand in mine. Her skin was fine and pale, her body just beginning to bud beneath her blue dress. Her hand was cold and she trembled.

'"I'm Christian. I will not hurt you. I'm a friend of Peter's."

'She nodded and seemed to calm down a little.

'"I saw you a few weeks ago. Do you remember?" I asked.

'"Yes," she replied softly. "I remember."

'"What is your name?"

'"Rosalind."

'"I'm Christian. Do you live here too?"

'"Yes, I live here with Papa."

'"Papa?" I could barely form the word. She was Owling's daughter. "Do you have a mother?"

'She shook her head. "I don't think so. Are you living here now?"

'"Apparently. Peter brought me home and said I was to stay with him. I don't know why he hasn't introduced us."

'"I'm not supposed to leave my room."

'"And I'm not supposed to be upstairs. What do you do all day?"

'She seemed to be warming to me. "I read, sometimes I play. Would you like to play?"

'"What would we play?"

'"I make up games, like stories in a book. Sometimes I pretend I'm a lady pirate. Or a queen. Or a horse. Would you like to play pirates?"

'She beamed at me so beautifully that I would not have been able to refuse even if my silly childish brain had remembered that I was somewhere I wasn't supposed to be. She dressed me up with a patch over my eye and we spent the morning pretending that her bed was the Good Ship *Rosalind*, fighting Spanish sailors and amassing a huge stockpile of coloured wool as treasure. We laughed and squealed like . . . well, like children, which was something I had never been before. Every now and then she would press her warm, soft body against mine and kiss my cheek or whisper in a secretive voice, and her sweet, hot breath would tickle my ear. I very quickly became besotted.

'When I heard the door slam downstairs and I realised Peter must be home, I was less concerned about being in trouble than I was about having to stop playing. At the sound of the door, Rosalind gasped and said, "Papa," in an urgent, low voice. We looked at each other, far too young to decide on any kind of solution before we heard his footsteps on the stairs.

'"Christian, where are you?" he was calling.

'I decided honesty would perhaps get me through. "I'm up here, Peter. I'm playing with Rosalind."

'The footsteps suddenly doubled their speed and Peter thundered along the hall before appearing at the door to Rosalind's room, beet-red with rage.

'"What the devil is going on here?" he demanded.

'"Papa, don't be cross . . ." Rosalind offered softly. "Please, don't be cross."

'I remembered I had the silly pirate patch on my eye, and I was pulling it off when I felt Peter's hand close on my upper arm and I was yanked violently into the hallway. With one swift movement he slammed Rosalind's door behind him, shutting out the light. It was too dark for me to see properly at first, and as he threw me against the wall I lost my bearings. I struggled to my feet weakly, unsure where Peter was. The blow came from behind me, slamming my head into the wall. I heard Rosalind scream from the other side of her door. I leaned against the wall for support. A massive blow to my lower back brought me to my knees. A high-pitched whining rang in my ears and I could taste blood in my mouth. Peter was an enormous man and I was just on the threshold of puberty. I had no way to defend myself, and as the blows rained down on me I accepted with the fatalism I had learned on the streets that I would probably die now. But Rosalind saved me. Through her sobs on the other side of her door, she managed to shout, "But Papa, his face. His beautiful face."

'Peter paused long enough for me to struggle into a sitting position and look up at him. I spat some blood from my mouth. He reached one of his fat, white hands towards me and gently touched my swollen, bleeding lip. I winced, but I was unafraid. All the violent rage seemed to have left him and he was once again his loving self.

'"Oh, Christian, forgive me." He leaned over me and scooped me easily into his arms. I was still too shocked to speak, so I let him press me to him and carry me downstairs. He placed me in the armchair in front of the fire and kissed my broken lip tenderly. "Forgive me, my beautiful boy. I will explain one day. Of course you were curious. I'm sorry, I'm sorry."

'Of course I forgave him. He was dearer to me than . . .' Christian trailed off, his full lips pressed together to hold back a tide of emotion. Holly, however, was glad for the interruption. Her nausea had been steadily worsening and now it had become unbearable.

'Christian, I think I'm going to throw up.'

'I should go.'

'Don't go.'

'You can call me again. Any time you want. And if you don't want to listen to my story, I can make love to you.'

The thought of his making love caused her to shiver. But a far more pressing issue was her stomach's threat to disgorge its contents.

'I'll speak to you again soon,' she said. 'Go now.'

The image shivered and disappeared, leaving her by herself in the dim candlelight. Almost instantly the nausea subsided, the pain in her head receded.

And she had never felt so lonely in her life.

CHAPTER EIGHT

~

'**J**ustin?'

Justin was halfway to his bedroom door when his aunt called him from the top of the stairs. He took a few paces back and paused, looking up at her.

'Hi, Emma.' Today had been a strange day. Holly hadn't been in at all and Prudence had been chatty. She was nice, but a bit exhausting. And he was more than a little concerned about how disappointed he had been that Holly hadn't shown up. The last thing he needed was to go getting a stupid crush on somebody, especially somebody in the middle of a divorce. He just wanted to lie on his bed, stare at the ceiling and blank all his feelings out. Some days it was the only way to cope.

Emma descended the stairs with a smile playing across her lips. She was pretty, for an older woman, round and soft with blonde streaked hair and large brown eyes. But she was one problem too many for Justin. The attention she paid him was progressing beyond maternal concern. He felt himself flinch away from her.

Emma didn't seem to notice. 'Did you have a nice

day?' she asked, putting her arm around Justin's shoulder and leading him to the kitchen.

'Yeah, fine,' he replied flatly.

'Have a cup of coffee and a chat with me,' she said, ushering him to a stool at the kitchen bench before filling the electric kettle and switching it on. She came to stand beside him and idly stroked his hair. He wanted to get away from her but didn't know how to. Any movement or rebuff would be acknowledging that she made him uncomfortable. It seemed more polite, more prudent to ignore her attention and hope it would go away. Not an effective method for handling problems, as he knew from tragic experience, but the only one he could think of.

'How are things going with your work at the college?' she asked, stepping away from him to make two cups of coffee. She had never asked him how he liked his coffee or tea, and always made it very white and very sweet. He preferred black and unsugared, but it had been going on too long now for him to change. She placed a cup in front of him and he sipped it while she settled on the stool next to his.

'Quite well, thanks. Holly's been very helpful and Jane's a good supervisor.'

'Ah, all the women in your life, Justin.' Then she added in a muffled veil of sadness, 'Jane's such an attractive woman —I rather think Lucien prefers her to me sometimes.'

Justin looked across at his aunt. 'I'm sure that's not the case.' Justin couldn't imagine Lucien experiencing any kind of human emotion, let alone love or desire. But he didn't clarify his point, he let Emma think it was a compliment to her.

She smiled. 'Are you sure you're not going to change your mind about coming away with us next week? You'll be lonely by yourself.'

The Easter break was a couple of days away and Lucien

and Emma were off on a trip to Queensland. Although Emma wanted him to go, the way Lucien's mouth had tightened at the suggestion left Justin in no doubt as to where he was to spend Easter. Right here, in the happy Humberstone abode. 'No, I won't be lonely. I'll get some work done, I'll have a look around the city.'

She twisted her lips in thought. 'Perhaps I should stay here with you . . .'

'No,' he said, hoping it wasn't too quickly. 'Really, Emma, you go away and have a nice time with your husband.' He immediately regretted his choice of words. By using 'husband', had it seemed he was trying to put her back in her place? Talking to her was like negotiating a minefield.

'Lucien and I . . . well, we don't get on as well as we used to.'

Justin didn't want to risk saying the wrong thing, so he remained silent.

'Just between you and me, we haven't made love for months,' she continued in a conversational tone as she set her coffee cup back in its saucer. He looked into his lap and felt the blush spread across his cheeks.

'Am I making you uncomfortable, Justin?' He looked up. She had him trapped in her gaze.

He shook his head mutely. 'I've really got some work to get done,' he said, shooting out of his seat and leaving his coffee half finished. He was almost to the safe haven of his bedroom when she caught him around the wrist.

'Justin, don't shut me out,' she said softly, close to his ear. 'You and I could be so close, wouldn't you like to be close to somebody? You're such a sad, serious thing. I just want to be your friend, your confidante.'

'Emma, I . . .' Now was the time to spell out how uncomfortable her concept of friendship made him, in simple assertive terms. But his tongue was leaden. She was so close he could smell her warm, coffee-scented breath.

103

'I'm a woman, Justin. Please don't look at me as your fat old aunt. I'm a woman.'

'I have to get some reading done before tomorrow,' he said in the most ordinary voice he could muster. 'Jane's expecting me at nine, I don't want to let her down.'

Emma released his arm. 'No. Don't let her down.' He watched her turn on her heel and walk away, humming as though nothing had happened. Thankfully, he pushed his bedroom door open and collapsed on his bed, preparing to zone out for a few blissful hours.

Concentrate, Prudence. She admonished herself for getting carried away in the moment. As had won this time, summoning her to his office and giving her a bunch of flowers—no doubt bought for five bucks at a service station, but it was the thought that counted—and getting her skirt up around her ears before she could say, 'You're forgiven.' But now, with her hair splayed out on his desk calendar, her legs around his waist, and her hands reaching out to grasp his master keys, she felt a sense of triumph. His eyes were shut tight and his groans of passion masked any sound she made as she closed her fingers around his keys and hid them under her panties, which were discarded on the mahogany desk top. Mission accomplished.

He let out a huge sigh and collapsed on her breasts, the fingers of his right hand idly grazing her nipples. 'I'm so glad you came back, Prudence. After Monday I thought we were . . . you know, finished.'

'Of course not,' she murmured, her hand twining in his hair.

'I wanted to get this all sorted out before the break. I won't see you for nearly two weeks. I'll miss your gorgeous body.' She knew he was only pretending to be sad about not seeing her. Over Christmas they had been apart for two months and it had nearly killed her, while it hadn't seemed to bother him at all. As was just worried about getting his end in before he went away to Sydney with his family for the Easter break. She accepted his compliment, however, delighted about having a set of keys and an empty college to play in over the holidays.

He lifted himself off her and turned his back to rearrange himself. She surreptitiously tucked the keys into her underwear as she dressed and smoothed her skirt down. Not real comfortable, but worth enduring for the long-term benefits.

Aswell turned to her and kissed her forehead. 'Very fond of you, Prudence.'

She smiled mutely. Not the sentiment she'd been hoping for, but it would do.

'What time are you leaving in the morning?' she said as he walked her to the door.

'Our flight leaves at nine. My wife screwed up as usual—I wanted a much later flight. Now we have to fight with peak-hour traffic to get to the airport. Shall we go for a smoke?'

She shook her head and opened the door. 'No, I've got a few things to get together before the break. Have a good time away.'

He looked slightly surprised but let it slide. 'Sure. You have a good holiday.'

She walked carefully to the stairwell—difficult with keys stuffed in her knickers—then made it thankfully to her office. Justin and Holly were in, but both had their heads bent over their work. She swivelled her chair to the window, inched her fingers up under her skirt and secretly fished the keys out of her underwear. Dropping them into her tote bag, she turned once more and said loudly, 'Holiday time!'

Holly put down her pen and looked up. Prudence had noticed that Holly had been very quiet all week, but she put it down to the shock of having her husband threaten to kill himself. Justin swung around in his chair and gave her one of those looks that would have been a smile if his face hadn't been made of stone. She was starting to find it endearing.

'Are you guys going away anywhere?'

Holly shook her head and Justin said, 'No.'

'Neither am I. I've got a whole house and a wine cellar to myself. Interested?'

Holly seemed to be considering the offer very carefully. Finally she said, 'That sounds like fun.'

Justin, who had been watching Holly to see her response first, nodded slowly.

And what was that all about, by the way? thought Prudence. *Justin interested in Holly?*

'Do you want us to come over one night?' he asked.

'You can come over for the entire weekend for all I care,' Prudence replied, not sure why she felt mildly annoyed by the idea that Justin might like Holly. After all, Holly hadn't got pissed and passed out on his bed, Holly was smart and pretty and slim, Holly had manners and knew when to shut up. 'I have a surprise for you guys if you do come.'

'What is it?' Holly asked.

'Not telling. It's a surprise. You can't find out until tomorrow. Come by about six and bring clothes to stay over. I'll make dinner and we'll stay up all night, just like a slumber party.' Prudence felt the excitement wind up as she planned their weekend. 'Come on, it'll be so fun.'

'I'll be there,' Holly said firmly.

'I guess I will too,' Justin added.

Prudence grinned. 'Just wait until you see what I've got in store.'

For the few moments after Holly woke every morning, everything was okay. As she drifted up through the layers, she was only aware that she was somewhere soft, somewhere warm—thanks to the electric blanket she had bought last week—and that the wind was sighing lightly in the trees. Then a sharp tack on the muted, velvety path of her half-sleeping thoughts. That's right, she was going mad.

Holly sat up and shook her hair out of her eyes. *I'm going mad.* The notion had been preoccupying her since first thing Tuesday morning. Monday night she had believed that Christian was real, that a ghost really was making contact with her. In a kind of sensual daze she had slept that night, believing it all. But she had woken on Tuesday charged with the certainty that she had completely lost her grip on reality. It couldn't have been a ghost. She couldn't have seen it because ghosts didn't exist. She had imagined it all in a deluded fit, which threw doubt on her continuing sanity. Perhaps she should get help. How did she know it wouldn't happen again?

But Christian, Christian. The last time she had felt like this about somebody . . . Well, the truth was she had *never* felt this way about anybody. She had given up on the idea of love, decided it was nothing but a biological necessity that had garnered certain fictitious qualities through wishful thinking. To fall in love now, with somebody that wasn't even real . . .

She sighed and heaved herself out of bed. It was Good Friday. Prudence's dinner was on tonight. It would provide a useful diversion. Even so, even so. Perhaps it was time to admit that she was out of her depth. Perhaps she should book a plane back to Townsville, go back to Michael, back to the school and her family. The thought, though it made her wild with frustration, also offered some kind of strange comfort. She was convinced that the upheaval, Michael's letter, her awful accommodation were all contributing factors to her minor breakdown on Monday night. If she got away from all of that, surely it would put things right again.

The stupid thing was that she felt perfectly sane. She felt as though everything she had experienced was entirely real. But then, if she were mad, she *would* think that, wouldn't she?

She pulled on a robe and slippers and padded out to the kitchen. The tap dripped slowly and persistently into the sink. A bug scurried under the bench as she opened an airtight container of tea bags. The wallpaper was peeling behind the kettle and she pulled off a sad, grey strip while waiting for the water to boil. She fixed herself some breakfast, then picked up the phone and dialled her mother's number.

'Hello?'

'Mum? It's Holly. Happy Easter.'

'How lovely to hear from you,' her mother said. 'Are you well?'

'Thanks, yes I am. I'm busy at the college and I've got some friends to visit tonight.'

'You still like it there then?' Her mother had been trying to get her to come home since the moment she arrived in Melbourne. Her place was with her husband, according to the Beck family. And Michael's family. Holly wasn't prepared to admit defeat just yet, not on the phone to her mother anyway.

'Yes, I still like it.'

'Michael's here.'

Holly froze. 'At your place?'

'He and his family have come by to take me to church. Would you like to speak to him?'

'No, I can't speak to him.'

'Sure you can. Hold on, I'll put him on.'

'No, Mum, I—' Holly heard a thump as the phone was dropped on a table and her mother went in search of her husband. She briefly considered hanging up, but the suicide threat weighed heavily on her. Perhaps she owed it to him to talk.

Finally he came to the phone. 'Hello?'

'Happy Easter, Michael,' she said, trying to sound cheerful and failing.

'Happy Easter, Holly,' he said softly.

There was a long, uncomfortable silence.

'I got your letter,' she said at length. 'Did you really mean what you said?'

'I meant some of it.'

'You're not really thinking about killing yourself? Not over me, I'm hardly worth—'

'Holly, don't tell me how to feel. We belong together and I know that. I just want you to wake up and realise it too. We belong together.'

This was really uncomfortable. Holly wanted to crawl back into bed and sleep until she was thirty. 'Michael, I have to go.'

'Go where?'

'I . . . I'm getting together with a couple of friends.'

He didn't reply.

'Michael? You still there?'

'Goodbye,' he said. The phone clicked and it was over. At least for the time being. She wished his goodbye hadn't sounded so ominous. She wished she didn't have roughly eight hours to kill before she was in company again.

Lucien was just drifting into a much needed afternoon nap. Last night it had been impossible to get any rest—it was always difficult for him in a strange bed. He had spent the morning indulging Emma in a shopping trip and finished it off with an expensive lunch, thinking it would placate her for a few hours. She seemed to require so much attention. So he was surprised to feel a pair of warm, wet lips touch his own. He fought the inexorable tide of consciousness and tried to press himself back into dark slumber. There it was again, lips moving over his face, nuzzling at his neck.

'Lucien? Are you awake?' It was Emma, her voice jarring him.

'Emma? I just got to sleep. What are you doing?'

She was pulling the covers off him and kissing his chest, her tongue flicking over his nipples, her hands moving down to cup his balls. 'Come on, it's three o'clock in the afternoon. Why do you want to sleep when you have a willing sex slave here for you?'

He could see her outline against the drawn curtains of their hotel room—the huge hump of her shoulders and torso. He felt himself shudder as he pushed her away. 'Emma, I just want a little nap.'

She sat up petulantly. 'Lucien, we haven't made love in—'

'I know how long it is, you needn't remind me.' Now he was angry. Angry at her for waking him, for not being the slender, beautiful woman he had married. Angry at himself for not being able to suppress the anger and perform his duty as a husband. Anger was simply not conducive to lovemaking.

'Just forget about it, all right? I'm in no mood for being amorous.'

She lay down next to him again, brooding silently. Then suddenly she piped up, 'Are you feeling threatened?'

'What on earth are you talking about?'

'Justin. Does he make you feel old?'

Lucien was completely unprepared for this. 'No, of course not. He's just a slack, spoiled—'

'He's young and beautiful. You're approaching fifty.'

He could have hit her for that. Not because he was insulted, but because she had clearly formed an attachment to the boy. Times like these he wondered how they had ever found enough in common to marry each other in the first place. How could her judgement be so skewed?

'Emma, you're forty-four years old and hardly a sylph. Surely you don't harbour any fond fantasies that Justin would find you attractive?'

'Is it so unthinkable?'

He didn't answer, let the silence speak for him.

'He's a lovely lad, Lucien, and if you spent more than five minutes in his company you'd find that out for yourself.'

'Emma, that's wishful thinking. He's sullen and he says nothing to anybody. Don't interpret his silence as repressed desire for you. You'd be making a complete fool of yourself.'

She sniffed loudly and Lucien guessed he had brought her to tears. His exasperation with her only intensified. 'Just don't get too attached to him, whatever it is you think you feel for him. He's only passing through. He won't stay with us, I can guarantee it.'

Emma didn't reply. Lucien screwed his eyes shut to try to recapture the warm sleep she had interrupted. But it was proving impossible.

'He might stay,' she said softly, climbing off the bed and searching for her clothes on the floor. 'He might grow fond of us . . . or at least of me.'

Lucien sat up and reached for the book on his bedside table. Sleep had eluded him. 'Emma, just consider Justin a temporary fixture. It will be easier on all of us.' He gave her an insincere smile of reassurance. 'Trust me.'

'Justin? I wasn't expecting you.' Holly stood aside and let Justin in. He was wearing a dark green sweater and black cords, and he smelled of a delicious aftershave. If she were Prudence she'd be able to make a mildly flirtatious comment about it, but those things were better left to the experts.

111

'Yeah, I was on my way to Prudence's and I thought I'd come by and see if you'd left yet. We can walk down together.'

'Great. I'm just putting my shoes on. Um . . . sit down.' She indicated the single armchair in the corner that she called the living room and went to find her shoes. When she came back, Justin hadn't sat down and was looking over her bookcase.

'Did you make this?'

'Yes. Two packing crates and a few Besser bricks. Wait till you see Prudence's bookcases. You'll die of jealousy. Isn't this place ugly?'

He looked around, pushing his long curls out of his eyes. 'It's pretty dingy. But I've seen worse.'

'It's a bit warmer now I've got some draught blocks under the doors. But when it rains there's an awful smell. And it rains so much down here.'

He didn't respond and she bit her tongue to stop herself from filling the gap with mindless chatter. She just had to get used to him. It seemed Prudence had the hang of it, not caring if he seemed to hear her or not.

'Shall we go?' she said eventually.

'Sure.'

They trudged in silence down the hill and across the park, Holly making the occasional comment about the weather or other banalities. She wanted to ask him about so many things—about his aunt and uncle, his history, his plans—but she knew it was hopeless. Even Prudence hadn't managed to draw him out.

'This is it,' she said, steering him into Prudence's street and pointing to her house. 'Impressive, isn't it?'

He nodded. 'And she lives here alone?'

'Yes, her family are all overseas. I can't believe you missed hearing about that, it was her favourite gripe for a whole week.'

He shrugged. Night was falling and she couldn't see

112

his face clearly in the dark, just the streetlight reflecting in his glasses. 'Sometimes I tune out when Prudence talks. You don't think that's awful, do you?'

Holly was so stunned to hear him make such a frank, honest admission that she couldn't answer for a moment. 'No,' she said at last. 'No, she's a sweet girl but she does tend to—'

'Let's go in,' he said, cutting her off. 'It's cold out here.'

They walked through the gate, up the front path and knocked on the door. Prudence was playing some loud music inside. They waited a few minutes then knocked again. Still no answer.

'She's got her music up so loud she can't hear us,' Holly said.

Justin knocked again, louder. 'Prudence!' he called.

Holly and Justin looked at each other. 'Try the door,' he said.

Holly turned the handle. 'It's not locked. Shall we go in?'

'I guess so. She's expecting us, after all.'

A moment later they were standing in the tiled entranceway, calling for Prudence.

'God, that music's awful,' Holly remarked while they waited.

'Let's just go find her. Obviously she can't hear a thing.'

They followed the music into the lounge room. There they found Prudence, lying flat on her back with her head between two stereo speakers, eyes closed.

'Prudence?' Holly said, nudging her with her foot.

Prudence's eyes opened and she sat up with a start. 'God, you terrified me.'

'We knocked and knocked but you didn't . . . Can you turn that down,' Holly shouted.

Prudence turned and flicked the stereo off. 'Sorry. Robert Johnson. I always get carried away when I listen to him.'

'I've never heard of him.'

'Blues guitarist from the thirties. Really spooky. Hi, Justin. You guys came together?'

'Yeah, Holly's place was on my way.'

Holly was aware that Prudence was watching them closely, making her uncomfortable. It was as if the whole world were a source of perpetual stimulation to Prudence's imagination.

'Come through. I've decorated the dining room specially.' She stood and led them through. Two wrought-iron candelabras stood on the dining table, illuminating the otherwise dark room. A dark red tablecloth covered the table, and the napkins were black. In each place Prudence had placed a silver goblet. A delicious smell was wafting in from the kitchen.

'Mmm, dinner smells good,' said Holly.

'It's just pasta. But I'm an okay cook. Just one more reason why I should have been a suburban housewife, rather than aspiring to anything more intellectual. Sit down, sit down.'

They all sat around the dining table. Prudence had left a large chocolate egg for each of them, with 'Happy Pagan Fertility Festival' handwritten on the wrappers. Holly would have laughed but the candlelight was spooking her. It reminded her too much of Monday night, of her delusion of summoning Christian's spirit.

'Wine, anybody?' Prudence said, uncorking a bottle and filling her own goblet.

'These are beautiful cups, Prudence,' Holly said, holding hers out.

'Thanks. They were a twenty-first present. Justin?'

Justin looked up from under his fringe. 'I don't normally drink.'

'Come on, just one glass. I stole this from my father's cellar. It's got to be worth nearly five hundred bucks a bottle.'

114

Justin appeared to be considering for a moment, then finally pushed his goblet forward so Prudence could fill it. Holly realised she had been holding her breath. Tonight was going to be very awkward if Justin was bent on being surly.

Prudence raised her goblet and said, 'To the students of room 205.'

'Hear, hear,' said Holly. Justin clinked his cup to theirs and they all sipped their wine.

'So why don't you drink, Justin?' Prudence asked, picking up a bread basket and passing it round.

For a moment it didn't look like he was going to answer, but then he said, 'My mother drank. My worst memories stink of alcohol.'

'I'm sorry to hear that,' Prudence said, immediately subdued. 'Does she still drink?'

'She's dead. She died in January.'

Both Holly and Prudence gaped at him. Was this why he was so sullen? Holly felt her stomach tie itself in a knot.

'God, I'm so, so sorry,' Prudence said, reaching across and rubbing his wrist. 'Me and my big mouth.'

'That's just awful,' Holly added.

'Was it the alcohol that killed her?' Prudence asked.

'Kind of. She had an accident. Look, I'd rather not . . . I mean . . . we're supposed to be having an Easter party. I'm okay with it.'

'Yes, of course,' said Prudence. 'Let's have some music, shall we?' She shot out of her chair. As she was heading to the lounge room she called out, 'Any requests?'

'Something conducive to digestion,' Holly called back, then turned to look at Justin. She tried to muster a warm smile for him. He smiled back and Holly nearly fell off her chair. She had actually seen his teeth. She tried to hide her surprise and steer the conversation somewhere more cheerful.

'Have Lucien and Emma gone away?' she asked, just as soft music started up. Prudence came back in, humming along.

'Yes, they've gone up to the Gold Coast. You wouldn't believe what they've done. They've locked me out of every room with a door in the house, except my room and the bathroom.'

Prudence plopped back in her chair. 'You're kidding!'

'I'm as surprised as you are.'

'What a strange thing for them to do,' Holly said.

'Technically, I'll bet it's not *them*. It's him. Lucien did it, because Emma wouldn't dream of doing something like that. I wondered why there was a workman in the place on Wednesday. He was replacing all the door handles with lockable ones. Lucien must have been planning it for a while.' He shook his head lightly. 'It's pretty amusing, really.'

'He must have something to hide,' Prudence said enthusiastically, reaching for the wine bottle to top everybody up.

'I don't think so. I think he's just a bit anal. Doesn't want me to get into his things.'

'Still, there's such a romance in a locked door, isn't there?' Prudence replied. 'An open door is just an open door, but a locked one—well, that's an adventure waiting to happen, a story waiting to be told.'

Holly couldn't help feeling fond of Prudence. She was irrepressible. 'So, don't you and Lucien get on?' Prudence asked, turning back to Justin.

Justin shrugged and seemed to disappear back into his shell, clearly uncomfortable with being the centre of attention. 'I don't really know him, I guess,' he mumbled. 'Let's talk about someone else. I'm just boring.'

Holly could see Prudence struggle with her next sentence and swallow it. Perhaps she did have a bit of tact after all. 'I'll get the entrées,' she said.

Prudence was more than just an okay cook. Their meal was brilliant: a warm chicken salad for an entrée, a delicious creamy mushroom pasta for the main course, and a chocolate-mint cheesecake for dessert. The wine, too, was wonderful—Holly guessed any wine worth that much would have to be. And it had succeeded in loosening Justin up a little. He even laughed once or twice, though it was a bitter, ironic laugh compared to the screaming peals of laughter that periodically convulsed Prudence. Holly was feeling soft around the edges, her stomach pleasantly full, and her brain begging for a chance to lie down and drift to sleep, when Prudence shot out of her chair and said in an exaggerated whisper, 'Wait here. I'll get the surprise.'

Justin and Holly exchanged glances while Prudence disappeared. 'What do you think it is?' she said, her tongue heavy with slight drunkenness.

He shrugged. 'Knowing Prudence? It could be anything.'

'A dead body?' she giggled, realising that she sounded foolish but not bothering to check herself.

'Perhaps. More likely a dead *alien* body.'

'Or the whole flying saucer.'

They were laughing together when Prudence came back and dropped a heavy set of keys on the table in front of them.

'I've got to say, Prudence,' Justin remarked, 'that's rather an anticlimax.'

Holly shushed him. 'Keys, Prudence? Are they magic?'

She scowled. 'You people think I'm a fruit loop. No, they're not magic. They're As's master keys. To the college.'

It wasn't sinking in. 'But Prudence, we've all got keys to the college.'

'Yes, yes,' she said impatiently. 'To the front door and to our office. But these ones, they open *everything*.'

'You're not proposing we go up to the college?' Justin said. 'It's freezing outside.'

'God, you northerners have no stamina. The cellar, Holly. The tunnels. Like in the book I showed you. Don't you want to—'

Holly felt horror prickling her skin. 'No!' she almost shouted. 'Are you kidding? I can't think of anything I'd less like to do.'

'What tunnels?' Justin asked, intrigued.

'Howard Humberstone, who built the college, had a penchant for excavating tunnels under his buildings. I want to check out the college. I'm *dying* to check out the college.'

Justin nodded reasonably. 'That could be fun.'

'Are you two out of your minds?' Holly demanded. 'Anything could happen to us. We could . . .' She trailed off, unable to think of what bad thing could happen to them in a reasonable and sane world where there were no ghosts like the one she thought she had seen on Monday night. 'We could get caught and get kicked out of college,' she finished lamely.

'Ha! Everybody's away. It's not like Lucien would pay security to work on a public holiday. And we're allowed to go into the college—we all have keys anyway. We'll just be taking an extended tour. There's three of us, Holly. Nothing bad can happen to us. Unless . . .'

'Unless what?'

'Unless I'm not the only fruit loop who believes in the spirits of dead nuns.' She wriggled her fingers in front of Holly's face and made a spooky whistling noise, her eyes huge and black in the candlelight.

Holly gritted her teeth and bit back all her fear. No such thing as ghosts. She was not going to have another bout of Monday night's insanity with Justin and Prudence alongside. Just a bit of fun with her new friends. 'God,' she said weakly, 'I'm no good under peer pressure.'

'We'll go then?' Justin asked, reaching for his sweater.

Prudence looked at Holly expectantly. Excitedly.

Holly sighed. *I can't believe I'm doing this.* 'Yeah, we'll go.'

CHAPTER NINE

〜

'**R**ight,' Prudence said in her best drill-sergeant's voice, 'have we got everything?' She pulled the keys out and jangled them loudly in the dark. 'Keys.'

'Torch,' Justin responded obediently, producing the torch.

'Wine,' Holly added, patting the bulging pocket of an overcoat Prudence had loaned her. 'Can we go inside? It really is freezing out here.'

Prudence opened the front door of the college and ushered them inside, locking it behind her. She couldn't believe she had managed to convince them. She'd expected far more resistance, especially from Justin. Maybe she'd underestimated them. Or maybe there was a lot to be said for strategic inebriation.

The familiar stuffy smell of the college enfolded her. She felt wild, excited, delighted, delirious. She wanted to whirl in circles until the roof spun above her. God, this was *great*!

'Follow me,' she urged quietly.

'Why are we whispering?' Justin whispered.

'Because we're up to no good.' She couldn't help

herself bursting into loud laughter. Holly looked as though she wanted to be anywhere but here. 'You look so serious, Holly,' she said.

'Well, it's okay for you two. I'm on a scholarship, remember. I'm dependent on this college's goodwill for my continued stay here.'

'Relax. If we get caught, we'll make something up. We'll say we kidnapped you. Won't we, Justin?'

'If that's what it takes,' he responded quietly. He had switched the torch on and was swinging the beam up and down over the foyer. The light glinted here and there off shiny surfaces.

'Now, follow me.' Prudence led them across to the condemned stairwell and stepped under the yellow tape. They followed her to the cellar door and she searched for the right key while Justin trained the torchbeam unsteadily on the lock. The lock snicked and Prudence pushed the door open. A warm, dark tingle of excitement shivered through her. 'We're in,' she said. 'Justin, the torch.'

Justin handed her the torch and she pocketed the keys, then started warily down the few stairs to the floor of the cellar. Holly and Justin followed her, until the three of them stood in the cold, dusty cellar, gazing around them.

'You're taking advantage of the fact that I'm drunk,' Holly said, perhaps only half joking. 'I can't believe we're doing this.'

'It's one of those two-room cellars,' Prudence said, not taking any notice of Holly. She'd come too far to turn back now. 'We have to go around there.' She shone the torch on a red-brick wall with a dark entranceway gaping on either side. A musty, damp smell clung to everything. It seemed she could even taste it. The two doorways looked like black holes into nowhere. Or at least somewhere very spooky.

She advanced, holding the torch in front of her like a drawn sword. Justin and Holly were very close behind her, wanting to stay near the light. She led them around the brick wall, down five stairs and into the second cellar. Running the torch along the back of the brick wall, she stifled a squeal of distaste at the sight of a troop of vile black beetles scurrying out of the light. 'Oh God, bugs. I'd forgotten there would be bugs.'

'What's a few bugs,' Justin remarked casually, 'when there could be malevolent spirits down here?'

As usual, Prudence couldn't tell from his voice if he was joking or not, but she assumed he was. 'Don't make fun of me. Look.' She aimed the torchbeam at the opposite wall, illuminating a closed door set into the dark brick. 'I bet I know where that leads.'

'And I bet you want us to follow you,' Holly said softly.

'Well, it wouldn't be any fun without you,' Prudence replied warmly. She pulled the keys out of her pocket again, moved to the door and started trying the lock, the torch jammed unsteadily under her arm.

'What if the right key isn't on there?' Justin asked.

'It has to be. As once told me the keys to every door in the college except the other staff offices are on this ring.' Prudence was trying to be sober and steady as she went through the keyring, trying each key in turn. 'Ha! Got it!' she cried in triumph as the lock gave. Now there was only one door between her and whatever lay on the other side. She wanted to savour the anticipation and open it slowly, but Justin reached around her to turn the handle and pull.

'Good grief!' he breathed in awe.

Prudence found her torchbeam illuminating a long tunnel with a row of doors lining either side. She could barely contain herself. 'Yes! Yes! I *knew* it. I just knew it.' Without thinking of the others, she ran down the tunnel, singing at the top of her voice. '*When you wish upon a star, your dreeeeams come troooo . . .*'

'Prudence!' Holly called sharply from the door. But

Prudence was at the end of the tunnel, delighted to find that it split off in two directions. 'Guys, guys!' she called, spinning around and aiming the torchbeam at them. 'More tunnels. It's a whole fucking labyrinth. Oh, God, I think I'm going to come!'

'Bring the torch back,' Justin said, 'and let's explore it together.'

Prudence could see that Justin had squeezed Holly's hand in his own, and her grasp on his was white at the knuckles. Was Holly that frightened? In spite of her excitement and her loose grip on sobriety, Prudence felt very guilty. She came back with the torch and touched Holly's arm. 'I'm sorry. I got carried away.' She wanted to ask Holly why she was afraid of the dark, why this whole trip was spooking her out so seriously, but her mind was already on getting a look at the rest of the labyrinth.

Holly slipped her hand from Justin's and took the torch from Prudence. 'Do you mind if I take it?'

'That's fine. Come on.'

The doors in the first tunnel were all open, leading to small, dark empty rooms. Spiders were building permanent homes in the corners. The brickwork was crumbling everywhere, and in some places the hard-packed dirt that had originally been excavated showed through. At the end of the first tunnel, two arched doorways led off in different directions into darkness. A fancy mosaic crowned each arch.

'I wonder why he built all this,' Justin mused as they stopped to admire the pattern.

'He was almost certainly insane at the time he built St Anne's,' Prudence replied, running her fingers over the brickwork, which was freezing cold. 'Some of the underground passages he designed in other buildings were very convoluted, twisting and turning all over the place.'

'Symbolic of his state of mind, perhaps,' Justin suggested.

'Sure, Dr Freud,' Prudence remarked, urging them forward.

This time they found themselves walking around a slow curve. Once again dark rooms led off the passageway. The further they advanced, the deeper the cold, dank smell became. Eventually they came to the entrance to another, short tunnel, which they could see led off in two directions once more.

'Okay, which way?' Holly said, pointing the torchbeam up the new tunnel and around the curve.

'I think this one is just going to double back on itself,' Justin said. 'It's a ring. Let's go up there.'

Prudence shivered with excitement. 'How far have we come, do you think?'

'I'd say we're under the gardens now,' Justin offered. 'Do you think this will lead to an exit eventually?'

'None of the others I read about did,' she replied.

The short tunnel had no doors along it. They stood at the fork in the passage. This time they could see that it was curved much more sharply than the other ring.

'Another circle, I'll bet,' said Holly.

'God, look. Closed doors on these ones,' Prudence squealed, hurrying ahead. The rooms leading off this passage were shut off by thick stone doors. 'They're like dungeons, or something. Holly, hand me the torch.' She ran the beam over the crack where a door met the frame. An old-fashioned keyhole lock gave a view of a perfect blackness beyond.

'Well, I don't have any keys that match that on the ring,' Prudence admitted, disappointed.

'Maybe it's not locked.'

Prudence gave the door a little shove and it moved a few centimetres. 'No, it's not.' Her heart was thumping madly. 'I can't look! What if there's something in there? I'll just *die* of excitement!'

She noticed Holly hanging back behind Justin,

clutching the hem of his sweater. But Prudence was too delirious to spend time reassuring her.

'Go on, open it,' Justin said, and this time she could sense that he was caught up in the excitement himself. Prudence huddled close to them and stretched her leg out to push the door open with her foot. It swung inwards to reveal an empty room.

'Oh, how disappointing,' she sighed. 'Just like all the others. What on earth was he thinking? So many empty rooms.'

'Let's check them all,' Justin suggested.

They advanced around the ring, opening doors to a series of empty rooms. Prudence felt herself sag a little further every time a door swung open to reveal nothing except legions of bugs and spiders.

When they came to the point where the circle began to lead back towards the tunnel, they found one door on their right that wouldn't open as easily as the others.

'I can't open this one,' Prudence said, pushing hard with her shoulder.

'It must be jammed,' Justin said. 'Come on, let's look at the next one.'

'But I want to see in this one.' She pushed again.

'I guess it will be the same as all the others,' Holly said.

Prudence whirled around to look at them both. 'Perhaps it's not jammed. Perhaps it's locked.'

There was a beat of silence before Justin and Holly, guessing where this would lead if they didn't calm Prudence down, responded. 'I'm sure it's just jammed, Prudence,' Holly said dismissively.

'Yes,' added Justin, 'why would one be locked if all the others aren't?'

'Why indeed? That's *exactly* what I'm wondering.'

'The romance of the locked door,' Holly sighed. 'Why do I have a feeling we're never going to hear the end of this?'

Prudence tried the door a few more times while the others waited, getting more and more frustrated. 'I wonder where the key to this place is?'

'It's probably been lost for years.'

'Anyone here good at picking locks?'

They remained silent. 'Okay,' Prudence said. 'Let's open the wine and have ourselves a celebratory drink.'

'I don't know, Prudence,' Holly said. 'It's cold and it's dark and the torch will probably run out of batteries soon. Can't we just go home?'

'No, no, no! This has been a most disappointing journey. No dead bodies, no ghosts, no secrets. *Ergo*, we have to make it interesting. Let's choose one of these rooms and mark out some territory.'

She was about to push into one of the rooms when Holly stopped her by placing an icy hand around her wrist. 'If we must, can't we at least go back to the first ring? I don't like these rooms. What if the door shuts behind us and we can't get out? Nobody would ever find us.'

Prudence savoured the delicious, scary feeling. 'Ooh, you're right. How awful. Come on then, let's go back to the first ring.'

They were settled on the ground on Prudence's overcoat, a tea-light candle glimmering in each corner of the dark room. There had nearly been a serious fight over the candles—Prudence had wanted to go to their office to get them while Justin and Holly waited, but Holly had nearly scratched her eyes out at the thought of having to sit in the dark for ten minutes. It had nearly—not quite—ruined the evening. They had all gone together instead, Holly no less spooked in the warm halls of the college than she had been in the musty underground labyrinth. Justin knew it was the alcohol that had taken the edge off his social agony and allowed him to play big strong man to Holly's scared little girl. Tomorrow he was probably going to regret having taken her hand in his when Prudence rushed off with the torch, but it was such a soft hand, fingers icy with fear. It made him feel warm somewhere deep in his chest. Under normal circumstances he'd be pushing down these feelings, but in his soft haze of mild drunkenness, he felt happy to let them go.

'So, Prudence,' Holly was saying, in what seemed like mock lightness, 'aren't you worried that the candles will attract ghosts?'

Prudence took a swig of wine from the bottle and passed it to Justin. 'Christ, this floor's cold,' she said. 'Do you think it's true what they say about getting haemorrhoids from sitting on cold surfaces?'

'I don't think so,' said Holly, frowning in the dim light. 'I think it's something made up to scare kids. Like, If you swallow chewing gum, it'll get stuck in your digestive system.'

Prudence gasped. 'You mean that's not true? Christ, I've always believed that one.' She shook her head in amusement. 'Santa Claus and the Tooth Fairy you can figure out for yourself, but there really should be a fact sheet given out at puberty dispelling all those other myths of childhood.' She pulled her black cardigan tighter around herself. 'Anyway, in answer to your question, no. It takes more than a few candles to attract ghosts.'

'I read it in your book. Candles and a mirror.'

'A mirror only helps if you want to see them. It takes more than all that. Ghosts aren't drawn to candles. They're drawn to certain people. If you're not interesting to the ghost, it will leave you alone.'

'You really believe all this?' Justin couldn't help asking. Prudence knew too much about the supernatural for it to be just a passing fancy. And Holly had told him her bookcase was jammed full of occult books. Having never believed in anything except the ultimate horror of his own mortality, he found it hard to understand.

'Yeah, kind of,' she replied thoughtfully. 'Let's just say I'm open to any possibility. If a ghost suddenly popped out of the walls right now and said, Boo! I wouldn't be surprised. If scientists proved conclusively that other entities do not exist, again, I wouldn't be surprised. But think about it logically, what's more likely to happen? There's too much unknown in the universe already. It would take an eternity to delineate what does and what doesn't exist. On the other hand, millions of people throughout history have seen ghosts. The possibility is always there, in every second. Especially in old buildings like this, which have an interesting past.'

'So why would a ghost be drawn to one person and not another?' Holly asked.

Prudence shrugged, fished out her cigarettes and jammed one between her lips. 'I don't know.' Her lighter flared briefly, illuminating her face. 'Maybe because one person has the ability to help them or empathise with them where others don't. Why are you interested? Worried that it will happen to you?'

Holly shook her head. 'Here, give me the wine.'

Justin handed her the bottle.

'Okay,' said Prudence rubbing her hands together. 'We're in a cold, dark underground chamber, pissed. What do we do?'

Justin shrugged. 'I feel like going to sleep, actually.'

'No, no,' Prudence admonished him, waving her cigarette at him. 'We tell secrets. It's just the right pre-pubescent slumber-party kind of thing to do, don't you think?'

'What, like truth or dare without the dare?' Holly asked.

'Actually, I thought more like a true-confessions session. I'll go first. As didn't *give* me the keys.'

'Then how—?' Justin started.

'I stole them. When I was with him in his office on Thursday afternoon, he turned his back to get something and I pocketed them.'

'Prudence!' Holly gasped. 'Weren't you worried that he'd notice them missing?'

'Of course he'd notice them missing. But I know As. He would have wanted to get home for the holidays, so stopping to search for them would be out of the question. And he'd never admit to the Humberstones that he'd lost his keys. I'm pretty sure Lucien already thinks he's a bumbling idiot.'

'Lucien thinks everybody's a bumbling idiot,' murmured Justin. The mention of the word 'confession' had brought reality lurching back through his drunken haze. Damn Prudence, always trying to prise secrets out of people.

'Come on, Holly, your turn,' Prudence said.

'I don't know . . . I . . .'

'Not fair. I confessed. Now it's your turn.'

'God, I feel like a teenager again. I'm supposed to be a grown woman.'

'Please. It's just a bit of fun.'

'Okay.' She looked into her lap for a moment, then looked up. 'I'm thinking about going home, going back to Daybrook.'

Prudence was shocked. 'Back to Michael?'

'Well, I don't know. It's . . . I'm pretty confused.'

'But why?' Justin asked, passing the bottle around again. This was a surprising confession. Holly seemed so committed to her work and loved what she did so much, he never imagined she might be unhappy. And of course he was starting to develop his own selfish reasons for not wanting her to leave.

'I'm not handling things very well,' she said.

'Oh, rubbish,' snorted Prudence. 'You're As's pet. He thinks you're a genius.'

'Not the academic stuff. Other stuff. What with Michael threatening to top himself, and my family all wanting to know when my little adventure is going to end. And the flat I'm living in. And the upheaval. I'm so stressed out I'm starting to . . .'

There were a few beats of silence. 'Starting to what?' Justin urged.

She sighed deeply. 'Perhaps it would be easier all round if I just went home.'

'No!' Prudence wailed. 'Don't go. You have friends here now, and an exciting project to work on. You'll get used to it. If you went back to Daybrook, you'd regret it forever, I know. You have to do what you love, no matter what the cost, Holly. And don't you love it here?'

'It's weird,' Holly replied slowly, thoughtfully. 'I've never been more fulfilled in my life, but at the same time I've never felt more like I'm skating on thin ice. Dangerously close to some disaster.'

'That's just your fucked-up repressed psychology,' Prudence offered helpfully, handing the bottle to Holly. 'You're not used to being fulfilled so your mind has manufactured a feeling of dread to sabotage your happiness. Girl, you worked so hard to get in here. You took a huge risk, and look how it's paying off. Could you really go back to the way things used to be?'

Holly smiled. 'You're very perceptive, Prudence.'

'It's a gift,' she said, deadpan, lighting another cigarette. 'So, have I convinced you? Justin doesn't want you to go either, do you, Justin?'

Prudence had put him on the spot. Had she sensed already that Justin was fond of Holly? She really was perceptive. If not psychic. 'Of course not.'

'See? What do you say? Will you stay?'

Holly threw her hands up in the air. 'As I said, I'm no good with peer pressure. Okay, I'll stay. You're probably right. The mind can do strange things under strain.'

'Very strange,' agreed Prudence. 'Okay, Justin, your go. Confess or be damned.'

'Can't I just be damned?' he replied nervously, the old familiar panic rising up through the layers.

'What, you'd rather spend eternity in the flaming pit than tell us one little secret? Satan will set fire to your nuts every morning, you know.'

'So? I'd be used to it after a few days.'

'Come on, get in the spirit of things.'

Justin knew without doubt that he didn't want to give her one inch of any secret of his. What to do, then, without appearing surly? He'd have to tell a lie. Make something up. 'Okay,' he said. 'I heard Lucien and Emma having a heated discussion on Tuesday evening, so I put my ear against the door to listen.'

'Ooh, a domestic,' Prudence enthused. 'What was it about?'

Justin remembered what his aunt had told him. 'Emma wants sex and Lucien doesn't.'

Prudence squealed. 'Oh, how perfectly *sordid*.' She reached across and shook his hand. 'Congratulations, Justin. You managed to confess without telling us anything about yourself at all.'

'I thought the fact that I eavesdropped was the confession.'

She waved her hand dismissively. 'Who wouldn't listen in? That's not a secret, that's normal behaviour. So Lucien's not much of a stallion in the sack, eh? I must say I'm surprised. He's got that sexy domineering thing happening for him, don't you think, Holly?'

'I don't know. I've never seen him.'

'You surely don't think Lucien's attractive?' Justin asked, perplexed. He saw his uncle as a freakishly tall ogre, everything human about him squashed into manageable packages inside him.

'He has a certain appeal, but I certainly wouldn't fuck

him,' Prudence replied. 'Who's got the wine?'

Holly handed it back to Prudence. 'There's not much left, I'm afraid.'

'Justin, do you want to finish it?' Prudence offered him the bottle but he refused.

'No, you go ahead.'

She knocked it back and climbed to her feet. 'I'm cold and a bit sleepy. Shall we go home?'

'A warm bed sounds like a very good idea,' Holly said.

'Are you both coming to stay at my place?' Prudence asked.

'Sure,' said Holly.

Justin thought about the awkwardness of a single male staying overnight in the same house as two females. He was only just getting used to avoiding Emma in bathrooms and hallways at his new home. That was different though, because he suspected Emma was deliberately putting herself in his way most of the time.

'Well, I don't want to go home to my empty mansion,' he said. 'So I guess I will come. Anything good for breakfast?'

'I will make a breakfast you won't believe,' Prudence promised. 'And then we have another adventure to go on.'

'Another adventure?' Holly said wearily. 'I don't know if I'm up to it.'

'What adventure?' Justin asked.

'Somehow we have to convince a locksmith to cut us a set of these keys,' Prudence replied, dangling the bunch in front of them. 'Because I couldn't bear it if we never came back here.'

'Okay, do you know what to say?'

Holly sighed. 'Prudence, maybe you should do this.' The three of them were standing on the footpath across the road from a locksmith on Punt Road. As's keys were all stamped with 'Security key, do not copy', and Holly had been elected to sweet-talk the locksmith. It made her deeply uncomfortable but, like the whole weekend so far, the weight of Prudence's will was inexorable.

'Don't be ridiculous,' Prudence said. 'It has to be you. Who's going to do any favours for a girl with a nose ring, or a long-haired slacker like Justin?' She turned to Justin and added, 'Sorry, Justin.'

'I'm not good at this kind of thing,' Holly confessed.

'You'll do fine. You're pretty and you're dressed well, and this guy's obviously a junior.' She pointed across the road. Through the large front window, Holly could see a teenage boy flipping through a magazine behind the counter. 'It will be a cinch. Do you remember what you have to say?'

Holly nodded. 'Yes, I remember. Wait here for me.'

'Of course.'

'Good luck, Holly,' said Justin.

'Thanks.' She waited for a break in the traffic then hurried across the road to the locksmith's. A buzzer on the door sounded as she entered the shop and the junior looked up. She offered him her most disarming smile.

'Good morning,' she said.

'Hi. Can I help you?' he asked in a friendly voice, pushing aside his magazine.

'Yes, I'm from Peterson and Associates. My employer, Dick Peterson, called late on Thursday afternoon to authorise a new set of these to be cut.' She dropped the keys on the counter.

'Fine, I'll just check the register.' He turned his back to her and opened a book on the workbench behind him. Holly held her breath. She felt slightly overwhelmed, never having done anything like this before. An awful fear that it would somehow result in having her scholarship revoked lurked in her mind. And now that she'd had the talk with Prudence and Justin last night, she'd decided that more than anything she wanted to stay at Humberstone.

The boy turned to her and shook his head apologetically. 'I can't see anything for Peterson and Associates. Are you sure he called?'

'Yes, at least . . . I hope he didn't forget. It's terribly important and he's gone away for four weeks.'

'I'm sorry, but I can't cut a set without authorisation—see the engraving.' He pointed a dirty thumbnail at the security warning. 'If you'd like to come back on Tuesday the owner will be here and he'll be able to check it out for you.'

'Tuesday's too late, you see,' she said, heart thudding. 'I'm just new—it's only my first week on the job, and . . . you see . . . we need a set for the new CEO before closing time today and everyone's been working overtime and is stressed out and . . .' The words that Prudence had got her to rehearse were evaporating. Whose stupid idea was this? For the last twenty-four hours she had been a slave to Prudence's will. All night in that dark, horrible place, and now this, lying to a locksmith and endangering her scholarship. To her surprise, she started to cry.

'I'm sorry,' she said, palming the tears off her cheeks roughly. 'I'm really sorry, it's just that—'

'It's okay,' he said, startled. 'It's okay, I can cut you the keys. It's probably just a mistake. The guy who worked on Thursday was probably in a hurry to go home and forgot to write it down. Don't cry, okay, I can cut you the keys.'

She looked up at him. The tears had worked where lies had failed. She nodded and rummaged in her handbag for a tissue. He had turned back to his workbench and was busily cutting the keys.

'You'll just have to leave a name and address,' he

muttered over his shoulder. 'Just in case, you know.'

'Fine, fine. Thank you so much, you've saved me an awful headache.'

Presently he turned and dropped a handful of keys into her outstretched hand. 'That's twenty-eight dollars.'

She paid him dutifully, thanking him profusely. He wouldn't look her in the eye, maybe afraid that she was still weeping.

'And just write your name and address on the top of this invoice,' he said, turning a carbon-interleaved invoice book towards her. With a shaking hand, she filled in the blanks with fake details and took her copy.

'Thanks,' he said. 'I hope your day gets better.'

'I'm sure it will. Thank you.'

She heard the buzzer go off again as she left and hurried across the road. Prudence and Justin were hiding behind a tram shelter. She sat down heavily next to them.

'Did you get them?' Prudence asked.

Holly showed her the handful of keys. 'I sure did. It took me bursting into tears, but it worked.'

'Tears? Now why didn't I think of that?'

'Here's the invoice. You owe me. It was twenty-eight bucks.'

Prudence fished a purse out of her shoulder-bag and proceeded to count the money into Holly's hand. 'This is great,' she said. 'Access all areas.'

'I just hope nobody finds out,' Holly said nervously. 'I don't want to lose my place at the college.'

'If it's any consolation, we'd both go down with you,' Justin said. 'Whatever happens, from now on we're all in it together.'

CHAPTER TEN

....

~

'**W**ow.'
Holly dropped her bag next to her solitary armchair and turned to look at Prudence. 'Wow what?'

'Wow, it's just as bad as you said. I was leaving a margin for exaggeration.'

'No exaggeration necessary,' Holly sighed. 'Do you want a cup of coffee?'

'Thanks.' Prudence followed Holly into the tiny kitchenette. 'You could make something of it though.'

Holly busied herself making two cups of coffee. It was Sunday afternoon and she'd spent two nights at Prudence's. Her own flat was looking even more dingy than usual by comparison. Justin had left late on Saturday afternoon, but Holly had been unable to resist spending another night in comfort.

'I don't see how I could make something of it. The basics are missing—it's cold, it's bug-ridden.'

'So get some bug spray.'

'Mrs Partridge says—'

'Fuck Mrs Partridge and fuck her cats.' Prudence giggled. 'Not literally of course. How often do you see her?'

'Once a fortnight when I pay the rent.'

'Okay, so it's not like she's ever going to know that you've bombed the place. And if she does, well, she kicks you out. And you can go look for something better.'

Holly handed Prudence her cup of coffee. 'I can't afford anything better, Prudence. I'm living on a scholarship.'

'Don't you have any savings? You worked for a couple of years, right?'

Holly looked into her coffee and felt a blush start to spread up her throat. Prudence was going to eat her alive over this one. 'I left it all for Michael.'

'You what! Are you crazy? Why did you do that?'

'I don't know. I felt guilty about leaving and he did need my support to survive. He could never meet the rent without me.'

'Didn't he have a job?'

'Yes, but it wasn't well paid. He managed the local hardware store.' She couldn't bring herself to tell Prudence that the local hardware store in Daybrook was about the same size as Prudence's bathroom, or that Michael's job as manager really meant solo shop assistant when the owner was away for the weekend. It seemed disloyal to Michael, somehow, to reveal in this very different world what a small fish he was.

Prudence was clearly making an effort to bite her tongue. Holly smiled at her. 'I know what you're thinking. But it's done now. Maybe it wasn't the wisest thing to do.'

'Holly, trust me on this one. Buy a bug spray. Mrs Partridge will never know. And I've got an old bar heater at home that you can have. And we can go out on Tuesday and find some big cushions and throw rugs to liven the place up a bit. You can't live like this.' Prudence gestured around her with her free hand. 'No wonder you thought you'd be better off going home. Is there any-where to sit down?'

Holly shrugged. 'My bedroom, I guess.'

Prudence followed Holly to the bedroom and sat down next to her on the bed. 'You make your bed,' Prudence said, curious.

'Yeah.'

'Some people have strange habits. It never occurs to you that you'll just mess it up again?'

'Actually, I sleep very neatly.'

Prudence laughed out loud. 'Why doesn't that surprise me?' She put her coffee cup down on the floor and lay back on the bedspread. 'So, did you have a good weekend?'

Holly looked at her. The dark roots of her hair were growing out under the purple. 'What colour is your hair naturally?' she asked.

'Kind of dark brown. I was platinum-blonde the week before you arrived. You didn't answer my question.'

'I had a . . . mixed weekend.'

'Mixed? Ouch. I thought I'd organised the most fun agenda of entertainment that three people can have with their clothes on.'

'Well, yes, it was fun. But it was also a bit wild and scary for me. Within twenty-four hours of arriving at your place, I had broken into the college illegally, spent a couple of hours sitting in a freezing underground chamber, drunk more wine than I should have, confessed one of my darkest secrets, lied to a locksmith, and eaten roughly my own body weight in Easter eggs. Not bad for somebody who's always considered herself the queen of moderation.'

Prudence blushed with what appeared to be self-conscious pleasure. 'I'm like the girl your mother never wanted you to play with.'

'Exactly,' Holly replied, laughing. Then in her best impression of her mother's voice she added, 'You're not going over to that Prudence's! You always come back dirty and high on sugar!'

Prudence found this particularly amusing and giggled madly for a few moments. 'You're fun, Holly,' she said at last.

'No, I'm boring.'

'Rubbish. You and Justin are both fun, you've just never got in touch with your fun side. That's my job, to unleash the fun within you.'

'I couldn't believe it. Justin must have smiled about half a dozen times on the weekend,' Holly remarked, astonished.

'And laughed! I knew if we persevered we'd find him in there somewhere. And of course it helps knowing why he's so down all the time. It's only been a few months since his mother died.'

'Awful,' Holly murmured, leaning back on the bed next to Prudence and looking at the mouldy stains on the ceiling. They were quiet for a few moments.

'But I don't think that's all,' Prudence said.

'What?'

Prudence shifted onto her side. 'I think there's something else Justin hasn't told us. Some secret.'

'Only you would think that.'

'I notice things other people don't.' She tapped Holly playfully on the shoulder. 'Hey, do you like Justin?'

Holly groaned. 'Why do I feel like this is a trick question?'

'It's pretty clear to me that Justin thinks you're a potential object of love.'

'I don't know where you get these ideas from.'

'I'm unusually perceptive,' she replied, stretching out on her back. 'You said so yourself. He looks at you when you're not looking.'

Holly was momentarily dumbfounded, embarrassed and pleased all at the same time. 'Well, even if that did constitute some kind of crush, it's not reciprocated.'

'Come on, he's cute.'

'He's too short.'

'Only for an Amazon like you. I think he's nice. I've seen him shirtless.'

Holly flipped over and smiled at Prudence. 'Yeah? When?'

'The night I crashed at his place.'

'And?'

'And what?'

'And is he . . .? You know . . . how does he look?'

Prudence shook her head. 'You're wicked, Holly. You *are* interested in him, aren't you?'

Maybe under normal circumstances she would have been, but Holly was far too busy being in love with a spectral projection of her overwrought brain. Sad, sick, but true. 'He's nice, like you said. But I don't think it would be wise to make anything of it.'

'Okay. He's pale, and he's got a little bit of dark hair around his nipples and belly-button. A bit on the skinny side, but good clear skin. No acne scars.'

'Sounds like you looked closely. Why don't you go for it?'

'Two reasons. One, he wants you. Two, I'm not in the market for a man.'

'Why not?'

Prudence smiled ironically. 'It would interfere with my studies.'

Holly laughed. 'I wish you weren't joking.'

Holly was glad for Prudence's continued company that week. They spent the holidays redecorating Holly's flat with scraps and leftovers from remainder shops and Prudence's cupboard. As Prudence had predicted, Mrs Partridge did not notice the bug spray, and Holly spent each morning sweeping up dozens of dead bugs. By the end of the week, when it was almost time to go back to college, Holly had done no study at all, and her flat was trimmed in second-hand tie-dyed cushion covers and scented with burning rose oil. She suppressed the suspicion that she was turning into a Prudence Emerson clone.

'This is a lot better,' said Justin as he arrived on Sunday afternoon for dinner. Holly had decided on a house-warming dinner to celebrate her flat's facelift.

'Prudence is responsible.'

'Only partly,' Prudence protested from the floor where she was fiddling with an old portable stereo. She had found it in a cupboard at her place and had kindly donated it to Holly.

'Are Lucien and Emma back?' Holly asked as Justin followed her into the kitchen.

'They were pulling up just as I was leaving. I didn't stop to say hello.'

'So you won't have the mansion all to yourself any more?' Holly asked, placing a saucepan of water on a hotplate.

'No, but at least I'll be able to get into the pantry. Do you need a hand with anything here?'

'You could open a tin of tomato paste,' she said, handing him a tin and a can-opener. She watched him as he did it, long pale hands working, curls falling forward over his face. Yes, he was cute, and he seemed sweet and smart and funny. The brazen whirl of her week with Prudence had almost managed to banish her fear over Christian to a dark corner of her mind. Perhaps it was all just the product of a sad, overworked imagination. If that were the case, she could allow herself to be interested in Justin.

But Justin didn't have those achingly vulnerable blue eyes. Or that sad tilt of the lips. That was ridiculous, though. Christian wasn't a real person, Justin was.

A sudden loud burst of radio static from the living room interrupted her thoughts. Justin handed the open tin back to her. 'Sounds like Prudence got the stereo working.'

'God help us all,' Holly said. 'Let's just pray she hasn't brought any of her CDs.'

There was a short silence, and then Holly's flat filled with the scratchy tones of Robert Johnson at twice the sonic-pain threshold.

Justin raised his eyebrows. 'I think you should have started praying earlier.'

To Lucien's eternal torment, they were five. If there were any reasonable way he could work on this project alone, he would gladly do it. But no, he had his four co-conspirators for better or for worse.

He looked around the room, his back turned to the window. Emma and Jane gossiped while drinking tea; Aswell sat on the edge of Lucien's desk staring vacantly into space—late nights did not agree with him.

Lucien was tired of feeling crowded, not in perfect control. It had been an error, anyway, having five of them. The trouble with Owling's grimoire was that it was a living record of his experiments, and the rules changed the further he wrote. Owling, too, had started out with a group of five—one for each point of the pentagram. In the middle section of the Guyana fragment, Owling had decided he didn't need his four companions and had rid himself of them. Their method of dispatch was not discussed in the book, and Lucien sometimes wondered if Owling had murdered them. It would have been the most effective way to ensure their continued silence, but out of the question for Lucien. For a start, Randolph saw himself as the leader of the group, although it was never discussed openly. And then Emma was involved, and lovely Jane who had been brought in to replace Magnus at Randolph's behest. Aswell he wouldn't miss, the man was practically a simpleton. If it wasn't for Aswell and Randolph being close friends, Aswell might never have been allowed into the project to replace Graham, around two months before it was known that a fifth member was not needed at all.

Still, although they were his cohorts, they didn't know everything. Lucien kept a great deal to himself. The problem was going to be keeping information from Randolph when he came back from Israel. Lucien didn't want to reveal his plans for Justin until it was absolutely necessary. And then, hopefully, expedience would win out. When their own mortality was on the line, surely none of them would flinch at the small matter of Justin's fate.

'Lucien,' Emma called from the other side of the office, breaking into his reverie, 'what's the name of that restaurant we love in Carlton?'

'Restaurant?'

'Yes, the Nepalese place. I'm telling Jane that she should go there one evening. With her new *boyfriend*,' she added with significant emphasis.

Lucien set his jaw. 'I don't remember, Emma. You're the expert on food consumption, after all.' This was ridiculous, sparring with his wife over cups of tea at what was supposed to be a ritual of black magic. Just one more reason why he wished he could relieve himself of the lot of them. How had Owling done it?

He finished his tea and sighed. He hoped that Randolph would be back soon with the last fragment of the grimoire. He didn't want to die waiting, like Magnus had. A cold, black glove of fear grabbed at his stomach. *Please, anything but that.*

'Laurence, perhaps you should read us Randolph's latest letter,' Lucien suggested as they moved to sit down in their circle.

Aswell pulled out the letter and smoothed it on his lap. It vexed Lucien acutely that Randolph would only write to Aswell and not to himself. It was Randolph's way of keeping complete control out of Lucien's hands. The rivalry between the cousins went back a long way. While

Lucien and his older brother Graham had never been close to their father Magnus, Randolph had ingratiated himself at every opportunity. The old man hadn't known the difference between real affection and a shameless grab for an inheritance, and he made a habit of including Randolph like a third, and favoured, son in all the family business. Lucien had won out in the end, of course, inheriting the college and the controlling share of the family wealth after Graham had died prematurely. But Randolph still refused to see himself as anything but Lucien's equal.

'I think you'll be pleased, Lucien,' Aswell was saying. 'He sounds like he's getting pretty close.'

'Read, read,' Lucien urged him impatiently.

'Sure.

Dear Laurence, et al.

This city is filled with tourists! All the silly pilgrims are flocking to Jerusalem for Easter, and I'm confident that every single one of them has got in my way at some time during the last few days. The taxi drivers have taken the influx as a sign to increase their fares, and I've found myself walking a lot of places instead. And a marvellous advantage that has been.

While trying to get to Jaffa Road, I became completely lost. I had my street map upside down, and you know how poor my sense of direction is. Remember the time we lost ourselves on the way to Canberra through my appalling navigational skills? It's a good thing you have some kind of inner radar, Laurence, or else I think we would have been halfway across the Nullarbor before I knew anything was wrong! Anyway, shortly after I realised I was not getting any closer to Jaffa Road, I happened to pass a little bookshop tucked away between a dreary makolet and a boarded-up computer store. I would never have found it if I hadn't been lost. You know, sometimes I think these things are small gifts for all the work we do. You must all be working hard at your rituals in my absence, because some kind of black energy seems to be dragging me along with it over here.

I went into the bookshop of course—I've made it my mission to search out every book trader in this city. It was small and poky, and the owner was burning incense in an attempt to cover a damp, musty smell. It has been raining heavily on and off for the last week, and a bucket between two shelves was being used to catch a slow but steady drip from the ceiling The owner was a long, lean man bent almost double over a magnifying glass, which he was using to inspect the print on the back of an old book. I leaned on the counter and waited for him to notice me.

'Excuse me,' I had to say eventually.

He looked up with a start. 'I'm sorry,' he said, 'I didn't notice you there. You came in very quietly.' His English was good, but clearly not his first language.

'I'm looking for a very rare book and I'm led to believe I'll find it somewhere in Jerusalem.'

He shrugged and spread his hands on the counter. 'Jerusalem's not so small as you might think. There are many places for books to hide. Maybe you tell me about the book and I can help a little, eh? Its name? Its publisher?'

'This book was never released commercially. It's a handwritten one-off, about a hundred and fifty years old. Have you heard of anything like that in your dealings?'

'You need an antique shop, not a bookshop. I trade second-hand books, so you can bring in old ones you don't want. Three of yours for one of mine, straight swap. I have many titles.'

'I'm really only interested in this one. Have you heard anything about a book like this circulating amongst the traders in Jerusalem? Some people call it the dark fragment.'

At this he blinked and looked away too rapidly. 'Dark fragment? Who is the author? I can maybe find it in my catalogue.' He began to search around amongst the papers under his counter. 'I haven't heard of it before.'

I could tell he knew something, so I reached into my wallet and laid three hundred NIS on the counter. 'If you can remember something about the dark fragment, you can put this towards getting your roof fixed.' I pointed up at the mouldy stains on the ceiling.

He shook his head. 'I cannot remember what I do not know.'

I doubled the amount and leaned in closer. 'There's more where this came from. I'll pay a very good price for information about the dark fragment.'

Briefly, I thought he would take the money. His eyes rested on it for a moment, but soon he looked away. 'I do not know this dark fragment. Please look over my other books. There are many fine titles to choose from.'

I collected the money and put it back in my wallet. 'You just lost a sale,' I said, turning to leave. I expected him to come after me but he let me go without a word.

I ducked next door into the makolet. A sullen Jewish girl of about fifteen minded the counter while styrofoam boxes of vegetables wilted all around her. I grabbed a copy of the Jerusalem Post and went to the counter to pay.

'What time do you close?' I asked as she took my money from me.

'Seven o'clock,' she said.

'That's a long day. Do you have to do the whole shift alone?'

'No. My father comes in at four. If it's not busy we close early.'

'Do you know about the bookshop next door? Does he close at seven too?'

She sniffed in dismissal. 'Some days he closes at one, some days he's still there when we're gone. Why don't you go ask him?'

'Thanks, I think I will.'

I walked across the road. About a hundred metres up I found a bus shelter to protect me from the drizzle, and which provided me with a sliver of a view of the bookshop's front door. I sat back to wait.

It was shortly after five and growing dark before I saw the old man come to his front door and shoot the bolt. I could faintly see him moving around inside the shop, a pale figure in the darkness. I quickly crossed the road and rounded the corner of the closed computer shop. I found myself standing on a concrete path, overgrown with grass. Rubbish from the makolet *lay rotting in the alley. I hid in the doorway of the computer store and listened. Eventually I heard the back door of the bookshop opening and peered out. The owner had his back to me as he locked the door. I sprang out and put my hand over his mouth, drawing him back into the shadows. I shoved the point of my penknife into the soft flesh around his kidneys and told him to be quiet. Slowly I removed my hand from his mouth. He was breathing rapidly, terrified.*

'The book,' I said, 'the dark fragment. You know where it is.'

'I swear I don't—'

I pushed the blade lightly. 'Yes, you do.' I was getting worried by then, wondering if maybe I'd misjudged him, maybe he didn't know anything about it. I was tired from waiting in a bus shelter for six hours with only the Jerusalem Post *for company, and I doubted he was going to cooperate.*

'Why do you want it? It's evil,' he said, fear cracking his voice.

So he did know after all. 'You tell me everything you know about it, old man, or I'll disembowel you right here in the alley.' Of course he didn't know that all I had was a penknife. He could only feel the point of a blade and he feared the worst.

'I want nothing to do with that thing. It's an abomination.'

'Just tell me where I can find it. Or I will kill you, you understand.'

He gulped loudly. 'An antique dealer in the Old City, the Christian quarter, told me—'

Suddenly, a fat man opened the back door to the makolet

and wandered out to dump some more rubbish. My victim took it as an opportunity to call out for help. There were a few moments of noisy confusion, but I dropped him and sprinted around the back of the store and into the street. The fat man from the makolet rounded the corner of his shop and started to chase me, but he was far too unfit to keep up. I disappeared down a side street and found my way back to my apartment.

Since then, I've been past the bookshop every day but he's not open. He knows I'll come back, so he's hiding from me. I'm going to give him another two days, and then I'm off to the Old City to introduce myself to all the antique dealers. One step closer, friends. I can't wait to be away from this place, and I'm sure it will be soon.

Yours, Randolph.

'One more story from the Randolph Humberstone adventure diaries,' Lucien remarked wryly. He despised the way Randolph had constructed himself as an action hero, and wondered how much the truth had been distorted for effect.

'Perhaps you should be glad that Randolph is willing to go to such lengths to get the information you need,' Aswell replied with barely disguised anger.

Lucien clenched his jaw. Everything was going wrong tonight. If only they would all just shut up and do exactly what he said, if only he could keep them in boxes and just get them out when he needed them . . . But patience. Randolph was getting somewhere.

'Get the lights, somebody,' he ordered. 'Let's do some work.'

Only when the lights were dimmed, the candles lit, and the four of them were seated around their circle breathing deep and slow did Lucien allow himself to relax. Ritual magic was enormously difficult, taking years of patience and practice, but also enormously rewarding. He let his eyes close and started murmuring the names of the Klipothic beings with whom they worked. 'Bael, Agares, Vassago, Gamigin . . .' His voice was low, vibrating on the air. The others joined him, all seventy-two names learned by heart. 'Marbas, Valefor, Amon, Barbatos . . .' Their voices floated warmly in the room, caressed his eyelids.

The temperature of the air shot up and Lucien felt beads of sweat forming around his eyes. As usual, it took only a few minutes before he found himself breathing in another landscape. This always happened to him but not to the others. One more reason, he knew, why he should be the leader of the group. A dark, alien panorama of black mountains surrounded him, a faintly glowing red sky low overhead. The Klipothic beings—essentially demons—shadowed around him. He recognised many of them: Ipos's headless figure, eyes glowing yellow in his palms; Belial's horrifically scarred face and back; Zagan and Asmodeus locked in an eternal, infernal combat. Was he seeing hell? Lucien did not know. Nor was he afraid, not even when the beings turned to gaze at him, some curious, some openly hostile. He had his mind set on the ultimate goal. When he had achieved it, hell could wait forever. He was staying alive.

He peered into the darkness, beyond the seventy-two beings, and could dimly make out the shifting shadows of countless other entities. Perhaps among those shadows was the demon that would betray Satan into their hands. For it was only Satan himself who could grant eternal life, and if evoked properly he would have to do their bidding.

They were coming to the end of the long chant. 'Decarabia, Seere, Dantalion, Andromalius.' He opened his eyes. Almost as soon as the chant finished the temperature in the room dropped, making them all shiver. The others looked at him expectantly, wondering if he had seen anything on the other side.

'There are shadows waiting on the horizon,' he said. 'It won't be long now.'

Justin hugged his overcoat tightly around him as he trudged up the hill. It was late and he was freezing, but he felt warm and happy inside. He and Prudence and Holly had enjoyed another evening of good food and great conversation. He had forgone the wine on this occasion, as had Holly, but Prudence could drink anyone under the table.

Anyone, except perhaps his mother. But he couldn't think about her now. She had made socialising impossible for the first twenty-seven years of his life, but he wasn't going to let her make a similar mess of the next twenty-seven. The lifestyle he had led with her, the constant dread of disaster, had meant that it was impossible for him to form friendships. It required too much energy just staying prepared for the next horrific mood-swing, the next all-night session of her begging for forgiveness, the next time he had to pick her up off the floor and get her into bed without having his face clawed.

All behind him now. And new friends to mark his new life.

But if they find out what kind of person I really am . . .

That was ridiculous. He was himself—perhaps for the first time ever—and he wasn't going to let the years of horror and their steadfast assault on his self-confidence undermine him now.

As he neared the house he was surprised to see Lucien and Emma letting themselves in at the front door. What were they doing out so late? It wasn't like Lucien to take Emma out on a date, especially not after a week away. He checked his watch. Nearly three a.m. He almost called out to them but changed his mind at the last minute. He didn't want to deal with Emma right now, didn't want to explain to her that he had been over at Holly's. Things were already too complicated where Emma was concerned, avoiding her seemed to be the best defence.

He ducked behind a tree and waited until they were inside and the light had gone on in their upstairs bedroom. Then he crept quietly into the house and took refuge in his bedroom, wondering where they had been so late on a Sunday night.

CHAPTER ELEVEN

~

'**H**i, Prudence. How are you this morning?'

Prudence yawned immodestly. 'Tired. I had a late night.'

As nodded. 'You and me both, sweetheart.'

A late night? On a Sunday? With the wife that he wasn't supposed to love any more? 'Why? What were you up to?'

As tried to shrug it off. 'Oh, just out with some friends.'

'Out with your wife?'

'No. Just friends. What have you got to show me this week?'

Prudence wished that people wouldn't bother trying to hide things from her. It was an insult to her intelligence. Quick subject changes, dismissive gestures, refusal to elaborate were all beacons that something was going on. But she wouldn't push it because she'd get it out of him later. When he wanted sex he became very malleable.

She searched in her bag and proudly pulled out eight typewritten pages. 'I've started my dissertation.'

'Hallelujah!' As said, looking genuinely pleased and

fond. Maybe she should have tried this months ago.

'But I don't want you to read it.'

'I have to read it.'

'I know, but I don't want you to. I'll never be as good as Holly.'

He came around the side of the desk and took the pages from her. 'Don't worry about Holly, just worry about Prudence. Should I read it now?'

'Whatever.'

He moved very close to her, his breath hot in her ear. 'I've missed you.'

Obviously he didn't want to read it now. Obviously he wanted to do something else now. She felt her stomach flutter as it always did around As. No matter how hard she tried not to love him, not to be dependent on the fluctuations of his approval, she was completely and hopelessly hooked. His fingers touched her chin and she felt herself cave in.

When he started kissing her neck, she said casually, 'So, what *were* you up to last night, As? You're being awfully secretive.'

'Prudence, don't talk.'

'The more you refuse to tell me, the more interested I'm—'

'Prudence!' He stopped caressing her and took a step back. 'I caught up with some old friends, okay? God, you see conspiracies everywhere. Sometimes I wonder if you're not paranoid.'

She was hurt and confused. Was that true? Tears welled up in her eyes and she took a shaky breath. 'Don't be so cruel,' she said. Mustering her best pout, she gazed at him with reproachful eyes. Damn, maybe she was paranoid. Maybe not everybody had a secret, even though she desperately wanted them to.

'I'm not being cruel,' he replied, instantly repentant. Maybe he thought he'd ruined his chances of getting laid.

At that moment the phone rang and As gave her a reassuring smile before turning to his desk.

'Hello? Lucien, hi.' He turned his back to her and continued the conversation in a quiet voice. Prudence made a pretence of going to the bookcase and looking at some volumes. But she was eavesdropping and fishing in her bag for As's keys at the same time.

'No, no, I haven't found them yet. Of course. Of course, Lucien. Yes, I understand that.'

As's keys! He was getting a roasting from Lucien about the keys. Prudence had meant to bring them back before the holidays were over, but in all the excitement she had forgotten. Clearing her throat to cover the jingle, she pulled As's keys out of her bag and jammed them behind a china vase on the second shelf, then pulled out a book and pretended to be reading it. As's voice had dropped to a low mutter, and as much as she strained her ears she couldn't hear what he was saying. Finally he put the phone down and turned to her.

'I'm in trouble with Lucien,' he said with a grimace.

'Why?'

'I've misplaced my keys. Allison had to let me in this morning. I only reported them missing an hour ago and already Lucien's phoned me three times. He thinks it's a security risk to—'

'Your keys? They're over on the bookcase.'

He looked incredulous. 'What?'

'Behind your blue vase. I saw them just a moment ago.'

He swept past her to his bookcase and his hand closed over the keys. 'How on earth did they end up here?'

'Who knows?'

'I'd better ring Lucien. God, now he's going to think I'm a complete idiot.'

If he doesn't already. 'Of course he won't. Anybody can make a mistake.'

'You'll have to excuse me, Prudence,' he said, opening

the door and gesturing for her to leave. 'I need to speak to Lucien in private.'

Prudence was startled. 'You want me to go? But we haven't even—'

'Perhaps tomorrow morning?' he said, smiling, turning on the charm.

'I'm busy,' she said angrily.

'Busy?'

'With Justin,' she lied. Though she didn't know why she thought it could make him jealous. She had to remember she was just a sex toy to him, nothing more.

'Fine,' he said curtly, closing the door in her face.

She stood outside it for a few moments, fighting back tears.

'Fine,' she said at length and walked down the stairs to the office.

'God, I'm so fat. I really should lose some weight.' Prudence was perched on the edge of Holly's desk, swinging her leg nervously and grabbing at handfuls of non-existent fat.

'You're not fat,' Holly said, despairing of getting any work done while Prudence was in a chatty mood. Being in each other's pockets over the holidays was one thing, but during term she needed to concentrate on her work.

'I'm not skinny.'

'If God had meant for you to be skinny, he wouldn't have given you hips and breasts.'

'I don't believe in God.'

'Jeez, you believe in everything else. Choose your deity then. You're shaped like a woman. Coincidentally enough.'

Prudence narrowed her eyes. 'Is that just a nice way of saying I'm fat?'

Holly sighed in exasperation. 'Prudence, you're not fat.'

155

'I'm no supermodel.'

'Good! You're far more interesting than a supermodel.' How was she going to end this conversation and get back to work? She reached for her bag and pulled two dollars out of her purse. 'Here, go buy a coffee and cheer yourself up.'

'Do you want to come?'

'I've got lots of work to do, Prudence.'

The light dawned on Prudence's face. 'Ah, I see. I'm sorry, I'm disturbing you.'

Feeling guilty, Holly nodded. 'I've got a couple of things I need to get read before I see As tomorrow, and as it's already four o'clock . . .' She certainly didn't want to be alone here this evening.

Prudence pushed Holly's offer of money away. 'I'll go get a takeaway coffee for both of us, my shout, and when I get back I promise I'll be well behaved.'

'Thanks,' Holly said. 'And Prudence,' she added as Prudence was nearly out the door, 'you're not fat.'

Prudence shrugged and disappeared into the hallway, closing the door behind her.

Holly leaned back in her chair and gazed at the ceiling. The Prudence experience was exhausting but rewarding. Kind of like having a puppy. Justin didn't seem to have any problems handling her, but that was because he could always retreat behind his sombre demeanour. She looked over to Justin's desk. He had gone home a couple of hours ago, tired and headachy. He had looked particularly appealing today, his hair unruly and his clothes slightly rumpled. But she wasn't going to think about possible romantic entanglements with anybody until the divorce was over. She wanted to know what it felt like to be Holly solo, not Holly as part of a couple.

Prudence had left some music playing on her portable tape-deck—some piano music with a pretty-voiced girl singing over the top. Holly quite liked it. Low, slanting sunbeams glimmered through the dusty window over Prudence's desk, giving the room a soft golden glow. She let her eyes close and drifted into a daydream.

Something touched her. Lightly, fingers in her hair.

Her eyes snapped open and she caught her breath. Nobody was in the room with her.

Christian.

But no, he wasn't real. He was a product of her imagination. Did she dare to tempt fate? She closed her eyes again. Hands in her hair, hot breath on her neck. A pressure built around her ears, as though a word were trying to form in the air around her. A word starting with an 'H'—perhaps her own name? Her pulse was racing but she couldn't bring herself to open her eyes. She wanted to savour her lover's touch.

But there was such a sadness in his hands this time. A longing, an aching that wasn't usually there. His touch was tentative, afraid of rejection.

'Did you miss me, Christian?' she whispered. The late-afternoon sunshine pressed red patterns on her closed eyelids. 'Do you think me awful not to have spoken with you again?'

The pressure around her ears changed. He was trying to tell her something but the words wouldn't form. Suddenly the pressure blasted to pieces, causing a sharp ringing in her ears. Prudence had opened the door.

'Tea lady,' she said merrily, placing a styrofoam cup of coffee in front of Holly.

Holly blinked in a daze. What had just happened? Her skin seemed to burn with Christian's touch still, though he was definitely no longer there. Panic formed in the corners of her mind, threatening to take over.

'Are you okay?' Prudence was leaning close, looking at her.

'I . . . I was just lost in thought. You gave me a start.' It was no use lying to Prudence and Holly knew it.

Prudence smiled. 'Are you sure that's all?'

Holly took a deep breath. She wasn't up to a battle over information with Prudence. 'I don't want to talk about it,' she said simply.

Her friend looked taken aback. 'Sure. Just ignore me, I'm paranoid. I have it on good authority.'

And I'm going crazy, Holly thought. Time to do something about this.

The bright light in the 24-hour medical centre seemed very warm and comforting to Holly after a long walk up a cold hill. She approached the receptionist, who offered her a perfunctory smile.

'Yes?'

'I'm Holly Beck. I have an appointment for seven.'

The receptionist checked her appointment book. 'With Dr Porter?'

Holly had chosen Dr Porter based solely on availability and gender. If she was going to confess to encroaching insanity, she wanted it to be to another woman. 'Yes, that's right.'

The receptionist handed her a form. 'Fill this out. She won't be a moment.'

Leaning on the counter, Holly dutifully filled in the form. She caught sight of herself in the two-way mirror behind the receptionist as she handed the pen back. Her nose and eyes were red from walking in the brisk night air. Her blonde hair spilled over a tatty overcoat and a crumpled scarf, both on permanent loan from Prudence. She suspected she looked a complete mess, which matched perfectly how she felt inside. Grabbing a magazine from the rack, she sat down and opened it at random.

Halfway through an article about a set of quintuplets' first day at school, she heard her name called out.

'Holly Beck?'

She looked up. A young female doctor stood at the entrance to the surgery. She smiled. 'Come through, Holly.'

Holly mustered her courage and followed the doctor into a small, tastefully decorated room. A tang of pine-scented disinfectant hung in the air. Dr Porter showed her a seat and Holly sat down, clutching her handbag against her lap.

'How can I help you, Holly?' Dr Porter said as she settled behind her desk. She was an attractive woman in her early thirties, a gold wedding band and diamond engagement ring the only jewellery she wore.

'I . . . I don't know quite where to begin,' Holly stammered, watching her hands fold and unfold nervously.

'At the beginning,' Dr Porter suggested.

'I think I'm going mad.'

'Why do you think that?'

Holly looked up at the doctor. She was smiling at her warmly, encouragingly.

'I've been seeing things,' she said at last. 'Things that aren't there.'

Dr Porter picked up her pen and jotted down some notes. 'What things are you seeing?'

'Not just seeing things, but feeling things, hearing things.' With a shaky breath Holly pushed a sob back down her throat. 'It's . . . I'm just so scared.' Her resolve gave and she started crying. Dr Porter passed her a box of tissues.

The doctor waited a few moments, then said again, 'What things are you seeing?'

'A ghost,' Holly replied, sniffing. 'The ghost of a young man. First I felt his presence. I . . . I dozed off and he touched me and then one night I used a mirror and I asked him to appear and . . . and he talked to me for hours. And he's beautiful.'

'What did you talk about?'

'His life. He was a prostitute in London in the 1800s. I know I'm only imagining it but it seems so real. I've been so stressed—I left my husband and I moved here and I have no money ... no ... no security. I probably just need something to relax me. Valium or something.'

'Where do you work?'

'I'm a Masters student. I'm writing a dissertation on Victorian poetry.'

The doctor nodded. 'You realise that if I prescribe you a relaxing drug it may have an adverse effect on your mental faculties?'

'Oh. I don't want that.'

'Go back a few paces. We have plenty of time. Tell me why you left your husband.'

Holly took a deep breath and explained the entire situation to the doctor, including the first two orgasmic experiences she'd had with Christian. Dr Porter kept nodding and smiling kindly, occasionally asking a question, making notes but no judgements.

'Well, Holly, if you like, I can recommend you to our consulting psychiatrist. He has quite a long waiting list, so you might not be able to see him for a month or two, by which time your problem may very well have sorted itself out.'

'Can you recommend me anyway?' Holly said desperately. She didn't want to be turned away with nothing, with flimsy reassurances that everything would be fine. She was scared and overwhelmed and had no more energy to draw on to deal with her anxieties.

'Of course I can. I'll write a referral and get his receptionist to phone with an appointment time as soon as possible. But I want you to consider something else, Holly. Are you sure you're imagining it?'

Holly's eyes widened in surprise. 'I must be. I mean, ghosts just aren't ... Well, they aren't real.'

Dr Porter nodded slowly. 'And are you sure about that?

There are more things in heaven and earth, Holly, than we'll ever be able to fathom. In all other respects, you are a perfectly well-adjusted woman. You have no history of psychosis, and your visions are limited and very specific. You say that this ghost—what was his name?'

'Christian.'

'You say that Christian wouldn't hurt you?'

'No, never. It's like . . . It's like we have a bond.'

'If that's the case then, ghost or no ghost, you have nothing to fear. You aren't going crazy, Holly. Now, that's not to say that there definitely isn't a psychological reason for what you think you saw, but generally you are quite a sane young woman.'

Holly shook her head. 'You're a doctor, I thought you'd . . . I don't know, I thought you would be looking for the most rational explanation.'

Dr Porter tipped her head back and laughed. 'Actually, Holly, studying science seems to raise more questions than it answers sometimes. Perhaps a ghost *is* the most rational explanation for such a coherent, isolated instance of an unexplained vision.'

Holly considered. Dr Porter was clearly trying to be helpful, but Holly couldn't shake the fear rattling cold and deep inside her. 'But you'll still refer me to the psychiatrist?'

'Of course, if that's what you want.'

'I think you'd better.'

'But still consider what I've said, Holly.'

Holly nodded, looking back into her lap. 'Sure, sure. I'll think about it.'

Sing choirs of angels.

Justin knew he was dreaming. Dark, velvet layers of warmth enfolding him.

Sing in exultation.

Christmas so soon? Standing outside on a warm, summer evening. Coloured lights in windows of houses. A choir singing—angels in white.

Sing all ye citizens of Bethlehem.

One of the angels approaching him. Holly. Hair the colour of wheat in the sun. Her hands stretched towards him.

Glory to God, in the highest.

She smiled, dropped her eyes shyly as she did in the real world. Green eyes, long black eyelashes.

O come let us adore him . . .

His hands closed over hers. Warm, soft hands. She pulled him close.

O come let us adore him . . .

Her breasts pressed up against his chest; a hot mouth pressed against his cheek, his chin, his lips. Divine. So long since he'd had any physical contact like this. So what if it was only a dream? Enjoy it, let it happen.

Where was that cold air coming from, creeping up his chest?

'I'm cold,' he said to the dream Holly.

O come let us adore him . . .

'I'll warm you up.' But it wasn't Holly speaking. The voice seemed to come from outside. A hot, wet pressure on his groin. Ah, God, how long had it been? He opened his mouth somewhere in another world, let out a groan.

'Does it feel good?' the outside voice asked.

'Yes,' he said, a long hiss of a word.

Someone was shaking him. 'Wake up. It's not her, it's *me.*'

'Who?'

'You're not dreaming,' the voice said. The choir had stopped singing, it wasn't Christmas any more. Dream Holly's warm hands were dissolving in his own.

The other voice spoke again. 'Justin, beautiful Justin.'

Wakefulness was upon him all at once. 'Christ!' He sat up, saw the blonde head at his lap.

Emma looked up, her hand firmly around his prick. 'Just lie down, Justin. Lie back and enjoy it.'

'Emma—no!'

But her mouth had closed over him again. It felt so good, so damn good. And he was already so close.

With a groan he fell back on his bed and let her finish, let himself finish. Hot circles of unstoppable ecstasy rang out through him. Then it stopped, leaving only the regret. He kept his eyes closed, fighting back little-boy sobs of confusion. The covers were tucked around him once more and he heard her depart wordlessly.

Christ. Oh Christ, what had he done?

The phone's ring pierced the darkness. Most hideous sound of them all—the late-night phone call. Holly threw back the covers and dashed to the kitchen, grabbing the receiver.

'Hello?' Heart beating fast, anxious. Perhaps it was just a wrong number.

'Holly, it's Mum.'

'Mum? Is everything—'

'Michael's in hospital. He tried to kill himself.'

'What? What happened?'

'You're coming home.'

Holly pressed her palm to her forehead. 'Mum, I can't, I've got—'

'Holly! This is your husband we're talking about. He's in intensive care and he might not make it. Now, do you want that hanging over your head?'

Surely this was a nightmare. 'I can't afford a plane fare. I left all my money for Michael.'

'We'll book it for you first thing. Be ready to leave tomorrow.'

'Will it be a return ticket?'

Silence on the other end of the phone.

'Mum?' Holly asked. 'You haven't answered.'

'You don't belong down there, Holly. Surely that much is obvious after what has happened.'

Holly steeled herself. 'I'm not coming if it's not a return ticket.'

'Fine, you'll get your return ticket.'

'And *I* get to decide when I come home.'

More silence.

'Mum?'

'Fine,' her mother answered. 'We'll call you first thing with your flight details.'

'Okay, I'll speak to you in the morning.'

The phone clicked and she found herself hugging herself for comfort in the freezing darkness.

CHAPTER TWELVE

··

~

The smell of her mother's car had an acute physical effect on Holly. While it should have been the reassuring scent of maternal comfort, to Holly it signified the erasure of the past two months and the return to a life which she had tried to escape but failed. She heard the boot lid slam and her mother got back in the car.

'How are you, Holly?' she asked, pulling out into traffic.

'Tired. It was a long flight. How's Michael?'

'He's out of intensive care. They transferred him back to Daybrook hospital this morning.'

Holly had to bite her tongue. Why hadn't she been told that on the phone this morning when her father had called with her flight details? If he was going to live, what was she doing racing up here to see him? But she thought she knew. Her parents were trying to convince her to come home and restore her marriage. To put aside these other capricious fantasies. She remembered her father's words when she had confessed that she was going to Melbourne to take up her place at Humberstone: 'Haven't you learned enough already, girl?'

She gazed out the window as her mother took the entry ramp onto the freeway and headed towards Daybrook. Her stomach seemed to itch with anxiety, but it wasn't related to Michael's wellbeing. She couldn't stop thinking about how much work she would have to catch up on when she got back to the college. She sighed deeply and leaned her head against the glass.

Her mother patted her knee. 'It's all right, dear. I know you're upset. But it looks like he will be okay.'

Holly turned, almost told her the real reason she was upset, but changed her mind. 'How did he do it?' she asked instead.

'He cut his wrists in the bath. The doctor says the reason he's still alive is that he missed his left artery. His sister found him and called an ambulance before he'd lost too much blood.'

Poor Michael. Couldn't even kill himself effectively. Familiar landmarks whizzed by and she tried not to hate them for being markers of a forsaken existence. The turn-off to Daybrook came into view. *Abandon all hope, you who enter.*

'We'll swing by home first and drop your bag off,' her mother said. 'Are you sure you brought enough clothes?'

'I won't be staying long.'

A tight line formed at the side of her mother's mouth. 'You might change your mind when you see Michael.'

Holly didn't respond. This was going to be tougher than she had anticipated.

Her family home seemed bigger and brighter than she'd remembered. Although autumn was well advanced, it was warm enough for the ceiling fan to be beating in the lounge room and all the windows to be pushed open. A stark contrast to the drizzly Melbourne she had left behind this morning. She dumped her bag in her childhood bedroom, redecorated as a guest room. A Holly Hobby sticker was still stuck to the bedhead. She sat on the bed and idly picked at the sticker, remembering the hiding that gluing it there had got her. How old had she been? Nine? Ten? Strangely, today that was how old she still felt. Her family didn't care that she was intelligent or gifted or mature. She was little Holly, and she belonged safely in their circle.

'Here you are, sweetheart.' Her mother was behind her with a cold drink. Holly took it gratefully.

'Can I make a phone call? I have to let the college know I'm away for a few days.'

'A few days?'

'Mum, please.'

Her mother led her to the phone and waited next to her while she called. So much for privacy. Picking up the receiver, she dialled Prudence's number. It rang four times and then the machine answered.

'Hi, it's Prudence. I can't come to the phone right now but leave a message. If I don't call you back, well, draw your own conclusions.'

Drowning in a sea of unpleasant yesterdays as she was, the sound of Prudence's voice was like a lifeline. 'Prudence, it's me. I'm in Daybrook. Michael's tried to kill himself. Um ... I don't know when I'll be back. Can you please let Dr Aswell know and say hi to Justin.'

Her mother was looking pointedly at her watch, so Holly left her phone number and hung up.

'We'd better get out to the hospital,' her mother said. 'Michael will be anxious to see you.'

If only the feeling were mutual. With heavy feet, Holly followed her mother to the car.

By four o'clock Justin couldn't stop himself saying something. He suspected Prudence already had an inkling of his interest in Holly anyway, and by now it was hardly the most momentous secret he had.

'Do you know where Holly is today?' he asked, trying to sound casual but probably sounding as stiff and awkward as he always did.

'No. I guess she's not well. Or maybe she's working at home. Why don't you call her?'

Justin looked at his desk. 'Maybe *you* could call her.'

'God, what a wimp!' Prudence exclaimed good-naturedly. 'I'll be back in a minute.' She grabbed her bag and headed down to the public phone on the ground floor.

Justin walked over to Prudence's desk and gazed out the window. The maples in the garden were shedding their leaves and huge drifts of autumn colours were raked up in neat piles along the fence. He yawned and leaned his forehead on the glass. No sleep. He had lain awake after Emma's surprise visit, staring at the ceiling and trying to blank out his emotions. Somehow it must have been his fault. As soon as he had let himself relax, as soon as he had let others into his inner circle, he had suffered the consequences. Hadn't he learned from bitter experience that it didn't pay to trust anybody? To love anybody? To let anybody see him weak?

He sighed and turned his back to the window. Hadn't he learned from bitter experience that a locked door is often the best preventative? What on earth was Emma thinking could come of this? He had avoided her this morning, but avoiding her for the rest of his life wasn't going to be easy.

'My God, Justin, you'll never guess what's happened!' Prudence burst back into the room and grabbed his wrist.

'What? Is she okay?'

'She's gone home!'

It took a second for this information to sink in. And the remnants of his happiness seemed to sink with it. 'Gone home? To her husband?'

'She wasn't at her place so I checked my message bank. Michael tried to kill himself so she flew back this morning.'

'For good?'

'She didn't say. She said she doesn't know when she's coming back. I can't believe it.' She sat heavily on the edge of her desk and put her face in her hands. 'I can't believe it. I wanted her to stay here.'

'So did I.'

Prudence looked up. 'She left a number, so I'll call her tonight and get the whole story.'

'And ring me afterwards to tell me?'

'Of course.' Prudence shook her head. 'Man, I hope she doesn't stay up there. She can do way better than a loser halfwit redneck husband like Michael.'

A sudden loud bang over by Holly's desk made them both turn round in surprise.

'What was that?' gasped Prudence, putting her hand over her heart.

Justin moved cautiously towards the desk. 'There's glass all over the place. Ah, I see. The light bulb in her lamp is broken.'

'How?' Prudence was behind him.

Justin shrugged. 'I don't know. It wasn't on, was it?'

'No.' Prudence carefully picked up a shard of glass. 'So it just exploded for no reason?'

Justin didn't answer. Prudence was examining the lamp. She turned to Justin with a smile. 'Wow.'

'What?'

'Are you angry that Holly's gone back to her husband?'

'No, not really. I'm disappointed of course. Why?'

'Psychokinesis. If you were really angry but couldn't express it openly, you might, you know, project your rage onto an inanimate object.'

Justin shook his head. 'Sorry, Prudence. You're way off the mark there. I'm not angry.'

'So if you're not angry, who is?'

'Prudence, just because the light bulb—'

'We're not talking about a dead light bulb,' she said, indicating the glass all over Holly's desk, 'we're talking about a dismembered one. Maybe there's an angry spirit around here.'

Under normal circumstances Justin would have humoured her. But he was too sick and desolate, too annoyed that Prudence's imagined ghost had become more important than Holly's sudden departure. He grabbed his coat off the back of his chair and went to the door. 'Call me when you've spoken to Holly,' he said flatly.

'Sure, sure,' she said, waving him away. She was earnestly inspecting the remnants of the broken bulb.

He tried not to be angry with her. What was Prudence's lunacy in comparison with Emma's lechery? He trudged down the stairs, hoping against hope that Emma wasn't home.

After a brief but heated argument, Holly's mother agreed to go back home while Holly went to see Michael alone. Daybrook hospital was a pleasant-smelling place with lemon-painted walls and yellow and green floral wallpaper decorating the rooms. She walked along the corridors to Michael's room. At seventeen she had spent a night here having her wisdom teeth removed, and it seemed it hadn't changed at all since then. She found the room and went in.

Michael lay in one of four beds—the others were all empty—with his back to the door, gazing out the window. It seemed odd to see him after all that had happened. He was a stranger to her now. A dark-haired man whom she had shared most of her adult years with, but still a complete and utter stranger.

'Michael?'

He rolled over as she came to sit on the seat beside his bed. He was pale, not the beautiful luminosity of Christian's skin, but the pallid, greyish shade of the very sick. He looked much bigger than she remembered him, with large square hands and hairy forearms.

'Holly, you've come back!'

How was she to bear this pain? She tentatively stroked his firmly bandaged forearm, felt tears pricking at her eyes. 'No, not for good. Just for the weekend.'

His face crumpled. 'Then there's no point in living.'

'That's ridiculous, Michael. You could . . . You could do anything. You could find somebody else—'

'Is that what you've done? Found somebody else?'

She thought of Christian, his warm, skilled touch. She even thought of Justin and his twisted, ironic smile. Attractive, interesting, intelligent, but emotionally crippled. 'No. I haven't found somebody else.' Nobody attainable anyway.

He sighed and shifted in his bed. 'There was no point in you coming, Holly. As soon as you're gone, I'm just going to do it again.'

'Look, Michael, you need to get some professional help. You need to speak to a counsellor or—'

'I'm not fucking mad!' he shouted. Then lowering his voice he continued, 'You want me to go to a shrink? Like a teary housewife who can't handle her problems?'

'It might help. It might be what you need.'

'I know what I need. I need you. And if I can't have you, then I'll have nothing.'

'Michael—'

'Just go. You've made things worse by coming.' He flipped over, turning his back to her.

Frustrated, Holly picked up her bag and stood. She wavered for a moment, desperately wanting to leave, but wondering if she should stay and try to talk some sense into him. What would Prudence say? *It's not your problem, Holly.* It certainly seemed as though she had been brought in to solve a problem in another galaxy. It felt as though this sad family drama had very little to do with her.

'I'll just be here if you need me,' she murmured, dropping her bag and lowering herself into the chair next to his bed. Unfortunately, it *was* her problem.

A knock at Justin's bedroom door made him jump. He had been lying on his bed with his nose in a book, blissfully forgetful for a few moments of the predicament he had got himself into with Emma. He stood warily and called, 'Who is it?'

'Lucien.'

His uncle. Justin went to the door and removed the chair he had jammed under the handle to keep Emma out. Lucien would never have opened the door and barged in uninvited—he had an inherent respect for personal space. One thing Justin and his uncle had in common.

Justin opened the door a crack, checking nervously over Lucien's shoulder for Emma.

'What's up?' he asked, wondering if his guilt were written all over him for Lucien to read.

'You have a phone call. Prudence Emerson.' Lucien delivered the message without expression.

'Thanks, I'll take it in the kitchen.' He could hear the television on upstairs and assumed his aunt was up there. The more distance he could put between himself and Emma the better.

'As you wish.' Lucien nodded once and was gone, heading up the stairs with a straight back and a dour aspect.

Justin watched him go, then went to the kitchen and picked up the phone.

'Prudence?'

'Hi. God, Lucien's all charm, isn't he?'

'It's one of his many fine qualities. Have you spoken to Holly?'

'Yep. She's a mess, Justin. It would be nice if you could call her some time.'

'Maybe. Lucien has a thing about making interstate calls. I've heard him hammering Emma over it before. Is Holly coming back?'

'She was vague about it, but yes, I think so. Her husband—Michael—slashed his wrists in a hot bath. He nearly died, but he's recovering now.'

Justin tried to imagine it—the blood pouring out, life growing dark around the corners. It terrified him. No matter how bad things got, he knew he could never kill himself. He was too afraid of dying.

'That's horrible. How is she feeling?'

'Confused, understandably. I think she feels responsible for him or something.'

'But that's ridiculous. He's a grown man, why doesn't he just get over it? Marriages break up all the time.'

'Hey, you're preaching to the converted here. But don't worry, I've been working on her. I'll have her back here in no time.'

For once Justin was grateful for Prudence's powerful drive to get everything her own way. If anybody could convince Holly to come back, it was Prudence. 'I hope you're right,' he said.

'Am I ever wrong?'

'Rarely. Give me her number.'

As Justin copied the number down he heard somebody come into the kitchen behind him. Without looking he knew from the faint tang of perfume that it was Emma. He shuddered involuntarily.

With trepidation he said his goodbyes to Prudence and put the phone down. Emma's arms snaked around his middle.

'Who was that?' she said.

'Prudence,' he replied, extricating himself from her embrace and heading for the door.

'Where are you going?' she asked, hurt.

'I've got lots of study to do,' he called over his shoulder. But she was following him. He got to his bedroom and closed the door before she could reach him.

Knocking lightly on the door, she said, 'Is there something going on between you and Prudence?' When he didn't answer, she called angrily, 'Justin, you can't avoid me forever, you know.'

Maybe not, but there was nothing to stop him trying.

Holly was completely disoriented when she woke. The smells and the sounds were familiar but didn't seem right somehow. It took her a moment or two before she remembered she was back at her mother's place. She opened her eyes and looked around her childhood bedroom. Cheap wood panelling and mismatched linen. It was Saturday morning. Magpies sang in the trees outside. It couldn't have been much after eight o'clock, but it was already too hot with the blanket over her. She kicked it off and pulled open the curtains, lay back in her nightdress in an early morning sunbeam, thinking about Christian.

It seemed she hadn't stopped thinking about him since she had been home. Of all the elements of her new life to obsess about, why an imagined entity? Why couldn't she be obsessed with her dissertation, or her new friends? All she knew was that she wanted to go back to Humberstone as soon as possible, but she couldn't see how to get away. Her family were exerting an unbearable amount of pressure. Even Michael's mother had been over, subjecting her to a long and embarrassing harangue about playing with people's emotions. She had made it quite clear that she held Holly responsible for Michael's brush with death. And being here, amongst all the markers of her childhood, made it impossible for Holly to react like the strong, independent woman she was, instead of a ten-year-old who caved under the slightest pressure. It had been four days since she arrived. Four days sitting for hours a day with Michael, who was alternately tight-lipped or begging for her to come back to him. Four days living under the continual barrage of reproaches from her family. Time seemed to be slipping away from her too swiftly, as though Daybrook were fairyland and for every hour she spent here, a week or two was going by in the real world. The world where she really belonged.

She closed her eyes and leaned her head back, imagined the flutter of Christian's fingertips on her body, recalled every detail of that sad, lost face. Was the doctor right? Was it possible that she hadn't imagined it? She ran her own hands over her body. What did she feel like to him? Flesh and hot blood?

The phone rang somewhere downstairs. Warm sun-shine seemed to permeate the thin fabric of her nightdress, pressing hot patterns on her skin. She was drifting back into a sensual doze when the door burst open and her mother came in screaming, 'Holly, get up! Get dressed!'

Holly sat up dazed. 'What? What's the matter?'

'He's gone and done it again.'

'I don't know what they were thinking, leaving him in a room alone,' Michael's mother spluttered through her tears. 'Somebody should have been watching him. I should sue. I should sue the hospital over this.'

Michael's father was comforting her. Holly tried to block them out. They stood around Michael's bed in a dimly lit intensive-care unit. Holly had Michael's freezing hand in her own, but he was barely conscious. Security at Daybrook hospital was not great, and Michael had managed to steal a letter opener from the nurses' station and shut himself in the shower, where he tried to finish the job he had started. He was a sickly grey creature on the hard white bed, surrounded by machinery and harried nurses, still too unstable to transport to Townsville hospital. They had run out of warm supplies of his blood type and had to transfuse him with refrigerated supplies. He shivered and shuddered convulsively. She thought of this morning, lying in bed having sexy fantasies about another man, while her husband was bleeding to death.

But no. Not her husband. Just a stranger, really. A pallid stranger in a world that she no longer understood.

'I hope you're satisfied, Holly,' Michael's mother was saying, obviously needing an outlet for her anger and frustration. 'You drove him to this. You with your silly ideas about poetry. Well, was it worth it? Is your poetry worth doing this to my son?' She broke down into shuddering sobs.

Holly looked at her, anger rising. *I deserve better than this.* There was more to life than this long, agonising nightmare. These people were draining her of every drop of her identity. She had to get away. Somewhere a beautiful spirit was waiting for her with cool, pale hands and eyes of watercolour blue.

'I have to go,' she said, placing Michael's hand gently on the bed.

'Well, don't be long,' his father said. 'You'll want to be here if he comes round.'

She took a breath and steeled herself. 'No, I mean I have to go. For good.'

Michael's mother stared at her open-mouthed. 'You're not going to leave him?'

'I've already left him. This time I'm not coming back.' She collected her handbag and took one last look at Michael's face, his dark hair, his big square workman's hands. He may die. If not this time, then perhaps the time after. But if saving him meant abjuring every dream and desire she cherished out of a misplaced pity, then she would have to let him save himself.

'Goodbye, Michael,' she said softly, close to his ear. 'I have a plane to catch.'

Justin sat in the kitchen, glancing through the morning paper and eating toast. He had successfully dodged Emma for a few days. Over meals, where Lucien was also present, his aunt could only attempt to make furtive eye contact which Justin easily deflected. Otherwise, he stayed in his room and didn't emerge unless he knew Lucien was around. But this morning would be different, because every Saturday he went shopping with his aunt. It was a habit that had pleased his uncle, so he had been reluctant to break it. Today he was going to refuse to go. He did not want to be alone with Emma.

'Justin, you're not ready,' Lucien said as he came in and took a coffee cup off the shelf, surveying Justin's track pants and T-shirt.

'I thought I'd stay home this morning.'

'I'm afraid that won't be possible.'

Justin looked up from the paper. 'Why not?'

'Because you will go shopping with your aunt. Because I say so.'

'But I—'

'What you want is hardly an issue.' His uncle's face was set in stern lines. Justin had to admit that he was frightened of Lucien. Emma stepped in behind him.

'Justin? Lucien? Is everything okay?'

Lucien turned to her. 'Everything is fine, Emma. I was merely reminding Justin that he had to go out with you this morning. You'll need help carrying the shopping.'

He went to the bench and switched on the electric jug.

Emma fixed an eye on Justin. 'Well, I'm going in ten minutes. You'd better get dressed.'

The weight of their combined wills was too much for him. He gave in. He went wearily to his room and pulled on jeans and a shirt, practising over and over what he would say to Emma. *What you did was wrong. It's not to happen again. It would be better if we both forgot the other night.*

'Jesus,' he muttered, flopping on his bed and covering his face with his hands. None of these things were what he wanted to say. What he wanted to say was *I'm sorry I came.* Because that was the truth. He felt entirely responsible for this mess, simply because he couldn't exercise control over his body at that crucial moment.

After the long years of pain with his mother, after that awful night she had died, he thought that perhaps things would look up for him. And when Lucien had stepped out of the shadows at his mother's funeral, standing out like a well-dressed sore thumb amongst her erstwhile drinking buddies, he had thought it was the start of something new and brilliant. To be claimed by a rich uncle he didn't even know he had, relocated to a new city, dropped in the lap of luxury, recruited by an elite institution—all of these things were the stuff of fairytales. But it was clear from the start that Lucien wasn't motivated by love and that Emma's interest in him was more carnal than maternal. Clear that he was going to have to pay a price for the freedom from his mother.

'Justin, are you ready?'

He took his hands away from his face. Emma stood there, plump but gorgeous in a blue dress, her hair loose and flowing around her shoulders. He wanted to weep.

'I'm ready,' he said.

He followed her to the car and she chatted casually, as if nothing were different in their relationship. 'Did Lucien give you a hard time about wanting to stay home?' she asked as she let him into the car and went around to her own side.

'Kind of.'

'He's a bit strange like that,' she said, buckling her seat belt. 'Always has to have his time to himself for his stupid book.'

'Is he writing a book?'

She smiled to herself as she reversed into the street. 'One day I just might tell you, Justin. For now, trust Aunty Emma and keep away from him on Saturdays.'

Trust Aunty Emma. That hadn't done him a lot of good so far. He had to say something, he had to sort this problem out. It took a few minutes before he could make himself speak.

'Emma, I want to ... We should talk about ... You know.'

'Save it, Justin. I know I've made you very uncomfortable and I'm sorry.'

'And you won't do it again?' he said in a tiny voice.

'I didn't say that, did I?' she replied, laughing.

'But ...'

She sighed, dropped her hand to his lap and squeezed his thigh gently. 'Justin, come on. You don't have to be shy with me.'

This was a nightmare. *Just say the words. Just say, Emma I'm not interested in you.*

'Emma, I'm ... You see, I'm not interested in you.' The words nearly got stuck in his throat but made it out at the last minute.

'What?'

'I'm not ... The other night, I was half asleep and I couldn't stop. I'm sorry. But I'm just not interested in you like that. You're my aunt.'

'We're not related. Your father was my husband's brother. It's not incest or anything.'

'No, I mean ... I don't see you like ... like *that*.'

'Oh.' Her face fell and she pressed her lips together, trying to hold back tears.

'I'm sorry. I really am.'

'Sorry? Is that supposed to make it better?' she said angrily.

He froze. He was not good with women or with mood swings. They paralysed him.

'The way I see it,' she continued, 'you *owe* me.'

'Owe you?' His throat felt tight, constricted.

'You got your pleasure. Where's mine?' She beat the steering wheel and coughed out angry tears. 'Where's mine? What does Emma ever get?'

'I'm sorry.'

She pulled the car over to the kerb and pulled out a handkerchief, sobbing openly. Justin gaped at her, trembling. Overwhelmed, his primary urge was to open the car door and run away. But she launched herself into his arms and he was forced to hold her, to comfort her.

'I'm sorry, I'm sorry,' she sobbed.

He held her stiffly, patted her back tentatively.

'I'm so unhappy with Lucien. I don't feel like a woman any more. I feel like . . . I feel like I'm invisible. A fat old bitch, that's what Lucien calls me. He says I'm a fat, ugly old bitch.'

'Of course you're not,' Justin said, aware that he had to say something. 'You're beautiful.'

She looked up at him. 'Do you think so? Do you really think so?'

He nodded stiffly. She grabbed the collar of his shirt and drew his face very close to hers. 'Just once, Justin. Can't you make love to me just once? So I can feel like a woman again?' Her lips were at his throat, her breath in his ear. He felt a reluctant stirring of his senses.

'I don't know, Emma . . .'

'You owe me,' she said, a bold hand creeping between his legs. 'Lucien's going out on Monday night for dinner at his accountant's. I'll say I'm sick, I'll stay home. Come *on*, Justin. Just once.'

She had picked her moment beautifully. His emotions were completely in shock. He sat bewildered as her hot body pressed his. 'Will you leave me alone after that?' he gasped, guilt, fear, confusion spinning him out of control.

'Yes, I swear,' she breathed.

'All right,' he conceded, regretting it almost instantly. 'Just once.'

Holly almost wept with relief when the cab pulled into Sheldon Street and she could see the towers of Humberstone College outlined against the cloudy night sky. She had been travelling since ten that morning, spent a torturous two hours held over at Brisbane airport, almost got on a plane straight back to Townsville twice, but finally made up her mind about something.

About Christian.

'You sure you want me to drop you here?' the cab driver said as she paid him. 'Doesn't look like there's anybody here.'

'It's fine thanks. I'm meeting a friend.' She counted out the last of her spending money for the fortnight and grabbed her bags.

The cab sped off into the darkness and she turned to look at the smooth stone entrance of the college, gleaming in pale blue moonlight. The wind was picking up, shaking the treetops.

'Do I really want to do this?' she murmured under her breath.

But what Prudence had told her had been the final, deciding factor. Holly had called her from Brisbane airport, as much to pass the time as to tell her she was coming home. Prudence, as always, was overspilling with exuberance.

'You'll never believe it, Holly. I think we have a ghost right in our office at the college!'

'What makes you think that?' Holly had asked, her breath a little short.

'A light bulb exploded—bang!—out of nowhere. For no reason. At first I thought it was some kind of psycho-kinetic energy from Justin—I'd just told him you were back with your husband—but he swears he wasn't angry.'

'One exploded light bulb is hardly evidence of supernatural intervention,' Holly said. Where was that excitement coming from? That lifting hope, like a golden light building in her chest?

'Hey, explain it some other way and I'll listen.'

Holly hadn't replied.

She was inside, the door slamming out the security lights behind her. She waited a moment for her eyes to adjust to the dark, then went straight up to the office. The smell of the place was intoxicating—wood and paper and stone, not the awful toilet-deodorant scent of her mother's house. Dropping her bags on the floor, she went to Prudence's desk and grabbed two tea-light candles from her top drawer. Her hands shook as she found the matches, lit the candles and set them up on her desk.

No need for the mirror yet. She could wait to see him. But now she needed to feel him touch her. She secured the lock on the inside of the office door and pulled her clothes off. Freezing, she lay on the floor among her discarded clothes. Gooseflesh rose all over her skin.

'I'm here,' she called into the dark. He was with her in an instant.

She closed her eyes as the first touch came. Light fingers on her belly, warm palms pressing against her breasts.

'I'm sorry,' she said. 'I'm sorry I thought you weren't real.'

Warm lips over her own. She put her arms out to find him but embraced nothing.

'Why can't I feel you?' she asked.

No reply. She would have to ask him later, when she could see and hear him. For now she resigned herself to being a passive lover. He knew exactly where to touch her, almost as though he could read her desires as they raced recklessly through her synapses. Warm, firm hands; a hot, wet tongue; the sensation of his hair tickling her face, her belly, her thighs. She let her legs fall apart and felt his face pressed between them, drawing her up into a circle of rapture, then making her fall, fall all the way down again. Until she lay gasping, naked and alone on the floor of her office.

She opened her eyes. Although he was no longer touching her, she could sense a warm zone in the room where she thought he might be.

'I'm going to get the mirror,' she said, dressing herself. 'Will you wait for me?'

Again, no reply. She hurried to the third floor and brought the mirror back down with her. Her face was flushed and hot, the tingling trail of her orgasm still burning in her limbs. Christian, she had to see Christian again. An addiction.

Setting the mirror up on her desk, she sat in front of it and focussed on the gloom behind her shoulder. A warm, dark frisson of fear shivered through her. Crazy behaviour. Perhaps she was mad.

It didn't matter.

'Christian,' she said softly, 'come to me.'

CHAPTER THIRTEEN

~

'**H**olly, why did you ignore me for so long?' His pale blue eyes were sad and reproachful. It stabbed at her heart, and she was staggered that one glance from him could do what seeing Michael near to death had not.

'I thought I must be imagining you, that I must be going mad. But you're real, aren't you?'

'I'm here with you. What else would I be but real?'

'But why can't I touch you? Why can't I feel you, hear you and see you at the same time?'

'We exist on two different planes, Holly. Your earthly plane won't accommodate me as an embodied creature any more. I am dead to your world. I am an unnatural being. While we meet at the limits of our planes, we can make a semblance of physical contact, but never full contact.'

'Could we ever . . .?'

He shook his head. 'It wouldn't be safe. I can never cross back to the earthly plane, so you would have to come here.'

'Where's here?'

'The Elysian plane.'

'Is it like heaven?'

'I don't know—for others perhaps. But I'm bound to earth.'

'Why are you bound to earth?'

'I'm looking for something. A book. It's a long story but I must tell it. Do you remember where I was up to last time?'

The nausea was already spreading clumsy fingers through her. Questions could wait. 'You spoke of Rosalind, of Peter finding you and thrashing you. What happened after that?'

'Rosalind,' he rolled the word on his tongue thoughtfully, slowly, as though tasting it. He turned his eyes downwards and resumed. 'Rosalind and I became friends. Peter conceded that as I already knew she was in the house, we may as well continue to play together. But he swore me to secrecy over her. I was to tell no-one of her existence. Of course, I had no-one to tell so it was very little to ask.

'I knew not, nor did I think to ask, why he wanted Rosalind kept a secret. You may think it strange that my curiosity was not piqued, but you must remember that I had never known normal family or social behaviour. Many times I left things unquestioned with Peter simply because it did not occur to me that they were unusual. However, I did gain some insight into his secret about Rosalind one Friday evening about two weeks later.

'On Fridays Peter treated himself to a few whiskies. He rarely drank apart from that, although he gave me wine with most of my meals. He would grow pleasantly drunk in front of the fire, then pull me into his lap for long, loving embraces. I loved to be cuddled against his fat, warm belly and feel his hands stroking my hair. This particular Friday he was drunker than usual, and quite talkative.

'"You and Rosalind are going to be friends. The three of us will live here together and the world will never have to know about our little family." On and on he spun his tale, a detailed fantasy of cosy family life for the three of us. After a while he fell silent and I thought he had dozed off as he often did on Fridays, but eventually he said, almost sadly, "The trouble is, she looks exactly like her mother."

'I lifted my head from his chest to look at him, and he was half dozing. A trail of drool shone on his chin and I wiped it off lovingly with my sleeve. He smiled and settled back into sleep. I assumed he meant Rosalind, and for the first time I began to speculate on why he wanted her hidden. Perhaps her mother's family were searching for her and he did not want her taken away. That seemed perfectly reasonable to me. I vowed silently to myself that I would do anything to protect Rosalind from the outside world.

'At first I only saw Rosalind at suppertime, when I was allowed to take up her supper tray and eat with her. Sometimes we played for hours afterwards, until midnight or later. Peter did not enforce regular hours with us, and we would often be delirious with sleep deprivation before he would come to make us go to bed.

'But after a month or so Peter relaxed and allowed Rosalind to roam the house as I did—under strict orders never to set foot outside. Friday evenings were made even more perfect, with Peter in his drunken haze and Rosalind and I taking turns in his lap, or sitting at his feet in front of the fire.

'Of course, I was besotted with Rosalind. But in a very innocent way. I thought she was unspeakably pretty and I lived to see her smile. She could have ordered me to do anything and I would have complied, but she was too sweet to make me act against my will. And although we were both young adults really, and not the children that we reverted to in each other's company, there was no glimmer of sexual feeling between us. We would push and wrestle with each other, completely oblivious to budding and sensitive body parts. If ever I brushed her breast or felt the curve of her waist by accident, it was to me as guileless an action as touching her shoulder or her arm.

'I believed Peter. I believed that the three of us would be together in our dusty, gilt-edged cocoon forever. But that was all to change shortly before my fifteenth birthday, when Peter began to invite his "associates" over.

'As we had never had visitors before, I was terrified the first time I heard a group of voices outside our front door and the loud chime of the doorbell. I shrieked and ran upstairs to call for Peter. He came out of his room, wrapped in a purple and gold silk robe, and ushered me down the stairs in front of him.

'"Now, Christian. Just stay here, say nothing and be well behaved. My associates are only here for a short time, and we must be good hosts or they won't wish to come back."

'I nodded, wide-eyed, went to my chair, picked up my letter book and began to copy my spelling words for the week. All the time, though, I was watching out of the corner of my eye, curious to see what Peter's associates looked like.

'Much to my disappointment, they were a quartet of rather ordinary-looking men, mostly in their forties. They passed hats and coats to Peter, who hung them carefully on a black oak hatstand by our front door before showing the men inside.

'"Who's the lad?" one of them remarked. I focussed hard on my letters, nervous that I had been noticed and wondering if Peter would be cross with me.

'"He must be Peter's son," commented a portly man, "he has his father's taste in clothes. Quite the young dandy, isn't he? Is it your son, Peter?"

'Peter joined them in front of the fire, where they had formed a curious circle around me. "No, he's not my son. He's an orphan. He can't speak, can you, lad?"

'I looked up at him shocked, then shook my head slowly. If he wanted me to be mute, then mute I would be. To me, Peter's wisdom supplanted the word of God.

'"So there will be no security problems, if you grasp my meaning," Peter continued, leading his associates upstairs.

'"Well done, Peter. Can't have the whole world knowing, can we?" I heard one of them say as their voices faded out of earshot.

'I knew the only place upstairs that Peter would take them was what he called his reading room, which I was forbidden to enter. I had not confessed to Peter that I had already seen this room on the day I had found Rosalind. It was the room with the strange star painted on the wall, and I would not have entered it again even if Peter had allowed it.

'These visits of Peter's associates fell into a regular pattern, and I knew it was Sunday night when I heard the doorbell chime. Apart from them, we had no other callers. After a few weeks I could easily tell them apart. There was Patrick, a friendly, round-faced man who wore a sheen of perspiration even on the coldest day; Edmund, the youngest, handsome and blond, always dressed immaculately, but often reeking of whisky; Thurber, the portly man who usually turned eyes of undisguised desire upon me when Peter was not looking; and Ezekial, a tall and powerfully built man with lizard eyes and a pointed chin. Of all of them, I liked only Patrick. He often brought me sweets and always stopped to say hello. The others were arrogant and would take any opportunity in Peter's absence to make jokes about the nature of our relationship, thinking I was unable to repeat them. In fact, I consciously decided not to tell Peter what they said, somehow convinced that it was my fault that they made up those jokes. I had been a bugger-boy for so long, perhaps they could tell.

'After a few hours upstairs in the reading room, they would all emerge with flushed faces, sometimes warily subdued, sometimes unnaturally ebullient. Peter would look glad to close the door on them and return to his dark, isolated space, muttering about it being unfortunate, yet "the only way" for him to proceed. I gathered from this that he did not enjoy the intrusion of his associates any more than I did, but I did not ask him why they were necessary to him. It was usually at this time that Peter would exclaim upon the lateness of the hour and lay out blankets and pillows for my bed, with all the fuss and fondness of a mother hen.'

'What did you think they were doing in the reading room?' A sharp pain throbbed over Holly's right eye. She tried to ignore it.

'Actually, it didn't occur to me to wonder. So many things I left unquestioned, presuming that Peter had a kind of divine purpose. It was Rosalind who brought it up and awoke my curiosity.

'My favourite time of the day was after supper, when Peter would go about his studies and I would sit with Rosalind in her room. During summer we would sometimes stand at the window, gazing out on the filthy rooftops and chimneys of the city. I had not set foot in the outside world for nearly a year, and Rosalind said she could not remember ever being out there. I told her stories about my experiences living on the streets in the freezing winters, and she would shudder and declare that she did not want to know the world if it were so cruel.

'Peter kept Rosalind confined to her room on Sundays, to keep her out of the sight of his associates. I took it as more proof that Rosalind's maternal family must be looking for her, that Peter was desperate to keep her himself. I imagined that Rosalind's mother was careless and callous like my own mother, that if she got hold of her daughter she would abandon her in a filthy squat, never to return. So I was just as particular as Peter about keeping Rosalind hidden.

'"What do they look like, Christian?" she asked me one evening.

'"Who?"

'"Papa's associates. Are they as noble and fine as he?"

'I described them to her in thorough detail, especially Patrick, my favourite. She closed her eyes as if trying to picture them.

'"Which one has the soft, rumbling voice?" she asked, her eyes blinking open.

'"That would be Ezekial."

'"And which the stentorian tone?"

'At this time, I did not know what stentorian meant, but not wanting to appear foolish I said, "I don't know. I pay no attention to their voices."

'"I do. I press my ear to my keyhole and listen as hard as I can. But after they have gone into Papa's reading room, I hear very little. The occasional cry or laugh, sometimes a voice raised in anger, but no words. What do you think they are doing in there, Christian?"

'"It's not for us to know."

'She hit my arm playfully. "Oh, Christian. You are too good. Just because Papa doesn't allow you to *know*, doesn't mean you aren't allowed to *wonder*. Perhaps they are pirates, planning a voyage to Spain. Come now, you make up a story."

'I thought hard. "Perhaps they are crusaders, investigating how to capture witches."

'"Or playwrights."

'"Or a secret royal family." I pretended to be enjoying our storytelling game, but it had occurred to me with sudden certainty that what Peter and his associates were doing involved buggery. I said nothing to Rosalind because

I knew she would neither understand nor approve. I kept it inside with a sick jealousy growing in my stomach. Peter harboured no desire for me, even though he repeatedly affirmed my beauty. I could not understand why he would wish to make love with the others but not with me. For my part, I would have given myself to him willingly and lovingly—I lived to please him. However, his taste clearly led him in a different direction.

'I could not stop thinking about it, I could not suppress the pictures that formed in my mind. I became obsessed and sulky. One Friday evening I shied away from him when he tried to hold me. He gave me a hard clip around the ear and told me sternly, "Christian, I own you. Do as I say immediately."

'I allowed myself to snuggle against his belly, hot silent tears springing to my cheeks. I felt as a lover betrayed.

'You must understand that my feelings for him were not sexual. I was not attracted to or aroused by him. I knew little of love, all I had was an aching desire never to be abandoned again. I thought that if I was perfect for Peter, if I fulfilled all his needs, I could relax and not fear exile.

'My curiosity, my obsession, grew too strong to resist. The following Sunday I watched his associates arrive, heard them disappear upstairs, waited a few minutes, then crept up after them.

'Holly? Are you ill?'

Holly had dropped her head into her hands with a soft groan. 'My head. It hurts.'

'Keep your eyes closed for a while, perhaps.'

She closed her eyes. The dull throb in her head seemed to ease marginally. 'Did you see anything?' she asked.

'I crouched against the door quietly and peered through the keyhole. The room was lit with dozens of candles. The flickering, shifting shadows of Peter and his friends stained the spines of books in the shelves lining the walls. To my relief, they were all still fully dressed, sitting in a circle on the floor, with Peter positioned underneath the painted star. He wore a black robe and hood, and his face was almost in complete darkness. They had their eyes closed and were speaking in a low hum, almost as though the words were vibrating on the air. It caused my ears to buzz and I found myself relaxing with each beat of the chant. The words they were saying made no sense to me. I thought they might be using another language.

'On and on they went, and I felt myself dropping into some kind of a daze, my own eyes rolling back in my head and the lids closing. I could still feel my hands pressed against the doorframe, but the field of vision in my mind seemed to be expanding. I began to feel as though I were somewhere else all together. The air seemed very close and steamy, even though it was nearly winter. In my mind I saw a field— barren dirt and blasted rocks. An orange glow on the horizon intensified and grew dim in random glimmers, and from there came the sound of horrible, muffled wails. Great clouds of smoke and steam oppressed me from above. From the direction of the orange glow, black figures were approaching me, not slowly, but inhumanly fast. They rushed upon me, some on foot and some with great batlike wings, all with their mouths open as though trying to say something.

'I was rooted to the spot in my half-trance. One being reached me before all the others—a hideous, headless corpse with blackened limbs and vile, gaping wounds in his chest. He stopped in front of me and slowly turned the palms of his hands towards me. In each palm glimmered a baleful golden eye. He thrust his hands at me with urgency, and the smell that rose from his rotten skin overpowered me. I screamed and felt myself fall, and only realised I was safe at home when my head thumped painfully against the floor.

'Peter and his associates were at the door in a second,

crowding around me. Senseless, I reached for Peter and groaned in terror. He scooped me into his arms and ordered the others back to the room, then took me to his own bedroom. It seemed very cool and dark in comparison to the place I had just visited. He dumped me on the dusty bedspread and sat heavily next to me, his hands shaking with anger.

'"What were you doing?" he demanded, his great hand closing roughly around my throat.

'I gasped vainly for air, then choked out, "I saw . . . I saw . . ."'

'He released me and leaned very close. "What did you see?"

'"I'm so frightened, Peter." I tried to curl up against him but he held me at arm's length.

'"Tell me what you saw, or I will thrash you until you are a bleeding pulp," he spat through gritted teeth. I knew from experience it was not an idle threat.

'"I saw hell," I replied.

'Hell?' Holly asked, opening her eyes again. Pain zoomed back into her head.

'Oh, yes. As ignorant as I was of theological matters, I recognised the infernal realm. Almost instinctively, as would you if you had seen it. There is no mistaking such a vision.

'Peter immediately went quiet. I think it was the first time I had seen him lost for words. A few minutes passed as he watched me closely in the dark, clearly weighing up what I had said. I was frightened of him, more frightened than I had ever been because normally his rage was articulate. When he reached out his hand to me, I winced in anticipation, but he merely stroked my hair once and said, "Wait here," before leaving me in his room and going back to his associates.

'I could hear him making excuses to them in the hallway, saying I had taken ill and they would have to cancel the evening's meeting. Old lizard eyes Ezekial began to complain bitterly, but Peter was insistent. I felt very important being the cause of their cancellation and lay on his dusty bed waiting for him to return and explain.

'When I heard the front door close behind them some minutes later, I crept up and waited at the door to the bedroom. Peter's footsteps echoed up the stairs and soon he was coming down the hall towards me. He scooped me into his arms and laid me gently on the bed, one hand tangling in my hair.

'"My beautiful, beautiful boy," he said. "Could it be you possess more gifts than your beauty?"

'I knew not how to answer so I remained silent.

'"What did you see, Christian? Describe it to me in perfect detail."

'I obediently recounted what I had seen, how it had felt to go into the trance, what smells and sounds I experienced. He asked me a thousand questions, made me repeat myself over and over. Finally, when he had exhausted his curiosity, he leaned into me and kissed me, lovingly, a kiss that went on for ages.

'At length he pulled away and smiled at me. "You are my gift from the Lord. I do love you, Christian."

'I was deliriously happy. Too happy even to speak.

'"We will train this second sight of yours, Christian." He chuckled quietly. "You will be a sorcerer's apprentice."'

CHAPTER FOURTEEN

~

Holly drooped her head and took a deep, shuddering breath. The nausea was overwhelming. Her mouth was dry and her stomach churned. She realised she hadn't eaten since breakfast that morning.

'Do you want me to go?' Christian asked.

She lifted her head to look at him. The pale, perfectly formed face gazed back at her in the mirror, blue eyes touched with concern. 'I never want you to go. I could listen to you forever if it wasn't for this sick feeling.'

'Perhaps we can meet again tomorrow night?'

'No, just keep going for now. I'll tell you if I'm going to be sick. Why did he say sorcerer's apprentice? Was he practising black magic?'

'At that stage his activities were still a mystery to me. He promised to include me the next time his associates came over, and I was thrilled and excited. However, before that could happen, Peter's financial situation took a turn for the worse. A merchant ship in which he had invested disappeared off the coast of India in a violent storm. He had borrowed the money for the investment from the Humberstone family, and they were less than sympathetic about his losses. As soon as the news about the ship had reached London, Philbert Humberstone was at our door demanding to know how payment was to be made on the loan. Peter did the only thing he knew how—he ran away.

'I hadn't been outside our house in over a year. Rosalind could not remember ever being outside. When the carriage came to take the three of us away, it was after midnight and we were hustled with urgent secrecy into it by a nervous Peter. For Rosalind and me it was a huge adventure.

'"Shall we ever come back here, Papa?" Rosalind asked, peering from left to right from her seat in the carriage.

'"Yes, yes, eventually," he replied as he settled me in and rearranged my scarf, which had come loose. "Depending upon Lord Burghley's generosity. Perhaps even depending on the charms of my Christian. Eh, Christian? What limits will you go to for me?"

'"Anything," I replied wholeheartedly, glad for the opportunity to tell him. "I'll do anything at all."

'"Well, that may not be necessary," he mumbled as we pulled away from Milton Close. "Let's just hope that the old dog remembers how much he owes me."

'The excitement kept us awake for an hour or two, but eventually the rhythmic jostling of the horses sent Rosalind and me to sleep. Two or three times I was jolted out of my slumber by a noise or a hole in the road, and I saw Peter was still wide awake and watching over us both. The journey seemed to take an interminable night, with the sound of the horses' hooves and the smells of the carriage and the dark world beyond it permeating my senses as I drifted in and out of sleep. In truth, we were probably travelling for around seven hours, and we arrived at Lord Burghley's shortly before dawn.

'Peter shook me awake gently. Rosalind was stirring

next to me, her warm little body heavy against my shoulder. "Christian, Rosalind. We're here."

'I peered out of the coach. The sky was pale grey-blue, and pinkish streaks of dawn stretched from the horizon over the tops of a forest of oak and ash. Beside me, Rosalind squealed.

'"Christian, look. Look." She grabbed my hand and pointed out her coach window. I turned and gasped, astonished. A giant manor house rose before me. Grecian columns and a marble entranceway framed a huge oak door. Shuttered windows closed out the early morning sun as it began to struggle over the horizon. I leaned past Rosalind and peered up at the front of the house.

'"Is it a castle?" I breathed in awe. I had never seen anything like it except in books.

'Peter chuckled. "I suppose you could call it a castle . . . of sorts."

'"Oh, Papa, it is beautiful. Who lives here?"

'"An old friend, my dear. Henry Clement, the eighth Lord Burghley. He and I were at Oxford together."

'"Is he expecting us?"

'Peter frowned. "Not precisely. Though he should have known that one day I would turn up. Come along, let's see if we can rouse somebody."

'The coachman helped us to unload our bags at the front entrance then went on his way. Peter tugged his gloves at his wrists nervously. A frosty bite hung in the air.

'"Wish me luck, children," he said as he approached the door and reached for the ornate brass knocker.

'The knocking seemed very sharp in the crisp morning air. It echoed loudly enough to frighten a group of birds that rose from a nearby copse and took to the sky. I had never smelled fresh air like this and I tried to take huge gulps of it. Rosalind, too, was wide-eyed, looking around her and hugging her shawl closer against the frost.

'Finally the door opened, and a middle-aged woman in a plain grey dress peered out. "Who is it?" she asked.

'Peter extended his hand but she didn't take it, merely eyed him suspiciously. "Who is it?" she repeated.

'"My name is Peter Owling. I'm an old friend of Lord Burghley. Could you please let him know I'm here?"

'"He's sleeping."

'"He won't mind being woken for me."

'She deliberated for a time, then opened the door wide and ushered us into a front parlour. "Wait here," she said, "I'll send somebody to stoke the fire."

'With relief we stepped out of the cold. Peter settled himself on an upholstered tapestry sofa as the housekeeper left us. Rosalind and I squeezed together in the window seat, gazing at the huge world outside.

'"No matter how wide I open my eyes, I can't fit it all in," Rosalind sighed, leaning into me. "I had no idea the sky was so big."

'After a few minutes a stooped man came in, palming sleep out of his eyes, to get a fire going in the grate. Rosalind and I watched him quietly and Peter appeared to be dozing into his chest. Soon the room began to warm up and we removed our gloves, scarves and overcoats. Rosalind and I tentatively moved closer to the fire to warm our faces. The stooped man nodded at us politely and left.

'"Do you think that was Lord Burghley?" I asked Rosalind in a whisper, not wanting to wake Peter.

'"Don't be silly. A lord would be tall and imposingly dressed. He was probably just a servant."

'I was embarrassed at my ignorance and fell silent. We sat together next to the fire and I began to feel sleepy again. Fine golden lines of sunlight squeezed through the cracks in the shutters, reaching across the room to where we sat. My head began to droop.

'"Are you tired, Christian?" Rosalind asked, her voice muted through a veil of approaching sleep.

'I nodded sleepily and she pulled my head down into her lap. "Rest while we wait for Lord Burghley. If he's terribly important, he might not come for ages."

'I needed little prompting. I curled my hand around her knee, closed my eyes and drifted off while she stroked my forehead with warm hands.

'Lord Burghley indeed took his time in coming. When Rosalind prodded me awake the sun was fully up. The housekeeper was advising Peter that Lord Burghley would be down in a few moments. Peter adjusted his clothes and tidied his hair, gesturing to us to do the same. We sprang up from our place near the grate and sat politely next to Peter on the sofa. Rosalind smoothed her skirts and folded her hands in her lap.

'Sure enough, soon a man—tall and imposingly dressed as Rosalind had predicted—entered the room. His hair was dark auburn, his eyes almost black and his skin pale gold. He wore a red silk waistcoat and his shirt sleeves, and though I had presumed he must be the same age as Peter, he appeared to be only in his early thirties. We all climbed uncertainly to our feet, looking at him expectantly.

'Lord Burghley stopped momentarily in front of Peter, a half-smile twitching at the corners of his lips. "By God," he said at last, "by God, Owling, it is you, isn't it? When Agnes told me you were here I wouldn't believe her. But it really is you."

'"Sorry to arrive so early, Clement, but I needed some quick relief from a . . . er . . . disadvantageous situation."

'Lord Burghley took a few steps forward and extended his hand to Peter, who shook it firmly and warmly. "Not at all, Owling. I'm delighted to see you. Just delighted. I'm surprised and disappointed you haven't been earlier than this. I haven't forgotten what you did for me, you know. Are these your children?"

'Peter turned to introduce us. "This is my daughter Rosalind."

'"Ah, she's the image of Madelaine. How do you do, Rosalind?"

'"Well, my lord," she replied, taking his hand and curtsying.

'"And who is this delightful creature?" Lord Burghley remarked as he took my hand. He studied my face closely. "He's really quite an angel, Owling. Not your son, I hope."

'"No, Christian is an orphan I have unofficially adopted. He's quite available for your pleasure, Clement."

'I looked at Peter in bewilderment, but he merely smiled at me and gave me a nod of the head to remind me of my manners.

'I bowed low. "An honour to meet you, my lord," I said.

'Lord Burghley seemed reluctant to let go my hand. "The pleasure is all mine, Christian." Finally he released me and turned to Peter. "Agnes is organising some rooms for you all. Would you care to join me for breakfast in the meantime?"

'Holly, I had never eaten such a sumptuous meal in my life. The table was crowded with dishes—hams, pastries, smoked fish, fresh fruit, hot tea. And two servants attended us the whole time, wiping up spills as soon as they were made, replenishing teacups without asking. I ate and ate and ate. And then Agnes, the housekeeper, showed us to our rooms and I collapsed for a few more hours' sleep, my stomach full and my mind at ease.'

'At ease?' Holly asked, astonished. 'But Peter had offered you to Lord Burghley "for his pleasure". Didn't he care about how you felt, or what you wanted to do?'

'I didn't mind. I had done worse things in my time, made love to worse men in worse situations than to Lord Burghley in his castle.'

'It's appalling. Peter professed to have saved you from prostitution. I don't think he had your best interests at heart if—'

'Don't!' Christian cried. 'Don't dare to say anything like that about Peter. He knew what he was doing. He was looking after all of us—myself and Rosalind as well as himself.'

Holly fell silent. Christian had clearly adored Peter unreservedly, and there was little point at this distance of years and on the other side of the grave in trying to show how outrageously he had been exploited. She felt sick and headachy and just wanted the story to continue.

'I'm very sorry, Christian. Please go on.'

'After two weeks at Lord Burghley's estate, it started to feel like home. My life fell into a regular pattern. I would sleep in Lord Burghley's bed most nights. Sometimes he just wanted to hold me as he went to sleep, sometimes he was more demanding. I liked him, he was very kind, though I was frustrated on occasion that I didn't get to sleep in my own bedroom. It was the first time in my life I'd had a comfortable space of my own. In the mornings after breakfast I would often go back to my own room and climb into my own bed for a few hours, to read or to doze or to daydream.

'Rosalind and I would play together in the afternoon, running wildly in the endless gardens until we dropped, exhausted and grass-stained. We would gaze up at the sky, make pictures in the clouds; she would press my hand in her own and call me her "dear, dear Christian". One afternoon she rolled over and placed her hands on my face, leaned down and kissed me on the lips. I had a brief taste of her warm, milky breath and a brief caress from her hair and then she was sitting back giggling. I felt strange and guilty, as though we had done something we oughtn't. That one chaste kiss from her brought all my senses alive like none of Lord Burghley's more intimate caresses could.

'Peter spent his afternoons with Lord Burghley in his study on some kind of business. I once asked Peter what kind of business they were doing and he told me Lord Burghley was teaching him to fish. Then he laughed and ruffled my hair.

'"Don't concern yourself, Christian. You and Rosalind go and play."

'After that first fortnight, the rain set in. Lord Burghley asserted that it was typical for this time of year to be unbearably damp. Rosalind and I, now used to letting our energy expand in the unlimited greenness outside, found it difficult to reign it in between the smooth walls of the manor. We tried reading, we tried making up stories, we tried hide-and-go-seek, we pestered the cook, we pestered the servants, we pestered poor Agnes until she went nearly out of her mind with vexation. Finally, as we sat in Rosalind's room gazing bored out the window at the eighth consecutive day of rain, Rosalind looked at me with a wicked gleam in her eye.

'"I know," she said quietly. "I know a fun thing to do."

'"What?" I asked.

'She shook her curls in mock sadness. "No, you wouldn't be brave enough."

'"Yes I would, yes I would," I protested. Rosalind's good opinion was everything to me.

'"You would need to be very brave," she repeated.

'"I'm brave."

'"What do you think Papa and Lord Burghley are doing?"

'"Business," I replied.

'"Yes, but what *kind* of business?"

'I was perplexed. "Peter said Lord Burghley was teaching him to fish."

'Rosalind laughed. "Silly. It's an old saying: Give a man a fish and you feed him for a day, but teach a man to fish and he'll be fed for a lifetime. Papa came here to borrow money from Lord Burghley, but Lord Burghley is teaching him a new way to earn money. I overheard them yesterday when we were playing hide-and-go-seek."

'"What's he teaching him?"

'She shrugged. "I don't know. That is why we have to spy on them."

'"Spy on them?"

'"You told me you were brave enough." And so the trap was closed.'

Christian paused, reached out a white hand in the darkness. 'But, Holly, you're ill.'

Holly, pale and shaking, got unsteadily to her feet. "Wait here," she said. "I'll be back directly."

'I'll go, I don't want to make you ill.'

'No,' she replied with some vehemence. 'No, wait here. I have to hear the rest.'

Suffocating nausea surged through her. She stumbled into the hallway and ran up the stairs to the ladies' room. She could feel a cold sweat beading her brow as she paused over the open mouth of the toilet. For an instant she felt as though she wouldn't throw up after all, but then her stomach seemed to turn inside out, her gullet switched into reverse gear and a stream of sour bile exploded from her throat.

She remained bent over the toilet for a few minutes, taking deep breaths and expelling sticky spit from her mouth. Finally she went to the basin, washed her face and ran a shaking hand over her lips. This really was making her ill—Christian was right, she should stop. But now that she had vomited, her stomach had started to settle. The headache was sharp and throbbing, although if she could bear to close her eyes and shut out the vision of Christian it would subside soon enough. She checked her watch. It was nearly ten o'clock. Just another hour, perhaps, and then she could go home to sleep it off.

The room appeared to be empty when she came back, except for the two little flames flickering by the mirror. But she could sense his presence, a warm assemblage of air particles near her desk. She sat back down and closed her eyes.

'Are you all right?' Christian asked with concern. She felt his hand touch the back of her head gently.

'I'm all right when I'm with you. The rest of the time I'm not. When I was with Michael—'

'Michael. I heard what he did.'

'How did you hear?'

'The purple girl was talking about it. And the other man who is here sometimes.'

'Did you break the light bulb?'

'I didn't intend to. Sometimes, under pressure, I can affect things in your world.'

'You were angry?'

'I thought you may not come back.'

'I came back for you.' She lifted her head and peered into the mirror. Christian's form appeared in the darkness, his dark hair falling over his shoulder as he tilted his head to look at her. A sharp pain pierced her right eye. 'Do you think that's crazy?'

'No. The only reason to be in any place at any time is love. Close your eyes, Holly. I don't wish to make you unwell.'

She closed her eyes and rested her head on her folded forearms on the desk. 'So you went to look in on Peter and Lord Burghley. What were they doing?'

'We knew that they were usually in Lord Burghley's study by about two o'clock, so shortly after dinner we declared that we were going upstairs for an afternoon nap. In actuality we crept into the study and tucked ourselves up in the window seat behind the heavy red drapes. Rosalind was on one side and I on the other. We were quite hidden from view, our backs pressed up against the window as the rain beat steadily upon it.

'We only waited for about twenty minutes before Peter and Lord Burghley arrived. I peered cautiously from behind the gold braid fringe on the side of the curtain. Rosalind did the same on her side.

'For some reason they had brought Mina, one of Lord Burghley's servants, with them. She was quite a young woman, whom Rosalind and I secretly made fun of. She had brown hair, brown eyes and brownish skin, and always wore a brown dress. It was as though she were one colour from head to toe. We had nicknamed her "Miss Brown".

'"Now, Mina," Lord Burghley said with kindly authority, "you aren't to worry. You just relax and go along with what Mr Owling says and there will be an extra treat in your wage at the end of the month."

'"Yes, my lord," she said warily as she was sat down in an upholstered chair.

'"Good. Now, Owling," here he turned to Peter, "do you have the crystal?"

'Peter felt in his waistcoat pocket and pulled out a ball of clear crystal, about the size of his palm. He and Lord Burghley stood close in front of Mina and Peter held up the ball near her face, just above her eyes.

'"Look at the crystal, Mina," he said.

'"Yes, sir," she replied. I could see her eyes turned upwards, watching the ball.

'"Just keep looking at the ball." He moved the crystal almost imperceptibly closer, then, with tiny movements, started to sway it from left to right. "Keep watching," he said in a soft, compelling voice. "Keep watching."

'I looked over at Rosalind but her face was firmly pressed up against the curtain, watching, fascinated. I turned back to observe Mina. Her eyelids were flickering from the effort of concentrating on the crystal.

'"Let go of the world, Mina," Peter said. "Cut yourself loose, let yourself drift. That's my girl. Watch the crystal, follow the crystal. Let yourself drift."

'He repeated himself over and over and even I began to feel torpid. I watched as Mina's eyes finally closed and she sagged back in the chair. Lord Burghley touched Peter gently on the back. "You've done it, Owling, she's under."

'Peter straightened up, looking satisfied. "And now?"

'"Now, you can do as you wish with her. She won't resist and she won't remember a thing when she wakes."

'"Are you sure?"

'"Yes. Watch this." Lord Burghley approached Mina and pushed her skirts around her waist, tugging her skinny brown legs forward so that she was naked from the waist down. He roughly shoved two of his fingers inside her. That strange, guilty feeling came over me again, and I was unbearably embarrassed for Rosalind. But she had not moved, and still watched as her father stepped in and joined Lord Burghley in crudely exploring the girl's private parts.

'"Go on, Owling, fuck her if you wish. You know I'm not interested," Lord Burghley asserted.

'I caught my breath, strangely jealous and disappointed in Peter, but he did not let me down. He smoothed Mina's skirts over her legs and turned away. "No, I'm not interested either."

'"Are you sure? Magic thrives on transgression, doesn't it? You are still dabbling in magic, aren't you, Peter?"

'"Come now, Clement. I'm a grown man. Magic is the province of college boys."

'"You seemed rather more serious about it than any other college boy I knew," Lord Burghley replied.

'"That's all in the past," Peter replied. "What do we do with young Mina now?"

'"That's the beauty of it—you can plant any suggestion you want," Clement said. "You can suggest that she crows like a rooster when she wakes up every morning, if you wish. It's useful for breaking bad habits, for relaxation, for being rid of nervous problems. There's not a hysterical wife in London whose rich husband won't pay good money to have her sorted out by Peter Owling. And if you *suggest* that she needs to come back again, well, there you have an unlimited source of income. Come, let's suggest something to Mina."

'They deliberated for a while before hitting upon the idea of having Mina jump and spit like a cat every time she saw or heard a dog. My nose was beginning to itch from having my face pressed against the curtain, so I sat back in the window seat and did not watch for a while. Rosalind did likewise, and she squeezed my hand and rolled her eyes excitedly. I knew this would not be the last time we would be playing our little game of espionage.'

'What happened to Mina?' Holly asked.

'She seemed quite normal the next time I saw her. Rosalind and I were mischievous and made a barking sound when we saw her passing in the halls, and she actually did jump and look around skittishly like a cat might, emitted a harsh hissing noise, then collected herself and went on her way, puzzled. After the third time we did it she burst into tears, so we left her alone. And a week later she appeared to be back to normal. But I saw her serving food to Peter and Lord Burghley and she never displayed a hint of embarrassment about the indignity they had put her through. I suppose she must, indeed, have been unaware of it.

'From then on, all Rosalind ever wanted to do was spy on Peter and Lord Burghley, but I was reluctant to go with her. First, I was afraid of being caught and thrashed. Rosalind would certainly not be punished as severely as

I, so she had less to fear. But I was also afraid that we would see the two of them performing some other intimate act with their experiments, and I wanted to prevent Rosalind from being exposed to that. In any case, on one particular day when she was bothering me and bothering me to go with her, I finally lost my temper and said that I would not go under any circumstances and then stormed off to my bedroom to sulk.

'That night was a rare night when Lord Burghley did not request my presence in his bed. I would often spend such nights struggling to stay awake so that I could savour my solitude and the fantasies that went with it. I would imagine in fine detail that I was lord of this manor, and this my bedchamber. Rosalind would be my lady. Ever since she had kissed me that afternoon, my innocent affection for her had started to transform into something more natural for a boy of fifteen. But out of respect for what she was—my dear, sweet Rosalind—I would stop myself from imagining what she and I would do as lord and lady in a bedchamber and instead concentrate on fantasies of recounting to her those business transactions I had made during my working day.

'When my fantasy started to blur into sleep I heard a knock at the door. I got up to answer it and Rosalind stood there.

'"Christian," she whispered, "let me in. I have the most awful secret to tell!"

'I ushered her in and closed the door behind her. I made to light a taper but she stopped me. "No, it must be very dark for you to hear this tale."

'We walked back to my bed and huddled under the covers together. "What secret?" I asked, dying of curiosity.

'"An awful, awful secret. I wanted to tell you earlier, but I thought you were still cross with me. And then when it became dark and I was alone in my room, I was far too scared to keep it inside any longer. Christian, Lord Burghley is a murderer!"

'"A murderer?"

'"Yes! I went to spy on him and Papa again this afternoon, and at first it was so dull—they smoked and they talked about Oxford and people I had never heard of before—but then . . .'

'"Then what?" I prompted.

'"Remember Papa has said a number of times that Lord Burghley owes him a favour? It seems that a young man who was a lover of Lord Burghley in his college days, before he was Lord Burghley and still just Henry Clement, had threatened to go to his father with the information that he was intimate with boys. The young man was broken-hearted over Lord Burghley's ending their relationship and wanted to avenge himself by having him disinherited. Imagine—the manor, the estate, the title, all would have gone to his younger brother."

'"So he killed him?" My breath had stopped in my throat. I shivered under the covers.

'"Yes! He and Papa were reminiscing, laughing about it. How the young man squealed when he saw Lord Burghley in his room. How he was bludgeoned to death with a rock which Lord Burghley later buried in the garden outside the young man's house. And worse, how Papa helped him dispose of the corpse!"

'I was speechless. "Are you sure you heard right?"

'"Absolutely. They talked about how Papa had taken his feet and Lord Burghley had ruined a velvet waistcoat supporting his bloodied head. Isn't it just awful?"

'I realised that, in actuality, Rosalind was more excited than horrified. If it were true, surely Peter would have only the best of reasons for getting involved in something so sordid. Surely he would have disapproved of Lord Burghley's activities and only helped him out of misplaced loyalty.'

'You don't still believe that, do you?' Holly couldn't help asking.

'I still believe that Peter only ever acted with the best interests at heart. No matter what things he . . . No matter what he did,' Christian replied hesitantly. He fell silent for a few moments, staring off into the distance, his lips turned down sadly.

'You miss him?' she asked, though she knew the answer.

'I miss him more than . . . more than I can ever express.'

Holly felt strangely jealous of the cruel and corrupt Peter, even though he was long dead. 'I'm very sorry.'

'In any case,' he said, resuming his story, 'we weren't much longer to stay with Lord Burghley. Thankfully. I was nervous to sleep next to him now, knowing what he was capable of, though he did not appear to notice my new-found apprehension of him.

'Of course Rosalind and I threw ourselves into our espionage with renewed enthusiasm. She for the thrill of horror—she really was excited to think that dashing Lord Burghley was a murderer. I, however, was more interested in hearing Peter clear himself of guilt. Either way, we never heard them mention the murder again. We did, nevertheless, hear the argument that led to Lord Burghley sending us packing.

'We overheard many business conversations which we found excessively tedious, and we would often roll our eyes and fake ostentatious yawns in our window seat, nearly giggling and giving the game away. It seemed clear to me that Peter wanted to borrow money from Lord Burghley, but Lord Burghley would deflect all his implied requests by steering the conversation back to good business strategies and investments that Peter could undertake to restore himself financially. Finally, Peter came out openly and asked for a sum of money to cover his debt to the Humberstones.

'Lord Burghley was quiet for a long time. Finally, he said, "Owling, you know I want to help you, but—"

'"Clement, you have it in your power to erase my debt completely and you would never miss the money. I'm not asking for that, I'm merely asking for a loan. I know that you'll be a kinder creditor than the Humberstones and give me time to get on my feet. Really, Clement, after all we've been through together . . ."

'"There is a way, Owling."

'"Name your terms."

'"You won't like them."

'"Go on, name your terms."

'Again Lord Burghley was silent. I was once more watching from behind the golden fringe. He paced the room, seeming to choose his words carefully.

'"You know it's my responsibility to produce the ninth Lord Burghley at some stage, but my interests have never been oriented towards marriage. Still, I have a duty to my family, to my genealogy."

'"What has this to do with—?"

'"I'm prepared to forward you all the money you require—as a bequest and not as a loan—in exchange for your daughter's hand in marriage."

'I could see Peter's face flush, his jowly cheeks quivering with anger. "You want . . . Rosalind?"

'"She would become Lady Burghley, and her duty would merely be to produce a male heir, after which time any physical contact between us would cease. She would have a life of unlimited luxury, you would have your money, and Christian would be able to visit regularly until his beauty is ravaged by age. It would profit us all nicely, Owling. Think about it."

'"How can you suggest such a travesty?" Peter roared. "My little girl."

'"Owling, she's nearly fifteen. She must be married

soon and, frankly, this is the best offer she'll get. Being Peter Owling's penniless daughter is not an enticing pedigree for prospective suitors. I'm willing to do this as a favour to a friend—"

'"How do you dare? How do you dare to suggest . . .? Rosalind will not marry you while I am alive to prevent it. After what I have done for you, you owe me far greater respect than—"

'Lord Burghley approached him and stood close, talking in a harsh whisper. "Owling, I owe you nothing. You are just as implicated as I in the whole event, and you know that. His blood was on your hands also. Do not dare to blackmail me."

'Peter looked as if he might burst with unexpressed anger. I was quivering in my window seat. He gathered his self-control and straightened his back haughtily. "We are leaving," he declared. "I will not stay here and have my entire family insulted by a wretched fop such as yourself." He stormed out of the study and Burghley ran after him. I could hear him faintly calling to Peter in the hall, and I even heard my name mentioned. Rosalind and I crept cautiously from our hiding place and clutched hands nervously.

'"You don't think he'll hurt Papa, do you?" she asked, pale with fright.

'"No, surely not," I replied, more to comfort her than out of any strong conviction. We stole upstairs to our rooms and waited for what would happen next. Even though I was disappointed about leaving the manor, I was pleased that Peter had been so adamant about defending Rosalind and myself from Lord Burghley's self-profiting plans. When a small knock on my door came I assumed it was Rosalind, so I called for her to come in.

'It wasn't Rosalind, it was Lord Burghley. I cringed involuntarily and cried out a little in fright.

'"What's the matter, Christian?" he said with some

concern, coming over to soothe me. "It's only me. I won't hurt you. Has Owling already been here warning you about what a scoundrel I am?"

'I merely shook my head and let him smooth my hair away from my face. "Christian, I've grown very fond of you, but now Owling is bent on taking you away from me. I want to tell you that if you wish to stay I won't let him do that."

'I stared at him for a while, then realised he was expecting an answer. "I belong with Peter," I said softly. Though the dusty, dark house in Milton Close did not seem very inviting after nearly two months at the manor.

'He nodded kindly. "I understand. But promise me this. If Owling . . . I mean if Peter's *activities*," he paused significantly on this word, "become too disturbing for you, you hop in a conveyance and you come to me. I'll pay the coachman when you get here. You can always run to me."

'I knew this offer had more to do with his immoderate desires than with kindness, so I shook my head firmly. "No. I belong with Peter."

'"Peter's a bad man," he said. "He has a capacity for great evil."

'I was angry beyond words, and my face seemed to twist with rage and tears. "Liar!" I screamed at him.

'He merely put his hands in the air and smiled. "You can always run to me," he repeated and left the room.

'Shortly after, we returned to London.'

'Christian,' Holly said unsteadily, putting a weak hand out. 'I have to stop you there. I'm not feeling—'

'I'll go.'

'Can I see you again soon?' Holly had started to feel dizzy and was concerned that she might faint if she didn't get relief from the nauseous pressure on her body and mind.

'Any time you call me. Goodbye.'

She watched as he dissolved in the mirror. The air in the room felt somehow clearer without him and she stood unsteadily, taking deep breaths. If she could just get home to bed, she knew she'd be fine.

Collecting her bags and her keys, she stumbled along the hallway and out into the keen night air. She made sure the door was locked behind her and began to walk unsteadily up the street, her fingernails pressed into her palms to keep her from fainting. The characters from Christian's story seemed to be crowding into her head. Henry Clement, Lord Burghley, the self-important cad who would murder to protect his title. And Peter Owling, a frightening figure in fop's clothes, exercising some kind of ungodly control over Christian's thoughts and opinions so that the poor boy couldn't see what a monster he really was. She had an overwhelming sick feeling in her stomach, a strange burning sensation behind her eyes. For a few moments she actually thought that Peter was behind her, seemed to sense a dark, evil shape a few paces into the distance. A low-level delirium had temporarily grasped her. She shook her head and blinked slowly.

When she opened her eyes, Holly became aware that the ground was approaching very fast. She only had time to drop her bags and put out her wrist to break her fall before she lapsed into a dead faint.

CHAPTER FIFTEEN

P rudence almost didn't recognise the tiny voice at the other end of the phone when it rang on Sunday afternoon.

'Hello?'

'Prudence, it's me.'

She hesitated for a moment. 'Holly? What's the matter?' Prudence immediately assumed Michael must be dead. It gave her a strange, sick thrill.

'I'm sick. I can't . . . Could you come over?'

'Sick? Oh. And Michael, is he all right?'

'I don't know, I haven't heard. I . . . I haven't eaten since Saturday morning and I've thrown up about eight times and I'm a little feverish. I can hardly . . .' Her voice trailed off into a feeble gasp.

'God, you sound terrible,' Prudence said with real concern. 'I'll be over in a few minutes. Hang tight. Get back into bed and don't move.'

'Okay. Bye.'

Prudence hung up. She grabbed her tote bag from where she'd left it on the entranceway floor and raced into the kitchen to retrieve a couple of tins of soup and a loaf of fresh bread from the pantry. Soup, that was sick people's food. Prudence really had no idea how to look after a sick person, but the prospect of playing Nurse Prudence appealed to her in a strange, almost childish way.

'Never let it be said that I'm not in touch with my inner eight-year-old,' she muttered as she scooped paracetamol tablets, diarrhoea pills and mineral-replacement sachets into her bag from the cupboard above the sink. All she needed was a little suitcase and a hat with a red cross on it. Come to think of it, there was probably a nurse's costume tucked away somewhere on the premises. Her mother couldn't bear to throw anything away, and so boxes and boxes of toys and children's books lined the walls of their garage.

Besides, who needed to throw stuff out when you could just move to the other side of the world to get away from it, Prudence thought bitterly. She grabbed her overcoat and keys and left.

Sunday afternoons always had a peculiar feel for Prudence. The world was very quiet and green, but something felt unfinished, some tiny buzz of anxiety itched in her stomach. It was probably the product of years and years of incomplete homework being written at the last minute before Monday swung around again. Procrastination had always been her curse. Sunday afternoons were when Prudence was most aware that time was ticking inexorably onwards and there were so many things still to do. Her dissertation, for example, was not writing itself. That would top it all off, if her two years ran out and she hadn't even managed to finish, or if she produced a work of such crap that the college failed her. Another two years of her life wasted. And what was she going to do when she finished the degree anyway? What careers were there for girls like her? Would she have to have a conservative makeover, learn to accept surrendering the hours of nine until five, five days a week, to a job? How could she bear that? To relinquish indefinitely Tuesday mornings at eleven o'clock, or Thursday afternoons at three o'clock, when the world was spinning and coffee was brewing and movies were showing to audiences of the leisure class. It nearly made her mad with frustration. There had to be more than wishing away five-sevenths of her waking life and being satisfied with weekends. She felt her lack of any remarkable skill acutely. That's what happened to girls like her—there were a few years of rebellion maybe, but eventually they all lapsed into mediocrity.

Now, why had she gone and made herself so depressed? She was approaching Holly's place and was aware she'd have to cheer up in order to play Nurse Prudence effectively. This was the problem—she felt she had no right to be depressed about her life when everybody else had it so much worse than her. No great tragedies had ever befallen her. She hadn't been through a divorce like Holly, or the death of an alcoholic mother like Justin. Life had gone swimmingly so far for Prudence Emerson.

The door was unlocked and Prudence let herself in. 'Nurse Prudence is here!' she called brightly.

'I'm in my bedroom,' Holly replied in a feeble tone.

Prudence peered into Holly's bedroom. Her friend's face looked pinched and pallid. 'Just wait there,' she said.

'I'm not going anywhere feeling like this,' Holly responded humourlessly.

Prudence went to the kitchen and bustled about, organising soup and toasting bread, getting Holly a glass of water and some paracetamol, all the while feeling moderately ridiculous.

'I feel like a grown-up doing all this,' Prudence told Holly as she brought in a tray with a bowl of pumpkin soup and toast. She nearly tripped over the phone which Holly had dragged in to have next to her bed.

'That's such a strange thing to say,' Holly replied, taking the tray gratefully. 'I've felt like a grown-up since I was seventeen and had to leave home to go to university.'

Prudence perched on the bed next to Holly. 'Can you eat?'

'I think so. I haven't vomited since about one o'clock. What time is it now?'

'It's after three. You should have called earlier.'

'I didn't want to bother you.'

'Yeah, like I've really got a lot to keep me occupied on a Sunday afternoon,' Prudence responded.

Holly dipped her toast in her soup and took a cautious bite. 'Don't you have other friends?'

'I know stacks of people, but not the kind that I'd phone or hang out with, or ... You know, I'm really not good at making friends.'

'I find that very hard to believe.'

'You and Justin and I are thrown together every day of the week, that's why it was easier with you. I always forget to call people, or I develop unfounded prejudices against them. People always end up disappointing me. I had a really close friend in my second year at uni, but when I rang one day and she said she couldn't chat because she was watching the Ashes—'

'The Ashes?'

'You know, the cricket. See, that's what I like about you, you don't even *know* what the Ashes are. I never phoned her again. I mean, choosing sport over me.'

'A cardinal offence.'

'Don't make fun.'

Holly took a few more spoonfuls of soup. 'Well, I hope I never disappoint you.'

'Of course you won't,' Prudence replied, hoping she was right. 'So, do you think the stress made you sick?'

Holly sagged back into her pillow. 'Perhaps.'

'Do you have any news about Michael?'

'I haven't answered the phone since I've been back. I only just brought it in here to call you. I might give Mum a call a little later on. But it was ugly, Prudence. I get the distinct feeling I won't be welcome back in Daybrook for a while.'

'I get the distinct feeling you don't want to go back anyway.'

'Maybe you're right.'

'Maybe? If I were you, I'd never go back.'

'But you're not me. *I'm* me.'

'I guess. I'd never want to go back to where I grew up. Sometimes I can't even bear to think about myself as a child—the stupid things I did. It's like I try to forget about it on purpose, like erasing myself so that there's only ever me in the now to worry about.'

'Prudence? You sound a bit down,' Holly said, placing her spoon in the empty soup bowl.

Prudence took the tray from Holly and smiled too brightly. 'Yeah, but I've got no reason to be, so it's all just middle-class boredom really.' She took the tray to the kitchen and turned the electric kettle on. 'Do you want a cup of tea?' she called.

'No, I—' Suddenly Holly raced out of the bedroom and into the bathroom, where Prudence heard her throwing up.

Prudence went in after her and put a hand on her shoulder as Holly leaned over the toilet.

'I'm sorry,' Holly whispered.

'Don't apologise. Why don't you have a warm shower and put some fresh pyjamas on?'

Holly took a deep breath and nodded. 'Okay,' she said, 'but the bathroom . . . I mean, there's no door.'

'It's fine. I'll sit by your bookcase and drink a cup of tea. Do you want me to get you anything?'

'No, no. Just . . .' She waved Prudence away.

The kettle was whistling, so Prudence made a cup of

tea and waited for Holly to finish in the shower. How strange for her to worry that there was no door on the bathroom. Modesty always intrigued Prudence.

When Holly was tucked back into bed, smelling fresh but still looking very pale, Prudence brought her a mineral drink and sat on the foot of her bed. Holly sipped the drink and turned up her nose in distaste.

'It tastes like orange juice with salt in it.'

'Mmm, my favourite.'

Holly giggled weakly and finished the drink. She settled back among the covers.

'Perhaps you should sleep for a while.'

'It's nice having you here. Tell me about the ghost.'

'The ghost?'

'The one that broke the light bulb.'

How could she have forgotten? 'Of course. Well, I haven't any more evidence since we last spoke. I'm still not convinced it wasn't Justin.'

'No, not Justin. Tell me about the ghost. What kind of ghost would do that?'

If Holly wanted to hear ghost stories, she had come to the right source. 'Well, I don't want to frighten you.' That was a lie.

'Go on, I won't be frightened.'

'It's just that . . . I mean, the light bulb exploded right when I was telling Justin about you going away. Perhaps there's a ghost in the office that has a . . . strange attraction to you, Holly.'

Holly smiled weakly. 'No way.'

'That's the conclusion I would draw.'

'I suppose light bulbs break all the time for no reason.'

'I guess so. But where's the fun in thinking about that? Where's the fun in the laws of physics?'

'But, I mean, if it was a ghost and it was interested in me, could that have made me ill?'

Prudence was completely taken aback by this question. 'Could it—? Why do you ask?'

'Well, last night I was feeling perfectly okay, and I got the cab driver to drop me at the college because I needed to pick up a book. I stayed at the college for . . . a while— maybe half an hour or an hour—and then when I was walking home I started to get sick and I fainted. It was very sudden, you know.' Holly didn't sound as if she were entirely convinced herself.

Prudence shook her head. 'You didn't see a ghost, did you?'

'No, of course not.'

'You would tell me if you did? I mean, you wouldn't keep *that* from me, would you?'

'Of course I'd tell you. I was just wondering.'

Prudence started to think that perhaps Holly was mildly delirious. 'No, I think you're sick from stress. Don't . . . I mean, what happened with Michael would understandably have put you under a lot of pressure. Don't trivialise it by thinking you're sick from something—'

'But can ghosts make people sick?'

'They have been known to. Their perceived presence usually puts a lot of pressure on the senses.'

'Has anybody ever died from it?'

Prudence laughed. 'No. God, Holly, you're really acting strangely. I think you'd better get some sleep.' Nurse Prudence had decided that Holly was in some kind of denial over what had happened with Michael. 'I'll wait in the lounge. Just call if you need me.'

Holly nodded weakly and settled back on her pillow.

There was a long, fevered darkness where Holly was convinced she was mortally sick. Ghostly fingers seemed to reach out to her from the shadows. A voice, which sounded a lot like her mother's, was admonishing her:

'You wanted to be with Christian—well, see how you like being with him permanently.'

The hands were dragging her into the shadows, her edges became blurred. 'It's only fair that it should be you and not Michael,' her mother said. 'He didn't run away and start messing around with books and ghosts.'

Her body felt unbearably heavy, as though it were being pinned down. Dark waves of cold surged through her. Was she dying? She tried to pull herself up but the bony fingers clutched at her more cruelly, pinching her.

'He's not really beautiful, you know,' her mother's voice whispered, very close to her ear, almost inside her head. Every word hissed and sizzled in her skull. 'By now he'd just be bones. A wasted skull grinning back at you. No watercolour-blue eyes, no porcelain skin, no sad lips. All gone, all surrendered to decay.'

A ringing, faint and far away. She felt like a hundred veils separated her from it, but that it was very important that she get to it. Then she could hear another voice, under water. Prudence's voice. She struggled weakly to open her eyes and a strangely out-of-focus world spun into her vision.

'I'm afraid that Holly's very sick,' Prudence was saying.

Holly opened her mouth to say she was awake but only a weak croak came out. Prudence spun around to look at her and her hazel eyes widened with concern. She put out a silver-ringed hand and pressed it gently to Holly's forehead.

'Yes, yes I'll tell her. Don't worry, I'll have her call you as soon as she's able. Yes, yes. Of course I will ... No, I'm sure she'll be fine, it's probably just a stomach bug or something ... Okay, bye.' Prudence put down the phone and sat on the edge of Holly's bed, smoothing the hair from her brow.

'I don't mean to alarm you, Holly, but you look worse.

And your temperature has gone up too. Perhaps we should get you to a doctor?'

'No, I don't want to go to a doctor. I'm fine. It's just stress, like you said. Who was on the phone?'

'Your mother. Sorry, I shouldn't have left the phone in here. I should have let you sleep.'

'Is Michael all right?'

'He's in Townsville and he's seeing a psychiatrist tomorrow morning. Don't worry about Michael. I'm going to get you a drink of water. Justin's here, do you want him to come say hello?'

'Justin?'

'He came by earlier to see if you were home yet.'

Although she was delirious, Holly was still healthy enough to be worried about her appearance. 'I'd probably rather not. But tell him thanks for coming.'

Prudence nodded and left. She could hear them talking in low voices in the lounge room. She didn't want to go to the doctor. Christian was making her sick; not stress, not a stomach bug, but a ghost. The illness would pass soon enough. And when it did, she knew without doubt she'd be back up at the college at night, calling for him. Whatever the cost.

'She's sleeping again,' Prudence said, emerging from Holly's room early that evening. Night had started to fall and Prudence switched on the light, flushing out the shadows hiding in corners. Justin was sitting in the only armchair, so Prudence flopped down on the floor with a cushion under her chest.

Justin looked up. 'I suppose I should go.'

'You don't want to go.'

He studied her for a second. 'And how do you know that?'

'Your voice, your choice of words. You "suppose"

you "should" go. Stay here with me. I'll probably hang here until later tonight, keep an eye on her.' Prudence realised she felt a slight thrill at the thought of sitting here all night with Justin in the quiet room. Was it the prospect of seeing if she could get him to talk, or was it something else? She hoped it wasn't something else. Her love-life was already unbearably complicated, her sexual history unbearably crowded.

He shrugged. 'I'll stay for a while.'

'Why don't you want to go home?'

'Don't you know? Didn't my voice and my choice of words tell you?'

She laughed, refusing to be intimidated by his humour-lessness. 'I'm perceptive but not psychic. Though I wish I were.'

Justin settled back into his chair. 'I'd hate to be psychic. I'd find out for sure how much everybody dislikes me.'

'Nobody dislikes you.'

'But people don't think the way they talk, Prudence. People don't think politely. Even if my friends . . . Even if you and Holly thought about just *one* of my faults, if I knew that, I would obsess about it, convince myself you hate me for it.'

Prudence considered. 'Never thought of it that way. I suppose you're right. But maybe after a while you'd get used to it, and you'd start to like it that people could still be fond of you despite your faults.'

'The transition period would be soul destroying.'

'I don't think you have any faults, for what it's worth.'

He shook his head. 'Now you're lying. Are you trying to tell me you've never thought, He's so rude, so uncom-municative, so terse?'

'I find those qualities intriguing. It makes you like a puzzle.'

'But you've thought those things?'

'Yes, I have. Look, nobody can blame you for

being . . . I mean, I understand why you're not the happiest being on the planet when it's only a few months since your mother . . .' She trailed off, realising she should never have started the sentence.

'Prudence, admit you don't really know what's wrong with me. There's stuff, dark stuff buried in me.'

'Are you trying to turn me on?' she giggled.

He smiled in spite of himself. 'No.'

'So why don't you want to go home?'

He sighed and leaned forward, resting his elbows on his knees, his chin cupped in his palms. 'Lucien and Emma.'

'What have they done?'

'Nothing. I'm just not comfortable with either of them.'

'Not even Emma?'

He pressed his lips together. 'No, not even Emma. I'm . . . unused to the kind of . . . I mean, I guess I don't know how to behave in a family.'

'You'll get used to it. If I got a chance to live in that house—shit, I could put up with anything.'

'Really? When they lock you out of all the rooms while they're away, and watch you like a hawk when they're home? Anyway, let's not talk about me.'

Prudence shifted into a sitting position, pulling the pillow into her lap and hugging it against herself. 'How about we organise a celebratory dinner for Holly's homecoming?'

'Okay, sure. When?'

'As soon as she's better. Tomorrow night?'

'Not tomorrow. I've promised to stay home and help Emma with something.'

Prudence paused. The way he looked away when he spoke made her curious. 'One of her charity things?' she said finally.

'Yeah, whatever. Holly won't be well enough for a dinner party by then anyway.'

'Which charity?'

'I don't know, I didn't ask.'

'She asked me to help her stuff envelopes one time, but I made up some excuse,' Prudence said.

'Yeah, that's what we're doing, stuffing envelopes.'

Prudence knew he was lying. The idea of Lucien or Emma being involved in any kind of charity work was ludicrous. Obviously Prudence knew them better than Justin did. So what was going on then? What dark stuff was buried in him?

God, she loved a mystery.

CHAPTER SIXTEEN

Lucien put aside the first Monday of every month as his day to visit the college. Apart from the Sunday black masses, he stayed away from Humberstone as much as he could. He had no taste for Victorian culture himself and could only see the students, even the fee-paying ones, as leeches sucking the blood out of Magnus's estate. If he could, he'd close the college, knock the building down and build an apartment block. Far more lucrative. No need to spend money on books and repairs and to give away thousands of dollars in scholarships for students to write pointless papers about dead people.

But he was strictly forbidden from doing so by Magnus's will. Magnus knew his sons well enough. Many stipulations had been made in his will to circumvent his heirs' more practical economic outlook. Inheriting Magnus's estate also meant inheriting the administration of the college and committing to run it well. Which Lucien did, albeit reluctantly.

He called out a forced hello to Allison, the receptionist, and began to ascend the stairs. Pausing on the second floor, he decided the professional thing to do would be look in on some of the students, especially his nephew. He hadn't even met the new girl, Holly Beck, who was claiming thousands of dollars a year from him in scholarship money. And perhaps he could get an idea of just how serious Justin was about staying at the college. After all, he did need him around for a while yet.

Lucien walked purposefully along the corridor, stopping at each office door to call a greeting to the students. The ones in the first room didn't even know who he was, he could tell by their blank faces, but they smiled and nodded to him nonetheless. A lone female in the next office looked up in shock when he greeted her, gathered her books about her and offered a respectful, 'Good morning, Mr Humberstone.' The next office was Justin's and the door was closed. He knocked lightly and opened it, to find Justin sitting with Prudence Emerson on the window sill, chatting.

'Lucien,' Justin said in surprise.

'Good morning, Justin. Good morning, Prudence.' He didn't like the girl at all. She showed no respect, and he was fairly certain that Aswell was knocking her off on the side. He spoke about her too much and too often, and the passionate way he had defended her place at the college, even when she hadn't met the academic requirements for the previous year, spoke volumes. He suspected Prudence was learning something at Humberstone College that wasn't literature. It was about how to service a weak-livered dolt suffering a midlife crisis.

'Hi, Lucien,' she said. 'To what do we owe this pleasure?'

There it was, that light, mocking tone. Didn't she realise that he could cancel her enrolment and send her packing back to her daddy with one signature? 'I wanted a chance to meet Holly, congratulate her on her scholarship.' Find out if she too sat on window sills gossiping. If so, he would have a closer look at her funding.

228

'She's sick. At death's door, really. She's come down with some stomach bug, but I told As—Dr Aswell,' Prudence replied.

'Fine.' He nodded. Justin looked at him with that same tongue-tied, dull-witted expression he always wore. 'Fine,' he repeated and offered a perfunctory smile. 'Goodbye.' He closed the door behind him and heard Prudence giggling. Perhaps he needed to have a word to Aswell about her. God only knew what the man saw in her anyway. She looked like a sideshow attraction.

He continued along the hallway and up the stairs, where he bumped into Aswell arriving at his office. Aswell held an airmail envelope in his hand but was too busy looking in his pockets for his keys to see Lucien standing beside him.

'Lost your keys again?' Lucien asked.

Aswell jumped and turned. 'Lucien? No, no, I—'

Lucien plucked the envelope out of his hand and peered at the return address. It was a letter from Randolph, as yet unopened. 'When did this arrive?'

'I just picked it up from my post-office box this morning.'

'But I suppose you weren't going to show it to me until next Sunday night?'

Angry defiance crossed Aswell's face, more the teenage-boy variety than the real challenge of an adult male. He opened his office door and ushered Lucien in ahead of him. When he'd closed the door he turned back to Lucien. 'That's how we usually do things. What's the problem?'

'Do you mind if I take it now?'

'But I haven't had a chance to read it yet.'

'I'll bring it back as soon as I'm finished.'

'I suppose you'll do whatever you want anyway,' Aswell muttered darkly.

'Don't be precious, Laurence. There's another matter we need to discuss.'

'And that would be?'

Lucien pointed to Aswell's chair, indicating for him to sit down. Lucien remained standing, back erect and hands folded.

'It's about Prudence Emerson,' Lucien began.

'What about Prudence?'

'Are you having sex with the girl?'

Aswell's face flushed deep red. 'What kind of a question is—?'

'Come on, Laurence. I've suspected for quite a while, and I'm sure Mandy suspects too if she has any brains. This is a warning—men do not think straight when their pants are off. Too much is at stake for you to accidentally let slip—'

'I can't believe I'm hearing this,' Aswell shouted. Then, checking his temper, he continued. 'This is insulting. I'm not sleeping with Prudence and I'm not divulging secrets to anybody. I certainly hope that Randolph gets back soon, because you're getting out of control. You may sign my pay cheques, but when we invoke that circle we do so as equals. You do not have the right to dictate to me where I put my dick.'

'Which is as much an admission that you—'

'Lucien, just stop. If this isn't about college matters, perhaps you should leave. I have some papers to mark.'

Lucien compressed his anger and tucked it away neatly. 'I'll bring this letter back when I'm done.'

'Just slide it under the door.'

'As you wish.' He left, his fingers itching to open the envelope and read Randolph's letter in the privacy of his office.

A misty rain was beginning to fall outside as Lucien locked his office door behind him. He didn't turn on his lamp, even though dark grey clouds smothered the sunlight. The room still smelled faintly of candle wax from the previous night's ritual, but that was the only sign that anything other than administrative duties had been performed in this room. Dropping his briefcase next to him, he settled behind his desk.

Lucien slit open the envelope and tipped out the contents. A postcard-size plastic square dropped onto his desk. He picked it up and examined it. It was a hologram of Mary and baby Jesus. Tilting it one way, Mary looked lovingly into her baby's face. Tilting it the other, both Mary and Jesus turned their faces to look at Lucien. It used the most vivid shades of blue and yellow, and the whole square was framed with gold embossing. He tilted it back and forth a few times, then turned to the letter.

Dear Laurence,
Do you like it? I can't believe the kitsch stuff you can buy in the Christian quarter. I've bought a large, glow-in-the-dark crucifix which I'll bring back with me. Jesus looks like he's on the point of an orgasm, and he has 'Made in Taiwan' stamped on his feet.

A tourist letter? Was this all it was? Lucien skimmed over the first page and a half as Randolph blathered on about day-glo rosary beads and faux-velvet prints of the crucifixion. Finally he came to the interesting part.

I'm in such a jolly mood because I feel we're very close now to finding the dark fragment. As I write, I'm sitting on the stone stairs across an alley from the residence of an antique dealer named Lily Kirkwood. She hasn't stepped out for a few days, but she'll have to go out eventually and I'm very patient.
The very first antique store I walked into led me to Lily. In fact, getting to the antique store in the first place proved about the hardest task in this whole new development. It's very easy to get lost in the Old City. At first I was hesitant about taking some of the narrower alleyways, which look more like gullies in places, afraid that I'd disappear forever down

one of them. Added to that was the number of wrong turns I took and the fact that my map is a cheap, nasty version, clearly drawn by somebody who has never actually been here. But I did eventually get to Wilson's Antiques in a cramped street behind the Muristan markets.

I thought that an antique shop in the Christian quarter might be peddling pieces of the true cross, but the stock in this place was rather lacklustre—mostly teacups and badly repaired upholstered chairs. The portly, bearded man behind the counter was friendly enough though.

'Good morning, sir. Are you looking for anything in particular?' he asked.

'Yes, actually,' I said, approaching the counter. 'I'm looking for part of an old book that I believe has been circulating here in the Old City. Some people refer to it as the dark fragment.'

'That thing? Lily Kirkwood handled that. I didn't want it.'

'Why's that?' I asked warily.

'Because it's worthless. A section torn from an old book— probably only late Victorian, like anything you can find in a library, and completely illegible. Looks like it's written in some secret language. But Lily seemed to think differently. When the old man came in to sell it I referred him to Lily straightaway. She deals in odd curios and bric-a-brac. I don't know how much she paid for it, but I had the distinct feeling the fellow wanted it off his hands. His father had found it under the floorboards of his house when he pulled them up to renovate and he blamed it for bringing him bad luck all his life. This fellow had dug it out when his father died—superstitiously, they'd had it buried in a box full of salt—and brought it in to see if it was worth anything. People get the strangest ideas in their heads, no?'

'And how long ago did all this happen?'

He pursed his lips as he considered. 'Hmmm . . . let me see . . . perhaps eighteen months ago.'

'Do you know if Lily found a buyer for it?'

'I don't know,' he said, shrugging. 'But I doubt it. Many people come to this part of the world because it's holy. The rumour is that the dark fragment is . . . well, unholy.'

'Unholy?'

'One only buries books in salt if they have something to do with the devil,' he responded cheerfully, 'or so I am told. Me, I'm not superstitious. Just a dirty old book with some mad Englishman's secret code in it. Probably outlines his sexual conquests.' He laughed loudly and I joined him, nearly hysterical with excitement—it seemed so close.

'Could you tell me where Lily lives?'

You would be proud of me, Laurence. I've had business cards made up with a false name and an address in Tel Aviv, to cover my tracks if anything should happen. I gave the antique dealer two, one on which to write Lily's address and draw a rough map of how to get there, and one for him to keep.

'Do you think she'd be home if I dropped by now?' I asked.

'Oh, yes, certainly Mr . . .' He peered at my card to read the name on it. 'Mr Clark. She rarely leaves home. A bit of a funny old thing, she is. Probably goes out once a month to get groceries and do a little business, but she usually shuts herself up in that house.'

'Thank you very much,' I said extending my hand.

He shook it firmly. 'Let me know how you get on.'

I took the hastily scribbled map he had drawn me and endeavoured to find Lily Kirkwood's house. It took me about ten minutes and a few wrong turns. Down gullylike streets and under bridges, past the cavernous food markets at the bottom of David Street and nearly into the Muslim quarter. She lived in an apartment which was part of a maze of stone buildings, stairwells and balcony rails popping out at unexpected places. I ascended the stairs and hesitated at her front door, hoping I had the right place.

I had to knock twice before she came. She looked nothing like I'd expected—the antique shop owner had made me think she would be a freakish octogenarian with chin hairs and hooded eyes. Instead I was greeted by a woman in her mid-fifties. Her hair was chestnut brown, streaked with grey, and piled on top of her head in an elaborate style. She wore a dark grey suit and a slash of red lipstick.

I had a business card at the ready. 'Ms Kirkwood? I'm Barry Clark. I believe you may have information on an antique book I'm looking for.'

She took my card and read it with an uninterested sniff before pocketing it.

'I don't normally deal in books.' She had an American accent.

'I think you'd remember this one. Some call it the dark fragment—an elderly gentleman sold it to you about eighteen months ago.'

Lily Kirkwood pulled her red lips into a thin line. 'Perhaps you'd better come inside, Mr Clark,' she said.

Her apartment was decorated eclectically with what looked like junk dating back centuries. A narrow window provided a view of the neighbouring building and little else. A potted palm, leaves curling brown and sad on the tips, sagged in a corner. It was dusty and dark, the smell of stone, mould and cat faint in the air. A grizzled moggy that looked as old as Lily peered at me warily from the couch, while another two cats slept curled together on a stack of old magazines.

She indicated for me to sit in a mismatched chair by a table that was covered in old books and newspapers. Her lips still pressed into a tight line, she sat across from me.

'I will start by saying up front that the dark fragment is not for sale,' she declared unequivocally.

I could barely control my excitement. She had it. Somewhere here, perhaps even under this pile of books in front of me, was what we have spent so long looking for.

At this point Lucien had to take a deep shuddering breath. His eyes refused for a moment to focus on the page, and his heart thudded rapidly. Forcing himself to be calm, he continued reading.

My experience with the old man at the bookshop had proved to me that not everybody can be bought. Still, I proceeded with my usual line of persuasion. 'I can make you a very wealthy woman.' I indicated around me. 'You're practically living in poverty. If you consent to sell the fragment to me, it could change your way of life permanently.'

She shook her head resolutely. 'Mr Clark, that book is worth more to me than any money you could ever offer me.'

I hadn't expected this. I began to suspect that perhaps she was studying the grimoire too, probably for the same reason that we do. If so, it was going to be impossible to get her to part with it.

'You do know that it is just a part of a larger whole?' I asked her, hoping to draw her out about its contents or its whereabouts.

'And I suppose you have other parts of that whole? Is that why you're interested?'

I nodded. 'I'm a scholar—Victorian literature.'

'I've managed to decode enough of the fragment to know I'm missing some. But I'm unconcerned at this stage because I also know that what I have is the last and by far the most important part of a powerful grimoire. Do you know what a grimoire is, Mr Clark?'

I shook my head in mock ignorance, willing her to tell me too much.

She stood and walked to a crowded kitchen bench, searched among dirty coffee cups for an ashtray and lit a cigarette. 'Though I'm sure a gentleman such as yourself is interested in the document for scholastic reasons, that book is not just a curiosity or a literary work to be surveyed coolly at the distance of a century. It is a working document of black magic.'

Clearly she meant to shock me, even scare me. I feigned surprise. 'Surely you don't believe in black magic,' I said.

She laughed, full of her own self-importance and enjoying what she thought was my fear of her. 'Perhaps I should explain. I'm a witch, Mr Clark. I've been studying necromancy for thirty-two years. I'm not one of these pagan peace-lovers, either,' she continued, spitting out her consonants with disdain, 'but the real thing. Black magic, voodoo, hexes, prophecy. I moved here five years ago on a presentiment that I would find the catalyst which would make me the master of black magic I know I am destined to be.'

Her transparent egotism was starting to annoy me, the way she spoke her words with heavy, dramatic emphasis. 'And you think the fragment is that catalyst?'

'I know it is, and as soon as I've cracked the code completely, the secrets within it will be mine.'

'What kind of secrets?'

'If I told you, they wouldn't be secrets any more. Do you understand now why I can't sell it?'

I nodded humbly. 'Of course. If you change your mind . . .'

'I won't change my mind,' she said.

I paused a moment before venturing, 'Could I see it?'

'Under absolutely no circumstances. It must only touch my hands, be viewed by my eyes.' And as she said this, she inadvertently turned her eyes to a room leading off the main living area, and I knew at once where she kept it.

'But why are you so certain it's the last part? Have you translated enough to know that for sure? There could be more, it might not be enough.'

'It's certainly the last part, Mr Clark, but I only know that for a very mundane reason. It has a back cover.'

'And you're not interested in the first part?'

'I have no need for it at this stage. If I find I do want it, I'll be sure to contact you and make an offer,' she replied condescendingly.

I resisted the urge to bind and gag the woman then and there and decided that breaking and entering was probably the lesser of two evils. I bade her goodbye and left.

My current hiding place has a view of her front door and is sheltered from the rain. The fellow in the antique shop was right—this woman never leaves her home. I've been waiting here every day, from dawn until dusk, for four days and, to make it worse, I've been plagued with awful headaches. Perhaps she's flying out the chimney for a witches' sabbat and I don't know about it. In any case, she'll have to go out eventually, and when she does I'm finally going to get my hands on the fragment. Perhaps even by the time you are reading this letter. Wish me luck.

Randolph

Lucien laid the letter on his desk, long pale hands shaking. Nearly there, nearly at the culmination of a thirty-year search for the parts of the grimoire, a search from which he was about to reap the rewards. He pressed his palms onto the desk, trying to get his nerves under control. *It has a back cover.* The last piece. He bent to his briefcase, unlocked it and pulled out the first three-quarters of the grimoire. A half-forgotten psalm from Sunday school came to mind, profane with diabolic irony. 'Though I walk through the valley of the shadow of death, I will fear no harm,' he ran his fingertips over the faded ink, 'for *thou* art with me.'

'Hey, As, what's this?' Prudence was buttoning up her top when she noticed the airmail envelope on the floor by the door.

'What's what?' He was busy dressing himself and smoothing his hair.

'This letter.' She picked it up. 'Someone must have slid

it under the door while we were—Hey, it's from Randolph.'

The letter was whipped out of her fingers in an instant. 'Don't read other people's mail, Prudence.'

It was too late—she'd seen the date, the stamp, the postmark. 'He's in Jerusalem,' she said, remembering As's earlier edginess about telling her where Randolph was.

'It's a stopover. He has friends there. He's bound to be back any day.' All said with a mock-casual air as As slid the letter into a drawer. 'Why are you so interested?'

She shrugged. 'I'm interested in anything. My life is pretty dull. Why are you so cagey?'

'I'm not. Prudence, I hope this isn't more of your misplaced paranoia.'

'Ouch,' she said, deadpan.

He gazed at her for a moment, then said with a sigh, 'Prudence, sit down.'

'I don't like this. I don't like any sentence that starts with "Prudence, sit down".' She laughed weakly, her heart suddenly thudding hard. Was he going to break it off? Had her 'paranoia' got too much for him? Damn it, she really had to learn when to keep her mouth shut.

He pulled out a seat for her and perched on the desk in front of her. She sat warily.

'Prudence, Lucien was in here this morning. He showed some . . . some concern about our relationship.'

'What? How does he know?'

'He doesn't know for sure. He just suspects. This is very bad for both of us. For you because you are so behind in your work, and for me because . . . well, because I have a family. Perhaps we should cool off for a while.'

Prudence tried to get angry, anything to stop herself from crying. 'I . . .' she started weakly, but couldn't finish.

'You know it makes more sense this way.'

'Is it because I asked too many questions about Randolph's letter?' she blurted out. 'Because I know I can be a pain, I know. I can stop, I can be more . . .' She trailed off, knowing that she would have to finish the sentence with a word she hated. Like meek, or pliable, or passive.

'No, it's not that. The discussion I had with Lucien has unsettled me, that's all. And I don't mean forever, I just mean for a short while.'

'But if you had the conversation with Lucien this morning, how come you fucked me before you broke it off?' Good, here came her temper—much more use to her. 'Wanted one last bite of the cherry?'

'Of course not, Prudence.'

'Bullshit. That's exactly what it was. You treat me like I'm not even a person, like I'm a wind-up toy or something.'

'Prudence, no. Really, I swear.' He put his hand over his heart. 'I swear,' he repeated softly.

She gathered up her bag and her books. 'Are you still going to be my supervisor?'

'Perhaps it would be best if I arranged for Jane to take over.'

'Or Randolph when he comes back?' she suggested, her heart heavy but unable to resist tweaking him for more information.

'We'll see. Come see me at the same time next week and I'll let you know what I've been able to arrange.'

'Gee, thanks,' she said, her voice heavy with irony.

'Goodbye, Prudence. I am sorry.'

'Yeah. Whatever.'

She closed the door behind her and stepped, empty, into the stairwell. Home was empty too. Perhaps she could go look in on Holly.

So this was it. She trudged up the hill towards Holly's place, going over the exchange with As in her head. It had to end eventually, she knew that. Only in her more deluded moments did she really believe he would leave his wife and take up with her officially. It was still unexpected though.

But why did he blame it on the conversation with Lucien? It was clear that he hadn't been thinking about that when she first arrived. He had handed back the first chapter of her dissertation, written all over in blue ink, then grabbed her and taken her almost violently on the desk. No hesitation, no uncertainty. It seemed to Prudence that it had been her finding the letter from Randolph that had set him off, made him uneasy. What was that about? Why lie to her about where Randolph was? What did it matter to anybody in the world whether he was in York or not?

But if it didn't matter, he wouldn't have been so anxious. It *did* matter. Randolph being in Jerusalem was supposed to be a secret.

How delicious—a secret.

She had arrived at Holly's. The gate squeaked as she pushed it open, and a sudden breeze made a tree shake the morning's raindrops out of its branches all over her. She brushed her hair back off her face and went to knock on Holly's door.

'It's me, it's Prudence,' she called as she knocked.

'Just come in,' Holly replied weakly from within.

Prudence pushed the door open and went straight through to Holly's bedroom. She still looked pale with dark rings under her eyes.

'Holly, you're not looking any better.'

'But I'm feeling a little better. I haven't thrown up today.' She reached a hand out for the wooden frame on her bed. 'Touch wood.'

'Have you eaten?'

'I had some toast this morning, but I've been sleeping most of the day.'

Prudence considered for a moment. Holly needed

somebody to look after her, and Prudence was lonely and heartbroken. A match made in hell. 'Why don't you come stay at my place for a few days? This place smells funny when it rains, and I can cook for you and help you get better.'

'I don't want to be a burden.'

'Really, Holly, I could use the company. I'm feeling a bit low today. We can catch a cab down.'

'Well, if you're sure. I mean, it is a bit depressing here by myself.'

'You'll be better in no time with me looking after you,' Prudence said. 'Trust me.'

Holly pushed back the covers and slowly sat up. 'Help me get my things together, then,' she said.

Prudence got her to her feet. Company, that's all she needed. Not to feel so alone. She would get over As soon enough. She just needed to stay busy, keep her mind occupied. Her dissertation could keep her employed.

Not to mention getting to the bottom of As's secret.

Justin took stock of his feelings. What was that twisting, churning sickness in his gut? Embarrassment, anxiety, regret. All of those things. But not desire, not excitement, not the thrill of anticipation. This was going to be impossible.

He heard Lucien upstairs, footsteps from the bathroom to his dressing room. A half-hour or so and he would be gone, leaving Emma, Justin and his hasty promise in the house alone.

He didn't want to do this.

Lying back on his bed, hands behind his head, he considered his options. Renege. But she wouldn't stop pursuing him. Move out. Sure, and use bottletops for money. Okay then, get a job and kiss his place at the college goodbye. And lose with it the only two friends he had ever managed to make, including a young woman he had more than a passing attraction to. But how could Holly, or even Prudence, like him if they knew what he was about to do with his aunt?

Was he really going to do it? Lucien's footsteps were on the stairs, he was calling out to Emma, 'Have you moved my watch? It was here by the phone.'

Emma's voice faint above. Justin couldn't make out what she said. She was lying upstairs in her bed, feigning illness.

Not like Holly, who really was sick. That's who he should be spending his evening with—warm, intelligent, pretty Holly. Probably in need of some company. He could sneak out before Emma even realised he was gone. And then avoid her for a while longer, put off the final showdown for as long as possible. He got up and opened the door a crack. Lucien was slamming the front door behind him, Emma was nowhere in sight. He crept out to the kitchen and picked up the phone, dialled Holly's number. Lucien's car started in the garage, pulled into the street.

'Justin!' Emma called from upstairs. The phone was ringing at Holly's place. It rang twice, three times. He hoped she wasn't sleeping. He had to see her, he had to get away from Emma.

'Justin! Come here, Justin, Lucien's gone.'

Five times, six times. *Answer the phone, answer the phone.*

Soft footsteps on the stairs. 'Justin, where are you?'

Eight, nine, ten times. She wasn't home. Damn it, she wasn't home.

'Justin, who are you calling?' Emma's arms were around him, her soft breasts pressed into his back. He felt his knees go weak.

'No-one,' he said, hanging up the phone and turning to face her. She was dressed in some flimsy, lacy item in deep red. Her smooth, pale flesh spilled out in voluptuous curves. He reached out and touched her shoulder, warm and soft under his fingers. She was beautiful, yes, but she was his aunt.

'Emma—'

She kissed his neck. 'Come upstairs.'

He nodded. 'You go up. I'll follow in a moment.'

She turned her face up for a kiss and he pressed his lips against hers gently. Smiling, she backed away. 'Don't be too long.'

He watched her go, waited a few moments until he was sure she would be in bed. His lips tasted faintly of cherry from where she had kissed him. He wavered. Perhaps it wouldn't be so bad. It had been such a long time, after all.

But with his aunt?

'Sorry, Emma,' he whispered under his breath.

He went out the front door, slammed it behind him and ran down to the main road to catch a tram.

CHAPTER SEVENTEEN

~

Friday morning was the first time Holly had been
in her office since her meeting with Christian.
Sunlit and populated, it seemed very different. Prudence
was working on a laptop computer on her window sill,
soaking up some morning sunshine. Justin had his nose
in a book.

'Good morning,' she said, coming in and dropping her
bag on her desk.

Justin looked up. 'Hi, Holly. Feeling better?' No smile,
but she was used to that.

'A lot better.'

'I tried to convince her to have a couple more days off,
but she's a terrible patient,' Prudence said. 'Ornery and
far too independent.'

'I had to get home eventually,' Holly remarked, picking
up a sealed envelope on her desk. In fact, while staying at
Prudence's had been great for her physical health, her
mental health had deteriorated moment by moment as Prudence's chatter had grown progressively more manic. As
dingy as her own place was, at least there was endless peace
to enjoy. She picked open the envelope.

'What's this?' she said, pulling out a handmade card decorated with a purple-glittered wine bottle.

'Read it,' Prudence urged.

Justin held up a similar card. 'It's an invitation.'

'Don't spoil it,' Prudence said to him.

Holly opened the card and read it. It was written in purple pen and decorated with stick-on love hearts. 'Prudence Emerson cordially requests the company of Holly Beck and Justin Penney for a grand piss-up at her place on Sunday night, followed by a trip to the Confessional.'

'Do you like it?' Prudence asked, now standing by Holly's shoulder. 'I went all eight-year-old—glitter and love hearts.'

'It's very pretty. But what's the Confessional?'

'You know, our room under the college. Where we confess our darkest secrets to each other.'

'Oh, of course.' Holly stood the card up on her desk. A whole weekend at home would have been nice—lots of long quiet hours to read, to write, to think about Christian.

'So, my place at six and we'll order pizza,' Prudence said, moving back to her seat.

'Sure, I'll be there.' Holly sat down and picked up a book, checking her watch. Only eight or nine hours and she would be able to call him. Her back tingled and her hands shook lightly. Soon, Christian, soon.

Holly stood by the window and watched the janitor's ute pull away from the front of the college. A strong wind had picked up that afternoon and the two trees that flanked the entrance to Humberstone shook their leaves furiously. She could hear the violent rustling even through the closed window.

She turned her back to the window and closed her eyes.

'Christian.'

The warm rushing of air and the feel of his hands on her ribcage. But something was wrong—his touch brought instant nausea, violent and overwhelming.

'Stop!' she shouted, opening her eyes. His hands were gone. She doubled over, her stomach cramping. 'Oh, God.'

'Holly?' a faint voice seeping out of the darkness around her.

'I've been sick. Perhaps I'm still not better.'

'I won't stay, then. I don't want to make you ill.'

Every word was a sharp jab to her brain. Involuntarily she put her hands over her ears. 'No, don't go. God, I've missed you. I want to be with you so much.'

'I don't want to hurt you, Holly. Goodbye.'

Then his presence was quite clearly gone. The air settled around her and the nausea ebbed slowly. 'No, Christian. Come back. Please, I don't care if I'm sick,' she whispered huskily in the gloom. 'Please come back.'

The darkness remained whole. He did not return.

This time they brought blankets. Walking through Fawkner Park, Prudence balanced her folded quilt on her head, arms out to steady herself. Justin was teasing her, trying to perch other items on her head—keys, the wine bottle, his own blanket. She squealed and giggled, pushing him away. Holly realised she was far more sober than either of them. Having been ill for so long, she had been wary of drinking too much. Prudence had more than made up for her, and she suspected that Justin had matched Prudence's excesses. He had come to her place early in the afternoon, asking if she minded him hanging out there for a while. Apparently some kind of uncomfortable situation had arisen around Lucien and Emma and he wanted to stay away from them as much as possible.

They had picked up a pizza on the way to Prudence's and had an early dinner. Justin was the first into the alcohol, urged on by an increasingly reckless Prudence. Still, Holly was glad she had come out after all. Sometimes she had to be reminded to have fun. Being responsible and hard-working wasn't everything. And thinking about Christian wasn't the only pastime available to her.

Prudence couldn't keep the blanket on her head as they walked up the hill to the college so she tucked it under one arm and took Holly's arm with the other. 'Having fun, sick girl?' she asked, a little too loudly but still good-naturedly.

'Of course I am.'

'Ooh, the fun's just starting. What's the time?'

Holly checked her watch, tilting it back and forth until the streetlight shone directly on its face. 'Just after seven-thirty.'

'The night is young.' They were approaching the college. 'Justin, are you sure you have the wine?' Prudence asked him for about the fourth time.

He held up the bottle. 'Yes, captain.'

'Holly, you're going to have to drink some more. You're too sober and you're making us feel stupid. Isn't she, Justin?'

'Yes, captain.'

Prudence handed her blanket to Holly as they stopped at the front entrance. Her hair was freshly tinted purple and she practically glowed under the security light. She plunged her hand into the bottom of her bag and felt around for the keys, found them and produced them with a flourish. 'Welcome, friends, to the Confessional.'

Twenty minutes later they were settled on their blankets. Justin lay on his side, almost dozing. Prudence was setting the last candle into the last corner and Holly was attempting to get into the spirit of things by swigging some wine straight from the bottle. The air was damp and earthy and the flickering candlelight occasionally illuminated dark shiny beetles scurrying into corners.

'So how do you do that, Prudence?' she asked as Prudence sat down across from her. 'How do you get your hair that colour?'

'I have to bleach it first, and then I put the purple in. Only it's not called purple, it's called Shrieking Violet. Fitting, yes?'

'Yes.'

'Never messed with your hair colour?'

Holly shook her head.

'That's an open challenge to me,' Prudence said, picking up a strand of Holly's wheat-blonde hair. 'You'd look great as a redhead—fire-engine red. Or how about black?'

'I'm quite happy with it this colour.'

'You never get bored with it?'

'No. The idea of getting bored with my appearance is kind of ludicrous. I get bored with activities, not with hair colour.'

Prudence suddenly squealed. 'Oh no, look, we've sent Justin to sleep talking about girl things. Justin, wake up!'

Justin opened his eyes. 'I'm awake. I'm just listening.'

'It's time to confess,' Prudence said, lighting a cigarette. As always she offered her packet around, and as always Holly and Justin refused.

'I don't know if I'm up to confessing,' Holly admitted. 'Can't I opt out?'

'You know you can't. Here, get some more wine into you. That'll help.' Prudence handed her the bottle, then settled back on her blanket. 'I have the biggest confession to make—it's really, really big.'

'Go on then,' Justin urged.

'Only on one condition. See, it's a sexy confession. So everybody else has to divulge something about their sex lives afterwards.'

'This sounds like a scam to me,' said Holly.

'No, it's not. When you've heard what I have to say . . .'

'Okay,' said Justin. 'Go ahead.'

Prudence took a deep breath. Holly had to admit that she was curious. Prudence's obsession with secrets was usually focussed on other people's, not her own. In fact, Holly was surprised she even had one. She didn't seem capable of repressing anything.

'For the past year,' she said slowly, 'I have been having an affair with As.'

There were a few seconds of stunned silence, then Holly whispered, 'Oh, my God.'

'Wow,' said Justin. 'He's married, isn't he?'

'Yes. We only ever did it in his office—'

'In his office? During the daytime? When we were just downstairs?' Holly asked, incredulous. She had not suspected this for an instant. The idea of Prudence and Dr Aswell together was unimaginable. How was she supposed to look her supervisor in the eye again? Every shred of respect for him had dissolved into nothing.

'Don't sound so shocked.'

'Prudence, that is a massive abuse of trust. He's your *teacher*. He should know better.'

'Well, it's all over. He broke it off on Monday.' Prudence was looking into her lap.

'He should never have started it in the first place. Prudence, are you okay?'

Prudence looked up and burst into tears. 'No, I'm not okay. I love him.' Her face crumpled and gave way to heaving sobs. Out of the corner of her eye Holly could see Justin flinch and draw his knees up to his chest. Holly went to Prudence and put her arms around her.

'There, it's all right,' she said, stroking Prudence's violet hair. 'You're better off out of that kind of relationship. You'll be feeling better soon.'

Prudence clung to her and sobbed like a child. 'I don't want to feel better. I want to feel like this forever. I always want to love him.'

Justin had moved closer and tentatively touched Prudence's forearm. 'I'm sorry that you're upset,' he said stiffly.

Prudence turned her face to him, eyes shiny and black make-up smudged. 'Thank you,' she said softly.

As Holly let her go she wiped her eyes and sniffed loudly. 'Well, there's my secret,' she said.

'It was a doozy,' Holly said, handing her the wine bottle. 'Here, drown those sorrows.'

'Thanks. Thanks, both of you. Now it's your turn.'

'Perhaps it's not the best time for all this if you're feeling down,' Holly suggested as Justin resettled on his blanket. He lay on his back with his arms crossed under his head.

'Are you kidding? It'll cheer me up no end to hear about other people's abortive love-lives. Come on, Holly. You intimated once before that you weren't a virgin bride—what happened there?'

'Do you ever forget anything?' Holly asked.

'Rarely. Come on, what happened?'

Ordinarily Holly would have refused to talk about this, but she didn't want to upset Prudence further. Besides, her own sexual history was pretty tame in comparison to her friend's. And, she had to admit, she was dying to find out what Justin would confess to.

'Okay. Well, Michael and I met in high school and his parents were pretty strict Methodists, so we never . . . you know . . .'

'No, we don't know.' Prudence was lighting another cigarette. 'Tell us, scientific terms and all.'

Holly took another sip of wine to fortify herself. 'Okay, we never went all the way. We never . . . We never had sex. Happy now?'

'Much happier, please go on.'

Holly was acutely aware of Justin's presence. But he hadn't moved or commented. Just lay there staring up into the darkness.

'When I got accepted into university, I had to move to Brisbane during term. It was the first time Michael and I had been apart, and at first I missed him terribly. But then I got to like the urban lifestyle. In my fourth year I was sharing a flat with these two gay guys. One of them had a brother named Daniel and we got close. I assumed that he was gay too—dumb country hick that I was—until the night he kissed me.'

'Ooh, illicit romance. I love it. And then?'

'I was guilty about it, but I was . . . well, I was totally turned on. He was gorgeous. We had . . . I guess you'd call it an affair. It lasted a few months and then he moved to Sydney and I went home to marry Michael. And on our wedding night, Michael thought I was still a virgin. God, I can't believe I'm telling you this.'

'So, let me get this straight,' Prudence said, flicking her hair off her shoulder. 'You cheated on Michael. You, self-proclaimed queen of moderation, fucked some guy who wasn't your fiancé?'

'Yes, and there's more.' Holly was starting to get a delicious, illicit thrill out of telling all this. 'Michael, who had never slept with anyone before, had no clue at all about how to make love to a woman. But Daniel had this stockpile of tricks. I taught them all to Michael. I re-created him sexually in Daniel's image.'

'God, Holly, you're making me blush,' Prudence said. 'I'm *so* shocked.'

'I felt really guilty about it. I guess I still do, after all that's happened.' Suddenly remembering the condition Michael was in at the moment damped down Holly's enthusiasm.

'Don't feel guilty,' Justin said quietly. 'It's not your fault, what Michael's done.'

They all fell silent.

'Great,' Prudence said at last. 'This was supposed to be a thrilling and exuberant exploration of naughty secrets. It's turning into a bit of a downer.'

'I don't know what that says about sex,' Justin offered.

'It's your turn, you know,' Prudence said, undeterred.

Justin sighed. 'Prudence, this isn't . . . I don't know if . . .'

'Come on, just one little forbidden secret. Ever done it in a lift? Fantasised about farm animals? Had two women at the same time?'

'Two women?'

'Yeah, that's the standard male fantasy, right?'

Justin shrugged. 'I don't know why, most guys only have one penis.'

Holly giggled and handed Justin the wine bottle. 'Here, fortify yourself. There's no escaping her.'

Justin took the bottle but didn't drink from it. He held it and looked at it for a few seconds. 'Okay,' he said. 'I probably need your help on this one anyway.'

'Our help? Oh, Justin, don't. You're getting me all hot and bothered,' Prudence giggled.

He smiled. The candlelight glinted off his glasses. 'No, Prudence, not that kind of help. It's Emma.'

'Emma?' Prudence gasped. 'You're not . . .?'

'No. But she wants to. She's made it very clear that her feelings for me are more carnal than maternal. The other night—Monday night—Lucien went out and she . . . she came on to me.'

'How strong?' Prudence asked.

'Perfumed and dressed in lingerie, asking me to come up to her room.'

'That's pretty strong.'

'But this is your aunt,' Holly said, shocked.

'Yeah, by marriage. And don't forget I've only ever known her as an adult.'

'But still—' Holly stopped her tongue. She was hardly qualified to comment on the depravity of the world when she was having an affair with an incubus.

'What did you do?' Prudence asked, wide-eyed.

'I told her to go up and I'd join her in a few minutes. Then I ran away.'

Prudence flinched. 'Ouch. Badly handled, Justin.'

'Where did you go?' asked Holly.

'I got on a tram and went into the city. Sat in a cafe all night until I was sure that Lucien would be home. Now I spend my entire life trying to avoid her. Yesterday I left the house at seven in the morning and didn't go home until seven at night. It's painful. And I know I should have handled it better, but my flight impulse is much better developed than my fight impulse.'

Again a short silence. Then Prudence said, 'Were you tempted?'

Justin shrugged. 'Perhaps. She's pretty and it's been . . .' He stopped for a moment. 'But not really. Holly's right, she's my aunt. It's too weird.'

'I know how to solve this problem and save Emma's dignity,' Prudence offered.

'How?'

'Tell her you have a girlfriend. That's why you ran. You were *so* tempted, because she's *so* gorgeous, but you had to remain faithful to your new partner.'

'But then she'll want to meet the girlfriend. It's all too complicated.'

'Silly, *I'll* be your girlfriend. Pretend girlfriend, of course. I ring your place often enough as it is. She'll believe that for sure. Don't underestimate my acting skills. And it would help solve my problem too—As was worried about getting in trouble with Lucien over our relationship. If Lucien thinks that you and I are going out, then he'll leave As alone. Making way for me to resume my sick and ultimately self-destructive affair with him.'

'You wouldn't, would you?' Holly asked, concerned.

'In a second. I love As. What do you think, Justin?'

Justin considered. 'I think I want to know what Holly thinks.'

Holly realised they were both looking at her, waiting for her to comment. 'There's something so twisted about all this,' she said. 'Can't you just tell her the truth?'

He shook his head. 'I'm not good with brutal honesty.'

Holly thought about it. Okay, so she was a bit jealous. What if this pretend relationship turned into a real one? But she had Christian, so she could hardly be jealous, nor could she comment about twisted relationships.

'Well, go ahead then. I'll be in on it.'

'See, it's all worked out perfectly,' Prudence said, settling back on her blanket. 'Aren't you glad you confessed?'

Prudence couldn't sleep. Justin and Holly hadn't come back to her place after the Confessional. The whole thing had been a bit depressing, really, and nobody much felt like kicking on until the wee hours. So she was home alone, half tanked and with a head full of secrets.

And she couldn't stop thinking about As. His warm hands, a little rough on the palms, pale blond hairs sprouting from the backs of his fingers. His lips, the way they curved up when he pushed them together, so it always looked like he was smiling when he was thinking hard. His eyes, that stormy shade of grey that was almost blue, almost green, depending on his moods. Not having him had made him suddenly ten times more desirable. There was no way she could sleep tonight. She turned on the light and looked at her clock. Only half past eleven. She threw back the covers and went to her wardrobe to dress.

She didn't really know where she was going when she stepped out of the house in a black dress and long overcoat, purple Doc Martens keeping her feet dry from dewy grass. But she wasn't surprised when she started heading towards As's house. She'd been there before, without him knowing of course. Just to look at it from the outside. To imagine the inside and a day when she might get to be there. All hopeless now.

An icy wind whipped strands of her hair into her face. The streets were in turmoil, the stiff breeze sending piles of leaves into whirlwinds, the windswept branches making shadows stir in the streetlight. Shopfronts glowed here and there and an occasional car went past. But it was Sunday night and most people were home in bed, so at times it seemed that she was the only person left in some post-apocalyptic world, walking forever down suburban streets looking for another living being.

She took a short cut through the back of a block of flats, resisting the impulse to steal some underwear left out overnight on a washing line. She was twenty-two now, too old for childish pranks. Sorting out the floundering mess of her love-life was a far more adult pastime.

Here was As's house, sitting silent in the dark. She sank down on the footpath behind a tree and gazed at it. Low-set, tiled roof, painted shutters. A picture of suburban happiness. As's car was in the driveway, but the wife's—Mandy's—was gone. Mandy spent a lot of time with her mother, who was sick with cancer. As said that Mandy took her mother to the oncologist most Monday mornings, so she was gone most Sundays, sometimes even for the whole weekend. The kid, apparently eager for an inheritance, usually went with her. When pressed about a possible weekend liaison with Prudence, As had back-tracked quickly. Too weird having her in his house. Too busy with other things. Neighbours would talk. Why on earth had she swallowed all that bullshit? For him it was fun having sex with her in his office at the college because it was dirty, taboo, and he didn't have to wake up next to her in the morning. Anything outside of work hours wasn't fun, it was a hassle. She sighed and leaned her head back against the tree. *Crazy, Prudence. You've been crazy.* Nothing good was ever going to come of this relationship, and to be honest the sex wasn't even that great.

But she couldn't help who she loved. She stood, meaning to take one last look at As's house, when she noticed there was a light on somewhere inside. Was he up still? It must be close to midnight. Perhaps he was just getting to bed. Perhaps he was reading, or making a cup of tea, or having a shower. Doing one of a million things from which she was excluded.

Then the front door opened and he stepped out. With a little gasp she ducked behind the tree, peering out cautiously. He locked the door behind him, went to the car and got in. He let the engine idle for a few minutes, then backed out into the street. Prudence pressed herself close against the tree and waited until she saw his tail-lights glow at the end of the street before she breathed again.

Where was he going?

With terrible jealous certainty it dawned on her. He had another woman. Of course. He was cheating on her as well as on Mandy. That was why he didn't want to see her on weekends. He had a girl for home, a girl for the office, and another for the weekend—the perfect set-up. If Prudence had had a car she would have followed him, but by the time she had run to the end of the street his car had disappeared from view. Off to some late-night liaison with a woman who, Prudence was certain, was slim, mature and beautiful. A woman who would laugh at Prudence if she saw her.

'Bastard,' she spat under her breath. 'You fucking bastard.'

★

The heat and the darkness. Sulphur and dusty earth. An icy, clawed hand, fingertips grazing his cheek.

'Lucien . . . Lucien.' A voice far away, miles into the darkness.

The hand grasping his shoulder. 'I'm waiting, Lucien. You won't let me down, will you?' The being's voice was raspy, spitting over broken glass.

'Who are you?' Lucien gasped, the heat leaping down his throat in smothering gusts.

Then a word starting with 'Ahh', but never forming wholly in his senses.

'Lucien, are you all right? Somebody turn on the lights.' The voice in the darkness again, a pebble in a swamp, fingers closing around it.

'I'm waiting, Lucien. You're the one. Not the others. You're the one I'm waiting for.'

'How do I find you again?' Lucien said hoarsely.

'You will. When the rest of the book is yours, you will find me again.' The demon was dissolving now, a red pattern pressed on Lucien's eyelids, the world rushing back in on his senses.

He opened his eyes. Jane was leaning over him, her dark hair falling forward. He rolled his eyes back and saw Emma behind him, cradling his head. Aswell was there, too. Memories came back to him. They were performing the mass, the temperature had gone up and he had pitched violently into the blackness, losing his usual thread to reality.

'Emma?' he said weakly.

She helped him sit up. 'Are you all right? You scared us, Lucien. What happened?'

'I . . . I don't know. I need a glass of water. My throat feels like . . .' Like he had been breathing in hell. But he wasn't going to tell them that. Aswell had a glass of water for him a few moments later and he drank it gratefully. 'Thank you,' he said, handing the glass back.

'What happened?' Emma repeated. Jane had moved back now and knelt on the floor a few metres away.

'I think I made direct contact with one of the shadow demons.'

'Then it worked,' said Jane.

The previous morning Lucien had decoded a section of the Guyana fragment, an invocation that Owling had crammed into a margin of his writing, but one that had proven to carry great import. 'To touch the other side,' it had promised, 'to join hands with the shadow beings.'

Lucien nodded slowly, his senses still reeling. 'Yes. Yes, it worked.'

CHAPTER EIGHTEEN

‘**E**mma, can I ... Can we talk?’ Justin fought down the fluttering in his chest as he stood in front of his aunt in the lounge room. She had her feet tucked up beneath her and was reading a novel, her blonde hair loose about her shoulders.

‘I don’t know that you could have anything to say to me,’ she said, feigning a lack of interest and not looking up from her novel.

‘Please, while Lucien’s not here. We need to get this sorted out.’

She put down her book and looked up at him. He wanted to run, but instead he forced himself to pull up a chair next to her and take her hand. ‘I need to explain what happened.’

‘I know what happened. I’ll never forget. I’ve never been more embarrassed, insulted or disappointed in my life.’

‘Emma, I wanted to. Really badly.’ Prudence had helped him rehearse this part, so it was coming out rather more smoothly than anything of this kind usually would. ‘But—I should have told you this earlier—I’m seeing someone.’

She looked surprised and hurt. 'How long has this been going on?'

'About a month. I didn't tell you because . . . I don't know. And I did . . . *do* find you attractive, but I didn't want to cheat on her. I like her a lot.' He held her gaze. 'I was so tempted, Emma.'

'I don't believe you.'

'You have to believe me. It's true. Lucien's crazy, you know. You're beautiful.'

She smiled, almost shyly. 'You think so?'

'Sure I do.'

She reached out and cleared a curl from his brow, sweeping the back of her hand along his cheek, across his shoulder. He let her, feeling himself blush.

'Who is it? Who are you seeing? Someone from the college?' she asked in a voice which, he realised, was too sweet.

'Prudence Emerson.'

It was as though she had been given an electric shock. All sweetness was suddenly gone from her voice. 'Prudence? That little piece of . . . Why her?'

He shrugged and averted his eyes. 'I don't know. Opposites attract, I guess.'

She set her jaw, her eyes steely. 'She's a stupid little tramp. How could you prefer her to me?'

Justin froze, not knowing what to do next. 'Emma, I—'

She pushed him away from her and stood, casting her book across the room so it hit the wall and came to rest bent backwards on the floor. 'You know Aswell's already been there before you, don't you?'

Justin remembered he had to protect Prudence's interests here too. 'No, that's not true. She and Dr Aswell have never—'

'You're deluded!' she shouted. 'She'll never be faithful to you, she's coarse and arrogant and—' Suddenly Emma burst into tears and dropped heavily back into her chair.

'Emma, I'm sorry,' Justin said, not sure whether to approach her or not.

'Get out of my sight. I'm insulted. More than Monday night. To pass me up for her. Get away from me and don't come near me or speak to me ever again.'

Justin realised with a kind of crazy relief that, while this was an ugly scene, it was probably the best thing that could have happened. She didn't want to see him, he was free.

'Whatever you say,' he muttered with as much contrition as he could summon. He backed out of the room and left her there crying into her fists like a little girl.

Prudence waited until late Tuesday afternoon to go and see As. She was still angry with him, still unsure of herself, wanted to ignore him one minute, talk him into realising what a huge mistake he had made the next. She practised long conversations in her head, conversations in which all her words were perfectly chosen and persuasive and As was convinced by her reasoning. Whether or not any of these conversations would happen was another thing.

With trepidation she rapped on his door.

'Come in.'

She let herself in, stopped herself from flicking the lock, and sat down across from him with as much composure as she could muster. 'Hi,' she said weakly.

'Hi, Prudence. I suppose we've got a few things to sort out with regards to a new supervisor for you—'

'Wait. I just wanted to tell you, Lucien thinks that Justin and I are an item.'

'His nephew?'

'Yes. And if he thinks that, he can't possibly think that you and I . . . you know. So we're safe . . . to continue.'

'I don't think that's very wise.'

'But you said—'

'Look, forget Lucien. This relationship had to end eventually, Prudence.' He looked down at his desk, trying to maintain a businesslike manner. 'I've spoken to Jane and she's happy to take over as your supervisor.'

'I don't want Jane. I want Randolph. Jane's into all that psychoanalytic bullshit—the id and the fucking superego. Boring.'

He kept his voice even. 'Randolph isn't here, Prudence.'

'You said he'd be back soon. I'll wait for him. I don't want Jane.' Jane bugged Prudence, all smoothed over and tidy-haired, with a supercilious tone and brown lipstick.

As realised he was defeated. 'All right, but if he's not back by the end of May I'm sending you to Jane.'

Prudence considered for a moment. 'You're not sleeping with Jane, are you?'

'What? No, of course not.'

'Are you seeing somebody else?'

He smiled. 'You give me credit for a lot of sexual energy, Prudence.'

'I mean, is that why you're splitting up with me, because there's somebody else?'

'No, Prudence. No.'

He must be lying. Of course he wouldn't tell her. The phone rang and he excused himself before picking it up. Prudence pretended to be busy pulling some papers out of her bag.

'Hello . . . Lucien, hi . . . No, no, I'd tell you if he had. I check it every morning . . . Lucien, really, I'll let you know as soon as something arrives . . . I have to go, there's somebody here with me . . . Yes, goodbye.' He put the phone down and Prudence looked up with a smile.

'Lucien giving you a hard time?'

'Nothing new there. Perhaps you should leave, Prudence.'

She tried to hand him a couple of pages. 'Could you look over these for me—it's an early draft of my second chapter.'

He hesitated, then shook his head. 'No. You're on your own until Randolph arrives. At your request.'

She pulled the papers back and stuffed them in her bag. 'That's it, then?'

'Yes. It would seem so.'

There didn't appear to be anything left to say, so Prudence quietly collected her things and left. Aswell saw her to the door, gave her a brief, weak smile and closed it behind her. The sound of the lock snicking into place almost broke her in two.

Justin had gone home but Holly was still in the office, her blonde head bent over a notepad, scribbling furiously. Prudence had never met anybody as industrious as Holly. It was almost freakish.

'Hey, study-girl,' she said, going to her desk to turn off her laptop. 'I'm off. Want to catch a tram into the city with me? We could go grab something to eat. Maybe we'll call Justin and see if he wants to meet us.'

Holly glanced up. 'Actually, I need to get this finished.'

'*Need* to?'

'Okay, I *want* to get this finished. Sorry.'

Prudence came over and perched on the edge of Holly's desk. 'You work too hard.'

'Not really. I don't usually get here until late, and then I spend half the day talking to you. I get most of my work done once everyone's gone.'

'How late do you stay in the evenings?' Prudence didn't like this vein of suspicion that was hardening inside her.

Holly looked back to her notepad. 'It depends.'

'Depends on what?'

'On lots of things. Sometimes I get hungry. Sometimes I run out of steam. Sometimes I can go for hours.'

'Is there ever anybody else around?' Like As, perhaps.

'Not that I'm aware of,' she replied a little too casually, not looking at Prudence.

God, why was she being so guarded about her answers? Prudence could feel her flesh prickle as her senses came alert. Could Holly—her best friend—be As's other woman? Could that be why she was so shocked by Prudence's confession?

No, that was ridiculous.

Wasn't it?

'Okay, I'll see you tomorrow,' Prudence said, stretching her legs and heading for the door.

'Sure. Bye, Prudence.'

Holly reached out and switched on her lamp. It had been an hour and a half since Prudence had left, and she still felt guilty. Poor Prudence, obsessed with ghosts, dying to meet one in person. And here was Holly, keeping it all secret from her. Clandestine encounters in the dark like a teenager. But she couldn't share Christian. He was hers.

If he would come. Holly shook her head. Of course he would come. It was just because she was sick on Friday that he had left. It wasn't forever. And she wasn't sick any more, even after eating greasy pizza and drinking wine at Prudence's on Sunday. He had to come.

She fetched the mirror and set it up on her desk, lighting candles and switching off the electric light. A deep breath. 'Christian?' Her voice wavered in the dark. Nothing happened.

'Christian?' A little more desperate this time. 'Please, Christian. I'm better now, really.'

She waited. The silence was heavy on her ears.

'Please.'

More silence, echoing into five minutes, ten minutes.

'Are you here anywhere? Can you hear me?'

A sudden breeze rushed past her ears, extinguishing the two candles and plunging her into darkness. Her heart picked up its beat. 'Then come to me. I'm well. You don't have to worry about hurting me.'

Nothing. She put her head in her hands, feeling her hair spilling over her fingers. 'How can I make you understand? All I want is to be with you.' The room remained still, dark and quiet. Christian did not come.

The phone was ringing when Holly let herself into her house. She dropped her keys on the kitchen bench and picked it up.

'Hello.'

'It's me.' Her mother.

'Hi, Mum. Everything okay?' She held her breath, expecting the worst news about Michael.

'I'm surprised you care. You haven't even called here since you got back.'

'I've been sick, Mum.' The truth was that she hadn't wanted to call. The whole trip had been so painful, her resentment towards her family considerable.

'So your friend told me.'

'Michael, Mum, how is he?'

'He's still in hospital and he's getting some help from a shrink. What he doesn't know, however, is that he won't have a home or a job to come back to when he returns to Daybrook.'

'What do you mean?'

'The hardware store is closing down. He'd been struggling financially since you left anyway, but now he's not been earning any money for the rent, the real-estate agent got in touch with his family to move his belongings from the house. Nobody has told him yet.'

'I left him all the money I had, Mum. It's not my fault.'

'I'm not saying it's your fault. Did you hear me say it was your fault?'

'It was implied.'

'I really think you should come back.'

Holly groaned inwardly, ran a hand through her hair. 'God, Mum, we've been through all this. I'm not coming back.'

'He has nothing.'

'If I come back, then *I* have nothing.'

'Don't go getting all dramatic,' her mother said with disdain. 'Is that something you learn to do at college?'

'I love it here.'

There were a few beats of strained silence. She thought she heard her mother sniff quietly.

'Mum? Are you crying?'

'If you don't come back now, you can forget about ever coming back.'

Holly was astonished. 'What?'

'You heard me.' Tears in her mother's voice now. 'Your father and I didn't bring you up to be so cruel and so . . . irresponsible.'

'Mum, this is ridiculous. Marriages sometimes fail— often fail.'

'I've been with your father for twenty-eight years, Holly. It hasn't all been rosy, but we've stuck together. You have to work for your happiness. You can't just run away from a sticky situation and hope it never catches up with you.'

Holly was speechless for a few moments. The only light in her flat came from the green numbers on the microwave. She watched them floating in the dark, shaking her head. 'Mum . . . I don't know what to say.'

'Say you'll come home.'

Working hard to keep the annoyance out of her voice. 'No. I won't come home.'

'Then say goodbye.'

She paused. An empty, sick feeling was trapped like a bubble in her throat. 'Goodbye,' she said at last.

The phone clicked. She hung up and looked around her, bewildered, wishing that she had gone into town with Prudence and Justin after all. It looked as though they were about all she had left.

Justin was en route from the front door to his bedroom when Emma cornered him.

'Been out with Prudence?' she said, stopping him at the doorway to the lounge room.

'Yes. We went for dinner.' That wasn't a lie. Prudence had called him from the city and arranged to meet him at her favourite diner on Swanston Street. As usual, Prudence had filled every spare moment with her vigorous chatter. It was the perfect social arrangement for him, really. He didn't have to say a word.

'I hope you don't spend the money we give you on her. That money is to keep you in necessities while you're studying.'

'No, Prudence pays her own way.' What had happened to Emma's vow of everlasting hatred and silence?

'Do you even have time to be running around with her? Are you getting your work done? You do realise that your staying here with us is dependent on your fulfilling all your academic requirements, Justin.'

'Everything is going fine,' he said in a monotone, trying to get past her.

She put out an arm to stop him. He paused. Her eyes were narrowed. 'I can make things hard for you, you know. You'd better not think that she can stay overnight in my house.'

Justin shook his head. 'Fine. I don't care.'

'Emma?' Lucien's voice came from behind them. As soon as Emma turned around Justin ducked past her and continued on to his room. He heard Lucien say, 'What's going on?' and rather than closing the door behind him, he hung back near the entrance to listen. He could hear muffled voices, but no distinct words. He wanted to find out what Emma said about him, what she had meant by making things hard for him. What would Prudence do in this situation?

He came out of his bedroom and slammed the door to make it sound like he had gone to bed, then tiptoed into the dark hallway. A few metres from the entrance to the lounge he could hear them arguing.

'It's Prudence Emerson, Lucien. I wouldn't be concerned if he'd taken up with a decent sort of a girl—'

'So? She's a slut and he's a simpleton. It sounds like a perfect match to me. Admit it, Emma, you're not concerned about his welfare. You just can't believe that he doesn't return your interest. I warned you this would happen if you went on deluding yourself in this way.'

'No, it's not that at all.'

'Don't be a fool. You're twice Prudence Emerson's age, and nearly twice her size. Why does it surprise you that he's more interested in her than in you? Were you really witless enough to think that he would find you attractive?'

'I *am* attractive.'

'This whole conversation is inane. I won't be part of it. Get over your absurd self-obsession, Emma. There are more important things at stake than your sex appeal. We should hear from Randolph soon and then we'll be into the last phase of our plan.'

'You and your stupid book! What if it doesn't work, have you thought of that? Then what will you do? Things like family and . . . and love, they will matter.'

'Of course it will work.'

'What if it doesn't?'

Lucien's voice grew loud, each word articulated with vehemence. 'It—will—work!'

At the sound of Lucien's temper snapping, Justin decided to go back to his bedroom. What book and what plan were they talking about? Emma had suggested once that Lucien was writing something or translating something. His angry reaction suggested he had a lot of passion invested in it. Justin opened his bedroom door and closed it behind him quietly.

So Lucien thought he was a simpleton. Probably better that way. It made for an uncomplicated relationship if nothing was ever expected of him. He kicked his shoes off, picked up a book and crashed onto his bed. His eyes were heavy but he wanted to read a chapter before he saw Jane tomorrow. Perhaps he'd close his eyes, just for a moment. The darkness was soothing. He could hear his watch ticking softly where his wrist was stretched out near his ear. Counting off the seconds. All talk of books and plans was forgotten as he drifted into a sweet, accidental slumber.

A storm woke Lucien in the early hours of the morning. Thunder grumbled all around and the bedroom glowed periodically from reflected lightning. Rain lashed at the windows and a gale howled in the trees outside. He tossed and turned for half an hour before admitting that it was pointless. He was so anxious about hearing from Randolph that relaxing under any circumstances was difficult, let alone when the rain was deafening on the roof. Emma dozed happily next to him and Lucien watched her for a while. What on earth had she been thinking about Justin all this time? To get so jealous when the boy took up with Prudence, almost as if she took it personally. He was embarrassed for Emma, sad plump fool that she was. Or perhaps he was embarrassed for himself as her partner.

Despairing of sleep, he rose and pulled a dressing-gown around him. Perhaps he could get some work done on the grimoire. There were still a couple of pages that he had not decoded, though he was fairly certain at this stage that they were just extraneous rubbish. Still, it had been a marginal note that had led them into contact with the shadow demon on Sunday night. He reminded himself it didn't pay to be quite so dismissive.

At the bottom of the stairs he turned to look down the hallway. The light was still on under Justin's door. Lucien checked his watch. It was nearly two a.m. He padded down the hallway, the stone tiles cool under his feet, and approached Justin's door to knock lightly.

A few moments passed before a bleary-eyed Justin opened the door warily. He peered out and checked over Lucien's shoulder. Was he checking for Emma? What had she been putting him through when Lucien wasn't around?

'It's only me, Justin,' Lucien said. 'I saw your light on.'

'I fell asleep with it on. I'm sorry.'

'I wanted to apologise for Emma's behaviour this evening. She has no right to interfere in your private life.'

Justin looked at him, speechless as always. He didn't seem to have the least notion about manners, Lucien thought—accepting the apology would be a start. What had Graham been thinking, running off with this one's mother? Still, he had easily been brought back to the fold, as had Justin. Money was like a magnet.

'Goodnight,' Lucien said, turning to leave.

'Thanks, Lucien,' Justin managed to spit out.

Lucien hesitated. 'I want you to feel comfortable staying here, Justin. It's your home, the money we advance you is your money. It's all set out in Magnus's will.'

'Thanks,' he said again.

Lucien nodded and headed back down the hallway to his office. He heard Justin's door close behind him. He couldn't have the lad leaving now, not when he might be necessary to the group's future plans. It would be just like Emma to upset it all with her incessant need for attention.

The storm was rumbling off into the distance, the rain

now torrential, when Lucien sat down in his office, the grimoire in front of him and a pencil in his hand. The electric light aggravated his tired eyes and made it difficult to focus. He worked half-heartedly on a few passages, then pushed the book away and put his head on the desk and fell into a light doze. The sounds of the storm seemed to bleed into it, until he dreamed he was outside in the rain trying to work the elastic shape between his hands. It gaped into nowhere. He tried not to look inside the gap, knowing he would go mad if he saw the darkness spinning off into infinity. But with a huge rushing sound the gap opened up and swallowed him. He beat against the sides of a dark prison. His knocking went on and on, growing louder and louder.

Coming back to consciousness, Lucien realised the knocking was not in his dream. Somebody was at the front door. He gathered his wits about him, pushing down the terror of the dream and hurrying out of his office. Still the knocking went on. Who would be calling at this time of night? He nearly slipped on the tiles by the front door. The knocking came again, loud and insistent.

'Yes, yes, I'm coming,' he called, steadying himself and reaching up for the door handle. He peered through the peephole, but could see only a dark shape in a raincoat and hat, hiding under the eaves from the downpour. Warily, he flicked on the light and opened the door.

The man looked up and pulled his hat off. 'Hello, Lucien.'

Randolph.

His strange albinolike eyes glittered in his grizzled face, drops of rain jewelled his white beard. Lucien felt his heart hammering hard in his chest. 'Randolph . . . is that . . .?'

Randolph thrust a small plastic bag into Lucien's hands. 'All the way from Jerusalem,' he said with a twisted smile. 'Special delivery.'

CHAPTER NINETEEN

~

Lucien was speechless, literally speechless. He held the bag in his long hands, unsure what to do next.

'Perhaps you'd let me in out of the rain?' Randolph asked.

'Of course, of course,' Lucien said, remembering himself and ushering his cousin in.

Randolph stepped inside, dropped his suitcase and shrugged out of his raincoat. He still had a backpack over one shoulder. 'Can we go to your study and have a chat, Lucien?' he asked as he hung his coat over a hook by the door.

'Yes, yes. This way.' Lucien led him towards his study and locked the door behind them. Randolph placed his backpack on the floor and dropped into a leather chair while Lucien carefully laid the wrapped grimoire on the desk.

'Go on, open it,' Randolph urged.

'I'm savouring it.'

'Were you like this on Christmas morning as a child? Or did you rip straight into everything, like most kids?'

Lucien cast his mind back. Was he ever a child? It

seemed like remembering somebody else's life. 'I think I used to take my time, peeling off the tape and unwrapping carefully.'

Randolph snorted. 'That's unnatural.'

Lucien smiled at Randolph. 'But if this works, we have all the time in the world.'

'For God's sake, just open it,' Randolph said impatiently.

Lucien unfolded the top of the plastic bag and gently, lovingly, pulled out the grimoire. It did indeed have a back cover, as Lily had said. He ran his fingers over the leather.

'It's human skin, you know,' Randolph said.

Lucien recoiled, curling his fingers in distaste. 'Really?'

'Probably from an unbaptised child.'

'How do you know?'

'Lily Kirkwood had made quite a study of it.'

'So you spoke to her again?'

Randolph shook his head. 'Not exactly.'

Lucien lowered himself into his chair, flipped the book open and scanned some of the pages. All in the most illegible of codes. It gave him a headache just thinking about transcribing it.

'Why did you come here? Why didn't you go to Aswell first? You've addressed all your letters to him.' Lucien hadn't meant to sound so bitter and accusing, but his usual self-control had deteriorated with the excitement.

'I came here tonight because some secrets belong safely within the family.'

'What do you mean?'

'I mean that I'll never be able to tell Laurence Aswell what I'm about to tell you. The Humberstones protect each other, no matter what.'

Lucien felt a sick thrill darken his solar plexus. 'Randolph? What have you done?'

'How about a cup of coffee and something to eat? Then I can tell you exactly what I've done.'

Lucien nodded and left Randolph in the office. He went to the kitchen, where he made coffee in a plunger and assembled a couple of sandwiches, his hands shaking with excitement and apprehension. Randolph was standing by the window gazing out at the rain when he returned. The only light in the room came from the lamp over Lucien's desk. Lucien placed the plate and the coffee plunger on the desk and went to join Randolph by the window. The thunder and lightning had stopped but the deluge continued, making the gutters overflow.

'What happened?' Lucien asked.

Randolph turned and leaned back on the window sill. 'I waited outside her house every day for nearly two weeks, come rain or shine. I was nearly mad with boredom by the time she finally left. And I'd been having the most horrendous headaches imaginable, like migraines. Sitting there on the cold stone steps, waiting and waiting for the bitch to leave her house.' He sighed and made his way to Lucien's desk, pulling the leather chair with him. Taking a sandwich, he sat down and reached out to pour himself a coffee. Lucien settled opposite him.

Randolph took a bite of his sandwich and continued. 'She stepped out on a Sunday morning. I watched her until she disappeared down the alley, then I went across to her front door. It had one of those old-fashioned keyhole locks, so I was inside within a matter of seconds, slamming the door behind me. Her cats—God, I hate cats—were glaring at me, Lucien, I swear. Eyes glittering in the dark. I kicked the fat one and they soon got out of my way. The house smelled like stale cooked meat. I went straight to the room where I knew the grimoire would be hidden.' He paused to finish his sandwich and washed it down with a gulp of coffee.

'The room was like one of Grandma Humberstone's old rooms back in London, full of forgotten odds and ends and piles of musty clothes and papers. But there was an oak dresser, and I assumed the grimoire would be in there, under lock and key.

'This lock was a lot trickier than the front door, and I was conscious of not taking too much time. I went to the kitchen and found a hammer under her sink, amidst dozens of half-empty detergent bottles and piles of roach shit. A couple of swings with the hammer and the lock broke, the door gaped open.

'This was a witch's cupboard, Lucien. A shrunken head grinned at me from the top shelf. There were packages of powder and bottles of tincture, a collection of pins and needles, and there, on the bottom shelf, I found a voodoo doll of myself.'

'Of you?'

'Yes. It had a beard of cotton wool and wore exactly the outfit I had worn the first time I met her. With a pin—'

'In its head?'

'Yes, precisely. She'd given me the headaches. Probably because I hadn't treated her with the respect she thought she deserved. Now I was angry. Very, very angry. I took the pin out and pocketed the doll. See, here it is.' Randolph felt around inside his jacket and pulled out a doll. Lucien took it from him carefully. It bore an uncanny likeness to Randolph, the face drawn in careful caricature.

'What are you going to do with it?' Lucien asked.

'Keep it somewhere safe. I'm frightened to destroy it—for obvious reasons. Can you put it in the safe with the grimoire?'

'Of course.' Lucien laid the doll on the desk cautiously, wary of dropping it or hurting it accidentally. 'I'll take care of it. Please continue.'

'I searched through the cupboard but couldn't find the

grimoire. Just as I was about to give up, however, I noticed the cupboard had a false bottom. I felt about for the catch and had it open a few moments later. There were pages and pages of notes in the recess, the grimoire hiding underneath them. I pulled all the papers into my lap and had a cursory glance through them. You'll be happy, Lucien. Let me show you.' He bent to reach inside his backpack, pulled out a sheaf of papers and passed them over the desk to Lucien.

Lucien's fingers picked at the knot of the string tying them together. 'What are they?'

'Her notes on the fragment. Including her attempts to decode it.'

Lucien flicked through the papers. This was wonderful. Most of the work had been done. Lily's cramped hand-writing covered the sheets, all her observances, her research, her translations tabulated and codified. 'Perfect,' he said in a low voice.

'I was going through them when I heard a noise behind me,' continued Randolph. 'I turned and saw the cat—the fat old one—just sitting there looking at me. I tried to shoo it away but it wouldn't go. I was tense and the cat spooked me, so I picked up the hammer and threw it at it. The hammer struck the cat on the paw and it jumped and squealed, but it wouldn't leave. It settled itself down again, watching me. I didn't like to turn my back to it now that I was very much on edge. I looked down for just a few seconds, put the grimoire fragment and the notes in my backpack, and when I turned back to the cat Lily was there, watching me, the cat in her arms. I froze.

'In that supercilious tone, like she wasn't afraid of me, she said, "What are you doing, Mr Clark?"

'I didn't know whether to run or to talk myself out of the mess. All that was important was that I get out of there with the grimoire fragment still in my possession. She could have . . . You know, if she'd only been a little less arrogant, a little less egotistical, she wouldn't have made it necessary for me to do what I did. But she made my decision for me. She said, "I wouldn't advise your leaving here now, with my book, Mr Clark. It won't be just a pin in your head next time: perhaps it will be a tumorous lump in your abdomen, or a candle flame under your balls." The way she spoke, threatening me like that, not only made me realise that it was dangerous to leave her alive, it also made me lose my temper. I dropped the backpack and reached out to grab her. But her cat hissed and scratched me and she managed to slip out of the room, dropping the cat behind her.

'I chased her to her front door and she nearly got away, only she had locked the door behind her when she came in and she couldn't get it open in time. She didn't scream, she just made this loud, gulping noise. I grabbed her around the throat and . . .'

Lucien let him be silent for a few moments. 'Go on, Randolph.'

'Her throat was very pale and delicate, and my hands— we've all got such large hands in this family.' He splayed his fingers onto the desk to demonstrate. 'I strangled her. She fell limp in my arms and I threw her on the floor. Such a sickening thud. My heart was . . . I can't describe how I felt. Excited, terrified. I ran to the other room, picked up my backpack. The cat glared at me. I wanted to kill it too, but I think I was more afraid of it than I was of her.

'I was almost at the door when I heard a sound. I turned. She was still alive. Gasping and . . . and trying to get up. Her hands clawing at the carpet. I'm not much of a murderer, Lucien.' He hung his head, silent for nearly a full minute. The clock on Lucien's desk ticked quietly.

Randolph took a breath and continued. 'I went to the kitchen bench. There was a, a large carving knife in the sink, all covered in grease. I didn't have time to consider. I went to her. She was still on the floor, so I kneeled on . . . on her arms. On the joints. I thought I heard one of them crack. She cried out. Her eyes were not quite focussed, like maybe she didn't know what was going on. I could smell urine and I realised that she'd . . .' Randolph's hands started to shake. He placed his coffee cup on the desk. 'I stabbed her,' he said quietly, not looking up. 'In the chest, in the neck. About a dozen times. The blade was greasy and the blood streaked through it in uneven patterns. The knife point . . . so sharp.' He paused, then finished in a quiet voice, 'You have no idea how much blood is in a person until you let some out.'

Lucien realised he was holding his breath. He let it go and said quietly but firmly, 'You did the right thing, Randolph.'

'I know.'

'You had to get the fragment and you had to get away. She would have raised the alarm. You did the right thing.'

Randolph looked up. 'Yes. I did the right thing. Lucien, her cat, the big old one—as she died, it came to rest on her chest. It died too. Just lay there and closed its eyes and drew its last gasp.

'I was going to leave them both there, blood swirling onto the dusty Persian rug. The woman hardly leaves . . . hardly left the house. I thought nobody would notice she was missing for weeks, maybe months. I thought that by the time they found her she'd just be bones and old hair. But then it occurred to me. The body doesn't rot pleasantly, or without odour, and all the houses were so close together where she lived.

'I searched through her kitchen cupboards and found some large plastic garbage bags and a ball of string. I slipped the cat into one without difficulty, but then realised that putting her into another might cover me in blood. There was so much of it. I couldn't go back to my hotel room with my clothes covered in blood. So I stripped completely naked and left my clothes by the door.

'Lucien, being naked in the company of a woman I

had just stabbed to death was not how I expected to find myself that morning. I was suddenly overcome by a violent shaking, a strange dislocation of the mind. As I bagged her, it seemed like I was watching myself from a great distance. I watched myself ease her legs into the bag first and tie it tightly around her waist. Then I watched as I besmeared myself with blood, slipping another bag over her top half. The iron smell of it hovered in the air. All sounds were of my laboured breathing as I struggled with her body. And . . . I don't know whether to tell you this . . .'

'Tell me everything.'

'I was naked, her body was still warm, slippery with blood as I held her against me . . .' He shook his head and laughed cynically. 'I realised I had an erection. Again, it was like watching someone else. I remember being completely embarrassed for myself. At a time like that . . .' Again he shook his head before continuing. 'I used a second layer of bags, then a third, to make it as difficult as possible for any smell to escape. Then I took her to the room where she had kept the grimoire.

'I cleared out the oak cabinet, throwing bottles and jars haphazardly on the ground. I used the hammer to knock the shelves out of place and then I folded her in there, shoved the cat in with her and closed the doors. The lock had been smashed when I'd broken in, so I wound the string around the cabinet to keep the doors together. Round and around, until I had no string left, and until I realised I was doing it in something of a daze.

'Looking down at myself, I noticed I was covered in blood. I went to her bathroom. It was a tiny curtained corner of her bedroom. I got in the bath and turned the water on, scrubbed myself clean. Scrubbed my beard and my feet, then dried myself on what must have been her towel. It smelled faintly musky—the scent of a female.'

Randolph looked up, shrugged. Now the story was

told, he seemed to be regaining his normal bold demeanour. 'I dressed, I left unnoticed. And here I am.'

'And you've covered your tracks?'

'I used three different false names. The business cards have an address in Tel Aviv. They won't find me. Especially if we can use some of our . . . power to ensure my safety.'

'We'll work on it on Sunday night. Randolph, I want to reassure you, there are far uglier secrets in the Humberstone history.'

'I know. Really, I'm not so concerned any more. She was a bitch, she deserved to die.'

Lucien nodded, his lips pressed together. 'Of course she did. And sacrifices do have to be made, we're all aware of that.'

'Yes.'

'Graham's son is here.'

Randolph drew back, astonished. 'Really?'

'It's a long story. You're probably tired, want to get home.'

Randolph shook his head. 'Is he definitely . . .?'

'Without a doubt. He looks exactly like Graham.'

'How old is he?'

'Twenty-seven.' Lucien smiled to himself. 'Can you believe it's been that long? I was only twenty when it happened, Graham just a few years older.'

'And Magnus came wading into the mess, handing out cash and making more of his strange promises. I've never known anybody who cared so much about what happened after his death. It's like he's still controlling us all from beyond the grave. Even Graham's boy, whom he never met—what's his name?'

'Justin. We got word that his mother had died so I made an appearance at the funeral.'

'Did Justin have any idea he was a Humberstone?'

'No. His mother kept her end of the bargain. He'd

never even heard of us. His surname's Penney.'

'Are we going to get him to change it? Become one of us like Magnus wanted it?'

Lucien considered for a few moments. Somebody had to be told eventually and it might as well be Randolph. As much as he disliked him, he was family. Trust was called for. 'I don't think so. I have plans for him.'

'Plans? At the college?'

Lucien smiled. 'Hardly. He's practically a halfwit. I suppose I could explain to you, though I haven't spoken to the others about it yet.'

'Of course you can tell me. We are Humberstones, after all—secrets stay in the family.'

Lucien steepled his hands together and rested his chin on the tips of his fingers. It had been a strange night and he was far too excited to sleep. He wanted to stay up until dawn, talk about, think about, read about the grimoire. It was the most important thing in his world. 'There's a lot for you to catch up on, and a lot of plans to make for the future,' he said eventually. 'I'll get us some more coffee.'

CHAPTER TWENTY

~

While most people were enjoying their Saturday
evening in nightclubs, bars, restaurants or
cinemas, Prudence found herself walking up Laurence
Aswell's street for the second time in a week. She didn't
know what she expected to find—perhaps a gorgeous
redhead's car in the driveway, perhaps a view into a living
room where As would be sitting rubbing the feet of a tall
brunette. Hollywood scenes of sexual betrayal played
themselves out in her head, and for a full five minutes she
actually forgot that As wasn't even hers in the first place.
She was almost disappointed when she finally stood in
front of his house to see no cars around and no lights on,
except for the security light over the door.

She stamped her cigarette out on the pavement and
pushed her hands further into her overcoat. Too cold to
be indulging in this kind of lunacy, really. What did she
stand to gain from it anyway? 'Prudence, you're a fool,'
she said softly, her breath foggy in the air. Her fingers
fiddled with the keys in her pocket as she gazed across
the road at As's house, not wanting to go home but realising it was stupid and futile to stay.

The keys.

Prudence caught her breath. The set of master keys they'd had copied were As's. That meant that As's house keys were probably somewhere in the bunch. She pulled the keys out with a loud jangle and eyed them carefully. Did she dare?

Well, why not? She'd come here with hopes of proving for sure that As was fooling around with somebody else, and if she could get into his house she could probably find something incriminating. Love letters, maybe.

Gathering her determination, she crossed the street and walked up to his front door. She tried a few keys before finding the one that fit, nervous of the security light illuminating everything. But it was a quiet street and no cars went past. Besides, it wasn't like she was breaking in with a crowbar. She shut the cold night air out behind her, switched on the entranceway light, and turned to look at As's house.

Her eyes were adjusting to the dark when she realised that there was a cat sniffing at her toes. She reached down to scoop it up into her arms. As had a cat. How come he'd never mentioned it? How many other details of his life had he not told her?

'Hello there,' she said, rubbing the cat under the chin. 'Sooty would love to meet you one day.'

Taking the cat with her, she moved further into the house. It smelled faintly of jasmine from little bowls of potpourri placed here and there. The living room was large and comfortably furnished, a big-screen television in the corner, a modern stereo against the wall under a copy of Waterhouse's *Lady of Shalott*. Lots of healthy plants. Prudence switched on a lamp and perused the CD stack. Most belonged to As's teenage son, by the looks. Bad taste in music—death metal and American punk.

'See, kitty, this is what testosterone does to perfectly normal little boys,' she said as she surveyed a particularly grisly album cover. She slid it back into its slot and went on her way up the hall to the bedrooms. The first one was obviously the boy's—a television, a super Nintendo, clothes and game cartridges strewn from one end to the other, a Marilyn Manson poster grimacing from the wall. She continued along the hallway, found a tastefully decorated spare bedroom with a stack of storage boxes in the corner, another room with Mandy's sewing machine in it, bolts of cloth draped here and there, a dressmaker's dummy thrusting its breasts out, unaware that it had no head. And then, finally, she got to the bedroom. *His* bedroom.

She flicked on the light and looked around. Bed, dresser, mirrored wardrobe doors, an abnormally green potted palm. She let the cat go and lay down carefully on the bed. So this is what it felt like to lie in As's bed. She closed her eyes, imagined the weight of him on top of her. The cat mewed softly, either hungry or craving more attention. She sighed and opened her eyes, rolled over and caught sight of a packet of birth control pills on the dresser.

'Shit,' she said, getting up and moving to the dresser. As had told her that he and Mandy no longer had sex. Why take the pill when you were already taking abstinence? Prudence was staggered by how unbelievably naïve she had been. She picked up the box and read the sticker. Mandy Aswell.

Fuck Mandy Aswell.

But this wasn't getting her anywhere. She was looking for love letters from the other woman and so far all she had done was take a vicarious tour through As's daily life. The cat was winding around between her ankles so she picked it up again. It purred against her cheek. With her free arm she pulled open the drawers in the dresser one by one. Mandy's underwear, Mandy's sweaters. And in the third drawer As's things, folded neatly and smelling of laundry detergent.

'Kitty, what I'm doing now has gone beyond the curious and is firmly in the realm of the perverse,' she said as she sorted through socks and jocks, hoping every second to close her fingers around an envelope, a card, a token of love. Nothing. The closer she got to the bottom of the drawer, the more holey boxers and frayed heels she found. This was just stupid. She slammed the drawer shut and went to the wardrobe. It was full of Mandy's dresses. Prudence was happy to note that they were all in various shades of beige. How boring. Why anybody would wear beige was unfathomable to her. Did people who wore beige *want* to fade into the background?

She checked that she'd left everything as it was before moving into the en suite bathroom. Not quite as tidy. As's shaving things sitting in a soapy stain, hairspray and deodorant containers capless on the bench, dirty clothes draped over the side of the bath. And the window was open. Obviously they were not security conscious.

A sudden noise from outside made her ears prick up. The cat squeezed out of her arms like toothpaste and padded off into the dark. She hastily backed out of the en suite, turned the bedroom light off and moved nearer to the front door. Keys in the lock. He was home.

What to do now? Should she go out the bathroom window, or should she brazen it out? The cat sat impatiently by the front door. Prudence ducked into the living room, where the light was still on, sat on a couch and waited. She was nothing if not brazen.

First his voice, talking to the cat. 'Hello, Micawber. Have you been behaving yourself?' Then a clatter as he dropped his keys on a table by the door. Then a pause, probably as he realised that there was a light on where there hadn't been when he'd left the house. In a few cautious seconds he was standing at the door to the living room, a KFC bag in one hand.

'Prudence, what the——?'

'Hi. Sorry.'

'How did you get in?'

'Bathroom window. You should be more careful.'

He paused for a few moments, clearly bewildered. Then in an incredulous voice, 'What are you doing here?'

She sighed and rose to stand with him. 'I thought you'd gone out for the evening.'

'I went out to get some fried chicken.' He lifted the KFC bag to demonstrate. 'I always have it on Saturday nights when Mandy isn't here to nag me about heart disease.'

'You can get it skin-free now, can't you?'

'That kind of defeats the purpose of having fried chicken. You still haven't answered my question.'

'Just your standard break and enter. Except I wasn't going to steal anything. I just wanted to see . . . how you lived.'

He shook his head in disbelief. 'Paranoid Prudence on the prowl.'

'Nice alliteration. Ever thought of writing poetry?'

He sighed. 'Come sit in the kitchen with me. The cat seems to like you.' He nodded towards Micawber, who was winding around her legs, purring again.

'Cats always like me. Dogs are another story.'

'He wouldn't like you if he understood anything about human fidelity. He's Mandy's cat, you know. He dotes on her.'

'Cats are notoriously disloyal.'

'Come on.'

She followed him into the kitchen and sat with him at the table. He pulled out his fried chicken and a box of chips and went to the fridge. 'Would you like a drink?'

'Yes, please.'

He poured two glasses of lemonade and sat next to her, offering her some chips. She took some gratefully, remembering that she hadn't eaten since lunchtime.

'Prudence,' he said gently and slowly, 'this has got to stop.'

'I've only done it once.'

'No, not just you coming to my house. Your refusal to accept that our affair is over is . . . disturbing. You must let go.'

She looked down, tears welling in her eyes. 'I feel so stupid.'

'You're not stupid, Prudence. You just do stupid things sometimes.'

'Mandy wears beige. How can you love her?'

'I don't love her. But I like her. I'm used to her.'

'That's the most that a woman who wears beige can expect in the end, to have people get used to her,' she joked, wiping greasy fingers on a napkin. Then in a small voice, 'Is there somebody else?'

His eyes grew stormy. He was twice as attractive when he was angry. 'Prudence, ordinarily I would just say no, but given that our relationship is now strictly professional, I will say that that is none of your business.'

'Our relationship isn't even professional any more, remember?'

He took a fresh piece of chicken from the box. 'Which reminds me, Randolph is back. He'll be at work again on Monday and I've told him to expect you.'

Her heart sank. It was all over. 'Are you sure you're not sick of me because you've got somebody else?'

He set his jaw. 'That is none of your business.'

Infuriating. Why refuse to commit? He knew it would drive her crazy. She pushed back her chair violently, sending the cat scurrying. 'I'm sorry,' she said curtly. 'Goodbye.'

He didn't get up to see her out and she found her own way to the front door and back onto the street. What a foolish, fruitless enterprise this had been. Hands thrust in pockets, she began the long walk home.

The rhythm of her footsteps helped her to think. No evidence of any love affair, but then why would there be anything in his house where Mandy could stumble across it? What about his office, which Prudence still had the keys to? She wavered for a full five minutes, nearly heading straight for the college. But the embarrassment of her exchange with As weighed her down and she changed her mind. Paranoia was not a facility to be nurtured.

Perhaps it would do her good to forget about As for a while. She lit a cigarette and went on her way.

'I'm sure this isn't good for my eyes, Prudence.'

'Stop bitching and read. It's your turn.'

Holly focussed the torchbeam on the page in front of her and began to read. '"I had a dream, which was not all a dream. The bright sun was extinguished, and the stars did wander darkling."' Of all Prudence's imaginative social ideas, this was Holly's favourite so far. It was Thursday night, the three of them were in the Confessional, and they were taking turns reading their favourite spooky stories and creepy poems by the light of a fast-dying torch. As usual, the candles were in the corners and they were all tipsy on some to-die-for red wine stolen from Mr Emerson's ever-dwindling supply. So far Prudence had read them Poe, Poe, and more Poe, Justin had read parts from Goethe's *Faust*, and Holly had dug up some Coleridge and now some Byron.

The torch managed to hold out until the eleventh line before fading into nothing. Holly gave it a shake and it glimmered once, then died forever.

'Shit!' Prudence exclaimed, grabbing the torch from Holly and shaking it violently.

'I guess we should have brought spare batteries,' Justin remarked.

'I thought these ones were fresh. Damn, and the night's

still so young.' She cast the torch aside petulantly. 'What are we going to do now?'

'I suppose we could go home,' Holly suggested.

'But it was just getting interesting. I was just starting to get that hysterical prepubescent feeling. I *live* for that feeling.'

'Prudence, you must have a store of creepy stories in your head,' Justin said. 'Surely you could entertain us for hours.'

Prudence grinned. 'Yeah, I guess I could. Here's an idea—somebody put the candles out.'

'I don't know, Prudence, it would be pitch black,' Holly said, feeling a little chill walk over her.

'That's the whole idea. Go on, Justin, put the candles out.'

Justin turned to Holly. 'What do you think? Not too scary?'

Holly became aware that the whole mood of the evening depended upon her willingness to join in. 'Okay, put the candles out,' she said, 'but I get to hang onto the matches.'

Prudence passed Holly the matchbox as Justin went to each corner to blow the candles out. She pocketed the matches and waited for the darkness to engulf her. The last candle was extinguished and the sudden blackness almost took her breath away.

Justin's voice came from a few metres away. 'Now how am I going to get back without standing on somebody? I can't see a thing.'

'We're over here,' Prudence said. 'Follow the sound of my voice. Holly, give me your hand.'

Holly squirmed forward and reached out for Prudence. Her friend took her hand and squeezed tightly.

'Don't freak out,' Prudence said softly.

'You must think I'm such a wimp,' Holly said, laughing lightly. Justin nearly tripped over her.

'Sorry,' he said. 'Who did I kick?'

'Me,' Holly said. 'Sit down here.'

'Take one my hands and one of Holly's,' Prudence said.

Holly felt Justin's hand brush her knee and she grabbed it with her own hand. The three of them sat in a close circle in the absolute darkness.

'Our eyes will adjust soon, right?' Holly said.

'You won't be able to see much,' Prudence replied, giving her hand another squeeze. 'Relax. Trust me, trust Justin. This is a character-building experience.'

They were silent a few moments. Gradually Holly could make out the difference between her two friends and the darkness. But there were no details to focus on, just an eerie silence and an obscurity that seemed to reel away from her into infinity. She could hear her own heartbeat and breathing as if amplified, yet her mind felt strangely dislocated from her body. Prudence's warm fingers stroked her own, rings pressing into her palm. On the other side, Justin's hand held hers lightly but firmly.

'When I was eighteen,' Prudence began in a slow, sombre voice, 'my grandmother died. We'd been close when I was little, but since we'd moved to Melbourne I'd hardly seen her, and me being a teenager, Nana wasn't the coolest person in the world to hang with. We flew up north for the funeral. There was a service at a funeral parlour, then my parents and my aunts and uncles were all going to the cemetery to watch the interment. I couldn't bear to see them put her in the ground, so I said I'd go back to Nana's and get it ready for the wake. You know, open the windows and defrost the teacake. My Uncle Jim had inherited the house and he was already planning all these changes to it so he could rent it out. I thought it might be my last chance to be in Nana's house as it used to be, and I went on my own.

'I wandered through and I looked at everything.

Among her teacups was the tiny teaset she'd let Julia and me drink out of as children. In her dresser were the seventies-style earrings we'd played dress-ups with. Under her bed, where they had always been, were her drawings, neatly stacked one on another, separated by tissue paper. I leafed through them all, just like I did when I was a kid. Wishing that I could draw.' Prudence laughed derisively. 'Another fucking talent I didn't manage to inherit.

'It was late afternoon, overcast and dreary, an evening breeze quickening, coming off the sea. Just me and my memories. Dusk and dust and lavender. And I began to feel, so strongly, that Nana was there with me, sharing that last hour with me.' She paused and took a deep breath, as though trying to hold back tears. 'That's all.'

'Do you think it was her ghost?' Justin asked.

'Who knows? I just wanted to tell you guys that story. Today's four years since she died. I still miss her.'

The silent dark set in again, the black seeming to bleed into Holly's perimeter.

Prudence's voice rang out bravely in the obscurity. 'Do you miss your mother, Justin?'

The answer was immediate, cold. 'No.'

'No you don't, or no you won't answer?'

'No, I don't miss her.'

'But you loved her?'

Holly couldn't believe Prudence was being so forward.

'Of course I loved her,' Justin said softly, 'she was my mother.'

There was a long pause and Holly was glad she could feel her friends' hands. Otherwise she might have believed herself to have disappeared into forever.

'But I don't miss her,' Justin said at last. 'She was a constant source of misery. She was a sad, shambling wreck, shuffling through my life and turning everything to grey. I prefer her absence. It doesn't grow. It hurts but it doesn't move or act unexpectedly. I don't miss her at all.'

Holly realised she'd been holding her breath. She squeezed Justin's hand. 'I'm so sorry.'

He was silent again and she wished she could see his face. But she also knew that if she could see his face he would never have said what he had. The darkness gave them all a temporary anonymity. She wondered, a little cynically, whether Prudence had planned it that way.

'Ghost stories, Prudence,' Holly said gently. 'That's why we put the candles out. You were going to scare the pants off us with ghost stories.'

'But ghost stories *are* about death. About what happens on the other side of mortality. Just think, death is even darker than this room, right now. Because there's no Justin, no Holly. No matches to light if you get freaked out.'

'No getting freaked out,' Justin added softly. 'No nothing.'

'Please don't,' Holly said. 'It's too weird, it's too dark and too far underground to start talking about death.' Holly could honestly say that she went through life very rarely thinking about the big issues like death and God, but here, with her sight obliterated, the strange atmosphere, the charged emotions, talk of death scared her. She felt like she was wearing a coat of warm stars that ran over her skin in mad patterns. 'It's too big to think about,' she said in a whisper.

'All right, I'll tell a ghost story. It's a true one, I just read it the other day.'

'Can we have some candlelight again?' Holly asked.

'Sure,' Prudence said kindly. The circle broke and Holly relit the candles. As Prudence told her story—not particularly frightening, but highly imaginative—with her usual verve, Holly felt herself relaxing, laughing, enjoying herself.

When she had finished, Prudence turned to Holly and said, 'You'll be interested in something else I read in that book, Holly. Remember how you were going on when you were delirious about ghosts making you sick? A woman in Mexico had exactly that problem, and she treated it with motion-sickness tablets. Apparently it's a disturbance to the inner ear, just like motion sickness, that makes some people allergic to ghosts.'

Justin laughed cynically. 'Allergic to ghosts?'

'Hey, don't laugh at me. It was Holly who thought she had spirit-induced gastroenteritis.'

'I had an excuse, I was delirious,' Holly protested, her excitement growing. Motion-sickness tablets—was it that simple, that mundane?

Justin yawned and suggested they pack up and go home as he had a nine a.m. appointment with Jane.

'Sure,' Prudence said. 'I suppose I should try to get some work done in the morning. How about you, Holly? What time will you come in tomorrow?'

The question shook her out of her reverie. 'What?'

'Will you be in early enough for a cup of coffee with Justin and me before his meeting?'

'No,' Holly said casually. 'I'll be in a little later.' She had to pay a visit to the chemist.

The sweet twilight, the smell of old books, just Holly and the promise of Christian's presence. She swallowed a couple of the little tablets, washed them down with flat warm lemonade out of a can. She'd been saving it all afternoon. The mirror was ready, the light was out, the candles wavering.

'It's all right, Christian,' she said into the night. 'I promise I won't get sick this time. And you must have missed me as much as I've missed you.'

This time he came right away.

CHAPTER TWENTY-ONE

⁓

He said her name as he materialised in a sad breath. 'Holly.' She found she was on the verge of tears.

'Christian. I've missed you.'

'Close your eyes.'

She closed her eyes and felt his warm hands on her ribcage, hot lips on her neck. She savoured his touch, each point of contact making her nerves tingle and sing. As the caresses moved lower, she let her head fall back and gave herself up to the dark, lush sweetness.

When Christian had expertly taken her to a shimmering climax, she opened her eyes and watched his reflection for a few moments. A melancholy ache had begun to grow around her heart, a sad bruise under her ribs. She loved him, but she was separated from him by the most profound obstacle imaginable—the passage between life and death.

Finally, she said, 'What's it like to die?'

Christian looked surprised, then considered her question for a moment. 'It's very frightening to die. You lose control of your body. You want to make limbs and joints work but they won't. The instinct to survive is over-whelming, it prevails over everything else, and moments draw out forever as you desperately try to hang on to any last thread of being.'

'And then?'

'Then there are long stretches of darkness, spinning away into eternity. Moments of strange, disjointed consciousness. Then there is Elysium, or the abyss for some, nothing at all for others, and for me . . .' He lifted his hand and gestured around.

'And you're still here because of Peter?'

'Peter did something very bad, and I intend to atone for him.'

'How bad?'

'I have to tell you all of it. You'll judge Peter unfairly otherwise. He had good reasons for all he did. You love me, Holly, so perhaps you'll understand that he also loved me. That he sometimes took tortuous routes through convention and morality to protect me.'

'Go on then. You came back to London after seeing Lord Burghley.'

'Peter advertised a business in mesmerism, saying he specialised in treating nervous problems. Clients began to arrive sporadically. The chime of the doorbell was a sign for Rosalind to hide in her room. Usually I would hover nearby as Peter let the clients—always ladies—into his house. Together the three of us had cleaned and decorated the spare upstairs room. A leather couch and a compact bookcase took up most of the space. Peter had also bought three framed prints, and we had scrubbed the wallpaper back to its original dark green. It was by far the most appealing room in the house now that it was clean, and my job was to keep it that way. I dusted and tidied it every day.

'At first the clients weren't intrusive because there were so few. Later they would start to become bothersome, but back then there were barely enough for Peter to keep up the minimum payments to the Humberstones to prevent them sending him to debtor's prison.

'In fact, Lucy Humberstone—the wife to Philbert—had been one of Peter's earliest customers. Peter told me that she had not yet produced an heir, and Philbert was sure that some nervous disorder on her part was to blame. So he sent her along once a week, and Peter treated her and received no payment. Rather, the fee came off his enormous debt to the Humberstones.'

He stopped for a moment and seemed to be choosing his words carefully. 'There was something beautiful and yet sly about Lucy Humberstone. She was perhaps in her late twenties or early thirties. Her eyes were almost black, her hair yellow-blonde. The way she looked at me as she passed me in the parlour made me feel strangely thrilled. So much so that I began to have a superficial prejudice against any day of the week that wasn't Wednesday, which was the day she came. She was very independent and came alone in a hansom cab, dressed in expensive clothes and with jewellery dripping from her throat and ears and wrists.

'Look around you, Holly. Look at what the Humberstones have, over a century later. Peter's blood is in these walls. They drove him to do what he did, as surely as if they commanded him under threat of his life. They possessed so much, and yet they hounded him for what he owed until he became desperate.'

He paused, his eyes turned heavenwards. Holly's eyes drank in his angelic face. Her desire was almost an agony. What good could it do her to be in love with this being? But in love she was, for better or for worse.

With a slow blink, he continued. 'Peter resumed his Sunday night meetings with his associates. They were angry with him for leaving London for so long without telling them, but for the first few weeks they performed their ritual as usual. Only when their tempers had eased did Peter introduce to them the idea of my being part of the ritual.

'That first evening I took part, Peter led me solemnly into the ritual space, naked but for a long black robe. I was frightened of course. I didn't like the room; I liked his associates even less, apart from Patrick who gave me a reassuring smile. Peter sat me down in the middle of the circle they formed, and gave me a pen and ink. Then he opened up a bound book at an empty page and placed it in my lap. Peter wished to maintain the charade that I was mute, so I was under strict instructions not to say a word, merely to write down what I saw and heard.

'The five of them settled around me. Peter presided while his associates exchanged dubious glances, sure that I did not belong here in their ritual space. Edmund and Thurber wore their usual supercilious expressions, while Ezekial, cold eyes glittering, pointedly stared at me. I tried not to meet their eyes and kept my gaze focussed on the empty page in front of me.

'They began to chant lowly, voices humming and buzzing on the air. Sweat beaded my brow as the temperature in the room shot up. Even my mind seemed to grow hotter, my thinking less distinct; it was like trying to make sense through a cloud of steam. I didn't even notice when my eyes closed, and it seemed perfectly natural suddenly to be standing in the alien landscape again, in a valley between the mountains of hell.

'Like the last time, a throng of beings crowded about me, but this time I did not scream. I knew that I merely had to open my eyes to make the world return, but I had vowed to myself not to disappoint Peter. I held firm, bathed in sweat, my breathing laboured, while they examined me, their hot sulphurous breath toxic in my face.

'From behind me I heard a call—my own name—and

at first I thought it was the real world intruding, but the call sounded again and I spun around to see where it came from. On a black hill in the distance, the glow of fire silhouetting him against the infernal sky, a creature beckoned to me.

'I made to move my feet, but it wasn't necessary to move my feet in this place. Merely by willing it I approached the being. He was hideous—perhaps once a man, but now scarred and withered. Only a few tufts of powdery hair covered his shiny pate, his ears appeared to be melted into his head. One eye was half closed by a deformed eyelid, the other was a glimmering yellow. He stank of rotting flesh and burning hair.

'"I have a message for your master," he said.

'I tried to speak but couldn't make my tongue move.

'"Tell him Aathahorus is prepared to deal with him, but with him alone. There are terms which we need to discuss. You may be his intermediary, but the others must go."

'I nodded. My tongue was parched as I ran it over dry, cracked lips. Still words would not come. In fact, I couldn't think of any words at all. The longer I stayed there, the more I forgot about the outside world. It seemed to be only a watercolour illusion—pretty, but ultimately just a fantasy used to ameliorate a darker reality.

'A loud shouting and cursing brought me back to myself, and the feel of Peter's hand closing around my upper arm and shaking me. I suddenly remembered where I was. As I opened my eyes I could feel something burning my fingers and looked down in a kind of dazed curiosity. Peter and his associates were shouting about something.

'"Put it out before the whole book is destroyed!" Ezekial exclaimed.

'Somehow in my trance I had inked the pen and pressed it violently into the page. A strange sigil marked the page in splattered ink, and to my horror the sigil was smouldering, tiny flames licking along the intricate lines and curves. Without thinking, I threw the end of my cloak over the page and smothered the flames before they grew and consumed the entire book. Peter snatched the grimoire out of my hands and examined it closely. My fingers were still closed around the pen, ink splattered along my hand and wrist. My pulse raced and my breath was ragged. The room cooled suddenly, bringing me out in gooseflesh.

'Ezekial was shouting at Peter, his lizard eyes flashing. "This is what has become of your grand scheme, Owling. This is what happens to stupid men who let their desire override their common sense. The boy has almost destroyed the grimoire, now will you listen to reason and leave him in your bedchamber where he belongs?"

'Even Patrick, who was usually very affectionate with me, agreed. "Badly done, Owling. This has all been a bit of a fond notion. Send the boy back downstairs and let's get on with our work."

'The others agreed in angry mumbles and murmurs, and I was so mortified that I hung my head and began to cry. Peter put an arm around me and drew me to him, defending me from their insults.

'"You fools! Christian didn't set the book alight—something else did. Something from the other side. It could be the most valuable contact we have made, and the book is still intact, no harm is done." But they wouldn't listen to him. They thought that I had defaced the book on purpose through some kind of trickery. I was ashamed and insulted and I fled the room, sobbing with shock and humiliation, dropping my robe behind me.

'I ran naked into Peter's room and burrowed beneath the bedclothes. Loud shouts and recriminations were coming from the reading room, and I heard the associates breaking up and leaving. One of them, I could not tell which, stuck his head in at Peter's bedroom door and saw me huddled under the covers. He laughed and muttered something pejorative about Peter's sexual preference before going on his way. One by one the others left, Peter calling insults at them. Somebody knocked over a vase— probably on purpose—and I heard it smash to pieces in the hallway. I wondered if Rosalind was afraid of the ruckus, but then I remembered that Rosalind hardly seemed afraid of anything.

'Some time after that, Peter's bulky shadow darkened the doorway. I flinched instinctively, even though I knew that Peter was on my side. He came to the bed and shrugged off his robe, slipping naked under the covers beside me. I cuddled against him and he stroked my hair.

'"I'm sorry, Christian," he said at last. "I'm sorry that you had to endure their abuse."

'"I'm sorry that I broke up your group."

'"Oh, they'll be back. Next Sunday when they've cooled off. You're not to worry."

'We lay there silently for a long time, my face pressed into his soft shoulder, my fingers lost in the thick hair that grew on his chest. I was almost dropping off to sleep when he spoke again.

'"What did you see, Christian?"

'I started awake and shifted to a sitting position. "A devil spoke to me."

'"Who was he? Did he say a name?"

'I nodded, racking my brain but unable to remember the name. The memory of my trance had grown vague soon after I had returned to consciousness. "I've forgotten it. It started with A."

'"It's no matter. Come with me." He heaved himself out of the bed, threw his black robe around him and moved to the door. I followed him to the reading room, then hesitated at the door, nervous.

'"Don't be afraid, Christian. While you're with me, you're safe."

'I nodded and he led me into the room. He lit a lantern and I found my robe on the floor and gathered it around me. Dropping to his knees, he searched about on his bookcase for a large volume bound in leather. He pulled it out and reached for the grimoire, which still lay open at the burnt page.

'As he leafed through pages and muttered to himself, I looked around the room. Somehow I couldn't get accustomed to the feel of the place. The corners seemed dark and hot, the air somehow thicker, as though a million voices, just on the other side of audibility, murmured around me.

'"Christian, I think that this sigil is the name of the demon you encountered," Peter was saying. He had overlaid a sigil glyph on the page of the grimoire and was tracing it with a steady finger. "Aa—th—a—ho—ru—s. Does that sound right? Aathahorus?"

'It was the right name, but it sounded different in my head now. Like when you dream something that makes no sense upon waking. I nodded solemnly. "Yes, Peter, that was its name."

'"Good, good. And did this being, did this Aathahorus have anything to say for itself?"

'Hearing the being's name triggered my memory, and the sentences came to me, coherent and whole. "He said I had to pass on a message for my master, for you. He had terms to discuss, but he wants to deal with you alone. I can go between you, but the others cannot be part of it."

'Peter's eyes bulged in shock. "Me alone?"

'I nodded. Peter grabbed me around the upper arms and shook me. My cloak fell off my shoulders and pooled in my lap. "Why didn't you say earlier? My God, Christian. It wants to deal with me alone? My God, but that's wonderful. Then the others weren't necessary, were *never* necessary. What a fool I've been."

'Even though he was shaking me violently, I understood that he was more excited than angry. I felt proud to be the one to impart such important news to him and didn't try to remove his hands, despite the fact that they were pressed hard enough into my flesh to bruise. He let me go suddenly and dropped back to sit on his haunches.

'"But what to do now, my lad, what to do now?" Chin in hand, he pondered for a few minutes while I waited upon his wisdom. Slowly he lifted his eyes to meet mine, his mouth set in a hard line.

'"Christian, will you help me with something?"

'"I'll do anything for you, Peter."

'He smiled. "Yes, you will, won't you," he said, more to himself than to me. "My Christian will do anything for me. What a good lad you are. And for being such a good lad, you can sleep in my bed tonight."

'True to his word, he walked me back to his bedroom and tucked me in. However, he did not join me. I put my arms out to him. "Peter? Are you not coming to bed?"

'He shook his head and moved to his wardrobe, where he began to dress himself in his going-out clothes. "No, no, Christian. I'm very busy, I have things to organise. You sleep tight and I'll be back in a few hours. You've been a good lad, a very good lad." He approached the bed, fully dressed, and touched my face. "Look at you," he said, "you're nearly a grown man and here I am talking to you like a child. And you haven't lost an ounce of your beauty, my Christian. My angel."

'I pressed my lips into his palm and kissed it. He pulled his hand away gently. "Sleep well, my angel," he said as he left. I heard him on the stairs, then the sound of the front door closing behind him as he left the house.

'I stretched myself out in the big comfortable bed, but

sleep did not come easily. Every time I began to drift off I was visited by shadowy traces of my earlier vision in the reading room. The outline of the mountains against the burning sky would be pressed into my eyelids, or the echo of Aathahorus's hissing voice would murmur, muffled and rasping, in my ears. I felt profoundly that something about me had changed forever. Now I had seen those things, they would always be with me in some small way.'

He stopped and Holly gazed at his face.

'And was that true?' she asked. 'Were you changed forever?'

'Yes, I think I was. Certainly, I mark that point as the commencement of my adulthood—strange, stunted creature that I was. It was the first significant moment of self-consciousness, of realisation that there is no going back. That time passes, that life assails you with events that alter you in unpredictable ways, that only you can look from behind your eyes, and to the rest of the world you are an object held in its gaze.'

'How old were you when you . . .' Holly paused, not wanting the last part of the question to be true, but realising that there was no changing the facts, 'when you died?'

'Seventeen,' he replied. 'It happened shortly after my seventeenth birthday.'

'And how did you . . .?'

'Under the water, Holly. In the cold, cold Thames.'

Holly felt tears pricking at her eyes. 'Oh God, I'm so . . .' Sorry wasn't the right word. There were no right words for talking to a ghost. 'I wish you had been born one hundred years later.'

'I'm here now, with you.'

'I wish I could touch you,' she said in a small voice.

'Would you like me to continue the story?' he said gently.

She nodded.

'Peter came to me later in the week. Rosalind had just gone to bed, and I was dropping off to sleep in front of the fire when Peter shook me awake.

'"Christian," he said, "wake up, lad, I have something to show you."

'I sat up drowsily and pulled my blanket around my shoulders. "What is it?" I asked.

'"Come with me to the dining room."

'I followed him to the dining room and he sat me down at the large dusty table. He placed a small silver box in front of me. "There," he said, "have a look."

'I fiddled with the clasp and the small box sprang open. Inside was a fine white powder. "What is it?"

'"Don't touch it. It's a surprise for my associates. I need you to help me."

'I looked at him curiously. "What must I do?"

'"On Sunday, after we've performed our ritual, I'll invite them downstairs for drinks. I'll send you off to pour the wine and you must place one spoonful of the powder in each drink except mine. Do not touch the powder lest you contaminate it. Most importantly, make sure you serve me first and that I get an unadulterated drink. Understand?"

'"But what does the powder do?"

'"It's just a drug to make them relaxed."

'I eyed him dubiously.

'"People pay good money for this powder," he said, snapping the lid shut. "It's my gift to my associates, to make up for the argument last Sunday."

'"Is it opium?" Among Rosalind's many fantastic tales was one about opium pirates in the East Indies.

'"The less you know, the better," Peter said with a stern brow. "Just ensure that I get none. Those exotic medicines make me ill. You wouldn't want me to get sick, would you?"

'Not entirely convinced that what he was getting me to do was the beneficent act he was pretending it was, I concurred to his will.

'I thought little more upon the silver box of powder that week because Peter went on a sudden cleaning spree, dragging Rosalind and me out of bed every morning to don old clothes and help him clean up. Rosalind got kitchen duty and I was assigned the cellars. In all honesty I think Rosalind had drawn the short straw because our kitchen was a filthy, stinking mess. The cellar was damp and dusty but did not have the years of Peter's accumulated filth to excavate.

'I crept down the stairs with my lantern and surveyed the task. Old, broken furniture was cast haphazardly in there, and a half-dozen bottles of old wine that had probably turned to vinegar. Peter kept his good wine upstairs. Books and papers lay about, some spoiled by age and rising damp, their pages swelled and the words faded into illegible smudges. I leaned my broom against the stairs and went about organising it all.

'Peter came down later that evening to congratulate me. I had cleared away the furniture, stacked the books and papers neatly against one wall, and swept up the bodies of a thousand dead insects into a pile under the stairs.

'"Well done, Christian, well done," he said, giving me a hearty thump on the back. "Now you go on upstairs and keep Rosalind company. I've a few things to sort through down here and a few tasks to take care of."

'I left the lamp with him and went upstairs to find Rosalind.

'She was in the dining room, her hair tied up in an old scarf, her face smudged with dirt as she washed down the walls. The wallpaper was springing back to vividly coloured life wherever her soapy rag splashed and rubbed against it. When she saw me approach, her face lit up.

'"Oh, Christian, thank God! Papa has had me working

305

like a slave all day, but he said I could stop as soon as you came for me." She dropped her rag into a bucket of dirty water and threw her arms around me. I realised that I too must have been covered in dust and sweat. "Where is Papa now?"

'"He's in the cellar. I think he's sorting through his papers. There were a lot of old books and ledgers under there."

'She took a step back and examined me. "You're so dirty. We're both so dirty. We should bathe, you know."

'Bathing wasn't a practice that any of us took much interest in, even though Lord Burghley had insisted on us bathing regularly while we stayed with him. In the house on Milton Close, Peter had a small tiled room leading off his own chamber, with a stained enamel tub in it.

'Rosalind grabbed my hand and began to drag me into the freshly scrubbed kitchen. "Come on, we can make believe we're in Arabia, we can pretend the water is goat's milk. Yes, just like an Arabian queen and king."

'She set water on the stove to boil and made me begin to fill the bath. Up and down the stairs I went with the water jug. We took the hot water up last, careful not to spill any on ourselves. The old mirror in the bathroom began to steam up. Rosalind hunted in Peter's chest for soap and towels, then we stood facing each other on either side of the bath, both of us jolted out of our Arabian fancy by the sudden realisation that we would have to disrobe in front of one another. Somehow in the past few months we had learned the shame of adults.

'Rosalind giggled. "You undress first," she said.

'I shook my head. "Perhaps we should take turns bathing."

'She sighed and dropped her eyes. "I suppose we could, though it wouldn't be nearly as much fun." Suddenly she looked up brightly. "I know, I'll close my eyes and you get in the tub, and then you can close your eyes while I get in. Once we're in the water it won't matter, will it?"

'I suspected it would matter. But I was curious, I was excited. An illicit thrill spread through me. "You don't think Peter will be cross if he finds us?"

'"Oh no, of course not. We're like brother and sister, aren't we? I bet brothers and sisters bathe together all the time." She made a sweeping gesture with her hand that seemed to indicate the whole world beyond the walls of our house. "Besides, Papa will probably be in the cellar for hours yet. Go on, I'll cover my eyes."

'She put her hands firmly over her eyes and I quickly struggled out of my dirty clothes and sank into the warm bath. My arms and back, aching from all the work I had done that day, began to ease in the warm water.

'"I'm in," I said, drawing my knees up to my chest.

'Rosalind uncovered her eyes. "Now it's my turn," she said. "Don't you dare peek."

'I placed my hands over my eyes but couldn't resist parting my fingers a little way over my left eye. The sight of a small firm breast tipped with a pink nipple shocked me a little, causing me to close my eyes in embarrassment.

'"One more garment," I heard her say. Then she must have extinguished the lamp, because suddenly it was very dark. I felt her body slide into the water, her feet brushing my ankles as she settled herself in.

'"You can look now."

'I took my hands away. A small sliver of moonlight from a tiny high window was all that illuminated the room. Rosalind was little more than a pale glow across from me, a few tantalising shadows gliding over hollows and slopes on her body. Embarrassed, I began to scrub my arms and chest with purposeful energy. She leaned across and grabbed one of my hands.

'"Here," she said. I felt the slippery touch of soap in my hand. "Half the cake for you, half for me."

'Oh, how I wanted to touch her body, how I wanted

to slide the soap over those sweet, wet curves. I was glad it was dark, because there was no hiding my desire for her—it was physically manifest. But we washed ourselves in silence and in isolation from each other, apart from the occasional accidental brush of limb against limb, always accompanied by a murmured and hurried apology.

'The water had cooled considerably when we finished. Rosalind shyly instructed me to look the other way as she stepped out of the bath and into a waiting towel, then she handed me the other towel and told me to get out of the bath. I did so, wrapping the towel modestly around my hips. We turned our backs to each other while we dried. The air was cold on my wet skin and I rubbed myself hurriedly, only to turn and see that Rosalind was watching me.

'I was embarrassed, even though I knew I would be little more than a dark shape in the moonlit room.

'"Christian," she said, "take a step back."

'I covered myself with my towel and did as she said, looking at her curiously.

'"And another." Her voice was soft and warm among the cold tiles. I took another step back and she said with a sigh, "Ah, that's better."

'I realised that I was standing directly in the ray of moonlight that shot through the high window. I hung my head modestly, damp hair trailing on my shoulders. She was with me a moment later, her arms around my hips, pulling me to her.

'"You are so very beautiful, Christian," she murmured into my ear. "Look, look we are both beautiful."

'I lifted my head and gazed at us in the mirror. We were like two pale fallen angels in the moonlight. Her golden hair seemed to glow around her face, her white body pressed into mine. All my senses came alive, my heart thundered under my ribs. She loosened my towel and it dropped to the floor. Naked, we embraced for an instant, my hardened prick pressed momentarily into her soft belly. Then she was backing away, laughing lightly, collecting her towel around herself and shaking her damp curls. "Oh, Christian, you are wicked. I felt it, I felt it." And she giggled madly as I realised she meant my erection.

'"I can't help it," I said defensively.

'"Come, let's get dressed. We should never do this again, and we should never mention it. I felt it, Christian, and I know what it means when it's hard. I mean, I know what it's for. And that is something we can never do."

'Shaking with humiliation, I picked up my clothes and began to struggle into them before I realised they were still filthy from the day's work. Rosalind pulled on her chemise and gathered her other clothes up in a bundle against her chest. "I'm going to bed," she said quickly, almost breathlessly. "I'll speak to you in the morning."

'With that she was gone and I was left, my dirty clothes half on, half off, in the dark bathroom. I kicked off the garments once more and went to Peter's room to find something fresh to wear. I pulled out a red satin housecoat and slipped it on, then lay back on the bedspread. My loins ached, my prick was still half erect. I rolled onto my stomach and pressed my groin into the mattress. The satin slid against me with an unbearably light friction. I imagined her body again, fresh and soft. I moved my legs, making the satin rub me again. Guilty, panting in the dark, I rubbed myself against the satin, against the bed, until I soiled the inside of the housecoat with my seed. Then I flipped over onto my back to think about what Rosalind had said. "I know what it's for, and that's something we can never do." I knew without doubt that she was right. We were not destined to be lovers. But part of her sentence began to play on my mind—"I know what it's for." How did she know? She was barely fourteen, had spent her entire life in this house. Yes, she read widely and had an active imagination, but there was something too knowing, too impure about the way she had said it. And while I heeded her wish in never mentioning the event again, I found myself wondering many times after that just what she had meant. Just how she knew.'

CHAPTER TWENTY-TWO

~

'**W**ere you infatuated with Rosalind?' Holly
asked. 'Were you in love with her?'

'I loved her, yes,' Christian said. 'Not quite as a lover,
not quite as a brother. But now it was for me as though
a perfect tune had gone slightly false. Like one small
dissonant note had been played, and it would recur occasionally and without warning in amongst the sweet notes.
I did my utmost to keep her out of my guilty fantasies,
and I mostly managed—especially on the days after a visit
from Lucy Humberstone. I must admit that Lucy's narrow
black eyes often featured in my waking dreams. Not to
mention other parts of her that I had never seen.'

Holly laughed, and Christian smiled at her in the
mirror. 'It's lovely to hear you laugh,' he said.

'It's lovely to see you smile,' she replied.

He nodded, but the smile died on his lips. 'I should
not smile,' he said, 'for something very dark happened
next.

'Peter's associates came by on the following Sunday, and
there were apologies and self-recriminations in the air as
they ascended the stairs to attend to their ritual without me.

I had the little silver box of powder in the kitchen with the glasses and the wine, and I sat awaiting further instructions from Peter.

'The minutes ticked by on the clock over the mantelpiece, echoing through the empty ground floor of the house. I played with the glasses, lined them up like soldiers, viewed the world through their thick bases, stood them upside down and stacked them like a precarious pyramid. Candlelight glinted off the heavy crystal cut, reflecting things innumerable times and in strangely distorted shapes. At last I heard the sound of voices on the stairs.

'I rose and peeped into the parlour. Peter was laughing and talking with his associates. I thought that perhaps my fears were unfounded, perhaps the white powder really was an expensive treat to celebrate their regrouping. Peter caught my eye and smiled.

'"Christian, there you are, lad. How about pouring us all a glass of wine." Then turning to the others he said, "What do you say, fellows, shall we drink to our little magic circle?"

'They ayed and nodded, even Ezekial who was in an unusually good humour. Patrick smiled at me in his moon-faced way, and I smiled back. Yes, a drink for all of them to celebrate. My humiliation from the previous week was almost forgotten.

'I went back into the kitchen and poured five glasses of red wine. With a steady hand I spooned white powder into four glasses and stirred. I set those four glasses on a silver tray in a group and then placed Peter's wine glass at some distance from them, so I wouldn't forget which was his. I was very careful, watching his glass as I carried the tray through to the parlour, almost as though I were afraid the glasses would change places of their own accord if I took my eyes off them for a moment. I placed the tray on the mantelpiece and took Peter's drink directly to him.

He smiled and nodded and I was filled with pride that he trusted me with this task.

'One by one I gave the men their glasses. Peter waited until they had all been served, then raised his own drink.

'"A toast to the magic circle," he said, eyes burning bright with excitement.

'They lifted their glasses. I took the silver tray under my arm and hovered near the hallway. One by one they drank, they complimented the wine, they drank again. Peter urged them to finish their drinks like men, not to sip like women. They laughed and followed his lead. I relaxed. All were in merry spirits. My back was turned and I was halfway out the door when Patrick coughed loudly.

'I spun around. Patrick had a hand to his chest and he coughed and coughed convulsively. Speckles of blood sprayed from his lips. Edmund was reaching for him to help him when he too was doubled over with coughing. Thurber collapsed into a chair, his hands to his mouth, making a gagging, choking noise. Only Ezekial still stood, his face drained of blood, his eyes popping as horrible realisation dawned.

'He turned to me, pointed one long finger and shouted, "He's poisoned us. He's ..." But his voice trailed into an enormous cough. Blood and regurgitated wine spurted from his lips. He stumbled towards me, knocking over furniture and nearly slipping on the rug. I screamed and backed away, dropping the silver tray and putting my hands out before me defensively. Ezekial was too quick and too strong for me. His hands closed over my wrists and he jerked me violently towards him, his fingers pressed cruelly into my flesh.

'"You ..." he coughed again and blood spattered my face. "You ... killed ... me."

'His fingernails had drawn blood on my arms. He threw me with the last of his strength against the wall and

313

I slammed into it with a violent thud and slid to the ground. He landed on top of me, pummelling me with baby-weak fists; then, with a hacking cough and a toxic gasp, he died on top of me.

'I blacked out from shock and pain for I know not how long—perhaps minutes, perhaps only seconds—but eventually I became aware that Peter was laughing in the background. I looked up, shocked and dazed. Edmund, Thurber and Patrick were all dead, their lifeless bodies littered around the room like discarded playthings. I struggled out from beneath Ezekial's body, wiping blood from my face, bubbling hysteria barely repressed in my throat.

'"They thought you did it," he said, doubled over. "They didn't even know it was me. Hee, hee, hee, the perfect crime."

'I opened my mouth and wanted to find a word, the perfect word to say to him to express what I felt. All that came out was a long, hysterical scream. In seconds he was next to me, his hand clamped over my mouth.

'"Shh, Christian, shh there, boy. Quiet now. Be quiet for Peter. It's all right. Everything is all right. Shh, boy, shh." He calmed me down gently. I closed my eyes, the sight of the bodies too sick and awesome for my mind. Their hands outstretched, blood drying in a light crust on their chins.'

'Oh my God,' Holly said, tears in her eyes. 'Oh, Christian, poor Christian.'

'Peter took me into the kitchen and gave me a glass of brandy—I wouldn't touch the wine he offered me—and he sat stroking my hair for a long time. But I couldn't relax knowing their bodies were out there, waiting for me to see them again, the dark, blunt horror of the act lurking in the parlour.

'So Peter told me to fortify myself for the final round and I followed him to the parlour. One by one we dragged them through the kitchen and down the stairs to the cellar. I now knew what Peter had been doing down there on the night that Rosalind and I had bathed together. He had not been sorting papers, rather he had been removing the bricks in the cellar wall one by one, revealing the dark earth behind it. He had driven wooden stakes into the earth, and now we tied each body up, arms apart in a profane parody of a crucifixion, side by side in the cellar wall.

'It took forever. I worked in a strange delirium, dragging bodies, helping Peter hold them to the wall, tying knots, watching the bodies sag against their bonds, blocking my ears as Peter broke their knees with a mallet so that their legs wouldn't bend and protrude into the brickwork. Sick, thudding pain resided in my breast, and my life seemed glazed and unreal, a painting seen from afar.

'But Ezekial. Oh God, he was so big and so heavy. And his eyes . . . Peter rolled back a lid to check he was dead and it was as though he were still looking at me, still saying with that one dead eye, "You killed me." Because I knew as certainly as I knew that daylight would come again even after this night of horror that I had killed him. That I had killed all of them.'

'But it wasn't you,' Holly protested. 'Peter made you do it. He lied to you, he didn't tell you it was poison.'

'Acid, Holly. It was acid. It ravaged their gullets and their stomachs. He bought it from a crooked apothecary at St Giles who sweetened it to make it undetectable in wine. He told me all this much later. Their bodies were burned from the inside, their organs flaked to mush. The pain would have been excruciating.'

'Christian, it wasn't you. You just did as he said. Your only crime was trusting an evil man.'

He shook his head angrily. 'Peter was not evil, Holly. He did what he had to for a greater good.'

Holly dipped her head sadly. There was no point in

trying to convince him otherwise. 'But you didn't kill them.'

'I put the powder in the glasses. I gave them their drinks. Ezekial was right.'

Holly did not know what to say, so she said nothing.

'We bricked the wall in again, leaving their bodies trapped forever behind it. Their skeletons are probably still there, a collection of bones in the crevice inside the wall. Perhaps a bony wrist or two is still bound to a stake, dangling from rope. The smell was unbearable for nearly three weeks, and then it faded. I never went into the cellar again.'

'But did nobody suspect? Didn't the police come?'

'No. The magic circle had been a secret. Peter's associates were respectable men from good families and they had not told anybody about their Sunday night dalliances—probably none had ever admitted to knowing Peter.

'Peter sent me to bed very late that night and he cleaned the blood from the parlour alone. In the morning when I came down, it was as if nothing had happened. I picked up my reader and started where I had left off the previous day, burying my guilty secret as far down as I could inside my soul.

'Peter only waited a week before he dragged me into the reading room again, attempting to contact the spirit Aathahorus. It felt strange and empty without the others there, with just Peter and myself robed in black and huddled around his grimoire. He showed me the list of words he used to contact the other side and taught me how to say them, dropping the words lightly on the air so that they hummed and vibrated, rather than speaking them aloud.

'What happened next was very strange. I remember feeling the drowsy, darkening sensation, then I have only the corners of another memory—Aathahorus speaking to me, my saying something in return, and Peter's voice. But these seemed all less than a second in length. My next coherent thought came when I woke up in Peter's bed, some hours later.

'I was frightened and disoriented, but Peter was sitting next to me, waiting for me to wake.

'"What happened?" I asked, unable to lift my head from the pillow.

'"Aathahorus took you over briefly. He spoke to me through you. Christian, you are my angel. Who would have thought when I saw you on the doorstep all those years ago and took you with me, who would have thought that you would turn out to be my most valuable asset."

'"What do you mean, he took me over?"

'"He possessed you. He entered your body and spoke to me. The knowledge, the wisdom he has to impart to me, Christian—my God, it is priceless. And you made it possible."

'Of course I was pleased that Peter was so happy with me, but I was also frightened by the lapse of consciousness that the evening's endeavours had induced. Peter seemed to sense this and he pulled me to him, pressing me against his chest and smoothing my hair.

'"Christian, remember last week when I trusted you not to give me any of the powder? When I trusted you to get the drinks and not to poison me?"

'I nodded, wincing as I was forced again to consider the murders.

'"Well, just as I trusted you, you must trust me. We must trust each other."

'"Of course we must," I said softly.

'"And everything I do, I swear to you, Christian, everything I do is for the good of you and Rosalind and me. So that we can stay together forever, so that the rest of the world cannot interfere with our joy. I swear to you, Christian. Do you love anybody in the world as much as you love Rosalind and me?"

'I shook my head. "Of course not."

'"So if you trust me, and if you love Rosalind and me, and if you want us all to be together happily for good, then you have no need ever to ask questions, or to be frightened. Do you understand?"

'I understood.'

'And you trusted him,' Holly said. 'Despite everything he'd done, you trusted him.'

'If we cannot trust those we love, then there is very little for which we may hope.'

Holly winced slightly, remembering Michael. 'Go on.'

'Every Sunday Peter took me to his reading room. I would black out for an hour or so, then wake to his tender ministrations. He'd feed me soup and thick bread, and sometimes he'd even have sweets or a new book for me as a present. He appreciated my help. He sometimes showed me what I had written while under the influence of Aathahorus. To me it was unintelligible, but Peter understood it all.

'And so life continued in this way. The bodies rotted forgotten in the cellar, I aided Peter on Sundays, his mesmerism clients became more frequent, I still had my eye on Lucy Humberstone, my reading improved, and slowly the memory of the murders dulled, until I could forget about it for days on end.

'Rosalind and I became closer than ever as we grew out of childish games and started to read and study together. She had taken up sketching and I was her favourite subject. Every week she had me in some new pose for her. Her hand became steadier and steadier, her eye for proportion sharper and sharper. It was blissful, just as Peter had said it would be, and now that he had a little more money we ate better and had new clothes more often.

'My particular favourite item of clothing was a gold and red silk cravat, which I always wore on Wednesdays when Lucy Humberstone was coming. I made sure that I was in the parlour at eleven o'clock and Lucy would nod and smile, sometimes her eyes would linger momentarily, but then Peter would be ushering her upstairs and I wouldn't see her for another hour, when she would nod and smile again then disappear until the next week.

'Then one Wednesday, to my horror and delight, she stopped to talk to me on her way upstairs. She paused in front of my chair and smiled, reached out and fingered the silk cravat.

'"This is very pretty, Christian."

'I smiled shyly but did not reply. Peter had kept up the pretence that I was mute, and I was now well used to saying nothing.

'She pulled her hand away gently and took off her gloves, put them very deliberately on the mantelpiece, then followed Peter, who was waiting for her. As soon as she had gone I lifted one glove from the mantelpiece and breathed in the scent of her. Lavender and musk—divine. I held the glove for a few moments, then, concerned about spoiling it, I reverently laid it next to its twin and turned back to my book until her hour was up.

'When she came downstairs again, chatting to Peter, I rose and grabbed her gloves, preparing to give them to her. But she would not look in my direction and I could not call to her. And so she left without them.'

'She left them deliberately, didn't she?' Holly said.

'Yes. It was deliberate. Two hours later we received a post which requested that I bring her gloves to her at home that afternoon. She promised that she would endow Peter with a generous sum for his troubles, and without any deliberation he packed me off on my way.

'I knew my way well enough around the inner city of London, where I had once peddled my trade, but out at

Camden where I lived now I was not so sure. Peter had hastily scribbled me a map, and I followed it down Camden Road but where Camden Road ended I became confused, and was about half a mile down High Street before realising I was heading in the wrong direction. Then, when I was back on track, I was confounded by the Zoological Gardens, which Peter hadn't marked at all, and I followed the outer circle road all around the bottom of Regents Park—perhaps another mile out of my way—before I found Hanover Mews where the Humberstones lived. I was too tired and anxious to notice the splendour of their home on arriving. I merely went to the front door and rang the bell, then waited with a thudding heart.

'A servant opened the door to me and I handed her the post Lucy had sent. She scanned it briefly, handed it back, then ushered me in.

'"Mrs Humberstone won't be long," she said, dropping a small curtsy and leaving me in the parlour. I sat heavily on an overstuffed sofa. Every spare inch of the room seemed to be covered with something extravagant—gilt-edged frames, velvet-covered cushions, marble cigar boxes, fantastic oil paintings, fancy curtains. It made Lord Burghley's rooms look positively spartan.

'Presently the maid returned, Lucy in her wake. She nodded for the servant to leave and then it was just Lucy and me, alone in the parlour.

'Remembering my manners too late, I leapt to my feet and bowed, then held out the gloves to her.

'"Thank you, Christian," she said, taking the gloves and flinging them carelessly on a side table. "Please, sit down."

'I sat on the sofa again and she moved to the window to draw the curtain. The room was suddenly very dark. I looked around me in wonder, still naïvely having no idea what she had planned.

'She came to sit by me and turned to face me. "Poor

little mute boy," she said softly, touching a finger to my lips.

'I wanted to tell her that I wasn't mute, that it was all just a pretence, but Peter trusted me and I would not betray that trust. She took her hand from my face and reached down to the bodice of her dress.

'"I've seen the way you look at me, Christian," she said softly, almost inaudibly. Her black eyes were fixed on mine as she slowly unbuttoned her bodice. She took one of my hands gently and led it into the front of her blouse. Only then did she take her eyes off me, tilting her head back and moaning softly, one hand loosening her long yellow hair from its elaborate style.

'Apart from my brief embrace with Rosalind in the bathroom, I had never touched a woman before. I delved my hand into the front of her corset, finding a small peaked nipple under my fingertips. I touched her as much from curiosity as desire.

'"Undress me, Christian," she said in a husky voice.

'I had no idea where to begin to undress her, so I sat looking at her in dismay. She mistook my silence for reluctance and smiled to reassure me. "It's fine. Philbert is abroad and the servants wouldn't dare to interrupt me."

'I mimed unbuttoning my own shirt, then pointed to her bodice and shook my head.

'"Oh? You don't know how? Dear Christian, have you never been with a woman before?"

'I shook my head.

'"And you do desire women? Not men? Not Peter?"

'In reply, I took her hand and kissed it fervently, feeling the soft skin of her wrist under my lips and tongue.

'"Good Lord, you really are an angel," she said, her eyelids fluttering with desire. "Well, my angel, allow me to be your instructress. Allow me to show you how to keep a woman well satisfied. My husband is a cold fish, Christian. To him, making love is little more than an act of penetration, performed with as many clothes on as remains practical. Here ..." She took my hands and helped me remove her bodice and skirts, what appeared to me to be layers of undergarments, and even a set of lacy bloomers. The delicious stripping seemed to take forever, with each layer bringing me closer to her scented flesh. I was so hard that I thought I might explode, and in fact, when the pale triangle between her legs was finally revealed, its strange musky aroma teasing my senses, I felt that familiar tightening and releasing in my breeches, leaving me wet and embarrassed.

'She must have sensed what had happened, because she was very gentle and kind, assuring me that a man had more facilities for pleasing a woman than just that single appendage. She took me carefully over her entire naked body—I was still fully clothed—naming parts, demonstrating the best way to touch her, often stopping to moan and murmur, "My angel." For me, it was a journey into a mysterious and luscious new world. Only one brave beam of afternoon sun made it through the curtains. All else was warm and dark, the scent of her intoxicating.

'"Now," she said, "although you cannot speak, I sincerely hope there is nothing wrong with your tongue." She pushed my head between her legs and, with careful and gentle instruction, explained what to do. The smell of her and the seemingly illicit nature of the task served to make me hard again, but even after her own climax she did not move to undress me or return any favours. Rather, she dressed herself calmly, thanked me, and bade me farewell.'

'That was all she said?' said Holly, who had found the story made her both aroused and painfully jealous.

'There was no indication that I would even see her again, though I supposed she would return to Peter's house again the following Wednesday. I felt bewildered and disappointed, but also strangely ... strangely powerful. And, for the first time in my life, very much like a man, rather than an angelic boy.'

Holly laughed lightly. 'Poor Christian. Perhaps you were too beautiful to be taken seriously.'

'I often felt that, yes. And of course I did see Lucy again. The following Wednesday she arrived with her sister Catherine, an unattractive woman with lank brown hair and a sallow complexion. She arranged for her sister to have the appointment directly after her own.

'I sat in the parlour with Catherine for an hour while Lucy had her time with Peter. Catherine interpreted my muteness as tacit interest in the most tedious minutiae of her daily life. Needless to say, she was mistaken in doing so. However, I endured her with good grace, already suspecting what Lucy had planned.

'When Peter and Lucy came downstairs, Peter beckoned for Catherine and handed Lucy to me with a smile. "Please be so kind as to keep Mrs Humberstone happy while I attend to her sister," he said, and I nodded my assent. I doubt that Peter suspected just how much I now knew about keeping Mrs Humberstone happy.

'At first I was terrified of being caught with Lucy. But then I reminded myself that Peter would be busy with his appointment for the next hour, no doubt as Lucy had planned, and Rosalind would not leave her room at all during the day now that Peter had clients dropping by. It really was just Lucy, myself, and the ticking clock on the mantelpiece in the dusty room. And so a new custom was established.'

'She brought her sister every Wednesday?'

'Yes, and every Wednesday from noon until one, Lucy and I would make love in front of the fireplace in Peter's parlour. She showed me things that I never dreamed possible, gave me pleasures heretofore inconceivable, as did I for her. Within three months I knew every crevice of her body intimately, and Peter still suspected nothing.

Lucy ensured he was paid triple, saying it was for his commendable service, but it was actually for me, so that we could be out of debt sooner. Because, she said, she had grown very fond of me and didn't like to see me want for anything.'

Christian stopped for a moment, his face clouded by a shadow of sadness. 'All was well with the world then, Holly, just as Peter had promised. And although I had the occasional twinge of guilt over my affair with Lucy, I tried to make up for it by being well behaved and doing extra tasks to relieve Peter's burden. I even began to keep the house a little cleaner. And I spent hours with Rosalind, posing for her sketches and listening to her chatter, to fill those times when she was allowed to roam the house as freely as she desired. Yes, all was well, then. But, of course, not for ever.'

'What happened?'

'Rosalind was a woman, of course, but she had always had such a girlish quality about her. Part of it was due to her childish body, those skinny limbs and the modest bust-line. Come the autumn of that year, her body began to change rapidly. She rounded out, her skirts were too tight around her waist. By November it was clear that she was expecting a child.'

Holly gasped. 'She was pregnant? But how?'

'Your shock is merely an echo of mine. I had suspected for a few weeks, but one night, while we were sitting in her room reading, she confirmed it for me.

'Her little hand reached out and pushed my book away. "We must talk, Christian. I believe something very serious is happening."

'I put my book down and turned my full attention to her. She put her head in my lap, looking up at me with her huge eyes. I felt a strange sense of sadness, somehow knowing that things would change from that moment on, and I desperately wanted to hold on to that instant, with her eyes looking into mine, her head in my lap, her hand gently reaching up to touch my face. I loved her so much, Holly. Dear, dear Rosalind.' He shook his head sadly and Holly felt her heart twist in her chest.

'Looking up at me she said in a soft lisp, "Christian, it seems I am to expect a baby."

'And although I'd had my suspicions, the confirmation was like a sickening death knell to my joy. I couldn't bear the thought that she had known a man's body, as Lucy and I had known each other. But then, of course, the question was, Which man? For a few minutes, as I sat there silently, listening to her quiet tears and not knowing what to say next, I began to be very afraid that Peter would be so angry he would kill her. Or worse, kill both of us, suspecting that I was the father of his unborn grandchild. I was the most obvious culprit, after all. But I need not have worried. As I was soon to discover.'

'What do you mean? Did she tell you who the father was?'

'When I could speak again, it was the first thing I asked. I said, "Rosalind, who is the father?"'

'She replied, "Papa."'

'I misunderstood. Of course. I said, "Who is the papa?"'

'And she repeated herself. "Papa." And the realisation was awful. Truly awful.'

Holly's breath was stopped in her throat. 'What? Surely you don't ... Surely ... Not Peter? Not with his own daughter?'

'Yes. Peter and Rosalind had been lovers all along. It explained a great deal. Why I was made to sleep downstairs, why she knew things unseemly for a young woman, why Peter kept her hidden, why he was so infuriated by Lord Burghley's offer for her hand—everything. He loved her, but perhaps not in the usual fashion that a man loves his daughter.'

Holly found herself boiling over with disgusted

outrage. Without even realising what she was doing, she burst into angry words. 'That's sick. That's . . . evil. Christian, Peter was an evil man.'

'Don't say that, Holly. He did what he had to do.'

'My God, I can't believe I'm hearing this. He had you murder four men, he used you in his diabolical experiments, and he raped his own daughter. Can't you see? Can't you see that these are not the acts of a good person?'

In the mirror Holly could see Christian place his hands over his ears. 'Don't say that. Don't dare to say that. I thought you would understand, but perhaps I was wrong, perhaps I was wrong about you.'

'Christian, don't be foolish. The man was wicked. He used you, he used you both solely for his own convenience, for his own twisted desires. It's been over a century, how can you still defend him?'

Suddenly Christian vanished.

Holly held her breath. 'Christian?' she whispered.

In the silence, her temper dampened, his final few words came back to her. *I thought you would understand, but perhaps I was wrong about you.* What had she done?

'Oh, Christian, please. I'm sorry. Don't go. Come back and finish the story. I won't say anything else, I promise. I can't promise I'll understand and forgive Peter the way you do, but I'll listen and I won't pass judgement. Please, Christian.' Silence. 'Please?'

But she knew with horrible certainty that he was not coming back.

CHAPTER TWENTY-THREE

~

For four weeks Prudence successfully avoided Randolph. She had seen him once, head down in the hallway, as she had been emerging from her office. Ducking away from him before he could spot her seemed the best option. Not because she was afraid of him, not even because she was in a state of denial over her break-up with As. Simply because Randolph had a reputation for being a hard taskmaster, and she just didn't feel like working as hard as she knew he would make her. She was so behind in her work as it was, but had always managed to stick around with special favours from As. It didn't take much to figure out that Randolph was not going to be that kind of supervisor.

She had even made some significant headway on her dissertation. Due in part to Holly, who had suddenly come over very quiet and depressed. Some days, Justin actually out-talked her. Prudence's inquiries about Holly's melancholy had uncovered that the weather was getting her down. And to be fair, it had been a miserable start to the winter—freezing and wet—and Holly was used to blue skies and sunshine where she came from. If there was anything else, Holly was keeping it well guarded. With Holly not amenable to chatter and excess socialising, and with Justin his usual self, Prudence had little choice but to get some valuable work done.

So, first thing one Monday morning, when she finally did make it to Randolph Humberstone's door, she at least had a few chapters of her dissertation to give him. He was a Humberstone, had a direct line to Lucien who could cancel her place at the college on a whim. And while the rumours held that Lucien and Randolph were not fond of each other, she didn't want to risk getting kicked out of her course. The weight of her parents' disapproval would crush her, even on this side of the globe.

'Come in,' Randolph called when she knocked.

She took a deep breath and went in.

Randolph's office was the same as As's but backwards because it was on the opposite side of the building, one floor down. The same mahogany desk, the same bookcases behind the door. The view was different, however, looking out over the carpark and the bare branches of elms along the driveway. Prudence paused to take in the view and Randolph waited for her behind his desk.

'Good morning, Prudence,' he said at length.

She turned to him and smiled. 'Good morning, Professor Humberstone.'

'Call me Randolph.'

'Sorry. Randolph.' His hair and beard were white. Prudence couldn't see where platinum hair ended and grey hair began. His eyes were strange and pale, rimmed with pinkish-red. Usually Prudence looked for an attractive quality in everybody's face. Whether it was kind eyes or nice skin or good bones, there was usually something good to be found in any visage, and she liked to focus on the good and ignore imperfections. That way the world always seemed populated with beautiful people. But she was having a hard time with Randolph, and when he smiled and bared a set of crooked, tobacco-stained teeth, she gave up. He was an ugly man, plain and simple.

'I've been expecting you for some time, Prudence,' he said.

'Did As mention me?'

'Yes.'

'What did he say?'

'Laurence said you were in need of a change of supervisor.'

'Did he tell you why?'

'I didn't ask. I presume it's because he's too busy to give you the attention you require. With me being away for so long he's had to take on extra students.'

There was a cool polish about him. Her questions were just sliding off him. She thought she'd bring out the big guns.

'That's right, you were in Israel, weren't you?'

No signs of discomfort. He smiled lightly. 'Yes, I was, but not many people know that. It was a matter I rather wanted to keep to myself. I had a few very personal things to take care of. It seemed more prudent to allow my colleagues to believe I was in York at the university. I'd appreciate you not spreading it.'

Damn, he was a good liar. Or perhaps, Prudence realised with some disappointment, he was telling the truth. 'Of course not. None of my business,' she muttered, feeling like a fool for bringing it up.

'And so you're working on Mr Oscar Wilde, Prudence. Poetry? Plays? Criticism? Novels?'

She handed over some freshly printed pages of her dissertation. 'All of the above. Perhaps I can leave this with you and come see you again just before the holidays.' She wanted to get out. He was so unresponsive, it forced her to be serious. Nothing made her feel less like herself than having to be serious. She needed a coffee and a cigarette and a good dirty joke.

'Certainly. Let's make an appointment for nine o'clock on the twenty-fifth of June.' He made a mark in his desk diary. As had never once written an appointment in his desk diary. He had used it solely for finding stupid quotes or doodling.

'Um, okay,' she said, scribbling the date and time in a margin of her notebook. 'I'll see you then.'

'Put aside a couple of hours, Prudence. We'll have a really in-depth session and get you on track. I'm aware that you've fallen behind somewhat.'

She nodded, suddenly feeling teary. He was going to make her work hard, just as she had thought. And he wasn't As, and these meetings were sure going to be boring without a shag and a smoke to liven them up. Her life had suddenly been drained of all colour.

'See you next week,' she said quietly, letting herself out of his office.

Prudence looked so depressed when she walked into the room after her brief meeting with Randolph that Holly temporarily forgot about her own woes.

'Prudence, what is it?'

Justin rose and went to Prudence, putting a tentative hand on her shoulder. Holly had watched them become a lot closer in the past few weeks and she felt a bit left out. Even though it was her fault; she was opting out of a lot of Prudence's social proposals and leaving them to go as a pair.

'I hate him!' she sobbed. 'I hate him, he's awful!'

'Why?' Justin asked, concerned. 'What did he say to you?'

'He's going to make me work.'

Holly couldn't help laughing. Prudence glared at her with teary eyes.

'I'm sorry, Prudence, but he's supposed to make you work. He's only trying to help.'

'But he's so . . . he's so . . . nothing. He's not anything. There's no fun about him, it's like he's not even a real person.'

'Prudence, he has to be professional. It's just that Dr Aswell operates differently.' *Very* differently. 'You'll get used to him.'

'I don't want to get used to him. I want to run away.' She crouched next to Holly's desk, her chin resting on her folded arms. 'You have to help me—I have to get more work done on my dissertation. He's going to have expectations that I can't fulfil.'

'Well, I can't help you that much—'

'Yes, you can. How do you do it? How do you get everything done? Lord, there's so much to be done. I'm going to be kicked out of college.' She put her head down and sobbed loudly.

Prudence's plummet into the pit of despair was as loud and intrusive as her manic, hare-brained highs. But somehow it endeared her even more to Holly. She reached out and touched Prudence's hair, made soothing noises. 'It's okay, you'll be fine. We'll both help. You won't get kicked out.'

Prudence looked up and palmed fat tears from her face. 'How do I do it?'

'It's really just a question of time management.'

Prudence's face crumpled again. 'Oh, stop. I can't bear to hear those two words together. Minutes and seconds don't want to be bossed around. They want to hang out until fun comes along to take them places.'

Justin pulled up a chair nearby and gave Holly a smirk. Prudence noticed and looked taken aback.

'I'm being a drama queen, aren't I?' she asked quietly.

'No, of course not.'

'You're upset,' Justin said. 'You'll feel better after a cup of coffee.'

Prudence pulled herself to her feet. 'I suppose,' she said.

'But can we run away? Can we not stay at the college?'

'It's not a good start to . . .' Holly looked at Prudence's face and changed her mind. 'Of course we can run away. Justin?'

He nodded. 'Sure. We can all start being serious tomorrow.'

Prudence beamed at him. 'You don't say much, but when you do, you say just the right thing. Come on.'

They caught a tram into the city, Prudence's mood now definitely on the upswing. Holly tried to give her a few study tips, but she dismissed them all as obsessive.

'I hardly think you should be calling me obsessive, Prudence, when you're obsessed with other people's secrets.'

'That's not an obsession, that's a curious nature.'

'But curiosity kills cats, right?'

'Yes, but cats only have brains the size of golfballs.' She made a circle with her thumb and forefinger to demonstrate. 'I'm way smarter than a cat.'

Holly laughed and Prudence turned her attention to Justin. Facing the window to watch the passing scenery, Holly felt she would never get used to this cold weather and thought with a strange longing about the subtropical winters back home. Where the sky was blue and all she needed to get warm was a sunbeam on her wooden verandah, a cup of tea and a book. They passed the Arts Centre and Southbank and crossed the bridge over the river into the city. A cabal of Goths congregated on the stairs of Flinders Street Station, pulling their long overcoats tightly around them against the cold.

She sighed. Missing home was about more than the weather. Her mother hadn't phoned, just as she'd promised. Finally Holly had called home. Coolly, her father had informed her, 'Your mother isn't prepared to speak to you yet.' Her inquiries about Michael had brought noncommittal clichéd grunts about 'a long road back' and 'ongoing financial hardship'. Holly had wanted to scream that it wasn't her fault, but of course she wasn't being blamed. Not explicitly, in any case.

Estrangement from her family—even when they annoyed the hell out of her with their misplaced sanctimony—was wearing her down. A girl needed her mum and dad, needed security and unconditional love. Especially now that her love-life had gone so completely off the rails and she had no way of getting it back on track. Falling in love with a ghost was the stupidest thing she had ever done. Or perhaps the stupidest thing she had ever done was letting him slip through her fingers. What did it matter what he thought of Peter Owling after more than a century? Why couldn't she just let it go? Was it because she wanted Christian to be perfect, and perfection would never allow such a taint as poor judgement of character?

A million times she had gone over this ground in her head, and still she knew that Christian was never coming back. She had tried and tried, but he was not there. Her relationship with him had started to feel like a dream, an extended delirium. And her heart ached and ached and ached, but didn't break. Because a heart needs a sympathetic ear and a lot of loud tears to break, and her love for Christian could never ever be told. Her pain was a bruise buried in her chest, a sweet muffled pain that throbbed dully and perpetually.

'Holly, are you listening?'

Holly was startled out of her reverie as Prudence pinched her lightly on the arm.

'What? Sorry.'

'You were a million miles away. The view can't be that good.'

'Did I miss something?'

'Justin was just saying that Lucien, of all people, has invited me out to dine with the family. How's that!'

Holly looked from Prudence to Justin, who was his usual impassive self. 'Wow. How come?'

Justin shrugged. 'They think she's my girlfriend, remember. And . . . well, it's my birthday on Thursday.'

Prudence squealed. 'You didn't tell me that! We'll have to have a birthday party.'

'That's the whole point of Thursday's dinner. I hope you don't mind, Holly. I'd love to have you both there, but seeing as how it's Lucien's idea . . .'

'Of course I don't mind.'

'It'll probably be a small slice of social hell anyway, with Lucien frowning at us and Emma giving Prudence the evil eye.'

'But you're still going ahead with it?' Holly asked.

'I don't see that I have a choice.'

'I'm going to wear something outrageous,' proclaimed Prudence.

'Perhaps that's not wise,' Holly remarked. 'Perhaps you should try conservative.'

Justin shook his head. 'There's no need for that. I think she should be herself.'

'See,' Prudence said, poking Holly, 'Justin's more accepting than you.'

'Gee, Mum, don't make us compete for your love,' Holly said, deadpan.

'So how old will you be?' Prudence said, turning to Justin.

'Don't pretend you don't know,' he replied.

'Twenty-eight?'

'Yeah, close enough to thirty to be scary. And I still haven't done anything with my life.'

Prudence smiled. 'You've met us, haven't you?'

'Yes, I suppose.'

'Well,' she said, leaning her head on his shoulder and playfully batting long black eyelashes, 'that should be enough for any man.'

★

334

A slut and a simpleton. Justin had not forgotten Lucien's opinion of Prudence and him, no matter that he was paying for this quiet table in a quiet corner of a quiet restaurant, for the expensive wine in a bucket beside them, for the soft music and muted light to remind him how much atmosphere money could buy. But perhaps, as it was Lucien's suggestion to have dinner as a birthday gift, it could mean that his opinion was changing. He didn't appear to Justin to be a man who acted without deliberation or reason.

Emma's brightly forced friendliness was stretched thin over stormy resentment. She smiled and asked polite questions of Prudence but her hostility was palpable, evident in the long hard stares she aimed at Justin every time she thought nobody else was looking. Justin responded to nothing and let the social machinations of the evening jar and grind on without him. He had confidence that Prudence could hold her own in any situation, and she had promised to make it seem as though the two of them were blissfully in love to put paid once and for all to Emma's designs on him.

While Prudence chatted amiably with his aunt and uncle, he watched her with quiet admiration. She was dressed in cherry velvet and black lace, her hair glowed lilac in the dim light, and silver jewellery and moonstones were jammed onto every finger, thumb and earlobe. At one stage he had looked up from his meal to see her laughing, and Lucien was actually laughing with her. How did she do that? How could she be so comfortable with these strangers? Justin had lived in the same house with them for four months and he and Lucien had never shared a joke. He wondered how different the last few months would have been without Prudence around, resolutely ignoring all his surliness to bring the three of them together.

She reached over and squeezed his hand affectionately.

At first he was startled, then he remembered the charade and squeezed back. Sincerely.

'And how are you liking your new supervisor, Prudence?' Emma was asking as she genteelly scraped the cream off the top of her dessert.

'Randolph? He's fine. Very . . . very professional.'

'Why was it you changed supervisors again?'

Justin could tell she was deliberately trying to goad Prudence. To her credit, Prudence didn't bite. 'I'm not sure. It was As's decision. It hardly matters as they're both equally capable of doing the job.'

Emma shot Justin another stormy glance. Prudence pushed her chair back and excused herself to go to the ladies' room. Emma quickly threw down her napkin and declared she was going too. Justin and Lucien were left sitting together, half-eaten desserts and wine glasses littering the short distance between them.

Conscious he had to say something, Justin took a deep breath. 'Uh . . . thanks, Lucien. Thanks for the dinner and everything.'

Lucien nodded. 'You're welcome.'

Another silence settled. Finally Justin said, 'I know I'm not . . . I know I don't say much, but . . . thanks for what you've done for me. I mean, not just the dinner. All of it. Finding me and bringing me to Melbourne and . . .' He trailed off, feeling like a fool. Lucien looked no more comfortable than Justin felt.

'You don't have to thank me. You're entitled, as one of our family.'

'Uh . . . yeah.'

'And your reticence is appreciated, not abhorred,' Lucien muttered. 'I have Emma to keep my ears full enough of rubbish.'

It was the closest thing to a compliment Justin had ever had from Lucien. Embarrassed, he bent his head to gaze into his wine glass until Prudence and Emma returned.

Lucien wasn't one to linger over a meal. Practically the instant Emma had finished her dessert, he was asking for the bill, laying out his gold American Express card, and ushering them outside into the car.

Prudence chatted merrily all the way to her street, then pointed out her house for Lucien.

'Thank you so much for dinner,' she said graciously when they were idling in front of her house.

'You're welcome, Prudence,' Lucien replied mechanically.

'Justin, would you walk me to the front door?'

Justin turned to her, surprised. She gave him a meaningful nod of the head.

'Ah, sure. I won't be a minute, Lucien.'

He and Prudence stepped into the cold night air and closed the door to the warm car behind them. Prudence remained silent until at her front door. She unlocked it and turned to put her arms around Justin, her face close to his ear.

'Your aunt is nuts,' she whispered.

'Sorry, she was—'

'No, Justin. I mean it. She's fucking demented. She cornered me in the toilets and told me all this weird shit about you and her, like you're having a full-on affair or something, and how you were only using me to throw Lucien off the scent.'

'Christ.'

'Well,' she said with a giggle, 'you *are* only using me, remember?'

'I don't know what's got into her,' he said. He couldn't help feeling guilty. That one weak moment haunted him.

'She's infatuated with you, Justin. And she's deluded. She warned me that I couldn't compete with her and she gave me a few detailed descriptions of what you get up to.'

Justin groaned. 'This is too much.'

'Don't you want to hear them?'

'Maybe another time. Prudence, I . . .'

'What?'

He fortified himself. 'There was this one time. Okay, I'm trusting you with this. She came into my room while I was asleep and . . . you know.'

'Fucked you?'

'No.'

'Blow job?'

'Yeah. I was asleep. I woke up at the last minute and ever since she's been . . .' He could feel his face on fire with shame. 'God, you must think I'm such a sick bastard.'

'No, of course not. I feel sorry for you. She's trouble, Justin, watch out for her. You know you can always come and stay here if it gets too bad.'

'Thanks.'

Lucien beeped the horn.

'Gotta go,' he said.

She nodded and he started for the car. He was two metres from her when he turned and came back.

'Don't tell Holly.'

She raised an eyebrow. 'Her good opinion is important to you, isn't it?'

'Please.' Desperate, wishing he could call his confession back and have it never spoken.

'Of course I won't tell her. Or anyone. I can be discreet, you know. Here,' she turned her face up, 'Emma will be expecting a kiss goodnight.'

He kissed her lightly on the lips. She took a step back and smiled. 'Right move, wrong girl. Perhaps we should have enlisted Holly to play your girlfriend,' she said teasingly.

'Don't, Prudence. You promised to be discreet.'

'Only around other people. I can still taunt you mercilessly when we're alone.'

Lucien beeped again, and with as much of a smile as he could muster, Justin ran back to the car.

The letters swam in front of him, his head ached and his eyes screamed for mercy, but still Lucien kept working. He wondered briefly if he was becoming insanely obsessed with the translations, then comforted himself with the fact that insane people didn't worry about their sanity. Perhaps madness was lurking close by, but what were the lives of most, anyway, if not an anxious repression of the madness induced by full contemplation of mortality? At least he was engaged in honest pursuit of a cure for that madness.

Lily Kirkwood was an idiot. Without a doubt. Some of her translations, some of her tabulations had been very useful. Others had led him so far off track that he despaired of ever finding his way back.

Lucien leafed through the remaining pages. Some resembled pidgin English, some—too many—were covered in lines and lines of scrawled, unintelligible code. Overwhelmed, he closed the book and went over his notes so far. Lists of minor invocations; charts of demonic names across cultures; strange, half-sensical phrases that lurked close enough to meaning to be frustrating, yet not close enough to be useful. He underlined one sentence in his notebook because it referred again to the orphan boy: 'pay with this body this christian body this orphan boy'.

In the grimoire, Owling's clearly legible handwriting had been beneath the inscription, a solemn seal of agreement: 'I will'.

This Christian body? The necessity of the orphan boy's religious orientation had not been mentioned before, and Lucien found himself wondering how far the definition of Christian might stretch. Had Justin's mother ever had him baptised? He had already suffered numerous bouts of panic over Justin's suitability for sacrifice—could he be an orphan boy at nearly thirty years of age? If not, then what was Lucien to do? It was not as if abducting children from foster homes was a viable option.

Too many questions, not enough time to answer them all. Lucien was already forty-eight years old. With good health and luck he would perhaps last naturally for another thirty to forty years. Not enough. Time was a tiny, claustrophobic space, narrowing to a point in front of him. Distractedly, he fingered his top button. His breath seemed to be pressed flat in his lungs.

He simply had to decode it all. He had to succeed. And in the meantime he had to stay alive. Not like Owling, who had come so close, only to be murdered shortly before finishing the task. Although in some ways Lucien was glad he had not succeeded. He sensed acutely that there would not be room enough in the world for both him and Peter Owling. Lucien, taking a lesson from Owling's tragic example, was meticulous in his avoidance of premature death. He drove like an old woman, took care to dry his hands totally before using his electric razor, stayed well clear of boats and bad neighbourhoods. Emma complained continually about his excessive caution, equating it with timidity rather than wisdom. The staggering ignorance with which she missed the point caused him endless irritation.

He turned to the last ten pages of the book—blank, still awaiting the final few secrets of eternal life. Perhaps soon Lucien would be able to fill them in himself.

pay with this body this christian body this orphan boy

Lucien removed his reading glasses, pinched the bridge of his nose. 'I will,' he muttered under his breath, 'I will.'

He picked up his pen and kept working.

CHAPTER TWENTY-FOUR

⁓

The frosted-glass and oak-panelled doors of the library were pure nineteenth century, and sometimes the computer system seemed as though it wasn't much newer. The smell of old wood and the dusty tickle exuding from the books could only do so much to ameliorate the long wait as the computer thought about responding to Holly's request. Microform catalogue, nineteenth-century science periodicals. Perhaps she had just fed the thing too many search strings to consider at once. A cursor blinked on an empty screen in blank confusion. She sighed and leaned back in her chair to wait.

The library was her favourite place in the college, where the smell and the feel of history were strongest. Its recent volumes were kept in the more modern-looking, easy-access section on the second floor where most students preferred to work, while all the old periodicals and rare books were up here on the largely deserted third floor. The third-floor librarian was a strange but very friendly Scottish girl in her mid-twenties who was on a collision course with early eccentricity. She treated the books as though they were her children and had a bizarre nickname for every student she dealt with. Today she wore a fuzzy blue beret and a Winnie-the-Pooh T-shirt.

'Having problems, Hollywood?' she asked, after Holly had been keeping a lid on her frustration with the computer for nearly five minutes.

'I think it's crashed, Noni.'

Noni approached and savagely jabbed the enter key a number of times. 'When in doubt with technology, one should always resort to violence,' she said sagely in her thick Scottish brogue.

When the computer still didn't respond she took a step back and shook her head. 'I don't know what's wrong with it. Perhaps you should try another terminal. What were you after? I might know where it is.'

'A microform catalogue which might list nineteenth-century science periodicals.'

'Ah, you'll be wanting *Journals of Discovery*. He's over here.' She beckoned Holly to follow her. Holly wondered if Noni's bestowal of gender on different books was based on some kind of logic or if it was purely arbitrary.

'Now, let me see.' Noni pressed her lips together as she scanned a shelf at eye level. 'He's got a green back ... Ah, here.' She pounced on a loose-leaf binder and handed it to Holly. 'The microforms for this are at MF292. If you need any help, let me know.' She smiled and nodded before heading off in one direction, changing her mind and disappearing between the stacks.

Holly took the binder and sat at a corner bench, where a set of carved initials in the wood crowned a faded amateur diagram of anal sex. Holly couldn't imagine why anybody would enjoy defacing a place like this. She opened the book and leafed through the 'O's. Oswald, Ottager, Owen—there it was, Owling, Peter, born 1818, died 1867. Her hunch had paid off. He had published two papers on experimental science in scientific journals. In 1856 an inquiry into the possible effects of astrology on regional weather patterns, and in 1860 a survey of convicted murderers about the influence of paranormal agency on their crimes.

Holly scribbled down the reference numbers, not sure if she expected to find anything of use in either of the articles. What she really wanted to know was how Christian's story ended. She didn't even know what years Christian was living with Peter, or if Peter had died first. It occurred to her that perhaps her best chance of finding information about Peter was in obituary notices for the year he died. She abandoned the binder and went back to the on-line catalogue. This time it agreed to help her, throwing up a number of lists of microform newspapers originally printed in Victorian London. One title in particular jumped out at her—the *Camden New Town Mail*. Christian had told her that Peter's house was at Camden. Surely it was the most likely paper in which to find his obituary notice. At least it was a start. From there she might be able to find out whether Christian survived him and by how long, and then she could begin to search for notice of his death. A little pain sparked in her heart at the thought of reading about Christian's death, even though she knew that he was long dead.

She found the right microfilm with little trouble and was soon tucked away in a remote corner of the library, reeling through the pages on the microform reader. Thankfully the *Camden New Town Mail* had been a weekly newspaper, making it only fifty-two issues she had to search through. She spun through the pages, pausing to read the obits. At first they were all fascinating. After nearly thirty weeks of them, she was losing patience and getting a killer migraine. The second reel had run out so she pressed the rewind button and prepared to load the third.

'Everything all right?'

Holly jumped. She had almost forgotten that she wasn't alone in the world.

Noni smiled. 'Sorry, didn't mean to frighten you.'

'I'm fine,' Holly replied, bending her head to load the third reel, hiding her embarrassed blush with her long hair. The tape rattled noisily onto the reel.

Noni was gone, back among the stacks to bond with her children. Holly lifted her head to look at the screen, the first two pages of the 7 October edition of the *Camden New Town Mail* calmly waiting for her to notice them.

'My God,' she said under her breath. Under a 'Police News' headline was a single, bold-type line: 'Violent Murder of Local Man Peter Owling'.

She quickly skim-read the piece. His body had been found stabbed to death in his Milton Close home. His houseboy had been taken into custody but was of little help to police with their questions as he was mute.

'Christian,' she murmured, and she felt tears spring to her eyes. She blinked them back and kept reading.

> Mr Owling was an experimental scientist and hyp-notist. He was educated at Corpus Christi College, Oxford, and published a number of papers in sci-entific journals. At the time of his murder, Mr Owling owed thousands of pounds to various private creditors in London and abroad. He was a widower with no family to survive him.

Nothing more about Christian, and nothing about Rosalind. The article had raised more questions than it answered. Holly slowly reeled through the rest of the paper but found nothing further. The next week was also empty of news about the murder. She reeled listlessly through the 21 October edition, almost missing the 'Police News' headline and rewinding to find one small paragraph that shook her to her core: 'Murder Suspect Drowns'.

The houseboy of murdered scientist Peter Owling drowned at the Docks on Wednesday evening. He was widely though unofficially presumed to be his master's murderer. The apparently intentional drowning has aided in substantiating popular conjecture. Police Constable Charles Hallam, who was present both at the murder scene and at the discovery of the boy's body, confirmed that the houseboy was the most likely culprit of Mr Owling's murder. The police have now closed the case.

'Oh, Christian, no.' So he was a murderer, the spirited defence of Peter's actions merely a product of his awful burden of guilt. And his intentional death perhaps the only way he felt he could compensate for the murder. She was close to tears. How she longed to see him again, tell him that she didn't care if he had killed Peter. But it was over a month since she had last spoken with him, and her hopes of ever speaking with him again died a little every day.

She fed thirty cents into the machine and made a copy of the article, folded it carefully and tucked it away. A quick scan of the rest of October's and November's papers revealed no further information, and she finally rewound the microfilm and headed back to the computer catalogue.

Using the word 'Humberstone' in a search string pulled up every book on the catalogue, overwhelming the computer for a second time that afternoon and sending it crashing. The word must have been on every entry, perhaps in the library location field. She went to the counter and rang the bell for Noni.

'Hi, what's up?' Noni asked, emerging from her back room with a half-eaten sandwich in one hand. Holly remembered that she had missed lunch. She desperately wanted to grab Justin and Prudence and head down to the cafeteria for some stodgy cauliflower au gratin and salty chips.

'Do we have any books about the Humberstone family?'

Noni took a bite from her sandwich and chewed thoughtfully. 'Hmm, let's see. Not about the family as such, although you could probably ask Lucien if he has anything in his private collection.'

'No, I don't want to do that. I'm curious, that's all. I don't want him thinking I'm—'

'Aha! I know.' She turned to her computer, fingers flying over the keys, sandwich perched on top of the monitor for safe-keeping. 'Here it is: *The Impact of the Private Banker on Colonial Economic Growth, 1850–1910*. It was Magnus's first history thesis. He researched four families, his own included. At the moment it's not in the stacks, though. Let me just check.' She hit a few more keys and Holly waited. 'Right, it's away being rebound. We sent a whole shipment for rebinding to a place in South Australia and it's among them.'

'South Australia?'

'This place does it cheap. Lucien's fastidious about saving money.'

'So I've heard.'

'It won't be back for a week or two. I'll put it aside when it comes in. Check with me after the holidays.'

'Okay, sure. Thanks.'

'No problem, Hollywood. Have a nice winter break.'

Feeling cold, sad and hungry, Holly grabbed her notebook and pen and prepared to find some live people to surround herself with. History was too full of the tragic and the dead to be comfortably immersed in for long.

Lucien had to admit to himself that he was excited. As the five of them gathered around the circle on Sunday just after midnight, his hands shook turning the pages of the grimoire. A breakthrough had come late on Saturday night. The letters on the page had long since become meaningless marks which mocked his efforts; then, with an almost supernatural suddenness, some of the letters had collected together to make sense.

Aathahorus.

A sigil burned into the Guyana fragment had given the same name when decoded. Its repetition in the Jerusalem fragment suggested to Lucien that Aathahorus was the name of the demon Owling was working with. The demon that had spoken to Lucien during the ritual when he had blacked out had pronounced a name starting with an A. Perhaps this was it. Perhaps this was the key he needed to find the demon again, to start asking it questions about the summoning. To break the unintelligible code that the rest of the grimoire was written in.

He had not told the others. What he saw and heard in his trances was best summed up in as few words as possible. None of them had any idea of the depth or intensity of his visions—they thought the knowledge he brought back with him was vague and indistinct, like prophecies given by tea-house fortune tellers. Only he knew about the burning landscape and the grotesque beings that peopled it. And keeping that information to himself felt like holding the advantage over his cohorts. It made him feel powerful, in control.

Candlelight flickered and the room grew quiet. Lucien looked around him. Jane, her eyes large and dark in the dim light, smiled at him. Emma and Laurence gazed at the circle, centring their thoughts. Randolph had his eyes closed. Lucien was still having difficulty getting used to Randolph being back in the circle. His presence alone seemed challenging, dangerous to Lucien's continued control. Lucien banished his fears with a deep breath. Randolph was one of the family, and they had to maintain loyalty among themselves. He hadn't even blinked at Lucien's proposal to offer Justin's body to their traitor demon. 'If that's what is necessary,' he had said simply.

'Now,' said Lucien, his voice soft in the muted gloom, 'whatever happens, do not bring me out of my trance early. Keep your eyes closed and keep the chant going. Do not be alarmed. I have a key to use tonight, and I think I can make contact with our traitor.'

The others nodded solemnly. Was that a glint of challenge or of jealousy in Randolph's eye? Lucien and Graham had inherited Magnus's ability to go into trance where Randolph had not. But perhaps Randolph's expression was nothing more than a trick of the light.

'Let us begin.' Lucien closed his eyes. One by one they revoked their saviour and began the chant.

The rise in temperature was sudden and violent. Lucien felt his breath torn out of his throat, burning his tongue and lips. He coughed and gasped for air. Finally, their breathing shallow and laboured, his lungs resumed their work. The imprints of candle flames against his dark eyelids faded and, with a strange sigh, gathering intensity, the infernal landscape rushed upon his senses. Time seemed to slow down slightly. He stood looking out over the mountains of hell. Hot gusts of orange smoke blasted into the air along the horizon. The Klipoth danced madly in the distance, dark silhouettes against the glowing sky, no longer interested in Lucien Humberstone. He had made it clear that he did not mean to enlist them for anything. They awaited the arrival of other, less daring magicians.

Lucien looked around him, the sense of his material body dissipating with every second. He appeared to be alone.

'Aathahorus!' His disembodied voice echoed sharply around the hills. He could not hear its vibration in his material body though, and wondered if it was because he had not spoken out loud back in the room at Humberstone College, or because he had lost so much of his thread to reality.

No response. Sounds of fires burning in the distance. Beyond that, an echoed groaning and weeping, which slipped beyond audibility every time he attempted to focus on it.

'Aathahorus!'

This time an inhuman screech greeted his cry. The piercing sound pushed into his brain, reverberating painfully. It grew louder and louder. Lucien was afraid it would go on forever and split his skull open. He was about to cry out in agony when it suddenly stopped.

'Don't ever, *ever* utter that word again!'

Lucien spun round. The demon, the one he had spoken to once before, stood before him. Barely recognisable as a human shape, he had withered stumps for arms, a big bald head that was misshapen as though it had melted down one side like candle wax, and a great, burnt belly that hung over grotesquely disfigured genitals.

'Isn't it your name?'

The creature screamed again and Lucien recognised it as a scream of rage.

'No,' it said finally, its voice husky and grating, 'it is not my name. It is the name of my enemy. If you wish to summon me, you must call, "Traitor, come." It's very simple, magus.'

'The code in the grimoire is not simple,' Lucien replied. 'It's impossible.'

'You will work it out.'

'So what is your name?' Lucien knew that the key to commanding demons started with naming them.

'I cannot tell you while you have a betrayer in your midst.'

'I don't understand.'

'Come with me, magus. Let's sit in the park and discuss a few things. You have questions and I have answers.'

'The park?'

With one of its stumps, the creature gestured towards

a blackened, blasted tree, clinging resolutely to the dusty ground with roots as tangled and sinister as the thoughts of a madman. The creature laughed hideously. 'This is a pretty park, is it not?'

They moved towards it. Lucien was growing adjusted to the disembodied feeling. He rested with the creature under the tree. The sky had turned a yellowy grey. Sulphuric swirls misted through the empty branches.

'Whatever we say is inaudible to the others,' the creature said, as though anticipating Lucien's thoughts, 'so whatever we say is in confidence. And that is the way I prefer it, because I do not wish to deal with the others, only with you.'

'Why?'

'I don't like the others. I only like you,' it said. Its tone struck Lucien as almost petulant.

'But I don't understand—'

'What I say goes!' it screamed. Lucien checked himself. He was not dealing with a reasonable human being here and it would serve him well to remember that.

'You know my price?' the creature asked, resuming its quiet, rasping tone.

'The body of an orphan boy to inhabit. I have chosen someone but I'm unsure as to his suitability.'

'He's male? He's parentless?'

'Yes.'

'Then he's suitable. You'd serve the turn just as well, magus. Your parents are no longer alive.' The creature laughed again, a sound like breaking glass. 'Although I would prefer a young and handsome body. It has been too long since I knew the pleasures of the flesh.'

'It's my nephew. He's young and handsome enough.' Compared to the creature's current form, there were few bodies that wouldn't prove suitable.

'Ah, yes. It will be good. I look forward to working with you, magus.'

'You mentioned a betrayer.'

'The woman, the one you have the fantasies about. Hmm.' And shimmering before him was an image of Jane, as though stolen from his mind and projected onto the landscape.

'Jane? Jane is betraying us?'

The image vanished. 'You, magus. She's betraying you. Or at least she intends to. You are too naïve. You help these people draw on black magic and do not check what they are using it for. She wants it all for herself. When you've done all the work decoding the grimoire, she intends to work a hex on you, steal the book and disappear. Throw her out of the circle immediately, cut off her power. She won't be able to hurt you after that.'

Lucien felt sick. Jane intended to betray him? He had thought her the one he could rely on the most. 'Of course. I'll get rid of her immediately.'

The creature leaned forward, an eager glint in its eyes. 'Will you kill her?'

'There's no need to kill her.'

It snorted disdainfully. 'There was a time when a magus like yourself would perform a heinous act every day just to prove his loyalty to the Prince of Darkness.'

'I'm not a murderer.'

'Oh, really?' The creature grinned hideously. 'You are too faint-hearted, magus. It's a failing I have noted in you for a long time.'

'How long have you been watching us?'

'I have little concept of time now. Months. Years, maybe.' Then he added dismissively, 'I grow tired of your questions. It's time for you to go back now.'

'Wait! You have to help me with the code in the grimoire. It's taking too long. I need your help, I need the summoning ritual.'

The creature's face twisted into the ugly smile again. 'Months and years, magus. There's a clue.'

351

'But why can't you—'

'Suffer! Suffer, magus, as I have suffered. Don't expect to work with a creature such as me and have things made easy for you. Bitterness can taste almost sweet when it is shared generously among others.'

'Wait!' Lucien called. The landscape was fading from his mind's eye. His limbs grew heavy around him as the sense of his embodied presence returned. The chanting of his companions grew slowly more audible, until finally he was sitting again around the circle, his tongue dry and swollen, his heart thudding.

'Water!' he cried as he came to full consciousness, a raging thirst tearing at his throat. 'I must have water.'

It was an incontrovertible fact of life that Prudence had to walk past As's office to get to the ladies' room, and she was hardly to be expected to hold her bladder just to avoid seeing him. But his door was always resolutely closed or open only a crack, crushing all her hopes for a chance meeting. Crushing all her hopes that one of the much-practised conversations she had with him in her head would actually take place. In her head she was witty, sexy, irresistible, and the exchanges usually ended with a reconciliation. In really stupid moments she even imagined them ending in a permanent relationship, Mandy left destitute with the kid in a housing commission apartment, and Prudence magically five kilograms lighter. But only when she allowed herself to be really stupid.

Like now, hovering near the top of the stairs, listening hard. The door was ajar about ten centimetres and she could hear Randolph's voice as well as As's. Hardly anything they said was audible, but she felt sure they must be talking about her.

Yeah, Prudence. What else of importance could they have to talk about? She marvelled at her uncontrollable self-obsession, chastening herself as an egotistical moron. Still, it didn't stop her listening.

Straining her ears, she heard the words 'Mandy' and 'away for the weekend'. Then Randolph's voice, louder for a moment as he paced past the open door: '. . . have to sort it out, Laurence.'

God, this was killing her. Was it to do with her? With the other other-woman? What needed sorting out? She checked behind her, noted that the stairwell was still empty and crept up to the landing, pressed close to the wall.

'. . . grow suspicious. If I'm away from home that late . . .' That was As, ending his sentence somewhere in his collar.

Randolph walked past the door again, clearly audible. 'It's rotten timing, her mother dying now.'

So this was about Mandy. Her mother had finally died and As was fretting because now Mandy would notice his late-night weekend absences. Had to be another woman. And while Prudence was delighted that she'd guessed, it was a rather tainted victory given that it also signed the death warrant for her hopes of reconciliation.

Their voices faded out for a few moments and then she heard Randolph approach the door again. 'Good luck with it all, Laurence.'

'Thanks, I'll need it. What's he doing up here today anyway?'

'Lucien moves in mysterious ways, my friend.'

Suddenly the door swung open and just before they spotted her, Prudence backed down two stairs. Randolph and As stepped out of the office, and Prudence walked up the stairs as though she had just arrived.

'Hello, Prudence,' Randolph said, smiling that nothing smile of his.

'Hi, Randolph. Hi, As.'

Randolph excused himself and brushed past Prudence on the stairs. She stood in front of As, every witty opening to a seductive conversation eluding her grasp.

'How are you, Prudence?' he asked.

'Okay, I guess,' she said.

'Have you come up here to see me?'

'No. I have to pee.' *Real good, Prudence, that'll turn him on.*

'Oh. Well, don't let me stop you.' He moved past her and went purposefully up the hall.

She waited until he was gone and kicked the top step. 'Shit!' she said. 'Shit, shit, shit!'

'Dr Jane Macintyre'. Lucien pulled out the neatly labelled employee file and placed it on the desk in front of him. Her resumé, her academic records, her quarterly reports. He thumbed through them all. Everything was perfectly in order, of course; she had been a model employee. Which made what he had to do no easier.

Lucien fed a sheet of Humberstone College letterhead into his printer and started typing a letter to Jane.

He was sealing the letter in an envelope when Aswell knocked at the door. With some reluctance, he let him in.

'Glad you're here, Lucien, I need to discuss something with you.'

'Please, sit down.' Lucien closed the door behind him and returned to his desk, turning the envelope over and over between his long fingers.

'Mandy's mother has passed on.'

'I'm very sorry. Do you need time off for the funeral?'

Aswell scowled. 'The circle, Lucien. I've been free to leave my home and come to the college on Sunday nights only because Mandy hasn't been there to ask me what I'm up to, where I'm going. I propose that we move the meeting to a time that's more—'

'It's out of the question and you know it.'

'But how am I—?'

'You'll just have to come when you can.'

'Won't it weaken the circle?'

'Randolph was away for months. We can manage without you.' Lucien began to feel almost hysterically light and unencumbered. Jane was going. Aswell was going. He was getting rid of them. Slowly but surely. And the smaller the group, the easier it would be to impose his will.

Aswell nodded. 'I suppose I can still keep up with the news.'

'Of course. And we'll save the important work for when you're there.' It was a lie, and Aswell probably knew it as well as Lucien did.

'Randolph will keep me informed,' Aswell said, deliberately goading Lucien by reminding him of Randolph's divided loyalty.

'I'm sure he will. Tell me, is Jane in today?'

'I haven't seen her. Why?'

'Could you take this letter to her?' He handed the envelope across to Aswell. 'If she isn't there, just slip it under the door to her office.'

Aswell took the letter without looking at it. 'Yes, sir. Any other errands I can run for you? Perhaps I can do your grocery shopping.'

'Goodbye, Laurence. It won't be the same without you on Sunday.'

'I'll be there this Sunday,' Aswell said hotly. 'Mandy's away organising the funeral.'

Lucien shrugged. One more week mattered little. He bent his head to Jane's file. He heard the door open and close. When he looked up, Aswell was gone.

Chapter Twenty-five

~

Justin was dreaming about his childhood dog, Jack, in a blue and green world of sunshine and wind in the trees. The dream was so happy and uncomplicated that he found himself clinging to it, even when the part of his conscious mind that stood sentinel signalled the alarm.

There's someone breaking in.

The game of fetch in the endless childhood landscape would have to end. He woke, his senses alert, listening. A rattle near his door, like somebody was trying to get in. But he had flicked the lock across, as he always did since the last time with Emma. The handle moved up and down almost imperceptibly in the dark.

'Emma?'

No response. What if it was a burglar? He was on the ground floor, perhaps the burglar thought his room was an office with a safe in it. The Humberstones must surely be well known for their wealth.

A scratching against the metal made him sit up. Somebody was picking the lock. Easy enough, really. It wasn't one of the key locks that Lucien had had fitted to every other door. Anybody with a bread knife could unlock his door from the outside. His heart was beating hard. Should he call out? Who would hear? And then if the burglar was armed . . .

He climbed out of bed and looked around for a weapon. If he was a jock he'd have a cricket bat, a set of martial arts weapons, or a football trophy to brain burglars with. But he wasn't that kind of guy. Wryly, he mused on how little damage a book could do to an intruder.

He scanned the room in the dark. A shape on his desk caught his eye. His laptop. He crept to his desk and picked it up, hefted it in his hands. Heavy enough to do some damage? Perhaps. It was about five years old, a lot heavier than the newer ones. The lock was moving slowly to the right. Positioning himself by the door, he raised the laptop and waited.

The door swung open and of course it was only Emma.

'Jesus Christ!' he cried, exasperated. 'What the fuck are you doing?'

She looked up and registered his stance, laptop upraised in his hands, and she actually had the gall to look insulted.

'Don't swear at me.'

Justin rarely lost his temper. Perhaps four or five times in his entire life. But with his heart still racing, weak at the knees, relief that the intruder was only Emma turning into exasperation at her continual harassment, he felt a hot, indignant fury growing. He was too close to happy in his life now to put up with this. When he had lived with his mother his whole life had been shades of grey and misery, and getting angry over anything was pointless. But now, with a chance that things could go right, the constant intrusion rankled him beyond all endurance.

'Get out!' he screamed, throwing the laptop across the room. It slammed loudly into a wall, cracking the plaster. 'Get out! How dare you break into my room while I'm sleeping?'

She stepped back, shocked. 'Don't speak to me like—'

'I'll speak to you however I want. You're driving me mad. I don't want to sleep with you. Leave me alone.' Already his anger was dissipating, leaving behind an unbearable sense of guilt and fear. 'Leave me alone,' he repeated in a softer tone. 'Please, Emma.'

Lucien was on the stairs, calling down. 'What's going on down there?'

Emma backed into the hallway. 'It's all right, Lucien, go back to bed.' She came back in and confronted Justin. 'It was only a bit of fun. You didn't have to go getting all worked up about it.'

Regretting every word that had just flown out of his mouth, he found he could not speak. He took her arm gently, and with a delicate push moved her into the hallway. He closed the door in her face and, rather than locking it, shoved a chair under the handle and went back to bed.

She's fucking demented. Perhaps Prudence was right. So here he was living with his contemptuous uncle and his demented aunt in unrivalled luxury. He'd rather live in a dingy flat like Holly's and never see them again.

He turned over and gazed at the trees beyond his window, tall and dark in the moonlight. Slowly it dawned on him. He didn't have to stay. Lucien hated having him around—he'd made that quite clear. Prudence had offered him a place to stay, at least for the short term. He had to be due some money—even the barest minimum—as Graham's son. Lucien wouldn't have brought him back from Sydney and told him about his genealogy if there wasn't some provision for him. And even if there wasn't, he could always get a part-time job. Perhaps he and Holly could find a flat to share—she seemed to hate her accommodation as much he did.

He checked himself before his imagination went too far. But there was nothing stopping him moving out, not really. There had to be a way. He had stayed with his mother because she needed him. Lucien and Emma didn't need him. He was free to go.

Closing his eyes, he vowed to speak to Lucien in the morning.

He waited until eleven before he took the short but unnerving walk up the hallway to Lucien's office. Emma wasn't around anywhere that he could see. Perhaps his rebuke last night had actually managed to make her feel ashamed of what she had done and she was deliberately staying out of his way.

But he doubted it.

He knocked and waited. No answer. Just as he was about to knock again the door opened a crack and Lucien peered down at him.

'Yes?'

'I need to talk to you.'

'I'm busy.'

Justin nearly backed off. But the prospect of having nothing sorted out before he ran into Emma again panicked him. 'It's really important.'

Lucien nodded and opened the door. 'All right. Come in.'

The office was well lit, tastefully decorated, almost unnaturally tidy, with plenty of space and clear surfaces. The desk was bare and Justin realised that Lucien had carefully put away whatever he was working on before opening the door. Was it that book Emma had spoken of? It hardly mattered any more. Lucien could be masterminding an international diamond heist from this office and Justin wouldn't care. He was getting out.

They sat facing each other on either side of the large desk.

'What is it, Justin?'

'I want to move out.'

There was a beat of silence. Justin couldn't read Lucien's face.

'I'm afraid that's not possible,' his uncle said.

Taken aback, Justin couldn't assemble a meaningful response. 'What?' was all he managed to say.

'It's not possible, Justin. You must stay here.'

'I don't have to.'

'You do.'

'Why?'

'Why don't you tell me why you want to leave?'

Justin shrugged. 'I just want my own place. I feel like I'm imposing. I—'

'It's Emma, isn't it?'

Not knowing what to say, Justin said nothing.

'I heard you fighting last night. I think I know what's been going on. And I apologise. I will speak to Emma and ensure that she leaves you alone from now on. You don't have to leave.'

'But I want to leave,' Justin blurted. 'I want to be on my own.' This was too weird. What possible reason could Lucien have for wanting him to stay? He had always assumed that his uncle hated having him in the house.

'No. You can't leave.'

Exasperated, Justin repeated his earlier question. 'Why not?'

Lucien paused, considering. Finally he spoke. 'I was acquainted with Dale Emerson when he still lived in Melbourne.'

'Who?'

'Prudence's father.'

'Oh.' What did this have to do with anything?

'Prudence is a constant source of vexation to her parents, as you can probably imagine. Dale had some concerns that Prudence had become spoiled and lazy. Her place at the college is her last opportunity to redeem herself in their eyes. I remember Dale saying to me before he left for Hong Kong that this was her last chance. If she screwed this up, they were going to have to cut her off. I presume he meant financially.'

Justin shook his head. 'I don't understand why you're telling me this.'

'Prudence did not meet her academic requirements last year, but on the embarrassingly fervent assurances of her supervisor at the time, she was allowed to continue. I can reverse that decision at any time.'

It took a few moments to sink in. The realisation was as unpleasant as it was puzzling. Lucien was blackmailing him.

'So if I leave . . .?'

'Prudence loses her place at the college. And everything that goes with that, including the luxury home which I'm sure you're convinced you'll be invited to live in. But if you stay, I guarantee you that Prudence will not only be allowed to keep her place at the college, but that she will be passed at the end of the year, no matter what meandering dross she manages to hand in by way of a dissertation.'

Justin was stupefied.

'Will you stay?' Lucien asked.

'I don't have a choice. I just don't know why you want me here.'

'My father wished for you to be part of the family.'

It was hardly an explanation, but Justin was still recovering from the shock of Lucien's proposal. He had thought his uncle arrogant, disdainful, remote, but not corrupt, not sinister.

'Ask no more questions and mention this to nobody. Please don't forget the power I have over your girlfriend, even though she pretends to be unaware of it.'

Justin put up his hands helplessly. 'Fine.' He began to back out of the room. 'Fine.'

'And I will take care of Emma. She won't bother you again.'

'Fine.' He let himself out of the office, closed the door behind him and sagged against the wall in the hallway. The burden of his newly bestowed responsibility for Prudence weighed heavily on him. A small shutter of sunshine in his life had just been closed, plunging him back into darkness. He should have just kept his mouth shut, he should have just put his head down and left things the way they were.

But it was too weird. Why had Lucien reacted like that? Was there something strange going on that Justin was implicated in? An inheritance problem, a family legal battle? He had been hanging around Prudence too much not to be suspicious.

Ask no questions and mention this to nobody. Under the threat of ruining the life of one of his best friends. Lucien needn't worry. If there was one thing Justin knew, it was how to keep quiet.

The door closed behind Justin, and Lucien was halfway back to the safe to fetch the grimoire when the phone rang. He almost ignored it, but it was his private line and only trusted business contacts had the number.

'Hello?'

'What is the meaning of this letter?' It was Jane.

'Exactly as it says. You're no longer needed at the college. You're fired.'

'Why? What have I done wrong?' Her voice told him that she was on the verge of tears.

'Are you alone?'

'Yes, I'm in my office at the college. Why?'

'It's a delicate matter. I have inside information of your disloyalty to me.'

'Lucien, you're not making sense. Just tell me what's going on.'

'I know what you've been planning to do, Jane. Work some black magic on me. Make me ill. Take the grimoire.'

A meaningful silence was his answer.

Finally, she said, 'I don't know what you're talking about. You know that I'm behind you one hundred percent. You know that. I'm the only one you can count on, Lucien. Don't get rid of me.'

'It told me.'

'It?'

'I have made contact with the other side, Jane. I was told that until you are gone it will not work with us. Betrayer, it called you.'

'You can't do this.'

'I can. It's on my side. Who knows what power it possesses? You don't want to cross me now. There could be danger in upsetting me or my plans.'

Another silence. Then, 'Are you threatening me?'

'I believe I am.'

'You can't—'

'I can. You know I can. Clear your desk out and be gone by the end of the week, and let me be sure never to hear from you again. It told me your innermost thoughts, Jane, I'm sure it could also punish you for them if I commanded it.'

She didn't speak for a few moments.

'Jane? Do you agree to my terms?'

'I do,' she said softly. He almost weakened then, remembering her beautiful eyes, her calm intelligence.

'Goodbye then, Jane,' he said, his voice wavering between resentful and tender.

The phone clicked as she hung up.

He leaned back in his chair. Wielding his power over others twice in one morning certainly agreed with him. Perhaps it was time to exercise his advantage over Emma.

★

363

After the third night, re-runs of bad American sitcoms and just-add-water meals were getting Prudence down. Listlessly changing channels with the remote and twirling instant noodles onto her fork, she wondered if her brain would atrophy before or after she developed scurvy.

It had been over six weeks since As had called the relationship off, so why was it hurting the most now? None of that cheerful denial she indulged in had paid off. She was used to getting what she thought she deserved from life. But now she was forced to admit that As had some other desperate bimbo to shag. Prudence had been retired, made obsolete, her body too familiar to be thrilling any more.

Why was every sitcom set in New York? Prudence felt as though she knew that cityscape better than she knew Melbourne. Yellow cabs and hot-dog vendors, good-looking Americans cracking jokes of inconsistent cleverness. She hit the off button and the black screen swallowed them all. Sooty looked up at her from the floor, as though upset that she had turned the television off.

'Die, Yankees,' she muttered, finishing her instant noodles. Eight o'clock Wednesday and she wasn't happy yet. How long was this grieving process going to take? She felt bloated from too much MSG, and her nerves were jangled from the litre of Coke and four coffees she had drunk that day.

Only one thing could make her feel better—a smoke.

Her tote bag was cast inelegantly behind the sofa. Rummaging through it for a packet of cigarettes, she found only shopping dockets, tissues in various stages of decomposition, stray tampons and a hairbrush in need of a good clean. Now she remembered smoking her last cigarette on the balcony at college before coming home. She'd forgotten to stop off and buy more. Luckily for her, she had emergency supplies upstairs in her wardrobe.

She marched upstairs and went to the wardrobe. On the top shelf, amongst clothes she would never wear again and unwanted Christmas presents from relatives, her hand closed over the long paper carton. But it crushed too easily. Perhaps there was one packet nestled up the end.

'Please, God. Please, God,' Prudence breathed as she pulled the carton down. Empty. No emergency supplies. No cigarettes in the house. Her craving increased proportionate to her distance from having it satisfied.

Only one thing to do—never mind that it was dark, cold and drizzling outside. Expedition to the milk bar. Reluctantly she pulled on her shoes and overcoat again, told Sooty to clean up the house before she got back, and locked the front door behind her.

She thought about As on her way to the milk bar, torturing herself over his new girlfriend. Was it another student? Somebody from outside the college? An old flame back on the scene? Who, who, who? It was going to drive her mad not knowing. If she wasn't already mad. The milk bar was bright and warm compared to outside. She grabbed a can of Coke and a Violet Crumble and went to the counter for cigarettes.

Outside again, under the awning of the milk bar, she wasn't sure which of her three treats she wanted to open first. Her craving for nicotine won out and she stuffed the Coke and chocolate into her overcoat pockets. She stood under the awning and smoked, watched cars spin past over the wet bitumen and made up her mind. Time to go up to the college and check out As's office. And that would be it. The last time she would do something mad and borderline illegal where As was concerned. She'd just check quickly for evidence—all she wanted to know was his new woman's identity, perhaps what she looked like—and then she'd leave it alone. Be adult about it. Let him go.

Let him go.

She polished off the chocolate and the Coke on the way to the college and chased it with another cigarette. She was feeling decidedly ill. Perhaps tomorrow she would starting eating right too. After all, she was a great cook, she should treat herself more often.

The college stood quiet and still between the huge trees that flanked it. The security lights lit up the edifice from below. Raindrops free-fell into the light beams, lit up like fairy dust. She let herself into the college, closing the drizzle out behind her. The fridges in the cafeteria hummed loudly. After checking the door was locked properly, she headed up to As's office.

A torch would have been a lot of use to her right about now. She stood in As's office, the door closed quietly behind her, not daring to turn the light on. With a bit of reflected help from the security lights, her eyes gradually adjusted to the dark and she went to As's desk and sat behind it. Top drawer. Locked. Of course. She pulled out her lighter and held a wavering light over her keys. The smallest one on the ring looked like her best bet. It fitted and she turned the lock. The drawer opened.

With only the flame of her cigarette lighter to assist, she began sifting through the things in the drawer. Pens, pencils, paper clips multiplying like rabbits, wipes for the reading glasses he never wore out of vanity, stationery request forms ... Boring, all boring. She slammed the drawer and started on the next one. It too was locked. This time she was rewarded with a stack of folded papers. She pulled them onto the desk and leafed through them. More stationery request forms, class schedules for coursework subjects, a list of students' names and phone numbers—hers was on it, as was Holly's—but nothing incriminating. No photos, no love letters, no nothing.

Bottom drawer. She turned the lock. This time she found condoms—the ones she had bought for them. He wouldn't go into a chemist and buy condoms himself in case somebody saw him. Like the whole world cared about his dick. She pushed them aside, found an expensive pen set in a box, and below that some letters still in their envelopes.

Her thumb was getting sore from holding the lighter on. She pulled out the first envelope and examined it by the light of the little flame. It was from Randolph, when he had been in Israel. Not a love letter, but intriguing all the same.

She pulled it out of its envelope, unfolded it and read:

I have come to Jerusalem on the advice of a very strange fellow I met in Eilat. He was a one-eyed Jew, whose grandfather practised magic in Germany . . .

Prudence caught her breath. Magic? She wondered if Randolph's scrawled handwriting and the darkness were playing tricks on her eyes. She held the letter a little closer to the lighter and kept reading.

The old man is dead now, but apparently he had often mentioned to his grandson the existence of a strange set of papers—the 'dark fragment' he called it—which was supposedly somewhere in the Old City of Jerusalem.

Prudence felt her heartbeat pick up, felt a strange, ecstatic joy bubbling up in her throat. Magic. Strange papers. The 'dark fragment'. A mystery, right here under her nose.

She skimmed the rest of the letter but found nothing more interesting until the second-last line: 'I want to find this fragment and bring it home.'

Prudence's mind was racing with half-formed questions as she placed the letter back in the envelope with shaking hands. What? When? What if? She reached for another letter, barely able to control her excitement.

That's when she heard the footsteps on the stairs.

She let out a little gasp, shoved the letter back into the drawer, the condoms and the pen set on top, and quickly locked it all away. The door was closed, so whoever it was wouldn't see her. Unless of course they were coming in here. Unless of course it was As. That would top it off, if As found her—once again—snooping in his private affairs. She slid off his chair and went to listen by the door.

The footsteps seemed to have stopped, and Prudence was suddenly overcome by the horrible sense that whoever it was stood on the other side of the door, listening too.

A few heartbeats passed like that, then the footsteps moved away. Prudence let out a relieved sigh. She waited a few minutes, then opened the door a crack and peered out. The hallway was clear. She tiptoed out and closed As's door behind her. The wrench she felt leaving her secrets behind was only marginally less painful than being dumped by As. But she could come back, check out the other letters later. Perhaps at one o'clock one morning when she was bound to be undisturbed. For now, she wanted to get out of the college quietly, without whoever was there noticing her.

She crept down the stairs—tiny, cautious steps—and peered along the second-floor hallway. There was a light coming from under her office door which she was pretty sure hadn't been there on her way up. Holly or Justin must be here. She put her money on Holly.

As she neared the door she thought she could hear crying. She stopped for a few moments to listen. Yes, it was definitely a muffled sobbing. She knocked tentatively.

'Holly?'

The crying stopped. 'Prudence?' came the reply from the other side of the door.

Prudence pushed the door open and went in. Her friend sat at her desk, no books open, no pen in hand, just sitting there as if waiting for something to happen.

'What are you doing here?' Prudence asked.

'I came to get a book. How about you?'

Prudence calmly sidestepped the question. 'Were you crying?'

Holly looked down at her desk, as if considering whether to answer the question honestly. Then, probably realising she didn't stand a chance with Prudence, she nodded slowly. 'Yes.'

'Why?'

'I'm just . . . Things aren't going so great.'

'So you come up to the college to cry your eyes out when I would've been happy to give you a cup of tea and a sympathetic ear?'

'Sorry. I didn't know I was going to . . . I . . . Sorry.'

'It's okay.' Prudence was suspicious of course. But she didn't want to push Holly with questions when she was so clearly upset. Something had been bugging her for the last month or so, but Prudence had no idea what it was. Surely not still the husband who couldn't even kill himself right? The family that wouldn't talk to her? Hell, Prudence's family didn't talk to Prudence either. At least Holly's family had the decency to announce it in advance and provide a reason.

'Come on,' Prudence said, 'get your book and let's go to my place. I'll stick a frozen apple pie in the oven.'

'Yeah, okay.' Holly grabbed a book off the top of her desk—it didn't look to Prudence as though she cared which one—and stood up. Too many questions crowded Prudence's head. Her thoughts were still up there in As's third drawer, among the other letters.

Holly put an arm around Prudence's waist. 'You're good to me, Prudence.'

'You deserve the best,' she said, leading Holly out of the office. Prudence cast a longing glance back up the stairs to the third floor, but Holly had rested a sad head on her shoulder. Secrets could wait for now. Apple pie was calling.

CHAPTER TWENTY-SIX

．．．

〜

As per the invitation she had found on her desk first thing Friday morning, Holly waited on the steps outside Humberstone College at seven o'clock on Sunday night for the next session in the Confessional. She hugged her newly purchased woollen overcoat around herself and watched the trees toss their branches in the chilly wind. Her fingers felt like they were brittle little sticks of ice. She hoped Prudence wouldn't be late.

Prudence arrived about five minutes later, a large blanket folded under her arm and Justin in tow. Holly felt another small twinge of jealousy, though she couldn't say why for sure. It wasn't about whether or not Justin preferred Prudence as a potential girlfriend, it was more to do with worrying that she, Holly, was the spare, the friend that hung around unwanted when the two of them would rather be alone together. Silly, really. But now she felt so acutely that Justin and Prudence were the most important people she had and she couldn't bear to imagine herself excluded from them in any way. She stood up and greeted them too brightly.

'Have you been waiting long?' Prudence asked.

'About five minutes.'

'We've got food. Show her, Justin.'

Justin held up a plastic bag with takeaway containers in it. 'Thai,' he said, 'my favourite.'

'And plenty of wine to wash it down with,' Prudence said, patting her tote bag. 'Two bottles tonight. I estimate roughly eight hundred dollars worth.'

Holly felt a small misgiving over drinking all Prudence's father's good wine. Sometimes Prudence dragged her along so cheerfully she didn't even notice how many lines of decency, legality or morality they crossed together. Still, Holly had never known anybody as warm and loving, despite her sometimes brittle exterior and her unconscious bouts of self-obsession. The other night when Prudence had found Holly sitting in the office crying her eyes out—after another unsuccessful attempt to contact Christian—she had taken her home, fed her apple pie and hot chocolate (with whipped cream out of a can), and not asked one single question. Holly knew the effort that took Prudence. She expected to be asked tonight, however, and had prepared a plausible lie for the time being. She wasn't prepared to share Christian's story with the world just yet. The whole thing felt so intensely private, she wanted to cherish it on her own in quiet moments. More often than not lately, those moments had been melancholy and cheerless.

'Follow Team Captain Prudence,' Prudence was saying as she unlocked the front door and led them in. 'Hey, were either of you any good at sport?'

The door closed behind them and they crossed the foyer and headed for the cellar.

'No,' Justin admitted. 'I was always shorter than everybody else, I wore glasses and I was good at art. I was the quintessential geek.'

'Geeks always grow up to be the coolest people,' Prudence assured him. 'Take me as an example. How about you, Holly?'

'Um . . . not really. Although, my dad paid for my membership at a tennis club until I was twelve. I'm almost ashamed to admit it to you two.'

'So you should be,' Prudence said, switching on the torch and closing the cellar door behind them. 'I'm sure I would have been good at school sport if they'd had a hundred-metre underground tunnel for a racetrack.'

'I came second-last in every race I was ever in,' Holly said.

'I came third-last,' Justin replied.

Prudence turned and smiled at them. 'I came dead last. But then, I wasn't trying. Ever notice they never made the sporty kids try out for the debating team? Or the school play? Always pissed me off that sport was compulsory.' She unlocked the door and shone the torch down the hallway. 'Come on, let's go eat.'

Holly felt a little queasy at the idea of eating food in the Confessional. The place smelled funny and the bugs were never far away. What if one fell into her food and she didn't see it?

'Do you think it's sanitary to eat down here?' she asked as Prudence led them round the first bend and into the Confessional.

'No worse than a lot of diners we've eaten in.' Prudence placed and lit a candle in each corner and switched the torch off. She shrugged off her overcoat and spread the blanket on the ground. 'Sir, madam, your table.' With a flourish of her arm, she crossed her ankles and sat on the blanket. Justin and Holly followed suit.

Holly cautiously started her food, careful to keep it covered as much as possible against free-falling bugs. Prudence uncorked the wine.

'This is a celebration, by the way,' Prudence said as she took a swig and passed the bottle round.

'Celebrating that we've never caught hepatitis off each other?' Holly remarked, taking a mouthful herself.

'No. We're celebrating three things. Number one—Justin's birthday, even though it was over a week ago. But the dinner with the rellies didn't really do justice to the great event. Am I right, Justin?'

Justin shook his dark curls. 'It was painful in the extreme.'

'And included a bizarre diatribe from Emma to me about . . . Well, we can go into that later. Number two—we're celebrating being on holidays, which officially start today as it's the first day of the first week of the mid-year break. Which brings me to number three. We're celebrating the fact that we've been friends for one whole semester. Here's to us.'

'Here's to us,' Holly and Justin responded. The bottle was passed around and suddenly Holly couldn't imagine any other circumstances she'd rather dine in.

Dinner finished, Holly stretched out on the blanket in the candlelight, a pleasantly full feeling in her stomach accompanying the pleasantly drunk feeling growing in her head.

'Before we start confessing tonight,' Prudence said, carefully sealing her plastic fork in her empty takeaway container, 'I want to go check out that locked door at the end of the second loop in the tunnel again. See if it's still locked, you know. I brought a screwdriver from home and thought I might try to jimmy the lock. What do you think?'

'Dumb idea,' Holly said. 'But no doubt you'll convince us to go along with you.'

'You don't have to,' Prudence said, frowning, 'but if you do, I'll let you in on a *huge* secret when we come back.'

'Yours or somebody else's?' Justin asked nervously.

Prudence punched his arm lightly. 'Not yours. Don't sweat.'

Justin shrugged. 'Sure. I'll come. Holly?'

Prudence turned to her. 'Holly?'

'You guys must think I'm so boring,' Holly said, exasperated. 'You always check with me before you do anything daring. Like I'm this boring old lady that hangs out with you.'

Prudence looked taken aback. 'Where did all that angst come from?'

'Of course I'll go,' Holly muttered, standing and brushing a stray grain of rice from her lap.

Justin had picked up the torch and switched it on, and Prudence was rummaging in her bag for the screwdriver. They headed up the tunnel, up the short walk and through to the second loop. Prudence gave her hand a squeeze.

'Sorry if we offended you.'

Holly sighed. 'I'm just feeling a bit . . . You know I'm not as brave as you two.'

'Brave? Are you kidding? You're probably the bravest of all of us. You risked everything to come to Melbourne. I've never risked anything in my life. Except, of course, the condition of my hair.'

'You don't mean that,' Holly said. The air seemed to grow much darker and closer in this part of the labyrinth. They stopped outside the locked door.

'Sure I mean it. I'm a moving target, Justin's an invisible one. You—you're just you and you do what you have to and you take the consequences. We both think you're great.' She turned to Justin. 'Don't we, Justin?'

He nodded briefly by way of a response and bent to shine the torch into the keyhole. 'Can't see anything, Prudence.'

'Here, hold the beam steady and let me try the lock.' She pulled the screwdriver out of her bag, jammed it into the lock and wriggled it up and down for a few moments. 'You know,' she said, pulling the screwdriver out and peering through the keyhole, 'I really have no idea what

I'm doing. I'm as good at picking locks as I am at catching soccer balls.'

'You don't catch soccer balls,' Justin remarked. 'You're not supposed to touch them with your hands. Even I know that.'

'I would have thought lock-picking would be part of your trade in secrets and mysteries, Prudence,' Holly said as they headed back down the tunnel.

'I've always found it easier to extort a set of keys than to force locks.' She giggled. 'That's my *modus operandi*. It would serve you both well to remember it.'

They went back to the Confessional. Prudence and Holly lay down on the blanket, while Justin sat cross-legged on his overcoat, hands resting on his knees. Prudence reached for the wine and took a swig.

'Okay, so I've got a secret.'

'Tell us,' Holly said.

'Well, remember the other night when I ran into you up here, Holly?'

Holly nodded.

'I'd been in As's office.'

'I thought I heard someone in there,' Holly said, snapping her fingers. 'Was that you?'

'Yep. I've got his keys, as you both know. I went through his drawers and I—'

'Prudence! You didn't!' Holly exclaimed.

'It's a long story. I had good reason to be there, honestly. Anyway, I found these letters in his bottom drawer and I read one of them and—'

This time Justin interjected. 'God, Prudence. You've got no morals.'

'I'll take that as a compliment,' Prudence replied, in a voice that made it clear she didn't. 'Do you guys want to hear what I found out, or would you rather just sit up there on high and judge me like sanctimonious twats?'

Holly and Justin exchanged a chastened glance.

'Sorry, Prudence,' Justin said.

'Sorry, Prudence,' Holly echoed. 'Please go on.'

'Right. Earlier this year I found out that Randolph was in Israel, but every time I asked As about it, he'd deny it. I've since got Randolph to admit that he was, but he's a bit coy about saying why.'

Holly couldn't believe what she was hearing. It was as though Prudence thought she was entitled to know, as though some crime against humanity were being committed when people didn't answer her questions.

'It all seemed a bit strange to me, because officially Randolph was supposed to be in York on a research project. So, the other night I found this letter that Randolph wrote As while he was in Jerusalem.' She sat up and wriggled closer to them both on the blanket. Her eyes were huge and black in the candlelight, her excitement palpable, almost contagious. 'This letter spoke about a strange set of papers, the whereabouts of which Randolph discovered from some magician guy. He called it the "dark fragment", and the letter seemed to indicate he was there to find it and bring it back here with him. Randolph came back six weeks ago and I'm willing to bet he found it, whatever it was.'

The mention of magic unnerved Holly for a moment, reminding her of Peter Owling and his experiments with spirit-raising. But once a logical explanation had occurred to her, it was hard to overlook in favour of Prudence's mysterious imaginings.

'Prudence, I hate to be a wet blanket, but Randolph is a specialist in Victorian texts. Couldn't it be that he was after these papers for their academic research value?'

Prudence's face quite visibly fell. Holly felt like a bitch. Obviously this explanation hadn't occurred to her.

'But . . . But he said that he'd been there for personal reasons. And As wouldn't admit that he was there at all. Why be so cagey if it was just a typical research thing?'

'Occam's razor, Prudence,' Justin said kindly. 'Don't multiply your entities unnecessarily. The most simple explanation is usually the right one. Maybe Randolph is possessive about his discovery—it could be important or momentous in his field: You know how academics are.'

'I'm sorry, Prudence, I didn't mean to upset you,' Holly said, stretching out a hand to touch Prudence's shoulder.

'God, I'm such an idiot!' Prudence wailed. 'I thought I'd uncovered a black-magic ring or something. I could cry I'm so disappointed.'

Holly squirmed. 'It's my fault, I shouldn't have—'

'No, it's not your fault. It's mine. I've got to stop thinking like an eight-year-old.'

'Still,' Justin said, trying to cheer Prudence up, 'the papers still sound interesting. Perhaps when Randolph starts working on them he'll let you assist him with his research. Could be an old spell book or something.'

'Oh, I don't care any more. I'm making a mid-year resolution. From this moment on I'm going to act like a reasonable human being.'

'Please don't,' Holly begged. 'Please just keep being you.'

'No, I'm determined. You guys have to stop me if I get out of hand. Just slap me or something.' Then, entertained by her own notion, Prudence looked up at Holly. 'What's your mid-year resolution, Holly?'

Holly was taken by surprise. 'Um . . . I haven't thought of one.'

'Well, think of one now. It'll cheer me up.'

'Okay. I resolve, for the rest of the year, to stop being a boring old lady and start having fun.' The bottle passed around again. Holly noticed it was getting very empty very quickly.

'Justin?'

'I resolve to be exactly the same as I ever was,' he said dryly.

Prudence clapped her hands together and laughed. 'If it's not broke, don't fix it, I suppose. Hey, Justin, how're things going with Emma?' Prudence lay down on her side again, lighting a cigarette and watching Justin. 'Is she still nuts?'

'Surprisingly, Prudence, she's not. She's left me alone for . . .' he counted in his head, 'six days.'

Prudence looked astonished. 'Really?'

'Why so surprised, Prudence?' Holly asked. 'Wasn't that the plan?'

'When we went to dinner for Justin's birthday, Emma cornered me in the ladies' room and ordered me to leave Justin alone. Threatened me. I thought she'd gone all *Fatal Attraction* or something.'

'Well, I had a quiet word with Lucien,' Justin said. 'It did the trick. She hasn't spoken to me—except the usual polite stuff—since Monday. And I was given a new laptop on Friday.'

'How come?'

'I broke my last one in a fit of pique,' he muttered, dropping his head.

'No way.'

'It's true. Emma made an unscheduled stop-off at my bedroom and I . . . kind of lost my temper.'

Holly and Prudence smiled at each other. Holly couldn't imagine Justin losing his temper or raising his voice, let alone breaking something in a rage.

'That's actually kind of exciting,' Prudence said, giving voice to Holly's thoughts.

'Exciting?'

'Never mind. It's a girl thing.'

'So you don't have to pretend to be my girlfriend any more,' Justin continued in a mildly embarrassed voice. 'I think my problem's solved.'

'Well, don't announce it officially or anything. We don't want them to know it was a scam.' Prudence drained the dregs of the wine bottle and uncorked the next. Holly almost said that they'd probably had enough to drink, but in keeping with her mid-year resolution she grabbed it from Prudence and downed a few gulps.

'Bravo, Holly,' Prudence said. She lit another cigarette and passed it to Holly. 'Come on, here's a new vice for you.'

Holly hesitated then took the cigarette. 'What the hell. No doubt I'll think better of this mid-year resolution thing in the cold hard light of tomorrow.' She took a careful drag and exhaled it elegantly. No coughing fits, but a bit of a head rush.

'But, Justin,' Prudence was saying, 'you really have to make a resolution.'

'I don't like to, Prudence. I hate to think about the future. Nothing scares me more.'

'Why?'

'Because . . . I don't know. Because it's going to run out one day and I don't know when.'

Prudence smiled at him. 'Okay, I'm starting to get the idea that you're given to morbid thoughts. Am I right?'

'It's not morbid, it's the truth. Life is like this tenuous spark trapped between two cold poles. It moves from nothing to nothing and it's so . . . it's so fucking aimless.'

'Please don't talk about death again,' Holly begged, starting to feel nauseous from the tobacco. 'Can't we talk about something fun?'

'We haven't confessed yet,' Prudence declared. 'We're all drunk enough to do that by now, aren't we?'

'So what's it going to be tonight?' Holly asked, happy to be on a more shallow subject.

'I don't know . . . Let me see . . . How about, What's the meanest thing you ever did to another person? Justin, you go first.'

'When I ran out on Emma, that was pretty mean,' he said, not meeting her eyes.

'No, make it something before we all knew each other.'

Justin pressed his lips together, thinking. At length he said, 'Okay. When I was seventeen my mother had a boyfriend. Some crusty old drunk that I hated. I hated all her boyfriends. He had this rare Frank Sinatra record that he'd bring over and play on my mother's old turntable. I always knew they were having sex when Frank started singing. I got to hate it so much that one day when they were out, I got a pin and scratched the record beyond repair. Apparently it was irreplaceable, and when he found out he actually cried. Wept like a baby.'

'Did you feel bad?'

Justin shook his head. 'I thought it was funny. He broke up with my mother shortly after that, so it was like mission accomplished, really.'

Prudence turned her eager gaze towards Holly. 'Holly? What's the meanest thing you ever did to another person?'

Holly thought about it. Leaving her husband? Slandering Christian's most beloved? Withholding evidence of a ghost from Prudence?

'Come on,' Prudence said.

'I'm thinking.'

'You can't be that virtuous.'

'Does stuff you did as a child count?'

'Hell, no. We're all selfish little demons as children. Look, forget it. What I really want to know is why you were up here at the college on Wednesday night, crying your eyes out.'

Holly butted her cigarette and closed her eyes. Her head was spinning and she didn't feel so well. She had known the question would come. 'I've been a bit down lately, that's all. What with Michael, and the weather, and my parents not talking to me. I got a little tired and emotional.'

'That's all?'

'Isn't that enough? Haven't you ever cried when things got too much?'

'Me cry? I never cry. I'm tough. Another cigarette, Holly?' Prudence was leaning over her. Holly opened her eyes to see her wafting a lit cigarette in the air above her face. Holly parted her lips and let Prudence jam the cigarette between them.

'Justin?' Prudence had turned her attention to Justin now, was holding out another cigarette.

'She won't be happy until she's given us all lung cancer,' Holly said.

'Sure.' He took the cigarette and leaned forward while Prudence lit it for him.

'I wish we had music,' Prudence said. 'We should put some batteries in that portable stereo from Holly's place. Hey, we should sleep down here one night.'

Holly shook her head. 'I don't know how much longer I can keep up with you, Prudence. It's only been half an hour since my resolution and I'm already exhausted and nauseous.'

They lay on their backs and stared into the darkness, long companionable silences broken by confessions, giggles, snatches of drunken conversation, Prudence's instructions for blowing smoke rings. The only sign that time was passing was the slow burning down of the candles in the corners of the room. When one of them spluttered and died, Holly was almost asleep and Prudence was singing quietly to herself.

Justin sat up and surveyed the three remaining candles. 'It's going to be real dark in here very soon,' he said. 'Want me to go get some more candles?'

'Do you know where they are?' Prudence asked. 'In my top drawer.'

'Sure. I hope you don't mind if I read any mail you've got lying around while I'm up there.'

'Don't make fun. What's the time?'

Justin checked his watch. 'Nearly midnight.'

'Yeah, let's get more candles. Let's pull an all-nighter. There's still some wine left. What do you say, Holly? What does the new you say?'

'More candles, more wine, more cigarettes,' Holly declared, wanting none of those things as much as she wanted a good, long sleep in a warm, soft bed.

'You heard her. Go, candle-boy.'

Justin rose, pushing his long hair back from his face. 'Back in a minute,' he said, grabbing the torch and heading out the door.

Holly watched him leave then turned to Prudence. She smirked at Holly.

'What?' Holly asked.

'You like him, don't you?'

'I'm drunk. Everybody starts to look good. You're not looking bad yourself.'

Prudence laughed that gorgeous belly laugh of hers, then wiped her eyes carefully, trying not to smudge her make-up. 'Well, just between you and me, you're Justin's favourite girl.'

Holly could feel herself blush and had trouble keeping a delighted smile off her face. 'How do you know?'

'He told me. Not in so many words, but in words enough. He's yours for the taking.'

'I'm not taking.'

'I don't know why not.'

Suddenly Justin stuck his head back in the doorway. 'There's somebody out there,' he hissed urgently.

Prudence and Holly sat up in shock.

'Who? Where?' Prudence asked.

Holly felt her heart thudding. Found out, they were

going to be found out. End of the scholarship, end of the dream.

'They're upstairs. I got halfway out the cellar door when I heard the front entrance open.' He stopped and ran a hand through his hair. 'This is going to sound crazy, but I think it was Lucien and Emma. I heard them talking. Though I don't know what they would be doing up here so late on a Sunday.'

Prudence stood and dragged Holly to her feet. 'Come on. Let's go peek out the cellar door and see who it is.'

'What if they find us?' Holly asked, panic-stricken.

'They won't come near the cellar. That part of the stairwell is condemned. I'm dying to find out what they're doing here.'

'They went upstairs, Prudence,' Justin said. 'You won't be able to see anything.'

'Well, we might hear something then. Come on, I'm curious.'

Prudence commandeered the torch and then they had no choice. They were going where she was going. Holly's nausea was now accompanied by a headache and dizziness. She stayed close to Justin going down the tunnel and back to the cellar. The three of them crowded by the door to the outside world and Prudence turned the light off. She cautiously opened the door a crack and peered out. Nothing happened for long moments, nor could they hear anything.

Then the front entrance opened again and Holly heard two male voices.

Prudence ducked back and closed the cellar door, plunging them into total blackness. 'Shit! It's Randolph and As. What the hell is going on? Midnight staff meeting?'

'You know, I remember once before coming home late one Sunday and seeing Lucien and Emma arriving,' Justin said.

Prudence's eyes widened. 'Yes! And I saw As leaving his house at around midnight a couple of Sundays ago. Do you think this is a regular thing?'

'Whatever it is, it's pretty strange.'

'Justin, have you heard Emma and Lucien leaving the house late on Sundays before?'

He shook his head. 'I don't think so, but then they could go out through the courtyard and I'd never hear a thing. The garage is on the other side of the house.'

Prudence snapped her fingers as she remembered something. 'Of course! I heard As complaining to Randolph that his wife was making it difficult for him to go out on weekends. I thought he must have another woman, but it was probably about these get-togethers.' She shivered noticeably. 'I've gone cold all over.'

Prudence opened the door again and peered out for a few more minutes. Holly had to remind herself to breathe.

'What do we do?' she asked. 'Do we sneak out?'

'No. We don't know who else will be arriving. I think we're going to have to have our little slumber party after all.'

'God, Prudence. I've been drinking all night and I need to pee,' Holly said, close to tears. She didn't want to stay all night in the underground chamber with no light while the people who decided her future were upstairs.

'So go in one of the chambers around the bend. It's not like anybody's going to care if it smells a bit pissy. I've got tissues in my bag.'

Holly closed her eyes and leaned back against the wall. 'I'm in hell.'

'Hey, it's not so bad. Come on, back to the Confessional.'

They trudged back to the chamber, where another of the candles had died. Holly—embarrassed, afraid, mortified—took a trip around to the second circle of rooms and speedily relieved herself, never taking her eyes off the door. She didn't know what she dreaded most, the appearance of an evil spectre, her academic supervisor, or Prudence with a smart remark.

When she returned, Prudence had positioned her tote bag as a pillow and laid her overcoat over herself like a blanket. Justin was stretched out on his back. Holly joined them with a sigh.

'I'm really uncomfortable about this.'

'What happened to the new you?' Prudence asked.

'She turned her toes up right about when she started picturing herself getting kicked out of college.'

Prudence shook her head. 'I don't understand. What is it all about? It may be the piss talking, but do you think it could have something to do with that letter from Randolph?'

'I thought we'd dismissed that notion.'

'Fuck Occam's razor. Occam was an unimaginative bastard. Listen, that letter was addressed to "Laurence, et al", which means it was intended for a group of people. What you've got upstairs is a group of people, including Randolph and As. And Lucien and Emma, who Justin says he's seen coming home very late on a Sunday before.'

'I can't believe I'm going to say this,' Justin said, turning onto his side. 'I'm sure I'm going to regret it because you'll never shut up.'

'What?' said Prudence. 'You know something?'

'No, it's just . . . Lucien locks himself in his study a lot. I don't know what he does in there, but he has been doing it a lot more often since Randolph came back. And Emma has hinted more than once that Lucien is working on some kind of book or translation.'

Prudence's eyes nearly popped out of their sockets. Holly would have laughed if she could have shaken the feeling of impending doom that had settled on her.

'Really? Oh, Justin.' Prudence pressed a hand to her

forehead as if trying to keep inside the million specu-
lations that had just sprung up in her mind. 'I'm going
to blow a fuse. A book, or a strange set of papers. A
dark fragment of something. And they're all up there
doing ... What are they doing? God, it's going to kill
me.'

'It won't kill you,' Holly said, trying to calm her down.

'I shouldn't have said anything,' Justin sighed. 'At least
not until it was daylight and we were sober.'

'There has to be a logical explanation,' Holly offered,
realising she sounded like a cliché.

'There doesn't have to be,' Prudence snapped.

Prudence was right, of course, there didn't have to be.
And a girl who spent some of the best nights of her life
in the company of a ghost should know that better than
anybody.

'Well, what's your explanation, Prudence?' Holly asked
gently.

'I don't know.' Prudence downed the last of the wine,
lost in thought. The third candle went out. Only a last
brave flame glowed in the black room. Holly lay back
and closed her eyes.

'I want to go to sleep before the last candle goes out,'
she said, not realising that she'd said it out loud until
Prudence replied.

'It'll be just as dark when you wake up in the morning.'

'I hadn't thought of that.'

'Anyway, there's nothing much else we can do tonight.
Here, cuddle up close so you don't get scared.'

Holly opened her eyes. Prudence held up one side of
her overcoat, making a space for Holly beside her. Holly
wriggled into the space gratefully, her friend's warm body
close against her own.

'Justin?'

'I'm fine over here.'

'Goodnight then,' Prudence said. 'Although it's not

like I'm going to be able to sleep with such a big mystery so close by.'

'Try your best,' Justin said, making himself comfortable.

'Goodnight, Justin,' Holly said.

'Goodnight, Holly.'

Holly closed her eyes just as the last candle went out.

CHAPTER TWENTY-SEVEN

$\sim$

Infinity started in his hands, spinning away from him in every direction, a nothingness that threatened to open up a gap in his mind, tearing him apart.

It's coming. Soon.

His hands touched a wall—cool earth. At first he was relieved to grasp something in the void, but then the icy certainty shuddered through him. *This is my grave.* His other hand stretched out to find an opposite wall, a third, a fourth wall. A tiny space, narrowing off to a point of light above him. And like the moon moving over the sun in eclipse, a dark shape began to move over the light. The earth began to shake beneath him. An infinity of nothingness was waiting just beneath his feet.

Lucien woke with a start. Terror's grip released him slowly. He touched his pillow, dug his fingers into the soft material.

It's okay, it's okay. Only a dream.

He needed a cup of tea and a good bright light to calm him down.

'Emma?' Feeling behind him for her soft body, he found only a cold space in the bed. He turned over and sat up. Where was she? Perhaps she hadn't been able to sleep and was downstairs having a warm drink herself. Sometimes it was hard to wind down after their Sunday night sessions.

Lucien slipped out of bed, put on his slippers and robe and went downstairs.

Emma was nowhere to be seen. He boiled the kettle and made tea for himself, musing on her whereabouts. Briefly, he wondered if she'd left him, and was ashamed at the sense of relief the thought gave him. Of course she hadn't left him. Though the argument they'd had over Justin had been particularly nasty.

On Tuesday he had taken her out to lunch, knowing that she wouldn't make as much of a scene in a public place. After their meal, when they were sipping coffee and Emma had seemed malleable enough, he had told her in no uncertain terms that she was to leave Justin alone. She had pretended she didn't know what he was talking about, conceded that perhaps Justin had developed a crush on her that had made him moody, and flippantly agreed that she would try to keep out of his way.

It wasn't enough for Lucien. He couldn't have Justin leaving, but at the same time he couldn't tell Emma why. Not yet. So he had played on her stupid vanity and let her believe he was jealous.

'You're my wife, Emma. You have no business flirting with my nephew.'

She had practically glowed over that remark. 'There's nothing wrong with flirting,' she had said.

Having tried everything else, he decided to state his advantage in simple terms. Magnus—ever the paranoid parent, concerned more for his fortune than for his sons' wellbeing—had disapproved deeply of Lucien and Emma's marriage, as they had both been very young. The marriage had only been permitted upon the signing of a contract by Emma, stipulating that should Lucien wish to separate from her on any reasonable grounds—adultery, for example—she would not be eligible to claim any Humberstone money. In the stupid, vainglorious certainty of young love, she had signed it, declaring that the contract would never again see the light of day. Indeed, she probably thought that it had long ago been lost or destroyed. Of course it hadn't. The Humberstones were nothing if not meticulous.

Lucien finished his tea and rinsed the teacup. He winced as he remembered the ensuing argument, not even the elegant surroundings of the restaurant able to make her keep check on her vicious tongue. But all her railing and ranting had come to nothing in the end, because he had her and she knew it. Finally he had leaned across and said in a soft, firm voice, 'I merely ask that you leave Justin alone from now on.'

To which she had replied, solemn as a marriage vow, 'I will.'

So if she hadn't left him, where was she at four o'clock in the morning? He checked the lounge room, wondering if she'd fallen asleep reading a book, but she wasn't there. Perhaps she was already back upstairs in bed.

He went up the stairs and stopped on the landing. His bedroom was on the left, the guest room on the right. From the guest room he thought he saw a faint glow of light. Curious about what she was doing, he padded up the hallway and quietly entered the room. It was dark in here, but from under the closed door of the en suite he could see a flickering glow. A rich, cloying scent hung on the air. He moved to the door and slid it open.

'Emma?'

It was a curious sight, and it took him a moment to comprehend what was going on. Emma sat naked before the bathroom bench. In front of her, arranged at four points on the bench, were a bowl of water, a bowl of salt, a candle and some burning incense. In the centre, between the four points, was a collection of objects he could not see properly. With a sharp scalpel Emma had sliced her thumb open, and was just dropping blood onto the objects. At the sound of her name she jumped and looked around, her eyes filled with shame.

'Lucien . . . I . . .'

He took off his robe and handed it to her. 'Cover yourself. Don't get blood on it.' He reached up and flicked the light switch, casting a harsh yellow light on everything.

'What are you doing?' he asked, although he thought he already knew.

'Just an experiment,' she said sheepishly, shrugging into the robe.

'You know we dispensed with these kind of experiments very early on in our studies.' In the opening parts of the grimoire, Owling had listed various ways to perform acts of minor magic—low witchcraft, really—and Lucien thought he recognised Emma's activity as the compilation of a gris-gris, a charm fetish.

'Trying to make Justin fall in love with you?' he asked, leaning forward to peer at the objects she had laid out in front of her.

'It doesn't matter. I'll stop,' she said, placing her body between his peering eyes and the bathroom bench. She was trying to hide something.

'Emma, move.' He put a hand on each of her shoulders and pushed her aside so he could examine what she was working on.

A scrap of red material. A pile of dust. A folded piece of paper. A few drops of blood and— He gasped as he recognised one single hair. Purple hair.

'Emma, you're not . . .' He picked up the hair. 'This isn't a hex fetish, is it?'

Emma let her silence speak for her.

He unfolded the piece of paper. It had been cut out of

an old Christmas card: 'Merry Christmas, Emma and Lucien, from Prudence Emerson.'

'Are you planning to work some black magic on Prudence?'

'You told me to leave Justin alone.'

He turned on her, couldn't believe she thought it a decent excuse. 'This is not what working magic is about, Emma. It's not about low hexes and spells.' He turned back to the gris-gris. 'What did you think, that you could wrap this all up and place it under her pillow?'

'I was going to tape it under her desk at the college.'

'And what's this?' He poked a finger into the handful of dirt.

'Just dirt.'

He turned back to her. 'The truth, Emma. Every part of the fetish has a purpose.'

She shook her head resolutely. Her refusal to speak made him fear the worst.

'Emma, is it graveyard dust?'

Again no response.

'Emma?' He tried not to raise his voice and it shook with the effort.

She sighed. 'Yes, Lucien, it's graveyard dust.'

'You were trying to kill her?'

'Just to make her sick.'

'You fool. You . . .' The force of his emotion dislodged his ability to speak. All the work they had done had come to this. His wife making jealous hexes in the guest bathroom, hexes that could bring about the death of his nephew's girlfriend if they were worked with enough power and focus. And Emma, as a long-time participant in their magical rituals, could certainly evoke the power and focus. He remembered what the creature had said to him. 'You help these people draw on black magic and do not check what they are using it for.' Would he have to throw Emma out of the circle too? She was his wife.

Yes, but he had the advantage over her.

He brushed the objects into the sink and turned the tap on, rinsing away what he could and shoving the rest, dripping and ruined, into Emma's hands.

'Destroy all these things.'

'Are you going back to bed?' she asked. The robe was too big for her, had started to fall off her shoulders.

'No, I'm going to my office. I have a lot to think about.'

Justin woke when a harsh light shone in his eyes. He opened them blearily to see Prudence kneeling over him, holding the torchbeam on his face.

'Your wake-up call, Mr Penney.'

'Thanks,' he croaked, feeling decidedly seedy. 'God, my throat's sore. Do you always feel like this when you wake up in the morning?'

'Nah, years of abuse have hardened me,' Prudence replied, sitting back and shining the torch on Holly's face to wake her up too.

'It's okay, it's okay, I'm awake,' Holly said. 'Any idea what time it is?'

Prudence shone the light on her watch. 'It's just after six. I couldn't sleep any more. My back is killing me.'

Justin sat up and looked around the dark chamber. By torchlight he could see the evidence of the previous night's entertainment. Takeaway containers, empty wine bottles, cigarette butts. No wonder he felt like hell. He wondered if this mixture of queasiness and muffled guilt had been his mother's constant companion during all her years of excess.

'God, I'd kill for a glass of water,' he said, dropping his head into his hands.

'Well, I guess we need to make sure that there's

nobody up there still, and then we can use the toilets upstairs,' Prudence said.

'I doubt they'd still be there,' Holly said uncertainly.

'I want to get out of here,' Justin agreed. He wanted to see some daylight. His sleep had been fitful and shot through with dark threads of nightmare.

'Okay, let's pack up and go,' Prudence said, already scooping their rubbish up into the takeaway bags. Justin and Holly helped her, and soon they were moving back down the hallway and through to the cellars. Prudence opened the door into the college and paused for a few moments, listening.

'I don't think there's anyone around,' she said. 'Justin, hang on to this stuff and I'll go check.' She shoved the rubbish and the blanket into his arms. 'If someone sees me, I'll just say I'm up here getting a book or something.'

She ducked out into the stairwell and disappeared. Justin waited with Holly. She looked tired and pale. He wished he could think of something witty or clever to say to her, but silence was easier. Prudence returned a few minutes later.

'There's no-one around,' she said. 'It's safe.'

They emerged from the stairwell and crossed the foyer to the opposite corner, stopping along the way to dump their rubbish in a bin.

'My teeth feel like they're wearing little fuzzy sweaters,' Prudence declared as they made their way up to the toilets on the third floor.

'You got your wish, anyway—we spent a night in the Confessional,' Holly said.

They paused at the top of the stairs outside As's office. Prudence jingled her keys. 'I think I'm going in,' she said.

'Is that wise?' Justin asked.

'I've got to check out the other letters. For more clues. I've got to find out what they were doing up here. You guys don't have to be part of it.'

'Fine, we'll meet you downstairs in our office,' Holly said. 'And pretend we know nothing.'

'Sure thing. But if I find something amazing, I just may withhold it from you,' she declared as she headed towards As's office.

Holly looked at Justin. 'As if she could.' She disappeared into the ladies' toilets and Justin went into the men's room to splash his face with cold water. Holly wasn't in the hallway when he emerged again, so he went downstairs to their office. He unlocked the door and found the room empty. A library notice addressed to Holly had been slipped under the door. He bent to pick it up.

Just then Holly came in. 'Prudence not back yet?' she asked.

He shook his head. 'Here, you've got a library notice.'

'Oh no, not an overdue fine. What does it say?'

He unfolded the notice and read it out. 'It's from Noni. It says, "Dear Hollywood, that book you were after came in last thing Friday. Thought you might need him over the break so I've left him in the pigeonhole outside the third-floor library." She calls you Hollywood?'

'Yeah. She's got a name for everybody.'

'She calls me Justin Case. I don't think she calls Prudence anything.'

'I guess her real name is ironic enough. I've got to go get that book, want to come?'

'Sure.'

They headed back up the stairs, and Holly found her book in a yellow envelope in a pigeonhole outside the locked library doors. The library would remain closed over the break, as would all of the other services at the college. Another way Lucien saved money. Holly was fiddling with the seal on the envelope when Prudence slammed the door of As's office behind her, scowling.

'What's up?' Justin asked.

'No luck. He's moved them.'

'Moved them?'

'Maybe he could tell they'd been disturbed, maybe he just cleaned out his drawers. Our condoms were gone too.'

'Oh,' Holly said. 'I'm sorry.'

'I don't care about that any more,' Prudence declared. 'As is interesting for far different reasons now. He's at the centre of a mystery.'

The three of them headed down the stairs and made to leave the college.

'Well, take care unravelling it, Prudence. You don't want to get yourself in any trouble,' Holly advised.

Prudence sighed. 'With my luck, it will probably turn out to have one of those logical explanations you're always going on about. Hey, Justin, reckon you could keep an eye and an ear on Emma and Lucien for me? I'm determined to get to the bottom of this.'

'Okay, I'll be extra attentive.' He was kicking himself for ever having brought Lucien's work up. Under ordinary circumstances her curiosity was exhausting. Now she was going to be unbearable.

'What do you think the chances are of you getting into Lucien's office at home?'

'Nil.'

'Still, don't turn down an opportunity to get in if one arises, will you?'

'I'll do my best.'

They were on the ground floor again, passing the information desk and opening the front door. As they stepped out into the cold dawn, Prudence turned to Holly and Justin. Her make-up was smudged around her eyes and she looked pallid.

'Breakfast at my place, anyone? We can go over the evidence.' Her breath was a cloud of steam in the air.

'You read too much Secret Seven as a child,' Holly said.

'I want to get home, get some proper sleep.' Justin yawned and palmed his eyes. The daylight had made them ache after hours in the dark chamber.

Prudence shrugged. 'Whatever. Holly and I can work alone. What do you say, partner?'

'I'm with Justin. I'll think a lot more clearly once I've spent a few hours in a soft bed. Come by later this afternoon.'

'Okay,' Prudence said. 'I'm going to buy a special notebook. I'll bring it with me.' She turned and headed off.

Justin and Holly watched her go, then started up the hill towards their homes. 'Is she really going to start a notebook about this business?' he asked.

'What do you think? Of course she is. She's unstoppable. I hope you don't have any secrets, Justin, because they'll come out eventually,' Holly said lightly.

Of course, he could not take it lightly. Some things were too serious to be made light of. 'Well, Holly,' he replied in a subdued voice, 'the same goes for you.'

As Lucien unlocked his office door, preparing to spend another frustrating day in the company of Owling's indecipherable grimoire, he felt something akin to a pang of nausea. The anxiety, the headaches, the nightmares were wearing him down. Added to that, the previous Sunday's ritual had been more than useless. He'd had bad nights before, when he'd failed to fall into a trance, but to have such a night this close to the consummation of his work was agonising. His anxiety was getting in the way, starting to interfere with his ability to relax into the magic vibrations. To be undone by his own uncontrollable feelings would be the most intolerable failure of all.

The door slammed behind him. His office was completely silent except for his own footsteps as he went to the safe and removed the grimoire and his notes. He longed to have a day off, to go back to bed and sleep until the jagged, unintelligible characters dissolved from his mind. Or watch television, the brightly coloured images shoving the obsession with those words out of his head.

He sat, opened the grimoire, went over his notes, tried not to weep with frustration. The summoning instructions, for bringing the traitor demon through to the earthly plane, were all encrypted. Occasionally a line here or there offered hope, but most of the important text remained as far from his grasp as it had been in a box of salt in Jerusalem.

He found himself scribbling boxes within boxes in the margin of his notes and dropped his pen in exasperation. Head in hands, he groaned. The most important thing in the world had been promised to him, and now it seemed it was to be denied. His only hope was the creature he had made contact with. If he could only relax enough to cross over at next Sunday's ritual, he could ask for help. That was if the creature decided to help. It had been obstinate and cruel. He felt a small chill of fear at the thought of working with such a creature. But once Lucien had its name and had complied with its request, it would be his to command. Or rather, theirs. The other three had a stake in the summoning too, much to his discomfort.

Lucien lifted his head and stared into middle distance. But the creature had said something, hadn't it? Something that Lucien had assumed was just perverse double-speak. It had said it had been watching the group for months and years. And when Lucien had asked it for help with the code, it had simply repeated, 'Months and years.'

Was it a clue, then? If so, what did it mean? He opened his top drawer and pulled out his diary. Important dates were marked throughout. He thumbed through, found August. The first magic ritual had taken place on 14 August, nearly seventeen years ago. He wrote the date down, looked at the numbers. Calculated the number of months between the first ritual and now. Divided it by the number of years. Got another number that he didn't know what to do with. He dropped the diary back into the drawer and slammed it angrily. This was hopeless.

The grimoire lay open in front of him. He thumbed back through the book, back to where it all began. The pages of the early sections were so familiar to him now. The experimental spells, the advice for consecration, the rigid methodology—most of which had been abandoned by Owling as he went further and further into the dark side of magic, where chaos sometimes achieved better results than focus. Magnus's occasional pencil notes in the margins caught Lucien's eye. Magnus was a brilliant man, lucid and almost painfully intelligent. What would he advise in Lucien's current situation?

With a bitter smile Lucien realised that Magnus wouldn't have helped him. He had died without knowing the secret of eternal life and would consequently have preferred that nobody else found it either. Lucien remembered sitting by Magnus's hospital bed, the old man's skin yellow and papery, his breath smelling like approaching death.

'You'll have to disband the group,' he had said. 'You can't go on without me.'

But of course they had. It was just lucky that Magnus's sudden illness and death meant that he couldn't stipulate in his will financial ruin for all those who dared to continue working magic after his death. Magnus had gone off into that void from which he would never return, the one Lucien was now so assiduously attempting to elude.

Lucien ran his fingers lightly over a page. At that moment, something occurred to him. Owling always dated his experiments—here 22 December 1860, further on 19 July 1862, on it went, years of work labelled. In the later sections, however, the dates stopped appearing as he lapsed into pages of automatic writing. But were they really undated?

Months and years, magus. There's a clue.

With shaking hands he leafed through towards the end of the book. The last dated experiment was October 1866. He turned to the encrypted section. Owling started a new page for every experiment. Here was a new page, the mute hieroglyphs etched into the paper. The second collection of characters numbered four. The only months spelled with four letters were June and July. He tried June, marking in his notes the characters and how they matched up with other letters in other words. He marked Es in, Ns—finding words. This two-letter word beginning with N, was it 'no'? If so, then he had Os. Words were starting to reveal themselves slowly. He scrabbled for a sheet of clean paper and wrote the alphabet down one side, the numerals on the other. With growing excitement, he started to see the same characters appearing in words and sentences.

His initial elation began to cool as he finished transcribing all he could of the first lines of the encrypted text. Even with educated guesswork he had managed to decode only a quarter of the letters and just a handful of complete words. He flipped forward, found another date. Eight letters—November or December? It could have even been February. The sudden realisation of how much there was to do pressed heavily on his shoulders. Pages and pages—it would take forever.

With hardening resolve, he took a deep breath and reached for fresh paper. If he managed this properly, he might soon have forever on his side.

CHAPTER TWENTY-EIGHT

~

I t took until Tuesday, on the other side of a decent
night's uninterrupted sleep and twenty-four hours of
detoxification, for Holly to start feeling marginally human
again. Monday had turned out to be rainy and cold and
she had spent the whole day in front of the television,
dozing and catching up on Ricki Lake. She had forgotten
about the book Noni had left for her until Tuesday
morning when she was making her bed. The library envelope was jammed down the side of her bedside dresser
with her handbag. She finished smoothing over the bedspread, then lay on her bed with the envelope. She didn't
really know what she was looking for. Any mention of
Peter Owling or Christian, she supposed, although she
had to concede she would be surprised to find it.

As she tipped the envelope up, two books fell out. One
a bound thesis with Magnus Humberstone's name on the
front. The second a slim handbook entitled *History of Humberstone Library*. Noni had stuck a Post-it note on the front.
'I remembered this later. Might be of some use to you.'

Holly picked up the thesis first. Private banking and
colonial development. Boring, as Prudence would say.

She leafed through it. Pages and pages of double-spaced typing, with headings, subheadings and graphs. One chapter was about the Humberstones but it still failed to hold her interest. She flicked through to the end and found an appendix. It featured a Humberstone family tree and some old photographs. Carefully she folded the book open and traced a finger backwards along the family line. Graham and Lucien. Graham was Justin's father—still alive when the thesis had been written. No date of death was recorded. Magnus himself, of course, and his brother Dominic, who was Randolph's father. The tree branched off to the right and left. She traced back to Magnus's father Quincy, the single offspring of Philbert. In small print next to Philbert's name, almost as if she'd had very little to do with the production of an heir, was 'Lucy Humberstone, née Mancini, b. 1838, d. 1902.' Lucy, Christian's lover.

Holly felt a strange frisson, seeing confirmation that these people were real and not just characters in some deluded fiction her brain had spontaneously created. Lucy Humberstone was Justin's great-great-great-grandmother. She desperately wanted to tell somebody, especially Justin, but how could she? It was not as though she could tell him she was having an affair with the same young man one of his ancestors had had sex with over a century ago.

Remembering that Christian had said Lucy was in her late twenties or early thirties, she performed some quick calculations in her head. That would date Christian's story to the mid to late 1860s. And as he had died in 1867, he must have been getting very close to the end of his tale the last time they had spoken. A pain went to her heart. Too long without Christian. He seemed more and more like a dream every day.

She turned the page and leafed through the photographs. Mostly pictures of ships and shopfronts, but one picture in particular caught her eye. It was a portrait of Philbert and Lucy, and Holly stared at it for a long time. Lucy was blonde and dark-eyed, just as Christian had described her, but Holly could see none of the sly sexuality in her face that he had spoken of. She posed, unsmiling, in a dark velvet dress and diamond jewellery. Her face was pretty, but not uncommonly so. Momentarily, Holly found it impossible to comprehend that Lucy had looked into the camera in 1864 and that now she, Holly, was looking back at her so long after she was dead and gone. It scared her, making her think of all the photos she had posed for, smiling in her present, only for it eventually to become somebody else's past. She shook her head and made a quick check of the index for Peter Owling's name, but did not find it. Casting the book aside, she picked up the other one.

She flipped over onto her back with the tiny Humberstone Library history in her hands and idly flicked the pages. More self-congratulatory Humberstone egotism. It was as though they thought they were the royal family or something. Once again she went to the back for the index and was surprised to see, under O, mention of the 'Owling collection'. She backtracked to the right page. Under the heading, a small paragraph read:

> Mr Peter Owling was a debtor to the Humberstones until his death in 1867. His assets were commandeered upon his death, and his books were sent to Humberstone Library shortly after. Among the collection were first editions and poetry, as well as a number of books on experimental science and mysticism, none of them rare. Intershelved on the third floor.

Owling's books had come to Humberstone College. Perhaps even the books from which Christian had learned to read and write. The pages that his live fingers had touched and turned. Maybe he had even left a note or a scribble in the margins. What a shame the library was closed. She would dearly love to hunt the books down, pore over the pages, make the connection with Christian that she burned for.

Then a colder, darker thought settled on her. Owling's books. The grimoire that Christian had spoken of. Prudence had been talking about Randolph tracking down a strange set of papers, perhaps even something to do with magic.

She shook her head and put the book down. For a start, the history said none of Owling's books were rare, so she was probably worrying needlessly. She didn't even know if it had been a proper bound volume. Something like that would surely be lost or destroyed by time. More importantly, Randolph had been in Jerusalem, not London. It was fine to believe in black magic in Victorian London, but among her teachers in modern-day Melbourne? That was ridiculous. She'd been hanging out with Prudence for too long. And she would pull her own teeth out before she'd mention a word of this to Prudence. It would cause her less pain in the long run.

She was reaching for Magnus's thesis again when she heard a knock at the door. She expected to open it to Prudence, who hadn't made good on her promise to drop by yesterday afternoon; to find her bright-eyed on the doorstep, a fresh notebook in her hands and a mind brimming over with delirious speculation. Instead she found Justin.

'Justin?' she said.

'Hi. You're not busy, are you?'

'No, I was just reading. Come in.' She showed him in and he stood uncertainly in her lounge room. 'Would you like a tea or a coffee?'

'A coffee would be nice. Black, no sugar.'

Holly didn't remind him that by now she knew how he took his coffee. 'Coming right up. Sit down.'

She made coffee in a plunger Prudence had given her and took it out to the lounge room. He sat on the floor among the tie-dyed cushions and she sat with him, pouring two cups of steaming coffee. Even after all this time she still felt slightly uncomfortable alone with him. She didn't have Prudence's gift for unstoppable chatter, and she still had trouble interpreting his silence as anything other than boredom with her, though she knew by now it was just his way.

She sipped her coffee, stealing a glance at him over the top of her cup. Prudence had assured her that Justin had a crush on her, but that could just be Prudence's fertile imagination.

'So, um . . . did you have fun Sunday night?' she said, knowing as soon as the words left her lips that it was the most inane way she could have opened a conversation.

'Yeah, I guess. I was pretty uncomfortable sleeping on the floor.'

'Yes. Me too.'

Silence, awkward and self-conscious, lumbered between them. She started to wonder why he had come by, but didn't dare ask in case it made matters more uncomfortable.

He seemed about to say something then changed his mind. She scoured her brain for a good topic of conversation, but all she could think about was whether his eyes were like Lucy Humberstone's in the photograph. They were very dark behind the small, round glasses. Did genetic traits carry that far down the line?

'What?' he asked, noticing that she was looking at him closely.

'Sorry, just looking at your eyes,' she replied without thinking. A blush started to spread up her neck and across her cheeks as she realised how it must have sounded. 'I mean . . .'

'That's okay.'

Another silence. Holly bit her lip, felt embarrassed and ill at ease.

'I like it that you don't talk all the time like Prudence,'

he said in one quick breath, as if he'd been planning to say it for a while but had been afraid.

She laughed. 'That's good. I was starting to worry.'

'It's nice just being with you,' he said, his voice perhaps a little too serious. She watched him watching her. He reached out and, for a second, time slowed down as she wondered what he was going to do. But he just touched her once on the shoulder, very lightly, then withdrew his hand. What had Prudence said? *He's yours for the taking.* And that was right, she'd have to take him if she wanted him. That touch on the shoulder was probably the boldest thing he'd ever try. She thought about Christian and how much she loved him. But that was hopeless. And here was a real live man, attractive and intelligent and sensitive. She looked up, was about to say something, murmur a word of encouragement, but before it could pass her lips there was a loud knock on the door and Prudence shouted, 'Open up! Inspector Prudence is on the case!'

'Come in, Prudence,' Holly called. 'It's not locked.'

Justin had settled back on his cushion, sipping his coffee like nothing had passed between them. Perhaps it was better that way.

Politics marred Sunday night's meeting before the ritual had even begun. Randolph, incensed by Jane's forced departure from the group without his prior knowledge, seemed out to prove a point. Lucien was explaining to them the breakthrough in decoding when Randolph interrupted.

'You'd get it done much quicker with my help,' he said. 'I think I should be allowed to leave work and help you with it.'

'That's not possible, Randolph. Now Jane's gone I need you at the college more than ever. I can manage by myself.' Of course Randolph was right, and the worst that would happen at the college might be a couple of rich kids writing letters of complaint until Lucien had found a new teacher to replace his cousin. But he couldn't bear the thought of Randolph working on the transcription as well. What if he got something vital incorrect? Or worse, found something important and didn't share the knowledge? It was simply out of the question in the manic obsessive state that Lucien had worked himself into.

'Then I expect to be consulted more often about what you're decoding. Perhaps I should call you every night. Once a week is not enough.'

Lucien felt a tightness growing in his belly. He nodded stiffly. 'If you wish.'

Randolph smiled and continued. 'And you'll be happy to know that Laurence and I have solved another problem.'

'Which problem?'

'Remember I told you about the difficulty I was going to have getting away on Sundays with my wife at home?' Aswell said. He too was grinning. Lucien braced himself against the worst. 'Well, would you believe that even as we speak Randolph and I are out fishing?'

'What?'

Randolph explained. 'Mandy thinks Laurence is with me. Which he is, really. He'll spend Sunday nights at my house before heading off for fictitious early-morning fishing trips. A few Monday morning visits to the fish market will authenticate the story. Laurence is staying with us, Lucien.'

A challenge was expressed in this last sentence, subtly but unmistakably. Lucien squeezed his anger down inside him. 'I'm pleased,' he said shortly. He had come so close—it would have been just the three of them, just him, his wife, his cousin. Close and controllable. He would never be able to understand Randolph's fondness for a fool like Aswell, but he suspected Randolph's insistence on Aswell's continued inclusion in the group was his cousin's way of keeping control out of Lucien's hands.

But he had to relax now. The ritual would not work if he was tense, and then he'd have to wait another week to talk to the being. Now that Jane was gone, it would tell him its name. Then the work could begin in earnest.

With supreme self-control, Lucien pushed aside his emotions and the ritual began.

It took longer than usual, but eventually the world broke up and disintegrated around him and he found himself on a rise, surveying the grey, blasted landscape.

'Traitor, come!' he cried.

The creature was there a moment later. 'Good to see you again, magus,' it said. 'Last time you didn't quite make it through.'

'Jane is gone,' Lucien said. 'Your name, please.'

'It's not as easy as all that. You see, you have a decision to make.' It rubbed the top of its shiny, misshapen head with a withered stump. 'If I say my name, I'm going to say it out loud.'

'Out loud?'

'Yes, so the others can hear it. Understand?'

'I understand. I command you to say your name.'

'If they know my name, they can command me too.'

'I know.'

'You think you know almost everything, magus. On that you are mistaken.'

After the frustrations of the evening so far, the creature's ambiguity was exasperating.

'What should I know that I don't?' he asked.

'Only one of you can have it.'

A horrible realisation pressed its restless edge into Lucien's mind. 'Only one of us can have what?'

'Eternal life. He'll only grant it once. Now, my name is—'

'Wait! Don't say it.' Lucien was frantic, his mind ticking

over with possibilities. 'I'll have to think about this. Laurence I could happily excise from my life, but the others are family. My wife, my cousin.'

The creature grinned. 'It sounds to me as though you need to make a decision. Do not think to ask for me again until you have made it.'

'The grimoire,' Lucien said. 'I've cracked some of the code. I'll soon have the summoning incantations translated.'

'Good. You will need them. And, of course, you will need me. When it's time, you will be able to find me.' It leaned close, its rancid breath thick. 'It's you I want, magus. Not the others. You have the spark in you, they don't. They are fools and weaklings.'

The landscape faded and Lucien came back to the hot room. Although he was completely conscious, he waited for long minutes before opening his eyes. He did not want to gaze on the abhorred people who stood in his way.

Prudence could not remember a better holiday in her life. Not even those school holidays as an eleven-year-old when a set of guilty parents, noticing their daughter's escalating insolence and defiance, had tried to smooth it over with expensive treats. They had given up by the time she hit her teens, but it was too late by then. They had trained her well and she could easily extract negligence compensation from them, sometimes without them even knowing.

Now, aged twenty-two, she had found that unlimited consumer goods had nothing like the appeal of two good friends and an unsolved mystery.

The fun started most mornings around ten, when she would phone Justin and Holly and organise to meet. Sometimes they would meet in the city and the day would be filled with cafe lunches, espresso, stupid jokes,

Italian food on Lygon Street, hiding from the bitter cold in heated cinemas. Or on days when Holly was stressed about finance, they would sit in front of the pot-bellied stove at Prudence's place with a video and a bag of chips, ordering pizza delivery—Prudence's shout. Holly would make an occasional meal at her place, but they never went to Justin's. The idea of running into Lucien and Emma appealed to none of them.

And for Prudence the brightly coloured thread running through all of it was the secret. In a hard-covered note-book she had jotted down all the pieces of her puzzle. An inexplicable midnight meeting, probably regular. The likelihood that Randolph had brought a strange set of papers with him back from Jerusalem. Lucien locked away in his office, working on some kind of book or transla-tion. Prudence's certainty that these things were all related was not shared by Justin or Holly, but they listened to her speculation—which ranged from international drug smuggling to alien contact and covered everything in between—with patience if not encouragement. All her ideas were scrawled into the notebook. Half the time she was only making up rubbish to amuse herself, but half the time the frisson of excitement would grab her for real and she would be convinced that something very strange was taking place right under her nose. In those moments she was so full of desperate curiosity that her skin could barely contain her any longer.

She often cast her mind back to last year's mid-year break. She had hated the other students sharing her office—two stuck-up bitches in Country Road sweaters—and had spent the break reading in her bedroom and mourning As's absence. Now the only time she thought about As was when she pondered what part he played in her mystery. Desire could direct itself into many avenues.

The last Saturday of the holidays they were at Holly's

place for dinner. Holly was in the kitchen cooking, so Prudence took the opportunity to quiz Justin again on what Emma had said about Lucien's book.

'So she said he was writing a book?'

'I can't remember the exact phrasing. Perhaps "working on" a book. It struck me as odd because I know Lucien's not interested in anything academic.'

'And that's it? That's all she ever said?'

Justin shifted in his seat. 'I overheard her and Lucien arguing one time. She was saying something like, What if the book doesn't work, or maybe, What if the plan doesn't work. But I definitely got the idea that the book was mentioned again.'

'A plan? What plan, I wonder?'

'I don't know. I didn't know then and I don't know now.' He ran a hand through his hair. 'Look, Prudence, these people have a lot of money. That kind of wealth can make people do strange things.'

'You think this is about money?'

'You know as well as I do how tight Lucien is. I've been thinking it might even have something to do with . . . well, with me.'

Prudence watched him carefully. 'Why?'

'Money—inheritances—my father being Lucien's brother. Lucien has been very adamant about me not moving out.'

'Did you ask to move out?'

'No, he's just dropped a few hints.'

She nodded slowly. 'You might be on to something, there. Your father, Graham, must have been worth quite a bit. Money which I presume has gone to Lucien. Graham never married, right?'

'As far as I know, I'm his only child.'

'But then why would Lucien bother to find you at all? You had no idea who your father was before he came along, did you?'

'No. My mother refused to tell me.'

'So why would he alert you to your family connections if it was better for him financially not to?'

'I don't know. I don't understand this family, and it unnerves me that I've got their genes.'

Holly came into the room and Justin switched his attention to her, apparently gratefully. 'Anything I can do to help?'

'No, it's under control. I heard all that, by the way. What do you make of it, Inspector Prudence?'

Prudence scribbled notes in her book. 'I have no idea. But maybe Justin better hire himself a lawyer. It's a pity Julia's gone.'

Justin shook his head. 'I don't care about money. Especially not their money. I wish you wouldn't write all this down, Prudence.'

She waved a dismissive hand. 'Don't worry. Your secrets are safe with me.' Prudence was vaguely disappointed. Her imagination had been focussed very squarely on a more esoteric mystery than illegal wrangling over inheritances, but now Justin had mentioned it, it did seem an obvious answer. Though it didn't explain why midnight on Sundays was a good meeting time, or why As was involved.

Holly poured them each a glass of wine and sat on the floor between them. 'Here's to semester two,' she said.

'Girlie swot,' Prudence replied.

'Cheers,' said Justin.

The phone started ringing in the kitchen. 'Back in a sec,' Holly said, rising again.

Prudence swirled the wine in her glass thoughtfully. 'You could just ask Lucien outright, you know,' she said. 'You're entitled to. You might be worth a fortune and not even know it.'

'Maybe some day,' Justin said evasively.

Suddenly, there was a cry from the kitchen. Prudence sat up straight. 'Holly?'

'No,' Holly was saying. 'Oh God, please, no.'

Prudence and Justin were on their feet in an instant. Prudence reached the kitchen first. Holly had the phone pressed hard to her ear, her hand clutched to the collar of her shirt. Her face was red and contorted. Prudence rushed to her and grabbed her around the waist.

'What? What is it?'

Holly went on crying into the phone, listening to the voice at the other end. Prudence already suspected she knew what had happened.

'Yes,' Holly said at last. 'Yes, I'll be there.' She hung up and crumpled into Prudence, sobbing loudly.

'Michael?' Prudence asked.

'He succeeded at last.'

'He's dead?'

Holly nodded into Prudence's shoulder.

Justin smoothed Holly's hair with a tentative hand. 'I'm so sorry, Holly,' he said.

'They've booked me a flight for tomorrow morning. Five a.m. They booked it before they rang me so I couldn't say no. What kind of person do they think I am?'

'Sshhh, it's okay,' Prudence said.

Holly's sobs were subsiding. 'He didn't bother with his wrists this time. He put a gun in his mouth and . . .. His father found him this morning. Christ, he's been dead all day and they only just phoned me. He's been dead all day and *I didn't even know*.' She broke free from Prudence and pushed her hair from her face, began to pace the room. 'I've been having fun. I've been hanging around with you guys and he's been lying there with his . . . brains . . .' More sobs.

This time Prudence stood back and let Justin hold her. Holly's pasta sauce had started to burn, so Prudence turned off the stove. 'Take her to the lounge room,' she told Justin. She filled the electric kettle to make tea. Holly cried and cried as Justin led her away. Prudence braced herself for a long night.

Surprisingly, after as little as an hour of tears and bland reminiscences of her now dead husband, Holly was impatient for them to go.

'I have an early plane to catch,' she said.

'But will you even be able to sleep?'

'I don't know.'

'I can stay here. I don't mind sleeping on the floor. Or you can come to my place. I can make you breakfast before you call a cab.'

'No, really. I want to be alone, Prudence. I'm sorry.'

Prudence touched her arm gently. 'Hey, don't be sorry. I just want what's best for you.'

'I want to be alone. I need to think.'

'Okay. But promise you'll call me if you need anything.' Suddenly conscious that her company could be overbearing at the best of times, Prudence continued, 'Or call Justin. He lives closer, after all.'

Holly looked at Justin and smiled a crooked smile. 'Okay. I promise.'

Justin pulled his overcoat on and offered Holly a brief, embarrassed squeeze. Prudence was more demonstrative, holding her in a long bear hug. Holly's skin was hot and her pulse was racing. 'Take care,' Prudence said, reluctant to go. 'Call me the instant you get back from Townsville.'

'I will. Goodnight.'

Prudence and Justin left her standing at her door, bravely waving goodbye. Mysteries and secrets were forgotten, Prudence's excitement dissolving into the frosty wind. Tragedy had made its first serious intrusion into her endless pursuit of fun.

Holly waited half an hour to be sure that Prudence and Justin were nowhere around before throwing on her overcoat and scarf and locking her flat behind her. The hot, sizzling shock had passed, leaving the sickening lurch of guilt and grief residing like a cold stone in her stomach. There was only one thing that could alleviate her distress. She had to try.

Her breath made warm puffs in the night air. The cold breeze was welcome on her hot skin.

Michael. Gone.

Who was he anyway? She felt she couldn't remember him properly, even though they had spent most of their adult lives together. The incomprehensibility of death momentarily overwhelmed her. It was too big to think about, would not fit into her brain.

Gone.

And even though she hadn't loved him for a long time, the pain was acute, relentless. She was a widow for Christ's sake. A widow at twenty-five.

The front of the college appeared to glow at the top of the rise. She started up the driveway. *He has to come.* He couldn't ignore her pain, her grief.

Her fingers fumbled with the keys. Finally she had the door open and was inside. The scent of old wood and paper. She took the stairs to the third-floor bathroom, came back to her office with the mirror and closed the door behind her. Lit candles, dry-swallowed a motion-sickness tablet. *He has to come.*

'Christian.' A cry in the darkness. Too many beats of silence followed. Her body was shaking. She took a deep breath. 'Please. Michael is dead. I need you. I *need* you.'

Still nothing. She remembered something he had said to her once, and repeated it into the dark. 'The only reason to be in any place at any time is love. If you love me, you have to come. Please, Christian, this is killing me.' Her voice dissolved into sobs.

The air shivered around her. Her heartbeat picked up. There was a warm caress on her cheek.

'It's all right, Holly,' he said, 'I'm here.'

CHAPTER TWENTY-NINE

~

His ghostly touch tangled in her hair and on the back of her neck.

'I want to see you,' she said softly.

He appeared in the mirror behind her. The sight of him—black locks and sad blue eyes—took her breath away. Had she forgotten so quickly how beautiful he was? How luminous and angelic?

'God, I've missed you,' she said.

He merely nodded, a trace of reproach in his eyes.

'I'm sorry, Christian. I'm sorry for what I said last time we spoke.'

'Peter was my saviour,' he said in a firm voice.

Holly bit her tongue, held back all the comments she wanted to make about Peter. 'Of course, of course,' she said instead. 'You loved him and you trusted him.'

'I'm sorry that your husband is dead,' he said, his eyes softening.

Michael. For five seconds she had forgotten about him. The guilt made her squirm. 'He took his own life. I feel as though it's my fault.'

Christian shook his head. 'No. When somebody takes

their own life, it can only be their own fault.'

'Is that what you did, Christian? Did you drown yourself on purpose?'

Christian looked taken aback. 'No. Of course not. It was an accident. I was knocked off a gangway.'

Holly said nothing for a few moments, trying to think of the best way to broach the next topic. 'Did you . . . Christian, how did Peter die?'

His lips turned down sadly. 'You have to let me finish my story. Peter's death is part of it.'

'I looked in some old newspapers. They say that you killed him.'

'I did no such thing!' he cried, suddenly angry.

'After your . . . drowning, the police confirmed that you had been his murderer.'

'That is an abominable lie. The police knew I did not murder Peter. A few of them suspected what had really happened, but they could never reveal it to the public.' He stopped, gazed at her mirror image for a few moments. 'Holly, you didn't believe that I—?'

'No, no. Of course not,' she lied, giving him what she hoped was a reassuring smile.

'Let me tell you, then, the real story behind Peter's death. Last time I told you of Rosalind's pregnancy?'

Holly nodded.

'I was shocked and . . . yes, I think I was angry with Peter. I tried to avoid him for a few days after I had found out, but finally, at one of our Sunday night rituals, he brought the subject up himself.

'"Rosalind has told you, I presume, that she is expecting a child." He said it like that—"a" child, not "my" child.'

'Did he ever admit responsibility?' Holly asked.

'Much later. At first it was as though he were pretending it was an immaculate conception. He said to me, "We need not be afraid that having a child in the house will change anything. We will go on as we always have, and we will teach this child to be one of us." He convinced me, of course, and I had many fond fantasies of having a small child around the house, playing with it, teaching it things. I would sometimes lie down next to Rosalind before she went to sleep at night and I would place my hand over the curve of her belly, imagine the little being growing within. Rosalind would sleepily chatter to me about her plans. If it was a girl she would call it Emmeline, after one of her favourite characters in a book. She hadn't chosen a name for a boy. She hoped to teach the child to draw and paint, and perhaps send it to a good school so it would have a future. Sadly, none of that would come to pass.'

'She lost the child?'

'It was the middle of winter. Dirty sleet fell most days. The sun came up late, sometimes it didn't feel like it had come up at all. Long, bleak days where the sky was low and grey outside. The day we lost her was one of those days. We had lamps burning all day, fires in every grate. Christmas had just passed and New Year was not quite upon us. Shortly after dinner, Rosalind became very ill.'

He paused, as though fortifying himself for what was to come. 'At first she complained merely of stomach pains and went upstairs to her room to lie down. But an hour or so later, she began to call for Peter. I can still hear it in my head, "Papa, Papa, it's very bad. Please come." Peter and I were sitting downstairs in front of the fire when she began to cry out. To my dismay, he ignored her and continued reading his book, pretending he couldn't hear. As her cries became more desperate, I could stand it no longer. I shot out of my seat and stood in front of him.

'"Please, Peter, you must go to her. If you don't, then I will."

'"Calm down, lad. She's not having the baby yet. It

isn't due for another three or four months. She has just eaten too much, that is all."

'"But she sounds as though she's in pain."

'Peter waved his hand dismissively and told me to sit down. Periodically Rosalind would call to him, but he steadfastly refused to go to her. When she started calling my name, I nearly died with pain.

'"Christian, please come. Somebody, please come."

'"Let me go to her, Peter. Perhaps she is ill."

'"You can if you want, but I won't be disturbed." He turned a page casually. I stood and began towards the stairs. At that instant, Rosalind appeared on the balcony screaming. Her skirt was soaked in blood.

'"Papa!" she screamed. "Papa, you must help me!"

'"Peter!" I cried as I ran up the stairs. "Peter, come quickly, she's bleeding."

'I raced towards her and gathered her in my arms. "Come, Rosalind, back to bed."

'Peter was lumbering up the stairs behind me.

'"What's all this, Rosalind?" he asked, almost as though she was bleeding purposely to be disobedient.

'I had her through her bedroom door and onto her bed in seconds. She was crying and her face shone with perspiration. "Oh, it hurts, Christian. Please make it stop hurting."

'I smoothed her hair from her face and began to undress her. Peter pushed me out of the way.

'"Go, lad. I'll take care of her."

'"Do you want me to find a doctor?"

'"No. It won't be necessary."

'I was almost certain that a doctor was necessary, but I backed away and Peter closed the door behind me, shutting out the sight of Rosalind writhing on the bed in the lamplight, soaked in blood.

'I waited outside her door all evening. She cried and cried. I barely heard two or three words from Peter, but

Rosalind's voice continued for hours. "It hurts." "Send for a doctor." "Please, Papa, don't let me die." I sat in the hallway with my head leaning against the door and I wept to hear her in so much pain. Still Peter didn't send for a doctor. I was desperate. I thought about going to Lucy Humberstone's to ask for help, but it would have been an immense betrayal of Peter. Nobody knew I could speak, nobody knew that Rosalind even existed. I had to trust that Peter had made a good judgement in not sending for a doctor.'

Christian stopped. Holly sensed what was coming next. She knew that Christian was wary about continuing. 'It wasn't good judgement, was it?' she said quietly.

He shook his head. His eyes were achingly sad. She would have given everything she owned to be able to hold him just for a moment, to press his body against hers and make his pain go away.

'No, it was not good judgement. He was protecting himself. Too many questions would be asked if he sent for a doctor. And perhaps, also, he sensed that it would be futile.

'Peter allowed me to see her at about ten o'clock in the evening. The room stank of blood, and she was very pale. I sat warily on her bed. She was not about to die quietly, that much was clear. She cried out and she railed against her fate, sometimes beating at her stomach as if to punish the small life that had flickered briefly and was about to take her with it into the dark.

'She kept saying the same thing, over and over. "Who will remember me? Who is to remember me? Nobody knows I exist. Once I am dead, I am nothing."

'"I will remember you," I said to her.

'"No, you won't, Christian. No, you won't." Then she turned to Peter. "I trust you with my memory, Papa. Please make sure that I am not nothing."

'This shook Peter's cool, accepting demeanour. He

nodded solemnly, eyes glistening with tears. "Of course, Rosalind. Of course you may trust me. You won't be forgotten by the ages."

'I repeated myself. I said, "I will remember you, too, Rosalind." She said the strangest thing in reply. "You can't."'

'What do you think she meant?' Holly asked.

Christian shook his head. 'She may have been delirious with pain. She could have meant anything, though I still find myself wondering.'

'Did she die?' Holly asked, the memory of her own recent loss acute.

'At eleven. She raged until the final moment. Crying out, accusing Peter of letting her die needlessly, beating her fists and shaking her head. Then a series of convulsions shook her. Her eyes rolled and she flailed her arm towards me. I grasped her hand and said her name, but if she heard me she gave no sign. With an almost animal-sounding cry, she let go of her last breath.'

Holly saw Christian close his eyes in the mirror. 'It seemed so strange to see her lying there, lifeless. But, Holly, it was the first time I had ever been totally certain that there is life after death. To see the difference between Rosalind alive and Rosalind dead, to see how much had left her, all that energy—it must have gone somewhere. Energy does not just disappear, it transforms.' He spread his hands in front of him as though to demonstrate, then let them fall at his sides.

'Peter was very calm. I wept like a madman over her bed. I felt sure that happiness would be a stranger to me forever, sure that I would lose my mind with grief. Peter pulled me up by the shoulders, marched me out of the room and told me to go and sleep in his bed. I hovered outside the closed door for a few minutes, calling to Peter and crying her name over and over. I leaned near the door, weeping, banging my head lightly on the wall, pressing the wallpaper under my lips to try to stop the cries that kept leaping from my throat. Finally Peter stepped out and landed one heavy whack across my face.

'"Go to bed," he said. "Let me take care of it."

'I nursed my jaw. Blood trickled from my nose. "But Rosalind's dead!" I cried, as if that statement alone were the cause of every ill in the world.

'"She is indeed," he said gravely, stepping back from me. He stared at the floor for a long moment, his jaw clenched tightly. "If it weren't for the Humberstones. If it weren't for their endless greed, I might have been able to afford proper treatment for her," he said with quiet anger.

'"What?" I asked, wondering why the Humberstones were suddenly the topic of conversation.

'"Always bothering me for their payment. I could have got her away—a quiet place for girls like her. Hell, I might have got her away somewhere before she grew curved enough to tempt me. But no, they had to have their money. Their dirty, filthy money. Damn them all." He looked up at me. He was clearly working himself into a rage. "Damn them all. Damn the Humberstones. Rosalind's death is on their hands, damn them. I said damn them, boy."

'"Yes, Peter," I replied warily.

'He drew back and thumped the wall, giving vent to his feelings. "Damn them. I shall avenge myself on them. I shall avenge Rosalind's death, by God. By all the demons of hell, Rosalind," he cried, lifting his head as tears coursed over his cheeks, "I swear I shall avenge your death." With a huge effort of self-control he turned to me and pointed down the hallway. "You, go to bed before I beat you again. Let me take care of everything."

'I did as he told me. During that night, while I tried to sleep, he . . .' Here Christian's voice dropped almost to a whisper. 'He walled her up in the cellar . . . with the others.'

Holly's eyes pricked with tears. 'I'm sorry.'

'Misery is a great seductress, Holly. She elicits promises of eternal devotion with one wicked sweep of her black arms—because she is intricately tangled with the object from which you are separated, yet desire so much to own. I venerated Misery that night, Holly, I promised that I would keep her close to my heart, as long as she still had Rosalind folded in her embrace.

'Peter did not come to bed. I heard him bathing very early in the morning, and then his footsteps led down the stairs. I imagined he was sitting in front of the fire, perhaps drinking whisky, perhaps reading calmly as he had done earlier that evening. Dry-eyed.'

'He didn't cry?'

'No. After his outburst against the Humberstones, he returned immediately to a calm, unexpressive demeanour. But do not interpret that as a lack of sorrow. His actions in the months after Rosalind's death most eloquently interpreted his anguish.'

'Why? What did he do?'

Christian did not answer immediately. His gaze held Holly's for a full minute before he responded. 'I don't know quite how to describe what happened to Peter. I suppose the facile thing to say is that he went mad. Insane with grief.

'At first it was only apparent in small ways. He became forgetful, distant, lost in a sad grey world of his own. He never mentioned Rosalind during this stage, and if I dared to use her name he would merely stand and walk away from me. During a meal, in the middle of a conversation, or as we sat in front of the fire on a Friday night. He'd just get up and leave, as though he had matters far more pressing in another room.

'And while his silence and his detachment saddened me

deeply, at least he managed to be . . . rational is the word I'm looking for, I think. He continued with his business—cheerlessly, but to his clients unremarkably so—and we managed to eat and sleep in a regular sort of way.

'My affair with Lucy Humberstone continued. I wanted so much to tell her what had happened, but when I thought logically about it I realised that was never going to be. Questions would be asked, Peter would be accountable; if anybody wanted to view Rosalind's body, the other four would be found. Only trouble would come from my breaking my vow of silence. And to be honest with both you and myself, Lucy Humberstone was not interested in me as anything other than a mute object. Her warmth went only as deep as her skin, and I took succour from that shallow warmth as much as I could, wordlessly, silently.

'The familiar, though fainter, scent of rotting flesh filled our kitchen for a second time. We had to keep that whole side of the house closed off when clients came. Again, it did not last long, though I'm sure if I had gone into the cellar the smell would have been so overpowering I would never have been able to banish it from my senses.' Once more, his voice dropped to a whisper. 'It affected me deeply, the smell of Rosalind rotting. It is not something anybody wishes to know about a loved one, how frail their flesh is. The imagination conjures up nightmare impressions of a pretty face and pale curls now subject to decay and putrefaction. Once, just seeing those features darkened by the slightest melancholy had been enough to torment me. Now, picturing the blue eyes dim and sightless, the full bottom lip limp and grey, it was—'

'Christian, please.' Holly's own imagination had been triggered by his words. 'It's too soon after Michael . . . Please.' Her voice cracked and the tears began to flow.

Christian disappeared from the mirror and Holly

suddenly felt his hands on her shoulders, fingertips grazing her throat, hot lips near her ear.

'It's not enough,' she murmured. 'Until I have my arms around you, until I can feel your body against mine, it's not enough.'

'Then it will never be enough.' That strange, disembodied voice echoed around her.

'But why?'

'Because I am not in the world. I reside in your mind, at the extremities of your perception. Without you, Holly, I am a sad shadow on the margins of the world. I exist only as an impression or an attachment to your senses.'

'Why did you choose me, Christian?'

'Because you were sad and alone. I felt you would understand me.'

'Is that all?'

His touch withdrawn, he appeared again in the mirror. 'Why do any two beings ever fall in love? Perhaps they each see a need that the other can fulfil. Perhaps it's just an excessive interest in another's beauty.'

'That's a cynical way of looking at love.'

'Many claimed to love me, Holly, for no reason other than they liked to gaze at me.'

Holly dropped her head, a strange and unexpected guilt spreading through her.

'Would you like me to continue?'

'Yes,' she said.

'Peter's thread to reality grew weaker and weaker as the months passed. I began to be afraid of him. My misery was incomprehensible—he was the only person I had left to love in the world and I had to shy away from him for fear he would grab me and hold me for hours, making improbable claims about his magical powers and what he intended to do with them. Not much of it made sense—double-speak and gibberish were his rhetorical tools. I dreaded Sundays. I dreaded going up with him to the reading room and feeling the cold chill of Aathahorus possessing me, leaving me to come to consciousness hours later, weak and disoriented. Sometimes I would spend those hours locked in the hellscape, frozen as I watched and listened to the business of the damned. Sometimes, thankfully, it was all blackness. But I did what I had to for Peter.

'After one Sunday night's ritual I awoke to find him dancing around the reading room naked, smeared with his own faeces, blood running in rivulets from two slashes he had made below his armpit.

'Looking up at him in horror, I said, "Peter, what are you doing?"

'"That is no longer my name," he hissed, leaning close so that his blood began to drip onto my chest. The stench of him was violent. "I have a spirit name, a demon name. I am going to command Satan to give me eternal life."

'"I don't understand, Peter," I said.

'"Do not call me that!" he screamed. His face was red from some kind of mad rage in the blood. "From now on you must only call me Archimago, the arch magus."

'Archimago?' Holly repeated.

'Yes. I knew the name from a poem he loved and had read to me often. I think he had forgotten that it was a fictional name and believed it to be his true identity.'

'Did he still manage to keep his clients?'

'For a while. He could put on a facade of normality, but not for extended periods. Soon he no longer needed his clients, due to an unlucky circumstance of which I was unfortunately the cause.

'My seventeenth birthday was on the first Monday in June. We had always celebrated birthdays before, the three of us, with a little party, a cake that Rosalind baked and a handmade gift of some description. Of course I wished for nothing more on my birthday than to be ignored. When you love someone, adore them with your whole being, revere them as the only creature who can grant you complete happiness, the shock of their loss is acute but bearable. But I could not endure seeing Peter still walking, talking, living, breathing, yet changed. So horribly, horribly changed, a mockery of the man he once was. All his intelligence, his depth, his potential transformed into a sad wreck who could not tell the difference between reality and the murky world of madness which he inhabited. And all I prayed was that he didn't know, that he didn't know how far he had fallen, that some kind of obliviousness was his partner in this appalling decline. But then I'd see it sometimes, a flash in the eye, a flicker of awful realisation, and I knew that he knew. He knew that he had become a tragedy. In the end, that was the primary reason I stayed away from him. I didn't want to see those all-too-brief glimmers of awareness when his pain and his shame were like daggers to my heart.

'Unfortunately I was not to be ignored on this birthday. As the previous night had been a ritual night, I had slept in Peter's bed. He had risen much earlier than I, and I woke with a sense of doom laid over my heart, hearing him downstairs moving furniture and whistling, an awful, too bright, too cheerful whistle that paid no regard to rhythm or melody.

'I hastily dressed and crept downstairs. I could not ignore him, because I was always afraid at this time that he might hurt himself unwittingly. I paused at the bottom of the stairs and watched him. He was dressed in his best going-out clothes—gold and purple silk waistcoat, a deep red cravat, a black coat over the top, his shoes shined to a mirror. Around the time of Rosalind's death, he had begun to put on a lot of weight, and his fat belly strained at the buttons on his waistcoat. He was rearranging all the chairs in a circle around a table he had brought in from the kitchen. The only chair still in its original place was the one facing the fireplace. On the table were two crystal bowls filled with something I could not see properly. The room was decorated with limp and dusty Christmas streamers.

'He turned and saw me on the stairs and sprang to pull me against him. His stale-sweat smell was overlaid with an expensive cologne. The combination of scents took my breath away.

'"Happy birthday, lad. Happy birthday, my Christian, my orphan boy." He often called me that in those days, his "orphan boy". I presumed it must have come from a poem also, and I certainly preferred it to hearing him call me "my angel", which was what Lucy called me. Those words for me had become acquainted with the dark, sweet world of Lucy's body.

'He released me and I took a few steps back to catch my breath.

'"We're going to have a little party," he said. "Just the three of us."

'I nodded and smiled, although I knew there were only two of us. Clearly the memory of our previous parties had become muddled in his head. "Thank you, Archimago," I said.

'"Sit down, sit down. Let me pour the wine." He pushed me into an armchair and gestured towards the crystal bowls. "Help yourself to some of these lovely treats and dainties."

'As he went to pour the wine, I leaned forward and examined the contents of the crystal bowls. In horror. They were filled with dead and dying insects, like the ones whose bodies I had swept up in piles the day I cleaned out the cellar. A large, black spider flexed its seven remaining legs and curled them up to die as I watched. I tried not to let Peter see me recoil from his dainties. He brought me a glass of wine.

'"Here's to my orphan boy's seventeenth birthday," he

said, in that perfectly normal voice he summoned from time to time.

'I tipped my glass and drank the wine. Peter dipped his fingers in one of the crystal bowls and stirred the insect corpses around. Thankfully he did not eat any.

'"I have a surprise for you, lad," he said, again in a reasonable tone. I had no cause to expect anything other than an ordinary birthday gift.

'"What is it, Archimago?" I asked.

'"A special visitor."

'"A visitor?" Perplexed, I considered the possibilities. Lord Burghley and Lucy Humberstone were the only other people who knew me well. Peter had vowed never to speak to the former and knew nothing of my relationship with the latter. He had walked to the chair by the fireplace, its back still turned to me. My heart stopped and went cold.

'He turned the chair around. There, old dried blood on the ruins of the dirty chemise she had died in, was Rosalind. Or rather, the remains of her. I think I screamed. I know that when I looked down I had dropped my glass in my lap and my wine had splattered like blood all over my clothes. I had only glimpsed her for a moment before covering my eyes, but the image was burned forever into my mind. She was little more than a raggedly clothed skeleton, some tufts of blonde hair knotted around her skull as though Peter had tried to fix them there, some flaky grey substance still clinging in places to the mossy brown bones, black holes for eyes, a skeletal leer for a mouth.

'"Aren't you going to say hello?" Peter asked. When I uncovered my eyes, I saw him standing close and peering at me.

'"No, Peter. No." I often forgot to call him Archimago, but he had long ago tired of beating me as a reminder.

'"But why not, Christian? It's your birthday. She had to come to the party."

'In a quiet, controlled voice, I merely said, "Peter . . . Archimago. She's dead."

'"Dead?" he said, as if finding out for the first time. And there was one of those moments, one of those glimmers of sanity. "Of course," he said, "of course she is dead."

'"Please, Peter . . ."

'"I'll take her to her room." He moved to the chair and began to gather her remains in his arms. A chunk of bone fell from under her skirt and landed with a thud on the ground.

'"Put her back in the cellar."

'"What? My little girl in the cellar? With those evil men? They'll kiss her, they'll touch her, they'll say it's all right and it won't hurt. Because she's such a sweet little treasure, such a little treasure. And they'll rape her and she'll cry out a little but she won't say no because I'm her papa." He tenderly cradled her in his arms and headed for the stairs. "I'm her papa."

'"Peter, you must be reasonable. You must be clear-headed. You can't put her up there in her room."

'"Why not?" he bellowed. "It's *her* room. You've always wanted her room as your own. Well, you shan't have it, orphan boy. Not even on your birthday."

'It was pointless to try to stop him, so I let him go. I remained seated, eyes closed, wishing I had never risen that day. It was only when Peter had been gone nearly half an hour and hadn't returned that I became curious and went upstairs to see what he was doing. When I reached the landing I could hear him quite clearly, sobbing in Rosalind's room. I crept along the hallway and listened from the door.

'He wept as though his heart would break, and I thought mine would break with it. Then he paused.

There was a long silence, broken suddenly by a wail. A long, single howl like a dog in a trap. It chilled me to my core. He took a breath, another pause. Then another wail. This went on for some time and I was riveted to my spot outside the door.

'The last wail turned into a word. At first I could not make out what he was saying, then I realised he was crying, "Me, me." He began to speak in a high, strained voice. He said, "Me, me. I did this to you. Me and my child. My child inside my child. Me, me. I killed you. I killed you." I slid to the floor, clutching my heart in agony. To hear him reduced to such a noise, the voice of a tiny child crying for a scraped knee, was more than I could endure.

'Then his voice grew louder, stronger. He began to curse and swear, and I heard a loud thumping as though he were throwing something around the room, perhaps Rosalind's books and toys. "Infernal bitch. Infernal whore. Whore like your mother. Damn you, damn you, whore."

'Tears ran in hot rivers down my face. My throat ached from holding back the sobs which would betray my presence outside the room.

'"I don't want to remember you. I want your memory out of my head, it pains me so. I will forget you. I will forget you, whore. Filthy harlot." More thumps and bumps. I backed away, hovered near the top of the stairs, afraid that he would emerge at any moment in a rage, and I would pay for overhearing his loss of control.

'My timing was excellent, for the very next moment he slammed out of her room and locked the door behind him. He saw me at the top of the stairs and held my gaze for a few moments. Rather than coming for me and thrashing me, as I supposed he would, he merely said, "We do not mention Rosalind's name again in this house."

'"Yes, Archimago," I responded grimly.

'"Clean my study. I'm going downstairs to rearrange the parlour."

'"Yes, Archimago." His study was the room where he took his hypnotism clients. I dutifully moved into it and began to straighten books and papers as he walked past and down the stairs.

'Once I heard him downstairs moving furniture again, I walked to the end of the hallway and tried in vain to open Rosalind's door. Checking that Peter wasn't behind me, I knelt near the keyhole and peered through. A shaft of light from a partially open curtain lit up the scene inside. Rosalind's bed, the huge brown bloodstain still spread over the covers, sat in the middle of the room. Around it, scattered across the floor and cast haphazardly against the furniture, were her bones. Peter had torn her skeleton apart and flung it in every direction as he cursed her. I was too aghast to cry. I hurried back to the study and tried to forget that I had ever seen such a hideous sight.

'I pressed all my horror and my pain down inside me and told myself it was only two days until Lucy came. Then I could take a brief respite from woe in the curves of her body. I barely know how I got through those two days. The house felt to me to be bookended with horror. Downstairs in the cellar the traces of awful murders. Upstairs in Rosalind's room the shadows of an even greater tragedy. And stalking through the rest of the house the monster that my beloved Peter had become. I sat for much of my time in front of the fireplace, reading, trying to lose myself among the smooth and uncomplicated pages of a book.

'When eleven o'clock on Wednesday came around, I had an ear out for Lucy's carriage, for her light footstep at the door. It did not come. When half an hour had passed and I noticed Peter wandering around in his green satin housecoat as though he were not expecting anyone, my heart began to sink.

'Cautiously I asked where Lucy was that day.

'"Grown fond of her, have you, lad? I can't blame you. There have been times when she's been under and I've fancied giving her a thorough poking."

'"Is she ill today, Archimago? Is that why she is not here?"

'"The illness she's got will last the best part of a year, Christian. Mrs Humberstone has no need for my assistance any more. It seems she has fallen pregnant. She won't be coming back."

'It was like a punch to the stomach. I had to sit down. Lucy's presence was my last shred of comfort in the world. I had long ago given up hope that Peter would return to normal, but as long as I had Lucy to escape into every week I could continue somehow. Now even that was taken from me.

'"Do you want to hear a fine trick, lad? Do you want to hear a secret about Lucy Humberstone?" Peter was saying, leaning close with glittering eyes.

'"What?"

'"Philbert sent Mrs Humberstone to me because he thought her nerves were causing her difficulties in producing an heir. The trouble, if you ask me, is Philbert. His first wife died about five years ago, and she could not conceive either. A bit of a coincidence, don't you think?"

'"I don't understand what you mean."

'"Philbert. He can't do his duty as a man. He's impotent. His wife isn't frigid. In fact, I'd wager she's far from it. I'd wager that the little infant clinging to her womb is a gift from another man. Now do you understand?"

'Of course I did. Another shock passed through me.

'"I wonder who the lucky sod was," Peter continued cheerfully. "I'd wager she'd make a fine spread of those wealthy legs. Yes, I would. What's the matter, boy? Jealous?"

'"Nothing's the matter."

'"Well, here's a balm to ease your woes. I'm going to redecorate. I'm going to borrow some more money from the Humberstones and I'm going to buy us some trinkets."

'His change of tack bewildered me. "How? You already owe them so much. Surely they won't lend you any more."

'He winked. "Perhaps Philbert won't. But I anticipate that Mrs Humberstone will be very accommodating when I let on that I know her secret."

'My breath stopped in my throat. "What secret?"

'"That the heir won't be a Humberstone. It can't be. Philbert will fool himself only so far. When I threaten to go to him with the proof—"

'"What proof!" I cried, leaping from my chair. I knew that I was losing control of my emotions and coming dangerously close to revealing too much but I could not stop myself. Everything warm and comfortable in my life had been taken from me.

'"People will talk under hypnosis, if one knows the right questions to ask," Peter said quietly.

'I looked away quickly. "What did she say?"

'"Sit down," he said. "Your excessive interest has me intrigued."

'"What did she say?"

'"She told me half a tale of illicit love," he said slowly. "It seems you are now telling me the other half."

'I did not reply. I kept my gaze averted.

'"Oh, Christian," he said, grasping my face softly in a large, fat hand. "Oh, you are such a good, good boy. It was you. It was you, wasn't it? You were fucking her right here, weren't you, while I was upstairs with her ugly sister?"

'"No. Of course not."

'"Do not lie to me," he bellowed. "Remember who I am."

'He was my saviour. We had a vow of trust between us. I looked into his eyes, and, regretting each syllable as it passed my lips, I said, "Yes, Peter. It was I."'

Holly shook her head in amazement. 'You were Quincy's father?'

'I do not know what she named the child.'

'Christian, he was the only child she bore. The people who own this college now are all descended from him. My God, my friend Justin is your great-great-great-grandson. None of them are really Humberstones.'

'It hardly matters. It was always the name rather than the blood that conferred upon them their power. And Peter had cursed them all as arrogant fools, as the unwitting perpetrators of Rosalind's death. He used his knowledge about my relationship with Lucy to his advantage and blackmailed her into organising another loan from the Humberstones. Our lifestyle became very lavish. We suddenly had more gilt and velvet objects, more new silk shirts, trinkets from every place on the globe, shiny new plate, silver and crystal crammed into every expensive oak sideboard, more jewellery than we could ever wear at one time. And the food—Peter bought the most exotic foods and spices, spent hours cooking extravagant dishes that were far too rich for me to eat but which he gorged himself on regularly. He grew fatter and fatter. I grew thinner, too sick at heart to eat properly, picking at the dishes and leaving them for Peter to finish.

'Summer died and part of me died with it. I was just another pretty trinket among all the others in the house on Milton Close, trying not to shine brightly enough to catch Peter's eager eye. Our rituals continued on Sunday nights, and Peter spoke obsessively about having eternal life. I could think of nothing more dreadful than having to live eternally with such pain and misery as my constant companions. In some ways, I had been better off on the streets. I could still have comfortably peddled my trade and, provided I had not frozen to death, I could have led a simple existence. I would never have known Peter or Rosalind or Lucy. I would never have felt love and the black shadow at its heels—loss.' He looked up and met Holly's eyes. 'Is that how you feel about Michael?'

'Perhaps. I've been wishing so often lately that I had never married him,' Holly said. 'That I'd broken up with him after university like I should have. It would have been easier on him to split before we became so settled. But I didn't love him any more, Christian. Perhaps I never loved him. My pain is more self-focussed. It's guilt. It's fear.'

'Guilt and fear. How?'

'Guilt that I may have driven him to it. Fear at the reminder of my own inevitable death.'

'Neither of those things should be troubling you.'

'I'm hoping to bury them with him at the funeral.' Suddenly Holly sat up straight. 'Oh my God, the funeral. I have to catch a plane.' She checked her watch. It was three a.m. 'I have to go. I'm sorry, Christian.'

He waved a hand dismissively. 'Please don't apologise. It is I who should apologise, after ignoring you for so long.'

'You had good reason. I was very cruel to you.'

'I am almost at the end of my tale. Will you come for me when the funeral is over?'

'I'll be away for over a week. But as soon as I'm back I'll be here.'

'Goodbye,' he said, and his image disappeared from the mirror. A pair of warm lips pressed momentarily against her cheek, and then that sensation too was gone.

Holly took a deep breath and prepared to face Michael's funeral.

CHAPTER THIRTY

I f she were to be completely honest with herself, Prudence enjoyed bearing bad tidings. After the shock wore off and life looked like it was going to keep right on moving around her, Prudence realised that Michael's death affected her only so far as it had upset her best friend, and it provided Prudence herself with an interesting conversation opener. She climbed the stairs to the third floor. As had to be told, after all. Holly would be away from the college for at least a week. Prudence's heart beat a little faster than usual. She was excited about seeing him. There were questions to be asked.

'Come in,' he called after she had knocked.

She closed the door behind her and smiled at him. 'Hi, As,' she said.

He looked wary. 'Hi, Prudence. I wasn't expecting to see you.'

'I'm here on behalf of Holly. She's had to go away for a little while and she wanted me to let you know.' That wasn't entirely true, but if Holly had been able to think at all rationally on Saturday night, Prudence was sure informing As would have been one of her top priorities.

'Oh? Where has she gone?' His blond hair flopped maddeningly over one grey eye. She had to stop herself from crossing the room and gently brushing it back.

'Her husband's dead. She's gone home for the funeral.'

As looked shocked. 'Dead? What happened to him?'

'He fellated a gun barrel. You know what country boys are like.'

'Prudence, don't be flippant. This is very serious. Poor Holly. What an awful thing to have to deal with.' His eyes showed a deep concern. Prudence felt annoyed but couldn't quite say why.

'I'm sorry. Of course I'm upset for Holly. But, you know, they were getting divorced anyway.'

'Still, it's a terrible shock. I really feel for her. She's doing it tough.'

Prudence wanted to scream, 'What about me? I haven't seen my parents for eighteen months and my sister has only called me once since moving to the other side of the world. It's like they all want to pretend I don't exist.' But she said none of these things. Sympathy was reserved for death, and especially death affecting helpless but pretty country girls.

Disturbed by her own acidic thoughts, Prudence decided to get into the next part of the conversation quickly.

'So, As,' she said, perching on the edge of his desk, 'Randolph told me all about his trip to Jerusalem.'

'He did?'

'Yeah, it's okay. I know he didn't want anybody to know about . . . you know, the discovery.'

As shook his head. 'I don't follow, Prudence.'

She reconsidered. If she gave too much away, she would let on that she had been reading his letters. 'Perhaps I mis-understood him,' she said, twirling a lock of hair in front of her eyes in mock thoughtfulness. 'I thought there were some nineteenth-century papers he was searching for. Maybe I've got it mixed up with something else.'

'Maybe you have.'

She looked up. His eyes were flinty. She thought about how the letters had been moved the second time she had come looking for them. Did he suspect that they had been tampered with? Time to backtrack before he got too suspicious. 'It's hardly important. Randolph's a good supervisor; I'm glad I've switched over, actually. I'm getting a lot more done.'

'Really?'

She could tell he was offended and decided to twist the knife a little before she left. 'Yes, he's very different from you. Very ... professional.' She slid off the desk and headed for the door. 'Bye, As.'

'Prudence?'

She turned back. 'Yes?'

'Randolph can be ...' He ran a hand through his hair, as if deliberating on what to say. 'Please don't cross him. I may not be professional but at least I'm forgiving.'

She frowned. Was this some kind of a warning? 'I'm not going to upset him.'

'Don't ask him too many questions.' Then, realising that was the wrong thing to say, he added, 'You know, about personal things.'

'I won't.'

He smiled. 'Take care, Prudence.'

'Sure. Bye.'

She stood in the hallway, his office door closed behind her. No satisfaction there. In fact, more questions raised than answered. She was sick of this half-arsed Nancy Drew stuff. It was time to do something radical.

Nine o'clock Sunday night, Justin was typing up some notes on his new laptop when somebody knocked at his bedroom door. He stood and went to open it. Emma waited on the other side.

'Yes?' he asked warily. She had been the embodiment of the perfect aunt in the last few weeks. It was almost eerie.

'Prudence is on the phone,' she said.

'Oh.' He really wanted to get this piece of work finished, and Prudence would no doubt want a long chat.

'Do you want me to tell her you're not here?' asked Emma, sensing his reluctance.

'No. No, I'll talk to her.' She might have news of Holly. Neither of them had heard from her since the previous weekend. 'I'll take it in the kitchen.'

Emma nodded and backed away. Justin went to the kitchen and picked up the phone.

'Prudence?'

'Hi, Justin.'

There was a click as Emma hung up the phone at the other extension.

'Have you heard from Holly?'

'No,' she said, and he got the distinct feeling it was impatiently. 'Come over.'

'I'm working on something.'

'I need your help.'

'With what?'

There was a long silence.

'Prudence,' he said, 'what's up?'

'I'm not as brave as I thought I was.'

'Why do you need me?'

'I can't tell you over the phone. Just in case . . . you know.'

Justin checked the clock over the doorway. If he went to Prudence's now, it would mean he wouldn't get any more work done tonight.

'Please, Justin,' she said. 'Aren't I your best friend?'

'Only girls have best friends.'

She giggled. 'Whatever. Come on, it's not often I ask for help. You know me—terminally independent.'

He softened. 'Okay, I'm coming. You've got me curious now anyway.'

'Believe me, this is a doozy. You won't believe what I've got planned.'

'That sounds ominous.'

'I'll give you half an hour.' She hung up. Justin replaced the phone and went to his room to put his shoes on.

Prudence sat smoking a cigarette on the kerb about three blocks from Justin's house, her purple hair glowing in the sickly streetlight. She didn't see him approach at first but looked up as he called out to her.

'Sitting in the gutter?'

She smiled. 'Some would say it was a suitable place for me.'

He sat down next to her. 'So why are you waiting for me here?'

'Because I didn't want you to have to walk all the way back to the college.'

'We're going to the college?'

'Yup.' She mashed her cigarette against the kerb and threw it away from her in a graceful arc. 'Come on, it's freezing out here.'

She stood and put out a hand to help him to his feet. He noticed she was wearing jeans and a black T-shirt under her overcoat. It seemed strange, he had only ever seen her in dresses before. They headed for the college.

'So what's this all about, Prudence?' he asked.

'I'm going to do something a bit daring but I was afraid to do it alone.'

'What makes you think that I'll do something daring with you?'

She laughed. 'You have before.'

Justin was mildly annoyed, but she spoke again before

he could respond. 'It doesn't matter. You won't be doing anything, I just want you to wait for me.'

'Wait for you where?'

'In the clock tower.'

They were walking up the college driveway. He stopped under a tree and turned to her. 'Okay, Prudence, what's all this about?'

Her eyes, almost black in the shadows of the branches, met his evenly. 'I'm going to see what they get up to.'

'Prudence . . .'

'I've been good, Justin. I haven't mentioned this mystery for a whole week. I've kept a respectful silence for the dead. But I just *have* to know. I will die if I don't know.'

'You won't die.'

'I *will*. You're not me, you don't know how it feels. A secret is like a burr stuck in my brain tissue. It hurts me not to know. I have to pull it out and look at it. I have to *know*.'

Justin had to admit to himself that he was curious too, but he wasn't going to tell Prudence that. 'What do you plan to do?'

'Well, I've figured that whatever they're doing it must be taking place in Lucien's office. It's the only room in the college that nobody goes into regularly, so it's perfect for storing a secret.'

'That's a big leap of logic, Prudence.'

'I have a feel for these things. Let me continue.' She glanced up at the college, strands of her hair fluttering in the breeze. 'Lucien's office is directly above Randolph's. All the offices are laid out exactly the same; the ones on the east are mirror images of the ones on the west, et cetera. In every room, up high in the corner opposite the window, is one of those old air vents—you know, the fancy plasterwork ones?'

'I can't say I've ever noticed.'

'I notice everything. In As's office, which is on the third floor like Lucien's, you can see the silver curve of the airconditioning duct through the vent, but there's a gap. The ducts are shoved through the old airways in the ceiling. On the roof, past the clock tower, is the access door that the maintenance crew use if something goes wrong with the aircon. I'm going in there, I'm going to find Lucien's office, and I'm going to see what I can see through the vent.'

'You're nuts.'

'What about my nuts?' she said, grinning.

'No. You—are—nuts.' He tapped her temple gently.

Unexpectedly, she took his hand and pressed it fervently in her own. 'All you have to do is wait for me in the clock tower. If I'm not out by, say, two o'clock, I'm probably stuck or dead and you can call an ambulance.'

'Prudence, don't say that.'

'Hey, it's okay, I'm joking.' She let go of his hand. 'I'll be fine. I'm always fine. Come on, let's go.'

They walked up to the college and let themselves in the front door.

'It's going to be cold on the roof, Prudence,' Justin said as they went up the stairs to the third floor.

'Not in the clock tower. You can get quite snug in a corner, though it's a bit dusty.' They stopped outside a door which kept the unauthorised out of the stairwell to the roof. Prudence pulled out her magic keys and unlocked it.

'After you.'

Justin went up the stairs while Prudence locked the door behind them. He felt a low-grade panic building in his solar plexus. The line they were crossing seemed significant. Under the door to the roof, a cold breeze licked into the stairwell. Prudence was beside him again, unlocking the last door. They stepped out onto the roof.

'God, it's freezing,' Justin said, hugging his overcoat around him.

'Come on, to the clock tower.' She led him up the walkway. The metal creaked underneath their feet. They stopped just to the left of the old clock.

'It's a nice view, isn't it?' Prudence said, pulling out a cigarette.

Justin leaned on the cold railing and gazed out over the city, its lights glowing in the darkness. 'It's like we try to make starscapes here on the ground.'

'Yeah, like Christmas trees and fireworks. We're all so fascinated with those little glimmers in the darkness. Got any good philosophical reasons why?'

He shook his head. 'It's just pretty, I guess.'

She took his arm. 'Let's get out of the cold.'

Prudence unlocked the door to the clock tower and they went in. She took off her overcoat and laid it on the floor. She wore a long-sleeved Nick Cave T-shirt and black cords. 'Here,' she said, 'I won't be able to wear this, so you may as well sit on it.'

Justin sat down and Prudence crouched next to him. 'Okay, it's just after ten o'clock. Last time, they arrived just before midnight. I'm going to go in now, give myself plenty of time to find the right room.' She searched in her bag for her torch and turned back to Justin. 'Are you warm enough?'

He was out of the freezing wind but he still wouldn't call himself warm. 'I'll be fine. Take care, won't you.'

Her eyes met his, and she suddenly slid her arms around his neck and pressed her upper body against him. Instinctively his hands went to her back. She pressed her lips against his neck. 'Thank you so much,' she murmured, then she pulled away and he was left with an impression of how warm her skin felt beneath her thin T-shirt. It seemed to make his fingertips tickle.

'You're welcome,' he managed, looking into his lap.

'Okay, I'm off.'

She left him in the clock tower. He watched her through the door as she went up the walkway and to the airconditioning unit. She opened a metal hatchway and disappeared down a ladder, closing the hatch behind her and giving him a brief, excited grin.

Justin closed the door on the cold and sagged back against a wall. Above him two metres of cobwebs floated in the gloom. His nose itched from the dust. The clock's workings clunked and squeaked in the darkness, starting the lonely job of marking off the hours until Prudence's return.

Prudence crouched at the bottom of the ladder and flashed her torchbeam around her, trying to get her bearings. The beam illuminated the long, silver air-conditioning duct disappearing around a corner in the distance. There was room for her to crawl down the right-hand side of the duct, but not the left. And she would need the left to see into the air vent.

'Cross that bridge when you come to it, Prudence,' she said, dropping to her knees and forearms and crawling towards her destination. A long girder divided her path in two, and she had to keep a leg and an arm either side of it. Dust and cobwebs clung to her. Her knees thumped on the wooden beams. It was a good thing she had set off early, because anybody would be able to hear her in the third-floor rooms. She tried to gauge how far she had come, decided she was somewhere over the toilets and kept crawling. About four metres ahead the duct took a turn to the left. She expected to find Lucien's office just around the bend.

As she went, she stirred up dust motes that got stuck in her throat, making her cough. She hoped they would settle down before the meeting started. Coughing and sneezing coming from the air vents were a surefire give-away that something wasn't quite right with the world.

If there *was* going to be a meeting. If she had the right place and the right time.

She banished the ifs. Of course there was going to be a meeting, in Lucien's office, at midnight. And she was going to witness it all.

Around the corner, picking her way carefully over beams. She stopped and rested over the curve of the metal duct, shining her torch up and down the left wall. The beam lighted on a fancy plasterwork vent, about thirty centimetres by twenty. She hastened up to it and leaned over the duct, aiming the beam through the vent. Lucien's office was below her. Bingo.

She checked her watch by torchlight. About an hour and a half to wait. She tried a couple of different positions to see which would give her the best view with the most comfort, and decided that kneeling on one side of the duct, draped over the metal curve, was best. She flicked off her torch so her eyes could get used to the dark, and sat down with her back to the duct. A cigarette would be nice but it was out of the question. She thought about Justin waiting for her on the roof and hoped he wasn't as bored as she already was.

Prudence sat, shivering and uncomfortable, for what seemed like an age. She played word games in her head— name a band, a movie and a book starting with every letter of the alphabet—to keep herself occupied, and tried to ignore the corner of a roofbeam stuck in her butt. When she finally heard a voice, she was unprepared and momentarily froze.

The door to the office had opened and Lucien was talking to Emma.

'No, it wasn't because of that, Emma. I wish you wouldn't take everything so personally.' A light went on and shone through the decorative air vent. Slowly, carefully, Prudence rolled onto her knees and peered cautiously over the top of the metal cylinder. She couldn't see Lucien, who was standing just out of her range of vision, but she could see Emma, dressed in blue and with her hair loose, chewing her bottom lip thoughtfully.

'Personally? Of course it's personal. You may be a Humberstone but you're also my husband.'

Lucien stepped into sight, holding a long index finger in front of Emma's face. 'Enough. We'll continue this conversation later. Have a thought for the appropriate time and place for your domestic complaints.'

He turned his back to her and didn't see her make a face at him.

Both of them were out of Prudence's sight then, and it sounded as though they were looking in a cupboard for something. Already her knees were complaining about the hard surface. She slipped off her T-shirt and jammed it under her kneecaps, shivering in her bra and a thin black singlet top. The door to the office opened again and As and Randolph walked in. Prudence felt her blood pressure rise. What the hell were they all doing here?

'Hi,' Emma said to them. 'Do you want to get the carpet?'

'Has Lucien got any information about the translation?' Randolph replied as As began to push Lucien's desk out of the way.

Lucien moved to the desk to help As. 'No, nothing new. It's ponderous work and I think it could still take some time.'

'I'm willing to help, you know.'

'It's best at the moment to continue the way we are. It would only become confusing if the two of us were trying to decode it at the same time.'

Decode what? The dark fragment? Why the hell were they moving the desk and rolling back the rug? And what was that cut in the carpet, and—? Prudence almost wet herself as she recognised what was painted on the floor.

A magic circle.

Oh-my-god-oh-my-god-oh-my-god. It was all Prudence could do to stop herself from screaming with excitement as they lit black candles and settled around the circle. She started to feel light-headed and realised that she hadn't breathed for a full ten seconds. Emma turned off the light and joined the others on the floor. The candlelight was much dimmer, so Prudence edged forward a few centimetres, confident that they wouldn't see her. She saw Lucien pull a collection of papers, bound in a folder, into his lap and flick through the pages. The dark fragment, perhaps, the one that the old magician had helped them find.

Then, one by one, they all said, 'I revoke my saviour.'

Even better—a *black*-magic circle. Only in her wildest fits of imagination had Prudence believed that anything like this could be happening here at boring old Humberstone College, among droves of anal academic fusspots, each with their own ugly, ragged blade for dissecting beauty. She gazed for ages at Lucien, lit dimly by candles, his long fingers spread firmly over the book. Who would have thought that he'd be the centre of this? She could hardly wait to tell Justin. But first, she had to see what was going to happen.

Lowly, almost like praying, Lucien started a chant. Prudence couldn't make out the words but suspected it was something out of the book, which would make it a spell book, if not a full-scale grimoire. She listened hard. It almost sounded like a list. Demon names, perhaps? If so, if they were conjuring up demons, Prudence realised that she might not be so safe up in the roof after all. For the first time she started to feel afraid and shrank back into the shadows. She could still see Lucien's profile and Emma's face, but the other two were lost from sight.

The chanting went on, now they were making sentences. Again, she couldn't understand, but it seemed they were doing some kind of working. She thought of all the books about ritual magic she had read. Lucien and the others did not fit the profile—there were no black robes and consecrated items, there was no extended role playing, no dramatic gestures. They were either rank amateurs, not serious about what they were doing, or far, far worse. She had read about magicians of the dark path, the ones who scorned Levi and Crowley as misinformed dolts, magicians who used latent psychic ability to shortcut grand ritual and all its misplaced adherence to ethics, magicians who pulled evil spirits into the world and made diabolic pacts to the detriment of those around them. Was that what this was about?

Lucien's voice suddenly dropped out of the chant as his eyes rolled back and he was lost in a trance. The others continued, focussed on the words. Prudence realised it had grown warm in the room. Even from where she watched she no longer felt the bite of winter on her bare skin.

For about ten minutes, hardly believing what she was seeing, Prudence watched as Lucien gibbered and twitched below her and the chant went on. Suddenly, Lucien fell backwards and cried out for water. Emma raced to him with a bottle of spring water which she pressed to his lips. He gulped it as though nothing could quench his thirst. Emma slowly brought him into a sitting position and he shook his head as if to clear it. The temperature dropped rapidly, bringing gooseflesh with it.

'What did you see? Did it say anything to you?' Randolph asked, leaning forward eagerly.

'No, nothing. It's being uncooperative.'

It? Perhaps Lucien had made contact with some being from the other side. Prudence wondered how long this had been going on, and what they hoped to gain from it.

Was this the secret to the Humberstone fortune?

Randolph stood, looking disappointed. The others followed suit, Emma helping Lucien to his feet. He leaned on her heavily for a moment, then seemed to find his balance and was once again fine.

'Next Sunday, perhaps,' he said. 'It can't ignore us forever.'

They went about putting the carpet and the rug back and shifting the desk. Emma turned the light on and put the candles away. Once more it looked like an ordinary office. Only the faint smell of candle wax lingered to suggest that anything out of the usual had happened. Prudence was almost disappointed to see them leave one by one, Lucien being the last to turn out the light and lock the door behind him. All fell silent.

Was that it? Prudence eased herself back into a sitting position, wanting to be sure they were out of the building before she headed back. She didn't want to give herself away by clunking back down the air shaft while they were underneath. Maybe this was just some hobby of theirs, and they were neither very serious about nor very adept at it. Only the secrecy surrounding it made it seem sinister. But then, why would any middle-aged respectable member of the community want anybody to know about a dalliance with black magic? It was probably more embarrassing than shocking.

Just as she was about to move, she heard the door open again. Once more she slowly turned to watch. No light came on, but she could make out Lucien's tall figure in the darkness. For a moment her heart almost stopped— he had found her out. He was coming back to confront her. She held her breath and her pulse pounded behind her eyes. But he did not acknowledge her presence. He walked to the centre of the room, then stood there very steadily and quietly for a few moments, as if centring himself. The book was open in his hands and he read something out loud—it was a low mumble, but it was definitely English this time. Something about 'betrayal' and 'steady hands' and 'arise as I insist'. Prudence knew enough about magic to know that calling any kind of dark being without a circle was dangerous. They had to be evoked, entrapped. She wondered why Lucien hadn't uncovered the circle again. She certainly wasn't expecting anything to happen after the earlier ritual had produced nothing exciting or noteworthy. Lucien seemed as shocked as she was when the temperature shot up, the walls seemed to creak, and a pallid bluish-white light suddenly appeared in the air in front of him.

Prudence clapped a hand over her mouth to stop herself from crying out. Slowly the light began to take on a shape. Lucien took an uncertain step back. She thought about turning away and crawling as fast as she could out of the ceiling. All things considered, it might be the safer option.

The being materialised in the room below her. It was a hulking figure, probably male, with a bald misshapen head and deformed limbs. The stench of sulphur made her gag, as though the being had crept out of hell. Horror and shock overwhelmed her as she realised that that was probably precisely where it came from. She swallowed a desperate sob of terror.

'Your name,' Lucien said in a firm voice.

'Are you sure you want to know, magus?' the thing said, in a voice that could have come out of the walls.

'Yes.'

'The others are going?'

'It will be taken care of.'

'I will have my body?'

'You will.'

'And you trust me, magus? That's important. Do you trust me?'

'Of course I do,' Lucien replied evenly. The words of

a madman or a novice, surely, Prudence thought. Beings like this were never to be trusted.

'Eternal life will soon be yours, then. Keep working on your translation. As soon as you have the final summoning completed, call me again. I will deliver my master to you, and your wish will be granted.'

'Yes, yes. Your name?'

In a blue flash the being disappeared from sight, leaving an imprint on Prudence's eyes. Its presence, however, was still palpable, its stench hung on the air.

Lucien screamed, 'Your name? What is your name?'

Prudence held her breath, waiting for darkness and silence to solidify. But first a gravelled voice, coming from everywhere and from nowhere, broke against the soft spaces of the room.

'My name is Archimago.'

Quite suddenly, all sense of the being's presence vanished. Lucien cried out once in triumph and hurried from the room, slamming the door behind him. Prudence let out a long breath and pressed a hand to her forehead. This was a much bigger secret than even she had ever anticipated.

Up on the roof Justin watched from the dark end of the pathway as Randolph and Aswell left. Emma sat in the car for a few minutes, waiting for Lucien. When they finally pulled away, he turned slowly and returned to the clock tower. Prudence should be back soon. He didn't know what he'd do if she didn't return. In fact, he had spent the last two and a half hours in a state of mild panic, cursing himself for not stopping her. While he was curious about what his aunt and uncle were up to, finding out was hardly as important as his friend's safety. He hovered outside the clock tower door, watching the entrance to the airconditioning shaft. An icy breeze kissed his cheeks and tousled his hair. His hands were jammed hard into his overcoat pockets, but nothing seemed to make them warm. He suspected he wouldn't feel warm again until Prudence emerged, whole, from the ceiling.

After a few tense minutes, there was a thump against the hatch and it shot open. Prudence stuck her head out, eyes looking around wildly. When she saw him, she nearly burst.

'Oh my God, Justin, you will never believe this!'

He grabbed her bare upper arm—her T-shirt was now tied around her waist—and helped her out of the hatch. There were a couple of stray cobwebs in her hair, and her clothes wore patches of thick dust. 'Prudence, you must be freezing.'

She shook her head as she slammed the hatch closed. 'My blood's too hot. You won't believe what I just saw. Come on.' She led him to the clock tower and closed the door behind them. It was almost pitch black but for the reflected glow of the security lights struggling through a crack under the door and gaps in the clock's mechanism.

Justin allowed Prudence to push him down on her spread-out overcoat. She made no move to put her T-shirt back on. Instead she huddled stiffly against him. He could feel her body shaking and sensed it wasn't from the cold. Her hands reached for his and he grasped them firmly.

'Prudence? Are you okay?'

'I'm ... I'm shocked,' she said in a whisper. 'I can't believe what I saw.'

'Tell me.'

She gazed at him momentarily, her eyes huge and almost delirious. With an effort, she appeared to gather her reason and take a deep breath. 'Okay,' she said softly, 'okay.'

Justin listened as she gave him a detailed account of

everything she had seen. At first it was intriguing, then surprising, then astonishing. As she spoke, the tension slowly left her body, until finally she sagged softly against him. There was something intoxicating about those fifteen minutes—her palpable excitement, her warm body, the frozen wind prowling around outside where the lights of the city glimmered indifferently in the cold night, the way her eyes never left his—so intimate and so illicit, sharing the sinister secret in the dark. She finished her story breathlessly, still clutching his hands in her own.

'Christ,' he said, 'you must have been terrified.'

'It was too unexpected to be terrifying,' she replied.

'How am I going to look at my uncle again, knowing he ... It's too much for me to comprehend. Raising spirits? I'm speechless.'

'Raising demonic spirits, Justin. It's evil.'

Justin shook his head. 'Should we do anything?'

'You should get out of that house.'

A painful reminder. He was Prudence's protector. 'I can't.'

'Sure you can. Come live with me for a while.'

He didn't answer her. She had pulled one hand free and slowly, thoughtfully, began to tangle her fingers in his curls. 'It might not be safe for you there. I couldn't bear it if anything happened to you.'

He froze, didn't know what to say or do. She was so close, so warm, so soft. But she was Prudence. He had never desired her before. His body's response confused him. He tingled all over, a tangle of hot electricity sat at the base of his neck.

'Justin?' she said, and it was a question, as if she were checking that it was okay to proceed.

He opened his mouth to speak. At first the word would not come out, was trapped under layers and layers of something. But then it bubbled up, tripped off his tongue almost like a gasp. 'Yes.'

She took his face in her hands and kissed him, her warm tongue darting between his lips. He groaned and put both hands on her waist, under her singlet, fingers pressed into her back. He thought in conspicuous sentences: *I'm kissing Prudence*, or *This is Prudence's breast*, or *Prudence is rubbing my crotch*. It was like a weird dream. The idea that it might actually be real was almost terrifying. *Prudence is unzipping my jeans.* She was all over him, soft hands and big eyes and hot mouth. 'Oh, God,' he said, over and over, 'oh, God.'

His fingers fumbled at her clothes, hands shaking, buttons and hooks eluding him and eluding him, then finally springing open, Prudence spilling out. *Prudence is naked.* She felt so soft against him, he felt himself so hard, a collection of so many planes and jutting joints. She traced a hot trail all over him with her mouth; her body kept slipping through his fingers as he lay, stupefied, on her overcoat, progressively more naked.

'Oh, God. Oh, God.'

'It's okay, Justin,' she murmured against his skin.

'Oh, God.'

'It's okay.' She was bending away from him, rummaging in her bag, looking for something, not finding it, swearing. Her body was a pale shape in the dark. 'I've got it,' she said. He had no idea what she was talking about until he heard the packet rip and she started expertly fitting him with a condom.

I'm going to have sex with Prudence. 'Oh, God,' he breathed, all desire and strange, hyperventilating fear.

'It's okay,' she said again. 'Really, really, it's okay.' She eased herself on top of him and began to move. His entire body was a hot, throbbing heartbeat. Her hair hung in his face. His hands reached for her round, heavy breasts.

'Oh, God.'

'Please,' she said, 'call me Prudence.'

'Oh, Prudence. Oh, Prudence.' *I'm having sex with Prudence.* 'Oh, God, Prudence.' Suddenly he couldn't bear to be underneath her any more, lying there like the whole show was going on without him. He pushed her over firmly, closed his lips over hers, pinned her to the floor with his body and thrust hard into her, over and over. She cried out. He ran his lips down to her breasts. *Prudence's breasts.* It was too much, he was either going to come or die. Luckily, he came.

Regret came hard on the heels of his orgasm. His first thought was for her.

'Sorry,' he said, 'I'm sorry, I'm sorry. What about you, did you . . .? Do you want me to . . .?'

'I'm fine,' she said, her hand stroking his hair. 'I came before you did. Didn't you hear me?'

He shook his head. 'I was kind of self-absorbed at the time.'

'I come easily,' she said lightly. 'Just another one of the skills I have that won't find me employment.'

'I'm glad,' he said, aware he had to say something. He pulled out of her carefully and removed the condom. Once again she rummaged in her bag, this time for a tissue to wrap it in.

'I should say sorry to you,' she said quietly, dropping a gentle kiss on his shoulder. 'I know I'm not the girl you want.'

He sighed and pulled his jeans towards him. It was starting to get cold again. 'God, I'm such a fuck-up. Why can't I just enjoy myself? You're so . . . you're so comfortable with yourself.'

She shrugged and began to dress herself. 'That's a nice way of saying I'm a slut,' she said dismissively.

'No, no, of course not.' He pulled her against him again. 'I'm sorry, Prudence. I ruined it, didn't I? Guys aren't supposed to get all morose after sex.'

She laughed. 'Instant guilt, just add semen,' she said.

Unable to help himself, he broke into laughter. It felt good, like it was dispelling his discomfort.

'So,' she said, pulling her top over her head, 'what do we do now?'

'Don't ask me.'

'I think we can go on as usual.'

'What, pretend it didn't happen?'

'No. Just don't mention it. I mean, you and Holly . . . You know.'

'There's nothing between me and Holly.' And now he feared there never would be.

'Well, let's try to go on as before.'

'Okay.' He kissed her, but desire was gone. It felt like kissing a friend again.

'And when Holly gets back,' Prudence said, 'we'll have far more interesting things to tell her about than us shagging.'

'Right,' Justin said. The thought of Holly made him feel dirty and stupid. Like an animal that rutted indiscriminately, following its baser instincts without care or dignity. He pulled his shirt and coat on and opened the door to the clock tower. The frozen wind gusted in his face. A shard of it seemed to drive all the way down into his stomach and lodge itself there. Prudence, fully dressed, pulled him to his feet.

'Come on,' she said, 'we should go now.'

CHAPTER THIRTY-ONE

⌣

Aswell was going to be easy to get rid of compared to the other two. Lucien caught the ends of his overcoat as they parted in the breeze. The morning was brisk, icy dew lay everywhere. In his pocket his fingers toyed with an envelope addressed to Mandy Aswell. This letter he would post himself. Usually Emma took their mail to the post office once a week. Today, an early morning walk to the postbox seemed in order.

Easy really—an anonymous tip-off to Mandy that all might not be as it seemed with her husband, a cautious implication that the Sunday night fishing expeditions may be a cover for something else, a judiciously placed hint that a certain female student seemed to be on very intimate terms with Laurence. Lucien had met Mandy, she wasn't an idiot. She would have had twinges, suspicions. This letter would confirm them, and that would put an end to Aswell's involvement with the grimoire, if he wanted to save his marriage. Lucien would be ready with a sympathetic ear, with assurances that Aswell could still be part of the grand plan, but whether he believed it was not Lucien's problem. Aswell would be out of the meetings and that was all that mattered.

Now, what to do about the others?

Lucien slipped the envelope into the postbox. Goodbye, Laurence. Archimago had been quite clear in Sunday night's trance—the others had to go. He had suggested murder—strategic poisoning or suffocation—but Lucien was wary. As long as there were legal avenues open to him, he would be foolish not to use them. Murder was tricky, difficult to get away with.

And, of course, Emma and Randolph were related to him. They were an inconvenience but he didn't want them dead.

He shivered as he walked back to the house, partly from the cold and partly from the memory of Archimago's presence in his world, between the four ordinary walls of his office at the college. Lucien was so close now, so close. He had his traitor demon, he had nearly half of the final summoning translated, he had an orphan boy as payment. Most of all, he had the courage. Small sacrifices had to be made. This was a prize that was worth transgressing any moral code to obtain. Instinctively, he stepped over a crack in the narrow, mossy sidewalk. Emma was his next problem. He made calculations in his head. How he hated to part with money. But with forever on his side, his earning potential was significantly enhanced.

He walked up the drive and entered the house, slipping unnoticed into his study. The contract was at the back of the bottom filing-cabinet drawer. He pulled it out and laid it on his desk, smoothing over creases. Magnus's clauses all in a row. Lucien's father really was a most meticulous man. Emma's signature—round loops a presage of how her body would change in the years to come—signing away her rights to anything but unconditional love. Lucien rummaged in his top drawer for his chequebook. He did not believe in unconditional love, but he certainly believed in the power of money. It was time for Emma to take a little trip away.

'So, how long has she gone for?' Prudence spooned two heaped sugars into her coffee. She and Justin were sitting in an airport cafe, waiting for Holly's plane, which had been delayed.

Justin shrugged. 'I don't know. Lucien said that her sister was very sick and that she was going to take care of her. She's somewhere on Phillip Island. That's all I can tell you. You know how hard it is to get anything out of Lucien.'

Prudence shook her head, stirring her coffee rapidly. It was too weird, Emma suddenly disappearing from the Humberstone abode so soon after Lucien had agreed to the demon's demand that he ditch the other members of the group. 'I don't know, Justin. What if he's killed her or something?'

'Prudence, she's not dead. I spoke to her last night. She rang to talk to Lucien.'

'How did she sound?'

'She sounded fine. I didn't say much to her—I don't exactly have the most comfortable relationship with her.'

Prudence averted her eyes, guilty again about their encounter on Sunday night. In some ways she felt that she had been just as bad as Emma. She was still assessing the reasons why they had ended up having sex at all. With a kind of sick shame, she had started to suspect it had something to do with being jealous of Holly. Everybody loved Holly. Just once, Prudence wanted to be the centre of attention. She knew that loud girls like her usually came second, after more humble, sweet-tempered types.

She sighed. A touch of jealousy, a good dose of excitement, the right place and the right time—and she had notched Justin up as number twenty-four on her ever-growing list of conquests. He deserved better. And as much as she was keen for it, he would never do it again. She knew without asking, so she wouldn't embarrass herself by bringing it up.

'What's up?' he asked.

'Nothing. Just sick of waiting.'

'I'm glad Holly's coming back. It seemed like I was getting deserted by everybody. Did I tell you Jane left?'

'No. Did she?'

'Yeah, I went to see her last Wednesday and she wasn't there. I asked Allison when she was coming in and she told me that Jane had resigned over the break. She's getting married or something.'

'How fifties. Leaving work because you're getting married.' She sipped her coffee. It was stale and watery. 'Yuk. This is the worst coffee, it tastes like somebody stirred it with a burnt stick.'

'So Holly doesn't know we're coming to meet her?'

Prudence shook her head. Holly, Holly, Holly. 'Nope. I got the flight details off her mother this morning.'

'What does her mother sound like?'

'Like she hates my guts. I'm used to that. Nobody's mother ever liked me, not even my own.'

Justin slipped his hand across the table and touched her fingers softly. She pulled away and he withdrew his hand.

'Hey, look,' she said, pointing to the arrivals board, 'her plane's landing. Let's go up to the gate.'

'You haven't finished your coffee.'

'I don't want it. Come on.'

Holly nearly walked straight past them, not expecting to see them. Prudence had to grab her by the elbow.

'Prudence! Justin! Oh, thanks for coming.' She went eagerly into Prudence's embrace.

All petty resentment was forgotten as Prudence hugged her and kissed her cheek. 'Missed you heaps,' she said.

'Me too. And Justin, hi.'

Justin gave Holly a cautious hug then stepped back into his own space. Prudence felt another twinge of guilt. It looked like she had fucked things up between Justin and Holly. *Ah, he'll get over it.*

'We came on the bus,' Prudence said as they began to walk down to the baggage collection, 'but I brought enough money to get a cab home.'

'Thanks, guys. That's great.' Holly looked pale but not too grief-stricken.

'We've got the most amazing story to tell you,' Prudence continued. 'But I'll save it for later.'

'I'd appreciate that. I'm a bit tired.'

'How was it?' Justin asked carefully. 'Was it very painful?'

Holly pressed her lips together and shook her head, looked to be on the verge of tears, then blinked them back as though she'd had a lot of practice recently. 'It was pretty awful. His parents were very . . . Look, I'd rather not talk about it now. Perhaps later. Perhaps we can have dinner tomorrow night or something. I just want to get home and rest.'

'Okay then,' Prudence said. 'Dinner at my place tomorrow night.'

They were subdued but comfortable with each other's silence as they picked up Holly's baggage and caught a taxi home. Holly rested her head on Prudence's shoulder on the way back while Justin stared out the window from the front seat.

'Thank you,' Holly said softly. 'I need friends at the moment.'

'Friends forever,' Prudence murmured, touching Holly's hair, wishing she hadn't had bad, jealous thoughts about her. She was almost bursting, not telling Holly about the black-magic ring, but Holly didn't need to hear it at the moment. All she needed was a couple of quiet friends close by. At great effort, Prudence remained quiet. Death was a great silencer.

The taxi dropped the three of them off outside Holly's place. Prudence paid the driver and took one of Holly's bags, Justin took the other.

'Glad to be home?' Prudence asked as they walked around the side of the house and back to Holly's flat.

'Home? Yes, I guess this is home now. I usually think of my parents' house as home.' She felt around in her handbag for her keys and opened the door, then paused, looking down. 'What's this? Why is there water on the floor?' The small tiled entranceway was covered with water. 'What's that horrible smell?'

Prudence and Holly took a few steps into the house while Justin hung back with the bags. 'It's wet carpet. Holly, I think the flat is flooded.'

'How could it be?' They were in the living room now, their feet squelching over soaking wet carpet. In the kitchen the water was nearly two centimetres deep. 'Oh, shit. I don't need this. My bedroom. Oh, God, my books!'

Prudence carefully placed Holly's bag on a chair and bent to examine her bookcase while Holly checked out her bedroom.

'It doesn't look too bad. There are only a couple on the floor, the rest are out of harm's way,' Prudence said.

Holly emerged from the bedroom with a dripping wet exercise book. 'Great, just great. Two months' worth of notes ruined.'

Justin had dropped Holly's other bag outside and carefully picked his way over the wet floor. 'What happened?'

Holly flung the exercise book away from her. 'God knows. The plumbing or something.'

Justin went to the bathroom. 'It seems to be coming from the shower drain. You'd better tell your landlady. I think the plumbing's blocked and it's all backed up into here.'

Holly buried her face in her hands and sobbed. 'I don't need this. I don't need this.'

Prudence put an arm around her shoulders. 'It's okay, you can come stay with me until it's sorted out. Don't worry, really. It will be fine.'

'But I like being on my own.'

Prudence smoothed her hair, soothing her. 'You don't have much choice. Do you want me to go talk to Mrs Partridge? You're in no fit state to confront her.'

Holly looked up, pushed her hair from her face with a resigned sigh. 'I suppose so. I'll pack up some books and things if you're sure it's okay for me to stay with you awhile.'

'Of course.'

'Just until the plumbing's fixed and the flat has dried out.'

'You can stay as long as you want to. You can move out of here for good if you like.'

'No, just until it's fixed.'

Prudence shrugged. Why anybody would want to be by themselves was beyond her. 'Whatever.' She left the flat and headed up to Mrs Partridge's house while Holly and Justin began to pack. She reminded herself that bad luck was not something she should wish for, even if it did mean being the centre of attention.

All Holly wanted to do was be by herself at the college, to go to Christian and hear the rest of his tale. And be with him. It seemed the only thing that kept her from sinking was the prospect of being with him. But for the past day and a half Prudence, almost irritatingly solicitous, hadn't let Holly out of her sight. She spoke periodically about finally having got to the bottom of the Sunday night mystery, but at this point Holly couldn't have cared less. The past week had been hell. Half of Daybrook had turned out for Michael's funeral, and it seemed they all thought it was her fault he was dead. Old school friends snubbed her, Michael's relatives were acidic, his boss from the hardware store—probably trying to displace his own guilt—openly accused her of driving Michael to his death. By the end of the whole process Holly hated Michael with a passion that surprised her. She suspected that his primary motivation for killing himself was to ruin her life. Well, she wasn't going to let that happen.

At least her parents had been marginally more understanding. Her father's standard query about when her 'silly adventure' was going to end did not surface at any time, making her think that perhaps he had accepted that she was never coming back. Her mother, who had always been very fond of Michael, was cool but kept her recriminations to herself. Despite the warm sunshine and the blue sky, Holly had never felt colder in her life than during that week.

There was no hope of getting away from Prudence on the Thursday night she returned, and the following day Prudence had organised for Justin to come for dinner. Holly gritted her teeth and told herself to wait. Saturday night, maybe. Christian was waiting for her. Besides, some quality time with her friends would probably prove therapeutic.

Friday night was bitterly cold and the three of them huddled in front of the fire in Prudence's lounge, drinking red wine after dinner. Holly knew it was probably unwise to be drinking alcohol so soon after such an emotional upheaval—there was always the danger that she was drinking to blot out rather than to enhance—but, as always, Prudence was very persuasive.

'You've got to come back to the land of the living some time,' she said to Holly, refilling her glass for the second time.

Holly laughed to herself, thinking about how unwittingly

appropriate Prudence's comment was. The land of the living. It seemed she was emotionally locked in by two dead men. 'I know, I know.'

'You've been so sullen since you got back.'

'Prudence, she's just been at her husband's funeral,' Justin interjected.

Holly shook her head. 'No, no. She's right, Justin. I haven't talked about it, I haven't told you guys anything.' She waved a hand towards Prudence. 'I haven't even listened to Prudence's awful secret and I know that she's dying to tell me.'

Prudence nodded eagerly. 'I'm dying all right.'

Holly sagged against the back of her armchair. 'Okay, tell me everything.'

Prudence leapt to her feet. 'Not here.'

Justin groaned. 'No, not the Confessional.'

'Of course the Confessional. It's the only place for this kind of thing.'

'It's freezing out there, Prudence, and it was just starting to drizzle as I arrived,' Justin protested. 'Can't we talk in here? We can turn the lights out if it makes you feel better.'

'You have no real sense of drama, have you?' Prudence responded, already pulling on an overcoat, gloves, scarf and beret. 'We'll take a blanket each. I'll get another couple of bottles of wine. Come on, guys, it's nearly August. I have to hand in my dissertation in about three months. Fun times are coming to an end soon.'

Holly got to her feet. A night in the Confessional was what she needed. Perhaps it would loosen her up enough to talk about her awful week in Daybrook. And this time she didn't want to be the last one to agree. 'Justin, it looks like you're outvoted.'

He reached for his coat, which was lying behind his chair. 'Sure does,' he said.

'You guys get some blankets,' Prudence said as she

made to leave the room. 'I'm going to the cellar. Daddy's going to shout us a good night out.'

Lucien did not realise how late it was until the phone rang in his study and he looked up at the clock. Eleven. Who was ringing on his business line at this hour? It could only be one person.

'Hello, Emma,' he said as he answered the phone.

There was a brief silence. 'How did you know it was me?'

'Because in the five days since you've left, you have made a habit of interrupting me at inopportune moments.'

'I've spoken to a solicitor. She says it won't hold up in court.'

'Then take me to court.' That would take money she didn't have and time he could well use.

'Just let me come back. I don't understand why you've done this.' Crying again. He was sick of her crying. Once, a long time ago, the thought of her tears had melted his heart. A very long time ago. Now it was too common, a trick too often used to manipulate him.

'Because I have reason to believe you were unfaithful to me. Now, you have a nice place to live and a nice fat allowance to live on, so just stay out of my way.' He had given her a cheque and packed her off to an investment unit they owned on the bay at Cowes. It was a good two hours away from him—an hour and a half the way Emma drove.

'This isn't about Justin and me,' she remarked with uncharacteristic perception. 'This is about that stupid grimoire. You're trying to get rid of me, just like you got rid of Jane.'

'You can believe what you like, Emma. The end result is the same.'

She laughed cynically. 'End result. Well, Lucien, let me tell you something. The end result of all your labours is that you'll find you've wasted a great deal of time and money on a load of old papers that have no power whatsoever. Do you really think that you can work with the devil and get eternal life? Have you any idea how ludicrous that is?'

Lucien felt his temperature rise. A tight ball of anger clutched in his stomach. 'You've been there, Emma. You know it's not rubbish.'

'Perhaps it's not complete rubbish, but we all think you've placed too much hope in an outcome that is highly unlikely.'

'And who is "we all"?'

'The rest of the group. Laurence, Randolph, even Jane once confessed that she thought you were counting too much on—'

'Shut up!'

'Nobody wants to die, Lucien. What makes you think that you're the only person who will elude death? What makes you think you're the one?'

For an instant, despite the contact he had made and the solemn promise he had elicited from Archimago, he doubted himself. For an instant it all seemed as though it could be a delusion, and mortality was approaching like a black steam train, heavy iron bearing down on him. He hated her for creating that instant of doubt.

'You bitch!' he screamed. 'You're never coming back. You're lucky I don't—'

'I'll see you in court.' The phone clicked as she hung up.

He replaced the receiver and leaned back in his chair. He realised with some surprise that his heart was racing. They doubted him. They all doubted him.

But surely not Randolph. Randolph had killed for the grimoire. No, Randolph was a Humberstone, he believed all right. And Randolph was Lucien's next problem. His cousin's devotion to the task at hand, a quality that had once made him Lucien's greatest asset, had now made him his greatest liability. He hadn't yet told Randolph that Emma was gone but he had a plausible lie ready to explain her absence. No doubt they would soon hear from Aswell that he was unable to attend on Sundays any more, then it would just be the two of them. Lucien held out scant hope that Randolph would be convinced to abandon the meetings until everybody could once again be present. He was too sharp, he had too much at stake.

Lucien stood and paced his study for a few minutes. Finally he came to rest, gazing thoughtfully at the picture which hung in front of the safe. No, where Randolph was concerned, more drastic measures were called for.

CHAPTER THIRTY-TWO

~

'**H**ow are you feeling?'
'Comfortably numb,' Justin said.
Prudence smiled at him. 'Good.'

Holly lit candles and then came to sit with them. Prudence switched the torch off and lay back on her blanket. The wine they were drinking this evening was more potent than usual and Justin felt decidedly foggy. The three of them were probably already well on the way to being intoxicated before they had left the house. Walking the couple of kilometres to the college had only served to heighten the headspin. Once inside, he actually found the Confessional a comfortable place to be—anything had to be better than the cold drizzle on the street.

'Okay,' Holly said, settling down and taking a swig of wine. 'I'm ready for the big secret.'

Justin watched as Prudence wriggled forward and grasped Holly's wrist. 'You'll never believe it.'

Holly turned to Justin. 'Will I believe it?'

'Probably not,' Justin said. He couldn't believe it himself. It was one of a growing list of things about his life that were beyond belief, not least the fact that he and

Prudence had had sex in the clock tower. But as he felt now, half drunk, soft around the edges, it hardly seemed to matter. The world was full of unbelievable stuff. Normality was just a collective fiction.

'Okay,' Prudence said. 'I went to spy on Lucien and the others on Sunday night.'

'What? How?'

'I crawled into the ceiling—Justin waited for me at the clock tower—and I watched through the air vent.'

'I'm glad I wasn't here. I would have stopped you.'

'Nothing could have stopped me.'

'Nothing could have stopped her,' Justin echoed. 'She is unstoppable.'

Prudence grinned. 'He's right, you know.'

'Come on, come on—the secret,' Holly urged. Her tongue slurred over her words slightly. And there were two more bottles of wine to go. Justin nursed one in his lap while he listened.

'Holly, there's a black-magic ring operating right here in the college.'

Holly froze, speechless. Finally she said, 'You're kidding me.'

'I saw them, Holly, I saw them. Lucien reading out of a grimoire, black candles, a big magic circle drawn on the floor. They all chanted and then Lucien fell into some kind of a trance.'

'A trance?' Holly sounded frightened.

'Yeah, and then, after they'd all gone, Lucien came back in alone and, right in front of my fucking eyes, he called up some spirit.'

'Tell me you're joking,' Holly said, but she could see Prudence was deadly serious. 'Oh, God. No.'

'You think you're shocked. *I* saw it. I was there. For all I know, the thing could have seen me.'

'What did he . . . What did he ask the spirit for?'

'Eternal life.'

Holly pressed a palm to her forehead and looked around her wildly. 'Oh, my God.'

'And he didn't even have the spirit—I mean, technically it was some kind of demon—didn't even have it trapped. He's messing with some weird shit, Holly. Some very weird shit.'

Holly turned to Justin and grasped him urgently around the upper arm. 'You must get out of that house,' she hissed. 'You must.'

Justin patted Holly's fingers. 'It's okay. He's not going to hurt anybody but himself. I hardly ever see him, honestly. And now Emma's gone, it's almost like living alone.'

'Emma's gone?'

'Yes,' Prudence said, lighting a cigarette. 'That's the other thing. It seemed like the spirit-demon thing was asking Lucien to get rid of the others.'

'How many in the group altogether?' Holly asked.

'Four.'

'Only four?'

'Yes, only four. Why? What's the matter?'

Holly shook her head. 'This is really freaking me out, that's all.'

'Well, imagine how I felt. I watched the whole thing.'

'Prudence, you have to be more careful. You won't do it again, will you?'

Prudence shook her head vehemently. 'Hell, no. It's all too fucking weird for me. Justin, pass the wine.'

He passed her the bottle and their fingers momentarily touched. She gave him a little smile and he drew his hand away. He wished he had never gone to the college with her last Sunday. He wished there was no reason for her to give him an intimate smile. He looked at Holly. She was visibly pale.

'Hey, don't worry. It's okay,' he said. He wanted to say or do something more to comfort her, but Sunday night's little adventure had put paid to those kind of ideas. How could he, in good conscience, pursue Holly when he had already had sex with her best friend? There was a breach in the trio now, a nasty dark secret. He would do anything to go back in time and do things differently.

'I'm sorry,' Holly said. 'Prudence, I don't know how you kept that in all this time. I had no idea that it was so . . . so significant.'

They fell silent for a few moments. Prudence offered Holly and Justin a cigarette and they both accepted. Justin realised he must be very drunk when he lit up and the tobacco actually tasted good.

'Should we do something about it?' Holly ventured at last, exhaling an uncertain stream of smoke. 'Should we try to stop him?'

Prudence shook her head. 'No way. We stay out of it. And it's a rare occasion when I say that, believe me. No, this is serious shit. We're better off pretending we know nothing. I've tried to talk Justin into coming to live with me, but he won't.'

'That would be cosy,' Holly remarked wryly. 'All three of us in one house.'

'How long do you think you'll be staying at Prudence's?' Justin asked, grateful for a change of topic.

'I spoke to Mrs Partridge this afternoon and she's a bit reluctant about the repairs.'

'But you can stay with me forever if you want,' Prudence interjected loudly. 'Honestly, I'm glad for the company, and I can stay out of your way and give you privacy whenever you need it. I am capable of it. You just have to remind me.'

Justin cringed inwardly. If Holly was living at Prudence's, that would double the reason why he couldn't leave Lucien's house. Once Prudence lost her place to live, Holly would follow.

Prudence was passing the wine bottle to Holly. 'Okay, Holly. Want to talk about the funeral?'

Holly sighed. 'I don't know. It's all so morbid.'

'Hey, you're among friends.'

'Let me get a bit drunker first.'

'Okay then. Let's confess. Any ideas for a good topic?'

Holly shook her head and Justin shrugged.

Prudence threw her hands up in mock despair. 'Booooring. You guys never think of anything. How about, Who do you hate most in the world?'

'I don't know if I hate anyone,' Holly said.

Prudence rolled her eyes. 'Oh, you are *so* virtuous. Come on, you must hate somebody. There must be somebody out there who annoys the fuck out of you, who has done something mean or cruel that you never paid back. Somebody that you'd laugh at if they told you they had three months to live.'

'You sound vicious, Prudence,' Justin remarked, mildly disturbed.

'You're only uncomfortable because you've felt that way at some stage,' Prudence declared confidently. 'Hate is a really powerful emotion, but we never let ourselves feel it. We sit on it. We practise eternal forgiveness.'

'All right, then,' Holly said, 'you go first. Who do you hate most in the world?'

Her answer was immediate. 'My father.'

Justin and Holly were temporarily taken aback.

'Your father?' Holly asked.

'He's a mean-spirited prick whose only redeeming quality is his good taste in wine. *Salut*, Daddy.' She raised a bottle to her lips and took a long swig of wine.

'I had no idea,' Justin said. 'You've mentioned your sister and your mother, but never him.'

'He moved halfway across the fucking world to get away from me.'

475

'I'm sure he didn't want to get away from you,' Holly said.

'I am a total embarrassment to my family. They have old money. They have degrees and contacts and awards and sky-high salaries. Look at me. Just look at me.' She opened her arms so they could inspect her. 'I'm a fucking freak.'

'I'm really sorry you feel that way,' Justin said, strangely afraid that they had all drunk too much and their emotions were getting out of control.

'Don't be sorry. I think we should rejoice in our hate from time to time. It only means you're alive and you care. So come on, Holly. Who do you hate most in the world?'

Holly considered. 'Well, right now I'm pretty steamed up about Michael's boss from the hardware store. He told me that I had driven Michael to his death.'

'Arsehole,' Prudence muttered. 'Did you tell him to jam it?'

'No. I mean, he was just upset and guilty and—'

'Don't make excuses for him. He didn't make excuses for you. He's an arsehole. He deserves to be hated. Go on, hate him.'

'Prudence—'

'Hate him. You were having a bad enough time already. Hate the bastard.'

'Okay. I hate him.'

'And if you found out he was killed in a horror smash—'

'Prudence, that's going too far.'

Prudence smiled. 'No such thing as going too far. Go on, in truth. How would you feel if you heard this prick had wrapped his ute around a tree?'

'I would feel . . . sad.'

'And?'

Holly's fingers had tightened around the neck of the

wine bottle. Justin felt the muscles in his stomach contract anxiously. He knew hate. He knew it too well, and if he were forced to think about that treacherous black nugget inside himself, too much of the surrounding area would be exposed. A buzz of fear that he had not felt for months began to hum inside his head. He wanted to get out of the Confessional and go home. Instead, he tried to lighten the situation a little. 'Prudence, perhaps you should use your powers for good instead of evil.'

Prudence ignored him. 'Holly?'

'I'd be glad,' Holly said in a small voice. 'If he died in a car wreck, I'd feel he got what he deserved.'

'Right. If you feel it, there's no need to hide it. Especially not from us.' Prudence's keen gaze turned to Justin. 'Okay, who do you hate most in the world?'

'I'm not answering this one.'

'Why not?'

He met her eyes evenly. 'I don't like to speak ill of the dead.'

She bit her lip and averted her eyes. 'Sorry. I got carried away.'

'So what else happened at the funeral, Holly?' Justin asked. 'Was it really horrible?' Justin lay down on his blanket, watching the two girls in the candlelight. A dark, cold grain had worked its way into his cosy drunk mood.

Holly drank some wine and passed the bottle to Justin. She pushed her hair back off her forehead and began to speak. 'I wish I could say that I came away from the funeral feeling sad and . . . and sorry for Michael, and grieving like a widow should.' Her voice cracked but she took a deep breath and continued. 'But I didn't. Sometimes I feel . . . I feel angry with him for fucking everything up for me. It's better when I'm angry, because then I don't feel the awful, awful guilt.'

A shiver ran over Justin. This was sounding terribly

familiar. Anger, death, guilt. Damn Prudence, damn Holly. Damn himself for getting close to them. He had been better off hiding behind his impervious shield of unfriendliness.

'How could you feel guilty?' Prudence was saying. 'You didn't put the gun in his mouth, you didn't pull the trigger.'

'But I left him for dead, Prudence. Last time I was up there, I could have worked with him, spent time and . . . and talked and helped him. But I didn't. I left him for dead.'

Justin's legs were shaking. He stretched them out and tensed his thigh muscles, trying to get control. *You're just drunk,* he told himself. *You're just drunk and everything seems worse than it is. Nobody ever has to know.*

'It's a really misplaced guilt, Holly,' Prudence said. 'You have every right to be angry with him. It's not a crime to stop loving somebody. Right, Justin?'

'Huh?'

'She shouldn't feel guilty, right?'

'Oh, God,' Justin said, sitting up. An overwhelmingly dark feeling was bubbling up inside him, like cold black water in his stomach.

'What's the matter, Justin?'

'Justin?' Holly leaned over him and grasped his hands. 'What's the matter?'

'There's something I've never told you.' He heard himself say it as though he were a million miles away. A stern voice in his head was screaming, *You idiot, don't tell them, don't tell them!*

Prudence had moved closer too. He shuddered. Everything was spinning out of control inside him. Prudence's warm hands were pulling his head onto her shoulder, stroking his hair. 'Hey, it's okay. It's okay. You've just had too much to drink, that's all.'

'No, there's something I never told you. I never told

you.' His heart was pounding. Dim resonances of unbearable memories swam up through the layers. Was he really going to tell them? But if he didn't, he felt he'd explode, go mad, turn into a dark vapour and bleed into the walls around him.

Prudence sat back from him, gazing at him with those large, dark eyes. 'Justin?' This is how he always knew it would be. He knew she'd get it out of him sooner or later. It was as inevitable as death. He felt a warm hand enclose his own and looked to his left to see Holly.

'Are you all right?' she asked breathlessly.

In a tiny voice he said, 'I have to tell you what happened the night my mother died.'

'You don't have to tell us anything,' Prudence said, though he knew she didn't mean it.

He nodded. 'I do have to tell you. I feel like I've been lying to you all this time. That you think I'm a different person to how I really am.'

Prudence took one of his hands, Holly still held the other.

'I assure you,' Prudence said softly, 'that we will not think any differently of you.'

Justin realised he was shaking violently, as though his body conspired to keep inside the awful secret that was intent on liberating itself this evening. Without looking at either of them, he began to speak. His voice seemed to be very close and hot in his ears.

'My mother was . . .' He gulped, tried again. 'I hated my mother. With all my heart I hated her. My life was ruined by my mother. She drank and she stank of alcohol and she cried outside my door every other night and I couldn't leave her. My heart ached for the woman she had been—you know, she could play the piano beautifully, but she sold it when she ran into debt because of her drinking. She used to play "Autumn Leaves" and "Tenderly" for me and sometimes she'd sing to me.

479

When she became that drunken harpy, I couldn't stop remembering what she had been. And I couldn't leave her. I was all she had. She was a . . . like a ball and chain, you know. Except around my neck. My shoulders—always weighed down.'

'But you loved her too, right?' Holly said in a soft voice. 'You loved her as much as you hated her.'

'Of course. Of course I did.'

'What happened the night she died?' Prudence prompted.

Justin felt that reality had started to dissolve around him. This was just a nightmare and he was talking in his sleep. 'She came home, as always, drunk. She was making herself something to eat. Grilling lamb chops.' He gulped. 'I woke up like I always did because I was only ever half asleep anyway, wondering if she'd come home at all or if I'd get a phone call from the morgue instead. I smelled the greasy smell of lamb chops. And while they were cooking, she came to stand on the other side of my door and started crying. Saying all the usual stuff. "Justin, forgive me, forgive me. I'm your mother, come talk to me. I don't want to be alone. I don't want to be alone."' His voice broke but he stopped himself from sobbing. 'And I ignored her like I always did and she went back to cooking her dinner, and then I heard this horrible sound. Like a thump. I knew something wasn't right, so I got out of bed and I went to the kitchen.

'She had slipped on the kitchen floor, because she hadn't covered the griller and there was grease, you know, on the floor. And she'd hit her head.' Justin pressed a palm to his own temple unwittingly. 'At first I thought she was dead. And . . . Oh, God.'

'It's okay,' Prudence said, giving his hand a squeeze. 'You'll feel better once you've finished telling us.'

'I was so happy,' he said, his voice strained over unshed tears. 'I thought, at last she's gone. At last it's over. But she wasn't dead.' He shook his head, tears began to fill his eyes. 'She was still alive. She stretched a hand up to me and said, "Justin, help me. Call an ambulance. I can't move." Her head was bleeding and it was kind of . . . odd, not quite right. Like she'd maybe broken her neck. Her breathing was laboured. I stood there looking at her, still alive. Stretching out that hand and . . . I didn't know what to do. I turned the griller off. I touched her hand. She said, "Justin, please call an ambulance."' He closed his eyes, tears overflowed and ran down his cheeks. 'But I didn't.'

There was a short silence. Prudence said, 'You didn't what?'

'I didn't call an ambulance. I went back to my room, back to bed. She started to cry out—not very loudly, like a dog that'd been kicked. So I got up and turned on my stereo really loud so I couldn't hear her. I got back in bed and I lay there for hours and hours until dawn, dozing and waking up to the horror, and dozing again. When dawn broke I got out of bed and went to the kitchen. She was dead.'

He opened his eyes and looked up, surveyed both the girls' faces. Holly was teary, Prudence was shocked and speechless. 'I let her die,' he said. 'I let my mother die.'

'She may have died anyway,' Prudence said.

'She may have lived,' Justin replied. 'Don't think I haven't gone through every possible outcome in my head. I'm responsible for her death, Prudence. I'm well aware of that.'

Prudence shook her head. 'No, no, Justin. You aren't. You're not responsible for anybody but yourself.'

Holly had withdrawn her hand and sat back silently. That was it, then, he thought. She would never be interested in him now. Perhaps he had had a small chance before, but now he was known for what he really was. He couldn't love himself, how could he expect anybody else to?

Justin sighed and drooped his head. 'I can't believe I told you.'

'You're among friends,' Prudence said. 'We love you, Justin.'

'What I did was reprehensible,' he said, meeting her eyes. 'How can you even bear to be in the same room as me?'

As if in answer, Prudence drew him to her and held him tightly. His arms went around her back and he fell limp against her shoulder, crying like he had never cried before. The smell of her enveloped him. He wished it were Holly holding him, then cursed himself for wishing it. Holly remained conspicuously silent. Finally he drew back, removed his glasses and palmed tears from his eyes.

'I'm sorry,' he said. He turned to Holly. 'I'm sorry.'

To his surprise, she met his gaze. 'It's all right,' she said. 'Really, it's all right.'

He pushed his hair back from his face, his anxiety suddenly peaking. 'Oh, God, please don't ever tell anybody. I mean—'

'Of course we won't tell anybody,' Prudence said quickly. 'Of course we won't.'

'It's safe with us,' Holly said. '*You're* safe with us.'

He took a few deep breaths. 'Okay,' he said, more to himself than to anybody else. 'Okay.'

Prudence reached for the wine, then seemed to think better of it. 'I am never, *ever* going to go after a secret again,' she said. 'This is getting painful.'

'Prudence,' Holly said, 'before you give up, I think there's something I need to tell you both. Here . . .' She grasped one of Prudence's hands and one of Justin's. 'And you two, too. Go on.'

Prudence took Justin's hand so that they sat in a close circle, hands linked. Justin felt unbearably light, as though he had been relieved of a huge burden.

Holly smiled at him. 'You're not the only one who has a secret,' she said.

He shook his head. He did not understand, but he realised with some astonishment that neither Prudence nor Holly were judging him adversely for what he had done. In fact, his confession seemed to have prompted Holly to make one of her own. Dark places in everybody.

'Prudence,' Holly said, 'I need to make a special apology to you. Of all people, I shouldn't have kept this from you. But I want you to understand that it meant so much to me that I had to keep it to myself.'

Prudence's lips were parted in a little 'o' of surprise, but she said nothing, as if this were all a delirious dream where everybody's secrets finally made it to the surface.

In a soft but certain voice, Holly spoke. 'There is a ghost in our office. I know this because since March I have been involved in a kind of a relationship with him.'

Prudence was stupefied, her jaw slack. Justin felt a chill run over him. Ghosts? On top of everything, ghosts? He had never questioned the existence of the supernatural, but he had certainly never expected it to intrude so conspicuously into his life.

'The reason I'm telling you this is because I'm scared. I'm very, very frightened, but not of the ghost. His name is Christian and he has been telling me all about his life in the nineteenth century. He was kind of a sorcerer's apprentice to a man named Peter Owling. I'm frightened because I think it's Owling's grimoire that Lucien is using, though I don't know how it got to Jerusalem.'

Prudence finally found her voice. 'You've been talking to a ghost, right upstairs in our office?'

Holly nodded. Prudence was silent for a second, her lower lip trembling, then suddenly she burst into loud tears. 'Why you?' she sobbed. 'Why not me? Why not me?'

Justin and Holly exchanged glances. They were all very,

very drunk. The evening's events were becoming almost burlesque. With one movement Holly and Justin dropped Prudence's hands and the three of them were in a huddle in the middle of the Confessional floor. Justin had the sense of hands and long hair brushing against him, and wished for a moment that the three of them could all meld into one. At length they became self-conscious again and pulled away from each other. Eyes were dried and wine passed around.

'So, you can see why I'm frightened,' Holly said quietly. 'If this is Owling's grimoire. He was an evil man.'

'What happened to him?' Prudence asked.

Holly shrugged. 'I don't know. Christian promised to tell me next time I was with him. God, this feels so weird. It's been a secret for so long. I almost feel that telling you has made it less real somehow.'

'When will you see him again?'

'As soon as I can.'

'You're in love with him, aren't you?' Prudence asked. Justin felt a shock to his heart.

Holly dropped her eyes for a moment. 'Yes, I think I am.'

'You can't ever have him, Holly. You have to realise that.'

'I know. I know.'

More silence. Justin reached for the wine. Right now he wanted to blot out every single feeling he had.

'Owling used to let the demon possess Christian's body,' Holly said. 'Did it seem that Lucien was allowing some kind of possession to take place?'

Prudence shook her head. 'Perhaps it's not the same being.'

'It must be. Christian says all the summoning instructions were written in the grimoire. The demon's name was Aathahorus.'

'Well, this one wasn't called that.'

'Are you sure?'

'Of course I'm sure. It had the same name as the evil magician in that Spenser poem.'

Holly sat bolt upright, gaping at Prudence. 'No, no. Not . . .'

'Archimago,' Prudence said cautiously, 'the being said its name was Archimago.'

'Oh, my God,' Holly breathed.

'What is it?' Justin asked. The candles flickered in the dark room. The smell of damp earth seemed very close.

'I have to see Christian,' Holly said. 'I have to see him immediately.'

Holly shivered in the dark office. Prudence and Justin had gone home at her request, heading off together to Prudence's house because Justin didn't want to be alone. She tried not to think about what could happen between the two of them on a night like this when emotions ran as high as blood-alcohol levels and comfort was so desperately needed. Tried not to think about anything but Christian, his sad blue eyes, the end of his tale. An unspeakable terror had begun to spread through her from a small point under her ribs. Archimago—here at the college. His grimoire still intact. The quest for eternal life taking place again. Christian knew how it would finish. He had been there.

She felt foggy from too much alcohol, shocked and cold from everything that had transpired tonight. Prudence's confession, Justin's awful secret, her own reluctant disclosure tarnishing the most beautiful treasure she had ever held dear. Exposing him to the world—even if it was just to her two closest friends—seemed a massive betrayal.

'Christian?' she said, gazing into the mirror. The two candles flickered eerily in the silent room. 'Christian, I need to know how it ended.'

He appeared over her shoulder. The sight of him almost brought her to tears, his beauty as exquisitely moving as the tragedy that was slowly unfolding.

'Yes, Holly,' he said solemnly, 'it's time you knew.'

CHAPTER THIRTY-THREE

~

'Peter descended further and further into madness. In some ways it was a relief—he was surely by now oblivious to the extent of his fall. In other ways it was unbearable. He became frighteningly violent, crazed, inescapable. He wanted me with him at all times. I could not move out of his sight. He did everything short of binding me and locking me in a room. His clients no longer came. By October I had seen no other living being but Peter for two months. His twisted logic, his sudden rampages, slowly wore me down. I had two long bouts of sickness, where even raising my head in the morning took more energy than I could muster. My very bones seemed to ache with misery.

'Then one evening, it all began. The beginning of the end. I remember it well. It was a Tuesday and I had been well for three days after two weeks of illness. Peter sat with me and solicitously asked after my health.

'"Christian, how are you feeling?"

'"Well, Archimago."

'"Your body is all working properly? No bruises, no aches and pains, no creaking joints?"

'"Really, I'm quite well, thank you."

'"Good, good. You see, this Sunday is an important day. This Sunday is the first day of eternity."

'I was well used to him saying things that made little sense, so I merely nodded and smiled. "Yes, it is."

'He shook his head irritably. "You're very little impressed by such a grand declaration, my orphan boy. The first day of eternity, I said. My eternity. This Sunday I will be granted eternal life."

'Still thinking it was gibberish, but realising he wanted me to be impressed, I said, "Eternal life, Archimago? Only you could bring such an event to pass."

'"Yes, yes. I will command Satan to give it to me. Our friend Aathahorus has tutored me well. I must draw a circle and evoke him, entrap him within the circle and command him to do as I bid."

'I started to think that perhaps this was not a delusion. That perhaps it was possible he actually intended to go through with it. Perhaps it was even possible that he may succeed. The thought of Peter as he was then living eternally was terrifying to me, even more terrifying in some ways than the idea of him summoning Satan to our home. To me, all devils were equal, and one had been possessing me every week for nearly a year.

'But then, some fainter hope began to grow in me. Perhaps, when this transformation took place and Peter was given eternal life, perhaps he would be restored to his former self. In a strange way I began to look forward to Sunday.'

Christian stopped and hesitated over his next sentence.

'Go on,' Holly said, trying to keep her own fear in check. Surely this was not what Lucien intended? She had never met him, but she had never heard him described as a madman.

'Holly, I don't want you to think badly of what I might have done,' he said.

'I won't,' she said, feeling a cold chill up her spine.

'Being constantly in the company of Peter's insanity, and after two sicknesses that had left me dazed and weak, perhaps I was not thinking clearly either. In any case, I came to a decision. I concluded that if Peter were able to command Satan for eternal life, he might also be able to command him to bring Rosalind back.

'However, I was under strict orders not to mention her ever again. I did not want to upset Peter at this time, but I thought that perhaps in his restored state he might be reasoned with. I fixed upon the notion of collecting her bones and bringing them to Sunday night's ritual.

'Her room had been locked for months, and I needed to get out of Peter's sight long enough to pick the lock and gather her up. He rarely slept, and when he did he usually insisted on my being cradled in his arms. I needed to devise a way to get him out of the house. By Friday, when time was running out, I settled upon appealing to his most exploitable vice—greed.

'I still had Lucy Humberstone's first note—the one where she had asked for me to return her gloves—stored in the back of one of my copy books. While I pretended to read and copy one afternoon, I actually falsified a note from Lucy to Peter, inviting him to an assignation with her to discuss an ongoing stipend for him. With a steady hand, I mimicked the slope and curls of Lucy's writing. The letter asked for Peter to meet Lucy away from the Humberstone abode, at a coffee house in an obscure side street, so that nobody would witness their rendezvous. Then I picked the seal off Lucy's original letter and held the two pieces momentarily over a candle, gluing the break back together as convincingly as I could and sticking it to the back of my note.

'I left it half under the front door while Peter wasn't looking and went about my day, waiting for him to notice.

'I was sitting in the kitchen, playing with a dish of some unappetising leftovers, when Peter came in with a stern look across his brow. He held up the note. "When did this arrive?" he demanded.

'I shrugged, attempting to look guileless.

'"Don't take me for an imbecile, lad. The seal has been tampered with. Did you think it was a love letter for you? I'd be surprised if Mrs Humberstone didn't hate you passionately after the way you betrayed her." He unfolded the letter. "In any case, it's for me, and I have to go out for a few hours. You are not to leave the house."

'I nodded. "Of course not, Peter. What reason would I have to—"

'"Just don't. I need you here. You're very important to me." He brushed my cheek with his fingertips and I felt a tug of the old devotion I'd had for him. The devotion now buried under layers of sorrow.

'He left shortly after and I ran directly to Rosalind's room. As always, the hallway was pitch dark and I needed a lantern to light my way. I peered through the keyhole again, but it was late in the afternoon and only shadows were visible, very still in the dusty gloom. I tried the handle with some violence but it was definitely locked. Peter had taken his keys with him, so I would have to break the lock myself.

'I left my lantern burning in the hallway and went to the kitchen for a collection of knives. On my return I pushed a butterknife into the lock and tried unsuccessfully to move the barrel. Every time I heard the snick of the lock giving, it dropped back into place when I tried to turn the handle. So, using one knife, I held the barrel up while I fiddled in the keyhole with another. Balancing the two knives carefully, I tried the handle again. This time it turned and the knives clattered to the floor as I entered Rosalind's room.

'First I closed the small gap in the curtains, then I

grabbed my lantern from the hallway and surveyed the room. Her bones, now clean of any remaining flesh, lay scattered around. I began to pick them up, forcing myself to bite down nausea and feel only detachment, and I made a small pile of her bones on her bloodstained bedspread. I felt around under the bed and cupboards for bones that may have eluded me, brushing off small black beetles and dust. While under her bed, I found a canvas bag which she had used to store her dolls. I tipped them out and began to fill the canvas bag with her bones.

'I worked assiduously, keeping an eye out for any parts of her that might have escaped me. I put her poor skull in the bag last, trying not to remember how it had used to feel, covered in soft, plump flesh.

'My next problem was how to get the bones to Sunday night's ritual without being noticed. Peter always required me to be naked beneath my robe and was always eager to check that this was the case. I closed the door to Rosalind's room behind me and the lock fell back into place. I took my lantern down the hallway to the reading room, where Peter performed his magic acts. I hid the canvas bag behind a bookcase, moved a chair in front of it just in case, and ran back downstairs with my heart pounding. I returned the cutlery to its drawer, the lantern to its place in the dining room, and myself to the chair in front of the fire to wait for Peter's return.'

Holly saw Christian shake his head in the mirror. 'Of course I was not thinking straight,' he said. 'Rosalind no longer resided in that collection of bones. But in the depths of my loneliness and misery, I craved so much the company of another who would love and understand me. Unholy means became plausible if the end result was a return to the way things had once been, when I had known happiness. I fantasised about Sunday night. Peter would command Satan, his sanity would be granted along with his immortality, and then I would make my plea.

Restore Rosalind. And all would be as it had—the three of us, together forever in our dusty house, with the fire and our books for company.

'Peter came in later that evening, grizzling about Lucy not turning up for their meeting. He muttered darkly about getting his revenge when he was immortal, but I tried not to think about what would come after Sunday. Sunday was everything—the first day of eternity, just as he said. And I would deal with eternity one day at a time when it arrived.'

Christian's voice dropped. 'Holly, what happened next was very grim. My tongue trembles to tell it. Sunday dawned. Peter was excited beyond all reason. He sat me down and brushed my hair, made me bathe, made me dress in my best.' He lifted his arms to display his red frockcoat, white silk shirt and cravat, black and gold-embossed vest. 'You see, I still wear it.

'Peter fussed about all day. In the morning he repainted the circle in the centre of the reading room floor, but would not allow me to help in case my clothes got stained. I sat nervously in the chair that hid Rosalind's bones, praying that he would not notice them until I wanted him to. He hummed, he sang, he laughed at nothing. But mostly he gazed at me with eager eyes, telling me over and over how beautiful and valuable I was to him. How he loved me, how I had helped bring it all to pass.

'In the late afternoon he began to cook. We were in the kitchen and he threw ingredients together to make extravagant dishes and sweets. Once again I was instructed to sit by and watch, not to soil my clothes or mess my hair. I watched him, sweat trickling down his face, as he arranged a sumptuous feast on our dining table—hams, jellies, tarts, roasted lamb and beef, creamy gravies in porcelain boats, bottles of wine assembled like soldiers at the ready. I asked him who he was expecting, and he declared that all the most important people in the world would now want to venerate him. He was merely preparing himself for their arrival.

'Shortly before midnight he went upstairs, dragging me with him, and bathed. I sat sentinel as he scrubbed his pallid, naked flesh, soapy bubbles caught in his chest hair, the room full of the warm scent of clean, wet flesh. I helped him towel down, enduring his barked orders not to get myself wet, and then assisted him into his ritual robe.

'"Shall I change into my robe too, Archimago?" I asked as I followed him downstairs.

'"No, boy. You're fine just as you are. You look young and healthy and beautiful, and tonight that's exactly as I wish." He went to the dining room and lit candles. I hadn't eaten all day and the smell of the food, although most of the hot dishes had cooled and the gravies coagulated, made my stomach ache with hunger.

'"Come on upstairs, boy. It's time we got this happening."

'My pulse quickened as I followed him to the reading room. The room smelled faintly of the paint he had used that morning. He indicated for me to sit, and once again I sat in front of the bag full of Rosalind's bones, resting my heel carefully against it to reassure myself. I kept telling myself that Peter would surely comply with my request when he was back to his old self, but my secret, hideous fear was that he would never be his old self. That he would remain this grotesque madman for eternity.

'Peter lit a candle in each corner of the room. Where I was, tucked almost behind the bookcase, I was still in shadow. I watched Peter pull out the grimoire and open it. He began to read—a long, almost unintelligible tirade against Christ, an even longer veneration of Satan. Then his voice dropped to a murmur and he began the evocation.

'I knew this evocation was different. I was familiar with the one that brought Aathahorus into my body, but this wasn't it. He gestured towards the circle and a blue-white light began to grow in the centre of it, about three feet off the ground. I began to be very frightened. Peter was not looking at me, and I huddled further back into the shadows, moving my chair a fraction. As I did so, I heard a tiny crack and realised that I'd pushed my chair against the bag of bones and broken one. A little shock ran through me, but Peter hadn't noticed. I reached covertly behind me and pulled the bag out, pushed it through the legs of my chair and hauled it into my lap, cradling it against myself almost like a shield. Perhaps in a way it was.

'I thought the blue-white light must be Satan coming, but I was mistaken. Soon, Aathahorus's very familiar voice rumbled through the room. The light began to take on a nebulous human shape as he said, "Archimago. You are ready?"

'"Yes," Peter said. I could see rivers of sweat running over him again. His cloak had gaped slightly and his naked body flashed pale in the candlelight.

'"You must direct me," Aathahorus said. I was trying to figure what he meant when Peter lifted his hand and with a stream of unintelligible language reached into the circle and pushed the blue-white light in my direction. The light began to rush towards me, and without thinking I raised the canvas bag to protect myself.'

Christian paused, and Holly realised that she was holding her breath.

'And then?' she asked.

He shook his head. 'Oh, horror,' he said. 'Horror. Something began to move inside the bag. At first I thought it only a trick of the light, but no. The bag squirmed in my arms and with a scream I dropped it to the floor. An indignant cry came from within the bag. I pressed my hand against my mouth so I would not scream again, for Peter was bearing down on me, enraged. "What have you done? What have you done?"

'I shook my head mutely. He picked up the bag and opened the drawstring, tipped it upside down. Bones came tumbling out, joined inhumanly and animated by some foul sorcery. The skull perched atop ribs; legs, arms in jumbled order; hands for feet and joints for hands. It scuttled across the room and paused in a corner. It screamed like a banshee, and Peter approached it cautiously.

'"What happened?" he said.

'Right up until the horrible skeleton spoke, I thought that it was Rosalind back from the dead. I thought my wish had come true, although hideously contorted. But when the jaw moved and Aathahorus's voice emerged, relief flowed through me like warm oil.

'"My body! My body, Archimago! This body is not what was promised!"

'"There's been a mistake," Peter said quickly. "I'll kill the lad for this. The fool, what was he thinking? But we can rectify it, can we not?"

'I shrank even further into the shadows.

'"We've started the summoning," Peter continued, "we must finish it now."

'"I will not assist you!" the thing screamed. "You have not met your end of our deal."

'Peter paused and looked at the thing slyly. "But you are trapped inside that body now, are you not? Unless you help me, you will remain there, I will see to it."

'"I want my body," it said again, this time more subdued.

'"And you shall get it. Help me with the summoning and I promise it will be the very second thing I make him grant me."

'"You shall make it the first."

'Peter seemed to consider, then nodded. "All right.

Now come here and betray your master into my hands."

'The thing crouched at Peter's feet; both of them seemed oblivious to my continued presence in the room. I wanted to run but I did not wish to draw attention to myself. So I stayed in my dark corner and watched.

'The long evocation continued. Peter's voice was occasionally interrupted by Aathahorus's as he made solemn promises in some demonic language. The temperature in the room rose to even greater heights than those I had already experienced during Peter's rituals. Perspiration beaded on my forehead and ran down my stomach underneath my layers of clothes. I felt I could barely breathe. In the distance I heard rumbling, as though thunder were poised on the horizon, ready to swing in and plough all before it.

'Suddenly, an icy breeze shot up through the floorboards and unsecured papers began to fly about the room. The cool was at first an instant relief, but it soon brought a freezing discomfort of its own as I curled myself up in a ball in the chair and watched in terror.

'Still Peter and Aathahorus continued speaking. I watched Peter's face for any sign of fear. He repeatedly palmed sweat off his forehead, but his eyes were dark and glazed, his mouth moving almost unconsciously as he proceeded with the chant that would finish him.

'Slowly, faintly, something began to glow in the middle of the circle. It was like a luminous whirlwind of orange and gold, spinning violent and radiant in the centre. The icy wind had died off and the loose papers had arranged themselves haphazardly around the room, as though finding a good vantage point from which to watch. The thundery sound still rumbled in the distance. Almost mad with fear, I watched the whirlwind dancing in the centre of Peter's circle.

'"Arise, as I insist," Peter was saying over and over. "Arise, as I insist."

'With a strangely beautiful shattering sound, the whirlwind disintegrated spectacularly, sending tiny golden lights flying through the air. The embers did not fall beyond the circle, however.

'For a few moments there was silence. Nothing moved, and it seemed the circle was empty. I caught my breath, thinking that the experiment must have failed. But then, with a sudden, deafening screech, a being appeared in the centre of the circle, as though he were being tugged through from another dimension.

'Holly, he was both beautiful and hideous. He landed on his shoulder on the floor, then, with superhuman dignity, climbed to his feet and stood. At least seven feet tall, the being was made of long, perfectly formed muscles and limbs. His feet were cloven, but his legs were those of an Adonis. His fingers were clawed, but the shape of his hands and forearms was that of a sculptor or a magnificent lover. His bearing was majestic, his face a horribly scarred mess, eyes at uneven angles and a cruelly twisted mouth. He was completely naked and his skin was burnished red-brown. Two tiny horns protruded from his forehead, sharp and pearl white. He turned and surveyed us all. For an instant his eyes lay on me and then moved on, but that instant seemed to me to be an eternity. The irises were bright green like leaves in summer, the pupils huge and black, lashes long and curved, almost prettily. Holly, I have held the gaze of Satan and I know that the stories are true. He was once an angel.

'He soon dismissed me, however, probably sensing I was nothing in this diabolical game. He turned his attention to Peter and the creature that Aathahorus had become.

'"Who did this?" His voice boomed through the room and made the walls shake.

'Peter took a brave step forward, careful to stay out of the circle. "I did. I intend to command you. You are

497

trapped in my circle and you will clearly state your name."

'"You know who I am."

'"Make him state his name," Aathahorus said.

'"You will clearly state your name," Peter repeated.

'The great creature turned its attention to the collection of jumbled bones. With no warning he cast one glorious arm out and made a noise. I can barely remember what it was, but it sounded like the kind of dismissive noise someone would make when confronted with abject stupidity. Aathahorus exploded instantly and spectacularly, Rosalind's bones turning to fine white dust which disintegrated before it even touched the ground. Peter went visibly pale, clutching the grimoire to his chest.

'"You are trapped in my circle," he said, licking his lips nervously. "You are trapped in my circle and you will clearly state your name."

'I watched, transfixed in awe and terror, as the great creature lifted one perfectly formed leg and took a single step outside the circle, its cloven hoof coming to rest on the other side of Peter's futile painted line.

'"I am Satan," he said. "I am lord of misery. And I am trapped by no man."

'Peter screamed and ran, slamming the door behind him. The beast followed and I was left alone. I was stupefied and did not know what to do next, but Peter's screams ringing through the house brought me to my senses. He was all I had in the world and he was about to be destroyed.

'I clambered to my feet and raced out through the hall and down the stairs. I traced Peter's screams to the dining room and stood, horrified, as I watched the beast finish him off. He had Peter around the throat with one immense hand, the other stripped him of his robe and threw it aside. With a movement that resembled a caress, the great creature trailed his claws over Peter's white flesh, tracing thin lines of butchery in the fat. Blood oozed. Peter dropped the grimoire with an inhuman howl, caught my eye and reached a desperate hand in my direction.

'"Christian, help me! Help me!" he screamed, although he must have known that there was nothing I could have done. The beast had him above his head now, and with a massive swing of his majestic arms he slammed Peter onto the dining table, among the dishes and candles and wine bottles. I heard a sickening crunch as the back of his skull was crushed. Peter's eyes rolled wildly—he was still conscious, though clearly not for long. "I don't want to die!" he cried in a guttural voice. "I don't want to die!"

'The creature picked up the grimoire and began to tear it apart. He pulled off a quarter and threw it over his shoulder, where it disappeared as though being swallowed by the hot, hungry air that surrounded the great beast. Then another quarter, and another. All three vaporised into nothing. The final quarter he held on to. He found a large carving knife on the table, slammed the last few pages of the book into Peter's chest and with a swift, powerful movement, drove the knife through them and into his heart. Peter died upon that instant, silently and in great ignominy.'

Christian stopped and drooped his head. 'I screamed, I howled, I ran to him and tried to rub life back into his fingertips, careless of my own safety.' Once more he looked up and met Holly's gaze. 'But he was dead.

'The beast turned to me. "Here is the story you shall tell," he said. "The book has been sent to the four corners of the world. This man's death is a reminder that you fools will not attempt to command me. If this happens again, I will destroy you all. There will be a great undoing. Civilisations will tumble and my emissaries will claim the world as their own. This is the story you shall tell. For that, I will spare your life."

'In a blink he disappeared, and the only sounds I had for company were my own ragged breathing, Peter's blood dripping to the floor, and the clock on the mantelpiece. I began to scream. I screamed and screamed forever. Eventually somebody came—a police constable nearby—and I was taken into custody and given a meal and a cold corner to sleep in. I dreamed of Peter and of Satan, and I knew I would dream about them for the rest of my days.' He sighed. 'That is all.'

'No, it's not. It's not all. That's the end of Peter's story, but what happened to you?' Holly said. Cold fear had gripped all her organs and her pulse thumped through her like a wild horse. *A great undoing.* Surely not? Surely something of that much cosmic significance could not ride on so simple a transgression?

Christian sighed. 'After one night they wished to release me from custody. I could not answer their questions so I fell back on my show of muteness. They knew, though. The constable who found me knew that something unholy had happened that night, and he wanted no part of it. The section of the grimoire that had been left behind fascinated and repulsed him. He held it at arm's length when he spoke.

'But I did not want to go back to Peter's house, and I did not want to go back on the streets. In the holding cell I had a roof and sustenance, and I had time to think. When the constable came to let me free, I hung on to the bars of my cell and shook my head.

'"Come, lad. You're free to go."

'Again I shook my head. He came into the cell and tried to bully me out. "Come on, don't make a fuss." He pulled me and prodded me, but still I hung on, shaking my head.

'"You can't stay here," he said, standing back and surveying me as though I were crazy.

'On each finger of each hand I wore a ring—Peter had

bought them all for me since he had been extorting money from Lucy Humberstone. I picked the most ostentatious—a silver ring with a large ruby—and held it out to him. He eyed me suspiciously.

'"What's this, lad? What do you want?"

'I pushed the ring into his hand and sat back in the corner of my cell. He held the ruby up to the light coming through the tiny window, seemed to think it was a fair swap and backed out of the cell. "All right, stay there. If that's what you want."

'Every day I gave the constable a ring when he tried to remove me from my cell. But he knew and I knew that it would not continue, for I had only eight rings. Consequently, eight days after Peter's death, I was forced to leave.

'I wandered alone through London, dazed and cold, but not willing to go back to the house on Milton Close. My only option, as I could see it, was to go to Lord Burghley's. He had said he would take me in, and at that point the promise of a warm bed in a quiet house was very inviting, even if it did mean having to share my body with him. I went to a coach hire on Leighton Grove and booked a conveyance for that evening.

'In the few hours I had left, I wandered to and fro aimlessly, my mind likewise wandering from topic to topic and not settling on any one for longer than a few seconds. I was protecting myself from pain and terror, but finally one thought kept recurring often enough for me to take notice. The grimoire. It could not be reassembled and used again, lest it bring about the great undoing that the beast had spoken of. Even though I knew the pieces were scattered around the world, I imagined it was still possible for them to be gathered in time. Peter was most certainly not the only individual who possessed a great enough fear of death and a meticulous enough mind to pursue such diabolic secrets. I resolved on going back to the police and asking for the remains of the grimoire. I would destroy it somehow, or just keep it with me and have it buried with me as an old man. But it must not be allowed to circulate publicly.

'I arrived at the police station at dusk. Two constables stood on the front steps, smoking pipes and talking in quiet voices. I had intended to go inside and break my vow of silence, ask for the constable who had found me and convince him of the necessity of my taking the book. He was frightened enough of it to want to be rid of it, I knew. However, I did not get that far. I overheard a snatch of conversation between the two constables and I paused in the shadows to listen.

'"Hallam's taken care of it."

'"A good thing too. He said it was some kind of black-magic book. That Owling died from some kind of black magic."

'"I think Hallam's too superstitious for his own good. As are you."

'The second constable rubbed his hands together. "I don't think you can be too superstitious. So what has he done with it?"

'"The Humberstones were sending a shipment of books to Australia on the *Antiope*. Hallam put it in with those. He's going down to the Docks tonight to make sure it gets away—now *that* is too superstitious."

'The Docks were a good ten miles from where I was and I had a coach to catch in just over two hours. I wavered, wishing I could abjure the responsibility for Peter's actions. I could not. I made the decision to go to the Docks. I still do not know if it was the right decision or the wrong.'

'That was where you drowned?' Holly asked.

Christian nodded. 'Trying to run up the gangway. In desperation. A cargo hook hit me in the head and I was knocked into the water. It was very cold and very dark, and all I knew was that I had somehow failed.'

'When did you realise that you were . . . you know . . .'

'A ghost? I don't know. There were long grey periods of unawareness. Sometimes I would be here with the books in the library, sometimes I would still be under the water in the Thames, watching dark shapes move and waver above me. At first I was just a non-sentient sadness moving between rooms, hoping to find something but not knowing what. When you came along, something awoke in me. As though I had somehow found the one warm being who would listen and understand.'

Holly watched him in the mirror. He blinked slowly and gazed back. She wanted this moment to last forever. His story was told and now she had to reveal to him what had become of his attempts to stop the grimoire being reassembled, what had become of his beloved Peter. It was going to change everything but she couldn't keep it from him.

'Can we ever be together?' she asked, stretching the last quiet moment out for as long as possible.

He shook his head sadly.

'But what if I died?' she asked.

'It's not time for you to die yet.'

She sighed deeply. 'Christian, something very bad is happening here at the college. Your worst fears have been realised. Lucien Humberstone has reassembled the grimoire.'

'What?'

'There's more. Lucien has called up the help of a spirit demon. It says its name is Archimago.'

His eyes grew wide. 'Peter?' he whispered. 'Peter is here?'

'I don't know where he is now, but he was here.'

'I must see him,' he said, still in the quiet, breathy voice.

Holly was unsurprised. She knew how deep Christian's

503

devotion to Owling was. 'Christian, he's dangerous. He's a demon now, like Aathahorus.'

'But I love him,' he wailed. 'I must see him. Holly, you can take me to him.'

She had no intention of being anywhere near Lucien next time he summoned up demonic help. 'Christian, I can't.'

'You can. You know where this happened, don't you? It will happen again next Sunday, that's what the grimoire says.'

'I would put myself at great danger if I—'

His face contorted with rage. 'I can't do it by myself. I'm only attached to you.'

'No. I can't help you,' she said simply.

Suddenly he disappeared. A low whoosh flew past her and the mirror on her desk unexpectedly fell to the floor and smashed. The candle flames bobbed as if in a quick breeze and books began to drop from her desk. One volume hovered momentarily in the air before being flung against the wall.

'Christian? Are you doing this?' she asked, frightened.

'I ask so little,' he screamed, his voice coming from everywhere. At Prudence's desk, pens and pencils began to rattle and jump. 'I must see Peter.'

'I can't take you to him.'

'You can.'

'I *won't* take you to him. He's dangerous to both of us. Don't you understand? What happened to Rosalind's bones was supposed to happen to you. Aathahorus was supposed to take over your body.'

'He took over my body every Sunday.'

'Peter promised him your body as part of the deal. It seems to me that he meant permanently.'

An unearthly scream shook the walls. '*That—is— untrue!*'

The light bulb in the lamp over Holly's desk exploded,

sending tiny shards of glass everywhere. She put up her hands to protect her face. Blood trickled from a minute cut in her palm.

'I will haunt you,' he said, 'until you agree to my demands.'

'Christian, he was evil. He was responsible for his daughter's death, and he would have been responsible for yours also if things had gone as planned.'

The candles blew out and she was suddenly in darkness. She stood and felt her way to the window so that she had the glow of faraway streetlights to help her see. The room was quiet. She looked around her wildly, trying to sense whether or not Christian was still with her. From the other side of the room a low hum buzzed in the air and started to move towards her, gathering speed.

'Christian, don't hurt me,' she breathed.

The buzzing raced hot across the room, changing into an ear-piercing howl. She put her hands up to defend herself. At the last instant it diverted past her left ear and disappeared. Her ears rang and her heart thudded, but she was quite sure he was gone. Leaving the broken mirror and the fallen books all around her, Holly raced back to Prudence's house, a sense of deep terror growing in her breast.

CHAPTER THIRTY-FOUR

~

Both Prudence and Justin wanted to stay up and wait for Holly's return, but by two a.m., when alcohol and emotional exhaustion had taken their toll, Prudence finally had to concede defeat.

'She'll wake us when she gets in,' she said, yawning as she showed Justin to a guest room. She stopped short of asking if he required a sleeping companion.

'I hope she's okay,' he said.

'I'm sure she's okay. She can look after herself,' Prudence said, mildly annoyed.

'Goodnight, then.'

She was a few steps away when he called her back.

'Prudence?'

'Yes?' She walked back to where he stood, looking slightly rumpled in his green sweater and blue jeans.

'What I told you guys tonight—'

'It's all safe. Don't worry.'

'But how can you not . . . how can you not hate me?'

She reached out a hand and rested it on his shoulder. 'I can only speak for myself here, but I could never hate you.'

He fell silent, his eyes cast downwards.

'Well,' he said at length, 'goodnight.'

'Goodnight.'

He closed the door and Prudence trudged up the stairs to her room. Sooty was a black smudge against her bed covers, and the message light on her answering machine blinked in the dark. Somebody must have called while they were out at the Confessional. She collapsed on the bed with her arm around the cat and hit the play button.

To her surprise, it was As. A very, very angry As. In a harsh whisper, he said, 'Listen, you little slut, it's okay for you to ruin your own life but don't ruin mine as well. Stay away from me and from my family. And here's a word of advice that you're probably too stupid to follow—grow up and don't be a vindictive bitch.' The message abruptly cut out and Prudence released a long breath. What was that all about?

'How dare he?' she said, her anger rising. 'How dare he call me a slut?' She snatched up the phone and punched out his home number—learned by heart but never used—then hung up before it connected. It was after two in the morning and she was just as likely to get his wife. She folded Sooty in her lap, smoothing her fur slowly to try to calm herself down.

'Fuck him,' she said, picking up the phone again and hitting redial.

She was almost disappointed when, after eight long rings, As himself answered blearily. 'Hello?'

'What the fuck is your problem?' she said.

'What the fuck is *my* problem?' he responded, as though stunned she could have the gall to ask it. 'You're the one with the fucking problem.' He was talking in a low, harsh voice, clearly trying not to wake his wife.

'The message you left on my machine. How dare you say those things to me with no reason or provocation—'

'No provocation! That's rich. You only wrote a letter to my wife about our affair.'

'You're insane. I wouldn't do that.'

'Mandy produced a letter today, addressed to her, claiming that I was involved with a certain pretty Masters student. Only you would be vain enough to describe yourself as pretty.'

Prudence's blood boiled. 'You prick. I didn't write a fucking letter to Mandy, I'm not stupid. Nor am I vain, vindictive, or a slut for that matter. Other people knew we were shagging. You said yourself that Lucien—'

'Lucien!' The word came out in a gasp of realisation. A guilty silence followed.

'As?'

'I think I owe you an apology,' he said softly.

'Fuck your apology. Fuck you.'

'Prudence, I—'

She slammed the phone down, her heart thumping. Her sense of triumph was tempered with curiosity. Lucien wanted Mandy to know about As's dalliances. The creature had wanted Lucien to rid himself of the others. Emma was already gone, and As, if he wanted to save his marriage, was going to have to give up his Sunday night intrigues.

'Look out, Randolph,' she said under her breath as she stripped and slipped under the covers. The desire to sleep having deserted her completely, she lay gazing up at the ceiling, wondering how Holly was doing and feeling a barbed pain of jealousy in her chest. Her eyes followed the rows and rows of books around the room. She knew more than anybody she had ever met about the supernatural and the occult, so why had the ghost attached itself to Holly and not her? Did even ghosts prefer unassuming blondes? She sighed and turned over. Sooty squeezed out of the way before Prudence rolled on him. It was wrong to get all bitter and twisted about Holly. It wasn't Holly's fault if Justin found her more attractive, if As thought she was smarter, if the Humberstone College ghost chose to come out after all these years for her and nobody else. Prudence had a horrible suspicion it was her own fault that she was seen as loud, weird and forward in contrast.

She sat up and felt on her bedside table for cigarettes. None. Probably better not to smoke in bed anyway. She wished she could stop thinking about Justin. Her attraction to him grew the more he stuck to his original preference for Holly, and had almost tripled when she finally got to the bottom of his deep, dark secret. He had become like some kind of Byronic hero that no woman could ever make happy. That was the kind of challenge she loved to take on. She remembered the feel of his body against hers that Sunday night at the clock tower, the wonderful sensation of his hands on her skin.

'Great. Now I'm getting horny,' she muttered to the dark as she burrowed under the covers once more, determined to sleep.

She had drifted off for perhaps ten minutes when there was a light tap at her bedroom door. She sat up. 'Justin?'

'No, it's Holly.'

'Come in, it's not locked.'

The door swung in and Holly came in and sat on Prudence's bed.

'How did it go?' Prudence asked.

Holly put her head in her hands. 'Get Justin. I need to tell you everything from the beginning.'

The sun was peeking over the horizon when Holly finally finished telling her story. The three of them sat, pale and tired, on Prudence's bed. Christian's story was too fantastic to be believed, but too full of detail to be anything other than true. And if it was true, the three of them had just been handed an enormous responsibility.

'So if Lucien is just repeating Owling's mistake,' Prudence said, 'then all we need to do is tell him how it ended. Tell him that Owling is Archimago and that he's just playing with Lucien because of some vendetta against the Humberstones.'

'What if he won't listen?' Holly asked. 'Then we've let him know that we know what he's doing, and we put ourselves in danger. I don't want to be anywhere near that man. Justin, you have to get out of his house.'

'It would be too obvious if I left now. I'm safe, don't worry. I hardly even see Lucien,' Justin said.

'This isn't just about our own safety, anyway,' Holly said. 'Christian said the Devil told him of a great undoing.'

'Surely that's not possible,' Prudence said warily.

'What if it is? We can't risk it. We have to get the grimoire and destroy it. Without the grimoire, he can't do the summoning.'

'How do we get the grimoire then?' Prudence asked, looking pointedly at Justin.

'I don't know,' he said.

'You're the closest to Lucien. Where do you think it is?'

'Perhaps in his study. In a safe. Or it could be up at the college.' He ran a hand through his hair. 'Hell, he could sleep with it under his pillow for all I know.'

Prudence nodded, thinking. Holly was right, they had to get the grimoire and destroy it. 'How about Emma? Would she know?'

Justin considered. 'Yes, I think she would. But Emma won't talk to me. We don't have the best relationship, you'll recall.'

'She might talk to you. Especially if you . . . hint there might be something in it for her,' Prudence suggested slyly.

'Prudence!' Holly said, shocked. 'Don't even suggest it.'

'He doesn't have to go through with it. All he has to

do is call her and pretend he misses her and then pump her for the information,' Prudence said defensively, cursing herself for making it so easy for Holly to take the moral high ground and come out looking like Justin's champion.

Justin shook his head. 'I'm not you. I'm not a smooth liar.'

'Thanks,' Prudence said irritably.

'I mean, I don't have your ability to get people on side. Especially over the phone. It's so impersonal. Maybe if she was still at home, but—'

'Okay. Go see her then. I'll spot you the bus fare and the money for accommodation. Drop in on her unexpectedly. Be the dutiful nephew who's concerned about her. Take her to dinner, get her drunk, and then make her tell you everything.'

They sat silently for a few moments. Prudence could tell Holly wanted to dismiss the whole idea but had wisely realised it was their best hope.

'I'm not you, Prudence,' Justin said quietly. 'I can't get information out of people.'

'So let a bit of alcohol and a bit of lust and a bit of anger do the job for you. See, I don't think she's off looking after her sister. I think Lucien has consigned her to draughty old Phillip Island to get her out of the way. We know Owling killed his associates, and we know that the demon hinted to Lucien that the others had to go. If Emma wanted the rewards of the grimoire enough to get involved in black magic, then she must be pretty pissed off with Lucien right about now. If you can remind her how angry she is, she'll squeal like a stuck pig, trust me.' Prudence knew that if it were up to her, she could do it. But Justin wasn't a good communicator like her. What he had on his side was the fact that he had been Emma's object of lust for the past six months.

'Can you afford it?' Holly asked Prudence, sounding

wary but already convinced that it was the right solution.

'Are you kidding? It's cheap out there. Besides, Dad sent me an extra couple of grand to get the roof fixed and the patio retiled. I'm flush at the moment.'

'But won't he——?'

'Hey, I'm saving the planet here, aren't I? Let's talk priorities.' She turned to Justin. 'Will you do it?'

He smiled tightly. 'You always get me to do what you want,' he said, subtly resentful.

'You don't have to do anything you don't want to do,' she snapped. 'People can't make you act against your will.'

Holly sat bewildered between them. 'Guys, don't fight about it.'

'I'll go,' Justin said suddenly. 'If it's for the best, then I'll go.'

From the inside of his cab from the bus station, Justin watched the bay, grey and mournful, looking back at him. The driver turned left down a side street and pulled up outside an apartment building hiding behind palm trees.

'This is the one,' the driver said.

'Thanks.' Justin looked up at the front of the building where Emma was staying. It was stucco, painted blue, spread out over a corner block. Finding out where she was had been surprisingly easy. All he had was a phone number and a great reluctance to ask Lucien. But for once luck had been on his side, and Lucien had stopped in the kitchen with a handful of mail to be posted. He had dropped it on the kitchen bench while looking for his car keys, and Justin had memorised the front of a window envelope readdressed to Emma. Prudence booked his bus ticket with her father's renovation money, handed him two hundred bucks emergency money, and, with much coaching on what questions to ask to get the information he needed, had accompanied him to the bus station and wished him luck. It was Wednesday afternoon, and he wasn't feeling lucky.

He paid the driver and got out, hoisting his overnight bag onto his shoulder. Emma was in unit four—that is, if she was home at all. He checked his watch as the car slid back onto the road behind him. Four o'clock. Branches swayed in a late-afternoon breeze. The salty tang of the sea was fresh and cold in his nostrils. He walked up to the front door security intercom and rang unit four.

The silence was long enough to convince him she wasn't there, and he was about to turn and go looking for accommodation when her voice sounded warily over the intercom.

'Yes?'

He took a deep breath. 'Emma. It's Justin.'

'Justin? What are you doing here?' Surprised. Understandably so.

'I . . . I need to see you. Can I come up.'

Her answer was the sound of the security lock buzzing open. He pushed the door ajar and went to the stairs.

His stomach was full of butterflies as he walked up the two flights to her unit. He felt as though life had become unbearably complicated through no fault of his own, but it was somehow up to him to sort it all out. Which, in a way, was the case. For things to return to normal they had to destroy the grimoire, Emma was the key to the grimoire, and Justin was Emma's weakness. He could not let Holly and Prudence down. Not only were they the only friends he had, they were also custodians of his darkest secret. He was bound to them now, whether he liked it or not. For the millionth time he told himself he should have just shut up and never said a word. Probably he should never even have become friends with them in the first place. Life would have remained much simpler.

513

Unit four was on his left. He went to her apartment and knocked once. A second later, Emma opened the door. She stood gazing at him for a few moments, and he could see over her shoulder into a simply but tastefully decorated lounge room, a balcony view over the bay. His eyes met hers.

'Hi,' he said.

'I don't know why you're here.'

'Are you alone?'

'Yes.'

'Can I come in?'

She stood aside and he took two steps into the room and dropped his bag while she closed the door behind him. She turned to face him and he tried to smile. 'I've missed you.'

'Rubbish.'

Stiffly, he took a pace towards her and folded her in his arms. Her shock soon melted and her hands pressed softly into his back. 'Justin?' she said unsurely.

He took a deep breath, banishing the fluttering fear and guilt from his stomach. No matter what Prudence had suggested, he did not intend to lead Emma on and desert her this time. He was through with deserting people. 'I'm here,' he said, kissing the top of her head. 'I'm here, Emma.'

Lucien was just stepping out of a hot shower when somebody knocked at the door. He wondered if Justin had forgotten his key. He hadn't seen his nephew all day and had started to consider whether he should enforce some kind of minimum residence rule with him. He often went off to Prudence's for a night or two, and Lucien had become concerned that Justin might not be around at the time he was most needed. It would be soon, that much was certain. But enforcing such a

514

rule would only arouse suspicion. Best to keep an eye on him from afar as he had been doing, and when the time was right come up with a reason for Justin to be where he needed him.

Wrapping a robe around himself, Lucien went to the door. It wasn't Justin, but Randolph.

'I have to talk to you,' Randolph said, following Lucien to the kitchen.

Lucien made coffee, trying not to meet Randolph's eyes. 'What's the matter?'

Randolph sat heavily at the kitchen bench. 'You're the only person I can talk to. Only you know what happened in Jerusalem.'

Lucien turned to Randolph and handed him a cup of instant coffee. Dark shadows under his eyes made him look haggard. Lucien sat across from him and waited for him to tell.

Randolph ran a hand over his beard. 'Nightmares, Lucien. For the last week I've been plagued by the most hideous nightmares. I'm afraid to sleep. As soon as I drop off they start.'

Lucien nodded sympathetically. 'What are the nightmares about?'

'Lily Kirkwood. It's driving me mad.'

'You have nothing to fear from Lily Kirkwood. She is dead.'

'She's dead in my dreams as well, Lucien. Covered in blood and stab wounds, skin grey and eyes rolled back. I dream that I'm back in her house, looking in the cupboard for the grimoire, and when I turn around she's there staring at me. I try to get away from her, but she grabs me with hands like iron vices. She strips me and smears blood all over me and . . . and goes down on me. But her mouth is like a metal trap and I feel her sucking blood out of me. It starts running over her chin and—Christ, Lucien. It's so horrible.' He leaned forward and put his head between his hands. Weariness and emotional exhaustion had him close to tears. Lucien did not touch him or offer any words of comfort.

'But it's not just what happens in the dream,' Randolph continued. 'There's a feeling that goes with it. Like something black and wicked is inside my head, scratching over my thoughts and polluting them all. I wake with such a sense of desolation and hopelessness that it overwhelms me, but I can't even take comfort in sleep.' He shook his head and looked up at Lucien. 'What am I going to do?' he said, his voice breaking and his jaw clenched to keep back tears.

'Why do you think you're having the nightmares?' Lucien asked.

'I don't know.'

'Guilt? Fear? We're getting close to the end of our venture now.'

'Don't try to psychoanalyse me, Lucien.'

'But are you guilty about Lily Kirkwood? Afraid of her?'

'No, of course not.'

'Not guilty?'

Randolph averted his eyes. After a short silence he said, 'Yes, sometimes.'

'Are you afraid?'

'I don't know. I feel fear, but I don't know what I'm afraid of. I'm not thinking straight and the pressure on me is unbearable. I feel I'm going mad.'

'I'm sure you're not going mad.'

'What am I going to do?'

Lucien took his empty coffee cup to the sink and rinsed it without looking at Randolph. 'We could take a break from the grimoire.'

'What? When we're so close?'

'Aswell's out for the time being, Emma's with her sister. Perhaps we could take a break for a month or so until everybody is back on deck. Maybe the strain is making you have bad dreams, causing the depression.'

The silence behind him unnerved him. He was almost afraid to turn around and see Randolph's face.

'Lucien, I don't believe I'm hearing this.'

Lucien turned slowly. Randolph's strange, albinolike eyes were narrow, his mouth set in a grim line.

'It makes perfect sense to me.'

'That would be so convenient for you, wouldn't it? If I just stepped out of the way. Hell, you probably orchestrated Laurence's latest problem yourself. What about Emma? Did you send her away under some pretence?'

'I don't know what you're talking about.'

'Yes, you do. You will not get rid of me, Lucien. A few bad dreams are not going to discourage me from pursuing this. Emma, Laurence, even Jane—they were unsure that any of this would work, but I know it will, Lucien. I have killed for the privilege of keeping my own mortality forever at bay. I am with you until the bitter end.' He paused a moment then added in an acid tone, 'Cousin.'

'Randolph, you've misunderstood me. I only want what's best for you. I can't do anything without the rest of you. I'm merely suggesting a brief sabbatical, a month or two at most. Then we'll resume again, do things properly.'

Randolph stood. He was far shorter than Lucien, but his lack of stature didn't stop him from leaning close to Lucien's face with a threatening leer. 'Forget I came here. Forget the nightmares. I can deal with them. I am part of this project and I will stay that way. Don't dare even to imagine the final summoning without me. I don't care about Emma, I don't even care about Laurence. But I've killed for this. You'd do well to remember that.'

He turned and stalked out of the kitchen.

'Randolph,' Lucien called after him, 'you've let your emotions get the better of your good sense. Of course I want you there.'

'Good. I'll see you on Sunday night then.'

The front door slammed behind Randolph. Lucien's anger welled up inside him and he slammed his fist into the kitchen bench. The pain brought him back to his senses. No use getting angry. He had to act, he had to solve the problem.

He strode purposefully upstairs to get the key to his study, then let himself in and went to the safe. His hands were shaking too much at first to dial the combination accurately. He took deep breaths and tried again. Randolph was determined to stick around, and that wasn't good. And was that a threat he had expressed? Did he really think he could do the summoning without Lucien?

It didn't matter. He wouldn't be there. Lucien was clear on that point. He reached into the safe and pulled out a piece of white cloth. He laid it on his desk and with his long fingers unfolded it. Inside was the doll of Randolph that Lily Kirkwood had made. He unpicked the stitching in the side of its head with the sharp point of a pair of scissors, and folded back the face to dig inside the stuffing. His fingers caught the tiny leg of a fly.

'You didn't do me a lot of good,' he said to the fly as he dropped its black corpse in the rubbish bin. He felt around in his drawer for the needle and thread he had already used once on the doll and sewed up the side of the head. He had no choice but to employ a more ruthless solution.

He pulled a stone from the pot of a fake plant on his desk and ran his fingertips over it. Sharp edges, quite heavy. It should do the trick. Violently, he stabbed the pointed scissors into the doll's stomach, opening it up. He dropped the stone in, then went to work with his needle and thread again. Leaving the doll on his desk, he went to the bottom of a cupboard and pulled out a desk tray full of odds and ends for magical practice. Salt, incense, bottled water, a candle. Muttering simple incantations to himself, he began to perform the working that would get Randolph out of his way permanently.

Protected from a cold sea breeze and the restless beating of the waves by a closed glass balcony door and a roaring fire, Justin lay next to Emma, cosy in the firelight. She curled around him and he tried not to be too stiff and unresponsive. She was endlessly soft and warm, but even in the dark he couldn't pretend that she wasn't his aunt. The carton of a wood-fired pizza they'd had delivered and two empty bottles of white wine—of which Justin had only had one glass—were spread about the room among their clothes. Justin looked at his jeans, dropped carelessly on the floor, the legs as flat and empty as he now felt. Emma cooed softly and drunkenly into his ear.

'Thanks for everything.'

'You're welcome.'

'The wine, the food, the . . . other.' She laughed lightly.

'You're welcome.' He realised he should say something more. 'It was my pleasure.'

Her hand idly stroked the inside of his thigh. 'I hope it was.'

She was drunk, happy, full and sexually satisfied. There would be no better time to start asking questions.

'Emma, you're not up here visiting your sister, are you?'

She shook her head and her hair tickled his shoulder. 'No, I'm not. My sister lives in Scotland.'

'Then why are you here?'

She giggled. 'Because of you, actually.'

'Me?'

'Yes. I'm so glad you came, because now Lucien's charges of adultery are founded. I may as well have the fun if I'm going to be punished for it.'

'I don't follow.'

'Lucien's father—your grandfather—Magnus was a nasty little prick of a man who got me to sign a kind of pre-nuptial agreement. Lucien has kicked me out because he thinks I broke one of Magnus's holy tenets. They're a mean-spirited lot, the Humberstones. You're wise not to take their name.'

'I'm sorry.'

'Don't be sorry. It will never hold up in court. I'm going to sue him for everything.' She shifted beside him, her round shoulder pressing into his armpit. 'Lucien's a strange character, Justin. I think you should move out.'

'I can't.'

'Of course you can. You're Graham's son. You have a trust fund coming to you on your thirtieth birthday.' She giggled again. 'You didn't know that, did you?'

Justin shook his head. 'No, I didn't. But I don't care about the money.'

'Care about it, Justin. Lucien will find a way to get hold of it otherwise.'

Silence followed, the waves kept crashing to shore below the apartment. At length Justin said, 'Emma, you mentioned once that Lucien was working on a book.'

'Did I?' she said disingenuously. 'I don't know why I would have said that.'

Treading carefully now. 'I know something about it.'

'You do?'

'Lucien has dropped a few hints.'

'I suppose he wants you in the group now that I'm gone. Jane too. He got rid of her some time ago.'

Jane was part of it too? Justin told himself he had to become a better judge of character. 'I think that's what he wants,' Justin lied, 'but of course I'm not supposed to mention it to anybody. Especially not you.'

She wriggled closer and draped a leg over his hips. 'I won't tell. I'm kind to those who are kind to me. And you've been most kind this evening.'

'It wasn't kindness,' he said, hoping it didn't sound forced. She kissed him, tasting of alcohol and garlic.

'Where does he keep the book?'

'Hasn't he shown it to you yet?'

'No. I'm curious, that's all.'

'In his safe, behind a painting in his study. With my diamonds, which I suppose I'll never see again. Don't worry, you'll see it if he gets you along to one of the meetings. Has he proposed that yet?'

'Um . . . yes.'

She propped herself up on one elbow. 'Look, if you want my advice, don't get involved with it, Justin. It's a load of rubbish, it really is. Eternal life—you don't have to be a quantum physicist to figure out that it's never going to happen. The whole business is consuming Lucien, and he's heading for a big fall. It was fine when it was just magic and ritual and . . . you know, the drama of it. But then Lucien got tired of robes and consecrations. He has this innate psychic sympathy with spirits, which allowed him to get around a lot of the fun stuff. I stayed with him because I'm his wife, the others I don't know about. Perhaps Randolph still believes in it all, but not me. Lucien's not stable. Stay away from him.'

'Maybe I will,' Justin said, musing on what to ask next. The safe in the study. But how to get into the study, let alone the safe. If he started asking questions, Emma was going to get suspicious, but did that even matter?

'You know, Justin,' she said slyly, 'you could get my diamonds for me.'

'Your diamonds?'

'Yes, they're in the safe. Lucien would never even

know they were gone, especially if you left the box in there.'

Relief swept over him. 'Oh, of course. Of course I'll get your diamonds.'

'He keeps the key to the study in his bedside table, top drawer. The safe combination is 34–28–36, left four, right three, left two and back to zero. They used to be my measurements. A long time ago.'

At first he didn't know what she was talking about, but then it dawned on him. 'Oh, in inches.'

'Yes.' She took his hand and ran it over a full, heavy breast. 'Am I revolting to you, Justin? Am I too fat?'

'No. Of course not.'

'I suppose Prudence is slim and firm still.'

'You feel wonderful,' he said. It wasn't a lie. Although she looked lumpy and stretched out of shape in the light, her body was all curves and soft spaces in the dark. And the last thing he wanted to think about now was his ill-considered fling with Prudence. He turned to face Emma and touched her cheek. 'You're irresistible. Why else would I be here?' He thought it wise to play to her vanity.

'You're pretty irresistible yourself,' she said. 'When is your bus home?'

'Tomorrow at midday.'

'We'll plan what to do about the diamonds tomorrow, then. Don't worry, technically they are mine. And if anything comes of it, I'll take the blame. You won't get into any trouble over it.'

'I'm not worried.'

'Tomorrow,' she said, pressing her lips against his throat, her hand moving up his inner thigh. He felt a reluctant stirring in his groin. 'We'll think about all that tomorrow.'

'Sure. Tomorrow.'

CHAPTER THIRTY-FIVE

rudence was expecting Justin's knock at the door. He had already called from the bus station with two simple words: 'Mission accomplished.' She threw open the door and dragged him in by his wrist. 'I want to know everything,' she said.

'Where's Holly?' Justin asked as they went to the lounge room to sit down. He took off his overcoat and folded it over the arm of a chair.

'She's up at the college. She didn't want to take any more time off.' Holly's retreat to the college was more about getting refuge from her, Prudence realised. If there was somebody in the house, she couldn't help herself. She loved to chat.

'The grimoire is kept in the safe in Lucien's study. I have the combination here.' He felt in the front pocket of his jeans and pulled out a folded piece of paper.

'You didn't have any problems getting it out of her?'

'None at all. She has jewels in the safe that she wants me to take and courier down to her.'

Prudence clapped her hands with glee. 'Ha! That's perfect.'

He took a weary breath. His hair was messy and he had dark shadows under his eyes. 'Only problem is the key to the study is in Lucien's bedroom. He locks his bedroom when he goes out. You know how paranoid he is.'

'Well, now we know the reason.'

'Right. Anyway, I figured if we wait until Monday—it's the first Monday in August so he'll definitely go up to the college—I can sneak into his bedroom while he's in the shower and get the key. Then when he's gone, I'll go get the grimoire.'

'I want to be there.'

'You don't have to be there.'

'What, and miss out on all the fun?'

'This isn't fun. It could be dangerous.'

Prudence shrugged. 'Okay, then what do we do with the grimoire?'

'I don't know. I don't even know how soon Lucien will notice it's missing. It could be straightaway, it could be the following Sunday.'

'You'd better come stay with me after we've taken it. If Lucien suspects you, you won't be safe there.'

He shook his head. 'If I move out, Lucien will suspect me. He's just got rid of three other members of his magic circle, I'm sure he'll suspect them first. By the time he's worked out that it was us—*if* he works out that it was us—the book will be destroyed. We'll worry about the rest later. I've just discovered from Emma that I have an advantage over Lucien.'

'Really? What's that?'

'I have a trust fund from my father. It's mine when I turn thirty, but Lucien's been using it for investments. He'll have to liquidate them within two years.'

'A trust fund? But that's so cool. You can just collect it and go. Any idea how much it's worth?'

Justin shook his head. 'I didn't ask, but I presume it's

considerable. Emma says it's always pissed Lucien off because so many of his property investments are dependent on it.'

'Well, make sure you get it out of him.'

'I don't care about money, Prudence.'

'You're strange.' She stood and stretched her arms above her head, yawning. 'Want coffee?'

'Yes, please.'

She went to the kitchen and made a plunger of coffee. Everything seemed to be working out fine and she could hardly wait to see the grimoire. She had a feeling it would be the most thrilling moment of her life. The coffee smelled wonderful as she poured it into two cups. Justin waited for her in the lounge room. She was overexcited and had so many other questions that she wanted to ask him, especially about how things had gone with Emma.

'So,' she asked, handing a coffee cup to him and sitting down across from him, 'how's Emma?'

'All right,' he said guardedly. 'Same as always.'

'Did you . . . you know, did she help out easily enough or did you have to persuade her with your more subtle charms?' She knew it was a forward question, but she also knew that it was fairly normal for her. The last thing she expected was for Justin to get angry.

'Must you know everything?' he said sharply, putting his coffee cup down.

'Hey, sorry. I was just asking.'

'You're always asking. Will you be happy when you know everything about me?'

'Justin, don't get angry. Please.'

'Yes, I fucked her. Happy now? Is that what you wanted to know? Or do you want more details? Would that make your life better? I've already laid everything bare to you, body and soul. Where does your curiosity end?'

'Stop making it sound like I force you to do these things,' she snapped. 'You still have your free will. Perhaps you could try exercising it from time to time.'

'Don't pretend to be innocent. You're the queen of manipulation and you know it. All I know is that in the last fortnight I've had sex with two women I didn't want to have sex with, and none of it would have happened if I'd never met you.'

Prudence was speechless with anger. 'You make me sound like a rapist,' she breathed at last.

'You are. You rape people's minds.'

Hot tears filled her eyes. 'You're such a hypocrite. If you didn't want to fuck me, you should have told me at the time. You shouldn't have got a hard-on, and you definitely shouldn't have come. But you did all those things, and I suspect it was the same with Emma.'

Justin opened his mouth as if to say something, then clamped it shut again. 'This is fucked,' he muttered. 'Sex is fucked. It is the most fucked-up part of life.'

'I'll drink to that,' she said, palming the tears out of her eyes and trying to calm down.

'You'd drink to anything.'

'I'm not your mother.'

That shut him up.

'I'm sorry, Justin,' she said. 'I don't want to fight with you. I thought we were friends.'

He shook his head sadly. 'I'm sorry too.'

'I care about you so much. More than I should, if you know what I mean.'

He wouldn't meet her eyes. 'Then I'm sorry about that as well.'

'But I can put my feelings aside,' she said, not liking the pleading tone she had accidentally slipped into. 'I mean, I know you like Holly. I can help you guys get together. It would make me happy to see you with her.'

Actually, it would make her painfully jealous. She didn't

know why she'd said it, unless it was a way to get Justin to like her again.

To her surprise, he laughed bitterly. 'That's not going to happen.'

'Why not?'

'Because she deserves better.'

She wanted to scream. *Holly deserves better and I don't?* Holly wasn't a fucking angel. Prudence was getting pretty tired of being told she was. 'Better than what?' she said, fighting back jealous tears.

'Better than me. She doesn't know what I've been up to and she won't know, because you won't tell her, right?'

'Of course I won't. I can be the receptacle of all your dirty secrets, and Holly can go on being some kind of pure, unsullied male fantasy for you.' She sniffled loudly. 'I'm such a dumping ground, I'm such a dirty slut.'

'Prudence, don't say that.'

'You think it. As thought it. Probably every guy I've ever been with has thought it because not one of them has stayed with me.'

They sat looking at each other for a few moments, wavering between anger and tears. Prudence sensed that Justin was about to move towards her and hold her when the front door slammed and Holly called out.

'We're in here,' Prudence called. She and Justin exchanged another glance as Holly appeared in the doorway.

'Justin, you're back. How did it go?'

'Everything went fine,' he said lightly. 'We're going to get the grimoire on Monday.'

Holly sat down with them wearily. 'Problems at the college,' she said quietly.

'What's the matter?' Prudence asked.

'Christian. Now he's really behaving like a ghost. Whenever I go into our room, books start flying off desks and drawers open and close by themselves. It's frightening.'

'You shouldn't be frightened of him,' Prudence said. 'You know him. He won't hurt you.'

Holly shook her head. 'I don't know that. He's angry. It . . . causes me so much pain.'

The three of them sat in silence, each nursing some pain of their own.

'I just want this to be over,' Justin said, pressing a weary hand to his forehead.

'One way or another, it will all be over soon,' Prudence said softly. 'Then we can get back to normal.' She smiled tightly. 'Hopefully.'

When Justin woke on Monday morning, rain was clattering on the eaves and the sky was the heavy colour of slate on the other side of his window. His first concern was that Lucien wouldn't go up to the college today if the weather was too bad. The thought actually made him relieved, although he knew it meant they would have to get the grimoire at some other time. But the pressure was just too much for him at the moment, and he wanted to run away from it all. Away from Holly and Prudence and the college, and disappear into anonymity. The only thing stopping him was the certain knowledge that things would be very bad for the people he left behind. And if Holly's ghost was right about the consequences of Lucien's plans, things were going to be bad for everybody. The whole thing seemed too incredible to be true. He shook his head and tried not to think about it. The responsibility was too great for his shoulders.

He pulled on jeans and a shirt and went to the kitchen. Surprisingly, Lucien was up making coffee, wrapped in his robe. Justin checked the clock on the microwave. Eight-thirty. He had overslept because it was so dark and rainy outside. He had intended to be up well before his uncle so he could listen for the hum of the hot water pipes when he got into the shower. All was undone.

'Good morning, Justin,' Lucien said, sitting down with his coffee. 'I'm glad I've caught you. I need to have a word with you.'

Surely if he had showered he would have dressed in his suit for the office. 'What's up?' he asked.

'You've been spending a lot of time out of the house. With Prudence, I presume?'

Justin nodded. 'Yes.'

'You remember our deal? You must stay here.'

'It's only been a few nights.'

Lucien pushed his lips together, thinking. 'All right then, if you are going to be out, you need to tell me in advance or leave a note for me. I like to know where you are.'

'If I'm not here, I'm either at the college or at Prudence's.'

'What about Holly's place?'

'Yeah, sometimes at Holly's place.' He didn't want to let Lucien know that Holly was staying with Prudence. It was better his uncle didn't realise how much depended on Prudence being allowed to finish her course.

'So you will let me know where you are going?'

'Sure. Today I'm going to Prudence's. I might not be back till tomorrow.' Why did Lucien need to know where he was? Was it some way of protecting the money he held in trust for him?

'Good.' Lucien drained the last of his cup and put it on the sink. 'I'm going to take a shower and then I'll be at the college all day.'

'Whatever.' Justin stayed where he was until he heard Lucien's footsteps disappear up the stairs. Then, quietly and carefully, he followed him.

Justin paused in the hallway two doors down from Lucien's bedroom. He heard nothing for a few moments, then the sound of the hot water pipes coming to life and the shower running. He crept cautiously along to Lucien's bedroom and peered in the half-open doorway. The door to the en suite was closed. Taking a deep breath, he tiptoed into the room and went to the bedside table. In the top drawer he found the key, slipped it into his pocket and tiptoed out.

It was only when he reached the bottom of the stairs that he realised something. At some stage he would have to put the key back, but Lucien would go out in half an hour or so and lock his bedroom door. The key felt suddenly heavy and cold in his pocket. He wavered at the bottom of the stairs, paralysed with indecision.

With purpose he took a step to his right and headed for Lucien's study. He carefully unlocked the door. The handle turned. He left it closed and headed back up the stairs to Lucien's bedroom. At worst, Lucien might go to his study before leaving for the college and think that he had left it unlocked himself.

As Justin was halfway across Lucien's bedroom for the second time, he heard the taps turn and the shower go off. His heart leapt into his throat. He replaced the key with shaking hands and raced back out of the room, nearly tripping on a rug by the dresser. He heard the door to the en suite slide open just as his foot hit the top stair, and he raced downstairs and hid in his room.

Ten minutes later Lucien left without a goodbye. Justin breathed a short sigh of relief. The first stage was over, and Prudence and Holly would be with him for the rest of this ordeal. He went to the phone and dialled Prudence's number.

Despite the fact that they had been huddled together under an umbrella, Holly and Prudence were soaked by the time they arrived. The wind was strong and had blown their umbrella inside out twice, driving the rain into their clothes.

'Come in and get warm,' Justin said, showing them through to the lounge. 'I'll put the heater on.'

Prudence and Holly removed their shoes and overcoats in the hall before following Justin inside. He turned on the radiator.

'Do you need a towel?' he asked.

'I'll be fine,' Prudence said, pushing damp purple strands from her shoulders.

'Once I warm up I'll be okay,' Holly said.

'You'd better dry off before we go into Lucien's study,' Justin said. 'We don't want to leave any incriminating puddles.'

'Incriminating puddles? What about when I pee myself when I finally see this grimoire?' Prudence said with a laugh. She seemed to have recovered from the fight they'd had the previous week. Justin still cringed inwardly when he thought about some of the things he had said to her. They had all seemed justified at the time, but now he sorely regretted losing his temper. For the first time in his life he had met people who accepted him unconditionally. It had only served to highlight his failure to display the same quality.

'We'd better not leave it too late. How long does he usually stay at the college when he goes up?' Holly asked.

'Usually all day. But we shouldn't count on it. We should be cautious,' Justin said.

'I'll wait here. I'm wetter than Prudence—she's an umbrella hog.'

'Oink oink. Come on, Justin. Have you got the combination for the safe?'

He tapped his forehead. 'It's up here.'

She stood and with a cold, damp hand pulled him to his feet. 'Come on. I'm dying.'

Opening the study door and standing this side of the threshold looking in, Justin suddenly got cold feet.

'I don't know, Prudence. This seems like such a violation.'

'Justin, you've heard what he's up to. You know what he plans.'

'But how does it affect us? Maybe we should just leave him to make his own mistakes.'

'You don't care if he dies?'

Justin shrugged. 'Not really.'

'What if you're not safe?'

'He does whatever he does up at the college.'

'What if Christian was right and Satan plans some "great undoing" if Lucien goes ahead?'

'It seems impossible.'

'Hey, pretty much everything I've seen or heard in the last three weeks seems impossible. Do you want to risk it?'

Justin felt a sick fear blossoming in his stomach. 'It's all so hard,' he said in a quiet voice. 'I want to run away.'

'You're not running away from this one,' Prudence said. She nodded through to Lucien's study. 'After you.'

They crossed the threshold.

'Have you ever opened a safe before?' Prudence asked as they started checking under pictures for the face of the safe.

'Yes. I worked at a newsagent for a while when I was at uni. I had to lock everything up at the end of the day.'

'Bingo.' She removed a painting to reveal the safe. 'Come on, then, see what you can do.'

Justin paused in front of it.

'Don't think about it,' Prudence said, 'just do it.'

'You sound like a sports shoe ad,' he said, reaching for the dial. He scrambled it first, then four times to the left landing on 34, right three times to 28, left twice to 36—he was up to Emma's hips now. He knew from his own experience that she didn't measure thirty-six inches around there any more. Back to zero, and he heard the lock drop into place. 'Okay,' he said, just because he felt he should say something.

'Open it, open it,' Prudence urged.

He turned to look at her. 'How can you even bear to be near me after how horrible I was to you the other day?'

She was taken aback. 'This is an odd time to bring that up.'

'Well?'

'Justin, get over it. We're friends. We can withstand a few disagreements. Open the safe.'

He pulled the handle and opened the safe door. The grimoire was leaned up against the left side, attached with a large rubber band to a folder of notes. Justin removed them both and handed them to Prudence. Lucien had bound the grimoire in a black leather folder. It was neat but looked as though he had done it himself. Justin supposed it was impossible to send that kind of document to a book binder. He pushed aside a couple of other unidentified objects to find the black velvet box Emma had told him her diamonds were in. He slid the box out carefully, removed a diamond necklace and earrings, snapped the empty box shut and replaced it.

'What else is in there?' Prudence said, peering over his shoulder.

He slammed the safe door. 'Don't know, don't care. Let's get out of here.'

Justin didn't feel safe until they were back at Prudence's house, door locked securely behind them, curtains drawn and radiator on. The grimoire and the notes were spread out on Prudence's bed and Prudence pored over them enthusiastically.

'Look at this!' she squealed time and again as she found something else wildly interesting or exciting.

'I thought we were supposed to be destroying it,' Justin said nervously as Holly paced the room.

'Soon enough. I just have to have a good look. All this last section is automatic writing, almost completely encrypted. Lucien must have the patience of Sisyphus to have figured all this out.'

'I don't know if Sisyphus was patient, I think he was just unlucky,' Holly remarked.

'Whatever.' Prudence flicked through some pages of Lucien's notes, comparing them with the original entries. 'Here, listen to this. "It wants a body, a boy with no folk or family. It wants an orphan boy. It wants this Christian body." Sounds like he was planning some kind of Satanic sacrifice.'

Holly hurried over. 'This Christian body? That's got to mean Christian. The spirit Owling used was allowed to possess Christian at every ritual.'

'Well, it certainly looks like Owling loved him for more than his beauty. Listen. "Without the boy, without the body there is nothing for the magus. Dress him well and let him be beautiful. It shall have its orphan boy."'

'I have to take this to the college,' Holly said, suddenly desperate. 'I have to show this to Christian. I must make him believe me about Peter. Make him forgive me.'

Prudence touched Holly's shoulder. 'Holly, what does it matter? He's been dead over a hundred years anyway. Perhaps you should just let him go.'

Holly flinched away. 'I can't, Prudence.'

'This is all too much,' Justin said. 'You'd have to be crazy to go up to the college with the grimoire while Lucien's there.'

'Then I'll go tonight. Late, when there's certain to be nobody there.' Her stubbornness surprised and pained him.

'It's not wise,' Prudence said gently.

'I don't care about being wise. Don't you see it's my only chance?'

534

Justin and Prudence exchanged a glance. 'We have to destroy this as soon as possible,' Justin said.

'We can destroy it tomorrow. Or late tonight when I get back. I won't take no for an answer.'

Reluctantly, knowing it was foolish, Justin agreed. 'Just be really careful,' he said.

'In the meantime,' Prudence said, 'everybody try to act as though everything is totally normal.'

'But everything is the furthest from normal it's ever been,' Justin moaned.

'Just try. We've got a lot riding on it.'

Freezing at three a.m., Holly let herself into the college, the grimoire wrapped in a plastic bag and shoved into Justin's backpack for good measure. The rain had eased, but damp showers still shook themselves out of trees on stiff breezes. Holly gladly shut it all out and headed for her office.

She paused before opening the door. If the previous day was anything to go by, Christian would be with her within a minute. But not to offer loving caresses or tell sad stories. Instead there would be more havoc—items being flung and windows being rattled, a strange, oppressive heat around her ears, the hairs on the back of her neck rising from some undefinable chill.

Fumbling with her keys, she unlocked the door and pushed it open, stopping to peer into the darkness.

'Christian?' she said warily as she closed the door behind her and waited for her eyes to adjust to the dark. She didn't want to turn the light on in case somebody was nearby outside. She had a very real sense of how dangerous it was to have the grimoire in her possession. A few moments of silence followed, and she went to Prudence's desk and cautiously lit one candle. The office furniture glowed dimly, casting shadows

535

against the wall. Candlelight made just about anything seem creepy.

'Christian, I want to talk. I have something to show you, something that bears out the claims I have made against Peter. Please come and talk to me—calmly, reasonably.'

An enraged cry came from somewhere behind her, and the chair behind Prudence's desk rolled suddenly and violently towards her, knocking her knees and sending her staggering. She put a hand out on Justin's desk to steady herself.

'The grimoire, Christian,' she said bravely into the dark, though her heart was pounding and a chill had begun to creep up her spine. 'I have it here. You have to look at parts of it.'

'It's here?' His voice came from everywhere at once and left a strange, hot impression on her inner ear.

She dropped the backpack on Justin's desk and pulled out the grimoire and Lucien's notes. Warily, she pressed the grimoire against her body and with her free hand flicked through Lucien's translations. 'Here. Let me read to you. "It wants an orphan boy. It wants this Christian body." And again, "Without the boy, without the body there is nothing for the magus. Dress him well and let him be beautiful. It shall have its orphan boy." And further on, "The requirement must be met. It shall have the boy, the Christian boy."'

'That is not the grimoire.'

'These are Lucien Humberstone's translations of the grimoire. It's all encrypted.'

'He's a Humberstone—he's a liar. He's trying to malign Peter.'

'He's a Humberstone, and that's why Peter is trying to send him to his death. And the rest of us. But listen. I have more.' She put the notes aside and cautiously opened the grimoire. 'In this part, not encrypted—"Pay with this

536

body this Christian body this orphan boy," and underneath it, in Peter's handwriting, "I will." What do you make of that?'

'You're mistaken.'

'Christian—'

Suddenly the grimoire flew out of her hands and landed on the floor, spine open and face down. 'No!' she called.

'It must be destroyed.'

She bent to gather the pages. Some had come loose from their binding. One quarter had fallen out all together. 'We're going to destroy it,' she said, collecting the pages, recoiling at the way the ageing paper felt under her fingertips. Her love of old books had been almost extinguished through contact with the grimoire. She stood up again, the book pressed close to her chest. 'I just wanted you to know that Peter intended for you to die that night.'

'One does not die when one is possessed.'

'You might as well have been dead. Peter intended for Aathahorus to have your body permanently. The spark that was you would have perished eventually, crushed by his will.'

'It isn't true.' Another hot gust passed her ears, causing them to ache. Pens and pencils flew off Prudence's desk. Books danced and popped out of shelves.

'You're impossible!' Holly cried. 'I love you and I only want what's best for you.'

'As did Peter.'

'You're lying to yourself. You know that I'm right, Christian,' she said, frustrated beyond all reason.

'It's all I have.'

'What is all you have?'

'The memory of love.'

Holly bit back tears. 'You have my love,' she said softly.

'I do not want it.' A rush of icy air blasted up between

her body and the grimoire, nearly tugging it out of her hands.

'No,' she said, pulling it back against her. 'Won't you listen to reason?'

'I won't listen to lies. Take me to Peter.'

'I only want to help you.'

'Then take me to Peter!' he screamed.

The room was alive around her. She stuffed the grimoire and Lucien's notes back into the backpack and quickly unlocked the door. 'I tried, Christian,' she said with a trembling voice, 'but this is goodbye.'

'Don't dare to leave. Tell me where he is. Take me to him. Oh, I'm dying.'

'You're already dead,' she said cruelly as she slammed the door behind her, taking refuge in the quiet hallway. She listened at the door for a few moments as the air seemed to calm down behind it. She was taking one step towards the stairs when a great shattering sounded behind her.

She spun around. The frame on a Moore print had splintered, flinging glass for metres around. She caught her breath. Could he follow her beyond the bounds of the office?

'Christian?' she whispered into the dark. But all was silence. She slung the backpack over her shoulder and couldn't get out of the college fast enough.

CHAPTER THIRTY-SIX

··

~

P rudence stumbled into the kitchen at seven while
Holly was making toast and coffee.

'How did it go?' she asked, palming sleep out of her
eyes.

'Not good.'

Prudence noticed Holly had dark rings under her eyes.
'Have you slept at all?'

Holly shook her head. 'No. I just want to destroy the
thing and be done with it.'

'We'll do it tonight, when Justin's here. We've got to
act normal. Can't have all three of us failing to turn up
at the college two days in a row.'

'I guess. It just makes me uncomfortable knowing it's
here.' She nodded towards the kitchen table, where Justin's backpack lay.

'I'll put it upstairs in my room, jam it between some
of my other books. It'll be safe. If Lucien notices Emma's
diamonds are gone too, he's not going to come after us.
He'll suspect her immediately.' Justin had sent Emma's
jewels down to her the previous day by courier, as she
had requested.

'And when he finds out it wasn't her?'

'By then the book will be destroyed. It won't matter.'

'It will matter if Justin's determined to stay there. Surely Lucien will eventually find us out.' She shivered visibly. 'God, what if he sends that demon after us or something?'

'It can't happen, don't worry. He probably can't even call it up without the grimoire.'

'But Justin said Emma told him Lucien has some innate psychic ability. You've even hinted yourself that that's why things have got so out of hand here.'

'Don't stress. It's attached itself to Lucien. Unless it gets an earthly body, we have nothing to fear. And Lucien didn't have a little sorcerer's apprentice like Owling did, so obviously that's not part of the deal this time.'

'Then what does Owling—Archimago—want?'

Prudence shrugged. 'Revenge, maybe? I suppose it's in his best interests to be the one who brings the Prince of Darkness to rule over the earth,' she said, sounding more flippant than she actually felt. Making a joke out of it seemed to keep the screaming heebie-jeebies at bay.

'Maybe we should burn it now?'

Prudence went to the backpack and pulled out the grimoire. She turned over a few pages. She didn't want to destroy the thing at all; it was utterly fascinating and would make a great addition to her library. Only the danger she'd be putting them all in stopped her from begging to keep it. 'Nah. Wait for Justin. It will be symbolic.' She looked up and smiled at Holly. 'Symbolic is important where magic is concerned.'

Holly sighed and threw her half-eaten breakfast away. 'I'm going back to bed. You don't want me at the college, trust me. I cause more damage than a monkey in a china shop.'

'Sure, sure,' Prudence said, waving her away. A couple of hours looking over the grimoire before college was just what she fancied.

Try to act normal.

It was like a mantra in Justin's head as he sat at the library catalogue, waiting for its creaking, fatigued hard drive to respond to his search. Lucien had behaved perfectly as usual during the two minutes Justin had been unfortunate enough to encounter him in the kitchen that morning. Prudence said Holly had got home safely and they were all set to do the deed that night. So far, everything was going okay.

But knowing that did not dispel the awful sense of impending doom. He could not go on living with Lucien. When Lucien found out the grimoire was gone, he was going to go insane, and Justin was terrified of that. But if he left, Prudence and Holly were homeless.

Justin sighed. And if he exercised his only advantage over Lucien and let him keep the trust money, financial security in the future would remain nothing but a fond dream. He kept telling people he didn't care about money, but the more he thought about it, imagined having it, listed the things he could do with it, the less he believed himself.

'Are you okay, Justin?' The thick Scottish accent brought him back to himself.

'Oh hi, Noni. I'm fine. Just lost in thought.'

She pulled up a chair next to him. 'I thought the ghost had possessed you or something,' she said, eyes huge and round.

For a moment he was bewildered, frightened. 'The ghost?'

'Oh, don't concern yourself. Most people think it's nought but my imagination anyway. Only there's a few things broken around the college this morning, and I found eight—*eight*—books jumped off the shelves this morning.'

'You saw them jump off shelves?'

She shook her head. 'No, I saw them on the floor. But

how else would they get there? I wager there's a poltergeist around here. Gives me a chill just thinking about it.'

Holly's ghost. It wasn't going to do the three of them any good to act normal if Christian had suddenly decided to make himself loudly and widely known around the college.

'No such thing as ghosts, Noni,' he said, almost mechanically.

She smiled. 'I don't think you really believe that. You've gone white.'

He turned back to the computer screen. The hard drive had crashed. 'Shit,' he said.

'Looks like the poltergeist is computer literate,' Noni said with a wry smile. 'I'll see if I can reboot the system.'

He watched her go behind her counter then looked up at the clock. A couple more hours and it would all be over.

Or at least the first part would be over. He dreaded what would follow.

'You make a good fire, Prudence,' Holly said, warming her hands by the open grate of the pot-bellied stove.

'Of course I do. I'm a Melbourne girl. And I kind of had this weird fascination with fire as a teenager, but that's a whole other Oprah show,' Prudence said, carefully placing another log in the stove. Holly watched her. The time was drawing closer. The grimoire would be destroyed. And with it her last chance of winning Christian back. Once Lucien had no way of calling Archimago, Christian could not expect to meet with his one-time provider and would probably disappear from her life forever. She wished it didn't hurt so much. She wished she didn't want to convince Prudence to hang on to it for a little longer. Not that she thought her friend would take much convincing—Prudence had spent every moment since she had come home from college engrossed in the pages of the book. She even forgot to have dinner which, for Prudence, was spectacularly out of character.

'Okay, hand me Lucien's notes first,' Prudence said, resting on her haunches and putting a hand out.

Justin did as she asked, cradling the grimoire in his left hand. Holly watched as Prudence fed the pages in one at a time. They curled and blackened and turned to ashes.

'We should have a drink to celebrate or something,' Prudence said as she kept feeding in the pages.

'Maybe after we've done the grimoire too,' Justin suggested.

Prudence burned the last few pages of Lucien's notes and reached for the grimoire. 'God, I hate to do this. This is the most incredible document any of us is ever likely to see.'

'Do it, Prudence,' Holly said. 'Get it over with.'

'Okay, but I can't bear to watch.' With a hand over her eyes she shoved the grimoire into the stove. Justin reached across her and slammed the grate shut.

'I don't suppose your father has anything stronger than wine in that cellar?' he asked as he stood and helped Prudence to her feet.

'There's some cooking sherry in the kitchen. It's nasty, but it will do the trick. Come on, let's go drink to destroying a valuable antique.'

Holly cast one longing glance at the stove and followed them to the kitchen. Prudence poured them each a half-glass of cooking sherry. 'To us,' she said, raising her glass.

'To us,' they chorused, clinking their glasses against hers.

'All in one go, now,' Prudence said. 'Last one to finish is a geek.'

'To the rest of the world, we're all geeks,' Justin remarked dryly, putting his glass to his lips.

Holly downed her drink. Cheap and nasty didn't even begin to describe how it tasted.

'Urgh,' said Prudence.

'My sentiments exactly,' Justin replied.

'Let's call it a character-building experience,' Prudence said, putting her empty glass on the sink. 'Shall we go up to the Confessional tonight?'

'I think I've had more than enough excitement this week,' Justin said, running a hand through his hair. He had seemed tired and distant since his trip to see Emma, and Holly was worried he had sacrificed himself for their cause. She didn't want to seem rude, though, so she didn't ask. In truth she didn't want to know. She still found the idea of an aunt hitting on her nephew kind of revolting. In any case, Holly felt he had certainly cooled off towards her, which was frustrating. Now that Michael was dead and Christian was gone from her life, it might be nice to have a comfortable, sane relationship with a man.

'Do you think it's completely burnt yet?' Holly asked.

Prudence nodded. 'It should be. Go check.'

Holly lined up her empty glass next to Prudence's and went back through to the lounge room. She pulled the handle of the stove and checked inside.

'Oh, God,' she breathed.

'Are Lucien's plans a pile of ashes yet?' Prudence called cheerily.

'You'd better come and look at this,' Holly replied. In a moment Justin and Prudence were standing behind her, peering into the stove.

'I've never seen anything like that,' Justin said at last.

The grimoire was perfectly intact. Lucien's leather cover and binding had disintegrated, but the pages of the grimoire were still whole. Flames licked dispiritedly around it.

'Fuck!' Prudence cried. 'I should have thought of that.'

'How can it not be burning?' Justin asked. The flames were reflected in his glasses, but Holly thought she could see fear in his dark eyes behind them.

'The same way it calls up a fucking demon. Magic.'

'Then we can't destroy it?' Holly asked, frightened and relieved at the same time.

'Oh, I'll find a way. Just give me time to go through some books.' Prudence pushed her hair off her face. 'Will you look at that? I feel like I'm in some bad eighties horror film. We'd better get it out of there.'

With tongs they pulled the book out of the fire and dropped it smouldering on the tiled hearth.

'Let it cool off and then I'll stash it back up in my room.'

Justin groaned. 'What are we going to do now? It's nearly Wednesday. He's bound to notice it missing soon.'

'Hey, it's okay,' Prudence said, grasping his shoulder firmly. 'I'll figure something out. I always do.'

'But how are we supposed to destroy it if it's—?'

'Stop worrying. If we can't destroy it, we can at least put it out of commission permanently. Just give me some time.'

'We don't have time, Prudence,' Holly said, feeling for Justin, who was obviously frightened. 'And don't forget that Justin has to live with Lucien. He's in more danger than either of us.'

Prudence turned to Justin. 'Look, once and for all, get out of that house. Come live with me and Holly.'

Justin shook his head. 'It's not that simple.'

'It's real simple. Pack. Move. Simple.'

'No. If Lucien finds his grimoire missing the same week I move out, that's going to arouse his suspicion. I'd be better off riding out the storm, acting as though everything's normal, as you said. He has no idea that I know what's going on, and he's not about to blab it all to me in a fit of pique. The only way he could possibly be suspicious of me is if he finds out I went to see Emma, and I don't think she's going to tell him. She hates him at the moment.'

Holly sighed. 'I don't like it, Justin.'

'I don't like any of this,' he replied. 'But we're all doing what we have to do.' He turned to Prudence. 'You'd better start your research, Prudence,' he said. 'I want this over and done with as soon as possible.'

A ringing phone woke Lucien at one a.m. At first he felt annoyed. He'd come down with a head cold, and a sore throat and periodic sneezing fits had kept him awake until midnight. As always, the slightest illness reminded him of the frailty of his body, arousing other, deeper fears. It was probably only Emma calling anyway. Then he realised that a ringing phone at one a.m. was the universal signal that something bad had happened, and decided to pick it up.

He sat up and felt on the bedside table for the phone. Just as he was about to pick it up, the ringing stopped. He remained as he was for a few moments, wondering if it would start ringing again, but had decided to go back to sleep when there was a quiet knock at his bedroom door.

'Lucien?' It was Justin. He must have got to the phone first.

'Yes?'

The door opened and Justin stood silhouetted against the hall light. 'Phone call. It's somebody from St Andrew's.'

At first it didn't register. A church?

'The hospital,' Justin continued. 'It's about Randolph.' Lucien couldn't make out his face, so couldn't tell if Justin's quiet tone was reverential sympathy or just his usual deadpan idiocy.

Realisation dawned. 'Oh. Thank you.'

Justin backed out and closed the door, then Lucien snatched up the phone.

'Lucien Humberstone here.'

'Hello, Mr Humberstone. My name is Dr White. I'm from St Andrew's hospital. I was given your name as next of kin to Randolph Humberstone.'

'That's right. What has happened?' Lucien's breath seemed to be stuck in his chest.

'Randolph was admitted earlier this evening with severe abdominal pains. He has some kind of tumorous growth in his lower intestine. We've scheduled him for an emergency operation first thing in the morning, but he has expressed a wish to see you before the operation takes place.'

'Of course. Is it . . . serious?'

There was a cautious silence. Then the doctor said, 'It's hard to tell at this stage. It really depends on whether it's cancerous or not, and how much of the lower intestine is affected. He is certainly in a serious condition at the moment, and in a lot of pain.'

'I'll come down right away.'

'Thank you, Mr Humberstone.'

A frisson of tiny, jagged icicles ran over Lucien. Randolph sick. Maybe even dying. He thought of his declaration to Archimago that he was not a murderer, and the way the demon had leered at him knowingly. *'Oh, really?'* His stomach felt loose, and an icy memory rose in the back of his mind. Panic stopped his throat.

With effort, Lucien collected himself. Randolph would not die. He was in good hands. Lucien only needed him out of the way for a few weeks. This Sunday—alone—he would perform the summoning. The translation had been complete for two weeks. He had only needed to be alone. All the rest he would worry about later—when he was immune to the worst that could happen to him.

Hospital smells repulsed him, even in an expensive private hospital like this where the wards looked like country-club rooms. A nurse showed him through to Randolph's room, hovered around her patient for a few moments, then left the two of them alone.

Lucien approached the bed. Randolph was pale and shivering. His shoulders seemed bony beneath cotton pyjamas.

'Randolph?'

Randolph looked up at him, eyes murderous. 'Did you do this to me?'

'What? How could you suggest—?'

'Did you?'

'No,' Lucien replied resolutely. 'I'm offended by the suggestion.'

'It has worked out very conveniently for you then, hasn't it?'

'Conveniently for me in what way?'

'Now you can go on without me.'

'You'll be fine after the operation. It merely means we'll have a few weeks off. By then Emma will be back and Aswell might have resolved his marital difficulties. We'll go back to normal.' Even imagining that happening filled Lucien with a kind of sick dread.

Randolph spoke through gritted teeth. 'If I recover from this operation, things will be different with the grimoire—' He winced as a pain rocketed through him, and he clutched his stomach and fought for breath.

'Are you all right?' Lucien asked between two violent sneezes.

'Things will be different,' Randolph continued. 'I will have the grimoire with me, I will do the translations and the summoning. I don't trust you, Lucien.'

'Randolph, don't concern yourself over—'

'I killed for it, Lucien. And I would kill again.'

Lucien was about to reply when the nurse came back in and another spasm of pain gripped Randolph. Lucien left without a word, rage boiling in his belly. How dare

Randolph threaten him? He walked slowly down the hospital corridor. The operation would almost certainly be successful, and Lucien had intended to remove the stone from the doll's belly. But did he really want Randolph around, even after it was too late and he had attained his goal?

As he stepped out into the freezing morning, another fit of sneezes gripped him. One, two, three. He paused, handkerchief clutched in his right hand. Three sneezes, make a wish.

I wish that Randolph would die.

Justin spent Wednesday at the college dispiritedly taking notes and waiting for Prudence or Holly to come in. By four o'clock, when neither had turned up, he began to worry and headed for Prudence's house.

'Justin! You're here at last. We were wondering when you'd come by,' Prudence said, ushering him in.

'I was worried. How come neither of you came in today? What happened to acting as though everything is normal?'

'I've been going through my books for a solution to our . . . small dilemma. And Holly raises the dead without trying when she's up there, so we thought it best to stay out of the way.'

Holly was sitting on the floor in front of the fire, gazing at the flames and nursing a cup of hot cocoa. 'Hi,' she said weakly as he came in. She certainly looked like a girl with a broken heart, though it was beyond Justin how she had ever allowed herself to fall in love so impossibly in the first place. However, he was relieved to see both of them alive and well, and he was glad of the company. Rattling around in his uncle's mansion, alone for all intents and purposes, was depressing at times.

'You're just in time,' Prudence said, dropping into an armchair. 'I've got it.'

'Got what?'

'A way to get rid of the grimoire.'

'How?' Justin asked.

'Okay, we're not going to have any luck at all destroying it,' Prudence said. 'It will eventually decay, like any other book, but actually destroying it—burning it, shredding it, whatever—isn't going to work. It's designed to withstand righteous do-gooders like us. The only being that could possibly destroy it is one of its own kind, which is why Satan could run it through with a knife. But I'm not about to call up Satan to get rid of it for us. The other option is to store it in salt. Salt keeps away evil spirits, so it would lose its power to tempt people like Lucien. But just because it doesn't tempt people, doesn't mean it might not be happened upon accidentally.

'However, we can pull it apart—each page will come out because the binding is old and has disintegrated. Holly and I experimented with it this morning. The danger is that there will always be somebody who comes along willing to reassemble it. Look at what Lucien's done with it. So my solution is to make it impossible to find and reassemble. We'll pull it into pieces—as many as possible—and bury them in at least a dozen different locations, in bags full of salt. Bury them really deep. The grimoire will lie forgotten under the earth forever. We'll take parts of it out to old quarries, national parks, forests, the side of the highway—wherever. Just so long as it's scattered over as many remote locations as possible.'

'When and how are we going to do all this?' Justin asked, hopeful but sceptical.

'We'll have to hire a car and do it late at night,' Holly said.

'Tonight?'

'Tomorrow. Holly's the only one of us who can drive, so she's going out to pick up a car tomorrow.'

'It has to be tonight,' Justin said with emphasis. 'I can't

handle the stress of knowing it's still around.'

'Lucien hasn't noticed yet?'

'Not that I'm aware of. Randolph's in hospital. They called last night to tell him. That should distract him for a couple more days. But we have to get rid of it tonight.'

'Randolph in hospital? I'm sure that's no coincidence.' Prudence sighed. 'But there's too much to organise. We'll have to get to the supermarket and buy about thirty packets of salt, pull the grimoire apart, bag it all up, get a spade, work out where we're going ... If we leave it until tomorrow night, we'll know that it's done properly.'

Justin sighed and dropped his head in his hands.

'Tomorrow night's soon enough,' Prudence said dismissively. 'Lucien's busy with Randolph, and he's not going to suspect us anyway.'

Justin turned to Holly with pleading eyes.

'It'll be okay, Justin,' she said.

Damn it. Both of them were reluctant to let the thing go. He was fighting a losing battle.

'It'll give me a chance to look over it some more,' Prudence said, heading towards the kitchen. 'Do you want cocoa?'

'Yes. Thanks.'

'Stay for dinner?'

He looked at Holly, who was gazing once more into the fire. 'Yeah, okay.'

'I wish we hadn't burned Lucien's notes so soon. It would have been good to study them some more,' Prudence said from the kitchen.

Justin shook his head and slumped in his chair. 'I'm going crazy.'

Holly turned to him. 'Don't worry,' she said, touching his shoulder lightly. 'It will be okay.'

He looked at her hand on his shoulder, felt an ache move inside him. The one thing that would bring him relief amongst all this confusion and anxiety was now separated from him by Prudence's and Emma's bodies.

'Yeah, I guess you're right,' he sighed. 'It will all be over soon.'

Prudence outdid herself with dinner that night, whipping up the most glorious lasagne Justin had ever tasted. All three of them went easy on the wine this time, memories of the farce that the last Confessional had descended into persuading them to be cautious. They relocated back to the fireplace and sat by firelight, drinking more hot cocoa with marshmallows.

'God, I'm so full,' Holly groaned, stretching out on her back and placing her hands over her belly. 'That food was amazing. You're so talented.'

'I'll make somebody a good wife one day,' Prudence replied, sneaking a glance at Justin. 'Provided I can induce some guy to stay with me for more than twelve minutes.'

'Don't be silly. You're adorable,' Holly said, rolling over and taking Prudence's hand. 'You'll find somebody amazing. Probably a millionaire painter or a rock star or something.'

'Ah, nobody would take me on,' Prudence replied. 'I'm a handful. You both know that.'

'Someone will rise to the challenge,' Justin said softly.

Prudence met his eyes momentarily then looked away. 'We're all so hopelessly single. Relationships just don't work. Let's keep things the way they are forever. Just the three of us, celibate and sharing each other's secrets. We'll be fat and content and we'll live happily ever after in a cottage that my dad will pay for just to shut me up. What do you think?'

'I don't think you could be celibate,' Holly said playfully.

'Well, I'll have a pretty boy locked in a closet for my pleasure, painted gold and wearing only a loincloth and a wreath of violets.' Prudence set her empty cocoa cup on the ground and plunged her hand into the marshmallow bag. 'White ones are the best, aren't they?'

'I prefer pink,' said Holly.

'White,' said Justin.

'So which one of us do you think will die first?' Prudence asked.

'If we all die of old age—' Holly started.

'Of course we will. Old and toothless and happy.'

'Then I'll die first,' said Justin. 'I'm the oldest.'

'No. Don't say that. That would mean I'd die last. I hate being alone,' Prudence wailed.

'Perhaps a jumbo jet will crash into our cottage and kill us all at the same time,' Holly suggested. 'Let's be optimistic.'

The phone rang and Prudence got up to answer it. Justin stared into the fire as it crackled and popped in the dark. He was warm, his stomach was full, and according to Prudence he was going to die toothless and happy of old age. Not so bad, really.

'Justin?' Prudence stood in the doorway. 'Lucien's on the phone.'

Holly sat up in fright. 'Do you think . . .?' she whispered.

Prudence shook her head and put a finger to her lips. Justin stood, his knees feeling rubbery, and headed for the kitchen where he picked up the phone.

'Hello?'

'Justin, it's Lucien. You were supposed to leave a note if you were going to be out.' His uncle sounded wired, his syllables short and quick.

'Sorry. I came over after college and haven't been home since.'

'You haven't been home all day?'

'Not since eleven or so this morning. Why? Is everything okay? Is Randolph okay?'

'Randolph will be fine,' Lucien replied distractedly. 'Justin, have you seen your aunt recently?'

Justin felt a hot rush under his ribs. 'Emma?'

'Yes, Emma. Has she been here?'

'No. No, I haven't seen her there. I thought she was in—'

'You sure you haven't seen anybody here apart from myself? Not Randolph or . . . or anyone?'

'No, Lucien. But then I haven't been there much the last three days. Are you expecting someone?'

'It doesn't concern you,' Lucien snapped. 'Are you going to be out all night?'

Justin desperately wanted to be out all night. All week, in fact. But tomorrow night he would be out burying the grimoire, and he didn't want to arouse suspicion by being away from home too much. 'No. I'm coming home shortly.'

'Good.' The phone clicked. Justin replaced the receiver and went back to the lounge where Prudence and Holly were waiting for him.

'Well?' Prudence asked.

'He's frantic,' Justin said. 'He knows the grimoire's gone.'

CHAPTER THIRTY-SEVEN

L ucien slammed the phone down and looked around him wildly. The open safe—a gaping hole in the wall—too, too empty. His book, his precious book, gone. His key to eternal life. On the floor beneath it he had flung the Randolph doll and a velvet-covered jewel box. He went to the safe and checked again. Maybe it had just been a trick of his imagination. But no, it was empty.

'Ah, God. Empty. Empty.' He wept openly, pressed his mouth against the cold steel of the safe. 'Where is it? Who has it?'

He took a step back and accidentally stood on the jewel box. He bent to pick it up, gathered the doll as well, and laid them both on his desk. Sitting heavily, he turned the box over and over in his hands. 'Where? Where?' he said, aware at some small remove that he was losing his grip but unable to stop the rising hysteria.

The doll. He had come for the doll. The four points were marked on his desk, ready for his planned working. He had to finish Randolph. He picked up the doll and unwrapped it, saw the gaping wound in its belly. From his pocket he drew a small plastic vial. In it he had saved samples from the last two days' body fluids, mucus from his streaming head cold, a tiny shaving of rotten meat. Anything infectious, dirty, bacterial he could collect. Die, Randolph.

But what if Randolph had the grimoire? What if he had taken it on Monday or Tuesday? Before he fell sick? He put the vial aside and began to toy with the jewel box again, snapping the lid open and closed between two blind thumbs. It slipped from his hands and dropped from the floor, turning upside down and snapping open. He reached down, picked it up.

It, too, was empty.

'Emma,' he breathed. She had come for her jewels—probably Monday when she knew he would be at the college—and decided to work some extra mischief.

God forbid that she had damaged it.

With purpose he flipped the lid off the vial and poured the substance into the doll, wrapped it again securely, muttered his incantations. Back into the safe it went, and with one swift movement Lucien had his car keys out of his pocket and was heading for the garage.

Going after Emma.

'It's me, Prudence.'

Her voice was small at the other end of the phone. 'Justin?'

Justin looked around him at the dark kitchen. 'I'm home safe. He's not even here.'

'Not there?'

He tangled the phone cord around his fingers. 'Car's gone. He's gone. I've checked the whole house. I'm here alone. And quite relieved about it.'

'Lock your bedroom door, just in case.'

'I always do.'

'Okay. Holly will be around to pick you up about midday tomorrow. Please be careful.'

'I will.'

'And after we've buried the damned thing, you can come stay with me.'

'I'll probably stay tomorrow night.'

'No, Justin, permanently.'

'Prudence . . .'

'Your excuses all suck. If this is just because of what happened between us, I—'

He cut her off, spilling the secret before he could stop himself. 'Prudence, the reason I have to stay here with Lucien *is* because of you.'

She was silent a few moments. 'Why because of me?'

'He's going to cancel your enrolment if I move out. He thinks you're my girlfriend, remember?'

'He's blackmailing you?'

'Yes.'

'Fuck him. I don't care if he cancels my fucking enrolment. I'll do something else.'

'Lucien knows your father, doesn't he?'

'So what?'

'He told me your father was going to kick you out if you didn't finish this course.'

She laughed cynically. 'Yeah, that sounds like Dad.'

They were both silent for a few moments. The tap dripped mournfully into the sink.

'How long have you been carrying that burden around with you, Justin?' she asked at last.

'A while.'

'It doesn't matter, you know. I'll be fine. I'll get a job or something. Something will come up.'

'But Holly—'

'She doesn't want to stay here anyway. Let's face it, she's the only one of us who really cares about her dissertation. You and I are just marking time.' She paused a moment and then continued in a soft voice. 'We could run away together.'

'I guess we could.'

'I don't care, Justin. Just leave. Get out. Pack everything, and tomorrow when Holly comes to get you, throw it all in the car and vacate. I'll withdraw Dad's renovation money and we'll disappear for a while.'

It sounded so appealing he almost agreed. 'We'll see,' he said.

'Be brave, but don't be foolish,' she said.

'Goodnight. I'll see you tomorrow.'

'Goodnight, Justin.'

Lucien let himself into the apartment. The beating of the ocean continued dispassionately below. All was dark. Emma must be sleeping.

He waited a few breaths for his eyes to adjust to the dark, then crept into the bedroom. Her body was a hump under the covers. He shuddered and moved closer. She lay on her back, one arm over the covers, the other tucked beneath her. As he kneeled on the bed, her eyelids started to flutter open.

In an instant, he had her pinned beneath him. She cried out in terror.

'Who is it? Who are you?'

'Your husband.'

'Lucien?' she gasped. 'Lucien, let me go. You're hurting me.'

With great force he drew back and hit her across the face. Her head rocked to the side and she grunted in shock.

'Where is it?' he asked.

'Where's what?'

Another whack across the face. Blood began streaming dark from her nostrils and onto the covers.

'I don't know what you mean,' she screamed. 'Please don't hit me again. I don't know what you want.'

He went to take another swipe at her, but paused. What if she was telling the truth? 'The book,' he said.

'The book?' Light dawned in her eyes. 'The grimoire?'

'Yes, it's missing from the safe.'

'Oh, my God.'

'And so are your diamonds.'

'Oh, my—. Oh, the diamonds. I have the diamonds.'

He whacked her again, this time just because he felt like it. 'Then where is the grimoire?'

'It's still in the safe. It was still there when I took the diamonds,' she said, her voice catching on breathless sobs. 'Don't hit me again. I swear I didn't take the grimoire.'

'If you didn't take it, who did?'

'I don't know. Maybe I left the safe open by accident. Maybe a burglar took it.'

'Did you lock it?'

She shook her head. 'I don't remember. I was in a hurry. I just wanted to get my diamonds and get out.'

'You—stupid—fat—bitch!' he yelled, punctuating each word with a slap to the face.

Then he stopped and looked at her closely. 'Are you lying? Is this all a story to make me think you don't have the grimoire?'

'No, Lucien. I don't have it, I swear.'

He thumped her once again, this time in the side of the head. To his shock and irritation, she blacked out with a sick groan.

'Damn,' he said, leaping off the bed and turning a light on. Her blonde hair was spotted with droplets of blood, her face showed the red imprints of his knuckles. He turned her on her front so she wouldn't choke and started pulling the apartment to pieces, determined to find the grimoire.

Prudence was fast asleep when the phone rang. She pushed aside books and knocked over an ashtray to pick it up before the machine got it. It might be Justin.

'Hello?'

A familiar, though not recognisable, female voice. 'Prudence?'

'Yeah, who's this?' She switched on her lamp and looked at the clock. Ten past one.

'It's Emma Humberstone.'

Prudence sat up, rubbing her eyes. 'Emma? What's wrong?'

'Is Justin there?'

'No, he's at his place—your place.'

'I can't ring him there. Lucien might answer.'

'What's wrong?'

'I need to give him a message. It's urgent. Very, very urgent. Can I trust you?'

'Of course.' Prudence's pulse had quickened.

'I think he's taken something from Lucien. Something very, very precious to Lucien. I want to tell him to put it back while he still can. Lucien is . . . Tell him Lucien is not to be messed with on this issue.'

'Okay, okay, I'll tell him.'

'I'm serious,' Emma said, beginning to sob out her words incoherently. 'He's been here, he's . . . he's hit me and my face is swollen like a . . . like a . . .'

'Emma, are you okay? Do you need help?'

'No, no. I'm fine. I'm fine. He's been through the whole place. He's turned it all over. I don't know how long ago he left, but he's an evil man. It's an evil book. Please, please tell Justin to be careful. And tell him I didn't mention to Lucien that he'd been here. Lucien doesn't know but if he finds out . . . Tell Justin to be careful. Tell him to put it back.'

'I will, I will. Emma, you'd better call an ambulance. You sound like you're in shock.'

'He's done bad things. Very, very bad things. He's not above murder, Prudence. He's not above any evil. Tell Justin, tell him.' She broke down into loud sobbing.

'Okay, Emma,' Prudence said in a measured, calming tone. 'I have your message, I realise how important it is—'

'It's very important.'

'Yes, I know. I fully understand, trust me. Now, when I get off the phone, I want you to call an ambulance. How badly has Lucien hurt you?'

'I don't know, I don't know,' she cried. 'My face is all messed up. There's blood.'

'Will you call an ambulance?'

Emma sniffed into the phone. 'Yes. If you promise to tell Justin.'

'I promise. Get yourself seen to, okay?'

'He has the capacity for great evil,' she said. 'They all do. It's in their blood.'

'I understand. Go. Call somebody to come help you.'

The phone was hung up without further warning and Prudence was left holding the buzzing receiver to her ear in the dark. She looked at the clock. In just over ten hours the three of them would be safely together and she could stop worrying. But first she had to call Justin.

A strong wind had whipped up, blowing the rain clouds away. Lucien could see tiny frozen pinpoints of stars between clouds from the window of his office at Humberstone College. He pressed his face against the cool glass and told himself to get a grip.

Emma didn't have the grimoire. He had checked if she was still breathing and left her unconscious on her bed, driven back to Melbourne in a nauseous frenzy of anger and fear, wondering what to do next. What if she had carelessly left the safe open? What if a burglar had taken

561

it, thinking it an antique worth a lot of money? How could he ever find it again? He held in his hand the photocopy of his notes that he kept in his office at the college, but without the book the words had no power. Time was running out—his death drew inexorably closer. He needed a short cut. He needed help from the other side.

He turned his back to the window and surveyed his office. The magic circle was exposed and candles were lit. It wasn't the designated hour, nor did he have the grimoire, but he still had his innate psychic ability and he knew by heart the chant that could pull him into a trance. The danger was in not having others around to pull him out again if he lost his thread. Carefully, he sat at the head of the circle and closed his fist around a burning candle. A splotch of wax dribbled warmly onto his flesh. If worst came to worst and he could not get back, the candle would burn down and the flame would bite his skin, jerking him back to reality. With a deep breath, he began the chant.

Hell was shaded blue this time, a sick grey-blue like bruises on the flesh of babies. Steam rose from the ground as hard, icy raindrops hit the fevered soil.

'Traitor, come!' he called, and his voice sounded like a thin, compressed insect noise in the rain. No response.

'Archimago. Help me, Archimago. I'm ready to deal if you'll just help me.'

Rancid breath behind his left ear. 'Magus, why are you here now?'

Lucien spun round to confront him. 'The grimoire has been stolen.'

'Stolen? Have you been careless with it?'

'No. I don't think so. All I know is that it's gone and I don't know where it is.' He realised he sounded desperate and that he needed to be more guarded about his feelings in front of this creature, but he couldn't help himself. He *was* desperate.

'You want to know where it is?'

'Yes. I'm planning the summoning for this Sunday.'

'Ah, yes. The summoning. I'm looking forward to it so much.'

'Can you help?'

'Yes. I can help. But there will be a price.'

Lucien had known this would happen. 'Anything. I'll do anything within my power.'

'I want my body early. I want my orphan boy. I want to taste and to feel again.'

'You can have it whenever you wish.'

'I want it now. I want you to bring him here now.'

Lucien thought of Justin, probably asleep in his bed. How was he going to manage it? 'I'll think of a way. I'll get him here as soon as I can.'

'Before the sun rises, magus. Agreed?'

'Agreed.'

'Very well. Here is the custodian of the grimoire.' An image materialised beside the demon, a purple-haired girl with a mocking grin.

'Prudence Emerson,' Lucien breathed.

'I sense it amongst her books.'

'I have to—'

'Priorities, magus. I want my body now.'

'Of course, I'll—' A sudden sharp pain to his hand jerked him back to reality. He flung the candle away from him. The temperature had dropped and he found himself once again sitting on the cool floor of his office at the college.

So Prudence had his book. How on earth had *she* managed to get it? How did she even know about it? From Aswell? Justin? But surely he knew nothing. He was an uncommunicative dolt with no interest in anything.

It hardly mattered. He knew where the book was, and all that remained was for Lucien to deliver Justin's shell to Archimago, and to silence Prudence. He extinguished the remaining candles in the room and headed for his car.

A sound in the dark woke him, and for some reason Justin thought of Emma. Had he been dreaming about her? The sound came again, a faint knocking at his bedroom door.

'Who's there?' he said weakly, his voice trapped behind thick sleep.

'It's Lucien. Open the door.'

Lucien. What to do now? *He doesn't know, he can't know.*

'Justin, there's a phone call for you. It's Prudence.' Justin sighed in relief, Lucien sounded quite normal. He got out of bed, pulled on his jeans and headed for the door.

'Hang on a second,' he said, pausing with his hand near the lock, wondering if he was going to regret this. But if he didn't open the door, then Lucien was going to get suspicious. The truth was, he couldn't know that Justin had anything to do with the disappearance of his grimoire. He flicked the lock and opened the door.

Lucien wasn't waiting with a knife or a shotgun.

'I'll take it in the kitchen,' he said.

Lucien smiled stiffly and nodded, turning to go back up the hallway.

'Prudence?' Justin said quietly, picking up the phone.

'Has Lucien gone?'

Justin looked around, strained his ears. 'I can't hear him anywhere. He's probably back in bed.'

'I had a call from Emma. Lucien's been to see her, got violent with her. She thought you might be next.'

'Why? She didn't tell him anything, did she?'

'She says she didn't.'

'Well, I'm okay,' Justin said, then dropping his voice to a whisper he asked, 'How's Emma?'

'She was about to call a doctor. Don't worry.'

'But I feel responsible.'

'You aren't. Just worry about you, just stay safe,' Prudence said tenderly.

'Really, I'm fine. Lucien seemed completely normal when he came to wake me up, and now he's gone back upstairs.'

'I'm glad you're okay,' she said. 'We'd better get off the phone so he doesn't get suspicious.'

'Fine, see you in the morning.'

He hung up and headed in the dark back to his bedroom.

The blow to the back of his head was as surprising as it was painful. Something cracked against his skull with cold, solid force. He turned dizzily and saw Lucien holding a glass paperweight in his right hand. Even in the dark he could see it was smeared with his blood.

Addled and in shock, he couldn't even form a word of protest. Lucien's dressing-gown gaped, and Justin could see he was fully dressed beneath it. Lucien lifted his arm for another strike and suddenly everything greyed out.

A few snatches came to him after that. The smell of car upholstery. The sound of the front door of the college closing behind him. He thought of Prudence and Holly and the Confessional. He almost came to consciousness at that point, but Lucien had him around the neck and was dragging him up stairs that seemed to go forever. Then candles in the dark; a strange, oppressive heat; a sick, mumbling sound ebbing in and out like his consciousness.

And last, an icy hand touching his heart. An uncomfortable feeling of being pushed down too hard inside himself, as though he would burst out of his body and go plunging towards chaos. An awful blue-grey landscape waiting for him at the very bottom of his being, all he was compressed into a tiny square of space. Dark, trapped, suffocating, only despair as a companion, reduced to shadow. At leisure to witness the horrors of hell.

'I just called you a cab,' Prudence said as Holly appeared in the kitchen, dressed to go out and pick up the hire car.

'Thanks. I would have taken the tram.'

'Make it easy on yourself. Here.' Prudence counted out a handful of twenty-dollar bills for Holly. 'And buy some treats on the way back.'

'Treats? What kind?'

'We could use some more marshmallows. Or a big block of chocolate. Sustenance, you know, for our adventure tonight.'

Holly put the money in her bag. 'Okay.'

'So will you pick Justin up first on the way back?'

'Yes, so I guess I'll be about an hour all up. You won't get too bored and lonely, will you?'

'I have an evil magic book to keep me entertained,' Prudence replied.

'Well, don't call up any spirits.'

'The only person I'm calling up is Justin, to see if he's still okay. Emma's phone call freaked me out. The sooner Justin is out of that place, the better.'

A cab beeped out front. Prudence followed Holly to the door. 'Take care. Melbourne roads are a lot busier than Hicksville roads.'

'I'm sure the basic concept is the same.'

'See you soon.' Prudence closed the door behind Holly and went to the kitchen to make a cup of cocoa. She was dunking marshmallows when there was a knock at the door. Assuming Holly had forgotten something, she raced to the door, nearly tripping over Sooty, and flung it open.

'Did you forget your keys or—?' Her sentence died on

her lips as she recognised Lucien Humberstone.

'Lucien?' she gasped, frozen to the spot.

He took one step and grabbed her around the wrist. She screamed as loudly as she could, and he took the opportunity to shove a damp cloth into her face. The smell was overwhelming, the taste burning and sweet. She gagged. The front door closed behind them. She wanted to plead for her life, but the chemical was hot on her tongue. She reached out, her hand flailing near her overcoat which hung on a hook behind the door. It fell and she began to fall with it. The floor slipped from beneath her. She felt her legs collide with his ankles, saw his face hovering dark above her, then the world faded to black.

It was fun to be behind the wheel of a car again. Michael had never wanted her to learn to drive, had told her she would be no good at it. She had proved him wrong, as she had with so many things.

She sighed, indicating to pull into Justin's street. Poor Michael. She guessed she shouldn't think ill of the dead. Outside, the bitterly cold winter wind tossed bare branches and stalked up narrow side streets. The heating in the car was on full, drying out her face. Tonight was going to be freezing if the wind remained strong. She would have to remember to wear extra layers.

The Humberstone mansion rose at the end of the street. She pulled up in front of it and turned the engine off, bracing herself for the bite of the icy wind outside. It whipped her hair into her eyes and mouth as she walked up the front path and rang the doorbell. She checked her watch—midday. Just when she had told Justin to expect her. She waited a few moments and then rang again. Prudence had told her that Justin's room was towards the back of the house and he sometimes didn't hear the doorbell.

Eventually the door opened, but it wasn't Justin who answered it. Holly's first look at Lucien Humberstone was unnerving, now that she knew what kind of person he was. His height, his lean features, his eyes black like Justin's but with no trace of kindness or humility about them. She would have been intimidated under any circumstances, but with what was on her mind today it was all she could do to make herself speak.

'Hi, is Justin here?'

'Who are you?' he said simply.

'I'm Holly Beck. You must be Lucien.' She extended a hand, aware that she should make some effort. He was the man who was funding her scholarship, after all.

Her fingers were engulfed in a huge, cold hand. He shook firmly. 'It's nice to meet you at last. I'm sorry I haven't been in touch sooner. It's been a busy year for me.'

Holly was taken aback by his congeniality.

'Justin's not here,' he continued. 'Was he expecting you?'

A warning bell went off in the back of her mind. *Don't tell him anything.* 'No,' she said. 'I was just after a book of mine that he borrowed.'

'He may be with Prudence.'

'Sure,' she said nodding. 'It's not important anyway.'

'Do you know where Prudence lives?'

'I've been there once or twice.'

'Perhaps you could drop by there.'

'Perhaps.' She forced herself to smile. 'Thanks.'

'You're very welcome.'

She walked to the car without looking back. Where was Justin? Maybe he had gone to Prudence's already. She told herself not to panic, that everything was okay, that Justin was safely ensconced in front of the fire with Prudence and a cup of cocoa. The wind grazed her cheeks, and she imagined that Lucien was standing there, watching her go. Did he suspect anything?

'Pull yourself together,' she said to herself as she got in and started the car again. 'Everything's all right.' At least, as all right as it could be given the roller-coaster she had been on for the last six months. She drove to Prudence's house and parked out front, her heart beating hard. *Please let Justin be here, please.*

Letting herself in, she called out, 'Prudence? Justin?'

No answer. Warm fear trickled in her belly. She cautiously peered into the lounge. Empty. The kitchen. Empty. A cup of cocoa sat on the table. She dipped her finger into it. Stone cold.

A noise behind her made her whirl around. Sooty stood there, gazing up at her expectantly, then mewed loudly. 'Where's Prudence?' she asked the cat.

Sooty mewed again and then padded away. Holly started up the stairs. 'Prudence?' Her voice was starting to waver, her knees were rubbery. On the landing now. 'Prudence? Justin?' They should have answered by now. If they were here they should have answered. Were they together somewhere? Gone to buy cigarettes? Couldn't wait for Holly to bring the chocolate home?

Prudence's bedroom door was ajar. She pushed it open all the way and stopped with a gasp. Her stomach turned to water. Dozens and dozens of books had been pulled from the shelf and lay scattered on the ground, spines bent and broken at awkward angles. Somebody had been here looking for the grimoire. Prudence and Justin were gone. Holly's pulse thundered in her ears.

Then there was a knock at the door downstairs. She froze. Was it Justin? Prudence? Or somebody else, somebody who had just advised her to turn up here? She hurried out of Prudence's bedroom and up the hall to the master bedroom, which had a view over the front entrance. She cautiously peeped between curtains. A dark blue car was parked behind her hire car out the front. She had no idea what colour car Lucien drove, and an ivy-covered trellis obscured her view of the front door. Her breath was cold in her lungs. The knock sounded again. She waited. Then a man backed up a few paces and looked up at the front of the house. She ducked behind the curtain, her heart thumping madly. It was him, it was Lucien. And he knew she was here because he had seen the hire car parked out the front.

She had to get out. He wouldn't knock forever. He would eventually work out some way to get in. To get her and do to her whatever he had done to Justin and Prudence. She ran back to Prudence's room and checked out the window. A drainpipe ran from just below the bathroom window—two footholds and then a sheer drop. But a tree branch leaned close. She sized it up. Would it be strong enough to hold her? Paralysis took over her limbs, her mind raced in circles and would not decide.

'Oh, shit,' she said, tears coming to her eyes. 'Shit, shit.'

The knock at the door again. She had to get out. She pulled off her boots and socks and stuffed them in her bag, then strapped it over her shoulder and around her neck to secure it. On Prudence's dresser, next to an overflowing ashtray, were Prudence's magic keys. Impulsively, she grabbed them, shoved them in her bag. She pushed the window up and didn't give herself time to think before she climbed out.

She stretched out a leg and found foothold on a pipe than ran off the main drainpipe. One hand still clutching the window sill, she inched her other hand up to the bathroom window sill. *Got it.* Now the other hand. She stopped for a moment, almost hyperventilating with fear. Hands around the smooth drainpipe, she crouched down. One hand slid. A fingernail broke. She regained her grip and kept crouching. Now her hands were where her feet had just been and her feet were reaching for the next cross-pipe. Twigs from the branch poked her in the calves as if teasing her. Turning slowly, bare toes clutching at the cold, smooth pipe, she pressed her back against the wall and reached for the branch.

'Please, please,' she said under her breath. She couldn't stop and rest. Every second counted. One hand on the branch, then the other. Pulling her weight forward. Torso on the branch. She leaned forward, testing her weight on it. It looked like it would hold. She wriggled forward, lay panting for a second on the branch, then started climbing down the tree. She jumped the last short distance, earth and grass welcome beneath her feet.

She ran to the fence behind the house and climbed over it easily, through the neighbour's yard and then out onto the street. She stopped only long enough to put her boots back on, then caught the first tram that came along, planning to disappear, anonymous, into the crowded inner city until she could decide what to do next.

The warm oblivion of unconsciousness occasionally gave way to a colder darkness. Prudence moved in and out of awareness, memories flickering momentarily then disappearing down dark hallways in her mind. The cold. The smell. Familiar. She felt she had opened her eyes but still saw nothing. Still unconscious then. But if she were still unconscious, why was she thinking? A fluttering sensation moved across her arm. She twitched her shoulder. She still saw nothing. How could she be awake, eyes open, and still see nothing. The fluttering sensation returned, scratchy legs. A bug. She sat up suddenly with a gasp and brushed it off, looked around. Pitch blackness. She was on a cold stone floor. Her muscles were cramped from being in the same awkward position for so long. How long had it been? Where was Lucien? More importantly, where was she?

She tried to stand, got as far as balancing on her knees before an overwhelming bout of dizziness forced her back down. She felt her overcoat lying on the ground beside her. Lucien must have taken it to wrap her in. Stiff and aching, she shrugged into it then crawled along the floor, felt for a wall, felt her way around. Found a door and pulled herself to her feet. Two steps to the left, looking for the handle. Something crunched beneath her feet— old branches or debris, perhaps. She tried the door. Locked.

A cold tide of cognisance washed through her mind. The smell was familiar because it was the smell of the Confessional. She felt in her pocket for her lighter. Her trembling hand closed around it and held it in front of her. With a flick a small flame appeared, throwing a tiny orange circle of light. Holding it up to the keyhole, she tried to peer through.

'Lucien?' she called weakly.

She turned, holding the flame in front of her like a shield. Something caught the corner of her eye and she looked down at the pile of debris she had almost tripped over before. Fear gripped her around the ribs, squeezing a scream out of her lungs, tearing up through her throat and past her lips. Below her feet, clothed in rotten rags, was a human skeleton. She jumped, cast the lighter away from her and was plunged into darkness, obliterating the hideous sight.

She took a breath and screamed again. 'Help me, help me!' She hammered at the door, pulled at the handle, then reeled back to collapse sobbing in a corner. Finally she knew what was behind the locked door in the tunnels under Humberstone College.

CHAPTER THIRTY-EIGHT

H olly waited until nine that night before she decided she had to do something. Wandering between cafes and diners had exhausted her, and she just wanted to lie down and sleep. But where? Her own flat would be the first place Lucien looked, Prudence's house the second. She knew that he knew that she knew. Whatever he'd done with Justin and Prudence, he might also do with her.

Her heart twisted as she considered they might even be dead. But no, she couldn't afford to think that. She couldn't give up on them yet.

She checked her bank account but her scholarship payment for the fortnight hadn't gone in yet, so getting a motel room was out of the question. There was only one place she could go. The Confessional.

She bought herself a box of matches and a couple of candles, then caught a tram back from town. The walk uphill to the college nearly did her in after being on her feet practically all day. Her legs ached, her head ached, her brain ached from worrying about Justin and Prudence. She needed a space in which to think.

The college was quiet and empty. She fumbled with the keys, finding the right one to let her through the cellar and into the tunnels. With a candle in front of her, she made her way up to the Confessional. It was impossible to tell that anybody had spent serious amounts of time here. Holly was sad that they had always been so scrupulous in cleaning up behind them—there wasn't one empty wine bottle or gutted candle to provide her with a link to her friends. She laid out her overcoat, used her bag as a pillow and lay down.

Think, Holly, think.

Call the police? They would laugh at her. Prudence and Justin hadn't even been missing long enough to alarm anybody but herself. Go to Lucien's and snoop? That was certain danger. Whatever she did, she had to keep as much distance between herself and Lucien as possible.

She thought about Prudence, trying to imagine where she might be. All her life Prudence had been in search of excitement and now she had it in bucketloads. Holly was willing to bet she'd swap it all for a few mundane problems. And Justin, how awful for him. Growing up fatherless, losing his mother so horribly; then discovering his family, only to be pursued by his aunt and betrayed by his uncle.

Some buzz of recognition sounded in the back of her troubled mind. Justin and Lucien. Christian and Peter. Orphans drawn into a surrogate family, only to be horribly betrayed.

Surely not. Lucien was working without an assistant.

But Lucien was also working with Peter Owling. The man who had written the grimoire in the first place. Was revenge on the Humberstones all he really wanted? Or was it far, far worse? Was Justin earmarked as a vessel for the spirit of Peter Owling?

Holly sat up and drew her knees to her chest. She didn't want to cry, she wanted to stay strong and calm.

She took deep breaths. The last thing she wanted was to lose somebody else precious to her.

Sunday. It all depended on Sunday. Lucien had his grimoire back, and he had the body for Archimago. That meant the final summoning of Satan would not be far away, perhaps even this Sunday. Her blood froze, and she wished she was anywhere but in a dark cellar, being responsible for saving Justin, Prudence, the rest of the world. Her shoulders were weary from the weight she was carrying. She didn't want to do this alone. Her body cried out for sleep, but her mind would not turn off.

She lay down again, staring into nowhere, picking back through Christian's story for an answer to her dilemma, a way to stop Lucien and rescue her friends. Over and over the details she went, until she finally dozed off. It seemed to her that parts of Christian's story replayed themselves in her dreams, although she had never seen Rosalind, or Owling, or his four associates. Half asleep, she mused on Rosalind's fear that she would be forgotten, and here, over a hundred and thirty years later, she was being remembered in a dream.

Holly suddenly opened her eyes and gasped. When Rosalind died, she had tried to get Owling to promise to remember her. Christian had offered to be custodian of her memory and Rosalind had said, 'You can't.'

Rosalind must have known what Owling had planned for Christian. Holly could have wept with pity for him. He had been doomed from the beginning, no matter how much he thought Owling had given him. It was only ever for Owling's own benefit. And here she was, the only being in the universe who loved him, and he had pushed her away. She closed her eyes again, thought about his face, his touch, ached from missing him. Somehow, despite her fear and discomfort, she managed to fall into a deep, dreamless sleep.

'More food, magus!'

Lucien shuddered as the creature called him once again. He had ensconced himself in Lucien's bedroom and lay naked among the covers, eating everything Lucien brought him with great speed and relish. Lucien pulled out of the freezer some of the frozen junk that Emma liked to eat and set to preparing waffles and icecream. He took his time, not eager to see the creature again. It was Justin's body, Justin's face, apart from the glasses which Archimago had torn off out of vanity, but not Justin's voice, not his expressions. Archimago's gravelly voice emerged from Justin's mouth. The eyes were black and dead. The creature never stopped chatting to himself, indulging every sensuous pleasure of his new body, from gorging on food to idling with his private parts. It was unnerving.

All of this, at least, served to take his mind off Randolph. An infection had set into the wound after the operation, as Lucien had intended, and the doctors had phoned with grave fears for his recovery. Lucien was not immune to feelings of guilt and regret, so dealing with the hideous being in his bed afforded him a kind of strange relief from the concerns of ordinary men.

He carried a tray of hot, sweet food and chocolate drink upstairs. Archimago sat up in bed waiting, head leaning back against the pillow with long hair spread around him. Lucien presented the tray of food and the creature set to with gusto, using knife, fork and fingers in equal measures.

'You know, magus,' he said between bites, licking his fingers, 'there is one more thing you can get me.'

'What's that?'

'A woman. I want to feel a woman's body again.'

'It's out of the question.'

'Come, you can afford me a prostitute. It seems forever since I slid into flesh.'

Lucien did not want anybody seeing Justin—Archimago—like this. 'Wait until after Sunday,' he said. After Sunday he didn't care what happened.

'What am I supposed to do with this in the meantime?' Archimago said, throwing back the covers to reveal an erection.

'What you have been doing with it since early yesterday morning.'

The creature pouted and covered himself again. 'Very well. After Sunday I'm a free man. What's my name, by the way?'

'Justin.'

'Do I have a girlfriend?'

'She's the one who had the grimoire. I had to get rid of her.' Lucien's stomach tightened as he thought about Prudence. By now she had been imprisoned under the college for nearly twenty-four hours. Locked away at the back of his memory with other black things he didn't dare think about.

'Pity you couldn't have hung on to her for a few more hours. I could have practised my stroke.' Archimago smiled tightly. 'How do you think Justin and his girlfriend found out?'

Lucien shook his head. 'I don't know. But there's one other girl that I'm wary of. She shared an office with them at the college and I think they were friends. But I haven't been able to find her.'

'It matters little, magus. Or should I call you Uncle Lucien?' He laughed and Lucien felt the hairs on the back of his neck stand on end. 'Nobody can stop you now. You have the grimoire, you have the summoning chant, you have me. Next stop, immortality.' Archimago picked up his dish and slowly licked off the remaining maple syrup and melted icecream.

'I suppose you're right.'

'Of course I'm right,' the creature said. 'Trust me.'

577

When the hunger pangs came, they momentarily took the edge off her thirst. Prudence dozed, dipped in and out of consciousness, sometimes dreamed she was in her bed at home, sometimes dreamed that she had waded into a river and was drinking it with every pore in her body. Then the cold darkness would bite into her mind again and she would realise that all was lost.

She would give everything for a glass of water. Her mouth was like cloth, her stomach cramped and complaining. She didn't want to die this way. Not this young, not forgotten. Maybe Holly and Justin would find her. Maybe they'd come looking for her.

She closed her eyes, focussing her mind. 'Holly, Justin, please find me.' Send them a psychic message. She had heard of people dying without water in the desert in two or three days. At least the temperature was low, she wasn't losing any sweat, and she had only peed once. A fun-size box of M&Ms in her overcoat had kept hunger at bay on the first day, but now she was aware that time was starting to run out. And judging by the skeleton near the door, Lucien wasn't coming back for her.

A huge wave of terror rose up and threatened to engulf her. Nobody was coming for her. Nobody would ever find her. Lucien had probably dispatched Holly and Justin by now, too, and they were the only ones who would notice her missing. Unable to sit still another moment, she rose and pounded on the wall.

'Help me!' she screamed. Her voice was swallowed up by the dark. Her nerves all seemed to be burning and melting with fear. She banged again on the wall. 'Somebody help me!'

She collapsed once more into her corner, sobbing. Getting frantic was not going to help. She had to stay alive, she had to conserve all her energy. Somebody would save her, surely. She wasn't meant to die like this. She was too special in the world. Things like this didn't happen to girls like her. For the umpteenth time she craved a cigarette, but would not light one, knowing it would only dehydrate her quicker.

'Justin, Holly, please find me,' she said again, realising it was futile but trying to convince herself it was not.

She stood once more, determined to work on a solution. Her joints ached, her skin itched, her eyes felt dry and sore. She put a hand out to steady herself against the wall. More than anything, she wanted to avoid going near the skeleton. But she needed her lighter. She wanted to look at the lock again, not that she had any kind of sharp object to use, even if she knew how to pick a lock.

But doing something made her feel better. Crouching, she began to feel on the ground for her lighter. Here and there a bug scurried over her fingers. At long last her hand closed over the smooth sides of the lighter, and she picked it up and flicked it on.

Once more, grim shadows danced on the skeleton. She tried not to look at it as she headed for the door. Down on her knees, peering at the keyhole, trying to see inside it and figure out its mechanism. She examined the brickwork around the door. Ten centimetres of mortar and a tongue of steel kept her in her prison. If only she had a mallet, she could maybe bust her way out.

She sighed, leaning back on her haunches. And if she had magic dust she could turn herself into a fairy and fly out through the keyhole. She braced herself and looked down at the skeleton. The solution had clearly been beyond him too.

Still, he might have something on him that could help her. It was a long shot, but it was foolish not to try. Leaning over the body, she pulled at the ragged clothes. An intact scalp of hair had fallen off on the ground beside him, so filthy and mould-ridden that its colour was unrecognisable. He had been wearing jeans and a polyester button-up shirt. His watch, which lay beside him, was still ticking. She checked the time and date—it was six p.m. on Friday. Ragged, rotting denim clothes sagged over sad bones, but a squarish lump caught Prudence's eye. There was something in his back pocket.

Gingerly, she peeled back the pocket and pulled out a leather wallet. The contents were mouldy but largely intact. Four twenty-dollar notes, and plastic banking cards nestled in their slots. The top of a driver's licence caught her eye, and she pulled it out and held it up to her flame.

The man in the photo looked strangely familiar, and she knew why as soon as she read the name. Graham Humberstone. Justin's father. Same hair and eyes, just slightly more masculine around the mouth and nose. So it wasn't a tragic fishing accident that had claimed him. It was an evil younger brother. Now Prudence understood what Emma had meant when she said that Lucien was not above murder. How she wished she had taken heed, got herself, Justin and Holly out of this mess and run away somewhere, and hang what happened to the rest of the world.

She let the flame go out and sat there fighting down the abject panic which would make her lose her mind if she let it. She, like Graham, was intended to die down here to expedite Lucien's plans. She, like Graham, had no tools at her disposal to get her out.

Or did she?

Turning the lighter on again, she examined the bones of Graham's fingers. She pulled one free—it came quite easily. It was small enough, but not sharp enough. The lighter was starting to waver and she had to conserve the fuel in it as long as possible, so she put it back in her pocket. Feeling up the wall, she found a ridge of hard, rough mortar between two bricks. With care, she began to file the finger bone against it, sharpening it to a point, determined to pick a lock for the first time in her life.

Shortly after nightfall Holly cautiously rounded the corner into Prudence's street. She had her hair tucked into a black beret she had bought during another long day in town and had her scarf wrapped high up around her chin. She saw the silver hire car glowing dimly under a street-light. The blue car that Lucien drove was nowhere in sight, nor were there any lights on in the house.

She had to do it. She had to go in, because more than twenty-four hours had passed and, despite all her efforts, she still didn't know what to do. Prudence's books were her last hope. Sunday midnight was approaching rapidly and she had to have something planned before then.

All was silent in the entranceway as she shut the cold street out behind her. She waited a few beats, then advanced into the kitchen. Sooty leapt out at her with a loud mew, making her cry out in fear.

'Oh, Sooty, it's you,' she said softly, pressing a relieved hand to her chest. She picked the cat up but it scurried away from her, mewing and waiting in front of a cupboard.

'Are you hungry?' Holly asked, turning the light on. With some illumination and the cat for company, she didn't feel so scared. The kitchen didn't face onto the road, so nobody would be able to tell if there was anyone home. She opened a tin of cat food and dumped it into a bowl for Sooty, who then ignored her as he gulped down his dinner.

Putting the tin opener back in the drawer, Holly decided to take a knife with her upstairs. Just in case. She climbed the staircase in the dark because she didn't want any light shining into the street. She went along the hallway and with a deep breath pushed open the door to Prudence's room.

The window was still open, letting in a cold breeze. Holly turned the light on. The room was exactly as she had left it, the disturbed books still scattered everywhere.

She picked her way across the room and pulled the window shut, turned and surveyed the room. Like finding a needle in a haystack. She picked up one volume—*The Truth About Alien Abductions*—and cast it aside. Picking her way through them, from *Ley-Lines of Britain* to Aleister Crowley's *Diary of a Drug Fiend*, she sorted the books, reshelving some, putting others aside if they contained anything about ghosts, black magic, or working with spirits. In the end she had a stack of eighteen books to work her way through. She found a box full of old *Rolling Stones* in Prudence's wardrobe, tipped the magazines out and stacked the books in, adding a pillow for good luck. It was tempting to stay here where it was warm and comfortable, to have a shower and a change of clothes, but she already felt she had spent too much time here. Who knew when Lucien would come looking for her again? He could even be out the front now.

When she was ready to leave, she went round to the master bedroom to check that Lucien's car was not parked outside. The street was empty. In the kitchen she opened a bag of dry cat food and filled a big bowl with water for Sooty, grabbed a torch and spare batteries, balanced the box of books on her hip and cautiously stepped outside.

She didn't breathe easily until she had crossed the park and was only a short distance from the college. Checking over her shoulder frequently, she tried to stay out of the pools of streetlight on the way. The box seemed to get heavier the further she moved up the hill, then she was finally at the college, letting herself into the cellar and lighting her way with the torch down to the Confessional.

Setting the pillow on the ground, she crossed her legs and sat, lit some candles to read by and opened the first book.

By five a.m., eyes aching, she was almost more confused and unsure than she had been when she started.

Conflicting theories abounded about all things super-natural—spirits could be controlled by naming them, by drawing a circle around them, by ordering them in the name of God. Demons could be destroyed by saying The Lord's Prayer, by holding them to promises made in life, by throwing salt on them. And just as many sources said that spirits could not be controlled or destroyed at all, that humans should just stay well out of their way and not mess with them unless they were an adept of at least ten years' standing. If only she had Prudence to help her sort the religious lunacy from the juvenile speculation from the reliable sources.

She sighed, rubbing her eyes. The only thing all the books bar two had agreed upon was that the most effective weapon against an evil spirit was a good one. Christian. She had to find a way to make him help her. But she was terrified to go upstairs and face his wrath again. The angrier he became, the stronger he became. And even if she could persuade him to help her, she didn't have the magical knowledge to invoke him into the world. According to the books he would remain, as he had always told her, merely an extension of her senses, visible and audible to nobody else. Hardly an effective tool against two potent magicians, one of them imbued with demonic power.

But she had to try. Christian was her last hope. She packed the books in a far corner, picked up the torch and extinguished the candles. Taking a deep breath, she headed up to her office.

The room was quiet and soft and warm compared to the Confessional. She closed the door behind her and, in the most confident voice she could summon, called his name in the dark.

'Christian?'

No response. Her heart hammered in her chest. What if he was gone now? What if he thought that Holly had already destroyed the grimoire and his task was over?

'Christian, if you are around, you must come. I have to tell you something.' She paused, waiting. 'Something about Rosalind,' she added.

An angry shaking started on the bookcase.

'Don't get angry, just listen.'

The books became still. 'I am listening. What could you possibly know about Rosalind?'

She wished she could see him, but she didn't have time to get the mirror, and besides, he would probably refuse to appear out of spite. It unnerved her, the way his voice came from everywhere, but she thought she could sense his presence. Just a slightly warmer collection of air molecules vibrating in the corner beside her desk. She addressed herself in that direction.

'Rosalind said you couldn't be the keeper of her memory. Do you know why?'

'I told you. She was delirious.'

'But she said nothing else in delirium that night.'

There was an angry silence. 'What slur are you trying to make against Rosalind?'

'No slur. I think Rosalind loved you very much and was sorry for you.'

'Sorry for me?'

'Because she knew that Peter intended to sacrifice you to Aathahorus.'

Holly braced herself for the stream of invective. It didn't come. Instead he said quietly, 'I don't believe you.'

'You're my last hope, Christian,' she said. 'My friends have both disappeared, Lucien has taken back his grimoire and I'm sure that he's planning the final summoning for this Sunday. You must help me.'

'Rosalind loved me,' he said.

'I know. And I love you too.'

'Perhaps she was trying to warn me.'

Holly felt a surge of hope rush through her. 'Perhaps she was.'

'I don't know what to believe,' he said. 'I have had time to think, to consider all you've said. I'm confused and don't know what to do.'

'Help me,' Holly said again. 'If you don't help me, I don't know what will happen.'

More silence.

'I'll need you. I have to confront Lucien, and Archimago will be there. You will get a chance to speak to him, perhaps, to find out for certain if he intended to harm you or not.'

'You'll have to bring me through,' he said.

Holly's breath caught in her throat. He was going to do it. 'I don't know how.'

'I do.'

'I don't have any of the materials, any of the experience.'

'There is another way. It's dangerous.'

'I don't care. I have to stop him.'

'You'll have to come and get me.'

She swallowed down her fear. 'Is it possible?'

'It's the only way.'

'What do I need to do?'

'Come for me on Sunday, about five hours before the summoning is due to start. Fast until then, get some sleep, don't be afraid.'

'I'll be here,' she said. 'Whatever it takes, I'll be here.'

'See that you are.' Quite noticeably, his presence was gone. Should she trust him? Did she have a choice?

She went to the window and looked down at the street. Sleep called her, but she wanted to put her head down somewhere warm and soft and comfortable, not in the Confessional. One more trip to Prudence's would solve it.

Back downstairs, back into the cellar, collecting the books in the box again, bones weary and mind in turmoil.

She eyed the curve of the tunnel fearfully. Everything seemed dark and spooky around her. Prudence's magic keys firmly in her handbag, she hit the street and cautiously went back to Prudence's. Sooty slept quietly in a beam of reflected streetlight. She opened the fridge, went to the tin where Prudence kept her spare cash. Should be just enough.

She called a cab and got it to take her to the city. Half an hour later she closed the door to a hotel room behind her, turned the radiator up and showered, then slipped in between soft, warm sheets. She slept for a long time.

Using cigarettes like little torches, Prudence went back again and again to the door with her improvised lock-picking device. Inhale when she needed more light, exhale when she was going by feel. Anything to preserve the fuel in her lighter, which couldn't last forever.

Not that she had forever.

She realised with barely repressed horror that she was dying of dehydration. Her skin was flaky, felt stretched too hard over her bones. Her eyes were dry and seemed to be sinking back into her head. She hadn't passed any urine now for more than twenty-four hours, and her sense of direction was periodically swallowed by strange dizzy fits where she suddenly couldn't remember up from down, right from left. But she kept focussed on her task, telling herself over and over that she would get out, the sound of her voice warding off the horrible creeping fear that she would die here alongside Justin's father, deprived of the substance she never usually bothered to drink if there was something alcoholic or caffeinated nearby.

The cigarette between her lips burnt down to nothing. She spat it out and felt in her pocket for another. There were five left. The lighter flared briefly in the gloom, so much brighter than the faint ember of the cigarette. But her eyes were becoming adjusted to the dark. She had to keep working.

She went to put the lighter back in her pocket but was overcome by a sudden bout of dizziness. The precious object slipped from her fingers and she heard it land on the ground. She leaned her head against the door and waited for the dizzy spell to pass, then began to feel on the ground for the lighter.

For a few horrible seconds she feared it had slid under the door and was now on the other side, along with her freedom. But it wasn't. It was jammed in the crack, not thin enough to escape her completely. As she was grabbing the end of it, she felt the corner of something else under the door. A piece of paper.

With one hand she picked up the lighter and pocketed it, keeping the fingers of the other stretched over the corner of paper. What was it? It suddenly became the most important thing in the world that she find out. What if Lucien had intended to leave her with instructions for how to survive, or a promise to come back? What if this note had blown out of the cell when he was leaving?

She grimaced. What if it was a two-for-one McDonald's voucher that had fallen out of her coat pocket when Lucien had brought her down here?

But she had to know. Her fingers felt clumsy and she almost pushed the piece of paper further out into the hallway. She took a deep breath and tried again, managed to drag the corner towards her far enough to grab its edge. Two pieces, joined together by some old glue. She flicked her lighter on and examined them.

At first she thought her disorientated state was making her see things. Writing covered the pages but it was totally illegible. But then she realised that she had seen this kind of encrypted text before. The grimoire.

The book had been through so much trauma, having had its binding all but burned off in the fire, that some of the pages had worked loose. Lucien must have brought her here straight from her house, the grimoire still jealously clutched to him, perhaps tucked in the front of his shirt for safekeeping. But in the effort of carrying her and dumping her and locking the door, these two pages had escaped.

She gazed at them for a few moments, then realised she was wasting her light and flicked the lighter off. As addled and dizzy as she was, she realised he would have to come back for them. It didn't matter how many incantations he had memorised or written elsewhere, the power was in this book. He had to come back next time he intended to use it, which would be Sunday night.

And then she could escape. Hope shot up through her like a beam of light. A plan, that was all she needed. A plan to overcome him.

First she had to figure out what day and time it was. Her fitful dozes had upset her awareness of time. She briefly flicked on the lighter to check Graham's watch. Providing it was keeping time right after all these years— and it was an expensive Swiss number so it probably was . . . it was ten p.m. on Saturday. So there would be another twenty-four hours at least until he got there.

She groaned. What if she didn't live that long?

'Be optimistic, Prudence,' she said to herself. Three days without water might kill somebody in the Sahara, but she was safe in a cool underground chamber. As long as she stayed conscious, stayed alert, she would be fine. But how was she to overcome Lucien when dehydration and hunger had left her with the strength of a kitten? She had no weapon.

She remembered Graham's skeleton on the ground next to her. 'I'm sorry,' she said to him, 'I'm sorry that I've turned you into a toolbox.' She ran her hand along the ribs and down to the pelvis and legs. She extracted and hefted one thighbone. Not particularly heavy. She needed more. She pulled the other thighbone out, feeling something snap weakly as it came loose. She tried to break it in half with her hands. No luck—it was too hard. She stood, waiting for another dizzy fit to pass. With all her strength she pulled back and hit the bone against the corner of brickwork by the door. Nothing happened. She tried it again. This time something snapped and splintered off. She ran a hand up the bone, found a jagged point on the end of it.

Folding the grimoire pages neatly into her overcoat pocket, she extinguished her cigarette and sat back to wait for Lucien's return.

CHAPTER THIRTY-NINE

~

What had started as an early-morning winter drizzle had turned into a freezing downpour by six-thirty on Sunday night. The sky had been so dark all day that it almost felt like the sun hadn't risen at all. For Holly, on what she expected would be the most frightening day of her life, it seemed fitting.

She closed the door of her office behind her, shivering and wishing she knew where the override switch for the central heating was. Despite her umbrella, she had still managed to get parts of her body soaked. Her skirt stuck to her legs and her arms were all gooseflesh beneath damp sleeves.

Breathing quietly, she surveyed the room. So much had happened here between their three desks. More than anything she wished that things could be as they were, that Justin and Prudence were safe and that this horrible darkness that had crawled into her life would, like the heavy clouds outside, blow away overnight. Without her having to confront Lucien or Peter Owling, without her having to cross to Christian's realm of death, without the growing certainty that she was all that stood between her friends and terrible danger.

'Christian, I'm here,' she said steadily.

A small rush of breath near her ears, then the weird, disembodied voice. 'We must ensure you will not be disturbed. Can you move something across the door?'

Holly nodded. 'Sure.' She picked up her chair and jammed it under the door handle.

'What do I have to do?' she said, returning to the centre of the room.

'Lie down. Take a few deep breaths. No matter what happens, focus on my voice. Follow my voice.'

She lowered herself to the carpet, lay back and closed her eyes. The muscles in her legs were twitching with anxiety and her stomach was growling from lack of food.

'You must relax, Holly,' Christian said, and she felt his warm touch momentarily on her brow.

'I'm frightened.'

'Listen to me very carefully. Whatever happens, follow my voice. If you see something black, stay away from it. If you become lost in shadow, call my name.' Then he repeated with sombre emphasis, 'Follow my voice. Do not go near the shadows.'

Holly nodded solemnly, cold fear seeping through her limbs. 'I don't know if I'm going to be calm enough to go through with this.'

'That's why I'm pulling you through. Follow my voice, take all the comfort you can from it. When you can hear my voice you are safe.'

'Okay.'

'What can you hear now? Tell me everything you can hear.'

'I can hear the rain.'

'Try harder. What else can you hear?'

She strained her ears. Faintly she could hear traffic in the distance, leaves moving on branches, a clock ticking somewhere far away, her own heartbeat. She listed these things for him.

'One by one, let them go. Become deaf to them. You only hear my voice or silence.'

Holly drew an imaginary veil between herself and all the noises, until it did seem that the world had become very silent.

'Now, what can you feel?'

'I can feel the carpet under my skin. My damp clothes stuck to my legs. A slight itch below my left shoulder blade. My breath tickling the skin under my nose.'

'Let those go as well. Move beyond your body. Let my voice pull you through.'

Slowly she let each sensation go, beginning to feel a strange kind of disembodiment, as though she were floating about two centimetres above the carpet. It was pleasant, liberating.

'Holly.' The sound of Christian's voice was like a hook catching her soul and pulling her up and up and out. She thought she heard a cry of terror a long distance away.

'Christian!' she said, though it was less like saying it than thinking it aloud. 'I'm frightened.'

'Look around you, Holly.'

Her field of vision opened up around her. She was still in the office, but the angles seemed flat and the colours seemed bleached. Twisting around and looking down, she saw a pale body in black—herself—lying on the floor behind her. For a horrible moment she wondered if she was dead. Like a magnet, her fear seemed to pull her towards her body.

'Don't be afraid. Don't go back there,' Christian said, and his voice drew her away once more. 'Keep following my voice.'

As she turned and looked ahead of her, she caught sight of a silvery trail of vapour, glistening dim like icicles by firelight. It appeared to run from her body on the ground up to where she now was. Starscapes reeled above her.

'Come, Holly, come to where I am.'

'Where are you?'

'There are several more steps to take. We're still separated by many layers. Keep advancing towards my voice.'

'Then keep speaking, don't stop,' she said, frightened. 'Sing or recite poetry or something.'

'"My heart aches, and a drowsy numbness pains my sense, as though of hemlock I had drunk," he began. 'Are you with me?'

'"Yes, I am. Keep going. Don't stop.' The starscapes were fading behind her, sunrise glowed in a silent space above. She had an impression of a body, of skin and senses working, but it was profoundly different to the way she felt normally. A faint tingling ran around her limbs, as though she were made of glittering light instead of flesh.

'"That thou, light-winged Dryad of the trees, in some melodious plot of beechen green, and shadows numberless, singest of summer in full-throated ease."' His voice wound on and on, somewhere far above her. She listened and kept moving towards it. An earthy smell enveloped her and she found herself moving forwards in a great, dark forest.

'Don't go near anything black,' Christian warned again, then resumed his recitation.

Holly looked around her apprehensively. Shadows deepened around tree trunks. Were they the black places she was to be afraid of? Behind her, the silvery trail of swirling vapour still followed, bending off into endless distances.

'Where am I, Christian?'

'It's best not to ask. Come on. "But here there is no light, save what from heaven is with the breezes blown through verduous glooms and winding mossy ways."'

The intoxicating scent of fresh rain hung in every air molecule. She went further and further into the dark green, being drawn by Christian's voice as though he were reeling her towards him on a line. She felt alive, wondrously, brilliantly alive. Colours dripped cool on her tongue, silvery shivers of sound traced patterns over her.

'This place is beautiful, Christian. Can we stay here a little while?'

'Death can be seductive, but it is never beautiful. Come, we have another step to take.'

She felt herself rising again, saw the tops of the trees she had just been walking among. From above, she could see that a river ran through the forest, thick and black like tar, hot bubbles of sulphur popping as it ran over rocks and tree roots. She looked up ahead. The world around her now was misty, blue. Snatches of voices came to her.

'Who is that speaking?' she asked.

'Don't listen to any other voice but mine,' Christian said.

'I won't.'

'No matter what happens. No matter what you might hear. There are souls of the dead floating in these mists, souls who haven't yet come to rest. Some are in pain, some are angry. But none can hurt you if you just follow my voice.'

'I will. Keep speaking.'

'"Darkling I listen; and, for many a time I have been half in love with easeful Death, call'd him soft names in many a mused rhyme . . ."'

'Holly!' The voice, too familiar, too close by.

'Christian, I think I heard—'

'Holly! What are you doing here?'

'Michael?' Fear froze inside her.

'Don't listen to him, Holly,' Christian warned.

'Holly, what have I done?' Michael said. 'I don't want to be here. I didn't want to die.'

'Where are you? I can't see you.'

'Ignore him,' Christian said.

She hesitated, Michael's voice drawing her to him.

Her hesitation was long enough to undo her. Something had hold of the silver trail behind her and was pulling it savagely. She felt herself falling backwards through the thick mists, coming to a stop when a pair of square workman's hands caught her around the shoulders. She looked up in horror, into the face of her dead husband.

She screamed for Christian. As the mist swirled around Michael's head, he appeared first whole and normal, then violently disfigured by the gunshot wound that had killed him, the vision shifting and changing. One moment his eyes held her firmly in his gaze, the next moment the top of his head was little more than a collection of bloody chunks of bone and brain, one sad eyeball hanging limply over his cheek.

'Help me go back,' he pleaded. 'I don't want to be here. I'm sorry I did it.'

'Michael . . . I . . .'

'No, Holly.' Christian's voice. 'You must ignore him. You must follow me. There is nothing more you can do for him.'

The horrible guilt momentarily held her hostage.

'That's right,' Michael said, seeming to read her thoughts. A clear fluid streaked with blood oozed across the remains of his face. 'You're responsible.'

'I'm . . .'

'Holly!' Christian's voice, now fearful and moving into the distance.

'Where are you?' she screamed, trying to twist away from her dead husband's hands, turning her face from the grisly sight. 'I'm trapped.'

'"Forlorn! The very word is like a bell to toll me back to my sole self!"' Christian's voice again, forcefully resuming his recitation. The words pulled her from

Michael's grasp, up and away. As her hands left his, she felt a warm moist trickle between her fingers. She looked down, turned her palms over. They were smeared with blood.

'*Ho-lly!*' Michael screamed, distant now. 'Don't leave me again!'

'Oh, God,' she said softly. 'Oh, God.'

'My voice, Holly. Just follow my voice.'

'His blood, Christian. It's all over my hands.' But as she moved away from the sound of Michael's voice, the blood shimmered and vanished.

'Come to me Holly,' Christian said. 'You're almost here.'

Around her the blue mists were clearing. A cold landscape below her, houses, trees, narrow streets, but all strangely flat, strangely two-dimensional.

'Where are we?' Great stone houses rose on cobbled streets. In other places, cold slums huddled together on dusty alleyways. A dirty river moved through it all.

'We're in London. Keep coming. You're almost here, I can almost grab you.'

Figures moved below her like tiny cut-out dolls. Horses, carriages crowded the streets. The veiled sound of city noises—wheels on roads, children calling to each other, marketeers shouting. Chimneys blew odd, flat clouds.

'Got you!' Christian said suddenly, and down she came, plummeting towards the roof of a two-storey, red-brick house. Unable to stop herself, Holly let out a scream. Around her she saw tiles, then the inside of a ceiling, dusty beams, down through the roof, down through the first storey, glimpsing linen and paintings and china dolls, down again. She closed her eyes in terror.

Just as suddenly she stopped with a jolt. Something was clamped tightly around her left wrist. She opened her eyes with trepidation and looked down. It was Christian's hand.

'Christian?' her eyes flicked up and took him in, standing whole and solid in front of her.

'My God. You're even more beautiful than I thought,' he said. 'I've only ever seen you flat and sapped of colour.'

She gazed at him. He was tall, much taller than she'd expected. His face was that of an angel. Pale skin, a slight blush on perfect cheeks, eyes as blue as a watercolour ocean, black hair curling around his ears. She reached a hand up to touch his lips. They were warm.

'I can feel you,' she said. 'I can see you, I can touch you.'

'Yes. Here you can.'

She looked around her. 'Where are we?' Though she thought she already knew. She saw red wallpaper, every spare inch of space crammed with gilt and velvet and crystal, a red marble fireplace with a worn, high-backed armchair in front of it.

'It's Peter's house. As it was then.'

'Do you live here?'

He sighed. 'It's difficult to explain. Here isn't anywhere. It's me. This is all part of me, built of my memory. You're here because you have come to me. When I come back to the living world with you, this place will disappear.'

'Will you ever be able to get back?'

He shook his head. 'I don't want to come back. I want to rest, with the others lucky enough to have gone to the other side.'

Holly couldn't stop touching him, feeling the velvet of his coat, pushing up his sleeves to examine the long, pale limbs beneath. In person, three-dimensional, he looked younger, more like the seventeen-year-old he had been when he died.

'Can I hold you?' she breathed.

'Yes.'

Her arms went around him, felt the distance around his back, felt his ribs rise and fall with his breath. The only thing hinting that this was anything other than real was the strange, disembodied tingling that continued along her limbs. She ignored it and held him tight.

'I love you,' she said, knowing that the words were not enough to express the deep, sweet darkness that inhabited her.

'And I love you,' he said, his heart beating faster. 'But we have to go back.'

'Can't we stay here a little longer? I want to hold you forever.'

'We don't have much time. Hours pass differently over here. Your friends are in danger. The world is in danger.'

Holly began to sob. 'It isn't fair. You're all I want.' She felt velvet against her cheek. Her warm tears spilled onto it. For a moment she was tempted to stay. To abandon her friends and leave her old world behind.

'It is right, though,' Christian said, stepping back and looking at her with huge, blue eyes. The sad corners of his mouth turned down. 'We must do what is right.'

She turned her face up and his lips moved over hers. She sighed. His warm tongue moved into her mouth, his pale fingers pressed into her shoulders. Her head spun. His lips moved up to her cheek, to her ear.

'Are you ready?' he murmured against her hair.

'Hold me for a little longer. Five minutes. Just hold me for five minutes.'

'All right,' he said softly.

The clock on the mantelpiece ticked the countdown. She pressed her face into his chest, rubbed her cheek against his waistcoat, ran lips over his warm throat. He held her tightly, over one hundred and thirty years of desire compressed into five short minutes. She knew that after this, true happiness would elude her for the rest of her life, so she clung to it desperately, savoured the last five minutes of her life as a contented, optimistic being.

'Come,' he said, pulling away from her. 'It's time to go.'

He took her hand and a feeling of vertigo engulfed her. Peter's house disintegrated around her and they sped away. The return journey was quicker, their joint momentum pulling them along the silver vapour trail towards the here and now. Holly saw the world appear below her and closed her eyes, dreading the awful dizziness as she plunged down and down.

She seemed to land with a soft thump inside her own body, the rain on the roof outside telling her that she was back. She opened her eyes warily. She lay as she had on the carpet, freezing cold. Sitting up, she looked around for Christian, but she was alone. Had it all been a dream?

'Christian?'

Suddenly he materialised in front of her, the two-dimensional being he had always been in the mirror. 'I'm here. You can call and dismiss me as you please. Wherever you go, I have to go until you release me. And I can go nowhere without you.'

She looked at the clock on her desk. It was shortly before midnight. 'Including Lucien's magic ritual. I have to take you in, don't I?'

He nodded. She reached out to touch him, but her hand passed through air, slightly denser than the air around it, but still not flesh and blood. 'Christian,' she said, 'how can I ever be happy again?'

'You will. Some day you'll be happy again. You'll fall in love with somebody else. Somebody real and alive.'

She rose and went to the window, gazing down below her. Overwhelming feelings fought for supremacy within her. Love, fear, pain. Car headlights swept up the front driveway of the college. Lucien had arrived. She turned to look at Christian, who was watching her, awaiting her command.

'What can we do to stop him?'

'I can stop him.'

'How?'

'I am stronger than Peter now. A hierarchy exists among souls of the dead. He has become a demon, the lowest form. You must trust me.'

Did she trust him? He still loved Peter. He still hadn't admitted that Peter may have wanted to destroy him. She considered for a few moments.

'You can't appear to them until I command you?'

'That's right.'

'Very well. Disappear for now. In a few moments I'll go up to the office. Come with me, but do not reveal yourself until I call you.'

'As you wish.' He disappeared. She shivered.

She went to the door, removed the chair that had barricaded her in, and listened for Lucien's footsteps. He wasn't alone—there were quite clearly two pairs of feet on the stairs. Who had he brought with him? She strained an ear at the keyhole for any snatch of conversation.

'. . . excited by all this. It's been some time since I . . .' That was an unfamiliar voice, deep and raspy like a heavy smoker.

'. . . by me, Archimago.'

'No need to be afraid, magus.'

The voices moved up to the next floor, then faded. Archimago, already embodied, here with Lucien. Everything ready to go for the final summoning. Holly shuddered as she remembered Christian's account of Owling's failed attempt to command Satan, with the great beast stepping easily from the magic circle. Why did she have to be here, now, involved in this?

She pressed her back against the door, took a deep breath, pushed an unsteady hand against her solar plexus. She stood like that for five minutes, too afraid to move, too afraid to back down. Finally, on rubber legs, light-headed and almost quaking with fear, she opened the door and headed up the stairs.

It was time.

CHAPTER FORTY

hrough the gap under the door to Lucien's office,
Holly could see candlelight dancing within.
Voices rumbled quietly, Archimago laughed. She crept
close, listening hard. Lucien began to recite something
like a list of insults, directed against every Christian saint
and prophet imaginable. It had started. Her stomach had
turned to water, terror held her in thrall, her breath was
trapped in her lungs. It was like jumping off a cliff, not
knowing whether a safety net waited below.

She tried the door handle. Locked. Of course. How
was she supposed to get in?

Suddenly the door flung open and Lucien stood glaring
down at her. He must have noticed the handle move, or
perhaps Archimago had alerted him. She screamed and
took a step backwards, but a huge hand closed over her
shoulder, another around her wrist, and she was dragged
into the room. The door to escape slammed shut behind
her, and Lucien rough-handled her up against his desk.
Her eyes took in the circle, the candles, and sitting in the
corner . . .

'Justin!'

The creature laughed, a horrible glassy screech. It was not Justin. It was Archimago. Justin was already lost. Hot tears of terror and sadness pricked at her eyes. Holly looked wildly around the room for Prudence, but was soon brought back to her own plight when Lucien pressed the cold tip of a letter opener against her throat.

'What the fuck are you doing here?' he spat.

'You . . . you have to stop,' she stammered. 'You can't trust that thing.'

'And what would you know?'

'I know who he is. He's Peter Owling. He's trying to trick you.'

'What?' Lucien said, turning her to face him. 'How do you know about Peter Owling?'

'He calls himself Archimago, but it's Peter Owling.'

'It's true, magus,' the creature in Justin's body said. It was the most unnerving thing she had ever seen, Justin's eyes dead and flat, the other being speaking through him. 'I was Peter Owling.'

Lucien still had her in a vicelike grip, but his gaze was turned on Archimago. 'Why . . .? What . . .?'

'But I'm not trying to destroy you. I'm trying to help you.' Archimago's voice had become reasonable, even sympathetic. 'You've seen what I look like on the other side. All I wanted was a body again. All I wanted was eternal life on earth, as do you. Together we can achieve it.'

'You should have told me,' Lucien said.

'You wouldn't have trusted me. Come, magus, do you want to die? Do you want to feel death creep through your body, trailing cold in your veins? Do you want to go to hell? You've seen it, you know what it's like, you know what will happen to you there. And you've come too far for repentance. You're responsible for so much death, so much suffering. It's the only way to avoid your judgement.'

Lucien turned his attention back to Holly, drew his hand away a few centimetres to gather momentum before plunging the letter opener towards her throat. She cried out, but Archimago was next to Lucien in an instant, staying his hand.

'Don't kill her,' he said.

'Why not?'

Archimago pushed Lucien out of the way and dropped a caress on Holly's throat. 'Because I want her. She's the first woman I've touched in over a century. Don't kill her.' Holly's nerve endings began to shriek in horror, making her body hot.

'We don't have time for you to—'

'Then I'll have her afterwards. Make her watch. I wager you she screams when she sees what we have planned.'

Holly's breath started coming in harsh, quick gulps. It was more repulsive than she could imagine to be pawed by this creature, even if it was in Justin's body, even if they were Justin's hands drifting down to the front of her blouse, brutally closing over her breasts.

'I don't think that's wise,' Lucien said.

The creature snarled. 'I'll tell you what is wise. I am in control here. Without me you have nothing. I can betray Satan into your hands, I can entrap him and make him grant you eternal life.'

'Don't believe him,' Holly said. 'Nobody can entrap Satan. He's too powerful.'

'Shut up!' Lucien cried, slapping her hard across the face. 'You know nothing. You're just a girl. I am a magus.'

Holly felt a stinging trickle of blood run from the corner of her mouth. Archimago bent close to her, his tongue emerging to lick the blood from her chin. His breath was sulphurous and acrid. She shuddered, sickened. Nausea bubbled dully in her stomach. She could taste bile in the back of her throat.

'All right,' Lucien conceded. 'You hold her while I find something to tie her up with.'

Lucien passed her to Archimago, who continued idly groping her. He pulled one of her hands toward him, rubbing it over the stiff bulge in his pants.

'Don't!' she shrieked, her fingers recoiling. 'Where's Justin? What have you done with Justin?'

'Justin's gone,' he replied.

Holly tried to ignore the creature's insistent hands as she watched Lucien. He went to a cupboard and pulled out a length of black cloth, which looked like it might have been a ceremonial robe, and tore long strips off it to tie her up with. He arranged a chair just on the periphery of the magic circle and, with Archimago's help, pushed her into it and tied her down. Uncontrollable shudders of terror ran through her as she saw how close she was to the circle. She felt she might pass out from the overwhelming fear. She desperately wanted to call Christian to help, but held off. It wasn't the right time yet. She knew he must be waiting, watching, maybe frustrated that she hadn't already summoned him. Peter was there, after all, and she knew how desperate Christian was to speak to him again. But she had things to ask him. She tried to take a deep breath, to get her panic under control.

'Archimago, tell me about Christian,' she said as Lucien moved back to the circle. Her voice was thin and breathy with fear.

'What about Christian?' he asked, his eyes narrowing.

'Tell me what you intended to do with him.'

Lucien strode over and hit her again. Her head rocked to one side and dizzying stars of pain overcame her momentarily. 'Be silent.'

He strode to the desk where a few stray lengths of cloth huddled together like sinister black limbs. He brought them back to her, balled up a rag and shoved it in her mouth, used another to tie tightly around her face, keeping the ball in place. The cloth drained all the moisture from her mouth, made her feel as though she were choking. To her horror, she couldn't form any words, not even Christian's name to summon him. Had she lost her only chance? Had she endangered everybody just for the chance to prove to Christian she was right about Owling? Panic was alive in her veins. She tried to cough the gag out, to close her jaws, to use her tongue to work it even a little loose. In the meantime, Lucien went back to his chant. Archimago shot her a long, suspicious look, then turned his attention to Lucien.

'Come, magus, let's get Old Nick out of his comfortable routine.'

The stream of abuse against Christ began again, then he began to praise Satan. Still Holly worked the gag in her mouth.

'You can skip the next two pages,' Archimago said matter-of-factly. 'As I already have my body. Go straight to the summoning.'

Lucien hesitated, looked at Holly, looked at the boundary of the circle.

'Be not afraid, magus,' Archimago said. 'Don't die before your time as I did, and lose your chance.'

Lucien flipped over a few pages and then began an evocation in a low voice. Holly realised that she was beginning to sweat, that the temperature had risen ten degrees or more. Frantically she pulled at her bonds, mashed her jaws at her gag. Thunder rumbled far away. With a sweep of his hands, Lucien described a circle in the air. Both he and Archimago looked at the centre of the circle expectantly. Five seconds passed, ten. Then Lucien turned to Archimago.

'Why isn't it working?'

'Let me see the book.'

Lucien handed the book to Archimago. 'It has to

work,' he said, his voice like a scared little boy. 'It has to.'

Archimago looked over the open pages. 'What is this!' he roared. 'There are two pages missing!'

'What?'

'The grimoire is not complete. The invocation will not work.'

Holly savoured the small moment of relief.

'Where are they?' Lucien asked. 'Do you know where they are?'

Archimago let his head drop back and closed his eyes. For a second the creature looked like Justin, not some monstrous marionette. Holly's heart twisted.

'You dropped them where you left the girl,' Archimago snarled, opening his eyes and handing the book back. 'You idiot.'

Lucien's jaw twitched with barely suppressed anger. 'It's of no consequence. I'll go and get them now.'

'Well, hurry. I'm hungry and I may soon decide that I don't want to do any more work this evening.'

Lucien slammed the grimoire down on his desk, took a torch out of his bottom drawer and moved towards the door. 'I'll be back directly,' he said tightly. 'Ten minutes at most.'

Archimago gave Holly a leer. 'We'll enjoy ourselves while you're gone. Take your time.'

Lucien raced down the stairs two at a time, nearly tripping as he rounded the corner and hurried across the foyer. Damn Archimago. He should never have fulfilled his end of the deal first. And now the horror of finding out that it was Peter Owling. Lucien was very likely bound to him for eternity as the two of them wandered the earth— Archimago a demon in human form, Lucien a human made immortal by demonic power. Only his certainty that anything was better than death kept him moving ahead.

He fumbled with his keys for the cellar. He did not want to go down there. Last time, when he had been carrying Prudence, it had felt like he was walking down dark corridors in his own mind, coming back to a horrible memory that he had managed to suppress for nearly four years. His brother. What he had done to his brother for money and for power, and because Graham's principles tempered everything they did with the grimoire. It was a fit of anger, not premeditated or planned. A blow to the head, a trip to the tunnels under the college, and a walking away that had taken him to new lengths of self-control. No more anger, no more emotional outbursts, no more remembering who he had been in the past.

But walking back towards it was walking back towards an old version of himself, a sticky blotch on his memory of guilt and fear and the cold dread of losing control.

She would be dead by now, surely. If not dead, then nearly so. He flicked the torch on, lit his way up the tunnel. Round the first bend, right to the very apex of the second loop. Telling himself there was no need to be afraid of memories, he found the right key and began to unlock the door.

Archimago removed her gag almost as soon as Lucien had closed the door behind them. He pressed his face close to hers and forced a wet, inescapable kiss on her mouth. Worse than the gag. She felt her legs and arms go into involuntary convulsions, as her body recoiled from him. Finally, he drew back and looked at her evenly.

'What do you know about Christian?'

Heart racing, she licked her lips and forced herself to speak. 'I know that you used him for your own ends. I know that you intended to sacrifice him to Aathahorus.'

'Why does it concern you?'

'Because he loved you. He trusted you. You betrayed that trust. Isn't that right?' She just wanted him to admit it, to show Christian for certain that Owling did not now, had not ever deserved his love or loyalty.

'Of course it's right. He was a pretty boy and I like pretty things. But he was growing older and wouldn't have been beautiful forever.'

'Aathahorus required a body and you promised him Christian, didn't you? Forever. Just as you have taken Justin's . . . forever.' Her voice cracked as a wave of pain and fear overcame her.

Archimago laughed. 'You miss him, girl? Why, I can be just as good as your Justin. I can be strong and hard.' His hands were all over her again.

'But that's right, isn't it?' she said desperately. 'That's what you planned all along for Christian. You didn't care if he lived or died.'

He became impatient. 'Of course it's right. Of course I didn't care. A pretty bauble is a joy to look on, but one should not get oneself too attached.'

Holly leaned back in her chair, dropped her head with relief. 'Christian, come!' she called.

The cry of rage came first, then her ghostly lover appeared beside her. The shock sent Archimago reeling away from her.

'You!' he said.

'Appear as you truly are!' Christian demanded. 'Let me see you. Get out of that body.'

Archimago looked stunned for a moment, but then a sly grin came across his face. To Holly's surprise, he began to laugh. 'You didn't expect it, did you? You didn't know I'd be embodied. Hee, hee, hee. It delights me to think you had planned to overcome me. But look at you, you're nothing but a spirit. I'm not on your plane any more, boy. You know what that means?'

Holly looked up at Christian. 'What is he saying?' she said, terrified.

He looked from her to Archimago and back again.

'Is it right? Are you powerless against him?'

'Only while he's embodied,' Christian said. 'I have as much power over him as I have over you or anything else on the physical plane.'

'Is everything lost, then?' Holly gasped.

'Stupid, ineffectual little boy,' Archimago goaded, laughing harder and harder. 'You were never any use for anything. You were a pretty, yet empty, vessel.'

Christian howled with rage and began to sob. 'I hate you!' he screamed. 'I hate you, I hate you!'

Hands on his knees, bent over double, Archimago laughed and laughed.

She stood in a great echoing bathroom. In the distance hill springs trickled, the grass grew deep and green. Three great taps were mounted in the wall. With joy in her heart, Prudence ran towards them. White marble, cool, glowed all around her. She twisted the first tap. Nothing came out. The second tap. Nothing. Desperate anxiety scrabbled in her chest. The third tap. A noise as the pressure built up behind it—this time there would be water. This time.

But with a horrible hissing noise, sand began to pour from the faucet, covering her feet. She cried out.

And woke. Still dark, still hungry, still burning with thirst. She hadn't even felt herself drift off that time. Was that how it would be, dying this way? Would she be conscious one moment, then drift off into one of the terrible nightmares, fade out of the dream and into death without even knowing? Without even being able to fight?

She sat up, felt around for her weapons. One bone in

each hand. Dizziness rang through her head. Was this it? Was she dying this time?

No. It stopped. What time was it? What day? Had Lucien come yet? She felt in her pocket. No, the two pages were still there. But what if it was only Saturday still? What if there were hours and hours to go—?

Footsteps.

No, she must be imagining it.

Again, footsteps. Her breath caught in her throat. She almost sobbed. He was coming.

She positioned herself flat against the wall next to the door. The footsteps came closer. She stood as silently as she could, not wanting him to know she was still alive. Her heart was thumping so hard in her chest she began to fear that she would have a cardiac arrest before he even got in the door. A beam of light through the keyhole. She watched it with awe, as if seeing light for the first time in her life. The sound of the keys. *Gather all your strength, Prudence. This is it.*

The door swung cautiously inwards and Lucien, his torchbeam ahead of him, took a step inside. With all her might, she brought his brother's bone crashing down on his head. He cried out and staggered, dropping the torch. His hand went out for her and got her around the wrist forcing one of her weapons out of her hand. She struggled weakly as he regained his balance and tried to pull her towards him. Her only advantage was that he couldn't see in the dark as well as she could after three and a half long days. She pulled him a few centimetres to the right, sending him stumbling over Graham's remains and pitching towards the floor.

Weak and out of breath, Prudence started to fear that she would pass out. Her ears were ringing and her knees felt like rubber. She took one step towards the door, only to collapse, her free hand flailing for something to grab onto. In an instant Lucien stood above her, one of his feet reaching out to find her stomach, pinning her down. His breathing was ragged and she could vaguely see his silhouette in the reflected beam of the dropped torch. Just on the other side of him, a cool breath of freedom taunted her from the open door.

'Where are the pages?' he hissed.

She tried to speak, but her throat was raw and her tongue useless. Her right hand tightened around the remaining sharpened bone. He kneeled down, pinning her with one knee and one arm while his free arm reached out for the torch. Gathering the last of her strength, she came at him from below with the sharp edge of the bone, drove it as hard as she could into his stomach and pulled it out again. She felt cloth tearing, flesh puncturing. He fell on his side and she scrambled to her feet. Standing unsteadily over him, she smashed the heavy end of the bone into his head, turned and ran. Slammed the door behind her. He had left the key in the lock. She turned it, pocketed the key, and stumbled up the hallway.

'No! No!' he screamed, beating against the inside of the door.

She ignored his screams and kept running.

'No! Don't leave me. Come back! Come back!' His voice faded as she rounded the first loop and went through to the second. She pelted past the Confessional and headed for the cellar, stopping for breath and to still her thumping heart. Was that rain she heard outside? Careless of her dizziness, she ran to freedom out the front door of the college, stood in the rain, opened her mouth to catch the fat drops. Was this a dream? She fell over on her back, felt her wrist turn the wrong way. The pain was acute. No, this was not a dream. Her overloaded system could not cope. Consciousness slipped through her fingertips. The rain beat on above her.

★

611

Between Christian's sobs and Archimago's laughter, Holly thought she would go mad. Lucien had been gone for ages, and while she dreaded him coming back, she dreaded more the attentions of Archimago, who had dropped to his knees and was lecherously fondling her ankles while he laughed. Overwhelmed with a sense of hopelessness, she feared there was now no escape.

'Well, girl,' he said at long last, 'do you want to dismiss your little helper now? He's not much use to you, and I'm sure you don't want him to witness us making *love*.' He emphasised the word with a hideous leer. His fingers crept up her calf, around and over her knees, and were moving up her inner thigh. She shuddered involuntarily.

'We don't want him to be jealous, do we?' he continued. 'After all, I have a body I can use, not just ghostly caresses.' He squeezed her thigh cruelly. She was so dreading what Archimago intended that she almost missed the hint he was unwittingly giving her. But she had spent a good six months in the company of Prudence Emerson, to whom every remark had a second meaning.

'Why do you really want Christian to go?' she asked.

Christian fell silent beside her.

Archimago laughed. 'I don't want to embarrass the boy with my superior skill.' He was unbuttoning her blouse now. Her flesh crawled wherever he touched her.

He didn't want Christian to stay. There must be a reason. There must be something that Christian could do to overcome him. She thought hard. The books she had read suggested that a reminder of a broken vow was enough to banish a troublesome spirit. Perhaps it was true. Perhaps Archimago was uncomfortable with Christian's in-depth knowledge of his life as Peter Owling. She looked with pleading eyes at Christian, who had bent his head to his hands, his black hair falling forward and covering his face. He was of no use to her.

But Christian had related the whole story to her. What

he knew, she knew. She frantically combed over everything in her memory, looking for that one detail that would stop him. She endured his caresses with a frozen spine, desperately picking over Christian's story in her mind. What was Owling's weakness?

Of course. Rosalind.

'Is this how you raped your daughter?' she said bitterly.

His head snapped up. The flat, black eyes fixed unblinkingly on hers, unnerving her.

'How do you know about Rosalind?'

Realisation and hope sat with her now as she remembered his broken vow. 'Are you wondering how anybody would know about Rosalind? After you vowed to preserve her memory and you didn't. You went back on your word, and you promised instead to forget her.'

Archimago dropped his head and removed his hands to cover his face. Holly thought she had won. Seconds ticked by in silence. But when he uncovered his face and looked at her again, he was grinning. 'Oh yes, I remember now. Rosalind, the whore. The little girl with the tight body—she tempted me, made me service her. I remember. And she died and I tore her to pieces. Do you remember that, Christian?'

Christian did not reply.

'I was everything to that girl, I tell you. I fathered her, fucked her and killed her. Somewhere in the world you already have a father, girl, but I can perform the other two for you. In fact,' he said, pulling himself to his feet ominously, 'I might. I grow weary of you.' He ripped open the front of her blouse and started to push up her skirt. Leaning over her, dropping hideous kisses on her neck, his hands felt their way up between her legs, roughly prodding at her soft flesh.

She moaned in terror. It hadn't worked. She let her head fall back and, as a last resort, began to recite The Lord's Prayer. 'Our Father, who art in heaven.'

Archimago howled with laughter. 'Yes, yes, that's the girl. Make it even more profane.'

'Hallowed be thy name . . .' Tears began to run down her cheeks, sobs shuddered through her body. 'Thy kingdom come, thy will be done . . .' His mouth, his teeth rough at her nipples, 'on earth, as it is in heaven . . .' He pulled her legs forward, started at the buckle of his pants.

'Peter.' Christian had finally chosen to speak. Holly looked up at him. He appeared emotionless, drained.

'Don't call me that!' Archimago called. 'You of all people should know better.'

'You admit that you killed Rosalind?'

'Yes, yes. Get over it, lad. It happened a hundred and thirty-two years ago. I didn't love you and I killed Rosalind. Why do you think I headed straight to hell? It wasn't because I behaved like a choirboy.'

'I remember something you said to me once,' Christian continued. 'Would you like me to tell you what it was?'

Archimago's head snapped up.

'Would you like me to tell you?' Christian repeated.

Archimago shook his head. 'No, I'm finished with you. Girl, command him to disappear or I will rape you with that letter opener the magus had pressed to your throat.'

'Christian?' she said, desperate.

'You thought for a while that perhaps the Humberstones were responsible for Rosalind's death,' Christian said in the calm, emotionless voice.

Archimago crossed the room and reached for the letter opener. 'Last chance, girl,' he said, advancing across the room towards her. 'Nearly time to meet your new lover.'

She looked from Archimago, the letter opener glinting cruelly in the candlelight, to Christian, seemingly dispassionate beside her. Her flesh tingled in anticipation of the pain. Surely Christian would not let that happen to her.

'Go on, Christian,' she said softly, 'I trust you.'

'You said, "By all the demons of hell, Rosalind, I swear I shall avenge your death."'

Archimago dropped the letter opener and stood quaking.

'You swore, Peter. By all the demons of hell. So it seems to me that either you must destroy yourself, or they most certainly will.'

A sudden howl pierced the air. At first Holly thought it was coming from Archimago, but then the howl was joined by another, and another, until the space around him seemed it would be ripped to tatters by the awful shrieking. She looked about her. Flitting shadows caught her eye and then disappeared, only to reappear again in another place.

'Ah, they awake!' cried Christian. 'Look here, Peter, they awake. They know now, and they've come for you.'

With an eerie tearing noise, a clawed hand appeared in the air, as though it were reaching through from the other side of a shimmering body of water. As the space around the hand opened up, the howling became louder, more focussed. A withered arm followed the claw and touched Archimago once on the back of the neck. Archimago slumped to the ground. From Justin's body there arose a strange blue-white light. It formed into a spectre of a fat, bald man, mutated and deformed almost beyond recognition. His voice boomed from all four walls. 'No! Don't send me back there. Christian, no! Tell them you're lying! Tell them to leave me alone! Don't send me to hell! I can't bear to go back there. You love me, Christian, don't send me back there.'

The macabre shadows grew darker as they approached, gathering around the spectre of Archimago. The heat became unbearable and Holly thought she would faint. The walls trembled and cupboards and drawers opened; books, papers, candles, pens, innumerable items began to fly about. The diabolic howling grew louder and louder as more spaces in the air opened up and unearthly demonic bodies began to push into the room, the same blue-white light that surrounded their prey running over their limbs. Holly screamed, echoing Archimago's screams as they closed in on him. All different shapes and sizes, one headless, grotesque faces, gnarled and withered limbs, rancid breath and black spiky hair like spiders, they tumbled to the floor, got up again, clawed and scrabbled at Archimago and began to drag him away from Justin's body.

'Christian, call them off. Tell them you're lying.'

'It's too late,' he said, 'the truth is told. Goodbye.'

The demons gathered around Archimago and began to tear him to pieces. With a popping noise and a flash of light his right arm was separated from his body, then his left. Holly fought wildly against her bonds, every instinct screaming for her to get away. One beast dug a long claw into Archimago's eye socket and popped out the eyeball. As the pieces of him dropped towards the floor, they fizzed and flared and disintegrated before they hit the carpet. The demonic howling was accompanied by awful ungodly grunts and sighs, as though this were the only pleasure ever afforded these beings. Holly thought she would go mad from the monstrous noise. Archimago did not stop screaming until the bitter end, demanding Christian call the demons off. As the last part of him was mutilated and atomised, the scream abruptly ceased. The swarm of beasts parted, and Archimago had ceased to exist. One by one, howling, the demons jumped and tumbled back to their own realm, as though they were diving into a vertical lake. The sulphurous smell of their breath and skin hung in the air momentarily, then the room grew quiet and the only sound Holly could hear was her own shallow breathing. They were gone.

'Christian?' she said, finding her voice at last.

He stood before her, reached down to smooth her skirt. Once, twice he tried. On the third attempt he managed it. 'I'm not much use to you in the physical world,' he said sadly.

'You're everything to me.'

'I can't even untie you.' He held his hands up in front of him as though they were guilty of some crime.

'You saved me. You destroyed Owling.'

'I think your friend is waking.'

Holly looked down. Justin was stirring at her feet. She turned her eyes towards Christian. 'Lucien's been gone for nearly an hour. Maybe he's not coming back.'

'You must keep the grimoire away from him. You must destroy it.'

'I will. Trust me.'

He fixed his blue eyes on her and she saw them glisten with tears. 'I wish I could hold you again.'

'So do I.'

'You have to release me now.'

She fought back tears of her own. 'I know. If that's what you want.'

'I'm so tired, Holly. I want to go across to the other side, where Rosalind is. I want to tell her I forgive her for not warning me about Peter.'

'Will I ever see you again? When I'm ….' Holly couldn't finish the sentence.

'Perhaps. But don't wish for death, Holly. Live. And be happy.'

She closed her eyes and tears squeezed from beneath the lids. She felt his familiar caress on her cheek. 'Goodbye, Christian,' she said. The words trembled on her lips then finally, reluctantly, made it across them. 'I release you.'

His touch faded. Her cheek tingled momentarily, then she felt nothing. She opened her eyes. He was gone and with him all her happiness.

But what of Lucien? What if he returned? She summoned the last shreds of her will and turned her attention to Justin. 'Justin? Justin, wake up.'

He groaned and twitched.

'Please, Justin, please. I need your help.'

'Holly?' Justin's voice, not the horrible creature that had been inhabiting him.

'Please, Justin. Wake up. Lucien may come back. We have to get out of here.'

His eyes opened and he looked at the devastation around him, then looked at Holly, blouse open, tied to a chair. 'Holly? What happened?'

'Untie me, *please*. We have to get out of here!'

He stood unsteadily and came to her, untying Lucien's knots with clumsy, groggy fingers. She tried not to recoil, remembering Archimago's vile caresses. Finally she was free. She straightened her clothes, cursing herself as a prude for being embarrassed at a time like this.

'What day is it?' he asked.

'It's Sunday.' She grabbed the grimoire from Lucien's desk. 'We can talk about what happened later. Come on.'

She took his hand and dragged him to the door. She peered out into the dark hallway. Nobody around. Where the hell was Lucien? Would he be waiting for them at the entrance?

Leaning on each other for support, Holly and Justin cautiously made their way down the steps. Still all clear.

'I don't understand,' Holly said. 'Where did he get to?'

They scurried across the foyer and out the door into the freezing night. They ran as far as the front gardens when they spotted Prudence crashed out on her back in the rain.

'Prudence! Oh, my God, Prudence.'

Justin kneeled over her. 'She's alive. She's unconscious. Her arm's all bent, I think she's broken it.'

'Can you move her?' Holly said, leaning over him.

Justin hoisted Prudence up in his arms, staggered a few paces, then found his balance. 'We have to call an ambulance.'

'There's a phone box around the corner.' Holly cast a wary glance at the college over her shoulder. 'I'm not going back inside.'

'Okay. Let's go.'

In the pouring rain, the three of them left the dark college behind.

EPILOGUE

⁓

Guilt was a treacherous entity, best shared among friends.

Holly noticed that Prudence had grown very quiet as they settled between four glowing candles in the Confessional, even though it had been her idea to come here. Four weeks had passed since the last beautiful thing in Holly's life—Christian—had slipped through her fingers, on a night that she only remembered in vague snatches of hellish noise and incomprehensible dread. In that time Lucien had failed to turn up anywhere, Emma had moved back into the mansion, Randolph had died quietly in his hospital bed, Prudence's parents had returned to nurse their injured daughter, and Holly had shed a million hot tears over a love that had always been impossible. Sick, desolate, somehow she still managed to function.

Prudence uncorked the wine and took a swig, passed it to Holly. She took a sip. Cheap and nasty compared to what they were used to, but Mr Emerson had put a padlock on his cellar. Holly handed the bottle to Justin. He had speckles of white paint in his hair from renovating. One of the investment properties Lucien had bought with his nephew's money had become vacant. Justin had jumped at the chance to get away from Emma. Holly was staying with him until Prudence's parents went back to Hong Kong. Justin had dropped out of his course and had become even more withdrawn.

Prudence took the wine from him and said softly, 'So, Justin, tell us about hell again.'

'Prudence—' Holly started, the familiar fear coiling in her stomach.

'It's important,' her friend replied.

Justin shook his head. 'I've told you already. I know you think I'm crazy.'

Holly remembered sitting in the hospital after the event, the long cold morning hours when it seemed the sun would never rise as they waited for Prudence to regain consciousness. Justin had told her a tale of hell. While Archimago had used his body, he had resided in a hot, blasted place where trees were skeletal hands, where the screams of the damned echoed night and day, where the sun was a blank disk behind thick veils of infernal smoke. For the past month he had been coldly certain that it was a place he was destined to go one day. He dreamed about it, drew pictures of it, admitted that he thought about it obsessively.

'I don't think you're crazy,' Prudence said softly. 'I believe you. That's the problem.'

Holly believed him too. 'What's all this about, Prudence?' she asked. 'The Confessional can hardly be your favourite place in the world any more. Why bring us here?'

'To confess of course.' Prudence took a fortifying gulp of wine then placed the bottle carefully in front of her. The cast on her left wrist was decorated with purple glitter which glinted in the candlelight. 'I lied about Lucien.'

'What do you mean?' Justin asked.

621

Prudence had told them that Lucien had come to release her then run off before she had a chance to catch him. Holly had been bugging her about reporting it to the police, but her friend had been reluctant to do so.

Prudence tilted her head towards the tunnels. 'He's still down there.'

A chill passed over Holly. 'You mean . . .?'

'He'd be dead by now,' Prudence said in a low voice. 'I didn't want to tell you until I was sure there was no chance of saving him.'

There were a few moments of stunned, sick silence.

Justin shook his head, pressed a palm to his forehead. 'I can't feel sorry for him,' he said. 'It's too just. It's too right.' As soon as she was conscious, Prudence had told them how Justin's father had died. But how she had kept Lucien's fate secret for so long was a mystery to Holly.

'So it really is time to make a decision on this issue,' Prudence said. 'You can understand how I feel.'

'Holly?' Justin said, turning to her. 'You're the one with the misgivings.'

'I made a promise.'

'Christian's gone,' said Prudence. 'He's out of your life forever.'

Holly sighed. 'I'm always the one who gets in the way of these grand plans, aren't I?'

'It'll be safe,' Prudence said. 'It's not going to fall into the wrong hands. We're young, we've got our whole lives to decide for sure. But if we destroyed it, then one day decided that we needed it, discovered that there was a way we could work around the danger and succeed, we'd never forgive ourselves.'

Holly laughed a bitter laugh. 'None of us can forgive ourselves anyway.' And that's what this was all about, wasn't it? Justin's descriptions of hell had got to them all, each with some guilty secret lurking in their past, each feeling responsible in varying degrees for the death of another. Justin's mother, Michael, and now Lucien.

Prudence felt in her backpack, pulled out the grimoire and dropped it on the floor between them. 'Justin has a basement now—the perfect place for burying a few secrets. All we need is a barrel of salt and a padlocked door. Just in case.'

'I don't know about leaving it at my house,' Justin said. 'I don't want to be solely responsible for it.'

'But you're not living there alone,' Prudence said.

'I won't be staying there forever, Prudence,' Holly countered.

'For longer than you think, though. My mismanagement of family funds has been discovered—Dad gave me my marching orders this morning. Now we're both homeless, and I don't think Justin will let us freeze to death on the streets.'

Justin looked trapped, he could barely spit out the words. 'Of course you can stay at my place.'

It was hard for Holly to forget Archimago when she looked at Justin. It was hard for her not to recoil from him when he passed her in the hallway or sat next to her on the threadbare sofa. Her discomfort must have been dazzlingly evident, though he tried hard to patch up the breach. Too hard. And the harder he tried to get closer to Holly, the more resentful Prudence became. The more resentful Prudence became, the more it annoyed Justin. If everybody's overactive emotions didn't settle down soon, they would tear each other apart before the year was out. Holly didn't know how they were supposed to live in the same house under those circumstances.

'We can make a deal,' Prudence suggested. 'Twenty years from today we'll have this conversation again. Then we can decide whether to destroy it finally or hang on to it.'

'Twenty years?'

'Yeah,' Prudence said, flicking a strand of hair off her shoulder. 'I'll be old, fat and ugly by then, and probably in a real good frame of mind for making a deal with the devil.'

'Don't even joke about it, Prudence,' Justin said, frowning.

'What do you say, Holly?'

'Holly,' Justin said, 'remember what I told you. Remember what I saw. I don't want to spend eternity there.'

Prudence was right, of course. Christian was out of her life, which made it hardly a life worth living. And she'd be foolish to make any rash decisions concerning her eternal soul while she was drained and confused from nursing a broken heart, right? Perhaps time was what she needed. 'All right,' Holly said. 'All right, put it in the cellar. Mark your diary for 5 September 2018. We can decide then. Somebody once told me never to do today what you can put off until doomsday.'

'That would have been a very wise woman,' Prudence said cheerfully.

'More wine, Prudence?' Justin asked, picking up the bottle and offering it to her.

'Yes. More wine all around,' Prudence said. 'I kind of like the idea of us still being together in twenty years' time. I always knew real best friends last forever.'

Justin shook his head, smiling bitterly. 'And the guilty are always afraid to die,' he added.

'Trust you to put a damper on the event,' Prudence said, raising the bottle to her lips then passing it on. 'Cheers to us. Chained together for better or for worse.'

Holly didn't know whether to laugh or cry. 'Cheers,' she said.

'Yeah, cheers,' Justin echoed. 'Cheers to us.'

THE POEMS

‘Alone, alone, all, all, alone . . .’ from *The Rime of the Ancient Mariner* by Samuel Taylor Coleridge.

‘I think we are not wholly brain . . .’ from *In Memoriam, AHH* by Alfred, Lord Tennyson.

‘We caught the tread of dancing feet . . .’ from ‘The Harlot’s House’ by Oscar Wilde.

‘But when the feast is finished and the lamps expire . . .’ from ‘Cynara’ by Ernest Dowson.

‘Abandon all hope, you who enter . . .’ from *The Divine Comedy* by Dante.

‘I had a dream, which was not all a dream . . .’ from ‘Darkness’ by George Gordon, Lord Byron.

‘My heart aches, and a drowsy numbness pains my sense . . .’ from ‘Ode to a Nightingale’ by John Keats.